PENGUIN BOOKS

THE PENGUIN BOOK OF
MODERN BRITISH SHORT STORIES

Malcolm Bradbury was a novelist, critic, television dramatist, Emeritus Professor of American Studies at the University of East Anglia and co-founder there, with Angus Wilson, of the creative writing MA course. His novels include *Eating People is Wrong* (1959); *Stepping Westward* (1965); *The History Man* (1975), which won the Royal Society of Literature Heinemann Prize and was adapted as a famous television series; *Rates of Exchange* (1983),which was shortlisted for the Booker Prize; *Cuts: A Very Short Novel* (1987), also televised; and *Doctor Criminale* (1992). His critical works include *The Modern American Novel* (1984; revised edition, 1992), *No, Not Bloomsbury* (essays, 1987), *The Modern World: Ten Great Writers* (1988), *From Puritanism to Postmodernism: A History of American Literature* (with Richard Ruland, 1991), *The Modern British Novel* (1993) and *Dangerous Pilgrimages* (1995). He edited *Modernism* (with James McFarlane, 1976), *The Penguin Book of Modern British Short Stories* (1988) and *The Atlas of Literature* (1997). He was also the author of a collection of stories and parodies, *Who Do You Think You Are?* (1976), and several works of humour and satire, including *Why Come to Slaka?* (1986), *Unsent Letters* (1988; revised edition, 1995) and *Mensonge* (1987). He wrote many television plays, in particular the television 'novels' *The Gravy Train* and *The Gravy Train Goes East*, and he adapted several books for television and film, including Tom Sharpe's *Porterhouse Blue*, Kingsley Amis's *The Green Man* and Stella Gibbons's *Cold Comfort Farm*.

Malcolm Bradbury was awarded the CBE in 1991 for his services to Literature and was knighted in the 2000 New Year's Honours List. He died in November 2000.

THE PENGUIN BOOK OF
MODERN BRITISH SHORT STORIES

Edited with an Introduction by
Malcolm Bradbury

PENGUIN BOOKS

PENGUIN BOOKS

Published by the Penguin Group
Penguin Books Ltd, 80 Strand, London WC2R 0RL, England
Penguin Putnam Inc., 375 Hudson Street, New York, New York 10014, USA
Penguin Books Australia Ltd, 250 Camberwell Road, Camberwell, Victoria 3124, Australia
Penguin Books Canada Ltd, 10 Alcorn Avenue, Toronto, Ontario, Canada M4V 3B2
Penguin Books India (P) Ltd, 11 Community Centre, Panchsheel Park, New Delhi – 110 017, India
Penguin Books (NZ) Ltd, Cnr Rosedale and Airborne Roads, Albany, Auckland, New Zealand
Penguin Books (South Africa) (Pty) Ltd, 24 Sturdee Avenue, Rosebank 2196, South Africa

Penguin Books Ltd, Registered Offices: 80 Strand, London WC2R 0RL, England

www.penguin.com

First published by Viking 1987
Published in Penguin Books 1988
39

This selection and Introduction copyright © Malcolm Bradbury, 1987
All rights reserved

Pages 8–10 constitute an extension of this copyright page

Printed in England by Clays Ltd, St Ives plc

ISBN-13: 978–0–14–006306–6

CONTENTS

CONTENTS

CONTENTS

*A*CKNOWLEDGEMENTS

Thanks are due to the copyright holders of the following stories for permission to reprint them in this volume:
Kingsley Amis: for 'My Enemy's Enemy' from *Collected Short Stories* (Hutchinson & Co. Ltd), (reprinted by permission of Century Hutchinson Ltd). **Martin Amis**: for 'Let Me Count The Times' from *Granta* 4, © Martin Amis, 1981 (reprinted by permission of A. D. Peters & Co. Ltd). **Beryl Bainbridge**: for 'Clap Hands, Here Comes Charlie' from *Mum and Mr Armitage*, © Beryl Bainbridge, 1985 (reprinted by permission of Gerald Duckworth & Co. Ltd and Anthony Sheil Associates Ltd). **J. G. Ballard**: for 'Memories of the Space Age' from *Firebird 3*, © 1982 J. G. Ballard (reprinted by permission of the author c/o Margaret Hanbury, 27 Walcot Square, London SE11). **Julian Barnes**: for 'One of a Kind' from *New Stories 7, 1982*, © Julian Barnes, 1982 (reprinted by permission of A. D. Peters & Co. Ltd). **Samuel Beckett**: for 'Ping' from *Collected Shorter Prose* 1945–80 (John Calder, 1984), (reprinted by permission of the author and John Calder (Publishers) Ltd and of The Grove Press Inc.). © Samuel Beckett, 1974; all rights reserved. **Elizabeth Bowen**: for 'Mysterious Kor' from *The Collected Stories of Elizabeth Bowen*, © 1946 and renewed 1974 (reprinted by permission of Jonathan Cape Ltd., Alfred A. Knopf, Inc. and the Estate of Elizabeth Bowen). **Malcolm Bradbury**: for 'Composition' from *Encounter* and *Who Do You Think You Are?: Stories and Parodies* (Secker & Warburg Ltd, 1976). **Angela Carter**: for 'Flesh and the Mirror' from *Fireworks*, © 1974 Angela Carter (reprinted by permission of the author and Deborah Rogers Ltd). **John Fowles**: for 'The Enigma' from *The Ebony Tower*, © 1974 J. R. Fowles Ltd. **William Golding**: for 'Miss Pulkinhorn' from uncollected material (reprinted by permission of William Golding and Faber & Faber Ltd). **Graham Greene**: for 'The Invisible Japanese Gentlemen' from *Collected Stories* (reprinted by permission of Laur-

ACKNOWLEDGEMENTS

ence Pollinger Ltd). **Ted Hughes**: for 'The Rain Horse' from *Wodwo* (reprinted by permission of Faber & Faber Ltd). **Kazuo Ishiguro**: for 'A Family Supper' from *Firebird 2*, © 1982 Kazuo Ishiguro (reprinted by permission of Deborah Rogers Ltd). **B. S. Johnson**: for 'A Few Selected Sentences' from *Aren't You Rather Young to be Writing Your Memoirs?* (first published by Hutchinson & Co. Ltd, 1973), © the Estate of B. S. Johnson. **Doris Lessing**: for 'To Room Nineteen' from *A Man and Two Women*, © 1963 Doris Lessing (reprinted by permission of Jonathan Clowes Ltd on behalf of Doris Lessing). **David Lodge**: for 'Hotel Des Boobs' from *Cosmopolitan* 1986, © David Lodge, 1986 (reprinted by permission of Curtis Brown Ltd). **Malcolm Lowry**: for 'Strange Comfort Afforded by the Profession' from *Hear Us O Lord From Heaven Thy Dwelling Place* © Margerie Bonner Lowry (reprinted by permission of the Executors of the Malcolm Lowry Estate, Jonathan Cape Ltd and Literistic Ltd). **Adam Mars-Jones**: for 'Structural Anthropology' from *Quarto* magazine (reprinted by permission of A. D. Peters & Co. Ltd). **Ian McEwan**: for 'Psychopolis' from *In Between the Sheets*, © 1978 Ian McEwan (reprinted by permission of Deborah Rogers Ltd). **Edna O'Brien**: for 'Mrs Reinhardt' from *Mrs Reinhardt and Other Stories* (reprinted by permission of Weidenfeld & Nicolson Ltd). **V. S. Pritchett**: for 'A Family Man' from *On the Edge of the Cliff* (reprinted by permission of the author and Chatto & Windus Ltd). **Jean Rhys**: for 'The Lotus' from *Tigers Are Better Looking* (Andre Deutsch Ltd, 1978: first published in *Art and Literature*, no. 11, 1967), © Jean Rhys, 1967. **Salman Rushdie**: for 'The Prophet's Hair' (first published in the *London Review of Books*, Vol 3, No. 7 1981), © 1981 *London Review of Books* (reprinted by permission of Deborah Rogers Ltd). **Alan Sillitoe**: for 'The Fishing-boat Picture' from *The Loneliness of the Long Distance Runner* , © 1959 Alan Sillitoe (reprinted by permission of Tessa Sayle Agency and Alfred A. Knopf Inc.). **Clive Sinclair**: for 'Bedbugs' from the collection *Bedbugs*, © 1982 Clive Sinclair (reprinted by permission of Deborah Rogers Ltd). **Graham Swift**: for 'Seraglio' from the *London Magazine*, 1977 © Graham Swift, 1977 (reprinted by permission of A. P. Watt Ltd). **Muriel Spark**: for 'The House of the Famous Poet' first published in the *New Yorker*, 2 April 1966, © 1966 Copyright Administration Ltd (reprinted by permission of Harold Ober Associates Incorporated). **Emma Tennant**: for 'Philomela' from *Bananas*, © Emma Tennant, 1975 (reprinted by permission of the author). **Dylan Thomas**: for

INTRODUCTION

In setting out to collect the thirty-four short stories that make up this anthology of new British writing in probably the most difficult of all the prose forms of fiction, I had two main aims in mind. One was to display as well as I could the achievement of some of the best work produced by the strongest of our recent British writers, no easy task in a limited space, and one that tempts simplification and prejudice. The other and rather more difficult aim was to be broadly representative, so that the book might give not only a reasonable idea of the variety, but also the general trends and directions that have been taken by British fiction in the years since 1945.

It so happens that these two somewhat divergent intentions seemed to grow more reconcilable as I read through the many short stories from which this anthology has been collected. The short story has become one of the major forms of modern literary expression – in some ways the most modern of them all. For what we usually mean by the genre is that concentrated form of writing that, breaking away from the classic short tale, became, as it were, the lyric poem of modern fictional prose. The great precursors were Chekhov, Henry James, Katherine Mansfield, James Joyce, and Sherwood Anderson. It took on a strong modernist evolution in the work of Hemingway, Faulkner, Babel and Kafka which, in the period after 1940, was followed by a new wave of experiment led by Beckett and Borges, and provided the short story with a repertory of late twentieth-century forms. The modern short story has therefore been distinguished by its break away from anecdote, tale-telling and simple narrative, and for its linguistic and stylistic concentration, its imagistic methods, its symbolic potential. In it some of our greatest modern writers, from Hemingway to Mann to Beckett, have found their finest exactitude and most finished stylistic practice. In fact, for many prose-writers it has come closest to representing the most 'poetic' aspect of their craft.

INTRODUCTION

But if the short story is a major modern form, and if the above is the kind of thing it is, then it is sometimes argued that the British have not been especially good at it. We have owed as much to the tradition of direct narrative as of poetic narrative, to D. H. Lawrence as to James Joyce. The British short story has often seemed to resist those laws or conventions – about the story as an art of figures rather than adventures, or about the need for it to be committed to the single occasion or the single concentrated image – that have marked a good deal of its development elsewhere. The British have never been noted for respecting aesthetic skills in their authors, and the broad reputation of British writers in the form has been, with some striking exceptions, rather like that of British chefs in the field of *haute cuisine*; we may be able to imitate the practice but not generate great change or artistic originality. This may be one reason why only a few British writers have made the short story their first or only form, and why a good many of our finest short story writers also happen to be our finest novelists.

That fact has a convenience for this anthology, for it does, indeed, mean that many of the authors in this collection are our major writers of prose-fiction in general; hence the volume does display many of the striking directions and tendencies generally visible in British fiction since the War. But it also shows, I believe, that the short story has an importance and originality in the British line far greater than is often supposed. It is true that we have been somewhat short of those great magazines – consider the American tradition from, say, the *Kenyon Review* to the *New Yorker* – which encouraged the flourishing and development of the genre. But there have been moments, specifically during the 1940s when the pressure of wartime experience and the shortage of paper brought us *Penguin New Writing* and *Horizon* and the talents to fill them, when general interest in the short story has enlarged. We seem to be living in another such moment now, with a new wave of interest in short fictional forms. Though only a few recent writers have been short-story writers first, some of them have been of enormous importance. Writers of the thirties and forties like V. S. Pritchett and Elizabeth Bowen had major inheritors, such as William Trevor and Edna O'Brien, and the tradition seems particularly strong among new writers. Ian McEwan and Clive Sinclair, Adam Mars-Jones and Rose Tremain have made special use of the short story, and in a number of cases established their reputations with them, much as Angus Wilson did in the 1940s.

Perhaps it is that link between the novel and the short story that has made its development in Britain seem close to the same spirit of **13** argument that has fed the British novel. To say it crudely, that argument has been one between a notion of prose-fiction as falling into a long-standing tradition of realistic or reportorial narrative, and the notion of it as an art of language, of experimental form and symbol, a notion that has often led in the direction of the strange, the fantastic, the grotesque, the surreal and the mythic. In much post-war fiction these traditions have seemed to collide, producing new kinds of self-questioning and a fresh enquiry into the nature and the proper conditions of a fiction. That range is very obvious in this collection, reaching, as it does, from writers, like Samuel Beckett and Malcolm Lowry, who have been strongly marked by the modernist tradition, but who have taken it further, to writers who have largely practised the story as a social and anecdotal form, like Kingsley Amis, Alan Sillitoe and William Trevor. Equally it ranges from those writers who have stressed the self-questioning awareness of fiction (B. S. Johnson, John Fowles and David Lodge, for example) to those who, like Emma Tennant and Angela Carter, have explored the form's links with fantasy, fairy-tale and legend.

It seemed right to start this anthology at the close of the War, a time when there was indeed a revival of the short story and a marked sense of change in the spirit of writing, which we can sense in the fine, fragile manner of Elizabeth Bowen's story and which somehow seemed peculiarly appropriate to the experience of life during the War. V. S. Pritchett once called the short story 'the glancing form of fiction that seems to me right for the nervousness and restlessness of contemporary life', and his own work managed a reconciliation of form and experience which has been a mark of a good deal of post-war British fiction. It was Angus Wilson's appearance as a short-story writer at the end of the 1940s that suggested the post-war story had a new social experience to attend to, and that succession goes on still. Around the same time Samuel Beckett was developing a new form of experimental short story – exemplified by the difficult, exasperating and remarkable story 'Ping' in this collection; and in the work that followed we can sense not just the division of the modern British story into two traditions, one pre-eminently social and one predominantly experimental, but a sequence of constant attempts at reconciliation.

This, in a sense, is the 'enigma' of John Fowles's short story here, as a social fiction contends with an artistic one. And the extraordinary

14 flourish with which the form has developed over the 1970s and 1980s has surely something to do with the relationship between social and historical awareness and a revived fictionalist curiosity. The recent renewal of interest in the short story displays a very wide variety of preoccupations: the grotesque and fantastic modes of the stories of Ian McEwan and Angela Carter, the use of the oral story-telling tradition in Salman Rushdie, the exploitation of Jewish or Japanese inheritance in Clive Sinclair or Kazuo Ishiguro. In the short story as in the novel, it grows harder to suppose that there is a single or clear-cut tradition, just as it does to deny that the short story is serving us as a supremely artful form and a field of fictional experiment. One of the virtues of the story is that it shows us that in every serious work of fiction the writer is saying something crucial about the form he or she is using, as well as treating a subject or distilling an experience. Recent writers have emphasized this greatly and given the short story a remarkable contemporary promise. And so it is appropriate that this volume should not only display, as I think it does, that our major post-war writers have consistently explored the forms of short fiction but that it should give a large part of its space to the achievements of an outstanding young literary generation who are coming to dominate fiction and its future.

The aim of making this collection was to show that in Britain now the short story is an adventurous, inventive, very various and, above all, a discovering form. In creating it I have had great help from my wife Elizabeth, who did much of the collecting and organizing, from Martin Soames of Penguin Books, and from many of the writers included. I should also express my larger debts to others who have helped concentrate my notions of what the form can mean: my former colleagues Angus Wilson and David Lodge; other friends who are often former students, including Rose Tremain, Ian McEwan, Kazuo Ishiguro and Clive Sinclair, all of whom did much to expand my view of the story; and many present students who are working in the genre and doing exactly the same.

Malcolm Bradbury
Norwich, 1987.

STRANGE COMFORT AFFORDED BY THE PROFESSION

Sigbjørn Wilderness, an American writer in Rome on a Guggenheim Fellowship, paused on the steps above the flower stall and wrote, glancing from time to time at the house before him, in a black notebook:

> Il poeta inglese Giovanni Keats mente maravigliosa quanto precoce mori in questa casa il 24 Febbraio 1821 nel ventisessimo anno dell'età sua.

Here, in a sudden access of nervousness, glancing now not only at the house, but behind him at the church of Trinità dei Monti, at the woman in the flower stall, the Romans drifting up and down the steps, or passing in the Piazza di Spagna below (for though it was several years after the war he was afraid of being taken for a spy), he drew, as well as he was able, the lyre, similar to the one on the poet's tomb, that appeared on the house between the Italian and its translation:

Then he added swiftly the words below the lyre:

> The young English poet, John Keats, died in this house on the 24th of February 1821, aged 26.

This accomplished, he put the notebook and pencil back in his pocket, glanced around him again with a heavier, more penetrating look – that in fact was informed by such a malaise he saw nothing at all but which was intended to say 'I have a perfect right to do this', or 'If you saw me do that, very well then, I *am* some sort of detective, perhaps even some kind of a painter' – descended the remaining steps, looked around wildly once more, and entered, with a sigh of relief like a man going to bed, the comforting darkness of Keats's house.

Here, having climbed the narrow staircase, he was almost instantly confronted by a legend in a glass case which said:

> Remnants of aromatic gums used by Trelawny when cremating the body of Shelley.

And these words, for his notebook with which he was already rearmed felt ratified in this place, he also copied down, though he failed to comment on the gums themselves, which largely escaped his notice, as indeed did the house itself – there had been those stairs, there was a balcony, it was dark, there were many pictures, and these glass cases, it was a bit like a library – in which he saw no books of his – these made about the sum of Sigbjørn's unrecorded perceptions. From the aromatic gums he moved to the enshrined marriage licence of the same poet, and Sigbjørn transcribed this document too, writing rapidly as his eyes became more used to the dim light:

> Percy Bysshe Shelley of the Parish *of* Saint Mildred, Bread Street, London, Widower, *and* Mary Wollstonecraft Godwin *of* the City of Bath, Spinster, a minor, *were married in this* Church *by* Licence *with Consent of* William Godwin her father *this* Thirtieth *Day of December in the year one thousand eight hundred and sixteen.* By me Mr Heydon, Curate. This marriage was solemnized between us.
>
>   PERCY BYSSHE SHELLEY
>   MARY WOLLSTONECRAFT GODWIN
> In the presence of:
>
>   WILLIAM GODWIN
>   M. J. GODWIN

Beneath this Sigbjørn added mysteriously:

> Nemesis. Marriage of drowned Phoenician sailor. A bit odd here at all. Sad – feel swine to look at such things.

Then he passed on quickly – not so quickly he hadn't time to wonder with a remote twinge why, if there was no reason for any of his own books to be there on the shelves above him, the presence was justified of *In Memoriam, All Quiet on the Western Front, Green Light,* and the *Field Book of Western Birds* – to another glass case in which appeared a framed and unfinished letter, evidently from Severn, Keats's friend, which Sigbjørn copied down as before:

My dear Sir:

Keats has changed somewhat for the worse – at least his mind has much – very much – yet the blood has ceased to come, his digestion is better and but for a cough he must be improving, that is as respects his body – but the fatal prospect of consumption hangs before his mind yet – and turns everything to despair and wretchedness – he will not hear a word about living – nay, I seem to lose his confidence by trying to give him this hope [the following lines had been crossed out by Severn but Sigbjørn ruthlessly wrote them down just the same: *for his knowledge of internal anatomy enables him to judge of any change accurately and largely adds to his torture*], he will not think his future prospect favourable – he says the continued stretch of his imagination has already killed him and were he to recover he would not write another line – he will not hear of his good friends in England except for what they have done – and this is another load – but of their high hopes of him – his certain success – his experience – he will not hear a word – then the want of some kind of hope to feed his vivacious imagination –

The letter having broken off here, Sigbjørn, notebook in hand, tiptoed lingeringly to another glass case where, another letter from Severn appearing, he wrote:

My dear Brown – He is gone – he died with the most perfect ease – he seemed to go to sleep. On the 23rd at half past four the approaches of death came on. 'Severn – lift me up for I am dying – I shall die easy – don't be frightened, I thank God it has come.' I lifted him upon my arms and the phlegm seemed boiling in his throat. This increased until 11 at night when he gradually sank into death so quiet I still thought he slept – But I cannot say more now. I am broken down beyond my strength. I cannot be left alone. I have not slept for nine days – the days since. On Saturday a gentleman came to cast his hand and foot. On Thursday the body was opened. The lungs were completely gone. The doctors would not –

Much moved, Sigbjørn reread this as it now appeared in his notebook, then added beneath it:

On Saturday a gentleman came to cast his hand and foot – that is the most sinister line to me. Who is this gentleman?

Once outside Keats's house Wilderness did not pause nor look to left or right, not even at the American Express, until he had reached a bar which he entered, however, without stopping to copy down its name. He felt he had progressed in one movement, in one stride, from Keats's house to this bar, partly just because he had wished to avoid

17

signing his own name in the visitors' book. Sigbjørn Wilderness! The very sound of his name was like a bell-buoy – or more euphoniously a light-ship – broken adrift, and washing in from the Atlantic on a reef. Yet how he hated to write it down (loved to see it in print?) – though like so much else with him it had little reality unless he did. Without hesitating to ask himself why, if he was so disturbed by it, he did not choose another name under which to write, such as his second name which was Henry, or his mother's, which was Sanderson-Smith, he selected the most isolated booth he could find in the bar, that was itself an underground grotto, and drank two grappas in quick succession. Over his third he began to experience some of the emotions one might have expected him to undergo in Keats's house. He felt fully the surprise which had barely affected him that some of Shelley's relics were to be found there, if a fact no more astonishing than that Shelley – whose skull moreover had narrowly escaped appropriation by Byron as a drinking goblet, and whose heart, snatched out of the flames by Trelawny, he seemed to recollect from Proust, was interred in England – should have been buried in Rome at all (where the bit of Ariel's song inscribed on his gravestone might have anyway prepared one for the rich and strange), and he was touched by the chivalry of those Italians who, during the war, it was said, had preserved, at considerable risk to themselves, the contents of that house from the Germans. Moreover he now thought he began to see the house itself more clearly, though no doubt not as it was, and he produced his notebook again with the object of adding to the notes already taken these impressions that came to him in retrospect.

'Mamertine Prison,' he read . . . He'd opened it at the wrong place, at some observations made yesterday upon a visit to the historic dungeon, but being gloomily entertained by what he saw, he read on as he did so feeling the clammy confined horror of that underground cell, or other underground cell, not, he suspected, really sensed at the time, rise heavily about him.

MAMERTINE PRISON [ran the heading]
   The lower is the true prison
of Mamertine, the state prison of ancient Rome.
   The lower cell called Tullianus is probably the most ancient building in Rome. The prison was used to imprison malefactors and enemies of the State. In the lower cell is seen the well where according to tradition St Peter miraculously made a spring to baptise the gaolers Processus and Martinianus. Victims: politicians. Pontius, King of the Sanniti.

Died 290 B.C. Giurgurath (Jugurtha), Aristobulus, Vercingetorix – The Holy Martyrs, Peter and Paul. Apostles imprisoned in the reign of Nero. – Processus, Abondius, *and many others unknown* were:

> decapitato
> suppliziato (suffocated)
> strangolato
> morto per fame.

Vercingetorix, the King of the Gauls, was certainly strangolato 49 B.C. and Jugurtha, King of Numidia, dead by starvation 104 B.C.

The lower is the true prison – why had he underlined that? Sigbjørn wondered. He ordered another grappa and, while awaiting it, turned back to his notebook where, beneath his remarks on the Mamertine prison, and added as he now recalled in the dungeon itself, this memorandum met his eyes:

> Find Gogol's house – where wrote part of Dead Souls – 1838. Where died Vielgorsky? 'They do not heed me, nor see me, nor listen to me,' wrote Gogol. 'What have I done to them? Why do they torture me? What do they want of poor me? What can I give them? I have nothing. My strength is gone. I cannot endure all this.' Suppliziato. Strangolato. In wonderful-horrible book of Nabokov's when Gogol was dying – he says – 'you could feel his spine through his stomach.' Leeches dangling from nose: 'Lift them up, keep them away . . .' Henrik Ibsen, Thomas Mann, ditto brother: Buddenbrooks and Pippo Spano. A – where lived? became sunburned? Perhaps happy here. Prosper Mérimée and Schiller. Suppliziato. Fitzgerald in Forum. Eliot in Colosseum?

And underneath this was written enigmatically:

> *And many others.*

And beneath this:

> Perhaps Maxim Gorky too. This is funny. Encounter between Volga Boatman and saintly Fisherman.

What was funny? While Sigbjørn, turning over his pages toward Keats's house again, was wondering what he had meant, beyond the fact that Gorky, like most of those other distinguished individuals, had at one time lived in Rome, if not in the Mamertine prison – though with another part of his mind he knew perfectly well – he realized that the peculiar stichometry of his observations, jotted down as if he imagined he were writing a species of poem, had caused him prematurely to finish the notebook:

On Saturday a gentleman came to cast his hand and foot – that is the most sinister line to me – who is this gentleman?

With these words his notebook concluded.

That didn't mean there was no more space, for his notebooks, he reflected avuncularly, just like his candles, tended to consume themselves at both ends; yes, as he thought, there was some writing at the beginning. Reversing this, for it was upside down, he smiled and forgot about looking for space, since he immediately recognized these notes as having been taken in America two years ago upon a visit to Richmond, Virginia, a pleasant time for him. So, amused, he composed himself to read, delighted also, in an Italian bar, to be thus transported back to the South. He had made nothing of these notes, hadn't even known they were there, and it was not always easy accurately to visualize the scenes they conjured up:

> The wonderful slanting square in Richmond and the tragic silhouette of interlaced leafless trees.
> On a wall: *dirty stinking Degenerate Bobs was here from Boston, North End, Mass. Warp son of a bitch.*

Sigbjørn chuckled. Now he clearly remembered the biting winter day in Richmond, the dramatic courthouse in the precipitous park, the long climb up to it, and the caustic attestation to solidarity with the North in the (white) men's wash room. Smiling he read on:

> In Poe's shrine, strange preserved news clipping: CAPACITY CROWD HEARS TRIBUTE TO POE'S WORKS. *University student, who ended life, buried at Wytherville.*

Yes, yes, and this he remembered too, in Poe's house, or one of Poe's houses, the one with the great dark wing of shadow on it at sunset, where the dear old lady who kept it, who'd showed him the news clipping, had said to him in a whisper: 'So you see, *we* think these stories of his drinking can't *all* be true.' He continued:

> Opposite Craig house, where Poe's Helen lived, these words, upon façade, windows, stoop of the place from which E.A.P. – if I am right – must have watched the lady with the agate lamp: Headache – A.B.C. – Neuralgia: LIC-OFF-PREM – enjoy Pepsi – Drink Royal Crown Cola – Dr Swell's Root Beer – 'Furnish room for rent': did Poe really live here? Must have, could only have spotted Psyche from the regions which are Lic-Off-Prem. – Better than no Lic at all though. Bet Poe does not still live in Lic-Off-Prem. Else might account for 'Furnish room for rent'?

STRANGE COMFORT AFFORDED BY THE PROFESSION

Mem: Consult Talking Horse Friday.

– Give me Liberty or give me death [Sigbjørn now read]. In churchyard, with Patrick Henry's grave; a notice. No smoking within ten feet of the church; then:

Outside Robert E. Lee's house:
Please pull the bell
To make it ring.

– Inside Valentine Museum, with Poe's relics –

Sigbjørn paused. Now he remembered that winter day still more clearly. Robert E. Lee's house was of course far below the courthouse, remote from Patrick Henry and the Craig house and the other Poe shrine, and it would have been a good step hence to the Valentine Museum, even had not Richmond, a city whose Hellenic character was not confined to its architecture, but would have been recognized in its gradients by a Greek mountain goat, been grouped about streets so steep it was painful to think of Poe toiling up them. Sigbjørn's notes were in the wrong order, and it must have been morning then, and not sunset as it was in the other house with the old lady, when he went to the Valentine Museum. He saw Lee's house again, and a faint feeling of the beauty of the whole frostbound city outside came to his mind, then a picture of a Confederate white house, near a gigantic red-brick factory chimney, with far below a glimpse of an old cobbled street, and a lone figure crossing a waste, as between three centuries, from the house toward the railway tracks and this chimney, which belonged to the Bone Dry Fertilizer Company. But in the sequence of his notes 'Please pull the bell, to make it ring,' on Lee's house, had seemed to provide a certain musical effect of solemnity, yet ushering him instead into the Poe museum which Sigbjørn now in memory re-entered.

Inside Valentine Museum, with Poe's relics [he read once more]
Please
Do not smoke
Do not run
Do not touch walls or exhibits
Observation of these rules will insure your own and others' enjoyment of the museum.

– Blue silk coat and waistcoat, gift of the Misses Boykin, that belonged to one of George Washington's dentists.

Sigbjørn closed his eyes, in his mind Shelley's crematory gums and the gift of the Misses Boykin struggling for a moment helplessly, then he returned to the words that followed. They were Poe's own, and

formed part of some letters once presumably written in anguished and
private desperation, but which were now to be perused at leisure by
anyone whose enjoyment of them would be 'insured' so long as they
neither smoked nor ran nor touched the glass case in which, like the
gums (on the other side of the world), they were preserved. He read:

> Excerpt from a letter by Poe – after having been dismissed from West
> Point – to his foster father. Feb. 21, 1831.
> 'It will however be the last time I ever trouble any human being – I
> feel I am on a sick bed from which I shall never get up.'

Sigbjørn calculated with a pang that Poe must have written these
words almost seven years to the day after Keats's death, then, that far
from never having got up from his sick bed, he had risen from it to
change, thanks to Baudelaire, the whole course of European literature, yes, and not merely to trouble, but to frighten the wits out
of several generations of human beings with such choice pieces as
'King Pest', 'The Pit and the Pendulum', and 'A Descent into the
Maelstrom', not to speak of the effect produced by the compendious
and prophetic *Eureka*.

> My *ear* has been too shocking for any description – I am wearing
> away every day, even if my last sickness had not completed it.

Sigbjørn finished his grappa and ordered another. The sensation
produced by reading these notes was really very curious. First, he was
conscious of himself reading them here in this Roman bar, then of
himself in the Valentine Museum in Richmond, Virginia, reading the
letters through the glass case and copying fragments from these down,
then of poor Poe sitting blackly somewhere writing them. Beyond this
was the vision of Poe's foster father likewise reading some of these
letters, for all he knew unheedingly, yet solemnly putting them away
for what turned out to be posterity, these letters which, whatever they
might not be, were certainly – he thought again – intended to be
private. But were they indeed? Even here at this extremity Poe must
have felt that he was transcribing the story that was E. A. Poe, at this
very moment of what he conceived to be his greatest need, his final –
however consciously engineered – disgrace, felt a certain reluctance,
perhaps, to send what he wrote, as if he were thinking: Damn it, I
could use some of that, it may not be so hot, but it is at least too good to
waste on my foster father. Some of Keats's own published letters were
not different. And yet it was almost bizarre how, among these glass

cases, in these museums, to what extent one revolved about, was hemmed in by, this cinereous evidence of anguish. Where was Poe's astrolabe, Keats' tankard of claret, Shelley's 'Useful Knots for the Yachtsman'? It was true that Shelley himself might not have been aware of the aromatic gums, but even that beautiful and irrelevant circumstantiality that was the gift of the Misses Boykin seemed not without its suggestion of suffering, at least for George Washington.

> Baltimore, April 12, 1833.
>
> I am perishing – absolutely perishing for want of aid. And yet I am not idle – nor have I committed any offence against society which would render me deserving of so hard a fate. For God's sake pity me and save me from destruction.
>
> E. A. POE

Oh, God, thought Sigbjørn. But Poe had held out another sixteen years. He had died in Baltimore at the age of forty. Sigbjørn himself was nine behind on that game so far, and – with luck – should win easily. Perhaps if Poe had held out a little longer – perhaps if Keats – he turned over the pages of his notebook rapidly, only to be confronted by the letter from Severn:

> My dear Sir:
>
> Keats has changed somewhat for the worse – at least his mind has much – very much – yet the blood has ceased to come . . . but the fatal prospect hangs . . . *for his knowledge of internal anatomy . . . largely adds to his torture.*

Suppliziato, strangolato, he thought . . . *The lower is the true prison. And many others.* Nor have I committed any offense against society. Not much you hadn't, brother. Society might pay you the highest honors, even to putting your relics in the company of the waistcoat belonging to George Washington's dentist, but in its heart it cried: – *dirty stinking Degenerate Bobs was here from Boston, North End, Mass. Warp son of a bitch!* . . . 'On Saturday a gentleman came to cast his hand and foot . . .' Had anybody done that, Sigbjørn wondered, tasting his new grappa, and suddenly cognizant of his diminishing Guggenheim, compared, that was, Keats and Poe? – But compare in what sense, Keats, with what, in what sense, with Poe? What was it he wanted to compare? Not the aesthetic of the two poets, nor the breakdown of *Hyperion*, in relation to Poe's conception of the short poem, nor yet the philosophic ambition of the one, with the philosophic achievement of the other. Or could that more properly be discerned as negative capability, as opposed to negative achievement? Or did he merely wish to relate their melancholias? potations? hangovers? Their sheer guts – which commentators so obligingly forgot! – character, in a high sense of that word, the sense in which Conrad sometimes understood it, for were they not in their souls like hapless shipmasters, determined to drive their leaky commands full of valuable treasure at all costs, somehow, into port, and always against time, yet through all but interminable tempest, typhoons that so rarely abated? Or merely what seemed funereally analogous within the mutuality of their shrines? Or he could even speculate, starting with Baudelaire again, upon what the French movie director Epstein who had made *La Chute de la Maison Usher* in a way that would have delighted Poe himself, might have done with *The Eve of St Agnes: And they are gone!* . . . 'For God's sake pity me and save me from destruction!'

Ah ha, now he thought he had it: did not the preservation of such relics betoken – beyond the filing cabinet of the malicious foster father who wanted to catch one out – less an obscure revenge for the poet's nonconformity, than for his magical monopoly, his possession of words? On the one hand he could write his translunar 'Ulalume', his enchanted 'To a Nightingale' (which might account for the *Field Book of Western Birds*), on the other was capable of saying, simply, 'I am perishing . . . For God's sake pity me . . .' You see, after all, he's just like folks . . . What's this? . . . Conversely, there might appear almost a tragic condescension in remarks such as Flaubert's often quoted 'Ils sont dans le vrai' perpetuated by Kafka – Kaf – and others, and addressed to child-bearing rosy-cheeked and jolly humanity at large. Condescension, nay, inverse self-approval, something downright unnecessary. And Flaub – Why should they be dans le vrai any more than the artist was dans le vrai? All people and poets are much the same but some poets are more the same than others, as George Orwell might have said. George Or – And yet, what modern poet would be caught dead (though they'd do their best to catch him all right) with his 'For Christ's sake send aid', unrepossessed, unincinerated, to be put in a glass case? It was a truism to say that poets not only were, but looked like folks these days. Far from ostensible nonconformists, as the daily papers, the very writers themselves – more shame to them – took every opportunity triumphantly to point out, they dressed like, and as often as not were bank clerks, or, marvelous paradox, engaged in advertising. It was true. He, Sigbjørn, dressed like a bank clerk himself – how else should he have courage to go into a bank? It was questionable whether poets especially, in uttermost private, any longer allowed themselves to say things like 'For God's sake pity me!' Yes, they had become more like folks even than folks. And the despair in the glass case, all private correspondence carefully destroyed, yet destined to become ten thousand times more public than ever, viewed through the great glass case of art, was now transmuted into hieroglyphics, masterly compressions, obscurities to be deciphered by experts – yes, and poets – like Sigbjørn Wilderness. Wil –

And many others. Probably there was a good idea somewhere, lurking among these arrant self-contradictions; pity could not keep him from using it, nor a certain sense of horror that he felt all over again that these mummified and naked cries of agony should lie thus exposed to human view in permanent incorruption, as if embalmed evermore in their separate eternal funeral parlors: separate, yet not separate, for was it not as if Poe's cry from Baltimore, in a mysterious manner, in the manner that the octet of a sonnet, say, is answered by its sestet, had already been answered, seven years before, by Keats's cry from Rome; so that according to the special reality of Sigbjørn's notebook at least, Poe's own death appeared like something extra-formal, almost extraprofessional, an afterthought. Yet inerrably it was part of the same poem, the same story. 'And yet the fatal prospect hangs . . .' 'Severn, lift me up, for I am dying.' 'Lift them up, keep them away.' Dr Swell's Root Beer.

Good idea or not, there was no more room to implement his thoughts within this notebook (the notes on Poe and Richmond ran, through Fredericksburg, into his remarks upon Rome, the Mamertine Prison, and Keats's house, and vice versa), so Sigbjørn brought out another one from his trousers pocket.

This was a bigger notebook altogether, its paper stiffer and stronger, showing it dated from before the war, and he had brought it from America at the last minute, fearing that such might be hard to come by abroad.

In those days he had almost given up taking notes: every new notebook bought represented an impulse, soon to be overlaid, to write afresh; as a consequence he had accumulated a number of notebooks like this one at home, yet which were almost empty, which he had never taken with him on his more recent travels since the war, else a given trip would have seemed to start off with a destructive stoop,

from the past, in its soul: this one had looked an exception so he'd
26 packed it.

Just the same, he saw, it was not innocent of writing: several pages
at the beginning were covered with his handwriting, so shaky and
hysterical of appearance, that Sigbjørn had to put on his spectacles to
read it. Seattle, he made out. July? 1939. Seattle! Sigbjørn swallowed
some grappa hastily. Lo, death hath reared himself a throne in a
strange city lying alone far down within the dim west, where the good
and the bad and the best and the rest, have gone to their eternal worst!
The lower is the true Seattle . . . Sigbjørn felt he could be excused for
not fully appreciating Seattle, its mountain graces, in those days. For
these were not notes he had found but the draft of a letter, written in
the notebook because it was that type of letter possible for him to write
only in a bar. A bar? Well, one might have called it a bar. For in those
days, in Seattle, in the state of Washington, they still did not sell hard
liquor in bars – as, for that matter, to this day they did not, in
Richmond, in the state of Virginia – which was half the gruesome and
pointless point of his having been in the state of Washington. LIC-
OFF-PREM, he thought. No, no, go not to Virginia Dare . . . Neither
twist Pepso – tight-rooted! – for its poisonous bane. The letter dated –
no question of his recognition of it, though whether he'd made
another version and posted it he had forgotten – from absolutely the
lowest ebb of those low tides of his life, a time marked by the baleful
circumstance that the small legacy on which he then lived had been
suddenly put in charge of a Los Angeles lawyer, to whom this letter
indeed was written, his family, who considered him incompetent,
having refused to have anything further to do with him, as, in effect,
did the lawyer, who had sent him to a religious-minded family of
Buchmanite tendencies in Seattle on the understanding he be
entrusted with not more than 25c a day.

Dear Mr Van Bosch:
It is, psychologically, apart from anything else, of extreme urgency
that I leave Seattle and come to Los Angeles to see you. I fear a complete
mental collapse else. I have cooperated far beyond what I thought was
the best of my ability here in the matter of liquor and I have also tried to
work hard, so far, alas, without selling anything. I cannot say either
that my ways have been as circumscribed exactly as I thought they
would be by the Mackorkindales, who at least have seen my point of
view on some matters, and if they pray for guidance on the very few
occasions when they do see fit to exceed the stipulated 25c a day, they

are at least sympathetic with my wishes to return. This may be because the elder Mackorkindale is literally and physically worn out following me through Seattle, or because you have failed to supply sufficient means for my board, but this is certainly as far as the sympathy goes. In short, they sympathize, but cannot honestly agree; nor will they advise you I should return. And in anything that applies to my writing – and this I find almost the hardest to bear – I am met with the opinion that I 'should put all that behind me'. If they merely claimed to be abetting yourself or my parents in this it would be understandable, but this judgement is presented to me independently, somewhat blasphemously in my view – though without question they believe it – as coming directly from God, who stoops daily from on high to inform the Mackorkindales, if not in so many words, that as a serious writer I am lousy. Scenting some hidden truth about this, things being what they are, I would find it discouraging enough if it stopped there, and were not beyond that the hope held out, miraculously congruent also with that of my parents and yourself, that I could instead turn myself into a successful writer of advertisements. Since I cannot but feel, I repeat, and feel respectfully, that they are sincere in their beliefs, all I can say is that in this daily rapprochement with their Almighty in Seattle I hope some prayer that has slipped in by mistake to let the dreadful man for heaven's sake return to Los Angeles may eventually be answered. For I find it impossible to describe my spiritual isolation in this place, nor the gloom into which I have sunk. I enjoyed of course the seaside – the Mackorkindales doubtless reported to you that the Group were having a small rally in Bellingham (I wish you could go to Bellingham one day) – but I have completely exhausted any therapeutic value in my stay. God knows I ought to know, I shall never recover in this place, isolated as I am from Primrose who, whatever you may say, I want with all my heart to make my wife. It was with the greatest of anguish that I discovered that her letters to me were being opened, finally, even having to hear lectures on her moral character by those who had read these letters, which I had thus been prevented from replying to, causing such pain to her as I cannot think of. This separation from her would be an unendurable agony, without anything else, but as things stand I can only say I would be better off in a prison, in the worst dungeon that could be imagined, than to be incarcerated in this damnable place with the highest suicide rate in the Union. Literally I am dying in this macabre hole and I appeal to you to send me, out of the money that is after all mine, enough that I may return. Surely I am not the only writer, there have been others in history whose ways have been misconstrued and who have failed . . . who have won through . . . success . . . publicans and sinners . . . I have no intention –

*P*ING

Áll known all white bare white body fixed one yard legs joined like sewn. Light heat white floor one square yard never seen. White walls one yard by two white ceiling one square yard never seen. Bare white body fixed only the eyes only just. Traces blurs light grey almost white on white. Hands hanging palms front white feet heels together right angle. Light heat white planes shining white bare white body fixed ping fixed elsewhere. Traces blurs signs no meaning light grey almost white. Bare white body fixed white on white invisible. Only the eyes only just light blue almost white. Head haught eyes light blue almost white silence within. Brief murmurs only just almost never all known. Traces blurs signs no meaning light grey almost white. Legs joined like sewn heels together right angle. Traces alone unover given black light grey almost white on white. Light heat white walls shining white one yard by two. Bare white body fixed one yard ping fixed elsewhere. Traces blurs signs no meaning light grey almost white. White feet toes joined like sewn heels together right angle invisible. Eyes alone unover given blue light blue almost white. Murmur only just almost never one second perhaps not alone. Given rose only just bare white body fixed one yard white on white invisible. All white all known murmurs only just almost never always the same all known. Light heat hands hanging palms front white on white invisible. Bare white body fixed ping fixed elsewhere. Only the eyes only just light blue almost white fixed front. Ping murmur only just almost never one second perhaps a way out. Head haught eyes light blue almost white fixed front ping murmur ping silence. Eyes holes light blue almost white mouth white seam like sewn invisible. Ping murmur perhaps a nature one second almost never that much memory almost never. White walls each its trace grey blur signs no meaning light grey almost white. Light heat all known all white planes meeting invisible. Ping murmur only just almost never one second perhaps a meaning that much memory almost never. White feet toes joined like sewn heels together right angle ping elsewhere no sound. Hands hanging palms front legs joined like sewn. Head haught eyes holes light blue almost white fixed front silence within. Ping elsewhere always there but that known not. Eyes holes light blue alone unover given blue light blue almost white only colour fixed front. All white all known white planes shining white ping murmur only just almost never one second light time that much memory almost never. Bare white body fixed one yard ping fixed elsewhere white on white invisible heart breath no sound. Only the eyes given blue light blue almost white fixed front only colour alone unover. Planes meeting invisible one only shining white infinite but that known not. Nose ears while holes mouth white seam like sewn invisible. Ping murmurs only just almost never one second always the same all known. Given rose only just bare white body fixed one yard invisible all known without within. Ping perhaps a nature one second with image same time a little less blue and white in the wind. White ceiling shining white one square yard never seen ping perhaps a way out there one second ping silence. Traces alone unover given black grey blurs signs no meaning light grey almost white always the same. Ping perhaps not alone one second with image always the same same time a little less that much memory almost never ping silence. Given rose only just nails fallen white over. Long hair fallen white invisible over. White scars invisible same white as flesh torn of old given rose only just. Ping image only just almost never one second light time blue and white in the wind. Head haught nose ears white holes mouth white seam like sewn invisible over. Only the eyes given blue fixed front light blue almost white only colour alone unover. Light heat white planes shining white one only shining white infinite but that known not. Ping a nature only just almost never one second with image same time a little less blue and white in the wind. Traces blurs light grey eyes holes light blue almost white fixed front ping a meaning only just almost never ping silence. Bare white one yard fixed ping fixed elsewhere no sound legs joined like sewn heels together right angle hands hanging palms front. Head haught eyes holes light blue almost white fixed front silence within. Ping elsewhere always there but that known not. Ping perhaps not alone one second with image same time a little less dim eye black and white half closed long lashes imploring that much memory almost never. Afar flash of time all white all over all of old ping flash white walls shining white no trace eyes holes light blue almost white last colour ping white over. Ping fixed last elsewhere legs joined like sewn heels together right angle hands hanging palms front head haught eyes white invisible fixed front over. Given rose only just one yard invisible bare white all known without within over. White ceiling never seen ping of old only just almost never one second light time white floor never seen ping of old perhaps there. Ping of old only just perhaps a meaning a nature one second almost never blue and white in the wind that much memory henceforth never. White planes no trace shining white one only shining white infinite but that known not. Light heat all known all white heart breath no sound. Head haught eyes white fixed front old ping last murmur one second perhaps not alone eye unlustrous black and white half closed long lashes imploring ping silence ping over.

Translated from the French by the author

ELIZABETH BOWEN

MYSTERIOUS KOR

Full moonlight drenched the city and searched it; there was not a niche left to stand in. The effect was remorseless: London looked like the moon's capital – shallow, cratered, extinct. It was late, but not yet midnight; now the buses had stopped the polished roads and streets in this region sent for minutes together a ghostly unbroken reflection up. The soaring new flats and the crouching old shops and houses looked equally brittle under the moon, which blazed in windows that looked its way. The futility of the black-out became laughable: from the sky, presumably, you could see every slate in the roofs, every whited kerb, every contour of the naked winter flowerbeds in the park; and the lake, with its shining twists and tree-darkened islands would be a landmark for miles, yes, miles, overhead.

However, the sky, in whose glassiness floated no clouds but only opaque balloons, remained glassy-silent. The Germans no longer came by the full moon. Something more immaterial seemed to threaten, and to be keeping people at home. This day between days, this extra tax, was perhaps more than senses and nerves could bear. People stayed indoors with a fervour that could be felt: the buildings strained with battened-down human life, but not a beam, not a voice, not a note from a radio escaped. Now and then under streets and buildings the earth rumbled: the Underground sounded loudest at this time.

Outside the now gateless gates of the park, the road coming downhill from the north-west turned south and became a street, down whose perspective the traffic lights went through their unmeaning performance of changing colour. From the promontory of pavement outside the gates you saw at once up the road and down the street: from behind where you stood, between the gate-posts, appeared the lesser strangeness of grass and water and trees. At this point, at this moment, three French soldiers, directed to a hostel they could not find, stopped singing to listen derisively to the waterbirds wakened up by the moon. Next, two wardens coming off duty emerged from their post and crossed the road diagonally, each with an elbow cupped inside a slung-on tin hat. The wardens turned their faces, mauve in the moonlight, towards the Frenchmen with no expression at all. The two sets of steps died in opposite directions, and, the birds subsiding, nothing was heard or seen until, a little way down the street, a trickle of people came out of the Underground, around the anti-panic brick wall. These all disappeared quickly, in an abashed way, or as though dissolved in the street by some white acid, but for a girl and a soldier who, by their way of walking, seemed to have no destination but each other and to be not quite certain even of that. Blotted into one shadow he tall, she little, these two proceeded towards the park. They looked in, but did not go in; they stood there debating without speaking. Then, as though a command from the street behind them had been received by their synchronized bodies, they faced round to look back the way they had come.

His look up the height of a building made his head drop back, and she saw his eyeballs glitter. She slid her hand from his sleeve, stepped to the edge of the pavement and said: 'Mysterious Kôr.'

'What is?' he said, not quite collecting himself.

'This is –

> *"Mysterious Kôr thy walls forsaken stand,*
> *Thy lonely towers beneath a lonely moon –"*

– this is Kôr.'

'Why,' he said, 'it's years since I've thought of that.'

She said: 'I think of it all the time –

> *"Not in the waste beyond the swamps and sand,*
> *The fever-haunted forest and lagoon,*
> *Mysterious Kôr thy walls –"*

– a completely forsaken city, as high as cliffs and as white as bones, with no history –'

'But something must once have happened: why had it been forsaken?'

'How could anyone tell you when there's nobody there?'

'Nobody there since how long?'

'Thousands of years.'

'In that case, it would have fallen down.'

34 'No, not Kôr,' she said with immediate authority. 'Kôr's altogether different; it's very strong; there is not a crack in it anywhere for a weed to grow in; the corners of stones and the monuments might have been cut yesterday, and the stairs and arches are built to support themselves.'

'You know all about it,' he said, looking at her.

'I know, I know all about it.'

'What, since you read that book?'

'Oh, I didn't get much from that; I just got the name. I knew that must be the right name; it's like a cry.'

'Most like the cry of a crow to me.' He reflected, then said: 'But the poem begins with "Not" – "*Not in the waste beyond the swamps and sand* –" And it goes on, as I remember, to prove Kôr's not really anywhere. When even a poem says there's no such place –'

'What it tries to say doesn't matter: I see what it makes me see. Anyhow, that was written some time ago, at that time when they thought they had got everything taped, because the whole world had been explored, even the middle of Africa. Every thing and place had been found and marked on some map; so what wasn't marked on any map couldn't be there at all. So *they* thought: that was why he wrote the poem. "*The world is disenchanted*", it goes on. That was what set me off hating civilization.'

'Well, cheer up,' he said; 'there isn't much of it left.'

'Oh, yes, I cheered up some time ago. This war shows we've by no means come to the end. If you can blow whole places out of existence, you can blow whole places into it. I don't see why not. They say we can't say what's come out since the bombing started. By the time we've come to the end, Kôr may be the one city left: the abiding city. I should laugh.'

'No, you wouldn't,' he said sharply. '*You* wouldn't – at least, I hope not. I hope you don't know what you're saying – does the moon make you funny?'

'Don't be cross about Kôr; please don't, Arthur,' she said.

'I thought girls thought about people.'

'What, these days?' she said. 'Think about people? How can anyone think about people if they've got any heart? I don't know how other girls manage: I always think about Kôr.'

'Not about me?' he said. When she did not at once answer, he turned her hand over, in anguish, inside his grasp. 'Because I'm not there when you want me – is that my fault?'

'But to think about Kôr *is* to think about you and me.'

'In that dead place?'

'No, ours – we'd be alone here.'

Tightening his thumb on her palm while he thought this over, he looked behind them, around them, above them – even up at the sky. He said finally: 'But we're alone here.'

'That was why I said "Mysterious Kôr".'

'What, you mean we're there now, that here's there, that now's then? . . . *I* don't mind,' he added, letting out as a laugh the sigh he had been holding in for some time. 'You ought to know the place, and for all I could tell you we might be anywhere: I often do have it, this funny feeling, the first minute or two when I've come up out of the Underground. Well, well: join the Army and see the world.' He nodded towards the perspective of traffic lights and said, a shade craftily: 'What are those, then?'

Having caught the quickest possible breath, she replied: 'Inexhaustible gases; they bored through to them and lit them as they came up; by changing colour they show the changing of minutes; in Kôr there is no sort of other time.'

'You've got the moon, though: that can't help making months.'

'Oh, and the sun, of course; but those two could do what they liked; we should not have to calculate when they'd come or go.'

'We might not have to,' he said, 'but I bet I should.'

'I should not mind what you did, so long as you never said, "What next?"'

'I don't know about "next", but I do know what we'd do first.'

'What, Arthur?'

'Populate Kôr.'

She said: 'I suppose it would be all right if our children were to marry each other?'

But her voice faded out; she had been reminded that they were homeless on this his first night of leave. They were, that was to say, in London without any hope of any place of their own. Pepita shared a two-roomed flatlet with a girl friend, in a by-street off the Regent's Park Road, and towards this they must make their half-hearted way. Arthur was to have the sitting-room divan, usually occupied by Pepita, while she herself had half of her girl friend's bed. There was really no room for a third, and least of all for a man, in those small rooms packed with furniture and the two girls' belongings: Pepita tried to be grateful for her friend Callie's forbearance – but how could

she be, when it had not occurred to Callie that she would do better to
be away tonight? She was more slow-witted than narrow-minded – but
Pepita felt she owed a kind of ruin to her. Callie, not yet known to be
home later than ten, would be now waiting up, in her house-coat, to
welcome Arthur. That would mean three-sided chat, drinking cocoa,
then turning in: that would be that, and that would be all. That was
London, this war – they were lucky to have a roof – London, full
enough before the Americans came. Not a place: they would even
grudge you sharing a grave – that was what even married couples
complained. Whereas in Kôr . . .

In Kôr . . . Like glass, the illusion shattered: a car hummed like a
hornet towards them, veered, showed its scarlet tail-light, streaked
away up the road. A woman edged round a front door and along the
area railings timidly called her cat; meanwhile a clock near, then
another set further back in the dazzling distance, set about striking
midnight. Pepita, feeling Arthur release her arm with an abruptness
that was the inverse of passion, shivered; whereat he asked brusquely:
'Cold? Well, Which way? – we'd better be getting on.'

Callie was no longer waiting up. Hours ago she had set out the three
cups and saucers, the tins of cocoa and household milk and, on the
gas-ring, brought the kettle to just short of the boil. She had turned
open Arthur's bed, the living-room divan, in the neat inviting way she
had learnt at home – then, with a modest impulse, replaced the cover.
She had, as Pepita foresaw, been wearing her cretonne house-coat, the
nearest thing to a hostess gown that she had; she had already brushed
her hair for the night, rebraided it, bound the braids in a coronet
round her head. Both lights and the wireless had been on, to make the
room both look and sound gay: all alone, she had come to that peak
moment at which company should arrive – but so seldom does. From
then on she felt welcome beginning to wither in her, a flower of the
heart that had bloomed too early. There she had sat like an image,
facing the three cold cups, on the edge of the bed to be occupied by an
unknown man.

Callie's innocence and her still unsought-out state had brought her
to take a proprietary pride in Arthur; this was all the stronger,
perhaps, because they had not yet met. Sharing the flat with Pepita,
this last year, she had been content with reflecting the heat of love. It
was not, surprisingly, that Pepita seemed very happy – there were
times when she was palpably on the rack, and this was not what Callie

could understand. 'Surely you owe it to Arthur,' she would then say, 'to keep cheerful? So long as you love each other –' Callie's calm brow glowed – one might say that it glowed in place of her friend's; she became the guardian of that ideality which for Pepita was constantly lost to view. It was true, with the sudden prospect of Arthur's leave, things had come nearer to earth: he became a proposition, and she would have been as glad if he could have slept somewhere else. Physically shy, a brotherless virgin, Callie shrank from sharing this flat with a young man. In this flat you could hear everything: what was once a three-windowed Victorian drawing-room had been partitioned, by very thin walls, into kitchenette, living-room, Callie's bedroom. The living-room was in the centre; the two others open off it. What was once the conservatory, half a flight down, was now converted into a draughty bathroom, shared with somebody else on the girls' floor. The flat, for these days, was cheap – even so, it was Callie, earning more than Pepita, who paid the greater part of the rent: it thus became up to her, more or less, to express good will as to Arthur's making a third. 'Why, it will be lovely to have him here,' Callie said. Pepita accepted the good will without much grace – but then, had she ever much grace to spare? – she was as restlessly secretive, as self-centred, as a little half-grown black cat. Next came a puzzling moment: Pepita seemed to be hinting that Callie should fix herself up somewhere else. 'But where would I go?' Callie marvelled when this was at last borne in on her. 'You know what London's like now. And, anyway' – here she laughed, but hers was a forehead that coloured as easily as it glowed – 'it wouldn't be proper, would it, me going off and leaving just you and Arthur; I don't know what your mother would say to me. No, we may be a little squashed, but we'll make things ever so homey. I shall not mind playing gooseberry, really, dear.'

But the hominess by now was evaporating, as Pepita and Arthur still and still did not come. At half-past ten, in obedience to the rule of the house, Callie was obliged to turn off the wireless, whereupon silence out of the stepless street began seeping into the slighted room. Callie recollected the fuel target and turned off her dear little table lamp, gaily painted with spots to make it look like a toadstool, thereby leaving only the hanging light. She laid her hand on the kettle, to find it gone cold again and sigh for the wasted gas if not for her wasted thought. Where are they? Cold crept up her out of the kettle; she went to bed.

Callie's bed lay along the wall under the window: she did not like sleeping so close up under glass, but the clearance that must be left for the opening of door and cupboards made this the only possible place. Now she got in and lay rigidly on the bed's inner side, under the hanging hems of the window curtains, training her limbs not to stray to what would be Pepita's half. This sharing of her bed with another body would not be the least of her sacrifice to the lovers' love; tonight would be the first night – or at least, since she was an infant – that Callie had slept with anyone. Child of a sheltered middle-class household, she had kept physical distances all her life. Already repugnance and shyness ran through her limbs; she was preyed upon by some more obscure trouble than the expectation that she might not sleep. As to *that*, Pepita was restless; her tossings on the divan, her broken-off exclamations and blurred pleas had been to be heard, most nights, through the dividing wall.

Callie knew, as though from a vision, that Arthur would sleep soundly, with assurance and majesty. Did they not all say, too, that a soldier sleeps like a log? With awe she pictured, asleep, the face that she had not yet, awake, seen – Arthur's man's eyelids, cheek-bones and set mouth turned up to the darkened ceiling. Wanting to savour darkness herself, Callie reached out and put off her bedside lamp.

At once she knew that something was happening – outdoors, in the street, the whole of London, the world. An advance, an extraordinary movement was silently taking place; blue-white beams overflowed from it, silting, dropping round the edges of the muffling black-out curtains. When, starting up, she knocked a fold of the curtain, a beam like a mouse ran across her bed. A searchlight, the most powerful of all time, might have been turned full and steady upon her defended window; finding flaws in the black-out stuff, it made veins and stars. Once gained by this idea of pressure she could not lie down again; she sat tautly, drawn-up knees touching her breasts, and asked herself if there were anything she should do. She parted the curtains, opened them slowly wider, looked out – and was face to face with the moon.

Below the moon, the houses opposite her window blazed back in transparent shadow; and something – was it a coin or a ring? – glittered half-way across the chalk-white street. Light marched in past her face, and she turned to see where it went: out stood the curves and garlands of the great white marble Victorian mantelpiece of that lost drawing-room; out stood, in the photographs turned her way, the thoughts with which her parents had faced the camera, and the humble puzzlement of her two dogs at home. Of silver brocade, just faintly purpled with roses, became her house-coat hanging over the chair. And the moon did more: it exonerated and beautified the lateness of the lovers' return. No wonder, she said to herself, no wonder – if this was the world they walked in, if this was whom they were with. Having drunk in the white explanation, Callie lay down again. Her half of the bed was in shadow, but she allowed one hand to lie, blanched, in what would be Pepita's place. She lay and looked at the hand until it was no longer her own.

Callie woke to the sound of Pepita's key in the latch. But no voices? What had happened? Then she heard Arthur's step. She heard his unslung equipment dropped with a weary, dull sound, and the plonk of his tin hat on a wooden chair. 'Sssh-sssh!' Pepita exclaimed, 'she *might* be asleep!'

Then at last Arthur's voice: 'But I thought you said –'

'I'm not asleep; I'm just coming!' Callie called out with rapture, leaping out from her form in shadow into the moonlight, zipping on her enchanted house-coat over her nightdress, kicking her shoes on, and pinning in place, with a trembling firmness, her plaits in their coronet round her head. Between these movements of hers she heard not another sound. Had she only dreamed they were there? Her heart beat: she stepped through the living-room, shutting her door behind her.

Pepita and Arthur stood the other side of the table; they gave the impression of being lined up. Their faces, at different levels – for Pepita's rough, dark head came only an inch above Arthur's khaki shoulder – were alike in abstention from any kind of expression; as though, spiritually, they both still refused to be here. Their features looked faint, weathered – was this the work of the moon? Pepita said at once: 'I suppose we are very late?'

'I don't wonder,' Callie said, 'on this lovely night.'

Arthur had not raised his eyes; he was looking at the three cups. Pepita now suddenly jogged his elbow, saying, 'Arthur, wake up; say something; this is Callie – well, Callie, this is Arthur, of course.'

'Why, yes of course this is Arthur,' returned Callie, whose candid eyes since she entered had not left Arthur's face. Perceiving that Arthur did not know what to do, she advanced round the table to shake hands with him. He looked up, she looked down, for the first time: she rather beheld than felt his red-brown grip on what still seemed her glove of moonlight. 'Welcome, Arthur,' she said. 'I'm so glad to meet you at last. I hope you will be comfortable in the flat.'

'It's been kind of you,' he said after consideration.

'Please do not feel that,' said Callie. 'This is Pepita's home, too, and we both hope – don't we, Pepita? – that you'll regard it as yours. Please feel free to do just as you like. I am sorry it is so small.'

'Oh, I don't know,' Arthur said, as though hypnotized; 'it seems a nice little place.'

Pepita, meanwhile, glowered and turned away.

Arthur continued to wonder, though he had once been told, how these two unalike girls had come to set up together – Pepita so small, except for her too-big head, compact of childish brusqueness and of unchildish passion, and Callie, so sedate, waxy and tall – an unlit candle. Yes, she was like one of those candles on sale outside a church; there could be something votive even in her demeanour. She was unconscious that her good manners, those of an old fashioned country doctor's daughter, were putting the other two at a disadvantage. He found himself touched by the grave good faith with which Callie was wearing that tartish house-coat, above which her face kept the glaze of sleep; and, as she knelt to relight the gas-ring under the kettle, he marked the strong, delicate arch of one bare foot, disappearing into the arty green shoe. Pepita was now too near him ever again to be seen as he now saw Callie – in a sense, he never *had* seen Pepita for the first time: she had not been, and still sometimes was not, his type. No, he had not thought of her twice; he had not remembered her until he began to remember her with passion. You might say he had not seen Pepita coming: their love had been a collision in the dark.

Callie, determined to get this over, knelt back and said: 'Would Arthur like to wash his hands?' When they had heard him stumble down the half-flight of stairs, she said to Pepita: 'Yes, I was so glad you had the moon.'

'Why?' said Pepita. She added: 'There was too much of it.'

'You're tired. Arthur looks tired, too.'

'How would you know? He's used to marching about. But it's all this having no place to go.'

'But, Pepita, you –'

But at this point Arthur came back: from the door he noticed the wireless, and went direct to it. 'Nothing much on now, I suppose?' he doubtfully said.

'No; you see it's past midnight; we're off the air. And, anyway, in this house they don't like the wireless late. By the same token,' went on Callie, friendly smiling, 'I'm afraid I must ask you, Arthur, to take **41** your boots off, unless, of course, you mean to stay sitting down. The people below us –'

Pepita flung off, saying something under her breath, but Arthur, remarking, 'No, I don't mind,' both sat down and began to take off his boots. Pausing, glancing to left and right at the divan's fresh cotton spread, he said: 'It's all right is it, for me to sit on this?'

'That's my bed,' said Pepita. 'You are to sleep in it.'

Callie then made the cocoa, after which they turned in. Preliminary trips to the bathroom having been worked out, Callie was first to retire, shutting the door behind her so that Pepita and Arthur might kiss each other good night. When Pepita joined her, it was without knocking: Pepita stood still in the moon and began to tug off her clothes. Glancing with hate at the bed, she asked: 'Which side?'

'I expected you'd like the outside.'

'What are you standing about for?'

'I don't really know: as I'm inside I'd better get in first.'

'Then why not get in?'

When they had settled rigidly, side by side, Callie asked: 'Do you think Arthur's got all he wants?'

Pepita jerked her head up. 'We can't sleep in all this moon.'

'Why, you don't believe the moon does things, actually?'

'Well, it couldn't hope to make some of us *much* more screwy.'

Callie closed the curtains, then said: 'What do you mean? And – didn't you hear? – I asked if Arthur's got all he wants.'

'That's what I meant – have you got a screw loose, really?'

'Pepita, I won't stay here if you're going to be like this.'

'In that case, you had better go in with Arthur.'

'What about me?' Arthur loudly said through the wall. 'I can hear practically all you girls are saying.'

They were both startled – rather that than abashed. Arthur, alone in there, had thrown off the ligatures of his social manner: his voice held the whole authority of his sex – he was impatient, sleepy, and he belonged to no one.

'Sorry,' the girls said in unison. Then Pepita laughed soundlessly, making their bed shake, till to stop herself she bit the back of her hand, and this movement made her elbow strike Callie's cheek. 'Sorry,' she had to whisper. No answer: Pepita fingered her elbow and found, yes, it was quite true, it was wet. 'Look, shut up crying, Callie: what have I done?'

Callie rolled right round, in order to press her forehead closely under the window, into the curtains, against the wall. Her weeping continued to be soundless: now and then, unable to reach her handkerchief, she staunched her eyes with a curtain, disturbing slivers of moon. Pepita gave up marvelling, and soon slept: at least there is something in being dog-tired.

A clock struck four as Callie woke up again – but something else had made her open her swollen eyelids. Arthur, stumbling about on his padded feet, could be heard next door attempting to make no noise. Inevitably, he bumped the edge of the table. Callie sat up: by her side Pepita lay like a mummy rolled half over, in forbidding, tenacious sleep. Arthur groaned. Callie caught a breath, climbed lightly over Pepita, felt for her torch on the mantelpiece, stopped to listen again. Arthur groaned again: Callie, with movements soundless as they were certain, opened the door and slipped through to the living-room. 'What's the matter?' she whispered. 'Are you ill?'

'No; I just got a cigarette. Did I wake you up?'

'But you groaned.'

'I'm sorry; I'd no idea.'

'But do you often?'

'I've no idea, really, I tell you,' Arthur repeated. The air of the room was dense with his presence, overhung by tobacco. He must be sitting on the edge of his bed, wrapped up in his overcoat – she could smell the coat, and each time he pulled on the cigarette his features appeared down there, in the fleeting, dull reddish glow. 'Where are you?' he said. 'Show a light.'

Her nervous touch on her torch, like a reflex to what he said, made it flicker up for a second. 'I am just by the door; Pepita's asleep; I'd better go back to bed.'

'Listen. Do you two get on each other's nerves?'

'Not till tonight,' said Callie, watching the uncertain swoops of the cigarette as he reached across to the ashtray on the edge of the table. Shifting her bare feet patiently, she added: 'You don't see us as we usually are.'

'She's a girl who shows things in funny ways – I expect she feels bad at our putting you out like this – I know I do. But then we'd got no choice, had we?'

'It is really I who am putting you out,' said Callie.

'Well, that can't be helped either, can it? You had the right to stay in your own place. If there'd been more time, we might have gone to the **43** country, though I still don't see where we'd have gone there. It's one harder when you're not married, unless you've got the money. Smoke?'

'No, thank you. Well, if you're all right, I'll go back to bed.'

'I'm glad she's asleep – funny the way she sleeps, isn't it? You can't help wondering where she is. You haven't got a boy, have you, just at present?'

'No. I've never had one.'

'I'm not sure in one way that you're not better off. I can see there's not so much in it for a girl these days. It makes me feel cruel the way I unsettle her: I don't know how much it's me myself or how much it's something the matter that I can't help. How are any of us to know how things could have been? They forget war's not just only war; it's years out of people's lives that they've never had before and won't have again. Do you think she's fanciful?'

'Who, Pepita?'

'It's enough to make her – tonight was the pay-off. We couldn't get near any movie or any place for sitting; you had to fight into the bars, and she hates the staring in bars, and with all that milling about, every street we went, they kept on knocking her even off my arm. So then we took the tube to that park down there, but the place was as bad as daylight, let alone it was cold. We hadn't the nerve – well, that's nothing to do with you.'

'I don't mind.'

'Or else you don't understand. So we began to play – we were off in Kôr.'

'Core of what?'

'Mysterious Kôr – ghost city.'

'Where?'

'You may ask. But I could have sworn she saw it, and from the way she saw it I saw it, too. A game's a game, but what's a hallucination? You begin by laughing, then it gets in you and you can't laugh it off. I tell you, I woke up just now not knowing where I'd been; and I had to get up and feel round this table before I even knew where I was. It wasn't till then that I thought of a cigarette. Now I see why she sleeps like that, if that's where she goes.'

'But she is just as often restless; I often hear her.'

'Then she doesn't always make it. Perhaps it takes me, in some way

– Well, I can't see any harm: when two people have got no place, why not want Kôr, as a start? There are no restrictions on wanting, at any rate.'

'But, oh, Arthur, can't wanting want what's human?'

He yawned. 'To be human's to be at a dead loss.' Stopping yawning, he ground out his cigarette: the china tray skidded at the edge of the table. 'Bring that light here a moment – that is, will you? I think I've messed ash all over these sheets of hers.'

Callie advanced with the torch alight, but at arm's length: now and then her thumb made the beam wobble. She watched the lit-up inside of Arthur's hand as he brushed the sheet; and once he looked up to see her white-nightgowned figure curving above and away from him, behind the arc of light. 'What's that swinging?'

'One of my plaits of hair. Shall I open the window wider?'

'What, to let the smoke out? Go on. And how's your moon?'

'Mine?' Marvelling over this, as the first sign that Arthur remembered that she was Callie, she uncovered the window, pushed up the sash, then after a minute said: 'Not so strong.'

Indeed, the moon's power over London and the imagination had now declined. The siege of light had relaxed; the search was over; the street had a look of survival and no more. Whatever had glittered there, coin or ring, was now invisible or had gone. To Callie it seemed likely that there would never be such a moon again; and on the whole she felt this was for the best. Feeling air reach in like a tired arm round her body, she dropped the curtains against it and returned to her own room.

Back by her bed, she listened: Pepita's breathing still had the regular sound of sleep. At the other side of the wall the divan creaked as Arthur stretched himself out again. Having felt ahead of her lightly, to make sure her half was empty, Callie climbed over Pepita and got in. A certain amount of warmth had travelled between the sheets from Pepita's flank, and in this Callie extended her sword-cold body: she tried to compose her limbs; even they quivered after Arthur's words in the dark, words *to* the dark. The loss of her own mysterious expectation, of her love for love, was a small thing beside the war's total of unlived lives. Suddenly Pepita flung out one hand: its back knocked Callie lightly across the face.

Pepita had now turned over and lay with her face up. The hand that had struck Callie must have lain over the other, which grasped the pyjama collar. Her eyes, in the dark, might have been either shut or

open, but nothing made her frown more or less steadily: it became
certain, after another moment, that Pepita's act of justice had been 45
unconscious. She still lay, as she had lain, in an avid dream, of which
Arthur had been the source, of which Arthur was not the end. With
him she looked this way, that way, down the wide, void, pure streets,
between statues, pillars and shadows, through archways and col-
onnades. With him she went up the stairs down which nothing but
moon came; with him trod the ermine dust of the endless halls, stood
on terraces, mounted the extreme tower, looked down on the statued
squares, the wide, void, pure streets. He was the password, but not
the answer: it was to Kôr's finality that she turned.

V. S. PRITCHETT

A FAMILY MAN

Late in the afternoon, when she had given him up and had even changed out of her pink dress into her smock and jeans and was working once more at her bench, the doorbell rang. William had come, after all. It was in the nature of their love affair that his visits were fitful: he had a wife and children. To show that she understood the situation, even found the curious satisfaction of reverie in his absences that lately had lasted several weeks, Berenice dawdled yawning to the door. As she slipped off the chain, she called back into the empty flat, 'It's all right, Father. I'll answer it.'

William had told her to do this because she was a woman living on her own: the call would show strangers that there was a man there to defend her. Berenice's voice was mocking, for she thought his idea possessive and ridiculous; not only that, she had been brought up by Quakers and thought it wrong to tell or act a lie. Sometimes, when she opened the door to him, she would say, 'Well! Mr Cork', to remind him he was a married man. He had the kind of shadowed handsomeness that easily gleams with guilt, and for her this gave their affair its piquancy.

But now – when she opened the door – no William, and the yawn, its hopes and its irony, died on her mouth. A very large woman, taller than herself, filled the doorway from top to bottom, an enormous blob of pink jersey and green skirt, the jersey low and loose at the neck, a face and body inflated to the point of speechlessness. She even seemed to be asleep with her large blue eyes open.

'Yes?' said Berenice.

The woman woke up and looked unbelievingly at Berenice's feet, which were bare, for she liked to go about barefoot at home, and said, 'Is this Miss Foster's place?'

Berenice was offended by the word 'place'. 'This is Miss Foster's residence. I am she.'

'Ah,' said the woman, babyish no longer but sugary. 'I was given your address at the College. You teach at the College, I believe? I've come about the repair.'

'A repair? I make jewellery,' said Berenice. 'I do not do repairs.'

'They told me at the College you were repairing my husband's flute. I am Mrs Cork.'

Berenice's heart stopped. Her wrist went weak and her hand drooped on the door handle, and a spurt of icy air shot up her body to her face and then turned to boiling heat as it shot back again. Her head suddenly filled with chattering voices saying, Oh, God. How frightful! William, you didn't tell her? Now, what are you, you, you going to do. And the word 'Do, do' clattered on in her head.

'Cork?' said Berenice. 'Flute?'

'Florence Cork,' said the woman firmly, all sleepy sweetness gone.

'Oh, yes. I am sorry. Mrs Cork. Of course, yes. Oh, do come in. I'm so sorry. We haven't met, how very nice to meet you. William's – Mr Cork's – flute! His flute. Yes, I remember. How d'you do? How is he? He hasn't been to the College for months. Have you seen him lately – how silly, of course you have. Did you have a lovely holiday? Did the children enjoy it? I would have posted it, only I didn't know your address. Come in, please, come in.'

'In here?' said Mrs Cork and marched into the front room where Berenice worked. Here, in the direct glare of Berenice's working lamp, Florence Cork looked even larger and even pregnant. She seemed to occupy the whole of the room as she stood in it, memorizing everything – the bench, the pots of paintbrushes, the large designs pinned to the wall, the rolls of paper, the sofa covered with papers and letters and sewing, the pink dress which Berenice had thrown over a chair. She seemed to be consuming it all, drinking all the air.

But here, in the disorder of which she was very vain, which indeed fascinated her, and represented her talent, her independence, a girl's right to a life of her own, and above all, being barefooted, helped Berenice recover her breath.

'It is such a pleasure to meet you. Mr Cork has often spoken of you to us at the College. We're quite a family there. Please sit. I'll move the dress. I was mending it.'

But Mrs Cork did not sit down. She gave a sudden lurch towards the bench, and seeing her husband's flute there propped against the wall, she grabbed it and swung it above her head as if it were a weapon.

'Yes,' said Berenice, who was thinking, Oh, dear, the woman's drunk, 'I was working on it only this morning. I had never seen a flute like that before. Such a beautiful silver scroll. I gather it's very old, a German one, a presentation piece given to Mr Cork's father. I believe he played in a famous orchestra – where was it? – Bayreuth or Berlin? You never see a scroll like that in England, not a delicate silver scroll like that. It seems to have been dropped somewhere or have had a blow. Mr Cork told me he had played it in an orchestra himself once, Covent Garden or somewhere . . .'

She watched Mrs Cork flourish the flute in the air.

'A blow,' cried Mrs Cork, now in a rich voice. 'I'll say it did. I threw it at him.'

And then she lowered her arm and stood swaying on her legs as she confronted Berenice and said, 'Where is he?'

'Who?' said Berenice in a fright.

'My husband!' Mrs Cork shouted. 'Don't try and soft-soap me with all that twaddle. Playing in an orchestra! Is that what he has been stuffing you up with? I know what you and he are up to. He comes every Thursday. He's been here since half past two. I know. I have had this place watched.'

She swung round to the closed door of Berenice's bedroom. 'What's in there?' she shouted and advanced to it.

'Mrs Cork,' said Berenice as calmly as she could. 'Please stop shouting. I know nothing about your husband. I don't know what you are talking about.' And she placed herself before the door of the room. 'And please stop shouting. That is my father's room.' And, excited by Mrs Cork's accusation, she said, 'He is a very old man and he is not well. He is asleep in there.'

'In there?' said Mrs Cork.

'Yes, in there.'

'And what about the other rooms? Who lives upstairs?'

'There are no other rooms,' said Berenice. 'I live here with my father. Upstairs? Some new people have moved in.'

Berenice was astonished by these words of hers, for she was a truthful young woman and was astonished, even excited, by a lie so vast. It seemed to glitter in the air as she spoke it.

Mrs Cork was checked. She flopped down on the chair on which Berenice had put her dress.

'My dress, if you please,' said Berenice and pulled it away.

'If you don't do it here,' said Mrs Cork, quietening and with tears in her eyes, 'you do it somewhere else.'

'I don't know anything about your husband. I only see him at the
College like the other teachers. I don't know anything about him. If **49**
you will give me the flute, I will pack it up for you and I must ask you
to go.'

'You can't deceive me. I know everything. You think because you
are young you can do what you like,' Mrs Cork muttered to herself and
began rummaging in her handbag.

For Berenice one of the attractions of William was that their
meetings were erratic. The affair was like a game: she liked surprise
above all. In the intervals when he was not there, the game continued
for her. She liked imagining what he and his family were doing. She
saw them as all glued together as if in some enduring and absurd
photograph, perhaps sitting in their suburban garden, or standing
beside a motorcar, always in the sun, but William himself, dark-faced
and busy in his gravity, a step or two back from them.

'Is your wife beautiful?' she asked him once when they were in bed.

William in his slow serious way took a long time to answer. He said
at last, 'Very beautiful.'

This had made Berenice feel exceedingly beautiful herself. She saw
his wife as a raven-haired, dark-eyed woman and longed to meet her.
The more she imagined her, the more she felt for her, the more she
saw eye to eye with her in the pleasant busy middle ground of
womanish feelings and moods, for as a woman living alone she felt a
firm loyalty to her sex. During this last summer when the family were
on holiday she had seen them glued together again as they sat with
dozens of other families in the aeroplane that was taking them abroad,
so that it seemed to her that the London sky was rumbling day after
day, night after night, with matrimony thirty thousand feet above the
city, the countryside, the sea and its beaches where she imagined the
legs of their children running across the sand, William flushed with
his responsibilities, his wife turning to brown her back in the sun.
Berenice was often out and about with her many friends, most of
whom were married. She loved the look of harassed contentment,
even the tired faces of the husbands, the alert looks of their spirited
wives. Among the married she felt her singularity. She listened to
their endearments and to their bickerings. She played with their
children, who ran at once to her. She could not bear the young men
who approached her, talking about themselves all the time, flashing
with the slapdash egotism of young men trying to bring her peculiarity
to an end. Among families she felt herself to be strange and necessary –

a necessary secret. When William had said his wife was beautiful, she felt so beautiful herself that her bones seemed to turn to water.

But now the real Florence sat rummaging in her bag before her, this balloon-like giant, first babyish and then shouting accusations, the dreamt-of Florence vanished. This real Florence seemed unreal and incredible. And William himself changed. His good looks began to look commonplace and shady: his seriousness became furtive, his praise of her calculating. He was shorter than his wife, his face now looked hang-dog, and she saw him dragging his feet as obediently he followed her. She resented that this woman had made her tell a lie, strangely intoxicating though it was to do so, and had made her feel as ugly as his wife was. For she must be, if Florence was what he called 'beautiful'. And not only ugly, but pathetic and without dignity.

Berenice watched warily as the woman took a letter from her handbag.

'Then what is this necklace?' she said, blowing herself out again.

'What necklace is this?' said Berenice.

'Read it. You wrote it.'

Berenice smiled with astonishment: she knew she needed no longer defend herself. She prided herself on fastidiousness: she had never in her life written a letter to a lover – it would be like giving something of herself away, it would be almost an indecency. She certainly felt it to be very wrong to read anyone else's letters, as Mrs Cork pushed the letter at her. Berenice took it in two fingers, glanced and turned it over to see the name of the writer.

'This is not my writing,' she said. The hand was sprawling; her own was scratchy and small. 'Who is Bunny? Who is Rosie?'

Mrs Cork snatched the letter and read in a booming voice that made the words ridiculous: '"I am longing for the necklace. Tell that girl to hurry up. Do bring it next time. And darling, don't forget the flute!!! Rosie." What do you mean, who is Bunny?' Mrs Cork said. 'You know very well. Bunny is my husband.'

Berenice turned away and pointed to a small poster that was pinned to the wall. It contained a photograph of a necklace and three brooches she had shown at an exhibition in a very fashionable shop known for selling modern jewellery. At the bottom of the poster, elegantly printed, were the words

Created by Berenice

Berenice read the words aloud, reciting them as if they were a line from a poem: 'My name is Berenice,' she said.

It was strange to be speaking the truth. And it suddenly seemed to her, as she recited the words, that really William had never been to her flat, that he had never been her lover, and had never played his silly flute there, that indeed he was the most boring man at the College and that a chasm separated her from this woman, whom jealousy had made so ugly.

Mrs Cork was still swelling with unbelief, but as she studied the poster, despair settled on her face. 'I found it in his pocket,' she said helplessly.

'We all make mistakes, Mrs Cork,' Berenice said coldly across the chasm. And then, to be generous in victory, she said, 'Let me see the letter again.'

Mrs Cork gave her the letter and Berenice read it and at the word 'flute' a doubt came into her head. Her hand began to tremble and quickly she gave the letter back. 'Who gave you my address – I mean, at the College?' Berenice accused. 'There is a rule that no addresses are given. Or telephone numbers.'

'The girl,' said Mrs Cork, defending herself.

'Which girl? At Enquiries?'

'She fetched someone.'

'Who was it?' said Berenice.

'I don't know. It began with a W, I think,' said Mrs Cork.

'Wheeler?' said Berenice. 'There is a Mr Wheeler.'

'No, it wasn't a man. It was a young woman. With a W – Glowitz.'

'That begins with a G,' said Berenice.

'No,' said Mrs Cork out of her muddle, now afraid of Berenice. 'Glowitz was the name.'

'Glowitz,' said Berenice, unbelieving. 'Rosie Glowitz. She's not young.'

'I didn't notice,' said Mrs Cork. 'Is her name Rosie?'

Berenice felt giddy and cold. The chasm between herself and Mrs Cork closed up.

'Yes,' said Berenice and sat on the sofa, pushing letters and papers away from herself. She felt sick. 'Did you show her the letter?' she said.

'No,' said Mrs Cork, looking masterful again for a moment. 'She told me you were repairing the flute.'

'Please go,' Berenice wanted to say but she could not get her breath
to say it. 'You have been deceived. You are accusing the wrong
person. I thought your husband's name was William. He never called
himself Bunny. We all call him William at the College. Rosie Glowitz
wrote this letter.' But that sentence, 'Bring the flute', was too much –
she was suddenly on the side of this angry woman, she wished she
could shout and break out into rage. She wanted to grab the flute that
lay on Mrs Cork's lap and throw it at the wall and smash it.

'I apologize, Miss Foster,' said Mrs Cork in a surly voice. The
glister of tears in her eyes, the dampness on her face, dried. 'I believe
you. I have been worried out of my mind – you will understand.'

Berenice's beauty had drained away. The behaviour of one or two of
her lovers had always seemed self-satisfied to her, but William, the
most unlikely one, was the oddest. He would not stay in bed and
gossip but he was soon out staring at the garden, looking older, as if he
were travelling back into his life: then, hardly saying anything, he
dressed, turning to stare at the garden again as his head came out of his
shirt or he put a leg into his trousers, in a manner that made her think
he had completely forgotten. Then he would go into her front room,
bring back the flute and go out to the garden seat and play it. She had
done a cruel caricature of him once because he looked so comical, his
long lip drawn down at the mouthpiece, his eyes lowered as the thin
high notes, so sad and lascivious, seemed to curl away like wisps of
smoke into the trees. Sometimes she laughed, sometimes she smiled,
sometimes she was touched, sometimes angry and bewildered. One
proud satisfaction was that the people upstairs had complained.

She was tempted, now that she and this clumsy woman were at one,
to say to her, 'Aren't men extraordinary! Is this what he does at home,
does he rush out to your garden, bold as brass, to play that silly thing?'
And then she was scornful. 'To think of him going round to Rosie
Glowitz's and half the gardens of London doing this!'

But she could not say this, of course. And so she looked at poor Mrs
Cork with triumphant sympathy. She longed to break Rosie Glowitz's
neck and to think of some transcendent appeasing lie which would
make Mrs Cork happy again, but the clumsy woman went on making
everything worse by asking to be forgiven. She said 'I am truly sorry'
and 'When I saw your work in the shop I wanted to meet you. That is
really why I came. My husband has often spoken of it.'

Well, at least, Berenice thought, she can tell a lie too. Suppose I
gave her everything I've got, she thought. Anything to get her to go.

Berenice looked at the drawer of her bench, which was filled with beads and pieces of polished stone and crystal. She felt like getting handfuls of it and pouring it all on Mrs Cork's lap.

'Do you work only in silver?' said Mrs Cork, dabbing her eyes.

'I am,' said Berenice, 'working on something now.'

And even as she said it, because of Mrs Cork's overwhelming presence, the great appeasing lie came out of her, before she could stop herself. 'A present,' she said. 'Actually,' she said, 'we all got together at the College. A present for Rosie Glowitz. She's getting married again. I expect that is what the letter is about. Mr Cork arranged it. He is very kind and thoughtful.'

She heard herself say this with wonder. Her other lies had glittered, but this one had the beauty of a newly discovered truth.

'You mean Bunny's collecting the money?' said Mrs Cork.

'Yes,' said Berenice.

A great laugh came out of Florence Cork. 'The big spender,' she said, laughing. 'Collecting other people's money. He hasn't spent a penny on us for thirty years. And you're all giving this to that woman I talked to who has been married twice? Two wedding presents!'

Mrs Cork sighed.

'You fools. Some women get away with it, I don't know why,' said Mrs Cork, still laughing. 'But not with my Bunny,' she said proudly and as if with alarming meaning. 'He doesn't say much. He's deep, is my Bunny!'

'Would you like a cup of tea?' said Berenice politely, hoping she would say no and go.

'I think I will,' Mrs Cork said comfortably. 'I'm so glad I came to see you. And,' she added, glancing at the closed door, 'what about your father? I expect he could do with a cup.'

Mrs Cork now seemed wide awake and it was Berenice who felt dazed, drunkish, and sleepy.

'I'll go and see,' she said.

In the kitchen she recovered and came back trying to laugh, saying, 'He must have gone for his little walk in the afternoon, on the quiet.'

'You have to keep an eye on them at that age,' said Mrs Cork.

They sat talking and Mrs Cork said, 'Fancy Mrs Glowitz getting married again.' And then absently, 'I cannot understand why she says "Bring the flute."'

'Well,' said Berenice agreeably, 'he played it at the College party.'

'Yes,' said Mrs Cork. 'But at a wedding, it's a bit pushy. You wouldn't think it of my Bunny, but he *is* pushing.'

They drank their tea and then Mrs Cork left. Berenice felt an enormous kiss on her face and Mrs Cork said, 'Don't be jealous of Mrs Glowitz, dear. You'll get your turn,' as she went.

Berenice put the chain on the door and went to her bedroom and lay on the bed.

How awful married people are, she thought. So public, sprawling over everyone and everything, always lying to themselves and forcing you to lie to them. She got up and looked bitterly at the empty chair under the tree at first and then she laughed at it and went off to have a bath so as to wash all those lies off her truthful body. Afterwards she rang up a couple called Brewster who told her to come round. She loved the Brewsters, so perfectly conceited as they were, in the burdens they bore. She talked her head off. The children stared at her.

'She's getting old. She ought to get married,' Mrs Brewster said. 'I wish she wouldn't swoosh her hair around like that. She'd look better if she put it up.'

THE BURNING BABY

They said that Rhys was burning his baby when a gorse bush broke into fire on the summit of the hill. The bush, burning merrily, assumed to them the sad white features and the rickety limbs of the vicar's burning baby. What the wind had not blown away of the baby's ashes, Rhys Rhys had sealed in a stone jar. With his own dust lay the baby's dust, and near him the dust of his daughter in a coffin of white wood.

They heard his son howl in the wind. They saw him walking over the hill, holding a dead animal up to the light of the stars. They saw him in the valley shadows as he moved, with the motion of a man cutting wheat, over the brows of the fields. In a sanatorium he coughed his lung into a basin, stirring his fingers delightedly in the blood. What moved with invisible scythe through the valley was a shadow and a handful of shadows cast by the grave sun.

The brush burned out, and the face of the baby fell away with the smoking leaves.

It was, they said, on a fine sabbath morning in the middle of the summer that Rhys Rhys fell in love with his daughter. The gorse that morning had burst into flames. Rhys Rhys, in clerical black, had seen the flames shoot up to the sky, and the bush on the edge of the hill burn red as God among the paler burning of the grass. He took his daughter's hand as she lay in the garden hammock, and told her that he loved her. He told her that she was more beautiful than her dead mother. Her hair smelt of mice, her teeth came over her lip, and the lids of her eyes were red and wet. He saw her beauty come out of her like a stream of sap. The folds of her dress could not hide from him the shabby nakedness of her body. It was not her bone, nor her flesh, nor her hair that he found suddenly beautiful. The poor soil shudders under the sun, he said. He moved his hand up and down her arm. Only the awkward and the ugly, only the barren bring forth fruit. The flesh of her arm was red with the smoothing of his hand. He touched her breast. From the touch of her breast he knew each inch of flesh upon her. Why do you touch me there? she said.

In the church that morning he spoke of the beauty of the harvest, of the promise of the standing corn and the promise in the sharp edge of the scythe as it brings the corn low and whistles through the air before it cuts into the ripeness. Through the open windows at the end of the aisles, he saw the yellow fields upon the hillside and the smudge of heather on the meadow borders. The world was ripe.

The world is ripe for the second coming of the son of man, he said aloud.

But it was not the ripeness of God that glistened from the hill. It was the promise and the ripeness of the flesh, the good flesh, the mean flesh, flesh of his daughter, flesh, flesh, the flesh of the voice of thunder howling before the death of man.

That night he preached of the sins of the flesh. O God in the image of our flesh, he prayed.

His daughter sat in the front pew, and stroked her arm. She would have touched her breast where he had touched it, but the eyes of the congregation were upon her.

Flesh, flesh, flesh, said the vicar.

His son, scouting in the fields for a mole's hill or the signs of a red fox, whistling to the birds and patting the calves as they stood at their mother's sides, came upon a dead rabbit sprawling on a stone. The rabbit's head was riddled with pellets, the dogs had torn open its belly, and the marks of a ferret's teeth were upon its throat. He lifted it gently up, tickling it behind the ears. The blood from its head dropped on his hand. Through the rip in the belly, its intestines had dropped out and coiled on the stone. He held the little body close to his jacket, and ran home through the fields, the rabbit dancing against his waistcoat. As he reached the gate of the vicarage, the worshippers dribbled out of church. They shook hands and raised their hats, smiling at the poor boy with his long green hair, his ass's ears, and death buttoned under his jacket. He was always the poor boy to them.

Rhys Rhys sat in his study, the stem of his pipe stuck between his flybuttons, the bible unopened upon his knees. The day of God was over, and the sun, like another sabbath, went down behind the hills. He lit the lamp, but his own oil burned brighter. He drew the curtains, shutting out the unwelcome night. But he opened his own heart up, and the bald pulse that beat there was a welcome stranger.

He had not felt love like this since the woman who scratched him, seeing the woman witch in his male eyes, had fallen into his arms and kissed him, and whispered Welsh words as he took her. She had been the mother of his daughter and had died in her pains, stealing, when she was dead, the son of his second love, and leaving the greenhaired changeling in its place. Merry with desire, Rhys Rhys cast the Bible on the floor. He reached for another book, and read, in the lamplit darkness, of the old woman who had deceived the devil. The devil is poor flesh, said Rhys Rhys.

His son came in, bearing the rabbit in his arms. The lank, redcoated boy was a flesh out of the past. The skin of the unburied dead patched to his bones, the smile of the changeling on his mouth, and the hair of the sea rising from his scalp, he stood before Rhys Rhys. A ghost of his mother, he held the rabbit gently to his breast, rocking it to and fro. Cunningly, from under halfclosed lids, he saw his father shrink away from the vision of death. Be off with you, said Rhys Rhys. Who was this green stranger to carry in death and rock it, like a baby under a warm shawl of fur, before him? For a minute the flesh of the world lay still; the old terror set in; the waters of the breast dried up; the nipples grew through the sand. Then he drew his hand over his eyes, and only the rabbit remained, a little sack of flesh, half empty, swaying in the arms of his son. Be off, he said. The boy held the rabbit close, and rocked it, and tickled it again.

Changeling, said Rhys Rhys. He is mine, said the boy, I'll peel him and keep the skull. His room in the attic was crowded with skulls and dried pelts, and little bones in bottles.

Give it to me.

He is mine.

Rhys Rhys tore the rabbit away, and stuffed it deep in the pockets of his smoking coat. When his daughter came in, dressed and ready for bed, with a candle in her hand, Rhys Rhys had death in his pocket.

She was timid, for his touch still ached on her arm and breast but she bent unblushing over him. Saying goodnight, she kissed him, and he blew her candle out. She was smiling as he lowered the wick of the lamp.

Step out of your shift, said he. Shiftless, she stepped towards his arms.

I want the little skull, said a voice in the dark.

From his room at the top of the house, through the webs on the windows, and over the furs and the bottles, the boy saw a mile of green hill running away into the darkness of the first dawn. Summer storm in the heat of the rain, flooring the grassy mile, had left some new morning brightness, out of the dead night, in each reaching root.

Death took hold of his sister's legs as she walked through the calf-deep heather up the hill. He saw the high grass at her thighs. And the blades of the upgrowing wind, out of the four windsmells of the manuring dead, might drive through the soles of her feet, up the veins of the legs and stomach, into her womb and her pulsing heart. He watched her climb. She stood, gasping for breath, on a hill of the wider hill, tapping the wall of her bladder, fondling her matted chest (for the hair grew on her as on a grown man), feeling the heart in her wrist, loving her coveted thinness. She was to him as ugly as the sowfaced woman of Llareggub who had taught him the terrors of the flesh. He remembered the advances of that unlovely woman. She blew out his candle as he stepped towards her on the night the great hail had fallen and he had hidden in her rotting house from the cruelty of the weather. Now half a mile off his sister stood in the morning, and the vermin of the hill might spring upon her as she stood, uncaring, rounding the angles of her ugliness. He smiled at the thought of the devouring rats, and looked around the room for a bottle to hold her heart. Her skull, fixed by a socket to the nail above his bed, would be a smiling welcome to the first pains of waking.

But he saw Rhys Rhys stride up the hill, and the bowl of his sister's head, fixed invisibly above his sheets, crumbled away. Standing straight by the side of a dewy tree, his sister beckoned. Up went Rhys Rhys through the calf-deep heather, the death in the grass, over the boulders and up through the reaching ferns, to where she stood. He took her hand. The two shadows linked hands, and climbed together to the top of the hill. The boy saw them go, and turned his face to the wall as they vanished, in one dull shadow, over the edge, and down to the dingle at the west foot of the lovers' alley.

Later, he remembered the rabbit. He ran downstairs and found it in the pocket of the smoking coat. He held death against him, tasting a cough of blood upon his tongue as he climbed, contented, back to the bright bottles and the wall of heads.

In the first dew of light he saw his father clamber for her white hand. She who was his sister walked with a swollen belly over the hill. She touched him between the legs, and he sighed and sprang at her. But the nerves of her face mixed with the quiver in his thighs, and she shot from him. Rhys Rhys, over the bouldered rim, led her to terror. He sighed and sprang at her. She mixed with him in the fourth and the fifth terrors of the flesh. Said Rhys Rhys, Your mother's eyes. It was not her eyes that saw him proud before her, nor the eyes in her thumb. The lashes of her fingers lifted. He saw the ball under the nail.

It was, they said, on a fine sabbath morning in the early spring that she bore him a male child. Brought to bed of her father, she screamed for an anaesthetic as the knocking head burst through. In her gown of blood she slept until twilight, and a star burst bloody through each ear. With a scissors and rag, Rhys Rhys attended her, and, gazing on the shrivelled features and the hands like the hands of a mole, he gently took the child away, and his daughter's breast cried out and ran into the mouth of the surrounding shadows. The shadow pouted for the milk and the binding cottons. The child spat in his arms, the noise of the running air was blind in its ears, and the deaf light died from its eyes.

Rhys Rhys, with the dead child held against him, stepped into the night, hearing the mother moan in her sleep and the deadly shadow, filled sick with milk, flowing around the house. He turned his face towards the hills. A shadow walked close to him and, silent in the shadow of a full tree, the changeling waited. He made an image for the moon, and the flesh of the moon fell away, leaving a star-eyed skull. Then with a smile he ran back over the lawns and into the crying house. Halfway up the stairs, he heard his sister die. Rhys Rhys climbed on.

On the top of the hill he laid the baby down, and propped it against the heather. Death propped the dark flowers. The baby stiffened in the rigor of the moon. Poor flesh, said Rhys Rhys as he pulled at the dead heather and furze. Poor angel, he said to the listening mouth of the baby. The fruit of the flesh falls with the worm from the tree. Conceiving the worm, the bark crumbles. There lay the poor star of flesh that had dropped, like the bead of a woman's milk, through the nipples of a wormy tree.

He stacked the torn heathers in a circle. On the head of the purple stack, he piled the dead grass. A stack of death, the heather grew as tall as he, and loomed at last over his windy hair.

Behind a boulder moved the accompanying shadow, and the shadow of the boy was printed under the fiery flank of a tree. The shadow marked the boy, and the boy marked the bones of the naked

60 baby under their chilly cover, and how the grass scraped on the bald skull, and where his father picked out a path in the cancerous growths of the silent circle. He saw Rhys Rhys pick up the baby and place it on the top of the stack, saw the head of a burning match, and heard the crackle of the bush, breaking like a baby's arm.

The stack burst into flame. Rhys Rhys, before the red eye of the creeping fire, stretched out his arms and beckoned the shadow from the stones. Surrounded by shadows, he prayed before the flaming stack, and the sparks of the heather blew past his smile. Burn, child, poor flesh, mean flesh, flesh, flesh, sick sorry flesh, flesh of the foul womb, burn back to dust, he prayed.

And the baby caught fire. The flames curled round its mouth and blew upon the shrinking gums. Flames round its red cord lapped its little belly till the raw flesh fell upon the heather.

A flame touched its tongue. Eeeeeh, cried the burning baby, and the illuminated hill replied.

THE INVISIBLE JAPANESE GENTLEMEN

There were eight Japanese gentlemen having a fish dinner at Bentley's. They spoke to each other rarely in their incomprehensible tongue, but always with a courteous smile and often with a small bow. All but one of them wore glasses. Sometimes the pretty girl who sat in the window beyond gave them a passing glance, but her own problem seemed too serious for her to pay real attention to anyone in the world except herself and her companion.

She had thin blonde hair and her face was pretty and *petite* in a Regency way, oval like a miniature, though she had a harsh way of speaking – perhaps the accent of the school, Roedean or Cheltenham Ladies' College, which she had not long ago left. She wore a man's signet-ring on her engagement finger, and as I sat down at my table, with the Japanese gentlemen between us, she said, 'So you see we could marry next week.'

'Yes?'

Her companion appeared a little distraught. He refilled their glasses with Chablis and said, 'Of course, but Mother . . .' I missed some of the conversation then, because the eldest Japanese gentleman leant across the table, with a smile and a little bow, and uttered a whole paragraph like the mutter from an aviary, while everyone bent towards him and smiled and listened, and I couldn't help attending to him myself.

The girl's fiancé resembled her physically. I could see them as two miniatures hanging side by side on white wood panels. He should have been a young officer in Nelson's navy in the days when a certain weakness and sensitivity were no bar to promotion.

She said, 'They are giving me an advance of five hundred pounds, and they've sold the paperback rights already.' The hard commercial declaration came as a shock to me; it was a shock too that she was one of my own profession. She couldn't have been more than twenty. She

deserved better of life.

He said, 'But my uncle . . .'

'You know you don't get on with him. This way we shall be quite independent.'

'*You* will be independent,' he said grudgingly.

'The wine-trade wouldn't really suit you, would it? I spoke to my publisher about you and there's a very good chance . . . if you began with some reading . . .'

'But I don't know a thing about books.'

'I would help you at the start.'

'My mother says that writing is a good crutch . . .'

'Five hundred pounds and half the paperback rights is a pretty solid crutch,' she said.

'This Chablis is good, isn't it?'

'I daresay.'

I began to change my opinion of him – he had not the Nelson touch. He was doomed to defeat. She came alongside and raked him fore and aft. 'Do you know what Mr Dwight said?'

'Who's Dwight?'

'Darling, you don't listen, do you? My publisher. He said he hadn't read a first novel in the last ten years which showed such powers of observation.'

'That's wonderful,' he said sadly, 'wonderful.'

'Only he wants me to change the title.'

'Yes?'

'He doesn't like *The Ever-Rolling Stream*. He wants to call it *The Chelsea Set*.'

'What did you say?'

'I agreed. I do think that with a first novel one should try to keep one's publisher happy. Especially when, really, he's going to pay for our marriage, isn't he?'

'I see what you mean.' Absent-mindedly he stirred his Chablis with a fork – perhaps before the engagement he had always bought champagne. The Japanese gentlemen had finished their fish and with very little English but with elaborate courtesy they were ordering from the middle-aged waitress a fresh fruit salad. The girl looked at them, and then she looked at me, but I think she saw only the future. I wanted very much to warn her against any future based on a first novel called *The Chelsea Set*. I was on the side of his mother. It was a humiliating thought, but I was probably about her mother's age.

I wanted to say to her, Are you certain your publisher is telling you the truth? Publishers are human. They may sometimes exaggerate the virtues of the young and the pretty. Will *The Chelsea Set* be read in five years? Are you prepared for the years of effort, 'the long defeat of doing nothing well'? As the years pass writing will not become any easier, the daily effort will grow harder to endure, those 'powers of observation' will become enfeebled; you will be judged, when you reach your forties, by performance and not by promise.

'My next novel is going to be about St Tropez.'

'I didn't know you'd ever been there.'

'I haven't. A fresh eye's terribly important. I thought we might settle down there for six months.'

'There wouldn't be much left of the advance by that time.'

'The advance is only an advance. I get fifteen per cent after five thousand copies and twenty per cent after ten. And of course another advance will be due, darling, when the next book's finished. A bigger one if *The Chelsea Set* sells well.'

'Suppose it doesn't.'

'Mr Dwight says it will. He ought to know.'

'My uncle would start me at twelve hundred.'

'But, darling, how could you come then to St Tropez?'

'Perhaps we'd do better to marry when you come back.'

She said harshly, 'I mightn't come back if *The Chelsea Set* sells enough.'

'Oh.'

She looked at me and the party of Japanese gentlemen. She finished her wine. She said, 'Is this a quarrel?'

'No.'

'I've got the title for the next book – *The Azure Blue*.'

'I thought azure *was* blue.'

She looked at him with disappointment. 'You don't really want to be married to a novelist, do you?'

'You aren't one yet.'

'I was born one – Mr Dwight says. My powers of observation . . .'

'Yes. You told me that, but, dear, couldn't you observe a bit nearer home? Here in London.'

'I've done that in *The Chelsea Set*. I don't want to repeat myself.'

The bill had been lying beside them for some time now. He took out

64 his wallet to pay, but she snatched the paper out of his reach. She said, 'This is my celebration.'

'What of?'

'*The Chelsea Set*, of course. Darling, you're awfully decorative, but sometimes – well, you simply don't connect.'

'I'd rather . . . if you don't mind . . .'

'No, darling, this is on me. And Mr Dwight, of course.'

He submitted just as two of the Japanese gentleman gave tongue simultaneously, then stopped abruptly and bowed to each other, as though they were blocked in a doorway.

I had thought the two young people matching miniatures, but what a contrast in fact there was. The same type of prettiness could contain weakness and strength. Her Regency counterpart, I suppose, would have borne a dozen children without the aid of anaesthetics, while he would have fallen an easy victim to the first dark eyes in Naples. Would there one day be a dozen books on her shelf? They have to be born without an anaesthetic too. I found myself hoping that *The Chelsea Set* would prove to be a disaster and that eventually she would take up photographic modelling while he established himself solidly in the wine-trade in St James's. I didn't like to think of her as the Mrs Humphrey Ward of her generation – not that I would live so long. Old age saves us from the realization of a great many fears. I wondered to which publishing firm Dwight belonged. I could imagine the blurb he would have already written about her abrasive powers of observation. There would be a photo, if he was wise, on the back of the jacket, for reviewers, as well as publishers, are human, and she didn't look like Mrs Humphrey Ward.

I could hear them talking while they found their coats at the back of the restaurant. He said, 'I wonder what all those Japanese are doing here?'

'Japanese?' she said. 'What Japanese, darling? Sometimes you are so evasive I think you don't want to marry me at all.'

MORE FRIEND THAN LODGER

As soon as Henry spoke of their new author Rodney Galt I knew that I should dislike him. 'It's rather a feather in my cap to have got him for our list,' he said. The publishing firm of which Henry is a junior partner is called Brodrick Layland which as a name is surely a feather in no one's cap, but that by the way. 'I think Harkness were crazy to let him go,' Henry said, 'because although *Cuckoo* wasn't a great money-spinner, it was very well thought of indeed. But that's typical of Harkness, they think of nothing but sales.'

I may say for those who don't know him that this speech was very typical of Henry: because, first, I should imagine most publishers think a lot about sales and, if Brodrick Layland don't, then I'm sorry to hear it; and, secondly, Henry would never naturally use expressions like 'a great money-spinner', but since he's gone into publishing he thinks he ought to sound a bit like a business man and doesn't really know how. The kind of thing that comes natural to Henry to say is that somebody or something is 'very well thought of indeed', which doesn't sound like a business man to anyone, I imagine. But what Henry is like ought to emerge from my story if I'm able to write it at all. And I must in fairness add that my comments about him probably tell quite a lot about me – for example he isn't by any means mostly interested in the money in publishing but much more in 'building up a good list', so that his comment on Harkness wasn't hypocritical. And, as his wife, I know this perfectly well, but I've got into the habit of talking like that about him.

Henry went on to tell me about *Cuckoo*. It was not either a novel, which one might have thought, or a book about birds or lunatics, which was less likely, although it's the kind of thing I might have pretended to think in order to annoy him. No, *Cuckoo* was an anthology and a history of famous cuckolds. Rodney Galt, it seemed, had a great reputation, not as a cuckold, for he was single, but as a seducer; although his victories were not only or even mainly among married women. He was particularly successful as a matter of fact at seducing younger daughters and debs. Henry told me all this in a special offhand sort of voice intended to suggest to me that at Brodrick Layland's they took that sort of thing for granted. Once again I'm being bitchy, because, of course, if I had said 'Come off it, Henry' or words to that effect, he would have changed his tone immediately. But I did not see why I should, because among our acquaintances we *do* number a few though not many seducers of virgins; and if I made Henry change his tone it would suggest that he was *quite* unfamiliar with such a phenomenon which would be equally false. Fairness and truth are my greatest difficulties in life.

To return to Rodney Galt – the book he was going to write for Brodrick Layland was to be called *Honour and Civility*. Once again it was not to be a novel, however, like *Sense and Sensibility* or *The Naked and the Dead*. Rodney Galt used the words 'Honour' and 'Civility' in a special sense; some would say an archaic sense, but he did not see it that way because he preferred not to recognize the changes that had taken place in the English language in the last hundred years or so. 'Honour' for him meant 'the thing that is most precious to a man', but not in the sense that the Victorians meant that it was most precious to a woman. Rodney Galt from what I could gather would have liked to see men still killing each other in duels for their honour and offering civilities to one another in the shape of snuff and suchlike before they did so. He believed in 'living dangerously' and in what is called 'high courage', but exemplified preferably in sports and combats of long standing. He was, therefore, against motor racing and even more against 'track' but in favour of bullfighting and perhaps pelota; he was also against dog racing but in favour of baccarat for high stakes.

The book, however, was not to be just one of those books that used to be popular with my uncle Charles called *Twelve Rakes* or *Twenty Famous Dandies*. It was to be more philosophical than that, involving all the author's view of society; for example, that we could not be civilized or great again unless we accepted cruelty as a part of living dangerously, and that without prejudice man could have no opinion, and, indeed, altogether what in Mr Galt's view constituted the patrician life.

I told Henry that I did not care for the sound of him. Henry only smiled, however, and said, 'I warn you that he's a snob, but on such a colossal scale and with such panache that one can't take exception to it.' I told Henry firmly that I was not the kind of woman who could see things on such a large scale as that, and also, that if, as I suspected from his saying 'I warn you', he intended to invite Rodney Galt to the house, only the strictest business necessity would reconcile me to it.

'There *is* the strictest business necessity,' Henry said, and added, 'Don't be put off by his matinee idol looks. He's indecently good-looking.' He giggled when he said this, for he knew that he had turned the tables on me. Henry used to believe – his mother taught him the idea – that no woman liked men to be extremely good-looking. He knows different now because I have told him again and again that I would not have married him if he had not been very handsome himself. His mother's code, however, dies hard with him and even now, I suspect, he thinks that if his nose had not been broken at school, I should have found him too perfect. He is quite wrong. I would willingly pay for him to have it straightened if I thought he would accept the offer.

Reading over what I have written, I see that it must appear as though Henry and I live on very whimsical terms – gilding the pill of our daily disagreements with a lot of private jokes and 'sparring' and generally rather ghastly arch behaviour. Thinking over our life together, perhaps it is true. It is with no conscious intent, however; although I have read again and again in the women's papers to which I'm addicted that a sense of humour is the cement of marriage. Henry and I have a reasonable proportion of sense of humour, but no more. He gets his, which is dry, from his mother who, as you will see in this story of Rodney Galt, is like a character from the novels of Miss Compton Burnett, or, at least, when I read those novels I people them entirely with characters like Henry's mother. My parents had no vestige of humour; my father was too busy getting rich and my mother was too busy unsuccessfully trying to crash county society.

But it *is* true that Henry and I in our five years of marriage have built up a lot of private joking and whimsical talking and I can offer what seem to be some good reasons for it, but who am I to say? First, there is what anyone would pick on – that our marriage is childless, which, I think, is really the least of the possible reasons. It certainly is with me, although it may count with Henry more than he can say. The second is that everything counts with Henry more than he can say. 'Discerning' people who know Henry and his mother and, indeed, all the Ravens, usually say that they are shy beneath their sharp manner. I don't quite believe this; I think it's just because they find it easier to be like this so that other people can't overstep the mark of intimacy and intrude too far on their personal lives. You can tell from the way Henry's mother shuts her eyes when she meets people that she has an interior life and actually she is a devout Anglican. And Henry has an interior life which he has somehow or other put into his publishing. Well, anyhow, Henry's manner shy or not makes me shy, and I've got much more whimsical since I knew him.

But also there's my own attitude to our marriage. I can only sum it up by saying that it's like the attitude of almost everyone in England today to almost everything. I worked desperately hard to get out of the insecurity of my family – which in this case was not economic because they're fairly rich and left me quite a little money of my own, but social – and when I married Henry I loved every minute of it because the Ravens are quite secure in their own way – which Henry's mother calls 'good country middle class, June dear, and no more'. And if that security is threatened for a moment I rush back to it for safety. But most of the time when it's not in danger, I keep longing for more adventure in life and a wider scope and more variety and even greater risks and perils. Well, all that you'll see in this story, I think. But anyhow this feeling about our marriage makes me uneasy with Henry and I keep him at a humorous distance. And he, knowing it, does so all the more too. All this, I hope, will explain our private jokes and so on, of which you will meet many. By the way, about security and risk, I don't really believe that one can't have one's cake and eat it – which also you'll see.

To return to Rodney Galt; Henry did, in fact, invite him to dinner a week later. He was not, of course, as bad as Henry made out, that is to say, as I have sketched above, because that description was part of Henry's ironical teasing of me. In fact, however, he was pretty bad. He said ghastly things in an Olympian way – not with humour like Henry and me, but with 'wit' which is always rather awful. However, I must admit that even at that first dinner I didn't mind Rodney's wit as much as all that, partly because he had the most lovely speaking voice (I don't know why one says speaking voice as though most of one's friends used recitative), very deep and resonant which always 'sends' me; and partly because he introduced his ghastly views in a way that made them seem better than they were. For example:

Henry said, 'I imagine that a good number of your best friends are Jews, Galt.'

And Rodney raised his eyebrows and said, 'Good heavens, why?'

And Henry answered, 'Most anti-Semitic people make that claim.'

And Rodney said, 'I suppose that's why I'm not anti-Semitic. I can't imagine knowing any Jews. When would it arise? Oh, I suppose when one's buying pictures or objects, but then that's hardly knowing. It's simply one of the necessities. Or, of course, if one went to Palestine, but then that's hardly a necessity.'

And I said, 'What about Disraeli? He made the Tory party of today.' I said this with a side glance at Henry because he used then to describe himself as a Tory Democrat, although since Suez he has said that he had not realized how deeply Liberalism ran in his veins.

Rodney said, 'What makes you speak of such unpleasant things?'

And I asked, 'Aren't you a Tory then?'

And he answered, 'I support the principles of Lord Eldon and respect the courage of Lord Sidmouth, if that's what you mean.'

Henry said, 'Oh! but what about the Suez Canal and the British Empire? Disraeli made those.'

And Rodney looked distant and remarked, 'The British Empire even at its height was never more than a convenient outlet for the middle-class high-mindedness of Winchester and Rugby. The plantations and the penal colonies of course,' he added, 'were a different matter.'

Henry, who makes more of his Charterhouse education than he admits, said, 'Oh, come, Winchester and Rugby are hardly the same thing.'

Rodney smiled and said in a special hearty voice, 'No, I suppose not, old man.' This was rude to Henry, of course, but slightly gratifying to me. Anyhow he went straight on and said, 'The thing that pleases me most about coming to Brodrick Layland is your book production, Raven. I do like to feel that what I have written, if it is worth publishing at all, deserves a comely presentation.' This, of course, was very gratifying to Henry. They talked about books or rather the appearance of books for some time and I made little comment as I like the inside of books almost exclusively. It appeared, however, that Rodney was a great collector of books, as he was of so many other things: porcelain, enamels, Byzantine ivories and Central American carvings. He was quick to tell us, that, of course, with his modest income he had to leave the big things alone and that, again with his modest income, it was increasingly difficult to pick up anything worth having, but that it could be done. He left us somehow with the impression that he would not really have cared for the big things anyway, and that his income could not be as modest as all that.

'Heaven defend me,' he said, 'from having the money to buy those tedious delights of the pedants – incunables. No, the little Elzeviers are my particular favourites, the decent classical authors charmingly produced. I have a delightful little Tully and the only erotica worth possessing, Ovid's *Amores*.'

It was talking of Ovid that he said something which gave me a clue to my feelings about him.

'I know of no more moving thing in literature than Ovid's exiled lament for Rome. It's just how any civilized Englishman today must feel when, chained to his native land, he thinks of the Mediterranean or almost anywhere else outside England for that matter. "Breathes there a Soul", you know.' He smiled as he said it. Of course, it was the most awful pretentious way of talking, but so often I do feel that I would rather be almost anywhere than in England that he made me feel guilty for not being as honest as he was.

It seemed, however, that after a great deal of travel in a great many places, he *was* now for some time to be chained to his native land. He had, he said, a lot of family business to do. He was looking out for a house something like ours. He even hinted – it was the only hint of his commercially venturing side that he gave that evening – at the possibility of his buying a number of houses as an investment. Meanwhile he was staying with Lady Ann Denton. I ventured to suggest that this might be a little too much of a good thing, but he smiled and said that she was a very old friend, which, although it rather put me in my place, gave him a good mark for loyalty. (Henry scolded me afterwards and told me that Rodney was having an affair with Lady Ann. This surprised and disconcerted me. It didn't sound at all like 'debs'. Lady Ann is old – over forty – and very knocked about and ginny. She has an amusing malicious tongue and a heart of gold. Sometimes I accept her tongue because of her heart, and sometimes I put up with her heart because of her tongue. Sometimes I can't stand either. But, as you will have already seen, my attitude to people is rather ambiguous. However, Henry is very fond of her. She makes him feel broadminded which he likes very much.)

We had it out a little about snobbery that evening. 'Heavens, I should hope so,' Rodney said, when I accused him of being a social snob, 'it's one of the few furies worth having that are left to us – little opportunity though the modern world allows of finding anyone worth cultivating. There still do exist a few families, however, even in this country. It lends shape to my life as it did to Proust's.' I said that though it had lent shape to Proust's work, I wasn't so sure about his life. 'In any case,' he said with a purposeful parody of a self-satisfied smile, 'art and life are one.' Then he burst out laughing and said, 'Really, I've excelled myself this evening. It's your excellent food.'

Looking back at what I have written I see that I said that he wasn't as bad as Henry made out and then everything that I have reported him as saying is quite pretentious and awful. The truth is that it was his smile and his good looks that made it seem all right. Henry had said that he was like a matinee idol, but this is a ridiculous expression for nowadays (whatever it may have been in the days of Henry's mother and Owen Nares) because no one could go to a matinee with all those grey-haired old ladies up from the Country rattling tea-trays and feel sexy about anything. But Rodney was like all the best film stars rolled into one and yet the kind of person it wasn't surprising to meet; and, these taken together surely make a very sexy combination.

It was clear that evening that Henry liked him very much too. Not for that reason, of course. Henry hasn't ever even thought about having feelings of that kind I'm glad to say. As a matter of fact, Henry doesn't have sexy feelings much anyway. No, that's quite unfair and bitchy of me again. Of course, he has sexy feelings, but he has them at definite times and the rest of the time such things don't come into his head. Whereas I don't ever have such strong sexy feelings as he has, but I have some of them all the time. This is a contrast that tends to make things difficult.

No, the reason Henry liked him I could see at once, and I said as soon as he had left, 'Well, he's quite your cup of tea, isn't he? He's been everywhere and knows a lot about everything.' I said the last sentence in inverted commas, because it's one of Henry's favourite expressions of admiration and I often tease him about it. It isn't very surprising because Henry went to Charterhouse and then in the last two years of the War he went with the F S P to Italy, and then he went to the Queen's College, Oxford, and then he went into Brodrick Layland. So he hasn't been everywhere. In fact, however, he does know quite a lot about quite a number of things, but as soon as he knows something he doesn't think it can be very important.

We both agreed then that Rodney Galt was quite awful in most ways but that we rather liked him all the same. This is my usual experience with a great number of people that I meet, but Henry found it more surprising.

In the week that followed Henry seemed to see a good deal of Rodney Galt. He put him up for his Club. I was rather surprised that Rodney should have wanted to be a member of Henry's Club which is rather dull and literary: I had imagined him belonging to a lot of clubs of a much grander kind already. Henry explained that he did in fact belong to a lot of others, but that he had been abroad so much that he had lost touch with those worlds. I thought that was very odd, too, because I imagined that the point of clubs was that no matter how often you went round the world and no matter how long, when you came back the club was there. However, as I only knew about clubs from the novels of Evelyn Waugh, I was prepared to believe that I was mistaken. In any case it also seemed that Rodney wanted particularly to belong to this author's sort of club, because he believed very strongly that one should do everything one did professionally and as he was now going to write books, he wanted to go to that sort of place.

'He's a strange fellow in many ways,' Henry said, 'a mass of contradictions.' This didn't seem at all strange to me, because such people as I have met have all been a mass of contradictions. Nevertheless Rodney's particular contradiction in this case did seem odd to me. I had imagined that the whole point of his books would be that they should be thrown off in the midst of other activities – amateur productions that proved to be more brilliant than the professional. However, his new attitude if less romantic was more creditable and certainly more promising for Brodrick Layland. I decided indeed that he had probably only made this gesture to please Henry, which it did.

We dined once or twice with him and Lady Ann. She has rather a nice house in Chester Square and he seemed to be very comfortably installed – more permanently indeed than his earlier talk of buying houses suggested. However, this may well have been only the appearance that Lady Ann gave to things, for she made every effort short of absurdity to underline the nature of their relationship. I really could not blame her for this, for she had made a catch that someone a good deal less battered and ginny might have been proud of; and I had to admire the manner in which she avoided the absurdity for, in fact, looking at him and at her, it *was* very absurd, apart from the large gap in their ages – fifteen years at least, I decided.

Lady Ann as usual talked most of the time. She has a special way of being funny: she speaks with a drawl and a very slight stutter and she ends her remarks suddenly with a word or expression that isn't what one expects she is going to lead up to. Well, of course, one does expect it, because she always does it; and like a lot of things it gets less funny when you've heard it a few times. For example, she said she didn't agree with Rodney in not liking *Look Back in Anger*, she'd been three times, the music was so good. And again, she quite agreed with Henry, she wouldn't have missed the Braque exhibition for anything, but then she got a peculiar pleasure, almost a sensual one, from being jammed really tight in a crowd. And so on. Henry always laps up Lady Ann. She's a sort of tarty substitute mother-figure for him, I think; and indeed, if he wanted a tarty mother, he had to find a substitute. I thought, perhaps, that Rodney would be a little bored with her carry on, but if he was, he didn't show it. This, of course, was very creditable of him, but made me a little disappointed. Occasionally, it is true, he broke into the middle of her chatter; but then she interrupted him sometimes just as rudely. They might really have been a perfectly happy pair which I found even more disappointing.

I can't help thinking that by this time you may have formed some rather unfavourable views about the kind of woman I am. Well, I've already said that often I have very bitchy moods; and it's true, but at least I know it. But if you ask me why I have bitchy moods it's more difficult to say. In the first place life is frightfully boring nowadays, isn't it? And if you say I ought to try doing something with my time, well I have. I did translations from French and German for Brodrick Layland for a time; and I did prison visiting. They're quite different sorts of things to do and it didn't take long for me to get very bored with each of them. Not that I should want wars and revolutions – whenever there's an international crisis I get a ghastly pain in my stomach like everybody else. But, as I said, like England, I want security and I don't. However, what I was trying to explain about was my bitchy moods. Well, when I get very bored and depressed, I hate everyone and it seems to me everyone hates me. (As a matter of fact most people do like Henry better than me, although they think I'm more amusing.) But when the depressed mood lifts, I can't help feeling people are rather nice and they seem to like me too. I had these moods very badly when I was sixteen or so; and now in these last two years (since I was twenty-five) they've come back and they change much more quickly. When I talked to Henry about it once, he got so depressed and took such a 'psychological' view that I've never mentioned it again. In any case it's so easy to take 'psychological' views;

but I'm by no means sure that it isn't just as true to say like my old nurse, 'Well, we all have our ups and downs,' and certainly that's a more cosy view of the situation.

But enough about me, because all this is really about Rodney Galt. Well, in those few times I saw him with Lady Ann (it seems more comic always to call her that) I began to have a theory about him; and when I get theories about people I get very interested in them. Especially as, if my theory was right, then Lady Ann and Henry and Mr Brodrick and no doubt lots of other people were liable to be sold all along the line or up the river or whatever the expression is; but on the whole, if my theory was right it only made *me* feel that he was *more* fascinating. The best sort of theory to have. One thing I did want to know more about was his family. In such cases I always believe in asking directly, so I said, 'Where are your family, Rodney?' He smiled and said, 'In the Midlothian where they've been for a sufficient number of recorded centuries to make them respectable. They're the best sort of people really,' he added, 'the kind of people who've always been content to be trout in the local minnow pond. I'm the only one who's shown the cloven hoof of fame-seeking. There must be a bounderish streak somewhere though not from mother's family who were all perfectly good dull country gentry. Of course, there was my great-great-great uncle the novelist. But his was a very respectable middling sort of local fame really.'

Well there wasn't much given away there because after all there are minnows and minnows and even 'country gentry' is rather a vague term. It was a bit disingenuous about Galt the novelist, because even I have heard of him and I know nothing of the Midlothian. And that was the chief annoyance. I knew absolutely no one with whom I could check up. But it didn't shake my theory.

Now we come to the most important point in this story: When Rodney Galt became our lodger. But first I shall have to explain about 'the lodger battle' which Henry and I had been then waging for over a year and this means explaining about our finances. Henry had some capital and he put that into Brodrick Layland and really, all things considered, he gets quite a good income back. But the house which we live in is mine; and it was left to me by my Aunt Agnes and it's rather a big house, situated in that vague area known as behind Harrods. But it isn't, in fact, Pont Street Dutch. And in this big house there is only me and Henry and one or two foreign girls. They change usually every year and at the time I'm speaking of, about six or seven months ago, there was only one girl, a Swiss called Henriette Vaudoyer. Henry had long been keen that we should have a lodger who could have a 75 bedroom and sitting-room and bathroom of their own. He said it was because he didn't like my providing the house and getting nothing back from it. He thought, that at least I ought to get pin money out of it. This was an absurd excuse because Daddy left me quite a little income – a great deal more than was required even if I were to set up a factory for sticking pins into wax images.

I think Henry had, at least, three real reasons for wanting this lodger; one, he thought it was wrong to have so much space when people couldn't find anywhere to live, and this, if I had thought of it first I would have agreed with, because I have more social conscience really than Henry, when I remember it; two, the empty rooms (empty that is of human beings) reminded him of the tiny feet that might have pattered but did not; three, he had an idea that having a lodger would give me something to do and help with the moods I've already told you about. The last two of these reasons annoyed me very much and made me very unwilling to have a lodger. So Henry was rather shy in suggesting that we should let the top floor to Rodney Galt. He only felt able to introduce the subject by way of the brilliant first chapter of Rodney's new book. Henry, it seemed, was bowled over by this chapter when Rodney had submitted it and even Mr Brodrick, who had his feet pretty firmly planted on the ground, rocked a little. If it had been a feather in Henry's cap getting Rodney Galt before, it became a whole plumage now. Nothing must get in the way of the book's completion. Well, it seemed that living at Lady Ann's did. Henry pointed out that wonderful friend though Lady Ann was, she could be difficult to live with if you wanted to write because she talked so much. I said, yes she did and drank so much too. But I asked about the house that Rodney was going to buy. Henry said that Rodney hadn't seen the one he really wanted yet and he didn't want to do too much house hunting while he was writing the book which would require a lot of research. Above all, of course, he did not want to involve himself with what might turn out to be a white elephant. To this I thoroughly agreed. And, to Henry's surprise and pleasure, I said, yes, Rodney could come as a lodger.

I was a little puzzled about Lady Ann. I made some enquiries and, as I suspected, Rodney had thrown her over and was said to have taken up with Susan Mullins, a very young girl but almost as rich as Lady Ann. However, Lady Ann was putting a good face on it before the world. I was glad to hear this because the face she usually put on before the world, although once good, was now rather a mess. But I didn't say anything to Henry about all this, because he was so fond of Lady Ann and I was feeling very friendly towards him for making such a sensible suggestion about a lodger.

Hardly had the lodger idea taken shape and Rodney was about to take up residence, when it almost lost its shape again. All because of Mr Brodrick. I should tell you that Henry's senior partner was again one of the many people about whom my mood varied. He was a rather handsome, grey-templed, port-flushed old man of sixty-five or so – more like a barrister than a publisher, one would think. Anyway what would one think a publisher looked like? He was a determinedly old-fashioned man – but not like Rodney, except that both of them talked a bit too much about wine and food. No, Mr Brodrick was an old world mannered, 'dear lady' sort of man – a widower who was gallant to the fair sex, is how he saw himself, I think. He had a single eyeglass on a black ribbon and ate mostly at his Club. Sometimes I thought he was rather a sweet old thing and sometimes I thought he was a ghastly old bore and a bit common to boot.

At first, it seemed, he'd been delighted at Henry's capturing Rodney for their list, mainly because he was rather an old snob and Rodney seemed to know well a lot of people whom he himself had only met once or twice but talked about a good deal. He patted Henry on the back once or twice – literally I imagine though not heartily – and saw him even more as 'a son, my dear boy, since I have not been blessed with any offspring myself'. (I often wondered whether Mr Brodrick didn't say to Henry, 'When's the baby coming along?' He was so keen on heirs for Brodrick Layland.)

But suddenly it seemed that one day Mr Brodrick was talking to Mr Harkness of Harkness & Co., and Mr Harkness said that why they hadn't gone on with Rodney as an author was because they'd had a lot of financial trouble with him – loans not repaid and so on. Mr Brodrick didn't care for the sound of that at all and he thought that they should do what he called 'Keeping a very firm rein on Master Galt's activities'. And as he saw Henry as a son and perhaps me as a daughter-in-law (who knows?) he was very much against our having Rodney as a lodger. The more strictly commercial the relations with authors the better, he said.

Henry was upset by all this and a good deal surprised at what Mr Harkness had said. I was not at all surprised but I did not say so. I said that Harkness had no right to say such things and Mr Brodrick to listen to them. In any case, I said, how did we know that Mr Harkness had not just made them up out of sour grapes. And as to commercial relations I pointed out that Rodney's being a lodger was commercial and anyway the rent was being paid to me. So Mr Brodrick knew what he could do. But Henry still seemed a little unhappy and then he told me that he had himself lent Rodney various sums. So then I saw there was nothing for it but the brilliant first chapter – and I played that for all I was worth. Did Henry, I said, expect that anyone capable of that brilliant first chapter was going to fit in with every bourgeois maxim of life that people like Harkness and Mr Brodrick laid down in their narrow scheme of things? I was surprised, I said, that Henry who had a real flair for publishing because he cared about books should be led into this sort of 'business is business' attitude that, if persevered in, would mean confining one's list to all the dullest books produced. Anyway I made it clear I was determined that Rodney Galt should come if only as a matter of principle. When Henry saw that I was determined, he decided to stand on principle too and on the great coup he had made for Brodrick Layland as forecast by that brilliant first chapter. So Rodney moved in.

What with all the research Rodney needed to do for his book and what with Susan Mullins you may think that I was getting unduly excited about nothing. But if you have jumped to that conclusion, well then I think you can't have a very interesting mind and you certainly don't understand me. When I say that I had become interested in Rodney that's exactly what I mean and 'being interested' with me comes to this – that I don't know really what I want or indeed if I want anything at all, but I know for certain that I don't want to leave go. So for the first week or so Rodney went to the British Museum and read books about civility and honour of which they have lots there – intended when they were published in the seventeenth and eighteenth century for people who were on the social make, I think. I rather used to like to think that after all this time they were being read again by Rodney. When he was not at the British Museum, he was with Susan Mullins or on the telephone talking to her.

The British Museum fell out of Rodney's life before Susan Mullins. After only a fortnight it was replaced by books from the London Library which as Rodney had a sitting-room seemed only sensible. Then came a period when Susan did not telephone so often and once or twice Rodney telephoned to her and spoke instead to her mother (who was not called Mullins but Lady Newnham because she had been divorced and married again to a very rich Conservative industrialist peer) and then high words were exchanged. And finally one day when he rang he spoke to Lord Newnham and very high words were exchanged and that was the end of that. It became difficult then for Rodney to keep his mind even on the books from the London Library let alone going to the British Museum. It seemed somehow that his mind was diverted more by financial schemes than by study. None of this surprised me much either, but I thought I would not worry Henry by telling him in case he began to be afraid that there would only be a brilliant first chapter and no more. In any case it might have only been temporary, though I was not inclined to think that.

So Rodney and I used to go out in his MG (and perhaps it would have been more in keeping if he had refused to use any kind of motor-car later than a De Dionne but I was glad that he didn't). We went here, there and everywhere and all over the place. We saw a great number of lovely houses – a lot in London, but gradually more and more outside London. Rodney came very near to taking some of them, he said. And then since he proposed to turn some of the houses when he bought them into furnished rooms or flats, we looked at a great number of antiques. The antiques we looked at were rather expensive for this purpose, but Rodney said that only good things interested him and what was the good of his expertise if he never used it. But it was quite true – that he had expertise, I mean. We also had a lot of very good luncheons. On my theory Rodney would pay for these during the first phase, but later I expected I would have to pay. But I was determined to make the first phase last as long as possible and I succeeded. We took to going suddenly too to places like Hampton Court and Cambridge and Hatfield House and Wilton. We did not go to see any friends, though, partly because it wouldn't have done, but mostly because we really were very content to be alone together. However, often when we passed great parks or distant large houses, Rodney told me to which of his friends they belonged; and this was nice for him.

In fact we both had a wonderful time, although Rodney's time would have been more wonderful, he said, if I'd agreed to go to bed with him. Sometimes he cajoled; or at least he made himself as attractive and sweet as he could which was a lot; and this, I imagine, is what 'cajole' means. But often he took a very high-handed line, because in Rodney's theory of seducing there was a lot about women wanting to be mastered which fitted into his general social views. Then he would tell me that unless I let myself go and accepted his mastery which was what I really wanted, I would soon become a tight little bitch. I had, he said, all the makings of one already at twenty-six. 'You think,' he cried, 'that because you have attractive eyes and a good figure that you can go on having sex appeal just by cock-teasing every man you meet. But let me tell you it won't last, you'll quickly become a hard little bitch that no one will be interested in. It's happening already with your bitter humour and your whimsy and your melancholy moods. You're ceasing to be "civilized".' Civilization seemed to be his key to seduction, because he made light of my married position on the same grounds. 'In any civilized century,' he said, 'the situation would be sensibly accepted,' and then he talked of Congreve and Vanbrugh and Italian society. But I didn't care to decide too easily, because Vanbrugh and Congreve are no longer alive and this is not Italy of the Cicisbei and affairs of this kind aren't easy to control and even if life was often boring it was secure. Also I quite enjoyed things as they were, even the violent things he said about my becoming a bitch, but I wasn't sure that I would like all that masterfulness on a physical plane.

So we went on as I wished and I enjoyed managing the double life and if Rodney didn't exactly enjoy it he was very good at it. For example, one morning an absolutely ghastly thing happened; Henry's mother suddenly arrived as Rodney and I were about to set off for Brighton. I have already said about Henry's mother that you can feel two ways about her; I think that I would be prepared to feel the nicer way more often if she didn't seem to feel so consistently the nastier way about me. As it is, our relations are not very good and as, like most people, we find it easier to fight battles on our home grounds, we don't often meet.

Henry's mother doesn't bother much about dress and that day being a rather cold summer day she was wearing an old squirrel-skin coat over her tweeds. As to her hats, you can never tell much about these, because her grey hair gets loose so much and festoons all over them. It is said in the Raven family that she should have been allowed by her father to go to the University and that she would then have been a very good scholar and happy to be so. As it is, she has lived most of her life in a large red-brick Queen Anne house in Hampshire and the only way that you can tell that she is not happy like all the other ladies is that as well as gardening and jam making and local government, she does all the very difficult crossword puzzles very quickly and as well as the travel books and biographies recommended in the Sunday papers she reads sometimes in French and even in German. She closed her eyes when she saw me but this was no especial insult because as I have said she always does this when she speaks.

'You shouldn't live so close to Harrods, June dear, if you don't want morning callers,' was how she greeted me.

As Rodney and I were both obviously about to go out there was not much to answer to this. But the Ravens have a habit of half-saying what is on their minds and it immediately seemed certain to me that she had only come there because she'd heard about the lodger and wanted to pry. I said, 'This is Rodney Galt, our lodger. This is Henry's mother.'

Rodney must have formed the same conclusion for he immediately said, 'How do you do? I'm afraid this is a very brief meeting because I'm just off to the London Library.'

'Oh?' Henry's mother answered. 'You must be one of those new members who have all the books out when one wants them. It's so difficult being a country member. Of course, when Mr Cox was alive,' and she sighed, putting the blame on to Rodney but also making it quite clear to me that it was him she wanted to investigate. I thought it would be wise to deflect her so I said, 'You'll stay and have a coffee or a drink or something, won't you?'

But she was not to be deflected. 'What strange ideas you have about how I spend my mornings, June dear,' she answered, 'I haven't come up from Kingston, you know. I'm afraid you're one of those busy people who think everybody idle but yourself. I just thought it would be proper since I was so close at Harrods that we should show each other that we were both still alive. But I don't intend to waste your time, dear. Indeed if Mr Galt is going to the London Library I think I shall ask him if he will share a taxi with me. I'm getting a little old to be called "duckie" as these bus ladies seem to like to do now.'

So Rodney was caught good and proper. However, I needn't have worried for him, because when Henry came home I learned that his mother had been round to Brodrick Layland and had spent her time singing Rodney's praises. It appeared that he'd been so helpful in finding her the best edition of Saint Simon that she had offered him luncheon and that he had suggested Wheelers. His conversation must have been very pleasing to her for she made no grumble about the bill. She had only said to Henry, 'I can't think why you described him as a beautiful-looking young man. He's most presentable and very well informed too.' So we seemed to have got over that hurdle.

But Rodney was a success with all our friends; for example, with 'les jeunes filles en fleur'. This is the name that Henry and I give to two ladies called Miss Jackie Reynolds and Miss Marcia Railton and the point about the name is that although like Andrée and Albertine, they are Lesbian ladies, they are by no means jeunes filles and certainly not en fleur. Henry is very fond of them because like Lady Ann they make him feel broadminded. They are very generous and this is particularly creditable because they do not make much money out of their business of interior decoration. They have lived together for a great many years – since they were young indeed which must be a great great many years ago – and Henry always says that this is very touching. Unfortunately they are often also very boring and this seems to be all right for Henry, because when they have been particularly boring, he remembers how touching their constancy to each other is and this apparently compensates him. But it doesn't compensate me.

When the jeunes filles met Rodney, Jackie who is short and stocky with an untidy black-dyed shingle, put her head on one side and said, 'I say, isn't he a smasher!' And Marcia who is petite rather than stocky and altogether dainty in her dress, said, 'But of a Beauty!' This is the way they talk when they meet new people; Henry says it's because they are shy, and so it may be, but it usually makes everybody else rather shy too. I thought it would paralyse Rodney, but he took it in his stride and said, 'Oh! come, I'm not as good-looking as all that.' That was when I first realized that I preferred Rodney on his own and this in itself is a difficulty because if one is going to be much with somebody you are bound to be with other people sometimes. However, the evening went swimmingly. Rodney decided that, although he would always have really good objects in his *own* house, the people to whom he let furnished flats would be much happier to be interior decorated and who better to do it than les jeunes filles en fleur? Well, that suited Marcia and Jackie all right. They got together, all three in a huddle, and a very funny huddle it was. Rodney already knew of some Americans, even apart from all the people who would be taking furnished flats from him when he had them to offer, and the rest of the evening was spent in deal discussions. Henry said afterwards he'd never felt so warm to Rodney as when he saw how decent he was to les jeunes filles. I wasn't quite sure what the decency meant but still . . .

The truth was that much though I was enjoying Rodney's company,

I was beginning to get a little depressed by the suit he was so ardently pressing and the decision that this ardour was forcing upon me. It would be so much nicer if there was no cause and effect in life, no one thing leading inevitably to another, but just everything being sufficient in itself. But I could see that Rodney was not the kind of person to take life in this way and quite suddenly something forced this realization upon me rather strongly.

I have not said much about our Swiss, Henriette Vaudoyer, and I don't propose to say much now because nothing is more boring than talk about foreign domestics. I have to put up with it at three-quarters of the dinners we go to. Henriette was a very uninteresting girl, but quite pretty. There were only four of us in the house: Henry and me in one bedroom and Rodney and Henriette in two bedrooms. Well, no one can be surprised that Rodney and Henriette began to be in one bedroom sometimes too. I wasn't surprised but I was upset, it gave me a pain in my stomach. Clearly there were only two things I could do about that pain: get rid of Rodney or get rid of Henriette. The brave thing would have been to get rid of Rodney before I got worse pains; but already the pain was so bad that I was not brave enough. I gave Henriette notice. She said some very unpleasant, smug, Swiss sort of things to me and she began to say them to Henry which was more worrying. Luckily one of Henry's great virtues is that he never listens to tale-bearing and he did what is called 'cut her short'. However, he was a bit worried that I should decide to be without a foreign girl, because we'd always had one and sometimes two. But I explained that we had Mrs Golfin coming in, and she was only too pleased to come in even more, and for the rest, having more to do would be wonderful for my moods about which I was getting worried. So Henry saw the necessity and Henriette went. But I saw clearly too that I would have to decide either to accept Rodney's importuning or not, because soon he would take no answer as the same as 'answer – no'.

I think maybe I might have answered no, only at the time Henry annoyed me very much over the holiday question. This is a very old and annoying question with us. Every year since we were married Henry says, 'Well, I don't know why we shouldn't manage Venice (or Madrid, or Rome) this year. I think we've deserved it.' And first, I want to say that people don't deserve holidays, they just take them; and secondly, I want to point out that we're really quite rich and there's no question of our not being able to 'manage' Venice or Rome. I long, in fact, for the day when he will say, 'Well, I don't know why we shouldn't manage Lima this year, taking in Honolulu and Madagascar on the way home.' But if he can't say that – and he can't – then I would prefer him to ask, 'Shall we go to Italy or Spain or North Africa this year, June? The choice is yours.' However, just about the time that Henriette left, he came out with it. 'Well, I don't see why we shouldn't manage Florence this year.' So I said, 'Well I do, Henry, because I don't bloody well want to go there.' And then he was very upset and as I was feeling rather guilty anyway, I apologized and said how silly my moods were and Florence would be rather enchanting.

Henry cheered up a good deal at this. 'If that is so,' he said, 'I'm very glad, because it makes it much easier for me to tell you something. It's been decided on the spur of the moment that I'm to go to New York on business. It's only for a fortnight but I must leave next week.'

Now I wouldn't really have wanted to go to New York for Brodrick Layland on a rush visit but somehow everything conspired together to make me furious and I decided then and there that what I wanted was what Rodney wanted, physical mastery or no. And actually when the time came, the physical mastery wasn't such a trial. I mean there was nothing 'extra' or worrying about it. And for the rest, I was very pleased.

So that when Henry set off for New York, I was committed on a new course of life, as they say. But the weekend before Henry left, he insisted on running me down to a country hotel in Sussex and making a fuss of me. I suppose I should have felt very bad about it, because really he did his best to make the fuss as good as possible. But all I could think of was that I did hope cause and effect and one thing following another wasn't going to make life worse instead of better. After all I had made this committal to a new course in order to make life *less* boring, but if it meant that there were going to be more decisions and choices in front of me, it would be much *more* boring. One thing, however, I *did* decide was that I would try not to talk about Rodney to Henry even if I did have to think of him. After all, talking about Rodney would not have been a very kind return for the fussing.

In the end, however, it was Henry who raised the subject of Rodney. It seemed that Lady Ann had not been able to put a good face on all the time. One day at a cocktail party when even she had found the gin stronger than usual she had dropped her face in front of Henry. She said that the money she had spent on Rodney nobody knew – this I thought was hypocritical because she was just telling Henry how much it was – and the return he'd made had been beneath anything she'd ever experienced. I must say she couldn't have said worse, considering the sort of life she's led. Henry was very upset, because although he liked Rodney, Lady Ann was such a very old friend. But I said that age in friendship was not the proper basis for judgement (after all just because Lady Ann was so old!) and I also reminded him that hell had no fury. I succeeded in pacifying him because he didn't want his fussing of me to be spoiled, but I could see that things would never be the same between Rodney and Henry, as now indeed they were not between any of the three of us.

Well, there we were – Rodney and me alone for ten days. And Rodney did exactly the right thing – he suggested that we spent most of the time in Paris. How right this was! First there was the note of absurdity of adultery in Paris. 'That,' said Rodney, 'should satisfy your lack of self-assurance. Your passion to put all your actions in inverted commas.' It must be said that Rodney, for someone only my age, understands me very well, because I do feel less troubled about doing anything when I can see it as faintly absurd. Of course, the reasons he gives don't satisfy me very well; when I asked him why I was like that, he said, 'Because you're incurably middle class, June darling.' On the whole though, by this time Rodney gave me less of his 'patrician line'. However, things had not yet reached the pass that I could tell Rodney my theory about him.

This theory, you will already have guessed, was that he was little better or little worse or whatever than an adventurer, not to say, a potential crook. I did indeed know that his affairs had reached a serious state because of some of the telephone conversations that I overheard and because of the bills that kept arriving. The nicest thing was that Rodney paid the whole of the Paris trip. It is true that he hadn't paid for his rent for some weeks; it is also true that his trip to Paris was intended as an investment; nevertheless I think it was very lovely of him to have paid the Paris trip when he was up to his eyes in debts. Let me say that until the last day or so the Paris trip was everything I could ask or that money could buy. Also, though I don't think Rodney realized this, it was a great relief to me not to be committing adultery in Henry's house (for in a sense it *was* Henry's although it belonged to me).

It was only the last day but one of our trip, when we were sitting at a café looking at the Fontainebleau twiddly staircase and drinking

Pernod that Rodney began to press his further suit. I had been expecting it, of course; indeed it was the choice that lay ahead, the inevitable decision, and all the other things that I had so hoped would not happen but that I knew would. He asked me, in fact, to leave Henry for him. At first he just said it was what we both wanted. Then he said he loved me too much to see me go on living with Henry in such a dead, pretence life, getting more bitterly whimsical and harder every year. Then he said I was made like him to use life up and enjoy people and things and then pass on to others. It was all very unreal; but if he had only known it was exactly this confidence trick part of him that attracted me. I could quite clearly see the life of travel and hotels we should have on my money and the bump there would be when we got through my money which I think Rodney would have done rather quickly. But it was the bogusness, the insecurity and even perhaps the boue beneath, for which I had such a nostalgia.

Somehow, however, he didn't grasp this or perhaps he was too anxious to secure his aims. For he suddenly changed his tone and became a pathetic, dishonest little boy pleading for a chance. He was desperate, he said, and it must look as though he was after my money, for he was sure I had put two and two together. This I had to admit. 'Well,' he said, 'then you know the worst.' But he begged me to believe if he could have me with him, it would be different. He had real talent and he only needed some support to use it. Did I understand, he asked me, exactly what his life had been? And then he told me of his background – his father was a narrow, not very successful builder in a small Scotch town – he described to me most movingly his hatred of it all, his hard if dishonest fight to get into a different world, the odds against him. It was I, he begged, who could get him on to the tram-lines again.

I don't think I'm very maternal really, because I didn't find myself moved; I only felt cheated. If I hadn't been sure that in fact whatever he said, life with Rodney would have been much more like what I imagined than what he was now promising, I should have turned him down on the spot. As it was I said I must think about it. He must leave me alone in London for at least a fortnight and then I would give him an answer. He accepted this because anyway he had business in France, so I returned to London alone.

Henry was glad on his return to find Rodney absent, I think. And in a short while he was even more glad still. Or, at any rate, I was, because if Rodney had been in our house I think that Henry would have hit him. This, of course, might have fitted into Rodney's ideas of the violence of life, even if not into his view of civilization; and probably Rodney being much younger he would have won the fight, which would have made me very angry because of Henry. But it is just possible that Henry would have won and this would have made me very sad because of my ideal picture of Rodney.

What put the lid on it (as they used to say at some period which I'm not sure of the date of) for Henry was a visit he made to his mother shortly after his return, when he discovered that Rodney had borrowed money from her. I could only think that if Rodney could get money from Henry's mother he had little to fear about the future (and maybe if my future was joined to his, though precarious, it would not founder). But Henry, of course, saw it differently and so did I, when I heard of the sum involved which was only £50, a sum of money insufficient to prevent foundering.

Hardly had Henry's mother dealt Henry's new-found friendship a blow from the right, when up came les jeunes filles and dealt it a knockout from the left. It seemed that they had busily decorated and furnished two flats for American friends of Rodney's – one for Mrs Milton Brothers and one for Robert J. Masterson and family – and as these American people were visiting the Continent before settling in England, the bills had been given to Rodney to send to them. The bills were quite large because Rodney had told les jeunes filles not to cheese-pare. Now Mrs Brothers and Mr Masterson and family had arrived in London and it seemed that they had already given the money for les jeunes filles to Rodney plus his commission. Jackie said, 'You can imagine what it makes us look like,' and Marcia said, 'Yes, really it *is* pretty grim.' Then Jackie said, 'We look such awful chumps,' and that I think was what I agreed with most. Henry said he felt sure that when Rodney returned, he would have some explanation to offer. I didn't think this likely and I didn't think Henry did. 'Well,' said Jackie, 'that's just it. I'm not sure that Rodney ought to return because if Mrs Brothers goes on as she is now, I think there'll be a warrant out for him soon.'

I felt miserable when they had gone and so did Henry, but for different reasons. All I could find to do was to pray that Mrs Brothers should die in her bath before she could start issuing warrants. Henry said. 'I only hope he doesn't come near this house again, because I'm not sure what my duty would be.'

Then, the very next morning, at about eleven o'clock the telephone

rang and it *was* Rodney. I told him what Henry had said and we agreed
that it was most important that he should come to the house when
Henry was out. He came, in fact, just before lunch.

I had expected him to look a little haunted like Humphrey Bogart
sometimes used to in fugitive films; he did look a little hunted but it
wasn't quite like the films. Less to my taste. As I looked at him, I
suddenly thought of something. So I made an excuse and ran upstairs
and hid my jewel box. I would have hated to have been issuing
warrants for Rodney. Then we had a long chat and something more.
About that I will only say I have rather a 'time and a place' view and so
it ended things as far as I was concerned with a whimper rather than a
bang. As to the chat, I said that I had thought things over and the
answer was no, very reluctantly. And when people say 'you don't
know what it cost me', I think it's rather stupid because they could
always tell you. So I will tell what this cost me – it cost me the whole of
a possible, different life with someone very attractive. I shall always
regret it when the life I am leading is particularly boring, which it
often is. But that, after all, is the nature of decisions. The answer had
to be no. And I do not despair of other chances. But life is, indeed, a
cheat.

What Rodney said after my negative answer was a pity. He went on
again about how soon I would become a hard little bitch and rather
depressing with all my 'amusing' talk. He even said, 'I should think
you might go off your head. People who get the idea that they can
make a game of other people's lives often do.'

I must say that I thought, everything considered about Rodney's
own life, this was a bit too much. And in any case all this toughness
and bullying was all right when Rodney was pressing his suit, but now
that the suit had been pressed and sent back, I thought it all rather
boring. And so I changed the conversation to the warrant that might
be out at any moment. Rodney was well aware of this, he said, and he
had almost enough but not quite to get abroad that night. I said I
would see what I could find in ready cash, because obviously cheques
would be no good. He didn't seem sure about this, but I stuck to
my point, emphasizing how little he understood money matters as
evidenced in his life.

While I was looking for what cash I had, he went upstairs to the
lavatory and I heard him walking about in my bedroom so I was glad
for his sake that I had hidden my jewel box. And I did find enough to
help him overseas, because I had put some aside in case he turned up

although I did not tell him this. Away, looking rather hunted but still very handsome, he went out of my life.

It was all rather an anti-climax without Rodney, although his name was kept alive, what with Henry's mother, and les jeunes filles, and the Americans, and Mr Brodrick furious at only having a first chapter, however brilliant, after paying so much in advances. But all this was not the same for me as Rodney's physical presence, not at all the same.

It was only a month later that it got into the papers in quite a small column that he'd been arrested for stealing some money at the house of the Marchesa Ghirlaindini in Rome where he was a guest. It mentioned also about Mrs Brothers's warrant.

Well, I did miss the excitement of life with him and the decision that I hated so much when I had to make it; so I got talking to an old friend of mine – Mary Mudie who writes a long, gossipy column in a Sunday newspaper. And sure enough there was a featured bit about him the very next Sunday. All about the well-known people he'd dined with and about Lady Ann Denton, how he was one of the 'many fortunate young men of talent and charm who had profited by her friendship', and how valuable she was as a bridge between her generation and the young. Then there was a bit about Rodney's great brilliance as a writer and how few who knew him in this capacity realized his double life. It told us with what expectancy connoisseurs of the fresh and original in modern writing had awaited his new book and how ironic its title *Honour and Civility* now seemed. So brilliant was the first chapter of this, it said, that an old-established publishing firm, famed for its cautious policy, had gone to unusual lengths to assist its young author. Realizing the supreme importance to a writer of congenial surroundings in which to work, the enterprising junior partner Mr Henry Raven even installed their brilliant protégé as a tenant in his own house. Then came a block heading 'More Friend Than Lodger' and it was followed by a bit about me. '"I can hardly believe that Rodney was leading this double life," said almond-eyed, brunette June Raven, well-known young London hostess and wife of publisher Raven, "he was more of a friend than a lodger as far as I was concerned. He was not only clever and witty, but he had the rare gift of easy intimacy."'' Dear Mary followed this up immediately with a mention of Rodney's first book, *Cuckoo* – 'a study of married infidelity in history's pages as witty as it was scholarly.' The paragraphs went on with a little interview with Rodney's parents. '"Rodney never took to the building trade," his father told me in the front parlour of his typical unpretentious little Scots "hame", "he always wanted big things out of life."' And then Mary ended on a moral note, 'Rodney Galt got his big things – bigger perhaps than he imagined when an Italian court on Monday last sentenced him . . .' It was a sad little article, but I did think it was clever of Mary to have made so much of what I told her.

I'm afraid Rodney will be very upset by the piece about his parents, but he did say very nasty things to me. And Henry, too, won't like the 'more friend than lodger' part, but Henry ought to pay for my being faithful to him too, I think. At least that's how I feel, after life has presented me with such awful choices.

Sure enough Henry read Mary's article and got into a terrible rage. 'I'm pretty sure it's actionable,' he said. So I looked very nonchalant and said, 'I don't think so, darling, because I supplied Mary with all the information.' Then he looked at me and said, 'I think you should be very careful, June. This sort of mischievous behaviour is frequently a danger signal. It may seem a strange thing to say to you but you'd only have yourself to blame if you went off your head.' He was trembling when he went out of the room, so I think it likely that he'd known about me and Rodney for some time.

Well, there you are – both Henry and Rodney take a 'psychological' view of me. But as I said before I often think that common sense views are wiser. I spoke before of my old nurse and what she used to say of me was, 'Miss June wants to have her cake and eat it.' Well, so do most people one meets nowadays. But I think perhaps I want it more than the rest, which makes me think that in the end I'll get it.

THE LOTUS

'Garland says she's a tart.'

'A tart! My dear Christine, have you seen her? After all, there are limits.'

'What, round about the Portobello Road? I very much doubt it.'

'Nonsense,' Ronnie said. 'She's writing a novel. Yes, dearie –' he opened his eyes very wide and turned the corners of his mouth down – 'all about a girl who gets seduced –'

'Well, well.'

'On a haystack.' Ronnie roared with laughter.

'Perhaps we'll have a bit of luck; she may get tight earlier than usual tonight and not turn up.'

'Not turn up? You bet she will.'

Christine said, 'I can't imagine why you asked her here at all.'

'Well, she borrowed a book the other day, and she said she was coming up to return it. What was I to do?'

While they were still arguing there was a knock on the door and he called, 'Come in . . . Christine, this is Mrs Heath, Lotus Heath.'

'Good evening,' Lotus said in a hoarse voice. 'How are you? Quite well, I hope . . . Good evening, Mr Miles. I've brought your book. *Most* enjoyable.'

She was a middle-aged woman, short and stout. Her plump arms were bare, the finger nails varnished bright red. She had rouged her mouth unskilfully to match her nails, but her face was very pale. The front of her black dress was grey with powder.

'The way these windows rattle!' Christine said. 'Hysterical, I call it.' She wedged a piece of newspaper into the sash, then sat down on the divan. Lotus immediately moved over to her side and leaned forward.

'You do like me, dear, don't you? Say you like me.'

'Of course I do.'

'I think it's so nice of you to ask me up here,' Lotus said. Her
sad eyes, set very wide apart, rolled vaguely round the room, which
was distempered yellow and decorated with steamship posters –
'Morocco, Land of Sunshine', 'Come to Beautiful Bali'. 'I get fed up, I
can tell you, sitting by myself in that basement night after night. And
day after day if it comes to that.'

Christine remarked primly, 'This is a horribly depressing part of
London, I always think.'

Her nostrils dilated. Then she pressed her arms close against her
sides, edged away and lit a cigarette, breathing the smoke in deeply.

'But you've got it very nice up here, haven't you? Is that a
photograph of your father on the mantelpiece? You are like him.'

Ronnie glanced at his wife and coughed. 'Well, how's the poetry
going?' he asked, smiling slyly as he said the word 'poetry' as if at an
improper joke. 'And the novel, how's that getting on?'

'Not too fast,' Lotus said, looking at the whisky decanter. Ronnie
got up hospitably.

She took the glass he handed to her, screwed up her eyes, emptied it
at a gulp and watched him refill it with an absentminded expression.

'But it's wonderful the way it comes to me,' she said. 'It's going to
be a long book. I'm going to get everything in – the whole damn thing.
I'm going to write a book like nobody's ever written before.'

'You're quite right, Mrs Heath, make it a long book,' Ronnie
advised.

His politely interested expression annoyed Christine. 'Is he trying
to be funny?' she thought, and felt prickles of irritation all over her
body. She got up, murmuring, 'I'll see if there's any more whisky. It's
sure to be needed.'

'The awful thing,' Lotus said as she was going out, 'is not knowing
the words. That's the torture – knowing the thing and not knowing
the words.'

In the bedroom next door Christine could still hear her monotonous, sing-song voice, the voice of a woman who often talked to
herself. 'Springing this ghastly old creature on me!' she thought.
'Ronnie must be mad.'

'This place is getting me down,' she thought. The front door was
painted a bland blue. There were four small brass plates and bell-
pushes on the right-hand side – Mr and Mrs Garland, Mr and Mrs
Miles, Mrs Spencer, Miss Reid, and a dirty visiting-card tacked
underneath – Mrs Lotus Heath. A painted finger pointed downwards.

Christine powdered her face and made up her mouth carefully. What could the fool be talking about?

'Is it as hopeless as all that?' she said, when she opened the sitting-room door. Lotus was in tears.

'Very good.' Ronnie looked bashful and shuffled his feet. 'Very good indeed, but a bit sad. Really, a bit on the sad side, don't you think?'

Christine laughed softly.

'That's what my friend told me,' Lotus said, ignoring her hostess. '"Whatever you do, don't be gloomy," he said, "because that gets on people's nerves. And don't write about anything you know, for then you get excited and say too much, and that gets under their skins too. Make it up; use your imagination." And what about my book? That isn't sad, is it! I'm using my imagination. All the same, I wish I could write down some of the things that have happened to me, just write them down straight, sad or not sad. I've had my bit of fun too; I'll say I have.'

Ronnie looked at Christine, but instead of responding she looked away and pushed the decanter across the table.

'Have another drink before you tell us any more. Do, please. That's what the whisky's here for. Make the most of it, because I'm sorry to say there isn't any more in the kitchen and the pub is shut now.'

'She thinks I'm drinking too much of your Scotch,' Lotus said to Ronnie.

'No, I'm sure she doesn't think that.'

'Well, don't think that, dear – what's your name? – Christine. I've got a bottle of port downstairs and I'll go and get it in a minute.'

'Do,' Christine said. 'Let's be really matey.'

'That's right, dear. Well, as I was saying to Mr Miles, the best thing I ever wrote was poetry. I don't give a damn about the novel, just between you and me. Only to make some money, the novel is. Poetry's what I really like. All the same, the memory I've got, you wouldn't believe. Do you know, I can remember things people have said to me ever so long ago? If I try, I can hear the words and I can remember the voice saying them. It's wonderful, the memory I've got. Of course, I can't do it as well now as I used to, but there you are, nobody stays young for ever.'

'No, isn't it distressing?' Christine remarked to no one in particular. 'Most people go on living long after they ought to be dead, don't they? Especially women.'

'Sarcastic, isn't she? A dainty little thing, but sarcastic.' Lotus got up, swayed and held on to the mantelpiece. 'Are you a mother, dear?'

'Do you mean me?'

'No, I can see you're not – and never will be if you can help it. You're too fly, aren't you? Well, anyway, I've just finished a poem. I wrote it with the tears running down my face and it's the best thing I ever wrote. It was as if somebody was saying into my ears all the time, "Write it, write it." Just like that. It's about a woman and she's in court and she hears the judge condemning her son to death. "You must die," he says. "No, no, no," the woman says, "he's too young." But the old judge keeps on. "Till you die," he says. And, you see –' her voice rose – 'he's not real. He's a dummy, like one of those things ventriloquists have, he's not *real*. And nobody knows it. But she knows it. And so she says – wait, I'll recite it to you.'

She walked into the middle of the room and stood very straight with her head thrown back and her feet together. Then she clasped her hands loosely behind her back and announced in a high, artificial voice, 'The Convict's Mother.'

Christine began to laugh. 'This is too funny. You mustn't think me rude, I can't help it. Recitations always make me behave badly.' She went to the gramophone and turned over the records. 'Dance for us instead. I'm sure you dance beautifully. Here's the very thing – *Just One More Chance*. That'll do, won't it?'

'Don't take any notice of her,' Ronnie said. 'You go on with the poem.'

'Not much I won't. What's the good, if your wife doesn't like poetry?'

'Oh, she's only a silly kid.'

'Tell me what you laugh at, and I'll tell you what you are,' Lotus said. 'Most people laugh when you're unhappy, that's when they laugh. I've lived long enough to know what – and maybe I'll live long enough to see them laugh the other side of their faces, too.'

'Don't you take any notice of her,' Ronnie repeated. 'She's like that.' He nodded at Christine's back, speaking in a proud and tender voice. 'She was telling me only this morning that she doesn't believe in being sentimental about other people. Weren't you, Christine?'

'I didn't tell you anything of the sort.' Christine turned round, her face scarlet. 'I said I was tired of slop – that's what I said. And I said I was sick of being asked to pity people who are only getting what they deserve. When people have a rotten time you can bet it's their own fault.'

'Go on,' said Lotus. 'You're talking like a bloody fool, dear. You've never felt anything in your life, or you wouldn't be able to say that. Rudimentary heart, that's your trouble. Your father may be a clergyman, but you've got a rudimentary heart all the same.' She was still standing in the middle of the room, with her hands behind her back. 'You tell her, Mr What's-your-name? Tell the truth and shame the devil. Go on, tell your little friend she's talking like a bloody fool.'

'Now, now, now, what's all this about?' Ronnie shifted uncomfortably. He reached out for the decanter and tilted it upside down into his glass. 'It's always when you want a drink really badly that there isn't any more. Have you ever noticed it? What about that port?'

The two women were glaring at each other. Neither answered him.

'What about that port, Mrs Heath? Let's have a look at that port you promised us.'

'Oh yes, the port,' Lotus said, 'the port. All right, I'll get it.'

As soon as she had gone Christine began to walk up and down the room furiously. 'What's the idea? Why are you encouraging that horrible woman? "Your little friend", did you hear that? Does she think I'm your concubine or something? Do you like her to insult me?'

'Oh, don't be silly, she didn't mean to insult you,' Ronnie argued. 'She's tight – that's what's the matter with her. I think she's damned comic. She's the funniest old relic of the past I've struck for a long time.'

Christine went on as if she had not heard him. 'This hellish, filthy slum and my hellish life in it! And now you must produce this creature, who stinks of whisky and all the rest better left unsaid, to *talk* to me. To talk to me! There are limits, as you said yourself, there are limits . . . Seduced on a haystack, my God! . . . She oughtn't to be touched with a barge-pole.'

'I say, look out,' Ronnie said. 'She's coming back. She'll hear you.'

'Let her hear me,' said Christine.

She went on to the landing and stood there. When she saw the top of Lotus' head she said in a clear, high voice, 'I really can't stay any longer in the same room as that woman. The mixture of whisky and mustiness is too awful.'

She went into the bedroom, sat down on the bed and began to laugh. Soon she was laughing so heartily that she had to put the back of her hand over her mouth to stop the noise.

'Hullo,' Ronnie said, 'so here you are.'

'I couldn't find the port.'

'That's all right. Don't you worry about that.'

'I did have some.'

'That's quite all right . . . My wife's not very well. She had to go to bed.'

'I know when I've had the bird, Mr Miles,' Lotus said. 'Only give us another drink. I bet you've got some put away somewhere.'

There was some sherry in the cupboard.

'Thanks muchly.'

'Won't you sit down?'

'No, I'm going. But see me downstairs. It's so dark, and I don't know where the lights are.'

'Certainly, certainly.'

He went ahead, turning on the lights at each landing, and she followed him, holding on to the banisters.

Outside the rain had stopped but the wind was still blowing strong and very cold.

'Help me down these damned steps, will you? I don't feel too good.'

He put his hand under her arm and they went down the area steps. She got her key out of her bag and opened the door of the basement flat.

'Come on in for a minute. I've got a lovely fire going.'

The room was small and crowded with furniture. Four straight-backed chairs with rococo legs, armchairs with the stuffing coming out, piles of old magazines, photographs of Lotus herself, always in elaborate evening dress, smiling and lifeless.

Ronnie stood rocking himself from heel to toe. He liked the photographs. 'Must have been a good-looking girl twenty years ago,' he thought, and as if in answer Lotus said in a tearful voice, 'I had everything; my God, I had. Eyes, hair, teeth, figure, the whole damned thing. And what was the good of it?'

The window was shut and a brown curtain was drawn across it. The room was full of the sour smell of the three dustbins that stood in the area outside.

'What d'you pay for this place?' Ronnie said, stroking his chin.

'Thirty bob a week, unfurnished.'

'Do you know that woman owns four houses along this street? And every floor let, basements and all. But there you are – money makes money, and if you haven't any you can whistle for it. Yes, money makes money.'

'Let it,' said Lotus. 'I don't care a damn.'

'Now then, don't talk so wildly.'

'I don't care a damn. Tell the world I said it. Not a damn. That was never what I wanted. I don't care about the things you care about.'

'Cracked, poor old soul,' he thought, and said: 'Well, I'll be getting along if you're all right.'

'You know – that port. I really had some. I wouldn't have told you I had some if I hadn't. I'm not that sort of person at all. You believe me, don't you?'

'Of course I do.' He patted her shoulder. 'Don't you worry about a little thing like that.'

'When I came down it had gone. And I don't need anybody to tell me where it went, either.'

'Ah?'

'Some people are blighters; some people are proper blighters. He takes everything he can lay his hands on. Never comes to see me except it's to grab something.' She put her elbows on her knees and her head in her hands and began to cry. 'I've had enough. I've had enough, I can tell you. The things people say! My Christ, the things they say . . .'

'Oh, don't let them get you down,' Ronnie said. 'That'll never do. Better luck next time.'

She did not answer or look at him. He fidgeted. 'Well, I must be running along, I'm afraid. Cheerio. Remember – better luck next time.'

As soon as he got upstairs Christine called out from the bedroom, and when he went in she told him that they must get away, that it wasn't any good saying he couldn't afford a better flat, he must afford a better flat.

Ronnie thought that on the whole she was right, but she talked and talked and after a while it got on his nerves. So he went back into the sitting-room and read a list of second-hand gramophone records for sale at a shop near by, underlining the titles that attracted him. *I'm a Dreamer, Aren't We all? I've Got You Under My Skin* – that one certainly; he underlined it twice. Then he collected the glasses and took them into the kitchen for the charwoman to wash up the next morning.

He opened the window and looked out at the wet street. 'I've got you under my skin,' he hummed softly.

The street was dark as a country lane, bordered with lopped trees. It glistened – rather wickedly, he thought.

'Deep in the heart of me,' he hummed. Then he shivered – a very cold wind for the time of year – turned away from the window and wrote a note to the charwoman: 'Mrs Bryan. Please call me as soon as you get here.' He underlined 'soon' and propped the envelope up against one of the dirty dishes. As he did so he heard an odd, squeaking noise. He looked out of the window again. A white figure was rushing up the street, looking very small and strange in the darkness.

'But she's got nothing on,' he said aloud, and craned out eagerly.

A police whistle sounded. The squeaking continued, and the Garlands' window above him went up.

Two policemen half-supported, half-dragged Lotus along. One of them had wrapped her in his cape, which hung down to her knees. Her legs were moving unsteadily below it. The trio went down the area steps.

Christine had come into the kitchen and was looking over his shoulder. 'Good Lord,' she said. 'Well, that's one way of attracting attention if all else fails.'

The bell rang.

'It's one of the policemen,' said Ronnie.

'What's he want to ring our bell for? We don't know anything about her. Why doesn't he ring somebody else's bell?'

The bell rang again.

'I'd better go down,' Ronnie said.

'Do you know anything about Mrs Heath, Mrs Lotus Heath, who lives in the basement flat?' the policeman asked.

'I know her by sight,' Ronnie answered cautiously.

'She's a bit of a mess,' said the policeman.

'Oh, dear!'

'She's passed out stone cold,' the policeman went on confidentially. 'And she looks as if there's something more than drink the matter, if you ask me.'

Ronnie said in a shocked voice – he did not know why – 'Is she dying?'

'Dying? No!' said the policeman, and when he said 'No!' death became unthinkable, the invention of hysteria, something that simply didn't happen. Not to ordinary people. 'She'll be all right. There'll be an ambulance here in a minute. Do you know anything about the person?'

'Nothing,' Ronnie said, 'nothing.'

'Ah?' The policeman wrote in his notebook. 'Is there anybody else in the house, do you think, who'd give us some information?' He shone a light on the brass plates on the door post. 'Mr Garland?'

'Not Mr Garland,' Ronnie answered hurriedly. 'I'm sure not. She's not at all friendly with the Garlands, I know that for a fact. She didn't have much to do with anybody.'

'Thank you very much,' the policeman said. Was his voice ironical?

He pressed Miss Reid's bell and when no answer came looked upwards darkly. But he didn't get any change out of Number Six, Albion Crescent. Everybody had put their lights out and shut their windows.

'You see –' Ronnie began.

'Yes, I see,' the policeman said.

When Ronnie got upstairs again Christine was in bed.

'Well, what was it all about?'

'She seems to have conked out. They're getting an ambulance.'

'Really? Poor devil.' ('Poor devil' she said, but it did not mean anything.) 'I thought she looked awful, didn't you? That dead-white face, and her lips such a funny colour after her lipstick got rubbed off. Did you notice?'

A car stopped outside and Ronnie saw the procession coming up the area steps, everybody looking very solemn and important. And it was pretty slick, too – the way they put the stretcher into the ambulance. He knew that the Garlands were watching from the top floor and Mrs Spencer from the floor below. Miss Reid's floor was in darkness because she was away for a few days.

'Funny how this street gives me goose-flesh tonight,' he thought. 'Somebody walking over my grave, as they say.'

He could not help admiring the way Christine ignored the whole sordid affair, lying there with her eyes shut and the eiderdown pulled up under her chin, smiling a little. She looked very pretty, warm and happy like a child when you have given it a sweet to suck. And peaceful.

A lovely child. So lovely that he had to tell her how lovely she was, and start kissing her.

MISS PULKINHORN

This isn't a ghost story. I wish it were. What I personally believe doesn't come into this story. An organist has to subscribe to what the chapter believes or at least keep his mouth shut. Come to that, the chapter is rocky enough if you ask me, what with this reservation of the Sacrament and all the rest. Isn't that in a rubric or flat against the thirty-nine articles or something?

I suppose Miss Pulkinhorn knew them by heart. What a woman! Understand me, I can think of a dozen women, fifty women connected with the cathedral, and all sincere, devout, and good. But Miss Pulkinhorn was an oddity. A cathedral always collects one like that, crazy with opinions and hate. You can even see a couple like her, hats perched up, feathers a-quiver, nodding and whispering away the reputation of half the city. They always believe in their own privileged goodness, of course – want their pennies and their buns: want to keep pride and vanity and hate and yet remain God's own special chicken. She was one of that sort. She set about removing me because after all I'm a worldly creature even for an organist but she couldn't catch me up to anything. And when I got my knighthood and became Sir Edward, I was canonized, so to speak – part of the dignity of the diocese – and she couldn't touch me. Besides, I altered a little – what with music and glass for a hobby – I found it easy enough to conform. As I got interested in painted glass, year by year time slid away. Time doesn't count in a cathedral even though this story stretches over a whole generation. When I first knew her I thought a church window was a hole to let in light. By the end, I was a knighted organist and something of an authority on painted glass and our own windows in particular; though with one exception they're a shoddy lot. The exception is the Abraham window in the ambulatory and it's part of this story in a very subtle way. But the time factor in a cathedral doesn't affect the concentration, the unity of a story. Time ceases to be a dimension, drawing things apart. Two hundred years are nothing and what happened five hundred years ago is just round the corner. I see his strange involuntary association with Miss Pulkinhorn as a single thing that grew persistently and slowly as a great tree. When it was a seedling I was a cheerful young man with a tendency to – irregularities. When it ended, position and respectability lay on me like the dust on the tombs.

She was desperately poor, you know, and kept up appearances in a huge wreck of a house. Those were easy days for finding servants but all she ever had was a woman to help in the mornings. She was a great one for the cathedral and I don't suppose she ever missed a service, but sat out the lot, simmering with disapproval. Between whiles she came into the cathedral once a day and swept round it in a – possessive manner; though not only the weather but the vestments, the candles, the images, must have been purgatory for her. Between the two wars when they re-dedicated the chapel of St Augustine and reserved the Sacrament there, I'm told she nearly left the diocese. She carried an ebony cane with a silver top and she was so tiny it seemed to reach her shoulder. She wore a black silk dress and a black silk coat that reached her instep. Her neck was enmeshed in black netting stiffened at the nape with wire. The netting spread down in front under the short 'V' of her dress-front which was fastened with an enormous topaz brooch. Her hat was a round black thing set exactly on top of her head and gleaming with feathers. She would come through the north-west door, go up the north aisle, her stick clicking as she went, and into the ambulatory. When she passed the chapel of the Sacrament she would lift her chin higher, and come as near as a lady should to a sniff. A light burns there whenever the Sacrament is present, and is put out if it's not. She'd go on round the ambulatory, down the south aisle, across inside the great west door, and out again where she had come in. I labelled that round in my mind as 'Miss Pulkinhorn's tour of the estate'. I suppose she was going through the list of all the things that ought to be different, mentally removing everything that conflicted with her own peculiar conception of God.

Take a candle now. Is there anything prettier in the world than those little nests of lighted candles you'll see – say in Chartres cathedral? There they are, alive and twinkling in the darkness with those unbelievable windows smouldering above them. I had the luck to hear Miss Pulkinhorn on the subject of candles. She struck her cane on the floor and hissed: 'Like a Christmas Tree!' Precisely. Miss

Pulkinhorn didn't understand Christmas. Anything more than the bare date was pretty high up on the list of her 'superstitions'. She had some honorary position which gave her the chance to direct the future behaviour of fallen women, poor things. And she kept what she could of the city very, very clean. One night when I had her too much on my mind I totted up her list of triumphs; three wives, two school-masters, and a parson.

And, of course, him.

He was her masterpiece, her magnum opus, the crown of her life's work. I don't think she intended to do what she did. I'm sure she meant everything for the best. She wanted to teach him a lesson; and believe me, when so much bigotry and ignorance gets mixed up with jealousy on however high a plane, it curdles into a poison that can turn a woman into a witch. It can make a criminal trick feel like an act of charity. I'm sure she called it charity. She probably prayed for him with the dead top of her mind while everything underneath was festering.

Was he a saint? No, I'm certain he wasn't. Read about the saints, even the least spectacular among them, and somewhere in their characters you'll come across steel-sheer adamant, something that can't be driven. He was a good man but a weak man; immeasurably better than most of us, and he lived, you'll see, on the very fringe of lunacy. He was a self-deceiver, as successful in his line as Miss Pulkinhorn, but his deceit had a kind of innocence about it. I didn't believe in his illuminated face, of course. That rumour began to float about and maddened Miss Pulkinhorn. I watched him, so I ought to know. You can see from the organ-loft across the chancel right into the chapel of the Sacrament. Glancing in my mirror as I played – my driving mirror, I call it – I could see the choir or the decani at least, and beyond them the Bohun chantry and Bishop Winne holding up two stumps. Beyond that I could see the light flickering by the Sacrament and shining on his bowed bald head. That was my daily life for a generation. Fill in the summer differences for yourself. If he'd started shining or levitating or any of the stock things, I should have spotted him in my mirror.

Then there's the window. He didn't notice things as a normal man does but he might have noticed Abraham unconsciously. Mind, I'm not doubting his belief. Day after day, year after year, you'd see him shambling up the north aisle, his bright, silly face tilted a little, his patched overcoat flapping round him, his broken shoes scraping over the stones. In summer that coat looked like a piece of dusty carpet that daylight discovers crumpled somewhere in a shed. In winter he moved in it a shadow among shadows. He was old, thirty years ago when I saw him first and he changed no more than Miss Pulkinhorn. Three times a day he went into the chapel of the Sacrament, knelt at the back, and worshipped what was reserved there. He came for a while in the morning after consecration or perhaps during the service and sometimes followed the Sacrament into the chapel. He'd come back at midday for a longer spell and then exactly at half past six in the evening. If the light was out he'd go away. What point was there in his staying? But you could set your watch by his half past six visit.

This is an indecent story. It trespasses on the privacies of two most unfortunate people. Yet I was woven into it and can't escape my knowledge nor partial responsibility for what happened. What mercy we all need! Now I look back after these years I can feel nothing but remorse and shame for my lack of wit; and pity for them, pity for us all.

But this indecency – he wasn't properly conscious, you know. Sometimes when the fit was on him he'd give things away with a kind of frantic eagerness. And some of his visits to the chapel were more successful than others. He'd be there, bowed and kneeling and occasionally his head would lift and his arms – and he'd look ecstatic. You see that gesture here and there in religious art as a symbol of revelation. There's a figure like that in Chartres and one in Rheims. I've even seen it in a hieroglyphic four thousand years old and always meaning the same thing. But we've got it too, in the Abraham window. Some people object to the secondary colours, orange, purple, and mauve, that you get in fifteenth-century glass, but I enjoy it. There they are, God appearing from a great burst of colour, smiling in a friendly, fatherly way, and Abraham below in the right-hand light, smiling up with face and hands lifted.

Well, Miss Pulkinhorn disapproved of his habits publicly. I'm sure that privately she hated him. She came to hang all her feelings on his alleged superstition; and I think she was jealous – jealous of his simplicity and fervour; jealous of his devotion with all the dreadful energy of childless and ignorant women. She'd have called him an exhibitionist if she'd known the world, and perhaps in an innocent way he was. You see he *could* have got that gesture from Abraham. That was why I checked up on the rumour of his shining face. Like all people who don't believe in miracles, I was very ready to accept one. But he remained as he was, time drifted past, and the tree of their relationship grew.

One foggy December night I let myself out of my house and walked briskly across the close to the cathedral. Nobody was about except the precentor who passed me by Saint Swithin's Gate, and I felt chilly and lonely as I let myself in. The office had been said, as is usual on a Monday, and not sung. But Canon Blake was about as ill as he could be and next morning we were to have a special service of intercession for him. He was a great benefactor of the school and the hospital and a good friend to me, but Tuesday is my day in London, so our organ being what it is I was going to set the pistons for my new assistant and leave a note. Now I remember I wanted to try over an old prelude of mine that I'd turned up – yes, of course, otherwise I should never have warmed my hands as I did. I let myself in by the organist's door and walked gratefully into the warmth. We've got eight great stoves in the cathedral and one stands just where the Norman work ends and the fifteenth-century addition begins. It's by the chapel of the Sacrament and the flue goes straight up through the vaulting. I tucked my music under one arm, pulled off my gloves, and felt the stove gingerly. They're pretty nearly red hot sometimes but this one had been shut down for the night and was only a very little too warm. The light was flickering away in the chapel and someone was moving in there at the back. It was Miss Pulkinhorn. She came out of the shadows and walked quickly towards the light. Then she saw me and stopped. We were almost alone in the cathedral, for it shuts at seven. Only old Rekeby was prowling round somewhere, moving chairs, shutting doors, and shining his electric torch into corners. Miss Pulkinhorn turned and walked out of the chapel, passing me without a word, and vanished into the shadows of the east end. She held her stick away from the pavement too. It didn't click. Less than half a minute later the north-west door bumped and *he* came in, though it was long past his usual time. He fairly cantered up the aisle, talking to himself and fumbling with the buttons of his overcoat. He rushed past me into the chapel and slumped on his knees. Then and there with no preliminary cough or shuffle or settling down he went straight into that position, for all the world like Abraham in the window.

I stayed where I was, thinking less of music and more of what extraordinary things we are. And I was vaguely worried. Do you know those days of discomfort when you expect the worst without reason?

Standing there, still mechanically caressing the stove, I felt a kind of expanding worry that I was unable to pin down. Usually when I saw him so, even when I took Abraham into account, I maintained a kind of interior respect for something I couldn't understand. What was different now? I walked away across the chancel towards the steps that lead up to the organ loft, but my unformed worry went with me. I felt let down and didn't know why. Something was cheapened. That was it. Something was cheapened and diminished. Then as I reached the top step, I remembered the precentor pacing through the close, going to visit Canon Blake on his death-bed, pacing along, a bell-shaped figure in his black cloak, and under the cloak the silvery pyx; and in the silver pyx the Reserved Sacrament.

At that moment I was pulling my hind foot a little breathlessly on to the top step. I'm a ruminative character and lack presence of mind, but I understood the situation in a black flash. There was Miss Pulkinhorn swallowed up in the shadows of the east end. Old Rekeby had locked all doors but the north-west one where he would let himself out and was trotting across the chancel, flicking his torch here and there, going towards the chapel of the Sacrament – and there *he* was on the pinnacle of his secret happiness, hands lifted, face tilted towards the light.

I turned back and pretty well hurled myself down the wooden stairs. As I came out of the chancel Rekeby was standing in the doorway by the stove. He never noticed *him* there at the back – it was past half past six you see. He bustled forward, bobbed to the altar, went up to the aumbry and bobbed again a bit doubtfully. He fumbled for his keys, opened the door, peered into the empty cupboard, and said in a vexed voice: 'I thought so!'

He shut the door carefully. Completely unaware of the ecstatic at the back of the chapel he leaned forward and blew out the light.

I could have done something, I suppose, shouted 'Stop!' or 'One moment, Rekeby!' or thrown a fit. But while I was standing there, appalled and useless, Rekeby came out, said 'Good night, Sir Edward', and went back across the chancel, his torch flicking over the patterned stones. I suppose the chapel was silent for ten seconds. Then a voice laughed and choked and laughed and a shadow cannoned into the stove and reeled past me down the north aisle, laughing and crying till all the echoes got under way and answered. I groped after him, and Rekeby was shambling down the south aisle flashing his torch from the pavement to the roof and shouting, 'What is it? What is it?'

I found him inside the west door sitting on the step. I put my arm across his shoulders and Rekeby shone the quivering circle over his feet. After a while he stopped crying, but he was quite infantile, and his fingers were moving about. We got him outside between us. I remember a great red moon was detaching itself from the fog and gave next to no light. Rekeby locked the door behind him and we carried him like a long sack to the verger's cottage where we stretched him out on an old horse-hair sofa. Rekeby went to telephone the hospital so I myself had the job of getting the overcoat off him. He was nearly naked under it. All he had on was that pair of broken boots and his trousers and a cruel leather belt. And he knew nothing at all. The ambulance men were brisk and efficient – service couldn't have been better. At the hospital he was put to bed, bathed, and tucked up. I went with him but he noticed nobody. I visited him a couple of times after that but I don't suppose he noticed me. A month later he just guttered out.

When I got home from the hospital that first night I went to bed but I couldn't sleep. I went over and over the years and what I knew of them both till my throat was dry and my brain as useless as a pumpkin. I've told you I'm a fairly slow sort of fellow. Do you know, two o'clock struck before it dawned on me that she was still locked in the cathedral? I shot out of bed then and ran to the window. There the cathedral was, huge and squat, with the moonlight glistening icily on the windows. She was inside somewhere, a tiny upright figure in that vast darkness: and by the time I'd got my clothes on I'd come to see that I couldn't let her out.

I wonder how she did it? I suppose she nipped in when the Precentor left, lit the light, and sat right at the back waiting for him to come in. She'd have let him pray to it, I think, and then broken to him gently and lovingly that he was a superstitious fool for his pains and the cupboard was bare. But things went wrong for both of them – he didn't come, you see, so when she thought he was stopping away she went forward to blow out the light – and saw me. If her little wit had been quick enough she could have trumped up some excuse and still put it out – but she lacked presence of mind. She hurried past me not knowing what to say and hid in the east end, trying to think. Then he came after all – late but divinely happy with the one possible excuse for lateness at that appointment. Can you see? Imagine the tramp or labourer stopping him in the foggy back street, asking for the price of a bed, and backing away from the gift of a jacket and grubby shirt pulled off then and there, thrust upon him! So he was late – but think of the tidal wave of joy and triumph that hurried him up the aisle into the chapel and flung him on his knees!

I wonder what she thought standing there in the darkness listening to the end of his humanity? From where I stood in my bedroom I could see the east end and the chapel of the Sacrament. Of course, I thought, in sober fact she could get out whenever she wanted to – switch on the light or ring the five-minute bell. But no. How could so much warped respectability run the slightest risk of being connected with a scandal like that? And I could do nothing without letting her know that I was on to her game. I had to pretend ignorance. She must sit there, a tiny upright figure, while the moon moved down the walls and the effigies crept into the light.

I made tea and sat smoking. There is a kind of justice, isn't there? But I've never known it so apt to the occasion. So she kept her vigil and I kept it with her, so to speak, parallel, till the moon faded and you could see that roofs were red.

My assistant was surprised to see me next day. I'd forgotten the note and the pistons and in the end I put off the academy and played for the service myself. That wasn't entirely on Canon Blake's behalf either. I was too interested in Miss Pulkinhorn. I wanted to see if she would have the nerve to come, and what the night had done to her. And what effect was apparent, should you say? None. Absolutely none. Brave, blind, indomitable woman! She sat, stood, knelt, opened and closed her mouth exactly as she'd done for twenty years back – a timeless woman. Really I began to think I'd imagined the whole thing, and of course his death made no more stir than the fall of a sparrow. The shadows were much the same, the light burned peacefully in his chapel that was so often empty now.

A few months later the effect broke in Miss Pulkinhorn. I was coming up the north aisle, hurrying because I was near enough late for Evensong. I caught my heel on the step up to the ambulatory and the confounded thing came off and wrenched my ankle. I picked the heel up and went limping and muttering past his chapel, and I heard a little shriek inside and a chair fell over. Miss Pulkinhorn came out with great dignity and her usual lapidary expression. But the topaz brooch

shivered and jumped and would not be still. I stood back to let her pass
and we stopped for a moment, eye meeting eye. Nothing passed
between us and everything; an awareness, almost a mutual flinch; and
over us both the knowledge that I knew the whole dreadful story from
beginning to end. Miss Pulkinhorn in that chapel; Miss Pulkinhorn
kneeling before that light; Miss Pulkinhorn watching her defences
broken down, abandoning her one by one! Even a rock crumbles.
Little by little, day by day, the stick began to shake, and the head. The
dress was the same but the woman inside it was destroyed piece by
piece. I avoided her from a kind of shame at knowing so much. Going
about my business in the cathedral I took to circling and keeping an
eye lifted to see if she was in my path. But she made a meeting for us.

One night after I'd kept the choir back to run through the anthem for
Sunday morning I tried that prelude of mine over again; so the choir
had gone and the congregation when I had finished, and I thought the
way was safe. But when I came down the stairs from the organ loft
Miss Pulkinhorn was sitting on one of the rush-bottom chairs,
waiting. She lifted her chin and fastened her eyes on my face and we
stood so for – well, it seemed a long time even in a cathedral. There
was a little water on her chin which fell when she spoke.

Her words were very slow and distinct.

'Sir Edward. My conscience is perfectly clear.'

She turned to go, leaving me as still as the carven figures round us.
As she tapped shakily away over the stones I heard her repeating the
words to herself.

'– perfectly clear.'

A week later she was dead.

KINGSLEY AMIS

MY ENEMY'S ENEMY

I

'Yes, I know all about that, Tom,' the Adjutant said through a mouthful of stew. 'But technical qualifications aren't everything. There's other sides to a Signals officer's job, you know, especially while we're still pretty well static. The communications are running themselves and we don't want to start getting complacent. My personal view is and has been from the word go that your friend Dally's a standing bloody reproach to this unit, never mind how much he knows about the six-channel and the other boxes of tricks. That's a lineman-mechanic's job, anyway, not an officer's. And I can tell you for a fact I mean to do something about it, do you see?' He laid down his knife, though not his fork, and took three or four swallows of wine.

'Well, your boy Cleaver doesn't impress me all that much, Bill,' Thurston, who hated the Adjutant, said to him. 'The only time we've tried him on duty he flapped.'

'Just inexperience, Tom,' the Adjutant said. 'He'd soon snap out of that if we gave him command of the section. Sergeant Beech would carry him until he found his feet.'

'Mm, I'd like to see that, I must say. The line duty-officer getting his sergeant out of bed to hold his hand while he changes a valve.'

'Now look here, old boy.' The Adjutant levered a piece of meat out from between two teeth and ate it. 'You know as well as I do that young Cleaver's got the best technical qualifications of anyone in the whole unit. It's not his fault he's been stuck on office work ever since he came to us. There's a fellow that'd smarten up that bunch of goons and long-haired bloody mathematical wizards they call a line-maintenance section. As it is, the NCOs don't chase the blokes and Dally isn't interested in chasing the NCOs. Isn't interested in anything but his bloody circuit diagrams and test-frames and what-have-you.'

To cover his irritation, Thurston summoned the Mess corporal, who stood by the wall in a posture that compromised between that of an attendant waiter and the regulation stand-at-ease position. The Adjutant had schooled him in Mess procedure, though not in Mess etiquette. 'Gin and lime, please, Gordon . . . Just as well in a way he is interested in line apparatus, isn't it, Bill? We'd have looked pretty silly without him during the move out of Normandy and across France. He worked as hard as any two of the rest of us. And as well.'

'He got his bouquet from the Colonel, didn't he? I don't grudge him that, I admit he did good work then. Not as good as some of his chaps, probably, but still, he served his turn. Yes, that's exactly it, Tom, he's served his –'

'According to Major Rylands he was the linchpin of the whole issue,' Thurston said, lighting a cigarette with fingers that were starting to tremble. 'And I'm prepared to take his word for it. The war isn't over yet, you know. Christ knows what may happen in the spring. If Dally isn't around to hold the line-maintenance end up for Rylands, the whole unit might end up in the shit with the Staff jumping on its back. Cleaver might be all right, I agree. We just can't afford to take the risk.'

This was an unusually long speech for anyone below the rank of major to make in the Adjutant's presence. Temporarily gagged by a mouthful of stew, that officer was eating as fast as he could and shaking his forefinger to indicate that he would as soon as possible propose some decisive amendment to what he had just been told. With his other hand he scratched the crown of his glossy black head, looking momentarily like a tick-tack man working through his lunch-break. He said indistinctly: 'You're on to the crux of the whole thing, old boy. Rylands is the root of all the trouble. Bad example at the top, do you see?' Swallowing, he went on: 'If the second-in-command goes round looking like a shithouse detail and calling the blokes by their Christian names, what can you expect? You can't get away from it, familiarity breeds contempt. Trouble with him is he thinks he's still working in the Post Office.'

A hot foam of anger seemed to fizz up in Thurston's chest. 'Major Rylands is the only field officer in this entire unit who knows his job. It is due to him and Dally, plus Sergeant Beech and the lineman-mechs, that our line communications have worked so smoothly during this campaign. To them and to no one else. If they can go on doing that they can walk about with bare arses for all I care.'

The Adjutant frowned at Thurston. After running his tongue round his upper teeth, he said: 'You seem to forget, Tom, that I'm responsible for the discipline of officers in this unit.' He paused to let the other reflect on the personal implications of this, then nodded to where Corporal Gordon was approaching with Thurston's drink.

As he signed the chit, Thurston was thinking that Gordon had probably been listening to the conversation from the passage. If so, he would probably discuss it with Hill, the Colonel's batman, who would probably report it to his master. It was often said, especially by Lieutenant Dalessio, the 'Dally' now under discussion, that the Colonel's chief contact with his unit was through the rumours and allegations Hill and, to a less extent, the Adjutant took to him. A tweak of disquiet made Thurston drink deeply and resolve to say no more for a bit.

The Adjutant was brushing crumbs off his battledress, which was of the greenish hue current in the Canadian Army. This little affectation, like the gamboge gloves and the bamboo walking-stick, perhaps suited a man who had helped to advertise men's clothes in civilian life. He went on to say in his rapid quacking monotone: 'I'd advise you, Tom, not to stick your neck out too far in supporting a man who's going to be out of this unit on his ear before very long.'

'Rylands, you mean?'

'No no no. Unfortunately not. But Dally's going.'

'That's gen, is it?'

'Not yet, but it will be.'

'I don't follow you.'

The Adjutant looked up in Gordon's direction, then leaned forward across the table to Thurston. 'It only needs one more thing,' he said quietly, 'to turn the scale. The CO's been watching Dally for some time, on my suggestion. I know the old man pretty well, as you know, after being in his Company for three years at North Midland Command. He's waiting to make up his mind, do you see? If Dally puts up a black in the near future – a real black – that'll be enough for the CO. Cleaver'll get his chance at last.'

'Suppose Dally doesn't put up a black?'

'He will.'

'He hasn't yet, you know. The terminal equipment's all on the top line, and Dally knows it inside out.'

'I'm not talking about that kind of a black. I'm talking about the administrative and disciplinary side. Those vehicles of his are in a shocking condition. I thought of working a snap 406 inspection on one of them, but that wouldn't look too good. Too much like discrimination. But there'll be something. Just give me time.'

Thurston thought of saying that those vehicles, though covered with months-old mud and otherwise offensive to the inspecting eye, were in good running order, thanks to the efficiency of the section's transport corporal. Instead, he let his mind wander back to one of the many stories of the Colonel's spell as a company commander in England. Three weeks running he had presented his weekly prize of £1 for the smartest vehicle to the driver of an obsolete wireless-truck immobilized for lack of spare parts. The Company Sergeant-Major had won a bet about it.

'We'll have some fun then, Tom old boy,' the Adjutant was saying in as festive a tone as his voice allowed. He was unaware that Thurston disliked him. His own feelings towards Thurston were a mixture of respect and patronage: respect for Thurston's Oxford degree and accent, job at a minor public school, and efficiency as a non-technical officer; patronage for his practice of reading literary magazines and for his vaguely scholarly manner and appearance. The affinity between Thurston's unmilitary look and the more frankly ragamuffin demeanour of Dalessio could hardly explain, the Adjutant wonderingly felt, the otherwise unaccountable tendency of the one to defend the other. It was true that they'd known each other at the officers' training unit at Catterick, but what could that have to do with it? The Adjutant was unaccustomed to having his opinions contested and he now voiced the slight bafflement that had been growing on him for the last few minutes. 'It rather beats me,' he said, 'why you're taking this line about friend Dally. You're not at all thick with him. In fact he seems to needle you whenever he speaks to you. My impression is, old boy, for what it's worth, you've got no bloody use for him at all. And yet you stick up for him. Why?'

Thurston amazed him by saying coldly: 'I don't see why the fact that a man's an Italian should be held against him when he does his job as well as anyone in the sodding Army.'

'Just a minute, Tom,' the Adjutant said, taking a cigarette from his silver case, given him by his mistress in Brussels. 'That's being a bit unfair, you know. You ever heard me say a word about Dalessio being an Eyeteye? Never. You were the one who brought it up. It makes no difference to me if a fellow's father's been interned, provided –'

'Uncle.'

'All right, uncle, then. As I say, that's no affair of mine. Presumably he's okay from that point of view or he'd never have got here. And that's all there is to it as far as I'm concerned. I'm not holding it against him, not for a moment. I don't quite know where you picked up that impression, old boy.'

Thurston shook his head, blushing slightly. 'Sorry, Bill,' he said. 'I must have got it mixed. It used to get on my wick at Catterick, the way some of the blokes took it out of him about his pal Musso and so on. I suppose it must be through that somehow, in a way, I keep feeling people have got it in for him on that score. Sorry.' He was not sorry. He knew quite certainly that his charge was well-founded, and that the other's silence about Dalessio's descent was a matter of circumspection only. If anyone in the Mess admired Mussolini, Thurston suspected, it was the Adjutant, although he kept quiet about that as well. It was tempting to dig at his prejudices on these and other questions, but Thurston did his best never to succumb to that temptation. The Adjutant's displeasure was always strongly urged and sometimes, rumour said, followed up by retaliatory persecution. Enough, dangerously much, had already been said in Dalessio's defence.

The Adjutant's manner had grown genial again and, with a muttered apology, he now offered Thurston a cigarette. 'What about another of those?' he asked, pointing his head at Thurston's glass.

'Thank you, I will, but I must be off in a minute. We're opening the teleprinter to the Poles at twenty-hundred and I want to see it's working.'

Two more officers now entered the Mess dining-room. They were Captain Bentham, a forty-year-old Regular soldier who had been a company sergeant-major in India at the outbreak of war, and Captain Rowney, who besides being in charge of the unit's administration was also the Mess's catering officer. Rowney nodded to Thurston and grinned at the Adjutant, whose Canadian battledress he had been responsible for securing. He himself was wearing a sheepskin jacket, made on the Belgian black market. 'Hallo, William,' he said. 'Won the war yet?' Although he was a great chum of the Adjutant's, some of his remarks to him, Thurston had noticed, carried a curious vein of satire. Bentham sat stolidly down a couple of places along the table, running his hands over his thin grey hair.

'Tom and I have been doing a little plotting,' the Adjutant said.

'We've decided a certain officer's career with this unit needs terminating.'

Bentham glanced up casually and caught Thurston's eye. This, coming on top of the Adjutant's misrepresentation of the recent discussion, made Thurston feel slightly uncomfortable. That was ludicrous, because he had long ago written Bentham off as of no particular account, as the most uninteresting type of Regular Army ex-ranker, good only at cable-laying, supervising cable-laying and looking after the men who did the actual cable-laying. Despite this, Thurston found himself saying: 'It wasn't quite like that,' but at that moment Rowney asked the Adjutant a question and the protest, mild as it was, went unheard.

'Your friend Dally, of course,' the Adjutant answered Rowney.

'Why, what's he been up to?' Bentham asked in his slow Yorkshire voice. 'Having his hair cut?'

There was a general laugh, then a token silence while Gordon laid plates of stew in front of the new arrivals. His inquiry whether the Adjutant wanted any rice pudding was met with a facetious and impracticable instruction for the disposal of that foodstuff by an often-quoted route. 'Can't you do better than that, Jack?' the Adjutant asked Rowney. 'Third night we've had Chinese wedding-cake this week.'

'Sorry, William. My Belgian friend's had a little misunderstanding with the civvy police. I'm still looking round for another pal with the right views on how the officers of a liberating army should be fed. Just possess your soul in patience.'

'What's this about Dally?' Bentham persisted. 'If there's a move to give him a wash and a change of clothes, count me in.'

Thurston got up before the topic could be reopened. 'By the way, Jack,' he said to Rowney, 'young Malone asked me to remind you that he still hasn't had those cigarettes for the blokes he's lent to Special Wireless.'

Rowney sighed. 'Tell him it's not my pigeon, will you, Thomas? I've been into it all with him. They're under Special Wireless for everything now.'

'Not NAAFI rations. He told me you'd agreed to supply them.'

'Up until last week. They're off my hands now.'

'Oh no they're not,' Thurston said nastily. 'According to Malone they still haven't had last week's.'

'Well, tell him . . .'

'Look, Jack, you tell him. It's nothing to do with me, is it?'

Rowney stared at him. 'All right, Thomas,' he said, abruptly diving his fork into his stew. 'I'll tell him.'

Dodging the hanging lamp-shade, which at its lowest point was no more than five feet from the floor, Thurston hurried out, his greatcoat over his arm.

'What's eating our intellectual friend?' Rowney asked.

The Adjutant rubbed his blue chin. 'Don't know quite. He was behaving rather oddly before you blokes came in. He's getting too sort of wrapped up in himself. Needs shaking up.' He was just deciding, having previously decided against it, to inflict some small but salutary injustice on Thurston through the medium of unit orders. He might compel the various sections to start handing in their various stores records for check, beginning with Thurston's section and stopping after it. Nice, but perhaps a bit too drastic. What about pinching his jeep for some tiresome extra duty? That might be just the thing.

'If you ask me,' Bentham was saying, 'he's too bloody stuck-up by half. Wants a lesson of some kind, he does.'

'You're going too far there, Ben,' the Adjutant said decisively. He disliked having Bentham in the Officers' Mess, declaring its tone to be thereby lowered, and often said he thought the old boy would be much happier back in the Sergeants' Mess with people of his own type. 'Tom Thurston's about the only chap round here you can carry on a reasonably intelligent discussion with.'

Bentham, unabashed, broke off a piece of bread and ran it round his plate in a way that Thurston and the Adjutant were, unknown to each other, united in finding unpleasant. 'What's all this about a plot about Dally?' he asked.

II

'You got that, Reg?' Dalessio asked. 'If you get any more interference on this circuit, put it back on plain speech straight away. Then they can see how they like that. I don't believe for a bloody moment the line's been relaid for a single bastard yard. Still, it's being ceased in a week or two, and it never was of the slightest importance, so there's no real worry. Now, what about the gallant Poles?' He spoke with a strong Glamorganshire accent diversified by an occasional Italian vowel.

'They're still on here,' Reg, the lineman-mechanic, said, gesturing towards the test teleprinter. 'Want to see 'em?'

'Yes, please. It's nearly time to switch 'em through to the tele-printer room. We'll get that done before I go.'

Reg bent to the keyboard of the machine and typed:

HOW U GETTING ON THERE READING ME OK KKKK

There was a humming pause while Reg scratched his armpit and said: 'Gone for a piss, I expect . . . Ah, here he is.' In typical but inextinguishably eerie fashion the teleprinter took on a life of its own, performed a carriage-return, moved the glossy white paper up a couple of lines, and typed:

4 CHRISTS SAKE QUIT BOTHERING ME NOT 2000 HRS YET KKK

Dalessio, grinning to himself, shoved Reg out of the way and typed:

CHIEF SIGNAL OFFICER BRITISH LIBERATION ARMY ERE WATCH YR LANGUAGE MY MAN KKKK

The distant operator typed:

U GO AND SCREW YRSELF JACK SORRY I MEAN SIR

At this Dalessio went into roars of laughter, digging his knuckle into one deep eye-socket and throwing back his large dark head. It was exactly the kind of joke he liked best. He rotated a little in the narrow aisle between the banks of apparatus and test-panels, still laughing, while Reg watched him with a slight smile. At last Dalessio recovered and shouldered his way down to the phone at the other end of the vehicle.

'Give me the teleprinter room, please. What? Who? All right, I'll speak to him . . . Terminal Equipment, Dalessio here. Yes. Oh, really? It hasn't?' His voice changed completely, became that of a slightly unbalanced uncle commiserating with a disappointed child: 'Now isn't that just too bad? Well, I do think that's hard lines. Just when you were all excited about it, too, eh?' Over his shoulder he squealed to Reg, in soprano parody of Thurston's educated tones: 'Captain Thurston is tewwibly gwieved that he hasn't got his pwinter to the Poles yet. He's afwaid we've got some howwid scheme on over heah to depwive him of it . . . All right, Thurston, I'll come over. Yes, now.'

Reg smiled again and put a cigarette in his mouth, striking the

match, from long habit, on the metal 'No Smoking' notice tacked up
over the ventilator.

'Give me one of those, Reg, I want to cool my nerves before I go into
the beauty-parlour across the way. Thanks. Now listen: switch the
Poles through to the teleprinter room at one minute to eight exactly, so
that there's working communication at eight but not before. Do
Thurston good to bite his nails for a few minutes. Put it through one
number . . .' – his glance and forefinger went momentarily to a
test-frame across the aisle – 'number six. That's just been rewired.
Ring up Teleprinters and tell 'em, will you? See you before I go
off.'

It was dark and cold outside and Dalessio shivered on his way over
to the Signal Office. He tripped up on the cable which ran shin-high
between a line of blue-and-white posts outside the entrance, and
applied an unclean expression to the Adjutant, who had had this
amenity provided in an attempt to dignify the working area. Inside the
crowded, brilliantly lighted office, he was half-asphyxiated by the
smoke from the stove and half-deafened by the thumping of date-
stamps, the ringing of telephones, the enraged bark of one sergeant
and the loud, tremulous singing of the other. A red-headed man was
rushing about bawling 'Emergency Ops for 17 Corps' in the accents of
County Cork. Nobody took any notice of him: they had all dealt with
far too many Emergency Ops messages in the last eight months.

Thurston was in his office, a small room partitioned off from the main
one. The unit was occupying what had once been a Belgian military
school and later an SS training establishment. This building had
obviously formed part of the original barrack area, and Thurston
often wondered what whim of the Adjutant's had located the offices
and stores down here and the men's living-quarters in former offices
and stores. The cubicle where Thurston spent so much of his time had
no doubt been the abode of the cadet, and then *Unteroffizier*, in charge
of barrack-room. He was fond of imagining the heavily built Walloons
and high-cheeked Prussians who had slept in here, and had insisted on
preserving as a historical document the chalked *Wir kommen zurück* on
the plank wall. Like his predecessors, he fancied, he felt cut off from
all the life going on just outside the partition, somehow isolated.
'Alone, withouten any company', he used to quote to himself. He
would laugh then, sometimes, and go on to think of the unique
lavatory at the far end of the building, where the defecator was

required to plant his feet on two metal plates, grasp two handles, and curve his body into the shape of a bow over a kind of trough.

He was not laughing now. His phone conversation with Dalessio had convinced him, even more thoroughly than phone conversations with Dalessio commonly did, that the other despised him for his lack of technical knowledge and took advantage of it to irritate and humiliate him. He tried to reread a letter from one of the two married women in England with whom, besides his wife, he was corresponding, but the thought of seeing Dalessio still troubled him.

Actually seeing Dalessio troubled him even more. Not for the first time it occurred to him that Dalessio's long, matted hair, grease-spotted, cylindrical trouser-legs and ill-fitting battledress blouse were designed as an offensive burlesque of his own neat but irremediably civilian appearance. He was smoking, too, and Thurston himself was punctilious in observing inside his office the rule that prohibited smoking on duty until ten at night, but it was no use telling him to put it out. Dalessio, he felt, never obeyed orders unless it suited him. 'Hallo, Thurston,' he said amiably. 'Not still having a baby about the Poles, I hope?'

'I don't think I ever was, was I? I just wanted to make sure what the position was.'

'Oh, you wanted to make sure of that, did you? All right, then. It's quite simple. Physically, the circuit remains unchanged, of course. But, as you know, we have ways of providing extra circuits by means of electrical apparatus, notably by utilizing the electron-radiating properties of the thermionic valve, or vacuum-tube. If a signal is applied to the grid . . .'

Thurston's phone rang and he picked it up gratefully. 'Signal-master?' said the voice of Brigadier the Lord Fawcett, the largest and sharpest thorn in the side of the entire Signals unit. 'I want a special dispatch-rider to go to Brussels for me. Will you send him round to my office for briefing in ten minutes?'

Thurston considered. Apart from its being over a hundred miles to Brussels, he suspected that the story told by previous special DRs who had been given this job was probably quite true: the purpose of the trip was to take in the Brigadier's soiled laundry and bring back the clean stuff, plus any wines, spirits and cigars that the Brigadier's Brussels agent, an RASC colonel at the headquarters of the reserve Army Corps, might have got together for him. But he could hardly ask the Lord Fawcett to confirm this. Why was it that his army career seemed littered with such problems? 'The regular D R run goes out at oh-five-hundred, sir,' he said in a conciliatory tone. 'Would that do instead, perhaps?'

'No, it certainly would not do instead. You have a man available, I take it?'

'Oh yes, sir.' This was true. It was also true that the departure of this man with the dirty washing would necessitate another, who might have been driving all day, being got out of the section billet and condemned at best to a night on the Signal Office floor, more likely to a run half across Belgium in the small hours with a genuine message of some kind. 'Yes, we have a man.'

'Well, I'm afraid in that case I don't see your difficulty. Get him round to me right away, will you?'

'Very good, sir.' There was never anything one could do.

'Who was that?' Dalessio asked when Thurston had rung off.

'Brigadier Fawcett,' Thurston said unguardedly. But Dally probably didn't know about the laundry rumour. He had little to do with the dispatch-rider sections.

'Oh, the washerwoman's friend. I heard a bit about that from Beech. Not on the old game again, is he? Sounded as if he wanted a special D R to me.'

'Yes, he did.' Thurston raised his voice: 'Prosser!'

'Sir!' came from outside the partition.

'Ask Sergeant Baker to come and see me, will you?'

'Sir.'

Dalessio's large pale face became serious. He pulled at his moustache. Eventually he said: 'You're letting him have one, are you?' If asked his opinion of Thurston, he would have described him as a plausible bastard. His acquiescence in such matters as this, Dalessio would have added, was bloody typical.

'I can't do anything else.'

'I would. There's nothing to it. Get God's Adjutant on the blower and complain. He's an ignorant bugger, we know, but I bet he'd take this up.'

Thurston had tried this, only to be informed at length that the job of Signals was to give service to the Staff. Before he could tell Dalessio about it, Baker, the D R sergeant, arrived to be acquainted with the Lord Fawcett's desires. Thurston thought he detected a glance of protest and commiseration pass between the other two men. When Baker had gone, he turned on Dalessio almost savagely and said: 'Now

look, Dally, leaving aside the properties of the thermionic bleeding
valve, would you kindly put me in the picture about this teleprinter to
the Poles? Is it working or isn't it? Quite a bit of stuff has piled up for
them and I've been holding it in the hope the line'll be through on
time.'

'No harm in hoping,' Dalessio said. 'I hope it'll be working all right,
too.' He dropped his fag-end on the swept floor and trod on it.

'Is it working or is it not?' Thurston asked very loudly. His eyes
wandered up and down the other's fat body, remembering how it had
looked in a pair of shorts, doing physical training at the officers'
training unit. It had proved incapable of the simplest tasks laid upon
it, crumpling feebly in the forward-roll exercise, hanging like a
crucified sack from the wall-bars, climbing by slow and ugly degrees
over the vaulting-horse. Perhaps its owner had simply not felt like
exerting it. That would have been bloody typical.

While Dalessio smiled at him, a knock came at the plywood door
Thurston had had made for his cubicle. In response to the latter's
bellow, the red-headed man came in. 'Sergeant Fleming sent to tell
you, sir,' he said, 'we're just after getting them Polish fellows on the
printer. You'll be wanting me to start sending off the messages we
have for them, will you, sir?'

Both Thurston and Dalessio looked up at the travelling-clock that
stood on a high shelf in the corner. It said eight o'clock.

III

'That's just about all, gentlemen,' the Colonel said. 'Except for one
last point. Now that our difficulties from the point of view of
communication have been removed, and the whole show's going quite
smoothly, there are other aspects of our work which need attention.
This unit has certain traditions I want kept up. One of them, of
course, is an absolutely hundred-per-cent degree of efficiency in all
matters affecting the disposal of Signals traffic, from the time the
In-Clerk signs for a message from the Staff to the time we get . . .'

He means the Out-Clerk, Thurston thought to himself. The little
room where the officers, warrant-officers and senior NCOs of the unit
held their conferences was unheated, and the Colonel was wearing his
knee-length sheepskin coat, another piece of merchandise supplied
through the good offices of Jack Rowney in exchange, perhaps, for a
few gallons of petrol or a couple of hundred cigarettes; Malone's men's

cigarettes, probably. The coat, added to the CO's platinum-blond hair and moustache, increased his resemblance to a polar bear. Thurston was in a good mood, having just received the letter which finally buttoned up arrangements for his forthcoming leave: four days with Denise in Oxford, and then a nice little run up to Town for five days with Margot. Just the job. He began composing a nature note on the polar bear: 'This animal, although of poor intelligence, possesses considerable cunning of a low order. It displays the utmost ferocity when menaced in any way. It shows fantastic patience in pursuit of its prey, and a vindictiveness which . . .'

The Colonel was talking now about another tradition of his unit, its almost unparalleled soldier-like quality, its demonstration of the verity that a Signals formation of *any kind* was not a collection of down-at-heel scientists and long-haired mathematical wizards. Thurston reflected it was not for nothing that the Adjutant so frequently described himself as the Colonel's staff officer. Yes, there he was, Arctic fox or, if they had them, Arctic jackal, smiling in proprietary fashion at his chief's oratory. What a bunch they all were. Most of the higher-ranking ones had been lower-ranking officers in the Territorial Army during the thirties, the Colonel, for instance, a captain, the Adjutant a second-lieutenant. The war had given them responsibility and quick promotion, and their continued enjoyment of such privileges rested not on their own abilities, but on those of people who had arrived in the unit by a different route: Post Office engineers whipped in with a commission, older Regular soldiers promoted from the ranks, officers who had been the conscripts of 1940 and 1941. Yes, what a bunch. Thurston remembered the parting words of a former sergeant of his who had been posted home a few months previously: 'Now I'm going I suppose I can say what I shouldn't. You never had a dog's bloody chance in this lot unless you'd been at North Midland Command with the Adj. and the CO. And we all know it's the same in that Mess of yours. If you'd been in the TA like them you were a blue-eyed boy, otherwise you were done for from the start. It's all right, sir, everybody knows it. No need to deny it.'

The exception to the rule, presumably, was Cleaver, now making what was no doubt a shorthand transcript of the Colonel's harangue. Thurston hated him as the Adjutant's blue-eyed boy and also for his silky fair hair, his Hitler Youth appearance and his thunderous laugh. His glance moved to Bentham, also busily writing. Bentham, too, fitted into the picture, as much as the Adjutant would let him, which was odd when compared with the attitude of other Regulars in the Mess. But Bentham had less individuality than they.

'So what I propose,' the Colonel said, 'is this. Beginning next week the Adjutant and I will be making a series of snap inspections of section barrack-rooms. Now I don't expect anything in the nature of spit-and-polish, of course. Just ordinary soldierly cleanliness and tidiness is all I want.'

In other words, just ordinary spit-and-polish, Thurston thought, making a note for his sergeant on his pad just below the polar-bear *vignette*. He glanced up and saw Dalessio licking the flap of an envelope; it was his invariable practice to write letters during the Colonel's addresses, when once the serious business of line-communications had been got through. Had he heard what had just been said? It was unlikely.

The conference broke up soon afterwards and in the Mess ante-room, where a few officers had gathered for a drink before the evening meal, Thurston was confronted by an exuberant Adjutant who at once bought him a drink. 'Well, Tom,' he said, 'I reckon that fixes things up nice and neat.'

'I don't follow you, Bill.'

'Step number one in cooking your friend Dally's goose. Step number two will be on Monday, oh-nine-thirty hours, when I take the Colonel round the line-maintenance billet. You know what we'll find there, don't you?'

Thurston stared blankly at the Adjutant, whose eyes were sparkling like those of a child who has been promised a treat. 'I still don't get you, Bill.'

'Use your loaf, Tommy. Dally's blokes' boudoir, can't you imagine what it'll be like? There'll be dirt enough in there to raise a crop of potatoes, fag-ends and pee-buckets all over the shop and the rest of it. The Colonel will eat Dally for his lunch when he sees it.'

'Dally's got three days to get it cleaned up, though.'

'He would have if he paid attention to what his Commanding Officer says. But I know bloody well he was writing a letter when that warning was given. Serves the bastard right, do you see? He'll be off to the mysterious East before you can turn round.'

'How much does the Colonel know about this?'

'What I've told him.'

'You don't really think it'll work, do you?'

'I know the old man. You don't, if you'll excuse my saying so.'

'It's a lousy trick and you know it, Bill,' Thurston said violently. 'I
think it's completely bloody.'

'Not at all. An officer who's bolshie enough to ignore a CO's order
deserves all he gets,' the Adjutant said, looking sententious. 'Coming
in?'

Still fuming, Thurston allowed himself to be led into the dining-
room. The massive green-tiled stove was working well and the room
was warm and cheerful. The house had belonged to the commandant
of the Belgian military school. Its solid furniture and tenebrous
landscape pictures had survived German occupation, though there
was a large burn in the carpet that had been imputed, perhaps rightly,
to the festivities of the *Schutzstaffel*. Jack Rowney, by importing
photographs of popular entertainers, half-naked young women
and the Commander-in-Chief, had done his best to document the
Colonel's thesis that the Officers' Mess was also their home. The
Adjutant, in excellent spirits, his hand on Thurston's shoulder, sent
Corporal Gordon running for a bottle of burgundy. Then, before they
sat down, he looked very closely at Thurston.

'Oh, and by the way, old boy,' he said, a note of menace intensifying
the quack in his voice, 'you wouldn't think of tipping your friend
Dally the wink about this little treat we've got lined up for him, would
you? If you do, I'll have your guts for garters.' Laughing heartily, he
dug Thurston in the ribs and added: 'Your leave's due at the end of the
month, isn't it? Better watch out you don't make yourself indispens-
able here. We might not be able to let you go, do you see?'

IV

Early on Monday Thurston was walking up from the Signal Office
towards the area where the men's barrack-rooms were. He was going to find his batman and arrange to be driven some twenty miles
to the department of the Advocate-General's branch which handled
divorce. The divorce in question was not his own, which would have
to wait until after the war, but that of his section cook, whose wife had
developed an immoderate fondness for RAF and USAAF
personnel.

Thurston was thinking less about the cook's wife than about the
fateful inspection, scheduled to take place any minute now. He
realized he had timed things badly, but his trip had only just become
possible and he hoped to be out of the area before the Colonel and the

Adjutant finished their task. He was keen to do this because the sight of a triumphant Adjutant would be more than he could stand, especially since his conscience was very uneasy about the whole affair. There were all sorts of reasons why he should have tipped Dalessio off about the inspection. The worst of it was, as he had realized in bed last night, when it was too late to do anything about it, that his irritation with Dalessio over the matter of the Polish teleprinter had been a prime cause of his keeping his mouth shut. He remembered actually thinking more than once that a thorough shaking-up would do Dalessio no harm, and that perhaps the son of an Italian café-proprietor in Cascade, Glamorganshire, had certain disqualifications for the role of British regimental officer. He twisted up his face when he thought of this and started wondering just why it was that the Adjutant was persecuting Dalessio. Perhaps the latter's original offence had been his habit of doing bird-warbles while the Adjutant and Rowney listened to broadcast performances of *The Warsaw Concerto*, the Intermezzo from *Cavalleria Rusticana*, and other sub-classics dear to their hearts. Cheeping, trilling and twittering, occasionally gargling like a seagull, Dalessio had been told to shut up or get out and had done neither.

Thurston's way took him past the door of the notorious line-maintenance billet. There seemed to be nobody about. Then he was startled by the sudden manifestation of two soldiers carrying brooms and a bucket. One of them had once been in his section and had been transferred early that year to one of the cable sections, he had forgotten which one. 'Good-morning, Maclean,' he said.

The man addressed came sketchily to attention. 'Morning, sir.'

'Getting on all right in No. 1 Company?'

'Yes, thank you, sir, I like it fine.'

'Good. What are you fellows up to so early in the morning?'

They looked at each other and the other man said: 'Cleaning up, sir. Fatigue party, sir.'

'I see; right, carry on.'

Thurston soon found his batman, who agreed with some reluctance to the proposed trip and said he would see if he could get the jeep down to the signal office in ten minutes. The jeep was a bone of contention between Thurston and his batman, and the batman always won, in the sense that never in his life had he permitted Thurston to drive the jeep in his absence. He was within his rights, but Thurston often wished, as now, that he could be allowed a treat occasionally. He wished it more strongly when a jeep with no exhaust and with seven men in it came bouncing down the track from the No. 1 Company billet area. They were laughing and two of them were pretending to fight. The driver was a lance-corporal.

Suddenly the laughing and fighting stopped and the men assumed an unnatural sobriety. The reason for this was provided by the immediate emergence into view of the Colonel and the Adjutant, moving across Thurston's front.

They saw him at once; he hastily saluted and the Adjutant, as usual, returned the salute. His gaze met Thurston's under lowered brows and his lips were gathered in the fiercest scowl they were capable of.

Thurston waited till they were out of sight and hurried to the door of the line-maintenance billet. The place was deserted. Except in illustrations to Army manuals and the like, he had never seen such perfection of order and cleanliness. It was obviously the result of hours of devoted labour.

He leant against the door-post and began to laugh.

V

'I gather the plot against our pal Dally misfired somewhat,' Bentham said in the Mess dining-room later that day.

Thurston looked up rather wearily. His jeep had broken down on the way back from the divorce expert and his return had been delayed for some hours. He had made part of the journey on the back of a motor-bike. Further, he had just read a unit order requiring him to make the jeep available at the Orderly Room the next morning. It wasn't his turn yet. The Adjutant had struck again.

'You know, I'm quite pleased,' Bentham went on, lighting a cigarette and moving towards the stove where Thurston stood.

'Oh, so am I.'

'You are? Now that's rather interesting. Surprising, even. I should have thought you'd be downcast.'

Something in his tone made Thurston glance at him sharply and put down the unit order. Bentham was standing with his feet apart in an intent attitude. 'Why should you think that, Ben?'

'I'll tell you. Glad of the opportunity. First of all I'll tell you why it misfired, if you don't already know. Because I tipped Dally off. Lent him some of my blokes and all, to get the place spick and span.'

Thurston nodded, thinking of the two men he had seen outside the billet that morning. 'I see.'

'You do, do you? Good. Now I'll tell you why I did it. First of all, the Army's not the place for this kind of plotting and scheming. The job's too important. Secondly, I did it because I don't like seeing an able man taken down by a bunch of ignorant jumped-up so-called bloody gentlemen from the Territorial Army. Not that I hold any brief for Dalessio outside his technical abilities. As you know, I'm a Regular soldier and I disapprove most strongly of anything damn slovenly. It's part of my nature now and I don't mind either. But one glance at the Adj.'s face when he was telling me the form for this morning and I knew where my duty lay. I hope I always do. I do my best to play it his way as a rule for the sake of peace and quiet. But this business was different. Wasn't it?'

Thurston had lowered his gaze. 'Yes, Ben.'

'It came as a bit of a shock to me, you know, to find that Dalessio needed tipping off.'

'How do you mean?'

'I mean that I'd have expected someone else to have told him already. I only heard about this last night. I was the only one here later on and I suppose the Adj. felt he had to tell someone. I should have thought by that time someone else would have let the cat out of the bag to Dally. You, for instance. You were in on this from the start, weren't you?'

Thurston said nothing.

'I've no doubt you have your excuses for not letting on. In spite of the fact that I've always understood you were the great one for pouring scorn on the Adj. and Rowney and Cleaver and the rest of that crowd. Yes, you could talk about them till you were black in the face, but when it came to doing something, talking where it would do some good, you kept your mouth shut. And, if I remember rightly, you were the one who used to stick up for Dally when the others were laying into him behind his back. You know what I think? I don't think you care tuppence. You don't care beyond talking, any road. I think you're really quite sold on the Adj.'s crowd, never mind what you say about them. Chew that over. And chew this over and all: I think you're a bastard, just like the rest of 'em. Tell that to your friend the Adjutant, Captain bloody Thurston.'

Thurston stood there for some time after Bentham had gone, tearing up the unit order and throwing the pieces into the stove.

THE RAIN HORSE

As the young man came over the hill the first thin blowing of rain met him. He turned his coat-collar up and stood on top of the shelving rabbit-riddled hedgebank, looking down into the valley.

He had come too far. What had set out as a walk along pleasantly-remembered tarmac lanes had turned dreamily by gate and path and hedge-gap into a cross-ploughland trek, his shoes ruined, the dark mud of the lower fields inching up the trouser legs of his grey suit where they rubbed against each other. And now there was a raw, flapping wetness in the air that would be downpour again at any minute. He shivered, holding himself tense against the cold.

This was the view he had been thinking of. Vaguely, without really directing his walk, he had felt he would get the whole thing from this point. For twelve years, whenever he had recalled this scene, he had imagined it as it looked from here. Now the valley lay sunken in front of him, utterly deserted, shallow, bare fields, black and sodden as the bed of an ancient lake after the weeks of rain.

Nothing happened. Not that he had looked forward to any very transfiguring experience. But he had expected something, some pleasure, some meaningful sensation, he didn't quite know what.

So he waited, trying to nudge the right feelings alive with the details – the surprisingly familiar curve of the hedges, the stone gate-pillar and iron gatehook let into it that he had used as a target, the long bank of the rabbit-warren on which he stood and which had been the first thing he ever noticed about the hill when twenty years ago, from the distance of the village, he had said to himself 'That looks like rabbits'.

Twelve years had changed him. This land no longer recognized him, and he looked back at it coldly, as at a finally visited home-country, known only through the stories of a grandfather; felt nothing but the dullness of feeling nothing. Boredom. Then, suddenly, impatience, with a whole exasperated swarm of little anxieties about his shoes, and the spitting rain and his new suit and that sky and the two-mile trudge through the mud back to the road.

It would be quicker to go straight forward to the farm a mile away in the valley and behind which the road looped. But the thought of meeting the farmer – to be embarrassingly remembered or shouted at as a trespasser – deterred him. He saw the rain pulling up out of the distance, dragging its grey broken columns, smudging the trees and the farms.

A wave of anger went over him: anger against himself for blundering into this mud-trap and anger against the land that made him feel so outcast, so old and stiff and stupid. He wanted nothing but to get away from it as quickly as possible. But as he turned, something moved in his eye-corner. All his senses startled alert. He stopped.

Over to his right a thin, black horse was running across the ploughland towards the hill, its head down, neck stretched out. It seemed to be running on its toes like a cat, like a dog up to no good.

From the high point on which he stood the hill dipped slightly and rose to another crested point fringed with the tops of trees, three hundred yards to his right. As he watched it, the horse ran up to that crest, showed against the sky – for a moment like a nightmarish leopard – and disappeared over the other side.

For several seconds he stared at the skyline, stunned by the unpleasantly strange impression the horse had made on him. Then the plastering beat of icy rain on his bare skull brought him to himself. The distance had vanished in a wall of grey. All around him the fields were jumping and streaming.

Holding his collar close and tucking his chin down into it he ran back over the hilltop towards the town-side, the lee-side, his feet sucking and splashing, at every stride plunging to the ankle.

This hill was shaped like a wave, a gently rounded back lifting out of the valley to a sharply crested, almost concave front hanging over the river meadows towards the town. Down this front, from the crest, hung two small woods separated by a fallow field. The near wood was nothing more than a quarry, circular, full of stones and bracken, with a few thorns and nondescript saplings, foxholes and rabbit holes. The other was rectangular, mainly a planting of scrub oak trees. Beyond the river smouldered the town like a great heap of blue cinders.

He ran along the top of the first wood and finding no shelter but the thin, leafless thorns of the hedge, dipped below the crest out of the wind and jogged along through thick grass to the wood of oaks. In blinding rain he lunged through the barricade of brambles at the wood's edge. The little crippled trees were small choice in the way of shelter, but at a sudden fierce thickening of the rain he took one at random and crouched down under the leaning trunk.

Still panting from his run, drawing his knees up tightly, he watched the bleak lines of rain, grey as hail, slanting through the boughs into the clumps of bracken and bramble. He felt hidden and safe. The sound of the rain as it rushed and lulled in the wood seemed to seal him in. Soon the chilly sheet lead of his suit became a tight, warm mould, and gradually he sank into a state of comfort that was all but trance, though the rain beat steadily on his exposed shoulders and trickled down the oak trunk on to his neck.

All around him the boughs angled down, glistening, black as iron. From their tips and elbows the drops hurried steadily, and the channels of the bark pulsed and gleamed. For a time he amused himself calculating the variation in the rainfall by the variations in a dribble of water from a trembling twig-end two feet in front of his nose. He studied the twig, bringing dwarfs and continents and animals out of its scurfy bark. Beyond the boughs the blue shoal of the town was rising and falling, and darkening and fading again, in the pale, swaying backdrop of rain.

He wanted this rain to go on forever. Whenever it seemed to be drawing off he listened anxiously until it closed in again. As long as it lasted he was suspended from life and time. He didn't want to return to his sodden shoes and his possibly ruined suit and the walk back over that land of mud.

All at once he shivered. He hugged his knees to squeeze out the cold and found himself thinking of the horse. The hair on the nape of his neck prickled slightly. He remembered how it had run up to the crest and showed against the sky.

He tried to dismiss the thought. Horses wander about the country-side often enough. But the image of the horse as it had appeared against the sky stuck in his mind. It must have come over the crest just above the wood in which he was now sitting. To clear his mind, he twisted around and looked up the wood between the tree stems, to his left.

At the wood top, with the silvered grey light coming in behind it, the black horse was standing under the oaks, its head high and alert, its ears pricked, watching him.

A horse sheltering from the rain generally goes into a sort of stupor,

tilts a hind hoof and hangs its head and lets its eyelids droop, and so it
stays as long as the rain lasts. This horse was nothing like that. It was
watching him intently, standing perfectly still, its soaked neck and
flank shining in the hard light.

He turned back. His scalp went icy and he shivered. What was he to
do? Ridiculous to try driving it away. And to leave the wood, with the
rain still coming down full pelt, was out of the question. Meanwhile
the idea of being watched became more and more unsettling until at
last he had to twist around again, to see if the horse had moved. It
stood exactly as before.

This was absurd. He took control of himself and turned back
deliberately, determined not to give the horse one more thought. If it
wanted to share the wood with him, let it. If it wanted to stare at him,
let it. He was nestling firmly into these resolutions when the ground
shook and he heard the crash of a heavy body coming down the wood.
Like lightning his legs bounded him upright and about face. The
horse was almost on top of him, its head stretching forwards, ears
flattened and lips lifted back from the long yellow teeth. He got one
snapshot glimpse of the red-veined eyeball as he flung himself backwards around the tree. Then he was away up the slope, whipped by
oak twigs as he leapt the brambles and brushwood, twisting between
the close trees till he tripped and sprawled. As he fell the warning
flashed through his head that he must at all costs keep his suit out of
the leaf-mould, but a more urgent instinct was already rolling him
violently sideways. He spun around, sat up and looked back, ready to
scramble off in a flash to one side. He was panting from the sudden
excitement and effort. The horse had disappeared. The wood was
empty except for the drumming, slant grey rain, dancing the bracken
and glittering from the branches.

He got up, furious. Knocking the dirt and leaves from his suit as
well as he could he looked around for a weapon. The horse was
evidently mad, had an abscess on its brain or something of the sort. Or
maybe it was just spiteful. Rain sometimes puts creatures into queer
states. Whatever it was, he was going to get away from the wood as
quickly as possible, rain or no rain.

Since the horse seemed to have gone on down the wood, his way to
the farm over the hill was clear. As he went, he broke a yard length of
wrist-thick dead branch from one of the oaks, but immediately threw
it aside and wiped the slime of rotten wet bark from his hands with his
soaked handkerchief. Already he was thinking it incredible that the

horse could have meant to attack him. Most likely it was just going down the wood for better shelter and had made a feint at him in passing – as much out of curiosity or playfulness as anything. He recalled the way horses menace each other when they are galloping around in a paddock.

The wood rose to a steep bank topped by the hawthorn hedge that ran along the whole ridge of the hill. He was pulling himself up to a thin place in the hedge by the bare stem of one of the hawthorns when he ducked and shrank down again. The swelling gradient of fields lay in front of him, smoking in the slowly crossing rain. Out in the middle of the first field, tall as a statue, and a ghostly silver in the under-cloud light, stood the horse, watching the wood.

He lowered his head slowly, slithered back down the bank and crouched. An awful feeling of helplessness came over him. He felt certain the horse had been looking straight at him. Waiting for him? Was it clairvoyant? Maybe a mad animal can be clairvoyant. At the same time he was ashamed to find himself acting so inanely, ducking and creeping about in this way just to keep out of sight of a horse. He tried to imagine how anybody in their senses would just walk off home. This cooled him a little, and he retreated farther down the wood. He would go back the way he had come, along under the hill crest, without any more nonsense.

The wood hummed and the rain was a cold weight, but he observed this rather than felt it. The water ran down inside his clothes and squelched in his shoes as he eased his way carefully over the bedded twigs and leaves. At every instant he expected to see the prick-eared black head looking down at him from the hedge above.

At the woodside he paused, close against a tree. The success of this last manoeuvre was restoring his confidence, but he didn't want to venture out into the open field without making sure that the horse was just where he had left it. The perfect move would be to withdraw quietly and leave the horse standing out there in the rain. He crept up again among the trees to the crest and peeped through the hedge.

The grey field and the whole slope were empty. He searched the distance. The horse was quite likely to have forgotten him altogether and wandered off. Then he raised himself and leaned out to see if it had come in close to the hedge. Before he was aware of anything the ground shook. He twisted around wildly to see how he had been caught. The black shape was above him, right across the light. Its whinnying snort and the spattering whack of its hooves seemed to be actually inside his head as he fell backwards down the bank, and leapt again like a madman, dodging among the oaks, imagining how the buffet would come and how he would be knocked headlong. Half-way down the wood the oaks gave way to bracken and old roots and stony rabbit diggings. He was well out into the middle of this before he realized that he was running alone.

Gasping for breath now and cursing mechanically, without a thought for his suit he sat down on the ground to rest his shaking legs, letting the rain plaster the hair down over his forehead and watching the dense flashing lines disappear abruptly into the soil all around him as if he were watching through thick plate glass. He took deep breaths in the effort to steady his heart and regain control of himself. His right trouser turn-up was ripped at the seam and his suit jacket was splashed with the yellow mud of the top field.

Obviously the horse had been farther along the hedge above the steep field, waiting for him to come out at the woodside just as he had intended. He must have peeped through the hedge – peeping the wrong way – within yards of it.

However, this last attack had cleared up one thing. He need no longer act like a fool out of mere uncertainty as to whether the horse was simply being playful or not. It was definitely after him. He picked up two stones about the size of goose eggs and set off towards the bottom of the wood, striding carelessly.

A loop of the river bordered all this farmland. If he crossed the little level meadow at the bottom of the wood, he could follow the three-mile circuit, back to the road. There were deep hollows in the river-bank, shoaled with pebbles, as he remembered, perfect places to defend himself from if the horse followed him out there.

The hawthorns that choked the bottom of the wood – some of them good-sized trees – knitted into an almost impassable barrier. He had found a place where the growth thinned slightly and had begun to lift aside the long spiny stems, pushing himself forward, when he stopped. Through the bluish veil of bare twigs he saw the familiar shape out in the field below the wood.

But it seemed not to have noticed him yet. It was looking out across the field towards the river. Quietly, he released himself from the thorns and climbed back across the clearing towards the one side of the wood he had not yet tried. If the horse would only stay down there he could follow his first and easiest plan, up the wood and over the hilltop to the farm.

Now he noticed that the sky had grown much darker. The rain was heavier every second, pressing down as if the earth had to be flooded before nightfall. The oaks ahead blurred and the ground drummed. He began to run. And as he ran he heard a deeper sound running with him. He whirled around. The horse was in the middle of the clearing. It might have been running to get out of the terrific rain except that it was coming straight for him, scattering clay and stones, with an immensely supple and powerful motion. He let out a tearing roar and threw the stone in his right hand. The result was instantaneous. Whether at the roar or the stone the horse reared as if against a wall and shied to the left. As it dropped back on its fore-feet he flung his second stone, at ten yards' range, and saw a bright mud blotch suddenly appear on the glistening black flank. The horse surged down the wood, splashing the earth like water, tossing its long tail as it plunged out of sight among the hawthorns.

He looked around for stones. The encounter had set the blood beating in his head and given him a savage energy. He could have killed the horse at that moment. That this brute should pick him and play with him in this malevolent fashion was more than he could bear. Whoever owned it, he thought, deserved to have its neck broken for letting the dangerous thing loose.

He came out at the woodside, in open battle now, still searching for the right stones. There were plenty here, piled and scattered where they had been ploughed out of the field. He selected two, then straightened and saw the horse twenty yards off in the middle of the steep field, watching him calmly. They looked at each other.

'Out of it!' he shouted, brandishing his arm. 'Out of it! Go on!' The horse twitched its pricked ears. With all his force he threw. The stone soared and landed beyond with a soft thud. He re-armed and threw again. For several minutes he kept up his bombardment without a single hit, working himself into a despair and throwing more and more wildly, till his arm began to ache with the unaccustomed exercise. Throughout the performance the horse watched him fixedly. Finally he had to stop and ease his shoulder muscle. As if the horse had been waiting for just this, it dipped its head twice and came at him.

He snatched up two stones and roaring with all his strength flung the one in his right hand. He was astonished at the crack of the impact. It was as if he had struck a tile – and the horse actually stumbled. With another roar he jumped forward and hurled his other stone. His aim seemed to be under superior guidance. The stone struck and rebounded straight up into the air, spinning fiercely, as the horse swirled away and went careering down towards the far bottom of the field, at first with great, swinging leaps, then at a canter, leaving deep churned holes in the soil.

It turned up the far side of the field, climbing till it was level with him. He felt a little surprise of pity to see it shaking its head, and once it paused to lower its head and paw over its ear with its fore-hoof as a cat does.

'You stay there!' he shouted. 'Keep your distance and you'll not get hurt.'

And indeed the horse did stop at that moment, almost obediently. It watched him as he climbed to the crest.

The rain swept into his face and he realized that he was freezing, as if his very flesh were sodden. The farm seemed miles away over the dreary fields. Without another glance at the horse – he felt too exhausted to care now what it did – he loaded the crook of his left arm with stones and plunged out on to the waste of mud.

He was half-way to the first hedge before the horse appeared, silhouetted against the sky at the corner of the wood, head high and attentive, watching his laborious retreat over the three fields.

The ankle-deep clay dragged at him. Every stride was a separate, deliberate effort, forcing him up and out of the sucking earth, burdened as he was by his sogged clothes and load of stone and limbs that seemed themselves to be turning to mud. He fought to keep his breathing even, two strides in, two strides out, the air ripping his lungs. In the middle of the last field he stopped and looked around. The horse, tiny on the skyline, had not moved.

At the corner of the field he unlocked his clasped arms and dumped the stones by the gatepost, then leaned on the gate. The farm was in front of him. He became conscious of the rain again and suddenly longed to stretch out full-length under it, to take the cooling, healing drops all over his body and forget himself in the last wretchedness of the mud. Making an effort, he heaved his weight over the gate-top. He leaned again, looking up at the hill.

Rain was dissolving land and sky together like a wet water-colour as the afternoon darkened. He concentrated raising his head, searching the skyline from end to end. The horse had vanished. The hill looked lifeless and desolate, an island lifting out of the sea, awash with every tide.

Under the long shed where the tractors, plough, binders and the rest were drawn up, waiting for their seasons, he sat on a sack thrown over a petrol drum, trembling, his lungs heaving. The mingled smell of paraffin, creosote, fertilizer, dust – all was exactly as he had left it twelve years ago. The ragged swallows' nests were still there tucked in the angles of the rafters. He remembered three dead foxes hanging in a row from one of the beams, their teeth bloody.

The ordeal with the horse had already sunk from reality. It hung under the surface of his mind, an obscure confusion of fright and shame, as after a narrowly-escaped street accident. There was a solid pain in his chest, like a spike of bone stabbing, that made him wonder if he had strained his heart on that last stupid burdened run. Piece by piece he began to take off his clothes, wringing the grey water out of them, but soon he stopped that and just sat staring at the ground, as if some important part had been cut out of his brain.

*T*HE *F*ISHING-BOAT *P*ICTURE

I've been a postman for twenty-eight years. Take that first sentence: because it's written in a simple way may make the fact of my having been a postman for so long seem important, but I realize that such a fact has no significance whatever. After all, it's not my fault that it may seem as if it has to some people just because I wrote it down plain; I wouldn't know how to do it any other way. If I started using long and complicated words that I'd searched for in the dictionary I'd use them too many times, the same ones over and over again, with only a few sentences – if that – between each one; so I'd rather not make what I'm going to write look foolish by using dictionary words.

It's also twenty-eight years since I got married. That statement is very important no matter how you write it or in what way you look at it. It so happened that I married my wife as soon as I got a permanent job, and the first good one I landed was with the Post Office (before that I'd been errand-boy and mash-lad). I had to marry her as soon as I got a job because I'd promised her I would, and she wasn't the sort of person to let me forget it.

When my first pay night came I called for her and asked: 'What about a walk up Snakey Wood?' I was cheeky-daft and on top of the world, and because I'd forgotten about our arrangement I didn't think it strange at all when she said: 'Yes, all right.' It was late autumn I remember and the leaves were as high as snow, crisp on top but soggy underneath. In the full moon and light wind we walked over the Cherry Orchard, happy and arm-in-arm. Suddenly she stopped and turned to me, a big-boned girl yet with a good figure and a nice enough face: 'Do you want to go into the wood?'

What a thing to ask! I laughed: 'You know I do. Don't you?'

We walked on, and a minute later she said: 'Yes, I do; but you know what we're to do now you've got a steady job, don't you?'

I wondered what it was all about. Yet I knew right enough. 'Get married,' I admitted, adding on second thoughts: 'I don't have much of a wage to be wed on, you know.'

'It's enough, as far as I'm concerned,' she answered.

And that was that. She gave me the best kiss I'd ever had, and then we went into the wood.

She was never happy about our life together, right from the start. And neither was I, because it didn't take her long to begin telling me that all her friends – her family most of all – said time and time again that our marriage wouldn't last five minutes. I could never say much back to this, knowing after the first few months how right everybody would be. Not that it bothered me though, because I was always the sort of bloke that doesn't get ruffled at anything. If you want to know the truth – the sort of thing I don't suppose many blokes would be ready to admit – the bare fact of my getting married meant only that I changed one house and one mother for another house and a different mother. It was as simple as that. Even my wage-packet didn't alter its course: I handed it over every Friday night and got five shillings back for tobacco and a visit to the pictures. It was the sort of wedding where the cost of the ceremony and reception go as a down payment, and you then continue dishing-out your wages every week for life. Which is where I suppose they got this hire purchase idea from.

But our marriage lasted for more than the five minutes everybody prophesied: it went on for six years; she left me when I was thirty, and when she was thirty-four. The trouble was that when we had a row – and they were rows, swearing, hurling pots: the lot – it was too much like suffering, and in the middle of them it seemed to me as if we'd done nothing but row and suffer like this from the moment we set eyes on each other, with not a moment's break, and that it would go on like this for as long as we stayed together. The truth was, as I see it now – and even saw it sometimes then – that a lot of our time was bloody enjoyable.

I'd had an idea before she went that our time as man and wife was about up, because one day we had the worst fight of them all. We were sitting at home one evening after tea, one at each end of the table, plates empty and bellies full so that there was no excuse for what followed. My head was in a book, and Kathy just sat there.

Suddenly she said: 'I do love you, Harry.' I didn't hear the words for some time, as is often the case when you're reading a book. Then: 'Harry, look at me.'

My face came up, smiled, and went down again to my reading. Maybe I was in the wrong, and should have said something, but the **137** book was too good.

'I'm sure all that reading's bad for your eyes,' she commented, prising me again from the hot possessive world of India.

'It ain't,' I denied, not looking up. She was young and still fair-faced, a passionate loose-limbed thirty-odd that wouldn't let me sidestep either her obstinacy or anger. 'My dad used to say that on'y fools read books, because they'd such a lot to learn.'

The words hit me and sank in, so that I couldn't resist coming back with, still not looking up: 'He on'y said that because he didn't know how to read. He was jealous, if you ask me.'

'No need to be jealous of the rammel you stuff your big head with,' she said, slowly to make sure I knew she meant every word. The print wouldn't stick any more; the storm was too close.

'Look, why don't you get a book, duck?' But she never would, hated them like poison.

She sneered: 'I've got more sense; and too much to do.'

Then I blew up, in a mild way because I still hoped she wouldn't take on, that I'd be able to finish my chapter. 'Well let me read, anyway, wain't you? It's an interesting book, and I'm tired.'

But such a plea only gave her another opening. 'Tired? You're allus tired.' She laughed out loud: 'Tired Tim! You ought to do some real work for a change instead of walking the streets with that daft post bag.'

I won't go on, spinning it out word for word. In any case not many more passed before she snatched the book out of my hands. 'You booky bastard,' she screamed, 'nowt but books, books, books, you bleddy dead-'ead' – and threw the book on the heaped-up coals, working it further and further into their blazing middle with the poker.

This annoyed me, so I clocked her one, not very hard, but I did. It was a good reading-book, and what's more it belonged to the library. I'd have to pay for a new one. She slammed out of the house, and I didn't see her until next day.

I didn't think to break my heart very much when she skipped off. I'd had enough. All I can say is that it was a stroke of God's luck we never had any kids. She was confined once or twice, but it never came to anything; each time it dragged more bitterness out of her than we could absorb in the few peaceful months that came between.

It might have been better if she'd had kids though; you never know.

A month after burning the book she ran off with a housepainter. It was all done very nicely. There was no shouting or knocking each other about or breaking up the happy home. I just came back from work one day and found a note waiting for me. 'I am going away and not coming back' – propped on the mantelpiece in front of the clock. No tear stains on the paper, just eight words in pencil on a page of the insurance book – I've still got it in the back of my wallet, though God knows why.

The housepainter she went with had lived in a house on his own, across the terrace. He'd been on the dole for a few months and suddenly got a job at a place twenty miles away I was later told. The neighbours seemed almost eager to let me know – after they'd gone, naturally – that they'd been knocking-on together for about a year. No one knew where they'd skipped off to exactly, probably imagining that I wanted to chase after them. But the idea never occurred to me. In any case what was I to do? Knock him flat and drag Kathy back by the hair? Not likely.

Even now it's no use trying to tell myself that I wasn't disturbed by this change in my life. You miss a woman when she's been living with you in the same house for six years, no matter what sort of cat-and-dog life you led together – though we had our moments, that I will say. After her sudden departure there was something different about the house, about the walls, ceiling and every object in it. And something altered inside me as well – though I tried to tell myself that all was just the same and that Kathy's leaving me wouldn't make a blind bit of difference. Nevertheless time crawled at first, and I felt like a man just learning to pull himself along with a clubfoot; but then the endless evenings of summer came and I was happy almost against my will, too happy anyway to hang on to such torments as sadness and loneliness. The world was moving and, I felt, so was I.

In other words I succeeded in making the best of things, which as much as anything else meant eating a good meal at the canteen every midday. I boiled an egg for breakfast (fried with bacon on Sundays) and had something cold but solid for my tea every night. As things went, it wasn't a bad life. It might have been a bit lonely, but at least it was peaceful, and it got as I didn't mind it, one way or the other. I even lost the feeling of loneliness that had set me thinking a bit too much just after she'd gone. And then I didn't dwell on it any more. I saw enough people on my rounds during the day to last me through the evenings and at week-ends. Sometimes I played draughts at the club, **139** or went out for a slow half pint to the pub up the street.

Things went on like this for ten years. From what I gathered later Kathy had been living in Leicester with her housepainter. Then she came back to Nottingham. She came to see me one Friday evening, payday. From her point of view, as it turned out, she couldn't have come at a better time.

I was leaning on my gate in the backyard smoking a pipe of tobacco. I'd had a busy day on my rounds, an irritating time of it – being handed back letters all along the line, hearing that people had left and that no one had any idea where they'd moved to; and other people taking as much as ten minutes to get out of bed and sign for a registered letter – and now I felt twice as peaceful because I was at home, smoking my pipe in the backyard at the fag-end of an autumn day. The sky was a clear yellow, going green above the housetops and wireless aerials. Chimneys were just beginning to send out evening smoke, and most of the factory motors had been switched off. The noise of kids scooting around lamp-posts and the barking of dogs came from what sounded a long way off. I was about to knock my pipe out, to go back into the house and carry on reading a book about Brazil I'd left off the night before.

As soon as she came around the corner and started walking up the yard I knew her. It gave me a funny feeling, though: ten years ain't enough to change anybody so's you don't recognize them, but it's long enough to make you have to look twice before you're sure. And that split second in between is like a kick in the stomach. She didn't walk with her usual gait, as though she owned the terrace and everybody in it. She was a bit slower than when I'd seen her last, as if she'd bumped into a wall during the last ten years through walking in the cock o' the walk way she'd always had. She didn't seem so sure of herself and was fatter now, wearing a frock left over from the summer and an open winter coat, and her hair had been dyed fair whereas it used to be a nice shade of brown.

I was neither glad nor unhappy to see her, but maybe that's what shock does, because I was surprised, that I will say. Not that I never expected to see her again, but you know how it is, I'd just forgotten her somehow. The longer she was away our married life shrunk to a year, a month, a day, a split second of sparking light I'd met in the black darkness before getting-up time. The memory had drawn itself too far back, even in ten years, to remain as anything much more than a dream. For as soon as I got used to living alone I forgot her.

Even though her walk had altered I still expected her to say something sarky like: 'Didn't expect to see me back at the scene of the crime so soon, did you, Harry?' Or: 'You thought it wasn't true that a bad penny always turns up again, didn't you?'

But she just stood. 'Hello, Harry' – waited for me to lean up off the gate so's she could get in. 'It's been a long time since we saw each other, hasn't it?'

I opened the gate, slipping my empty pipe away. 'Hello, Kathy,' I said, and walked down the yard so that she could come behind me. She buttoned her coat as we went into the kitchen, as though she were leaving the house instead of just going in. 'How are you getting on then?' I asked, standing near the fireplace.

Her back was to the wireless, and it didn't seem as if she wanted to look at me. Maybe I was a bit upset after all at her sudden visit, and it's possible I showed it without knowing it at the time, because I filled my pipe up straightaway, a thing I never normally do. I always let one pipe cool down before lighting the next.

'I'm fine,' was all she'd say.

'Why don't you sit down then, Kath? I'll get you a bit of a fire soon.'

She kept her eyes to herself still, as if not daring to look at the old things around her, which were much as they'd been when she left. However she'd seen enough to remark: 'You look after yourself all right.'

'What did you expect?' I said, though not in a sarcastic way. She wore lipstick, I noticed, which I'd never seen on her before, and rouge, maybe powder as well, making her look old in a different way, I supposed, than if she'd had nothing on her face at all. It was a thin disguise, yet sufficient to mask from me – and maybe her – the person she'd been ten years ago.

'I hear there's a war coming on,' she said, for the sake of talking.

I pulled a chair away from the table. 'Come on, sit down, Kathy. Get that weight off your legs' – an old phrase we'd used though I don't know why I brought it out at that moment. 'No, I wouldn't be a bit surprised. That bloke Hitler wants a bullet in his brain – like a good many Germans.' I looked up and caught her staring at the picture of a fishing boat on the wall: brown and rusty with sails half spread in a bleak sunrise, not far from the beach along which a woman walked bearing a basket of fish on her shoulder. It was one of a set that Kathy's brother had given us as a wedding present, the other two having been **141** smashed up in another argument we'd had. She liked it a lot, this remaining fishing-boat picture. The last of the fleet, we used to call it, in our brighter moments. 'How are you getting on?' I wanted to know. 'Living all right?'

'All right,' she answered. I still couldn't get over the fact that she wasn't as talkative as she had been, that her voice was softer and flatter, with no more bite in it. But perhaps she felt strange at seeing me in the old house again after all this time, with everything just as she'd left it. I had a wireless now, that was the only difference.

'Got a job?' I asked. She seemed afraid to take the chair I'd offered her.

'At Hoskins,' she told me, 'on Ambergate. The lace factory. It pays forty-two bob a week, which isn't bad.' She sat down and did up the remaining button of her coat. I saw she was looking at the fishing-boat picture again. The last of the fleet.

'It ain't good either. They never paid owt but starvation wages and never will I suppose. Where are you living, Kathy?'

Straightening her hair – a trace of grey near the roots – she said: 'I've got a house at Sneinton. Little, but it's only seven and six a week. It's noisy as well, but I like it that way. I was always one for a bit of life, you know that. "A pint of beer and a quart of noise" was what you used to say, didn't you?'

I smiled. 'Fancy you remembering that.' But she didn't look as though she had much of a life. Her eyes lacked that spark of humour that often soared up into the bonfire of a laugh. The lines around them now served only as an indication of age and passing time. 'I'm glad to hear you're taking care of yourself.'

She met my eyes for the first time. 'You was never very excitable, was you, Harry?'

'No,' I replied truthfully, 'not all that much.'

'You should have been,' she said, though in an empty sort of way, 'then we might have hit it off a bit better.'

'Too late now,' I put in, getting the full blow-through of my words. 'I was never one for rows and trouble, you know that. Peace is more my line.'

She made a joke at which we both laughed. 'Like that bloke Chamberlain!' – then moved a plate to the middle of the table and laid her elbows on the cloth. 'I've been looking after myself for the last three years.'

It may be one of my faults, but I get a bit curious sometimes. 'What's happened to that housepainter of yours then?' I asked this question quite naturally though, because I didn't feel I had anything to reproach her with. She'd gone away, and that was that. She hadn't left me in the lurch with a mountain of debts or any such thing. I'd always let her do what she liked.

'I see you've got a lot of books,' she remarked, noticing one propped against the sauce bottle, and two more on the sideboard.

'They pass the time on,' I replied, striking a match because my pipe had gone out. 'I like reading.'

She didn't say anything for a while. Three minutes I remember, because I was looking across at the clock on the dresser. The news would have been on the wireless, and I'd missed the best part of it. It was getting interesting because of the coming war. I didn't have anything else to do but think this while I was waiting for her to speak. 'He died of lead-poisoning,' she told me. 'He did suffer a lot, and he was only forty-two. They took him away to the hospital a week before he died.'

I couldn't say I was sorry, though it was impossible to hold much against him. I just didn't know the chap. 'I don't think I've got a fag in the place to offer you,' I said, looking on the mantelpiece in case I might find one, though knowing I wouldn't. She moved when I passed her on my search, scraping her chair along the floor. 'No, don't bother to shift. I can get by.'

'It's all right,' she said. 'I've got some here' – feeling in her pocket and bringing out a crumpled five-packet. 'Have one, Harry?'

'No thanks. I haven't smoked a fag in twenty years. You know that. Don't you remember how I started smoking a pipe? When we were courting. You gave me one once for my birthday and told me to start smoking it because it would make me look more distinguished! So I've smoked one ever since. I got used to it quick enough, and I like it now. I'd never be without it in fact.'

As if it were yesterday! But maybe I was talking too much, for she seemed a bit nervous while lighting her fag. I don't know why it was, because she didn't need to be in my house. 'You know, Harry,' she began, looking at the fishing-boat picture, nodding her head towards it, 'I'd like to have that' – as though she'd never wanted anything so much in her life.

'Not a bad picture, is it?' I remember saying. 'It's nice to have pictures on the wall, not to look at especially, but they're company. Even when you're not looking at them you know they're there. But you can take it if you like.'

'Do you mean that?' she asked, in such a tone that I felt sorry for her for the first time.

'Of course. Take it. I've got no use for it. In any case I can get another picture if I want one, or put a war map up.' It was the only picture on that wall, except for the wedding photo on the sideboard below. But I didn't want to remind her of the wedding picture for fear it would bring back memories she didn't like. I hadn't kept it there for sentimental reasons, so perhaps I should have dished it. 'Did you have any kids?'

'No,' she said, as if not interested. 'But I don't like taking your picture, and I'd rather not if you think all that much of it.' We sat looking over each other's shoulder for a long time. I wondered what had happened during these ten years to make her talk so sadly about the picture. It was getting dark outside. Why didn't she shut up about it, just take the bloody thing? So I offered it to her again, and to settle the issue unhooked it, dusted the back with a cloth, wrapped it up in brown paper, and tied the parcel with the best post-office string. 'There you are,' I said, brushing the pots aside, laying it on the table at her elbows.

'You're very good to me, Harry.'

'Good! I like that. What does a picture more or less in the house matter? And what does it mean to me, anyway?' I can see now that we were giving each other hard knocks in a way we'd never learned to do when living together. I switched on the electric light. As she seemed uneasy when it showed everything up clearly in the room, I offered to switch it off again.

'No, don't bother' – standing to pick up her parcel. 'I think I'll be going now. Happen I'll see you some other time.'

'Drop in whenever you feel like it.' Why not? We weren't enemies. She undid two buttons of her coat, as though having them loose would make her look more at her ease and happy in her clothes, then waved to me. 'So long.'

'Good night, Kathy.' It struck me that she hadn't smiled or laughed once the whole time she'd been there, so I smiled to her as she turned for the door, and what came back wasn't the bare-faced cheeky grin I once knew, but a wry parting of the lips moving more for exercise than humour. She must have been through it, I thought, and she's above forty now.

So she went. But it didn't take me long to get back to my book.

A few mornings later I was walking up St Ann's Well Road delivering letters. My round was taking a long time, for I had to stop at almost every shop. It was raining, a fair drizzle, and water rolled off my cape, soaking my trousers below the knees so that I was looking forward to a mug of tea back in the canteen and hoping they'd kept the stove going. If I hadn't been so late on my round I'd have dropped into a café for a cup.

I'd just taken a pack of letters into a grocer's and, coming out, saw the fishing-boat picture in the next-door pawnshop window, the one I'd given Kathy a few days ago. There was no mistaking it, leaning back against ancient spirit-levels, bladeless planes, rusty hammers, trowels, and a violin case with the strap broken. I recognized a chip in the gold-painted woodwork near the bottom left corner of its frame.

For half a minute I couldn't believe it, was unable to make out how it had got there, then saw the first day of my married life and a sideboard loaded with presents, prominent among them this surviving triplet of a picture looking at me from the wreckage of other lives. And here it is, I thought, come down to a bloody nothing. She must have sold it that night before going home, pawnshops always keeping open late on a Friday so that women could get their husbands' suits out of pop for the week-end. Or maybe she'd sold it this morning, and I was only half an hour behind her on my round. Must have been really hard up. Poor Kathy, I thought. Why hadn't she asked me to let her have a bob or two?

I didn't think much about what I was going to do next. I never do, but went inside and stood at the shop counter waiting for a grey-haired doddering skinflint to sort out the popped bundles of two thin-faced women hovering to make sure he knew they were pawning the best of stuff. I was impatient. The place stank of old clothes and mildewed junk after coming out of fresh rain, and besides I was later than ever now on my round. The canteen would be closed before I got back, and I'd miss my morning tea.

The old man shuffled over at last, his hand out. 'Got any letters?'

'Nowt like that, feyther. I'd just like to have a look at that picture you've got in your window, the one with a ship on it.' The women went out counting what few shillings he'd given them, stuffing pawn-tickets in their purses, and the old man came back carrying the picture as if it was worth five quid.

Shock told me she'd sold it right enough, but belief lagged a long way behind, so I looked at it well to make sure it really was the one. A price marked on the back wasn't plain enough to read. 'How much do you want for it?'

'You can have it for four bob.'

Generosity itself. But I'm not one for bargaining. I could have got it for less, but I'd rather pay an extra bob than go through five minutes of chinning. So I handed the money over, and said I'd call back for the picture later.

Four measly bob, I said to myself as I sloshed on through the rain. The robbing bastard. He must have given poor Kathy about one and six for it. Three pints of beer for the fishing-boat picture.

I don't know why, but I was expecting her to call again the following week. She came on Thursday, at the same time, and was dressed in the usual way: summer frock showing through her brown winter coat whose buttons she couldn't leave alone, telling me how nervous she was. She'd had a drink or two on her way, and before coming into the house stopped off at the lavatory outside. I'd been late back from work, and hadn't quite finished my tea, asked her if she could do with a cup. 'I don't feel like it,' came the answer. 'I had one not long ago.'

I emptied the coal scuttle on the fire. 'Sit down nearer the warmth. It's a bit nippy tonight.'

She agreed that it was, then looked up at the fishing-boat picture on the wall. I'd been waiting for this, wondered what she'd say when she did, but there was no surprise at seeing it back in the old place, which made me feel a bit disappointed. 'I won't be staying long tonight,' was all she said. 'I've got to see somebody at eight.'

Not a word about the picture. 'That's all right. How's your work going?'

'Putrid,' she answered nonchalantly, as though my question had been out of place. 'I got the sack, for telling the forewoman where to get off.'

'Oh,' I said, getting always to say 'Oh' when I wanted to hide my feelings, though it was a safe bet that whenever I did say 'Oh' there wasn't much else to come out with.

I had an idea she might want to live in my house again seeing she'd lost her job. If she wanted to she could. And she wouldn't be afraid to ask, even now. But I wasn't going to mention it first. Maybe that was my mistake, though I'll never know. 'A pity you got the sack,' I put in.

Her eyes were on the picture again, until she asked: 'Can you lend me half-a-crown?'

'Of course I can' – emptied my trouser pocket, sorted out half a crown, and passed it across to her. Five pints. She couldn't think of anything to say, shuffled her feet to some soundless tune in her mind. 'Thanks very much.'

'Don't mention it,' I said with a smile. I remembered buying a packet of fags in case she'd want one, which shows how much I'd expected her back. 'Have a smoke?' – and she took one, struck a match on the sole of her shoe before I could get her a light myself.

'I'll give you the half-crown next week, when I get paid.' That's funny, I thought. 'I got a job as soon as I lost the other one,' she added, reading my mind before I had time to speak. 'It didn't take long. There's plenty of war work now. Better money as well.'

'I suppose all the firms'll be changing over soon.' It occurred to me that she could claim some sort of allowance from me – for we were still legally married – instead of coming to borrow half-a-crown. It was her right, and I didn't need to remind her; I wouldn't be all that much put out if she took me up on it. I'd been single – as you might say – for so many years that I hadn't been able to stop myself putting a few quid by. 'I'll be going now,' she said, standing up to fasten her coat.

'Sure you won't have a cup of tea?'

'No thanks. Want to catch the trolley back to Sneinton.' I said I'd show her to the door. 'Don't bother. I'll be all right.' She stood waiting for me, looking at the picture on the wall above the sideboard. 'It's a nice picture you've got up there. I always liked it a lot.'

I made the old joke: 'Yes, but it's the last of the fleet.'

'That's why I like it.' Not a word about having sold it for eighteen pence.

I showed her out, mystified.

She came to see me every week, all through the war, always on Thursday night at about the same time. We talked a bit, about the weather, the war, her job and my job, never anything important. Often we'd sit for a long time looking into the fire from our different stations in the room, me by the hearth and Kathy a bit further away at the table as if she'd just finished a meal, both of us silent yet not uneasy in it. Sometimes I made a cup of tea, sometimes not. I suppose now that I think of it I could have got a pint of beer in for when she came, but it never occurred to me. Not that I think she felt the lack of it, for it wasn't the sort of thing she expected to see in my house anyway.

She never missed coming once, even though she often had a cold in the winter and would have been better off in bed. The blackout and shrapnel didn't stop her either. In a quiet off-handed sort of way we got to enjoy ourselves and looked forward to seeing each other again, and maybe they were the best times we ever had together in our lives. They certainly helped us through the long monotonous dead evenings of the war.

She was always dressed in the same brown coat, growing shabbier and shabbier. And she wouldn't leave without borrowing a few shillings. Stood up: 'Er . . . lend's half-a-dollar, Harry.' Given, sometimes with a joke: 'Don't get too drunk on it, will you?' – never responded to, as if it were bad manners to joke about a thing like that. I didn't get anything back of course, but then, I didn't miss such a dole either. So I wouldn't say no when she asked me, and as the price of beer went up she increased the amount to three bob then to three-and-six and, finally, just before she died, to four bob. It was a pleasure to be able to help her. Besides, I told myself, she had no one else. I never asked questions as to where she was living, though she did mention a time or two that it was still up Sneinton way. Neither did I at any time see her outside at a pub or picture house; Nottingham is a big town in many ways.

On every visit she would glance from time to time at the fishing-boat picture, the last of the fleet, hanging on the wall above the sideboard. She often mentioned how beautiful she thought it was, and how I should never part with it, how the sunrise and the ship and the woman and the sea were just right. Then a few minutes later she'd hint to me how nice it would be if she had it, but knowing it would end up in the pawnshop I didn't take her hints. I'd rather have lent her five bob instead of half-a-crown so that she wouldn't take the picture, but she never seemed to want more than half-a-crown in those first years. I once mentioned to her she could have more if she liked, but she didn't answer me. I don't think she wanted the picture especially to sell and get money, or to hang in her own house; only to have the pleasure of pawning it, to have someone else buy it so that it wouldn't belong to either of us any more.

But she finally did ask me directly, and I saw no reason to refuse when she put it like that. Just as I had done six years before, when she first came to see me, I dusted it, wrapped it up carefully in several layers of brown paper, tied it with post-office string, and gave it to her. She seemed happy with it under her arm, couldn't get out of the house quick enough, it seemed.

It was the same old story though, for a few days later I saw it again in the pawnshop window, among all the old junk that had been there for years. This time I didn't go in and try to get it back. In a way I wish I had, because then Kathy might not have had the accident that came a few days later. Though you never know. If it hadn't been that, it would have been something else.

I didn't get to her before she died. She'd been run down by a lorry at six o'clock in the evening, and by the time the police had taken me to the General Hospital she was dead. She'd been knocked all to bits, and had practically bled to death even before they'd got her to the hospital. The doctor told me she'd not been quite sober when she was knocked down. Among the things of hers they showed me was the fishing-boat picture, but it was so broken up and smeared with blood that I hardly recognized it. I burned it in the roaring flames of the firegrate late that night.

When her two brothers, their wives and children had left and taken with them the air of blame they attached to me for Kathy's accident I stood at the graveside thinking I was alone, hoping I would end up crying my eyes out. No such luck. Holding my head up suddenly I noticed a man I hadn't seen before. It was a sunny afternoon of winter, but bitter cold, and the only thing at first able to take my mind off Kathy was the thought of some poor bloke having to break the bone-hard soil and dig this hole she was now lying in. Now there was this stranger. Tears were running down his cheeks, a man in his middle fifties wearing a good suit, grey though but with a black band around his arm, who moved only when the fed-up sexton touched his shoulder – and then mine – to say it was all over.

I felt no need to ask who he was. And I was right. When I got to Kathy's house (it had also been his) he was packing his things, and left a while later in a taxi without saying a word. But the neighbours, who always know everything, told me he and Kathy had been living together for the last six years. Would you believe it? I only wished he'd made her happier than she'd been.

Time has passed now and I haven't bothered to get another picture for the wall. Maybe a war map would do it; the wall gets too blank, for I'm sure some government will oblige soon. But it doesn't really need anything at the moment, to tell you the truth. That part of the room is filled up by the sideboard, on which is still the wedding picture, that she never thought to ask for.

And looking at these few old pictures stacked in the back of my mind I began to realize that I should never have let them go, and that I shouldn't have let Kathy go either. Something told me I'd been daft and dead to do it, and as my rotten luck would have it it was the word dead more than daft that stuck in my mind, and still sticks there like the spinebone of a cod or conger eel, driving me potty sometimes when I lay of a night in bed thinking.

I began to believe there was no point in my life – became even too far gone to turn religious or go on the booze. Why had I lived? I wondered. I can't see anything for it. What was the point of it all? And yet at the worst minutes of my midnight emptiness I'd think less of myself and more of Kathy, see her as suffering in a far rottener way than ever I'd done, and it would come to me – though working only as long as an aspirin pitted against an incurable headache – that the object of my having been alive was that in some small way I'd helped Kathy through her life.

I was born dead, I keep telling myself. Everybody's dead, I answer. So they are, I maintain, but then most of them never know it like I'm beginning to do, and it's a bloody shame that this has come to me at last when I could least do with it, and when it's too bloody late to get anything but bad from it.

Then optimism rides out of the darkness like a knight in armour. If you loved her . . . (of course I bloody-well did) . . . then you both did the only thing possible if it was to be remembered as love. Now didn't you? Knight in armour goes back into blackness. Yes, I cry, but neither of us *did anything about it*, and that's the trouble.

DORIS LESSING

TO ROOM NINETEEN

This is a story, I suppose, about a failure in intelligence: the Rawlings'
marriage was grounded in intelligence.

They were older when they married than most of their married
friends: in their well-seasoned late twenties. Both had had a number of
affairs, sweet rather than bitter; and when they fell in love – for they
did fall in love – had known each other for some time. They joked that
they had saved each other 'for the real thing'. That they had waited so
long (but not too long) for this real thing was to them a proof of their
sensible discrimination. A good many of their friends had married
young, and now (they felt) probably regretted lost opportunities;
while others, still unmarried, seemed to them arid, self-doubting, and
likely to make desperate or romantic marriages.

Not only they, but others, felt they were well-matched: their
friends' delight was an additional proof of their happiness. They had
played the same roles, male and female, in this group or set, if such a
wide, loosely connected, constantly changing constellation of people
could be called a set. They had both become, by virtue of their
moderation, their humour, and their abstinence from painful experience, people to whom others came for advice. They could be, and
were, relied on. It was one of those cases of a man and a woman linking
themselves whom no one else had ever thought of linking, probably
because of their similarities. But then everyone exclaimed: Of course!
How right! How was it we never thought of it before!

And so they married amid general rejoicing, and because of their
foresight and their sense for what was probable, nothing was a
surprise to them.

Both had well-paid jobs. Matthew was a subeditor on a large
London newspaper, and Susan worked in an advertising firm. He was
not the stuff of which editors or publicized journalists are made, but
he was much more than 'a subeditor', being one of the essential

background people who in fact steady, inspire and make possible the people in the limelight. He was content with this position. Susan had a talent for commercial drawing. She was humorous about the advertisements she was responsible for, but she did not feel strongly about them one way or the other.

Both, before they married, had had pleasant flats, but they felt it unwise to base a marriage on either flat, because it might seem like a submission of personality on the part of the one whose flat it was not. They moved into a new flat in South Kensington on the clear understanding that when their marriage had settled down (a process they knew would not take long, and was in fact more a humorous concession to popular wisdom than what was due to themselves) they would buy a house and start a family.

And this is what happened. They lived in their charming flat for two years, giving parties and going to them, being a popular young married couple, and then Susan became pregnant, she gave up her job, and they bought a house in Richmond. It was typical of this couple that they had a son first, then a daughter, then twins, son and daughter. Everything right, appropriate, and what everyone would wish for, if they could choose. But people did feel these two had chosen; this balanced and sensible family was no more than what was due to them because of their infallible sense for *choosing* right.

And so they lived with their four children in their gardened house in Richmond and were happy. They had everything they had wanted and had planned for.

And yet . . .

Well, even this was expected, that there must be a certain flatness . . .

Yes, yes, of course, it was natural they sometimes felt like this. Like what?

Their life seemed to be like a snake biting its tail. Matthew's job for the sake of Susan, children, house, and garden – which caravanserai needed a well-paid job to maintain it. And Susan's practical intelligence for the sake of Matthew, the children, the house and the garden – which unit would have collapsed in a week without her.

But there was no point about which either could say: 'For the sake of *this* is all the rest.' Children? But children can't be a centre of life and a reason for being. They can be a thousand things that are delightful, interesting, satisfying, but they can't be a wellspring to live from. Or they shouldn't be. Susan and Matthew knew that well enough.

Matthew's job? Ridiculous. It was an interesting job, but scarcely a reason for living. Matthew took pride in doing it well, but he could hardly be expected to be proud of the newspaper; the newspaper he read, *his* newspaper, was not the one he worked for.

Their love for each other? Well, that was nearest it. If this wasn't a centre, what was? Yes, it was around this point, their love, that the whole extraordinary structure revolved. For extraordinary it certainly was. Both Susan and Matthew had moments of thinking so, of looking in secret disbelief at this thing they had created: marriage, four children, big house, garden, charwomen, friends, cars . . . and this *thing*, this entity, all of it had come into existence, been blown into being out of nowhere, because Susan loved Matthew and Matthew loved Susan. Extraordinary. So that was the central point, the wellspring.

And if one felt that it simply was not strong enough, important enough, to support it all, well whose fault was that? Certainly neither Susan's nor Matthew's. It was in the nature of things. And they sensibly blamed neither themselves nor each other.

On the contrary, they used their intelligence to preserve what they had created from a painful and explosive world: they looked around them, and took lessons. All around them, marriages collapsing, or breaking, or rubbing along (even worse, they felt). They must not make the same mistakes, they must not.

They had avoided the pitfall so many of their friends had fallen into – of buying a house in the country *for the sake of the children*, so that the husband became a weekend husband, a weekend father, and the wife always careful not to ask what went on in the town flat which they called (in joke) a bachelor flat. No, Matthew was a full-time husband, a full-time father, and at night, in the big married bed in the big married bedroom (which had an attractive view of the river), they lay beside each other talking and he told her about his day, and what he had done, and whom he had met; and she told him about her day (not as interesting, but that was not her fault), for both knew of the hidden resentments and deprivations of the woman who has lived her own life – and above all, has earned her own living – and is now dependent on a husband for outside interests and money.

Nor did Susan make the mistake of taking a job for the sake of her independence, which she might very well have done, since her old firm, missing her qualities of humour, balance, and sense, invited her often to go back. Children needed their mother to a certain age, that both parents knew and agreed on; and when these four healthy wisely brought up children were of the right age, Susan would work again, because she knew, and so did he, what happened to women of fifty at the height of their energy and ability, with grown-up children who no longer needed their full devotion.

So here was this couple, testing their marriage, looking after it, treating it like a small boat full of helpless people in a very stormy sea. Well, of course, so it was . . . The storms of the world were bad, but not too close – which is not to say they were selfishly felt: Susan and Matthew were both well-informed and responsible people. And the inner storms and quicksands were understood and charted. So everything was all right. Everything was in order. Yes, things were under control.

So what did it matter if they felt dry, flat? People like themselves, fed on a hundred books (psychological, anthropological, sociological), could scarcely be unprepared for the dry, controlled wistfulness which is the distinguishing mark of the intelligent marriage. Two people, endowed with education, with discrimination, with judgement, linked together voluntarily from their will to be happy together and to be of use to others – one sees them everywhere, one knows them, one even is that thing oneself: sadness because so much is after all so little. These two, unsurprised, turned towards each other with even more courtesy and gentle love: this was life, that two people, no matter how carefully chosen, could not be everything to each other. In fact, even to say so, to think in such a way, was banal; they were ashamed to do it.

It was banal, too, when one night Matthew came home late and confessed he had been to a party, taken a girl home and slept with her. Susan forgave him, of course. Except that forgiveness is hardly the word. Understanding, yes. But if you understand something, you don't forgive it, you are the thing itself: forgiveness is for what you *don't* understand. Nor had he *confessed* – what sort of word is that?

The whole thing was not important. After all, years ago they had joked: Of course I'm not going to be faithful to you, no one can be faithful to one other person for a whole lifetime. (And there was the word 'faithful' – stupid, all these words, stupid, belonging to a savage old world.) But the incident left both of them irritable. Strange, but they were both bad-tempered, annoyed. There was something un-assimilable about it.

Making love splendidly after he had come home that night, both had felt that the idea that Myra Jenkins, a pretty girl met at a party, could be even relevant was ridiculous. They had loved each other for over a decade, would love each other for years more. Who, then, was Myra Jenkins?

Except, thought Susan, unaccountably bad-tempered, she was (is?) the first. In ten years. So either the ten years' fidelity was not important, or she isn't. (No, no, there is something wrong with this way of thinking, there must be.) But if she isn't important, presumably it wasn't important either when Matthew and I first went to bed with each other that afternoon whose delight even now (like a very long shadow at sundown) lays a long, wandlike finger over us. (Why did I say sundown?) Well, if what we felt that afternoon was not important, nothing is important, because if it hadn't been for what we felt, we wouldn't be Mr and Mrs Rawlings with four children, et cetera, et cetera. The whole thing is *absurd* – for him to have come home and told me was absurd. For him not to have told me was absurd. For me to care or, for that matter, not to care, is absurd . . . and who is Myra Jenkins? Why, no one at all.

There was only one thing to do, and of course these sensible people did it; they put the thing behind them, and consciously, knowing what they were doing, moved forward into a different phase of their marriage, giving thanks for past good fortune as they did so.

For it was inevitable that the handsome, blond, attractive, manly man, Matthew Rawlings, should be at times tempted (oh, what a word!) by the attractive girls at parties she could not attend because of the four children; and that sometimes he would succumb (a word even more repulsive, if possible) and that she, a goodlooking woman in the big well-tended garden at Richmond, would sometimes be pierced as by an arrow from the sky with bitterness. Except that bitterness was not in order, it was out of court. Did the casual girls touch the marriage? They did not. Rather it was they who knew defeat because of the handsome Matthew Rawlings' marriage body and soul to Susan Rawlings.

In that case why did Susan feel (though luckily not for longer than a few seconds at a time) as if life had become a desert, and that nothing mattered, and that her children were not her own?

Meanwhile her intelligence continued to assert that all was well.

What if her Matthew did have an occasional sweet afternoon, the odd affair? For she knew quite well, except in her moments of aridity, that they were very happy, that the affairs were not important.

Perhaps that was the trouble? It was in the nature of things that the adventures and delights could no longer be hers, because of the four children and the big house that needed so much attention. But perhaps she was secretly wishing, and even knowing that she did, that the wildness and the beauty could be his. But he was married to her. She was married to him. They were married inextricably. And therefore the gods could not strike him with the real magic, not really. Well, was it Susan's fault that after he came home from an adventure he looked harassed rather than fulfilled? (In fact, that was how she knew he had been *unfaithful*, because of his sullen air, and his glances at her, similar to hers at him: What is it that I share with this person that shields all delight from me?) But none of it by anybody's fault. (But what did they feel ought to be somebody's fault?) Nobody's fault, nothing to be at fault, no one to blame, no one to offer or to take it . . . and nothing wrong, either, except that Matthew never was really struck, as he wanted to be, by joy; and that Susan was more and more often threatened by emptiness. (It was usually in the garden that she was invaded by this feeling: she was coming to avoid the garden, unless the children or Matthew were with her.) There was no need to use the dramatic words 'unfaithful', 'forgive', and the rest: intelligence forbade them. Intelligence barred, too, quarrelling, sulking, anger, silences of withdrawal, accusations and tears. Above all, intelligence forbids tears.

A high price has to be paid for the happy marriage with the four healthy children in the large white gardened house.

And they were paying it, willingly, knowing what they were doing. When they lay side by side or breast to breast in the big civilized bedroom overlooking the wild sullied river, they laughed, often, for no particular reason; but they knew it was really because of these two small people, Susan and Matthew, supporting such an edifice on their intelligent love. The laugh comforted them; it saved them both, though from what, they did not know.

They were now both fortyish. The older children, boy and girl, were ten and eight, at school. The twins, six, were still at home. Susan did not have nurses or girls to help her: childhood is short; and she did not regret the hard work. Often enough she was bored, since small children can be boring; she was often very tired; but she regretted nothing. In another decade, she would turn herself back into being a woman with a life of her own.

Soon the twins would go to school, and they would be away from home from nine until four. These hours, so Susan saw it, would be the preparation for her own slow emancipation away from the role of hub-of-the-family into woman-with-her-own-life. She was already planning for the hours of freedom when all the children would be 'off her hands'. That was the phrase used by Matthew and by Susan and by their friends, for the moment when the youngest child went off to school. 'They'll be off your hands, darling Susan, and you'll have time to yourself.' So said Matthew, the intelligent husband, who had often enough commended and consoled Susan, standing by her in spirit during the years when her soul was not her own, as she said, but her children's.

What it amounted to was that Susan saw herself as she had been at twenty-eight, unmarried; and then again somewhere about fifty, blossoming from the root of what she had been twenty years before. As if the essential Susan were in abeyance, as if she were in cold storage. Matthew said something like this to Susan one night: and she agreed that it was true – she did feel something like that. What, then, was this essential Susan? She did not know. Put like that it sounded ridiculous, and she did not really feel it. Anyway, they had a long discussion about the whole thing before going off to sleep in each other's arms.

So the twins went off to their school, two bright affectionate children who had no problems about it, since their older brother and sister had trodden this path so successfully before them. And now Susan was going to be alone in the big house, every day of the school term, except for the daily woman who came in to clean.

It was now, for the first time in this marriage, that something happened which neither of them had foreseen.

This is what happened. She returned, at nine-thirty, from taking the twins to the school by car, looking forward to seven blissful hours of freedom. On the first morning she was simply restless, worrying about the twins 'naturally enough' since this was their first day away at school. She was hardly able to contain herself until they came back. Which they did happily, excited by the world of school, looking forward to the next day. And the next day Susan took them, dropped them, came back, and found herself reluctant to enter her big and beautiful home because it was as if something was waiting for her there that she did not wish to confront. Sensibly, however, she parked the car in the garage, entered the house, spoke to Mrs Parkes, the daily woman, about her duties, and went up to her bedroom. She was possessed by a fever which drove her out again, downstairs, into the kitchen, where Mrs Parkes was making cake and did not need her, and into the garden. There she sat on a bench and tried to calm herself looking at trees, at a brown glimpse of the river. But she was filled with tension, like a panic: as if an enemy was in the garden with her. She spoke to herself severely, thus: All this is quite natural. First, I spent twelve years of my adult life working, *living my own life*. Then I married, and from the moment I became pregnant for the first time I signed myself over, so to speak, to other people. To the children. Not for one moment in twelve years have I been alone, had time to myself. So now I have to learn to be myself again. That's all.

And she went indoors to help Mrs Parkes cook and clean, and found some sewing to do for the children. She kept herself occupied every day. At the end of the first term she understood she felt two contrary emotions. First: secret astonishment and dismay that during those weeks when the house was empty of children she had in fact been more occupied (had been careful to keep herself occupied) than ever she had been when the children were around her needing her continual attention. Second: that now she knew the house would be full of them, and for five weeks, she resented the fact she would never be alone. She was already looking back at those hours of sewing, cooking (but by herself) as at a lost freedom which would not be hers for five long weeks. And the two months of term which would succeed the five weeks stretched alluringly open to her – freedom. But what freedom – when in fact she had been so careful *not* to be free of small duties during the last weeks? She looked at herself, Susan Rawlings, sitting in a big chair by the window in the bedroom, sewing shirts or dresses, which she might just as well have bought. She saw herself making cakes for hours at a time in the big family kitchen: yet usually she bought cakes. What she saw was a woman alone, that was true, but she had not felt alone. For instance, Mrs Parkes was always somewhere in the house. And she did not like being in the garden at all, because of the closeness there of the enemy – irritation, restlessness, emptiness, whatever it was – which keeping her hands occupied made less dangerous for some reason.

Susan did not tell Matthew of these thoughts. They were not sensible. She did not recognize herself in them. What should she say to her dear friend and husband, Matthew? 'When I go into the garden, that is, if the children are not there, I feel as if there is an enemy there waiting to invade me.' 'What enemy, Susan darling?' 'Well I don't know, really . . .' 'Perhaps you should see a doctor?'

No, clearly this conversation should not take place. The holidays began and Susan welcomed them. Four children, lively, energetic, intelligent, demanding: she was never, not for a moment of her day, alone. If she was in a room, they would be in the next room, or waiting for her to do something for them; or it would soon be time for lunch or tea, or to take one of them to the dentist. Something to do: five weeks of it, thank goodness.

On the fourth day of these so welcome holidays, she found she was storming with anger at the twins; two shrinking beautiful children who (and this is what checked her) stood hand in hand looking at her with sheer dismayed disbelief. This was their calm mother, shouting at them. And for what? They had come to her with some game, some bit of nonsense. They looked at each other, moved closer for support, and went off hand in hand, leaving Susan holding on to the windowsill of the livingroom, breathing deep, feeling sick. She went to lie down, telling the older children she had a headache. She heard the boy Harry telling the little ones: 'It's all right, Mother's got a headache.' She heard that *It's all right* with pain.

That night she said to her husband: 'Today I shouted at the twins, quite unfairly.' She sounded miserable, and he said gently: 'Well, what of it?'

'It's more of an adjustment than I thought, their going to school.'

'But Susie, Susie darling . . .' For she was crouched weeping on the bed. He comforted her: 'Susan, what is all this about? You shouted at them? What of it? If you shouted at them fifty times a day it wouldn't be more than the little devils deserve.' But she wouldn't laugh. She wept. Soon he comforted her with his body. She became calm. Calm, she wondered what was wrong with her, and why she should mind so much that she might, just once, have behaved unjustly with the children. What did it matter? They had forgotten it all long ago: Mother had a headache and everything was all right.

It was a long time later that Susan understood that that night, when she had wept and Matthew had driven the misery out of her with his big solid body, was the last time, ever in their married life, that they had been – to use their mutual language – with each other. And even that was a lie, because she had not told him of her real fears at all.

The five weeks passed, and Susan was in control of herself, and good and kind, and she looked forward to the holidays with a mixture of fear and longing. She did not know what to expect. She took the twins off to school (the elder children took themselves to school) and she returned to the house determined to face the enemy wherever he was, in the house, or the garden or – where?

She was again restless, she was possessed by restlessness. She cooked and sewed and worked as before, day after day, while Mrs Parkes remonstrated: 'Mrs Rawlings, what's the need for it? I can do that, it's what you pay me for.'

And it was so irrational that she checked herself. She would put the car into the garage, go up to her bedroom, and sit, hands in her lap, forcing herself to be quiet. She listened to Mrs Parkes moving around the house. She looked out into the garden and saw the branches shake the trees. She sat defeating the enemy, restlessness. Emptiness. She ought to be thinking about her life, about herself. But she did not. Or perhaps she could not. As soon as she forced her mind to think about Susan (for what else did she want to be alone for?), it skipped off to thoughts of butter or school clothes. Or it thought of Mrs Parkes. She realized that she sat listening for the movements of the cleaning woman, following her every turn, bend, thought. She followed her in her mind from kitchen to bathroom, from table to oven, and it was as if the duster, the cleaning cloth, the saucepan, were in her own hand. She would hear herself saying: No, not like that, don't put that there . . . Yet she did not give a damn what Mrs Parkes did, or if she did it at all. Yet she could not prevent herself from being conscious of her, every minute. Yes, this was what was wrong with her: she needed, when she was alone, to be really alone, with no one near. She could not endure the knowledge that in ten minutes or in half an hour Mrs Parkes would call up the stairs: 'Mrs Rawlings, there's no silver polish. Madam, we're out of flour.'

So she left the house and went to sit in the garden where she was screened from the house by trees. She waited for the demon to appear and claim her, but he did not.

She was keeping him off, because she had not, after all, come to an end of arranging herself.

She was planning how to be somewhere where Mrs Parkes would not come after her with a cup of tea, or a demand to be allowed to telephone (always irritating, since Susan did not care who she telephoned or how often), or just a nice talk about something. Yes, she needed a place, or a state of affairs, where it would not be necessary to keep reminding herself: In ten minutes I must telephone Matthew about . . . and at half past three I must leave early for the children because the car needs cleaning. And at ten o'clock tomorrow I must remember . . . She was possessed with resentment that the seven hours of freedom in every day (during weekdays in the school term) were not free, that never, not for one second, ever, was she free from the pressure of time, from having to remember this or that. She could never forget herself; never really let herself go into forgetfulness.

Resentment. It was poisoning her. (She looked at this emotion and thought it was absurd. Yet she felt it.) She was a prisoner. (She looked at this thought too, and it was no good telling herself it was a ridiculous one.) She must tell Matthew – but what? She was filled with emotions that were utterly ridiculous, that she despised, yet that nevertheless she was feeling so strongly she could not shake them off.

The school holidays came round, and this time they were for nearly two months, and she behaved with a conscious controlled decency that nearly drove her crazy. She would lock herself in the bathroom, and sit on the edge of the bath, breathing deep, trying to let go into some kind of calm. Or she went up into the spare room, usually empty, where no one would expect her to be. She heard the children calling 'Mother, Mother', and kept silent, feeling guilty. Or she went to the very end of the garden, by herself, and looked at the slow-moving brown river; she looked at the river and closed her eyes and breathed slow and deep, taking it into her being, into her veins.

Then she returned to the family, wife and mother, smiling and responsible, feeling as if the pressure of these people – four lively children and her husband – were a painful pressure on the surface of her skin, a hand pressing on her brain. She did not once break down into irritation during these holidays, but it was like living out a prison sentence, and when the children went back to school, she sat on a white stone near the flowing river, and she thought: It is not even a year since the twins went to school, since *they were off my hands* (What on earth did I think I meant when I used that stupid phrase?), and yet I'm a different person. I'm simply not myself. I don't understand it.

Yet she had to understand it. For she knew that this structure – big white house, on which the mortgage still cost four hundred a year, a husband, so good and kind and insightful; four children, all doing so nicely; and the garden where she sat; and Mrs Parkes, the cleaning woman – all this depended on her, and yet she could not understand why, or even what it was she contributed to it.

She said to Matthew in their bedroom: 'I think there must be something wrong with me.'

And he said: 'Surely not, Susan? You look marvellous – you're as lovely as ever.'

She looked at the handsome blond man, with his clear, intelligent, blue-eyed face, and thought: Why is it I can't tell him? Why not? And she said: 'I need to be alone more than I am.'

At which he swung his slow blue gaze at her, and she saw what she had been dreading: Incredulity. Disbelief. And fear. An incredulous blue stare from a stranger who was her husband, as close to her as her own breath.

He said: 'But the children are at school and off your hands.'

She said to herself: I've got to force myself to say: Yes, but do you realize that I never feel free? There's never a moment I can say to myself: There's nothing I have to remind myself about, nothing I have to do in half an hour, or an hour, or two hours . . .

But she said: 'I don't feel well.'

He said: 'Perhaps you need a holiday.'

She said, appalled: 'But not without you, surely?' For she could not imagine herself going off without him. Yet that was what he meant. Seeing her face, he laughed, and opened his arms, and she went into them, thinking: Yes, yes, but why can't I say it? And what is it I have to say?

She tried to tell him, about never being free. And he listened and said: 'But Susan, what sort of freedom can you possibly want – short of being dead! Am I ever free? I go to the office, and I have to be there at ten – all right, half past ten, sometimes. And I have to do this or that, don't I? Then I've got to come home at a certain time – I don't mean it, you know I don't – but if I'm not going to be back home at six I telephone you. When can I ever say to myself: I have nothing to be responsible for in the next six hours?'

Susan, hearing this, was remorseful. Because it was true. The good marriage, the house, the children, depended just as much on his voluntary bondage as it did on hers. But why did he not feel bound? Why didn't he chafe and become restless? No, there was something really wrong with her and this proved it.

And that word 'bondage' – why had she used it? She had never felt marriage, or the children, as bondage. Neither had he, or surely they wouldn't be together lying in each other's arms content after twelve years of marriage.

No, her state (whatever it was) was irrelevant, nothing to do with her real good life with her family. She had to accept the fact that, after all, she was an irrational person and to live with it. Some people had to live with crippled arms, or stammers, or being deaf. She would have to live knowing she was subject to a state of mind she could not own.

Nevertheless, as a result of this conversation with her husband, there was a new regime next holidays.

The spare room at the top of the house now had a cardboard sign saying: PRIVATE! DO NOT DISTURB! on it. (This sign had been drawn in coloured chalks by the children, after a discussion between the parents in which it was decided this was psychologically the right thing.) The family and Mrs Parkes knew this was 'Mother's Room' and that she was entitled to her privacy. Many serious conversations took place between Matthew and the children about not taking Mother for granted. Susan overheard the first, between father and Harry, the older boy, and was surprised at her irritation over it. Surely she could have a room somewhere in that big house and retire into it without such a fuss being made? Without it being so solemnly discussed? Why couldn't she simply have announced: 'I'm going to fit out the little top room for myself, and when I'm in it I'm not to be disturbed for anything short of fire'? Just that, and finished; instead of long earnest discussions. When she heard Harry and Matthew explaining it to the twins with Mrs Parkes coming in – 'Yes, well, a family sometimes gets on top of a woman' – she had to go right away to the bottom of the garden until the devils of exasperation had finished their dance in her blood.

But now there was a room, and she could go there when she liked, she used it seldom: she felt even more caged there than in her bedroom. One day she had gone up there after a lunch for ten children she had cooked and served because Mrs Parkes was not there, and had sat alone for a while looking into the garden. She saw the children stream out from the kitchen and stand looking up at the window where she sat behind the curtains. They were all – her children and their friends – discussing Mother's Room. A few minutes later, the chase of children in some game came pounding up the stairs, but ended as abruptly as if they had fallen over a ravine, so sudden was the silence. They had remembered she was there, and had gone silent in a great gale of 'Hush! Shhhhh! Quiet, you'll disturb her . . .' And they went tiptoeing downstairs like criminal conspirators. When she came down to make tea for them, they all apologized. The twins put their arms around her, from front and back, making a human cage of loving limbs, and promised it would never occur again. 'We forgot, Mummy, we forgot all about it!'

What it amounted to was that Mother's Room, and her need for privacy, had become a valuable lesson in respect for other people's rights. Quite soon Susan was going up to the room only because it was a lesson it was a pity to drop. Then she took sewing up there, and the children and Mrs Parkes came in and out: it had become another family room.

She sighed, and smiled, and resigned herself – she made jokes at her own expense with Matthew over the room. That is, she did from the self she liked, she respected. But at the same time, something inside her howled with impatience, with rage . . . And she was frightened. One day she found herself kneeling by her bed and praying: 'Dear God, keep it away from me, keep him away from me.' She meant the devil, for she now thought of it, not caring if she was irrational, as some sort of demon. She imagined him, or it, as a youngish man, or perhaps a middleaged man pretending to be young. Or a man young-looking from immaturity? At any rate, she saw the young-looking face which, when she drew closer, had dry lines about mouth and eyes. He was thinnish, meagre in build. And he had a reddish complexion, and ginger hair. That was he – a gingery, energetic man, and he wore a reddish hairy jacket, unpleasant to the touch.

Well, one day she saw him. She was standing at the bottom of the garden, watching the river ebb past, when she raised her eyes and saw this person, or being, sitting on the white stone bench. He was looking at her, and grinning. In his hand was a long crooked stick, which he had picked off the ground, or broken off the tree above him. He was absent-mindedly, out of an absent-minded or freakish impulse of spite, using the stick to stir around in the coils of a blindworm or a grass snake (or some kind of snakelike creature: it was whitish and unhealthy to look at, unpleasant). The snake was twisting about, flinging its coils from side to side in a kind of dance of protest against the teasing prodding stick.

Susan looked at him, thinking: Who is the stranger? What is he doing in our garden? Then she recognized the man around whom her terrors had crystallized. As she did so, he vanished. She made herself walk over to the bench. A shadow from a branch lay across thin emerald grass, moving jerkily over its roughness, and she could see why she had taken it for a snake, lashing and twisting. She went back to the house thinking: Right, then, so I've seen him with my own eyes, so I'm not crazy after all – there *is* a danger because I've seen him. He is lurking in the garden and sometimes even in the house, and he wants to *get into me and to take me over*.

She dreamed of having a room or a place, anywhere, where she could go and sit, by herself, no one knowing where she was.

Once, near Victoria, she found herself outside a news agent that had Rooms to Let advertised. She decided to rent a room, telling no one. Sometimes she could take the train in from Richmond and sit alone in it for an hour or two. Yet how could she? A room would cost three or four pounds a week, and she earned no money, and how could she explain to Matthew that she needed such a sum? What for? It did not occur to her that she was taking it for granted she wasn't going to tell him about the room.

Well, it was out of the question, having a room; yet she knew she must.

One day, when a school term was well established, and none of the children had measles or other ailments, and everything seemed in order, she did the shopping early, explained to Mrs Parkes she was meeting an old school friend, took the train to Victoria, searched until she found a small quiet hotel, and asked for a room for the day. They did not let rooms by the day, the manageress said, looking doubtful, since Susan so obviously was not the kind of woman who needed a room for unrespectable reasons. Susan made a long explanation about not being well, being unable to shop without frequent rests for lying down. At last she was allowed to rent the room provided she paid a full night's price for it. She was taken up by the manageress and a maid, both concerned over the state of her health . . . which must be pretty bad if, living at Richmond (she had signed her name and address in the register), she needed a shelter at Victoria.

The room was ordinary and anonymous, and was just what Susan needed. She put a shilling in the gas fire, and sat, eyes shut, in a dingy armchair with her back to a dingy window. She was alone. She was alone. She was alone. She could feel pressures lifting off her. First the sounds of traffic came very loud; then they seemed to vanish; she might even have slept a little. A knock on the door: it was Miss Townsend, the manageress, bringing her a cup of tea with her own hands, so concerned was she over Susan's long silence and possible illness.

Miss Townsend was a lonely woman of fifty, running this hotel with all the rectitude expected of her, and she sensed in Susan the possibility of understanding companionship. She stayed to talk. Susan found herself in the middle of a fantastic story about her illness, which got more and more impossible as she tried to make it tally with the large house at Richmond, well-off husband, and four children. Suppose she said instead: Miss Townsend, I'm here in your hotel because I need to be alone for a few hours, above all *alone and with no one knowing where I am*. She said it mentally, and saw, mentally, the look that would inevitably come on Miss Townsend's elderly maiden's face. 'Miss Townsend, my four children and my husband are driving me insane, do you understand that? Yes, I can see from the gleam of hysteria in your eyes that comes from loneliness controlled but only just contained that I've got everything in the world you've ever longed for. Well, Miss Townsend, I don't want any of it. You can have it, Miss Townsend. I wish I was absolutely alone in the world, like you. Miss Townsend, I'm besieged by seven devils, Miss Townsend, Miss Townsend, let me stay here in your hotel where the devils can't get me . . .' Instead of saying all this, she described her anaemia, agreed to try Miss Townsend's remedy for it, which was raw liver, minced, between whole-meal bread, and said yes, perhaps it would be better if she stayed at home and let a friend do shopping for her. She paid her bill and left the hotel, defeated.

At home Mrs Parkes said she didn't really like it, no, not really, when Mrs Rawlings was away from nine in the morning until five. The teacher had telephoned from school to say Joan's teeth were paining her, and she hadn't known what to say; and what was she to make for the children's tea, Mrs Rawlings hadn't said.

All this was nonsense, of course. Mrs Parkes's complaint was that Susan had withdrawn herself spiritually, leaving the burden of the big house on her.

Susan looked back at her day of 'freedom' which had resulted in her becoming a friend of the lonely Miss Townsend, and in Mrs Parkes's remonstrances. Yet she remembered the short blissful hour of being alone, really alone. She was determined to arrange her life, no matter what it cost, so that she could have that solitude more often. An absolute solitude, where no one knew her or cared about her.

But how? She thought of saying to her old employer: I want you to back me up in a story with Matthew that I am doing part-time work for you. The truth is that . . . But she would have to tell him a lie too, and which lie? She could not say: I want to sit by myself three or four times a week in a rented room. And besides, he knew Matthew, and she could not really ask him to tell lies on her behalf, apart from being bound to think it meant a lover.

Suppose she really took a part-time job, which she could get through fast and efficiently, leaving time for herself. What job? Addressing envelopes? Canvassing?

And there was Mrs Parkes, working widow, who knew exactly what she was prepared to give to the house, who knew by instinct when her mistress withdrew in spirit from her responsibilities. Mrs Parkes was one of the servers of this world, but she needed someone to serve. She had to have Mrs Rawlings, her madam, at the top of the house or in the garden, so that she could come and get support from her: 'Yes, the bread's not what it was when I was a girl . . . Yes, Harry's got a wonderful appetite, I wonder where he puts it all . . . Yes, it's lucky the twins are so much of a size, they can wear each other's shoes, that's a saving in these hard times . . . Yes, the cherry jam from Switzerland is not a patch on the jam from Poland, and three times the price . . .' And so on. That sort of talk Mrs Parkes must have, every day, or she would leave, not knowing herself why she left.

Susan Rawlings, thinking these thoughts, found that she was prowling through the great thicketed garden like a wild cat: she was walking up the stairs, down the stairs, through the rooms into the garden, along the brown running river, back, up through the house, down again . . . It was a wonder Mrs Parkes did not think it strange. But, on the contrary, Mrs Rawlings could do what she liked, she could stand on her head if she wanted, provided she was *there*. Susan Rawlings prowled and muttered through her house, hating Mrs Parkes, hating poor Miss Townsend, dreaming of her hour of solitude in the dingy respectability of Miss Townsend's hotel bedroom, and she knew quite well she was mad. Yes, she was mad.

She said to Matthew that she must have a holiday. Matthew agreed with her. This was not as things had been once – how they had talked in each other's arms in the marriage bed. He had, she knew, diagnosed her finally as *unreasonable*. She had become someone outside himself that he had to manage. They were living side by side in this house like two tolerably friendly strangers.

Having told Mrs Parkes – or rather, asked for her permission – she went off on a walking holiday in Wales. She chose the remotest place she knew of. Every morning the children telephoned her before they went off to school, to encourage and support her, just as they had over Mother's Room. Every evening she telephoned them, spoke to each child in turn, and then to Matthew. Mrs Parkes, given permission to telephone for instructions or advice, did so every day at lunchtime. When, as happened three times, Mrs Rawlings was out on the mountainside, Mrs Parkes asked that she should ring back at such-and-such a time, for she would not be happy in what she was doing without Mrs Rawlings' blessing.

Susan prowled over wild country with the telephone wire holding her to her duty like a leash. The next time she must telephone, or wait to be telephoned, nailed her to her cross. The mountains themselves seemed trammelled by her unfreedom everywhere on the mountains, where she met no one at all, from breakfast time to dusk, excepting sheep, or a shepherd, she came face to face with her own craziness, which might attack her in the broadest valleys, so that they seemed too small, or on a mountain top from which she could see a hundred other mountains and valleys, so that they seemed too low, too small, with the sky pressing down too close. She would stand gazing at a hillside brilliant with ferns and bracken, jewelled with running water, and see nothing but her devil, who lifted inhuman eyes at her from where he leaned negligently on a rock, switching at his ugly yellow boots with a leafy twig.

She returned to her home and family, with the Welsh emptiness at the back of her mind like a promise of freedom.

She told her husband she wanted to have an *au pair* girl.

They were in their bedroom, it was late at night, the children slept. He sat, shirted and slippered, in a chair by the window, looking out. She sat brushing her hair and watching him in the mirror. A time-hallowed scene in the connubial bedroom. He said nothing, while she heard the arguments coming into his mind, only to be rejected because every one was *reasonable*.

'It seems strange to get one now; after all, the children are in school most of the day. Surely the time for you to have help was when you were stuck with them day and night. Why don't you ask Mrs Parkes to cook for you? She's even offered to – I can understand if you are tired of cooking for six people. But you know that an *au pair* girl means all kinds of problems; it's not like having an ordinary char in during the day . . .'

Finally he said carefully: 'Are you thinking of going back to work?'

'No,' she said, 'no, not really.' She made herself sound vague, rather stupid. She went on brushing her black hair and peering at herself so as to be oblivious of the short uneasy glances her Matthew kept giving her. 'Do you think we can't afford it?' she went on vaguely, not at all the old efficient Susan who knew exactly what they could afford.

'It's not that,' he said, looking out of the window at dark trees, so as not to look at her. Meanwhile she examined a round, candid, pleasant face with clear dark brows and clear grey eyes. A sensible face. She brushed thick healthy black hair and thought: Yet that's the reflection of a madwoman. How very strange! Much more to the point if what looked back at me was the gingery green-eyed demon with his dry meagre smile . . . Why wasn't Matthew agreeing? After all, what else could he do? She was breaking her part of the bargain and there was no way of forcing her to keep it: that her spirit, her soul, should live in this house, so that the people in it could grow like plants in water, and Mrs Parkes remain content in their service. In return for this, he would be a good loving husband, and responsible towards the children. Well, nothing like this had been true of either of them for a long time. He did his duty, perfunctorily; she did not even pretend to do hers. And he had become like other husbands, with his real life in his work and the people he met there, and very likely a serious affair. All this was her fault.

At last he drew heavy curtains, blotting out the trees, and turned to force her attention: 'Susan, are you really sure we need a girl?' But she would not meet his appeal at all. She was running the brush over her hair again and again, lifting fine black clouds in a small hiss of electricity. She was peering in and smiling as if she were amused at the clinging hissing hair that followed the brush.

'Yes, I think it would be a good idea, on the whole,' she said, with the cunning of a madwoman evading the real point.

In the mirror she could see her Matthew lying on his back, his hands behind his head, staring upwards, his face sad and hard. She felt her heart (the old heart of Susan Rawlings) soften and call out to him. But she set it to be indifferent.

He said: 'Susan, the children?' It was an appeal that *almost* reached her. He opened his arms, lifting them palms up, empty. She had only to run across and fling herself into them, onto his hard, warm chest, and melt into herself, into Susan. But she could not. She would not see his lifted arms. She said vaguely: 'Well, surely it'll be even better for them? We'll get a French or a German girl and they'll learn the language.'

In the dark she lay beside him, feeling frozen, a stranger. She felt as if Susan had been spirited away. She disliked very much this woman who lay here, cold and indifferent beside a suffering man, but she could not change her.

Next morning she set about getting a girl, and very soon came Sophie Traub from Hamburg, a girl of twenty, laughing, healthy, blue-eyed, intending to learn English. Indeed, she already spoke a good deal. In return for a room – 'Mother's Room' – and her food, she undertook to do some light cooking, and to be with the children when Mrs Rawlings asked. She was an intelligent girl and understood perfectly what was needed. Susan said: 'I go off sometimes, for the morning or for the day – well, sometimes the children run home from school, or they ring up, or a teacher rings up. I should be here, really. And there's the daily woman . . .' And Sophie laughed her deep fruity *Fräulein's* laugh, showed her fine white teeth and her dimples, and said: 'You want some person to play mistress of the house sometimes, not so?'

'Yes, that is just so,' said Susan, a bit dry, despite herself, thinking in secret fear how easy it was, how much nearer to the end she was than she thought. Healthy Fräulein Traub's instant understanding of their position proved this to be true.

The *au pair* girl, because of her own common sense, or (as Susan said to herself, with her new inward shudder) because she had been *chosen* so well by Susan, was a success with everyone, the children liking her, Mrs Parkes forgetting almost at once that she was German, and Matthew finding her 'nice to have around the house'. For he was now taking things as they came, from the surface of life, withdrawn both as a husband and a father from the household.

One day Susan saw how Sophie and Mrs Parkes were talking and laughing in the kitchen, and she announced that she would be away until tea time. She knew exactly where to go and what she must look for. She took the District Line to South Kensington, changed to the Circle, got off at Paddington, and walked around looking at the smaller hotels until she was satisfied with one which had FRED'S HOTEL painted on windowpanes that needed cleaning. The façade was a faded shiny yellow, like unhealthy skin. A door at the end of a passage said she must knock; she did, and Fred appeared. He was not at all attractive, not in any way, being fattish, and run-down, and wearing a tasteless striped suit. He had small sharp eyes in a white creased face, and was quite prepared to let Mrs Jones (she chose the farcical name deliberately, staring him out) have a room three days a week from ten until six. Provided of course that she paid in advance each time she came? Susan produced fifteen shillings (no price had been set by him) and held it out, still fixing him with a bold unblinking challenge she had not known until then she could use at will. Looking at her still, he took up a ten-shilling note from her palm between thumb and forefinger, fingered it; then shuffled up two half-crowns, held out his own palm with these bits of money displayed thereon, and let his gaze lower broodingly at them. They were standing in the passage, a red-shaded light above, bare boards beneath, and a strong smell of floor polish rising about them. He shot his gaze up at her over the still-extended palm, and smiled as if to say: What do you take me for? 'I shan't,' said Susan, 'be using this room for the purposes of making money.' He still waited. She added another five shillings, at which he nodded and said: 'You pay, and I ask no questions.' 'Good,' said Susan. He now went past her to the stairs, and there waited a moment: the light from the street door being in her eyes, she lost sight of him momentarily. Then she saw a sober-suited, white-faced, white-balding little man trotting up the stairs like a waiter, and she went after him. They proceeded in utter silence up the stairs of this house where no questions were asked – Fred's Hotel, which could afford the freedom for its visitors that poor Miss Townsend's hotel could not. The room was hideous. It had a single window, with thin green brocade curtains, a three-quarter bed that had a cheap green satin bedspread on it, a fireplace with a gas fire and a shilling meter by it, a chest of drawers, and a green wicker armchair.

'Thank you,' said Susan, knowing that Fred (if this was Fred, and not George, or Herbert or Charlie) was looking at her, not so much with curiosity, an emotion he would not own to, for professional reasons, but with a philosophical sense of what was appropriate. Having taken her money and shown her up and agreed to everything, he was clearly disapproving of her for coming here. She did not belong here at all, so his look said. (But she knew, already, how very much she did belong: the room had been waiting for her to join it.) 'Would you have me called at five o'clock, please?' and he nodded and went downstairs.

It was twelve in the morning. She was free. She sat in the armchair, she simply sat, she closed her eyes and sat and let herself be alone. She was alone and no one knew where she was. When a knock came on the door she was annoyed, and prepared to show it: but it was Fred himself; it was five o'clock and he was calling her as ordered. He flicked his sharp little eyes over the room – bed, first. It was undisturbed. She might never have been in the room at all. She thanked him, said she would be returning the day after tomorrow, and left. She was back home in time to cook supper, to put the children to bed, to cook a second supper for her husband and herself later. And to welcome Sophie back from the pictures where she had gone with a friend. All these things she did cheerfully, willingly. But she was thinking all the time of the hotel room; she was longing for it with her whole being.

Three times a week. She arrived promptly at ten, looked Fred in the eyes, gave him twenty shillings, followed him up the stairs, went into the room, and shut the door on him with gentle firmness. For Fred, disapproving of her being here at all, was quite ready to let friendship, or at least acquaintanceship, follow his disapproval, if only she would let him. But he was content to go off on her dismissing nod, with the twenty shillings in his hand.

She sat in the armchair and shut her eyes.

What did she *do* in the room? Why, nothing at all. From the chair, when it had rested her, she went to the window, stretching her arms, smiling, treasuring her anonymity, to look out. She was no longer Susan Rawlings, mother of four, wife of Matthew, employer of Mrs Parkes and of Sophie Traub, with these and those relations with friends, school-teachers, tradesmen. She no longer was mistress of the big white house and garden, owning clothes suitable for this and that activity or occasion. She was Mrs Jones, and she was alone, and she had no past and no future. Here I am, she thought, after all these years of being married and having children and playing those roles of responsibility – and I'm just the same. Yet there have been times I thought that nothing existed of me except the roles that went with being Mrs Matthew Rawlings. Yes, here I am, and if I never saw any of my family again, here I would still be . . . how very strange that is! And she leaned on the sill, and looked into the street, loving the men and women who passed, because she did not know them. She looked at the down-trodden buildings over the street, and at the sky, wet and dingy, or sometimes blue, and she felt she had never seen buildings or sky before. And then she went back to the chair, empty, her mind a blank. Sometimes she talked aloud, saying nothing – an exclamation, meaningless, followed by a comment about the floral pattern on the thin rug, or a stain on the green satin coverlet. For the most part, she wool-gathered – what word is there for it? – brooded, wandered, simply went dark, feeling emptiness run deliciously through her veins like the movement of her blood.

This room had become more her own than the house she lived in. One morning she found Fred taking her a flight higher than usual. She stopped, refusing to go up, and demanded her usual room, Number 19. 'Well, you'll have to wait half an hour, then,' he said. Willingly she descended to the dark disinfectant-smelling hall, and sat waiting until the two, man and woman, came down the stairs, giving her swift indifferent glances before they hurried out into the street, separating at the door. She went up to the room, *her* room, which they had just vacated. It was no less hers, though the windows were set wide open, and a maid was straightening the bed as she came in.

After these days of solitude, it was both easy to play her part as mother and wife, and difficult – because it was so easy: she felt an impostor. She felt as if her shell moved here, with her family, answering to Mummy, Mother, Susan, Mrs Rawlings. She was surprised no one saw through her, that she wasn't turned out of doors, as a fake. On the contrary, it seemed the children loved her more; Matthew and she 'got on' pleasantly, and Mrs Parkes was happy in her work under (for the most part, it must be confessed) Sophie Traub. At night she lay beside her husband, and they made love again, apparently just as they used to, when they were really married. But she, Susan, or the being who answered so readily and improbably to the name of Susan, was not there: she was in Fred's Hotel, in Paddington, waiting for the easing hours of solitude to begin.

Soon she made a new arrangement with Fred and with Sophie. It was for five days a week. As for the money, five pounds, she simply asked Matthew for it. She saw that she was not even frightened he might ask what for: he would give it to her, she knew that, and yet it was terrifying it could be so, for this close couple, these partners, had once known the destination of every shilling they must spend. He agreed to give her five pounds a week. She asked for just so much, not a penny more. He sounded indifferent about it. It was as if he were paying her, she thought: *paying her off* – yes, that was it. Terror came back for a moment when she understood this, but she stilled it: things had gone too far for that. Now, every week, on Sunday nights, he gave her five pounds, turning away from her before their eyes could meet on the transaction. As for Sophie Traub, she was to be somewhere in or near the house until six at night, after which she was free. She was not to cook, or to clean; she was simply to be there. So she gardened or sewed, and asked friends in, being a person who was bound to have a lot of friends. If the children were sick, she nursed them. If teachers telephoned, she answered them sensibly. For the five daytimes in the school week, she was altogether the mistress of the house.

One night in the bedroom, Matthew asked: 'Susan, I don't want to interfere – don't think that, please – but are you sure you are well?'

She was brushing her hair at the mirror. She made two more strokes on either side of her head, before she replied: 'Yes, dear, I am sure I am well.'

He was again lying on his back, his blond head on his hands, his elbows angled up and part-concealing his face. He said: 'Then Susan, I have to ask you this question, though you must understand, I'm not putting any sort of pressure on you.' (Susan heard the word 'pressure' with dismay, because this was inevitable; of course she could not go on like this.) 'Are things going to go on like this?'

'Well,' she said, going vague and bright and idiotic again, so as to escape: 'Well, I don't see why not.'

He was jerking his elbows up and down, in annoyance or in pain, and, looking at him, she saw he had got thin, even gaunt; and restless angry movements were not what she remembered of him. He said: 'Do you want a divorce, is that it?'

At this, Susan only with the greatest difficulty stopped herself from laughing: she could hear the bright bubbling laughter she *would* have emitted, had she let herself. He could only mean one thing: she had a lover, and that was why she spent her days in London, as lost to him as if she had vanished to another continent.

Then the small panic set in again: she understood that he hoped she did have a lover, he was begging her to say so, because otherwise it would be too terrifying.

She thought this out as she brushed her hair, watching the fine black stuff fly up to make its little clouds of electricity, hiss, hiss. Behind her head, across the room, was a blue wall. She realized she was absorbed in watching the black hair making shapes against the blue. She should be answering him. 'Do *you* want a divorce, Matthew?'

He said: 'That surely isn't the point, is it?'

'You brought it up, I didn't,' she said, brightly, suppressing meaningless tinkling laughter.

Next day she asked Fred: 'Have enquiries been made for me?'

He hesitated, and she said: 'I've been coming here a year now. I've made no trouble, and you've been paid every day. I have a right to be told.'

'As a matter of fact, Mrs Jones, a man did come asking.'

'A man from a detective agency?'

'Well, he could have been, couldn't he?'

'I was asking you . . . Well, what did you tell him?'

'I told him a Mrs Jones came every weekday from ten until five or six and stayed in Number 19 by herself.'

'Describing me?'

'Well, Mrs Jones, I had no alternative. Put yourself in my place.'

'By rights I should deduct what that man gave you for the information.'

He raised shocked eyes: she was not the sort of person to make jokes like this! Then he chose to laugh: a pinkish wet slit appeared across his white crinkled face; his eyes positively begged her to laugh, otherwise he might lose some money. She remained grave, looking at him.

He stopped laughing and said: 'You want to go up now?' – returning to the familiarity, the comradeship, of the country where no questions are asked, on which (and he knew it) she depended completely.

She went up to sit in her wicker chair. But it was not the same. Her husband had searched her out. (The world had searched her out.) The pressures were on her. She was here with his connivance. He might walk in at any moment, here, into Room 19. She imagined the report from the detective agency: 'A woman calling herself Mrs Jones, fitting the description of your wife (et cetera, et cetera, et cetera), stays alone all day in Room No. 19. She insists on this room, waits for it if it is engaged. As far as the proprietor knows, she receives no visitors there, male or female.' A report something on these lines Matthew must have received.

Well, of course he was right: things couldn't go on like this. He had put an end to it all simply by sending the detective after her.

She tried to shrink herself back into the shelter of the room, a snail pecked out of its shell and trying to squirm back. But the peace of the room had gone. She was trying consciously to revive it, trying to let go into the dark creative trance (or whatever it was) that she had found there. It was no use, yet she craved for it, she was as ill as a suddenly deprived addict.

Several times she returned to the room, to look for herself there, but instead she found the unnamed spirit of restlessness, a pricking fevered hunger for movement, an irritable self-consciousness that made her brain feel as if it had coloured lights going on and off inside it. Instead of the soft dark that had been the room's air, were now waiting for her demons that made her dash blindly about, muttering words of hate; she was impelling herself from point to point like a moth dashing itself against a windowpane, sliding to the bottom, fluttering off on broken wings, then crashing into the invisible barrier again. And again and again. Soon she was exhausted, and she told Fred that for a while she would not be needing the room, she was going on holiday. Home she went, to the big white house by the river. The middle of a weekday, and she felt guilty at returning to her own home when not expected. She stood unseen, looking in at the kitchen window. Mrs Parkes, wearing a discarded floral overall of Susan's, was stooping to slide something into the oven. Sophie, arms folded, was leaning her back against a cupboard and laughing at some joke made by a girl not seen before by Susan – a dark foreign girl, Sophie's visitor. In an armchair Molly, one of the twins, lay curled, sucking her thumb and watching the grown-ups. She must have some sickness, to be kept from school. The child's listless face, the dark circles under her eyes, hurt Susan: Molly was looking at the three grown-ups working and talking in exactly the same way Susan looked at the four through the kitchen window: she was remote, shut off from them.

But then, just as Susan imagined herself going in, picking up the little girl, and sitting in an armchair with her, stroking her probably heated forehead, Sophie did just that: she had been standing on one leg, the other knee flexed, its foot set against the wall. Now she let her foot in its ribbon-tied red shoe slide down the wall, stood solid on two feet, clapping her hands before and behind her, and sang a couple of lines in German, so that the child lifted her heavy eyes at her and began to smile. Then she walked, or rather skipped, over to the child, swung her up, and let her fall into her lap at the same moment she sat herself. She said 'Hopla! Hopla! Molly . . .' and began stroking the dark untidy young head that Molly laid on her shoulder for comfort.

Well . . . Susan blinked the tears of farewell out of her eyes, and went quietly up through the house to her bedroom. There she sat looking at the river through the trees. She felt at peace, but in a way that was new to her. She had no desire to move, to talk, to do anything at all. The devils that had haunted the house, the garden, were not there; but she knew it was because her soul was in Room 19 in Fred's Hotel; she was not really here at all. It was a sensation that should have been frightening: to sit at her own bedroom window, listening to Sophie's rich young voice sing German nursery songs to her child, listening to Mrs Parkes clatter and move below, and to know that all this had nothing to do with her: she was already out of it.

Later, she made herself go down and say she was home: it was unfair to be here unannounced. She took lunch with Mrs Parkes, Sophie, Sophie's Italian friend Maria, and her daughter Molly, and felt like a visitor.

A few days later, at bedtime, Matthew said: 'Here's your five pounds', and pushed them over at her. Yet he must have known she had not been leaving the house at all.

She shook her head, gave it back to him, and said, in explanation, not in accusation: 'As soon as you knew where I was, there was no point.'

He nodded, not looking at her. He was turned away from her: thinking, she knew, how best to handle this wife who terrified him.

He said: 'I wasn't trying to . . . It's just that I was worried.'

'Yes, I know.'

'I must confess that I was beginning to wonder . . .'

'You thought I had a lover?'

'Yes, I am afraid I did.'

She knew that he wished she had. She sat wondering how to say: 'For a year now I've been spending all my days in a very sordid hotel room. It's the place where I'm happy. In fact, without it I don't exist.' She heard herself saying this, and understood how terrified he was that she might. So instead she said: 'Well, perhaps you're not far wrong.'

Probably Matthew would think the hotel proprietor lied: he would want to think so.

'Well,' he said, and she could hear his voice spring up, so to speak, with relief, 'in that case I must confess I've got a bit of an affair on myself.'

She said, detached and interested: 'Really? Who is she?' and saw Matthew's startled look because of this reaction.

'It's Phil. Phil Hunt.'

She had known Phil Hunt well in the old unmarried days. She was thinking: No, she won't do, she's too neurotic and difficult. She's never been happy yet. Sophie's much better. Well, Matthew will see that himself, as sensible as he is.

This line of thought went on in silence, while she said aloud: 'It's no point telling you about mine, because you don't know him.'

Quick, quick, invent, she thought. Remember how you invented all that nonsense for Miss Townsend.

She began slowly, careful not to contradict herself: 'His name is Michael' (*Michael What?*) – 'Michael Plant.' (What a silly name!) 'He's rather like you – in looks, I mean.' And indeed, she could imagine herself being touched by no one but Matthew himself. 'He's a publisher.' (Really? Why?) 'He's got a wife already and two children.'

She brought out this fantasy, proud of herself.

Matthew said: 'Are you two thinking of marrying?'

She said, before she could stop herself: 'Good God, *no!*'

She realized, if Matthew wanted to marry Phil Hunt, that this was too emphatic, but apparently it was all right, for his voice sounded relieved as he said: 'It is a bit impossible to imagine oneself married to anyone else, isn't it?' With which he pulled her to him, so that her head lay on his shoulder. She turned her face into the dark of his flesh, and listened to the blood pounding through her ears saying: I am alone, I am alone, I am alone.

In the morning Susan lay in bed while he dressed.

He had been thinking things out in the night, because now he said: 'Susan, why don't we make a foursome?'

Of course, she said to herself, of course he would be bound to say that. If one is sensible, if one is reasonable, if one never allows oneself a base thought or an envious emotion, naturally one says: Let's make a foursome!

'Why not?' she said.

'We could all meet for lunch. I mean, it's ridiculous, you sneaking off to filthy hotels, and me staying late at the office, and all the lies everyone has to tell.'

What on earth did I say his name was? – she panicked, then said: 'I think it's a good idea, but Michael is away at the moment. When he comes back, though – and I'm sure you two would like each other.'

'He's away, is he? So that's why you've been . . .' Her husband put his hand to the knot of his tie in a gesture of male coquetry she would not before have associated with him; and he bent to kiss her cheek with the expression that goes with the words: Oh you naughty little puss! And she felt its answering look, naughty and coy, come onto her face.

Inside she was dissolving in horror at them both, at how far they had both sunk from honesty of emotion.

So now she was saddled with a lover, and he had a mistress! How ordinary, how reassuring, how jolly! And now they would make a foursome of it, and go about to theatres and restaurants. After all, the Rawlings could well afford that sort of thing, and presumably the publisher Michael Plant could afford to do himself and his mistress quite well. No, there was nothing to stop the four of them developing the most intricate relationship of civilized tolerance, all enveloped in a charming afterglow of autumnal passion. Perhaps they would all go off on holidays together? She had known people who did. Or perhaps Matthew would draw the line there? Why should he, though, if he was capable of talking about 'foursomes' at all?

She lay in the empty bedroom, listening to the car drive off with Matthew in it, off to work. Then she heard the children clattering off to school to the accompaniment of Sophie's cheerfully ringing voice. She slid down into the hollow of the bed, for shelter against her own irrelevance. And she stretched out her hand to the hollow where her husband's body had lain, but found no comfort there: he was not her husband. She curled herself up in a small tight ball under the clothes: she could stay here all day, all week, indeed, all her life.

But in a few days she must produce Michael Plant, and – but how? She must presumably find some agreeable man prepared to impersonate a publisher called Michael Plant. And in return for which she would – what? Well, for one thing they would make love. The idea made her want to cry with sheer exhaustion. Oh no, she had finished with all that – the proof of it was that the words 'make love', or even imagining it, trying hard to revive no more than the pleasures of sensuality, let alone affection, or love, made her want to run away and hide from the sheer effort of the thing . . . Good Lord, why make love at all? Why make love with anyone? Or if you are going to make love, what does it matter who with? Why shouldn't she simply walk into the street, pick up a man and have a roaring sexual affair with him? Why not? Or even with Fred? What difference did it make?

But she had let herself in for it – an interminable stretch of time with a lover, called Michael, as part of a gallant civilized foursome. Well, she could not, and she would not.

She got up, dressed, went down to find Mrs Parkes, and asked her for the loan of a pound, since Matthew, she said, had forgotten to leave her money. She exchanged with Mrs Parkes variations on the theme that husbands are all the same, they don't think, and without saying a word to Sophie, whose voice could be heard upstairs from the telephone, walked to the underground, travelled to South Kensington, changed to the Inner Circle, got out at Paddington, and walked to Fred's Hotel. There she told Fred that she wasn't going on holiday after all, she needed the room. She would have to wait an hour, Fred said. She went to a busy tearoom-cum-restaurant around the corner, and sat watching the people flow in and out the door that kept swinging open and shut, watched them mingle and merge, and separate, felt her being flow into them, into their movement. When the hour was up, she left a half-crown for her pot of tea, and left the place without looking back at it, just as she had left her house, the big, beautiful white house, without another look, but silently dedicating it to Sophie. She returned to Fred, received the key of Number 19, now free, and ascended the grimy stairs slowly, letting floor after floor fall away below her, keeping her eyes lifted, so that floor after floor descended jerkily to her level of vision, and fell away out of sight.

Number 19 was the same. She saw everything with an acute, narrow, checking glance: the cheap shine of the satin spread, which had been replaced carelessly after the two bodies had finished their convulsions under it; a trace of powder on the glass that topped the chest of drawers; an intense green shade in a fold of the curtain. She stood at the window, looking down, watching people pass and pass and pass until her mind went dark from the constant movement. Then she sat in the wicker chair, letting herself go slack. But she had to be careful, because she did not want, today, to be surprised by Fred's knock at five o'clock.

The demons were not here. They had gone forever, because she was buying her freedom from them. She was slipping already into the dark fructifying dream that seemed to caress her inwardly, like the movement of her blood . . . but she had to think about Matthew first. Should she write a letter for the coroner? But what should she say? She would like to leave him with the look on his face she had seen this morning – banal, admittedly, but at least confidently healthy. Well, that was impossible, one did not look like that with a wife dead from suicide. But how to leave him believing she was dying because of a man – because of the fascinating publisher Michael Plant? Oh, how ridiculous! How absurd! How humiliating! But she decided not to

THE HOUSE OF THE FAMOUS POET

In the summer of 1944, when it was nothing for trains from the provinces to be five or six hours late, I travelled to London on the night train from Edinburgh, which, at York, was already three hours late. There were ten people in the compartment, only two of whom I remember well, and for good reason.

I have the impression, looking back on it, of a row of people opposite me, dozing untidily with heads askew, and, as it often seems when we look at sleeping strangers, their features had assumed extra emphasis and individuality, sometimes disturbing to watch. It was as if they had rendered up their daytime talent for obliterating the outward traces of themselves in exchange for mental obliteration. In this way they resembled a twelfth-century fresco; there was a look of medieval unselfconsciousness about these people, all except one.

This was a private soldier who was awake to a greater degree than most people are when they are not sleeping. He was smoking cigarettes one after the other with long, calm puffs. I thought he looked excessively evil – an atavistic type. His forehead must have been less than two inches high above dark, thick eyebrows, which met. His jaw was not large, but it was apelike; so was his small nose and so were his deep, close-set eyes. I thought there must have been some consanguinity in the parents. He was quite a throwback.

As it turned out, he was extremely gentle and kind. When I ran out of cigarettes, he fished about in his haversack and produced a packet for me and one for a girl sitting next to me. We both tried, with a flutter of small change, to pay him. Nothing would please him at all but that we should accept his cigarettes, whereupon he returned to his silent, reflective smoking.

I felt a sort of pity for him then, rather as we feel towards animals we know to be harmless, such as monkeys. But I realized that, like the pity we expend on monkeys merely because they are not human beings, this pity was not needed.

Receiving the cigarettes gave the girl and myself common ground, and we conversed quietly for the rest of the journey. She told me she had a job in London as a domestic helper and nursemaid. She looked as if she had come from a country district – her very blonde hair, red face and large bones gave the impression of power, as if she was used to carrying heavy things, perhaps great scuttles of coal, or two children at a time. But what made me curious about her was her voice, which was cultivated, melodious and restrained.

Towards the end of the journey, when the people were beginning to jerk themselves straight and the rushing to and fro in the corridor had started, this girl, Elise, asked me to come with her to the house where she worked. The master, who was something in a university, was away with his wife and family.

I agreed to this, because at that time I was in the way of thinking that the discovery of an educated servant girl was valuable and something to be gone deeper into. It had the element of experience – perhaps, even of truth – and I believed, in those days, that truth is stranger than fiction. Besides, I wanted to spend that Sunday in London. I was due back next day at my job in a branch of the civil service, which had been evacuated to the country and for a reason that is another story, I didn't want to return too soon. I had some telephoning to do, I wanted to wash and change. I wanted to know more about the girl. So I thanked Elise and accepted her invitation.

I regretted it as soon as we got out of the train at King's Cross, some minutes after ten. Standing up tall on the platform, Elise looked unbearably tired, as if not only the last night's journey but every fragment of her unknown life was suddenly heaping up on top of her. The power I had noticed in the train was no longer there. As she called, in her beautiful voice, for a porter, I saw that on the side of her head that had been away from me in the train, her hair was parted in a dark streak, which, by contrast with the yellow, looked navy blue. I had thought, when I first saw her, that possibly her hair was bleached, but now, seeing it so badly done, seeing this navy blue parting pointing like an arrow to the weighted weariness of her face, I, too, got the sensation of great tiredness. And it was not only the strain of the journey that I felt, but the foreknowledge of boredom that comes upon us unaccountably at the beginning of a quest, and that checks, perhaps mercifully, our curiosity.

And, as it happened, there really wasn't much to learn about Elise. The explanation of her that I had been prompted to seek, I got in the **183** taxi between King's Cross and the house at Swiss Cottage. She came of a good family, who thought her a pity, and she them. Having no training for anything else, she had taken a domestic job on leaving home. She was engaged to an Australian soldier billeted also at Swiss Cottage.

Perhaps it was the anticipation of a day's boredom, maybe it was the effect of no sleep or the fact that the V-I sirens were sounding, but I felt some sourness when I saw the house. The garden was growing all over the place. Elise opened the front door, and we entered a darkish room almost wholly taken up with a long, plain wooden worktable. On this, were a half-empty marmalade jar, a pile of papers, and a dried-up ink bottle. There was a steel-canopied bed, known as a Morrison shelter, in one corner and some photographs on the mantelpiece, one of a schoolboy wearing glasses. Everything was tainted with Elise's weariness and my own distaste. But Elise didn't seem to be aware of the exhaustion so plainly revealed on her face. She did not even bother to take her coat off, and as it was too tight for her I wondered how she could move about so quickly with this restriction added to the weight of her tiredness. But, with her coat still buttoned tight Elise phoned her boy-friend and made breakfast, while I washed in a dim, blue, cracked bathroom upstairs.

When I found that she had opened my hold-all without asking me and had taken out my rations, I was a little pleased. It seemed a friendly action, with some measure of reality about it, and I felt better. But I was still irritated by the house. I felt there was no justification for the positive lack of consequence which was lying about here and there. I asked no questions about the owner who was something in a university, for fear of getting the answer I expected – that he was away visiting his grandchildren, at some family gathering in the home counties. The owners of the house had no reality for me, and I looked upon the place as belonging to, and permeated with, Elise.

I went with her to a nearby public house, where she met her boy-friend and one or two other Australian soldiers. They had with them a thin Cockney girl with bad teeth. Elise was very happy, and insisted in her lovely voice that they should all come along to a party at the house that evening. In a fine aristocratic tone, she demanded that each should bring a bottle of beer.

During the afternoon Elise said she was going to have a bath, and she showed me a room where I could use the telephone and sleep if I wanted. This was a large, light room with several windows, much more orderly than the rest of the house, and lined with books. There was only one unusual thing about it: beside one of the windows was a bed, but this bed was only a fairly thick mattress made up neatly on the floor. It was obviously a bed on the floor with some purpose, and again I was angered to think of the futile crankiness of the elderly professor who had thought of it.

I did my telephoning, and decided to rest. But first I wanted to find something to read. The books puzzled me. None of them seemed to be automatically part of a scholar's library. An inscription in one book was signed by the author, a well-known novelist. I found another inscribed copy, and this had the name of the recipient. On a sudden idea, I went to the desk, where while I had been telephoning I had noticed a pile of unopened letters. For the first time, I looked at the name of the owner of the house.

I ran to the bathroom and shouted through the door to Elise, 'Is this the house of the famous poet?'

'Yes,' she called. 'I *told* you.'

She had told me nothing of the kind. I felt I had no right at all to be there, for it wasn't, now, the house of Elise acting by proxy for some unknown couple. It was the house of a famous modern poet. The thought that at any moment he and his family might walk in and find me there terrified me. I insisted that Elise should open the bathroom door and tell me to my face that there was no possible chance of their returning for many days to come.

Then I began to think about the house itself, which Elise was no longer accountable for. Its new definition, as the house of a poet whose work I knew well, many of whose poems I knew by heart, gave it altogether a new appearance.

To confirm this, I went outside and stood exactly where I had been when I first saw the garden from the door of the taxi. I wanted to get my first impression for a second time.

And this time I saw an absolute purpose in the overgrown garden, which, since then, I have come to believe existed in the eye of the beholder. But, at the time, the room we had first entered, and which had riled me, now began to give back a meaning, and whatever was, was right. The caked-up bottle of ink, which Elise had put on the mantelpiece, I replaced on the table to make sure. I saw a photograph I hadn't noticed before, and I recognized the famous poet.

THE HOUSE OF THE FAMOUS POET

It was the same with the upstairs room where Elise had put me, and I handled the books again, not so much with the sense that they belonged to the famous poet but with some curiosity about how they had been made. The sort of question that occurred to me was where the paper had come from and from what sort of vegetation was manufactured the black print, and these things have not troubled me since.

The Australians and the Cockney girl came around about seven. I had planned to catch an eight-thirty train to the country, but when I telephoned to confirm the time I found there were no Sunday trains running. Elise, in her friendly and exhausted way, begged me to stay without attempting to be too serious about it. The sirens were starting up again. I asked Elise once more to repeat that the poet and his family could by no means return that night. But I asked this question more abstractedly than before, as I was thinking of the sirens and of the exact proportions of the noise they made. I wondered, as well, what sinister genius of the Home Office could have invented so ominous a wail, and why. And I was thinking of the word 'siren'. The sound then became comical, for I imagined some maniac sea nymph from centuries past belching into the year 1944. Actually, the sirens frightened me.

Most of all, I wondered about Elise's party. Everyone roamed about the place as if it were nobody's house in particular, with Elise the best-behaved of the lot. The Cockney girl sat on the long table and gave of her best to the skies every time a bomb exploded. I had the feeling that the house had been requisitioned for an evening by the military. It was so hugely and everywhere occupied that it became not the house I had first entered, nor the house of the famous poet, but a third house – the one I had vaguely prefigured when I stood, bored, on the platform at King's Cross station. I saw a great amount of tiredness among these people, and heard, from the loud noise they made, that they were all lacking sleep. When the beer was finished and they were gone, some to their billets, some to pubs, and the Cockney girl to her Underground shelter where she had slept for weeks past, I asked Elise, 'Don't you feel tired?'

'No,' she said with agonizing weariness, 'I never feel tired.'

I fell asleep myself, as soon as I had got into the bed on the floor in the upstairs room, and overslept until Elise woke me at eight. I had wanted to get up early to catch a nine o'clock train, so I hadn't much time to speak to her. I did notice, though, that she had lost some of her tired look.

I was pushing my things into my hold-all while Elise went up the street to catch a taxi when I heard someone coming upstairs. I thought it was Elise come back, and I looked out of the open door. I saw a man in uniform carrying an enormous parcel in both hands. He looked down as he climbed, and had a cigarette in his mouth.

'Do you want Elise?' I called, thinking it was one of her friends.

He looked up, and I recognized the soldier, the throw-back, who had given us cigarettes in the train.

'Well, anyone will do,' he said. 'The thing is, I've got to get back to camp and I'm stuck for the fare – eight and six.'

I told him I could manage it, and was finding the money when he said, putting his parcel on the floor, 'I don't want to borrow it. I wouldn't think of borrowing it. I've got something for sale.'

'What's that?' I said.

'A funeral,' said the soldier. 'I've got it here.'

This alarmed me, and I went to the window. No hearse, no coffin stood below. I saw only the avenue of trees.

The soldier smiled. 'It's an abstract funeral,' he explained, opening the parcel.

He took it out and I examined it carefully, greatly comforted. It was very much the sort of thing I had wanted – rather more purple in parts than I would have liked, for I was not in favour of this colour of mourning. Still, I thought I could tone it down a bit.

Delighted with the bargain, I handed over the eight shillings and sixpence. There was a great deal of this abstract funeral. Hastily, I packed some of it into the holdall. Some I stuffed in my pockets, and there was still some left over. Elise had returned with a cab and I hadn't much time. So I ran for it, out of the door and out of the gate of the house of the famous poet, with the rest of my funeral trailing behind me.

You will complain that I am withholding evidence. Indeed, you may wonder if there is any evidence at all. 'An abstract funeral,' you will say, 'is neither here nor there. It is only a notion. You cannot pack a notion into your bag. You cannot see the colour of a notion.'

You will insinuate that what I have just told you is pure fiction.

Hear me to the end.

I caught the train. Imagine my surprise when I found, sitting opposite me, my friend the soldier, of whose existence you are so sceptical.

'As a matter of interest,' I said, 'how would you describe all this funeral you sold me?'

'Describe it?' he said. 'Nobody describes an abstract funeral. You just conceive it.'

'There is much in what you say,' I replied. 'Still, describe it I must, because it is not every day one comes by an abstract funeral.'

'I am glad you appreciate that,' said the soldier.

'And after the war,' I continued, 'when I am no longer a civil servant, I hope, in a few deftly turned phrases, to write of my experiences at the house of the famous poet, which has culminated like this. But of course,' I added, 'I will need to say what it looks like.'

The soldier did not reply.

'If it were an okapi or a sea-cow,' I said, 'I would have to say what it looked like. No one would believe me otherwise.'

'Do you want your money back?' asked the soldier. 'Because if so, you can't have it. I spent it on my ticket.'

'Don't misunderstand me,' I hastened to say. 'The funeral is a delightful abstraction. Only, I wish to put it down in writing.'

I felt a great pity for the soldier on seeing his worried look. The apelike head seemed the saddest thing in the world.

'I make them by hand,' he said, 'these abstract funerals.'

A siren sounded somewhere, far away.

'Elise bought one of them last month. She hadn't any complaints. I change at the next stop,' he said, getting down his kit from the rack. 'And what's more,' he said, 'your famous poet bought one.'

'Oh, did he?' I said.

'Yes,' he said. 'No complaints. It was just what he wanted – the idea of a funeral.'

The train pulled up. The soldier leaped down and waved. As the train started again, I unpacked my abstract funeral and looked at it for a few moments.

'To hell with the idea,' I said. 'It's a real funeral I want.'

'All in good time,' said a voice from the corridor.

'*You* again,' I said. It was the soldier.

'No,' he said. 'I got off at the last station. I'm only a notion of myself.'

'Look here,' I said, 'would you be offended if I throw all this away?'

'Of course not,' said the soldier. 'You can't offend a notion.'

'I want a real funeral,' I explained. 'One of my own.'

'That's right,' said the soldier.

'And then I'll be able to write about it and go into all the details,' I said.

'Your own funeral?' he said. 'You want to write it up?'

'Yes,' I said.

'But,' said he, 'you're only human. Nobody reports on their own funeral. It's got to be abstract.'

'You see my predicament?' I said.

'I see it,' he replied. 'I get off at this stop.'

This notion of a soldier alighted. Once more the train put on speed. Out of the window I chucked all my eight and sixpence worth of abstract funeral. I watched it fluttering over the fields and around the tops of camouflaged factories with the sun glittering richly upon it, until it was out of sight.

In the summer of 1944 a great many people were harshly and suddenly killed. The papers reported, in due course, those whose names were known to the public. One of these, the famous poet, had returned unexpectedly to his home at Swiss Cottage a few moments before it was hit direct by a flying bomb. Fortunately, he had left his wife and children in the country.

When I got to the place where my job was, I had some time to spare before going on duty. I decided to ring Elise and thank her properly, as I had left in such a hurry. But the lines were out of order, and the operator could not find words enough to express her annoyance with me. Behind this overworked, quarrelsome voice from the exchange I heard the high, long hoot which means that the telephone at the other end is not functioning, and the sound made me infinitely depressed and weary; it was more intolerable to me than the sirens, and I replaced the receiver; and, in fact, Elise had already perished under the house of the famous poet.

The blue cracked bathroom, the bed on the floor, the caked ink bottle, the neglected garden, and the neat rows of books – I try to gather them together in my mind whenever I am enraged by the thought that Elise and the poet were killed outright. The angels of the Resurrection will invoke the dead man and the dead woman, but who will care to restore the fallen house of the famous poet if not myself? Who else will tell its story?

When I reflect how Elise and the poet were taken in – how they calmly allowed a well-meaning soldier to sell them the notion of a funeral, I remind myself that one day I will accept, and so will you, an abstract funeral, and make no complaints.

THE ENIGMA

Who can become muddy and yet, settling, slowly become limpid?
Tao Te Ching

The commonest kind of missing person is the adolescent girl, closely followed by the teenage boy. The majority in this category come from working-class homes and almost invariably from those where there is serious parental disturbance. There is another minor peak in the third decade of life, less markedly working class, and constituted by husbands and wives trying to run out on marriages or domestic situations they have got bored with. The figures dwindle sharply after the age of forty; older cases of genuine and lasting disappearance are extremely rare, and again are confined to the very poor – and even there to those, near vagabond, without close family.

When John Marcus Fielding disappeared, he therefore contravened all social and statistical probability. Fifty-seven years old, rich, happily married, with a son and two daughters; on the board of several City companies (and very much not merely to adorn the letter-headings); owner of one of the finest Elizabethan manor-houses in East Anglia, with an active interest in the running of his adjoining 1,800-acre farm; a joint – if somewhat honorary – master of fox-hounds, a keen shot . . . he was a man who, if there were an -arium of living human stereotypes, would have done very well as a model of his kind: the successful City man who is also a country land-owner and (in all but name) village squire. It would have been very understandable if he had felt that one or the other side of his life had become too time-consuming . . . but the most profoundly anomalous aspect of his case was that he was also a Conservative Member of Parliament.

At 2.30 on the afternoon of Friday, July 13th, 1973, his elderly secretary, a Miss Parsons, watched him get into a taxi outside his London flat in Knightsbridge. He had a board meeting in the City; from there he was going to catch a train, the 5.22, to the market-town headquarters of his constituency. He would arrive soon after half-past six, then give a 'surgery' for two hours or so. His agent, who was invited to supper, would then drive him the twelve miles or so home to Tetbury Hall. A strong believer in the voting value of the personal contact, Fielding gave such surgeries twice a month. The agenda of that ominously appropriate day and date was perfectly normal.

It was discovered subsequently that he had never appeared at the board meeting. His flat had been telephoned, but Miss Parsons had asked for, and been granted, the rest of the afternoon off – she was weekending with relatives down in Hastings. The daily help had also gone home. Usually exemplary in attendance or at least in notifying unavoidable absence, Fielding was forgiven his lapse, and the board went to business without him. The first realization that something was wrong was therefore the lot of the constituency agent. His member was not on the train he had gone to meet. He went back to the party offices to ring Fielding's flat – and next, getting no answer there, his country home. At Tetbury Hall Mrs Fielding was unable to help. She had last spoken to her husband on the Thursday morning, so far as she knew he should be where he wasn't. She thought it possible, however, that he might have decided to drive down with their son, a postgraduate student at the London School of Economics. This son, Peter, had talked earlier in the week of coming down to Tetbury with his girlfriend. Perhaps he had spoken to his father in London more recently than she. The agent agreed to telephone Mrs Fielding again in half an hour's time, if the member had still not arrived by then.

She, of course, also tried the London flat; then failing there, Miss Parsons at home. But the secretary was already in Hastings. Mrs Fielding next attempted the flat in Islington that her son shared with two other LSE friends. The young man who answered had no idea where Peter was, but he 'thought' he was staying in town that weekend. The wife made one last effort – she tried the number of Peter's girlfriend, who lived in Hampstead. But here again there was no answer. The lady at this stage was not unduly perturbed. It seemed most likely that her husband had simply missed his train and was catching the next one – and for some reason had failed, or been unable, to let anyone know of this delay. She waited for the agent, Drummond, to call back.

He too had presumed a missed train or an overslept station, and had sent someone to await the arrival of the next trains in either direction. Yet when he rang back, as promised, it was to say that his deputy had

had no luck. Mrs Fielding began to feel a definite puzzlement and some alarm; but Marcus always had work with him, plentiful means of identification, even if he had been taken ill or injured beyond speech. Besides, he was in good health, a fit man for his age – no heart trouble, nothing like that. What very tenuous fears Mrs Fielding had at this point were rather more those of a woman no longer quite so attractive as she had been. She was precisely the sort of wife who had been most shaken by the Lambton–Jellicoe scandal of earlier that year. Yet even in this area she had no grounds for suspicion at all. Her husband's private disgust at the scandal had seemed perfectly genuine . . . and consonant with his general contempt for the wilder shores of the permissive society.

An hour later Fielding had still appeared neither at the party offices nor Tetbury Hall. The faithful had been sent away, with apologies, little knowing that in three days' time the cause of their disappointment was to be the subject of headlines. Drummond agreed to wait on at his desk; the supper, informal in any case, with no other guests invited, was forgotten. They would ring each other if and as soon as they had news; if not, then at nine. It was now that Mrs Fielding felt panic. It centred on the flat. She had the exchange check the line. It was in order. She telephoned various London friends, on the forlorn chance that in some fit of absentmindedness – but he was not that sort of person – Marcus had accepted a dinner or theatre engagement with them. These inquiries also drew a blank; in most cases, a polite explanation from staff that the persons wanted were abroad or themselves in the country. She made another attempt to reach her son; but now even the young man who had answered her previous call had disappeared. Peter's girlfriend and Miss Parsons were similarly still not to be reached. Mrs Fielding's anxiety and feeling of helplessness mounted, but she was essentially a practical and efficient woman. She rang back one of the closer London friends – close also in living only two or three minutes from the Knightsbridge flat – and asked him to go there and have the block porter open it up for him. She then called the porter to give her authority for this and to find out if perhaps the man had seen her husband. But he could tell her only that Mr Fielding had not passed his desk since he came on duty at six.

Some ten minutes later the friend telephoned from the flat. There was no sign of Marcus, but everything seemed perfectly as it should be. He found and looked in the engagements diary on Miss Parsons's desk, and read out the day's programme. The morning had been barred out, it seemed; but there was nothing abnormal in that. It was the MP's habit to keep Friday morning free for answering his less pressing correspondence. Fortunately Mrs Fielding knew a fellow director of the company whose board meeting was down for three o'clock. Her next move was to try him; and it was only then that she learnt the mystery had started before the failure to catch the 5.22 train; and that Miss Parsons had also (sinisterly as it seemed, since Mrs Fielding knew nothing of the innocent trip to Hastings) disappeared from the flat by three o'clock that afternoon. She now realized, of course, that whatever had happened might date back to the previous day. Marcus had been at the flat at nine on the Thursday morning, when she had spoken to him herself; but everything since then was uncertain. Very clearly something had gone seriously wrong.

Drummond agreed to drive over to the Hall, so that some plan of action could be concerted. Meanwhile, Mrs Fielding spoke to the local police. She explained that it was merely a precaution . . . but if they could check the London hospitals and the accident register. Soon after Drummond arrived, the message came that there had been no casualties or cases of stroke in the last twenty-four hours that had not been identified. The lady and Drummond began to discuss other possibilities: a political kidnapping or something of the sort. But Fielding had mildly pro-Arab rather than pro-Israeli views. With so many other more 'deserving' cases in the House, he could hardly have been a target for the Black September movement or its like; nor could he – for all his belief in law and order and a strong policy in Ulster – have figured very high on any IRA list. Virtually all his infrequent Commons speeches were to do with finance or agriculture.

Drummond pointed out that in any case such kidnappers would hardly have kept silent so long. An apolitical kidnapping was no more plausible – there were far richer men about . . . and surely one of the two Fielding daughters, Caroline and Francesca, both abroad at the time, would have been more likely victims if mere ransom money was the aim. And again, they would have had a demand by now. The more they discussed the matter the more it seemed that some kind of temporary amnesia was the most likely explanation. Yet surely even amnesiacs were aware that they had forgotten who they were and where they lived? The local doctor was called in from in front of his television set and gave an off-the-cuff opinion over the line. Had Mr Fielding shown forgetfulness recently? Worry, tenseness? Bad temper, anxiety? All had to be answered in the negative. Then any sudden shock? No, nothing. Amnesia was declared unlikely. The doctor gently suggested what had already been done regarding hospital admissions.

By now Mrs Fielding had started once more to suspect some purely private scandal was looming over the tranquil horizon of her life. Just as she had earlier imagined an unconscious body lying in the London flat, she now saw a dinner for two in Paris. She could not seriously see the prim Miss Parsons's as the female face in the candlelight; but she had that summer spent less time in London than usual. At any moment the telephone would ring and Marcus would be there, breaking some long-harboured truth about their marriage . . . though it had always seemed like the others one knew, indeed rather better than most in their circle. One had to suppose something very clandestine, right out of their class and normal world – some Cockney dolly-bird, heaven knows who. Somewhere inside herself and the privacies of her life, Mrs Fielding decided that she did not want any more inquiries made that night. Like all good Conservatives, she distinguished very sharply between private immorality and public scandal. What one did was never quite so reprehensible as letting it be generally known.

As if to confirm her decision, the local police inspector now rang to ask if he could help in any other way. She tried to sound light and unworried, she was very probably making a mountain out of a molehill, she managed the man, she was desperately anxious not to have the press involved. She finally took the same tack with Drummond. There might be some natural explanation, a lost telegram, a call Miss Parsons had forgotten to make, they should at least wait till the morning. By then Peter could also have gone to the flat and searched more thoroughly.

The Filipino houseboy showed Drummond out just after eleven. The agent had already drawn his own conclusions. He too suspected some scandal, and was secretly shocked – not only politically. Mrs Fielding seemed to him still an attractive woman, besides being a first-class member's wife.

The errant Peter finally telephoned just after midnight. At first he could hardly believe his mother. It now emerged that his girlfriend Isobel and he had had dinner with his father only the evening before, the Thursday. He had seemed absolutely normal then; had quite definitely not mentioned any change of weekend plan. Peter soon appreciated his mother's worry, however, and agreed to go round to the Knightsbridge flat at once and to sleep there. It had occurred to Mrs Fielding that if her husband had been kidnapped, the kidnappers might know only that address; and might have spent their evening, like her, ringing the number in vain.

But when Peter telephoned again – it was by then a quarter to one – he could only confirm what the last visitor had said. Everything seemed normal. The in-tray on Miss Parsons's desk revealed nothing. There was no sign in his father's bedroom of a hurried packing for a journey, and the suitcases and valises had the complement his mother detailed. There was nothing on any memo pad about a call to the agent or to Mrs Fielding. In the diary sat the usual list of appointments for the following week, starting with another board meeting and lunch for midday on the Monday. There remained the question of his passport. But that was normally kept in a filing-cabinet in the office, which was locked – Fielding himself and Miss Parsons having the only keys.

Mother and son once more discussed the question of alerting the London police. It was finally decided to wait until morning, when perhaps the secondary enigma of Miss Parsons could be solved. Mrs Fielding slept poorly. When she woke for the fifth or sixth time, just after six on the Saturday, she decided to drive to London. She arrived there before nine, and spent half an hour with Peter going once more through the flat for any clue. None of her husband's clothes seemed to be missing, there was no evidence at all of a sudden departure or journey. She tried Miss Parsons's home number in Putney one last time. Nobody answered. It was enough.

Mrs Fielding then made two preliminary calls. Just before ten she was speaking to the Home Secretary in person at his private house. There were obviously more than mere criminal considerations at stake, and she felt publicity was highly undesirable until at least a first thorough investigation had been made by the police.

A few minutes later the hunt was at last placed firmly in professional hands.

By Saturday evening they had clarified the picture, even if it was still that of a mystery. Miss Parsons had soon been traced, with a neighbour's help, to her relatives in Hastings. She was profoundly shocked – she had been with the Fieldings for nearly twenty years – and completely at a loss. As he had gone out the day before, she remembered Mr Fielding had asked if some papers he needed for the board meeting were in his briefcase. She was positive that he had meant to go straight to the address in Cheapside where the meeting was to be held.

The day porter told the police he hadn't heard the address given the taxi-driver, but the gentleman had seemed quite normal – merely 'in a bit of a hurry'. Miss Parsons came straight back to London, and opened up the filing cabinet. The passport was where it should be. She knew of no threatening letters or telephone calls; of no recent withdrawals of large sums of money, no travel arrangements. There had been nothing the least unusual in his behaviour all week. In private, out of Mrs Fielding's hearing, she told the chief super-intendent hastily moved in to handle the inquiry that the idea of another woman was 'preposterous'. Mr Fielding was devoted to his wife and family. She had never heard or seen the slightest evidence of infidelity in her eighteen years as his confidential secretary.

Fortunately the day porter had had a few words with the cab-driver before Fielding came down to take it. His description was good enough for the man to have been traced by mid-afternoon. He provided surprising proof that amnesia could hardly be the answer. He remembered the fare distinctly, and he was unshakeable. He had taken him to the British Museum, not Cheapside. Fielding hadn't talked, he had read the whole way – either a newspaper or documents from the briefcase. The driver couldn't remember whether he had actually walked into the Museum, since another immediate fare had distracted his attention as soon as Fielding paid him. But the Museum itself very soon provided evidence on that. The chief cloakroom attendant produced the briefcase at once – it had already been noted that it had not been retrieved when the Museum closed on the Friday. It was duly unlocked – and contained nothing but a copy of *The Times*, papers to do with the board meeting and some correspondence connected with the constituency surgery later that day.

Mrs Fielding said her husband had some interest in art, and even collected sporting prints and paintings in an occasional way; but she knew of absolutely no reason whatever why he should go to the British Museum . . . even if he had been free of other engagements. To the best of her knowledge he had never been there once during the whole of her life with him. The cloakroom porter who had checked in the briefcase seemed the only attendant in the Museum – crowded with the usual July tourists – who had any recall at all of the MP. He had perhaps merely walked through to the north entrance and caught another taxi. It suggested a little the behaviour of a man who knew he was being followed; and strongly that of one determined to give no clue as to his eventual destination.

The police now felt that the matter could not be kept secret beyond the Sunday; and that it was better to release the facts officially in time for the Monday morning papers rather than have accounts based on wild rumours. Some kind of mental breakdown did seem the best hypothesis, after all; and a photograph vastly increased chances of recognition. Of course they checked far more than Mrs Fielding realized; the help of Security and the Special Branch was invoked. But Fielding had never held ministerial rank, there could be no question of official secrets, some espionage scandal. None of the companies with whom he was connected showed the least doubt as to his trustworthiness . . . a City scandal was also soon ruled out of court. There remained the possibility of something along the Lambton–Jellicoe lines: a man breaking under the threat of a blackmailing situation. But again there was nothing on him of that nature. His papers were thoroughly gone through; no mysterious addresses, no sinister letters appeared. He was given an equally clean bill by all those who had thought they knew him well privately. His bank accounts were examined – no unexplained withdrawals, even in several preceding months, let alone in the week before his disappearance. He had done a certain amount of share-dealing during the summer, but his stockbrokers could show that everything that had been sold had been simply to improve his portfolio. It had all been re-invested. Nor had he made any recent new dispositions regarding his family in his will; cast-iron provisions had been effected many years before.

On the Monday, July 16th, he was front-page news in all the dailies. There were summaries of his career. The younger and only surviving son of a High Court judge, he had gone straight from a First in law at Oxford into the Army in 1939; had fought the North African campaign as an infantry officer and gained the M C; contracted kalaazar and been invalided home, finishing the war as a lieutenant-colonel at a desk at the War Office, concerned mainly with the Provost-Marshal department. There had followed after the war his success as a barrister specializing in company and taxation law, his giving up the Bar in 1959 for politics; then his directorships, his life in East Anglia, his position slightly right of centre in the Tory Party.

There were the obvious kinds of speculation, the police having said that they could not yet rule out the possibility of a politically motivated kidnapping, despite the apparently unforced decision not to attend the scheduled board meeting. But the Fieldings' solicitor, who had briefed the press, was adamant that there was categorically no question of unsavoury conduct in any manner or form; and the police confirmed that to the best of their knowledge the MP was a completely law-abiding citizen. Mr Fielding had not been under investigation or surveillance of any kind.

On the assumption that he might have travelled abroad with a false name and documents, a check was made at Heathrow and the main ports to the Continent. But no passport official, no airline desk-girl or stewardess who could be contacted could recall his face. He spoke a little French and German, but not nearly well enough to pass as a native – and in any case, the passport he had left behind argued strongly that he was still in Britain. The abundant newspaper and television coverage, with all the photographs of him, provoked the usual number of reports from the public. All were followed up, and none led anywhere. There was a good deal of foreign coverage as well; and Fielding most certainly did not remain unfindable for lack of publicity. He was clearly, if he was still alive, hidden or in hiding. The latter suggested an accomplice; but no accomplice among those who had formerly known the MP suggested himself or herself. A certain amount of discreet surveillance was done on the more likely candidates, of whom one was Miss Parsons. Her telephone at home, and the one at the flat, were tapped. But all this proved a dead end. A cloud of embarrassment, governmental, detective and private, gathered over the disappearance. It was totally baffling, and connoisseurs of the inexplicable likened the whole business to that of the *Marie Celeste*.

But no news story can survive an absence of fresh developments. On Fleet Street Fielding was tacitly declared 'dead' some ten days after the story first broke.

Mrs Fielding was not, however, the sort of person who was loth or lacked the means to prod officialdom. She ensured that her husband's case continued to get attention where it mattered; the police were not given the autonomy of Fleet Street. Unfortunately they had in their own view done all they could. The always very poor scent was growing cold; and nothing could be done until they had further information – and whether they got that was far more in the lap of the gods than a likely product of further inquiries. The web was out, as fine and far-flung as this particular spider could make it; but it was up to the fly to make a move now. Meanwhile, there was Mrs Fielding to be placated. She required progress reports.

At a meeting at New Scotland Yard on July 30th, it was decided (with, one must presume, higher consent) to stand down the team till then engaged full-time on the case and to leave it effectively in the hands of one of its junior members, a Special Branch sergeant hitherto assigned the mainly desk job of collating information on the 'political' possibilities. Normally, and certainly when it came to meeting Mrs Fielding's demands for information, the inquiry would remain a much higher responsibility. The sergeant was fully aware of the situation: he was to make noises like a large squad. He was not really expected to discover anything, only to suggest that avenues were still being busily explored. As he put it to a colleague, he was simply insurance, in case the Home Secretary turned nasty.

He also knew it was a small test. One of the rare public-school entrants to the force, and quite obviously cut out for higher rank from the day he first put on a uniform, he had a kind of tight-rope to walk. Police families exist, like Army and Navy ones, and he was the third generation of his to arm the law. He was personable and quick-minded, which might, with his middle-class manner and accent, have done him harm; but he was also a diplomat. He knew very well the prejudices his type could only too easily arouse in the petty-bourgeois mentality so characteristic of the middle echelons of the police. He might think this or that inspector a dimwit, he might secretly groan at some ponderous going-by-the-book when less orthodox methods were clearly called for, or at the tortured, queasy jargon some of his superiors resorted to in order to sound 'educated'. But he took very good care indeed not to show his feelings. If this sounds Machiavellian, it was; but it also made him a good detective. He was particularly useful for investigations in the higher social milieux. His profession did not stand out a mile in a Mayfair gaming-house or a luxury restaurant. He could pass very well as a rich, trendy young man about town, and if this ability could cause envy inside the force, it could also confound many stock notions of professional deformation outside it. His impeccable family background (with his father still a respected country head of police) also helped greatly; in a way he was a good advertisement for the career – undoubtedly a main reason he was picked for an assignment that must bring him into contact with various kinds of influential people. His name was Michael Jennings.

He spent the day following the secret decision in going through the now bulky file on Fielding, and at the end of it he drew up for himself a kind of informal summary that he called *State of Play*. It listed the **199** possibilities and their counter-arguments.

1. Suicide. No body. No predisposition, no present reason.
2. Murder. No body. No evidence of private enemies. Political ones would have claimed responsibility publicly.
3. Abduction. No follow-through by abductors. No reason why Fielding in particular.
4. Amnesia. They're just lost, not hiding. Doctors say no prior evidence, not the type.
5. Under threat to life. No evidence. Would have called in police at once, on past evidence.
6. Threat of blackmail. No evidence of fraud or tax-dodging. No evidence of sexual misbehaviour.
7. Fed up with present life. No evidence. No financial or family problems. Strong sense of social duties all through career. Legal mind, not a joker.
8. Timing. Advantage taken of Parsons's afternoon off (warning given ten days prior) suggests deliberate plan? But F. could have given himself longer by cancelling board meeting and one with agent – or giving Parsons whole day off. Therefore four hours was enough, assuming police brought in at earliest likely point, the 6.35 failure to turn up for his surgery. Therefore long planned? Able to put into action at short notice?

The sergeant then wrote a second heading: *Wild Ones*.

9. Love. Some girl or woman unknown. Would have to be more than sex. For some reason socially disastrous (married, class, colour)? Check other missing persons that period.
10. Homosexuality. No evidence at all.
11. Paranoia. Some imagined threat. No evidence in prior behaviour.
12. Ghost from the past. Some scandal before his marriage, some enemy made during wartime or legal phases of career? No evidence, but check.
13. Finances. Most likely way he would have set up secret account abroad?
14. Fox-hunting kick. Some parallel, identification with fox. Leaving hounds lost? But why?

15. Bust marriage. Some kind of revenge on wife. Check she hasn't been having it off?

16. Religious crisis. Mild C of E for the show of it. Zero probability.
17. Something hush-hush abroad to do with his being an MP. But not a muck-raker or cloak-and-dagger type. Strong sense of protocol, would have consulted the FO, at least warned his wife. Forget it.
18. Son. Doesn't fit. See him again.
19. Logistics. Total disappearance not one-man operation. Must have hide-out, someone to buy food, watch for him, etc.
20. *Must* be some circumstantial clue somewhere. Something he said some time to someone. Parsons more likely than wife? Try his Westminster and City friends.

After some time the sergeant scrawled a further two words, one of which was obscene, in capitals at the bottom of his analysis.

He began the following week with Miss Parsons. The daughters, Francesca and Caroline, had returned respectively from a villa near Malaga and a yacht in Greece and the whole family was now down at Tetbury Hall. Miss Parsons was left to hold the fort in London. The sergeant took her once more through the Friday morning of the disappearance. Mr Fielding had dictated some fifteen routine letters, then done paperwork on his own while she typed them out. He had made a call to his stockbroker; and no others to her knowledge. He had spent most of the morning in the drawing-room of the flat; not gone out at all. She had left the flat for less than half an hour, to buy some sandwiches at a delicatessen near Sloane Square. She had returned just after one, made coffee and taken her employer in the sandwiches he had ordered. Such impromptu lunches were quite normal on a Friday. He seemed in no way changed from when she had gone out. They had talked of her weekend in Hastings. He had said he was looking forward to his own, for once with no weekend guests, at Tetbury Hall. She had been with him so long that their relationship was very informal. All the family called her simply 'P'. She had often stayed at the Hall. She supposed she was 'half-nanny' as well as secretary.

The sergeant found he had to tread very lightly indeed when it came to delving into Fielding's past. 'P' proved to be fiercely protective of her boss's good name, both in his legal and his political phases. The sergeant cynically and secretly thought that there were more ways of breaking the law, especially in the City, than simply the letter of it; and Fielding had been formidably well equipped to buccaneer on the lee side. Yet she was adamant about foreign accounts. Mr Fielding had no sympathy with tax-haven tricksters – his view of the Lonrho affair, the other Tory scandal of that year, had been identical to that of his prime minister's. Such goings-on were 'the unacceptable face of capitalism' to him as well. But at least, insinuated the sergeant gently, if he *had* wanted to set up a secret account abroad, he had the know-how? But there he offended secretarial pride. She knew as much of Mr Fielding's financial affairs and resources as he did himself. It was simply not possible.

With the sexual possibilities, the sergeant ran into an even more granite-like wall. She had categorically denied all knowledge before, she had nothing further to add. Mr Fielding was the last man to indulge in a hole-in-the-corner liaison. He had far too much self-respect. Jennings changed his tack.

'Did he say anything that Friday morning about the dinner the previous evening with his son?'

'He mentioned it. He knows I'm very fond of the children.'

'In happy terms?'

'Of course.'

'But they don't see eye to eye politically?'

'My dear young man, they're father and son. Oh they've had arguments. Mr Fielding used to joke about it. He knew it was simply a passing phase. He told me once he was rather the same at Peter's age. I know for a fact that he very nearly voted Labour in 1945.'

'He gave no indication of any bitterness, quarrel, that Thursday evening?'

'Not in the least. He said Peter looked well. What a charming girl his new friend was.' She added, 'I think he was a tiny bit disappointed they weren't going down to the Hall for the weekend. But he expected his children to lead their own lives.'

'So he wasn't disappointed by the way Peter had turned out?'

'Good heavens no. He's done quite brilliantly. Academically.'

'But hardly following in his father's footsteps?'

'Everyone seems to think Mr Fielding was some kind of Victorian tyrant. He's a most broad-minded man.'

The sergeant smiled. 'Who's everyone, Miss Parsons?'

'Your superior, anyway. He asked me all these same questions.'

The sergeant tried soft soap: no one knew Mr Fielding better, she really was their best lead.

'One's racked one's brains. Naturally. But I can still hardly believe what's happened. And as for trying to find a reason . . .'

'An inspired guess?' He smiled again.

She looked down at the hands clasped over her lap. 'Well. He did drive himself very hard.'

'And?'

'Perhaps something in him . . . I really shouldn't be saying this. It's the purest speculation.'

'It may help.'

'Well, if something broke. He ran away. I'm sure he'd have realized what he had done in a very few days. But then, he did set himself such very high standards, perhaps he would have read all the newspaper reports. I think . . .'

'Yes?'

'I'm only guessing, but I suppose he might have been . . . deeply shocked at his own behaviour. And I'm not quite sure what . . .'

'Are you saying he might have killed himself?'

Evidently she was, though she shook her head. 'I don't know, I simply don't know. I feel so certain it was something done without warning. Preparation. Mr Fielding was a great believer in order. In proper channels. It was so very uncharacteristic of him. The method, I mean the way he did it. If he did do it.'

'Except it worked? If he did mean it to?'

'He couldn't have done it of his own free will. In his normal mind. It's unthinkable.'

Just for a moment the sergeant sensed a blandness, an impermeability in Miss Parsons, which was perhaps merely a realization that she would have done anything for Fielding – including the telling, at this juncture, of endless lies. There must have been something sexual in her regard for him, yet there was, quite besides her age, in her physical presence, in the rather dumpy body, the pursed mouth, the spectacles, the discreetly professional clothes of the lifelong spinster secretary, such a total absence of attractiveness (however far back one imagined her, and even if there had once been something between her and her employer, it would surely by now have bred malice rather than this fidelity) that made such suspicions die almost as soon as they came to mind. However, perhaps they did faintly colour the sergeant's next question.

'How did he usually spend free evenings here? When Mrs Fielding was down in the country?'

'The usual things. His club. He was rather keen on the theatre. He dined out a lot with friends. He enjoyed an occasional game of bridge.'

'He didn't gamble at all?'

'An occasional flutter. The Derby and the Grand National. Nothing more.'

'Not gaming clubs?'

'I'm quite sure not.'

The sergeant went on with the questioning, always probing towards some weak point, something shameful, however remote, and arrived nowhere. He went away only with that vague hint of an overworked man and the implausible notion that after a moment of weakness he had promptly committed hara-kiri. Jennings had a suspicion that Miss Parsons had told him what she wanted to have happened rather than what she secretly believed. The thought of a discreetly dead employer was more acceptable than the horror of one bewitched by a chit of a girl or tarred by some other shameful scandal.

While he was at the flat, he also saw the daily woman. She added nothing. She had never found evidence of some unknown person having slept there; no scraps of underclothes, no glasses smudged with lipstick, no unexplained pair of coffee-cups on the kitchen table. Mr Fielding was a gentleman, she said. Whether that meant gentlemen always remove the evidence or never give occasion for it in the first place, the sergeant was not quite sure.

He still favoured, perhaps because so many of the photographs suggested an intensity (strange how few of them showed Fielding with a smile) that gave also a hint of repressed sensuality, some kind of sexual–romantic solution. A slim, clean-shaven man of above average height, who evidently dressed with care even in his informal moments, Fielding could hardly have repelled women. For just a few minutes, one day, the sergeant thought he had struck oil in this barren desert. He had been checking the list of other persons reported missing over that first weekend. A detail concerning one case, a West Indian secretary who lived with her parents in Notting Hill, rang a sharp bell. Fielding had been on the board of the insurance company at whose London headquarters the girl had been working. The nineteen-year-old sounded reasonably well educated, her father was a social worker. Jennings saw the kind of coup every detective dreams of – Fielding, who had not been a Powellite, intercepted on his way to a board meeting, invited to some community centre do by the girl on behalf of her father, falling for black cheek in both senses . . . castles in Spain. A single call revealed that the girl had been traced – or rather had herself stopped all search a few days after disappearing. She fancied herself as a singer, and had run away with a guitarist from a West Indian club in Bristol. It was strictly black to black.

With City friends and Parliamentary colleagues – or what few had not departed for their holidays – Jennings did no better. The City men respected Fielding's acumen and legal knowledge. The politicians gave the impression, rather like Miss Parsons, that he was a better man than any of them – a top-class rural constituency member, sound party man, always well-briefed when he spoke, very pleasant fellow, very reliable . . . they were uniformly at sea over what had happened. Not one could recall any prior hint of a breakdown. The vital psychological clue remained as elusive as ever.

Only one MP was a little more forthcoming – a Labour maverick, who had by chance co-sponsored a non-party bill with Fielding a year previously. He had struck up some kind of working friendship, at least in the precincts of the House. He disclaimed all knowledge of Fielding's life outside, or of his reasons for 'doing a bunk'; but then he added that 'it figured, in a way'.

The sergeant asked why.

'Strictly off the record.'

'Of course, sir.'

'You know. Kept himself on too tight a rein. Still waters and all that. Something had to give.'

'I'm not quite with you, sir.'

'Oh come on, laddie. Your job must have taught you no one's perfect. Or not the way our friend tried to be.' He expanded. 'Some Tories are prigs, some are selfish bastards. He wanted to be both. A rich man on the grab and a pillar of the community. In this day and age. Of course it doesn't wash. He wasn't all that much of a fool.' The MP drily quizzed the sergeant. 'Ever wondered why he didn't get on here?'

'I didn't realize he didn't, sir.'

'Safe seat. Well run. Never in bad odour with his whips. But that's not what it's all about, my son. He didn't fool 'em where it matters. The Commons is like an animal. You either learn to handle it. Or you don't. Our friend hadn't a clue. He knew it. He admitted it to me once.'

'Why was that, sir?'

The Labour MP opened his hands. 'The old common touch? He couldn't unbend. Too like the swindler's best friend he used to be.' He sniffed. 'Alias distinguished tax counsel.'

'You're suggesting he cracked in some way?'

'Maybe he just cracked in the other sense. Decided to tell the first good joke of his life.'

Jennings smiled; and played naïve.

'Let me get this right, sir. You think he was disillusioned with Tory politics?'

The Labour MP gave a little grunt of amusement.

'Now you're asking for human feeling. I don't think he had much. I'd say just bored. With the whole bloody shoot. The House, the City, playing Lord Bountiful to the yokels. He just wanted out. Me, I wish him good luck. May his example be copied.'

'With respect, sir, none of his family or close friends seem to have noticed this.'

The MP smiled. 'Surprise, surprise.'

'They were part of it?'

The MP put his tongue in his cheek. Then he winked.

'Not a bad-looking bloke, either.'

'*Cherchez la femme?*'

'We've got a little book going. My money's on Eve. Pure guess, mind.'

And it really was a guess. He had no evidence at all. The MP concerned was a far more widely known figure than Fielding – a pugnacious showman as well as professional Tory-hater – and hardly a reliable observer. Yet he had suggested one thwarted ambition; and enemies do sometimes see further than friends.

Jennings next saw the person he had marked down as theoretically a key witness – not least since he also sounded an enemy, though where friend was to be expected. That was the son, Peter. The sergeant had had access to a file that does not officially exist. It had very little to say about Peter; little more indeed than to mention who he was the son of. He was noted as 'vaguely NL (New Left)'; 'more emotional than intellectual interest, long way from hardcore'. The 'Temporary pink?' with which the brief note on him ended had, in the odd manner of those so dedicated to the anti-socialist cause that they are prepared to spy for it (that is, outwardly adopt the cause they hate), a distinct air of genuine Marxist contempt.

The sergeant met Peter one day at the Knightsbridge flat. He had something of his father's tall good looks, and the same apparent difficulty in smiling. He was rather ostentatiously contemptuous of the plush surroundings of the flat; and clearly impatient at having to waste time going over the same old story.

Jennings himself was virtually apolitical. He shared the general (and his father's) view that the police got a better deal under a Conservative government, and he despised Wilson. But he didn't like Heath much better. Much more than he hated either party he hated the general charade of politics, the lying and covering-up that went on, the petty point-scoring. On the other hand he was not quite the fascist pig he very soon sensed that Peter took him for. He had a notion of due process, of justice, even if it had never been really put to the test; and he positively disliked the physical side of police work, the cases of outright brutality he had heard gossip about and once or twice witnessed. Essentially he saw life as a game, which one played principally for oneself and only incidentally out of some sense of duty. Being on the law's side was a part of the rules, not a moral imperative. So he disliked Peter from the start less for political reasons than for all kinds of vague social and games-playing ones . . . as one hates an opponent paradoxically both for unfairly taken and inefficiently exploited advantage. Jennings himself would have used the simple word 'phony'. He did not distinguish between an acquired left-wing contempt for the police and a hereditary class one. He just saw a contempt; and knew much better than the young man opposite him how to hide such a feeling.

The Thursday evening 'supper' had arisen quite casually. Peter had telephoned his father about six to say that he wouldn't be coming home that weekend after all. His father had suggested they had a meal together that evening, to bring Isobel along. Fielding wanted an early night, it was only for a couple of hours. They had taken him to a new kebab-house in Charlotte Street. He liked 'slumming' with them occasionally, eating out like that was nothing new. He had seemed perfectly normal – his 'usual urbane man-of-the-world act'. They had given up arguing the toss about politics 'years ago'. They had talked family things. About Watergate. His father had taken *The Times* line on Nixon (that he was being unfairly impeached by proxy), but didn't try seriously to defend the White House administration. Isobel had talked about her sister, who had married a would-be and meanwhile impoverished French film director and was shortly expecting a baby. The horrors of a cross-Channel confinement had amused Fielding. They hadn't talked about anything seriously, there had been absolutely no hint of what was to happen the next day. They had all left together about ten. His father had found a taxi (and had returned straight home, as the night porter had earlier borne witness) and they had gone on to a late film in Oxford Street. There had been no suggestion of a final farewell when they said goodnight to him.

'Do you think you ever convinced your father at all? In the days when you did argue with him?'

'No.'

'He never seemed shaken in his beliefs? Fed up in any way with the political life?'

'Extraordinary though it may seem, also no.'

'But he knew you despised it?'

'I'm just his son.'

'His only son.'

'I gave up. No point. One just makes one more taboo.'

'What other taboos did he have?'

'The usual fifty thousand.' Peter flicked his eyes round the room. 'Anything to keep reality at bay.'

'Won't it all be yours one day?'

'That remains to be seen.' He added, 'Whether I want it.'

'Was there a taboo about sex?'

'Which aspect of it?'

'Did he know the nature of your relationship with Miss Dodgson?'

'Oh for God's sake.'

'I'm sorry, sir. What I'm trying to get at is whether you think he might have envied it.'

'We never discussed it.'

'And you formed no impression?'

'He liked her. Even though she's not quite out of the right drawer, and all that. And I didn't mean by taboos expecting his son –'

The sergeant raised his hand. 'Sorry. You're not with me. Whether he could have fancied girls her age.'

Peter stared at him, then down at his sprawled feet.

'He hadn't that kind of courage. Or imagination.'

'Or need? Your parents' marriage was very happy, I believe.'

'Meaning you don't?'

'No, sir. I'm just asking you.'

Peter stared at him again a long moment, then stood up and went to the window.

'Look. All right. Maybe you don't know the kind of world I was brought up in. But its leading principle is never, never, never show what you really feel. I *think* my mother and father were happy together. But I don't really know. It's quite possible they've been screaming at each other for years behind the scenes. It's possible he's been having it off with any number of women. I don't think so, but I honestly don't know. Because that's the world they live in and I have to live in when I'm with them. You pretend, right? You don't actually show the truth till the world splits in half under your feet.' He turned from the window. 'It's no good asking me about my father. You could tell me anything about him and I couldn't say categorically, that's not true. I *think* he was everything he outwardly pretended to be. But because of what he is and . . . I just do not know.'

The sergeant left a silence.

'In retrospect – do you think he was deceiving you all through that previous evening?'

'It wasn't a police interrogation, for Christ's sake. One wasn't looking for it.'

'Your mother has asked in very high places that we pursue our inquiries. We haven't very much to go on.'

Peter Fielding took a deep breath. 'Okay.'

'This idea of a life of pretence – did you ever see any awareness of that in your father?'

'I suppose socially. Sometimes. All the dreadful bores he had to put up with. The small-talk. But even that far less often than he seemed to be enjoying it.'

'He never suggested he wanted a life without that?'

'Without people you can use? You're joking.'

'Did he ever seem disappointed his political career hadn't gone higher?'

'Also taboo.'

'He suggested something like it to someone in the House of Commons.'

'I didn't say it wasn't likely. He used to put out a line about the back benches being the backbone of parliament. I never really swallowed that.' He came and sat down again opposite the sergeant. 'You can't understand. I've had this all my life. The faces you put on. For an election meeting. For influential people you want something out of. For your old cronies. For the family. It's like asking me about an actor I've only seen on stage. I don't know.'

'And you've no theory on this last face?'

'Only three cheers. If he really did walk out on it all.'

'But you don't think he did?'

'The statistical probability is the sum of the British Establishment to one. I wouldn't bet on that. If I were you.'

'I take it this isn't your mother's view?'

'My mother doesn't have views. Merely appearances to keep up.'

'May I ask if your two sisters share your politics at all?'

'Just one red sheep in the family.'

The sergeant gave him a thin smile. He questioned on; and received the same answers, half angry, half indifferent – as if it were more important that the answerer's personal attitude was clear than the mystery be solved. Jennings was astute enough to guess that something was being hidden, and that it could very probably be some kind of distress, a buried love; that perhaps Peter was split, half of him wanting what would suit his supposedly independent self best – a spectacular breakdown of the life of pretence – and half wishing that everything had gone on as before. If he was, as seemed likely, really just a temporary pink, his father's possible plunge into what was the social, if not the political, equivalent of permanent red must be oddly mortifying; as if the old man had said, If you're really going to spit in your world's face, then this is the way to do it.

When the sergeant stood to go, he mentioned that he would like to see the girlfriend, Isobel Dodgson, when she returned to London. She had been in France, in Paris, since some ten days after the disappearance. It had seemed innocent enough. Her sister had just had the expected baby and the visit had apparently been long agreed. Even so – someone else's vision of a brilliant coup – Miss Dodgson and the comings and goings of her somewhat motley collection of French in-laws had been watched for a few days – and proved themselves monotonously innocent. Peter Fielding seemed rather vague about when exactly she would return. He thought it might not be for another week, when she was due back at her job at a publisher's.

'And she can't tell you anything you haven't heard ten times already.'

'I'd just like to see her briefly, sir.'

Jennings went on his way then, with once more next to nothing,

beyond the contemplation of an unresolved Oedipus complex, for his
210 pains.

He descended next, by appointment, on Tetbury Hall itself;
though before he gave himself the pleasure of seeing its beamed and
moated glory, he called on a selected handful of the neighbours. There
he got a slightly different view of his subject, and an odd consensus
that something thoroughly nasty (if unspecified) had happened.
Again, there was praise without reservation for the victim, as if *De
mortuis* was engraved on every county heart. Fielding was such a good
master of hounds, or would have been if he hadn't been so often
unavoidably absent; so 'good for the village'; so generally popular
(unlike the previous member). The sergeant tried to explain that a
political murder without any evidence for it, let alone a corpse, is
neither a murder nor political, but he had the impression that to his
listeners he was merely betraying a sad ignorance of contemporary
urban reality. He found no one who could seriously believe for a
moment that Fielding might have walked deliberately out of a world
shortly about to enter the hunting and shooting season.

Only one person provided a slightly different view of Fielding, and
that was the tweed-suited young man who ran his farm for him. It was
not a world Jennings knew anything about, but he took to the laconic
briskness of the thirty-year-old manager. He sensed a certain reflection of his own feelings about Fielding – a mixture of irritation and
respect. The irritation came very clearly, on the manager's side, from
feeling he was not sufficiently his own boss. Fielding liked to be
'consulted over everything'; and everything had to be decided 'on
accountancy grounds' – he sometimes wondered why they hadn't
installed a computer. But he confessed he'd learnt a lot, been kept on
his toes. Pressed by Jennings, he came up with the word 'compart-
mentalized'; a feeling that Fielding was two different people. One was
ruthless in running the farm for maximum profit; another was 'very
pleasant socially, very understanding, nothing snobbish about him'.
Only a fortnight before the 'vanishing trick' happened, he had had
a major planning get-together with Fielding. There had not been
the faintest sign then that the owner knew he would never see the
things they discussed come to fruition. Jennings asked finally, and
discreetly, about Mrs Fielding – the possibility that she might have
made her husband jealous.

'Not a chance. Not down here, anyway. Be round the village in ten
minutes.'

Mrs Fielding herself did not deny the unlikelihood. Though he had mistrusted Peter, the sergeant had to concede some justice to the jibe about keeping up appearances. It had been tactfully explained to her that Jennings, despite his present rank, was 'one of our best men' and had been working full time on the case since the beginning – a very promising detective. He put on his public-school manner, made it clear that he was not out of his social depth, that he was glad of the opportunity to meet her in person.

After telling her something of what he had been doing on the case, he began, without giving their origins, by advancing the theories of Miss Parsons and the Labour MP. The notion that her husband might have realized what he had done and then committed suicide or, from shame, remained in hiding, Mrs Fielding found incredible. His one concern would have been for the anxiety and the trouble he was causing, and to end it as soon as possible. She conceded that the inevitable publicity might irreparably have damaged his political career – but then he had 'so much else to live for'.

She refused equally to accept that he was politically disappointed. He was not at all a romantic dreamer, he had long ago accepted that he lacked the singleminded drive and special talents of ministerial material. He was not good at the cut-and-thrust side of parliamentary debate; and he spent rather too much time on the other sides of his life to expect to be a candidate for any Downing Street list. She revealed that Marcus was so little ambitious, or foolishly optimistic, that he had seriously considered giving up his seat at the next election. But she insisted that that was not out of disillusionment – simply from a feeling that he had done his stint. The sergeant did not argue the matter. He asked Mrs Fielding if she had formed any favourite theory herself during that last fortnight.

'One hardly seems to have talked of anything else, but . . .' she made an elegant and seemingly rather well-practised gesture of hopelessness.

'At least you feel he's still alive?' He added quickly, 'As you should, of course.'

'Sergeant, I'm in a vacuum. One hour I expect to see him walk through that door, the next . . .' again she gestured.

'If he is in hiding, could he look after himself? Can he cook, for instance?'

She smiled thinly. 'One hardly lives that sort of life, as you must realize. But the war. No doubt he could look after himself. As one does if one has to.'

'No new name has occurred to you – perhaps someone from the distant past? – who might have been talked into hiding him?'

'No.' She said. 'And let me spare you the embarrassment of the other woman theory. It was totally foreign to his nature to conceal anything from me. Obviously, let's face it, he could have fallen in love with someone else. But he'd never have hidden it from me – if he did feel . . .'

Jennings nodded. 'We do accept that, Mrs Fielding. I actually wasn't going to bring it up. But thanks anyway.' He said, 'No friends – perhaps with a villa or something abroad?'

'Well of course one has friends with places abroad. You must have all their names by now. But I simply refuse to believe that they'd do this to me and the children. It's unimaginable.'

'Your daughters can't help in any way?'

'I'm afraid not. They're here. If you want to ask them anything.'

'Perhaps later?' He tried to thaw her with a smile. 'There's another rather delicate matter. I'm terribly sorry about all this.'

The lady opened her hands in an acquiescent way – a gracious martyrdom; since one's duty obliged.

'It's to do with trying to build up a psychological picture? I've already asked your son about this in London. Whether his political views weren't a great disappointment to his father?'

'What did he answer?'

'I'd be most grateful to have your opinion first.'

She shrugged, as if the whole matter were faintly absurd, not 'delicate' at all.

'If only he'd understand that one would far rather he thought for himself than . . . you know what I mean.'

'But there was some disappointment?'

'My husband was naturally a little upset at the beginning. We both were. But . . . one had agreed to disagree? And he knows perfectly well we're very proud of him in every other way.'

'So a picture of someone having worked very hard to build a very pleasant world, only to find his son and heir doesn't want it, would be misleading?'

She puffed.

'But Peter does want it. He adores this house. Our life here. Whatever he says.' She smiled with a distinct edge of coldness. 'I do think this is the most terrible red herring, sergeant. What worst there was was long over. And one does have two daughters as well. One mustn't forget that.' She said, 'Apart from Peter's little flirtation with Karl Marx, we really have been a quite disgustingly happy family.'

The sergeant began to have something of the same impression he had received from Miss Parsons: that the lady had settled for ignorance rather than revelation. He might be there because she had insisted that investigation went on; but he suspected that that was a good deal more for show than out of any desperate need to have the truth uncovered. He questioned on; and got no help whatever. It was almost as if she actually knew where her husband was, and was protecting him. The sergeant had a sudden freakish intuition, no more founded on anything but frustration than those Mrs Fielding herself had had during that first evening of the disappearance, that he ought really to be searching Tetbury Hall, warrant in hand, instead of chatting politely away in the drawing-room. But to suppose Mrs Fielding capable of such a crime required her to be something other than she so obviously was . . . a woman welded to her role in life and her social status, eminently poised and eminently unimaginative. The sergeant also smelt a deeply wounded vanity. She had to bear some of the odium; and in some inner place she resented it deeply. He would have liked it much better if she had openly done so.

He did see the two daughters briefly. They presented the same united front. Daddy had looked tired sometimes, he worked so *fantastically* hard; but he was a super daddy. The younger of the two, Caroline, who had been sailing in Greece when the event took place, added one tiny new – and conflicting – angle. She felt few people, 'not even Mummy', realized how much the country side of his life meant to him – the farm, it drove Tony (the farm manager) mad the way Daddy was always poking round. But it was only because Daddy loved it, it seemed. He didn't really want to interfere, he 'just sort of wanted to be Tony, actually'. Then why hadn't he given up his London life? Caroline didn't know. She supposed he was more complicated 'than we all ever realized'. She even provided the wildest possibility yet.

'You know about Mount Athos? In Greece?' The sergeant shook his head. 'Actually we sailed past it when I was out there. It's sort of reserved for monasteries. There are only monks. It's all male. They don't even allow hens or cows. I mean, I know it sounds ridiculous, but sort of somewhere like that. Where he could be alone for a bit, I suppose.'

But when it came to evidence of this yearning for a solitary retreat, the two girls were as much at a loss as everyone else. What their brother found hypocritical, they had apparently found all rather dutiful and self-sacrificing.

A few minutes later, Mrs Fielding thanked the sergeant for his labours and, although it was half-past twelve, did not offer him lunch. He went back to London feeling, quite correctly, that he might just as well have stayed there in the first place.

Indeed he felt near the end of his tether over the whole bloody case. There were still people he had down to see, but he hardly expected them to add anything to the general – and generally blank – picture. He knew he was fast moving from being challenged to feeling defeated; and that it would soon be a matter of avoiding unnecessary work, not seeking it. One such possible lead he had every reason to cross off his list was Isobel Dodgson, Peter's girlfriend. She had been questioned in detail by someone else during the preliminary inquiry, and had contributed nothing of significance. But he retained one piece of casual gossip about her at the Yard; and a pretty girl makes a change, even if she knows nothing. Caroline and Francesca had turned out much prettier in the name than in the meeting.

She came back from Paris on August 15th, in the middle of one of the hottest weeks for many years. The sergeant had sent a brief letter asking her to get in touch as soon as she returned, and she telephoned the next morning, an unbearably sultry and humid Thursday. He arranged to go up to Hampstead and see her that afternoon. She sounded precise and indifferent; she knew nothing, she didn't really see the point. However, he insisted, though he presumed she had already spoken with Peter, and was taking his line.

He fell for her at once, in the door of the house in Willow Road. She looked a little puzzled, as if he must be for someone else, though he had rung the bell of her flat and was punctual to the minute. Perhaps she had expected someone in uniform, older; as he had expected someone more assured.

'Sergeant Mike Jennings. The fuzz.'

'Oh. Sorry.'

A small girl, a piquant oval face, dark brown eyes, black hair; a simple white dress with a blue stripe in it; down to the ankles, sandals over bare feet . . . but it wasn't only that. He had an immediate impression of someone alive, where everyone else had been dead, or playing dead; of someone who lived in the present, not the past; who was, surprisingly, not like Peter at all. She smiled and nodded past him.

'I suppose we couldn't go on the Heath? This heat's killing me. My room doesn't seem to get any air.'

'Fine.'

'I'll just get my key.'

He went and waited on the pavement. There was no sun; an opaque heat-mist, a bath of stale air. He took off his dark blue blazer and folded it over his arm. She joined him, carrying a small purse; another exchange of cautious smiles.

'You're the first cool-looking person I've seen all day.'

'Yes? Sheer illusion.'

They walked over the little climb to East Heath Road; then across that, and over the grass down towards the ponds. She didn't return to work until the next Monday; she was just a general dogsbody at the publisher's. He knew more about her than she realized, from the checking that had been done when she was temporarily under suspicion. She was twenty-four years old, a graduate in English, she had even published a book of stories for children. Her parents were divorced, her mother now lived in Ireland, married to some painter. Her father was a professor at York University.

'I don't know what on earth I can tell you.'

'Have you seen Peter Fielding since you got back?'

She shook her head. 'Just talked over the 'phone. He's down in the country.'

'It's only routine. Just a chat, really.'

'You're still . . . ?'

'Where we started. More or less.' He shifted his blazer to the other arm. One couldn't move without sweating. 'I'm not quite sure how long you've known the Fieldings.'

They walked very slowly. It was true, though meant as a way of saying he liked her dress, in spite of the heat she seemed cool beneath the white cotton; very small-bodied, delicate, like sixteen; but experienced somewhere, unlike sixteen, certain of herself despite those first moments of apparent timidity. A sexy young woman wearing a dark French scent, who tended to avoid his eyes, answering to the ground or to the Heath ahead.

'Only this summer. Four months. Peter, that is.'

'And his father?'

'We've been down two or three times to the grand baronial home. There was a party in London at the flat. Occasional meals out. Like that last one. I was really just his son's bit of bird. I honestly didn't know him very well.'

'Did you like him?'

She smiled, and for a brief moment said nothing.

'Not much.'

'Why not?'

'Tories. Not the way I was brought up.'

'Fair enough. Nothing else?'

She looked at the grass, amused. 'I didn't realize you were going to ask questions like this.'

'Nor did I. I'm playing it by ear.' She flashed him a surprised look, as if she hadn't expected such frankness; then smiled away again. He said, 'We've got all the facts. We're down to how people felt about him.'

'It wasn't him in particular. Just the way they live.'

'What your friend described as the life of pretence?'

'Except they're not pretending. They just are, aren't they?'

'Do you mind if I take my tie off?'

'Please. Of course.'

'I've spent all day dreaming of water.'

'Me too.'

'At least you've got it here.' They were passing the ladies' pond, with its wall of trees and shrubbery. He gave her a dry little grin, rolling his tie up. 'At a price.'

'The lezzies? How do you know about them?'

'I did some of my uniformed time up the road. Haverstock Hill?'

She nodded; and he thought, how simple it is, or can be . . . when they don't beat about the bush, say what they actually think and know, actually live today instead of fifty years ago; and actually state things he had felt but somehow not managed to say to himself. He had grown not to like Fielding much, either; or that way of life. Just that one became brainwashed, lazy, one swallowed the Sunday colour-supplement view of values, the assumptions of one's seniors, one's profession, one forgot there are people with fresh minds and independence who see through all that and are not afraid . . .

Suddenly she spoke.

'Is it true they beat up the dirty old men there?'

He was brought sharply to earth; and was shocked more than he showed, like someone angling for a pawn who finds himself placed in check by one simple move.

'Probably.' She had her eyes on the grass. After a second or two he said, 'I used to give them a cup of tea. Personally.' But the pause had registered.

'I'm sorry. I shouldn't have asked that.' She gave him an oblique glance. 'You're not very police-y.'

'We're used to it.'

'Something I heard once. I'm sorry, I . . .' She shook her head.

'It's okay. We live with it. Over-react.'

'And I interrupted.'

He hitched his coat over his back, and unbuttoned his shirt. 'What we're trying to discover is whether he could have got disillusioned with that way of life. Your friend told me his father hadn't the courage – either the courage or the imagination to walk out on it. Would you go with that?'

'Peter said that?'

'His words.'

She didn't answer for a moment.

'He was one of those men who sometimes seem to be somewhere else. You know? As if they're just going through the motions.'

'And what else?'

Again that pause. 'Dangerous isn't the word – but someone – very self-controlled. A tiny bit obsessional? I mean someone who wouldn't be easily stopped if he'd argued himself into something.' She hit her head gently in self-remonstrance. 'I'm not putting this very well. I'm just surprised that Peter –'

'Don't stop.'

'There was something sort of fixed, rigid underneath. I think that could have produced courage. And this abstracted thing he showed sometimes. As if he were somewhere else. And that suggests a kind of imagination?' She grimaced. 'The detective's dream.'

'No, this is helpful. How about that last evening? Did you get that somewhere-else feeling then?'

She shook her head. 'Oddly enough he was much jollier than usual. Well . . . I say jolly. He wasn't that kind of person, but . . .'

'Enjoying himself?'

'It didn't seem only politeness.'

'Someone who's made up his mind? Feels good about it?'

She thought about that, staring down. They walked very slowly, as if at any moment they would turn back. She shook her head.

'I honestly don't know. There certainly wasn't any buried emotion. Nothing of the farewell about it.'

'Not even when he said goodbye?'

'He kissed me on the cheek. I think he touched Peter on the shoulder. I couldn't swear about the actual movements. But I'd have noticed if there'd been anything unusual. I mean, his mood was slightly unusual. I remember Peter saying something about his getting mellow in his old age. There was that feeling. That he'd put himself out to be nice to us.'

'He wasn't always?'

'I didn't mean that. Just . . . not simply going through the motions. Perhaps it was London. He always seemed more somewhere-else down in the country. To me, anyway.'

'That's where everyone else seems to think he was happier.'

Again she thought, and chose her words. 'Yes, he did enjoy showing it all off. Perhaps it was the family situation. Being *en famille*.'

He said, 'I've got to ask you something very crude now.'

'No. He didn't.'

The answer came back so fast that he laughed.

'You're my star witness.'

'I was waiting for it.'

'Not even a look, a . . . ?'

'I divide the looks men give me into two kinds. Natural and unnatural. He never gave me the second sort. That I saw.'

'I didn't mean to suggest he'd have made a pass at you, but whether you felt any kind of general . . .'

'Nothing I could describe.'

'Then there was something?'

'No. Honestly not. I think it was just me. Psychic nonsense. It's not evidence.'

'Do I get on my knees?'

Her mouth curved, but she said nothing. They moved up, on a side-path, towards Kenwood.

He said, 'Bad vibes?'

She hesitated still, then shook her head. The black hair curled a little, negligently and deliciously, at its ends, where it touched the skin of her bare neck.

'I didn't like being alone with him. It only happened once or twice. It may have just been the political thing. Sympathetic magic. The way he always used to produce a kind of chemical change in Peter.'

'Like how?'

'Oh, a kind of nervousness. A defensiveness. It's not that they used to argue the way they once apparently did. All very civilized, really. You please mustn't say anything about this. It's mostly me. Not facts.'

'The marriage seemed okay to you?'

'Yes.'

'You hesitated.'

She was watching the ground again as they mounted the grassy hill. 'My own parents' marriage broke up when I was fifteen. I sort of felt something . . . just the tiniest whiff. When the couple know and the children don't. I think in real relationships people are rude to each other. They know it's safe, they're not walking on ice. But Peter said they'd always been like that. He told me once, he'd never once heard them have a row. Always that façade. Front. Perhaps I just came in late on something that had always been there.'

'You never had chat with Mrs Fielding?'

'Nothing else.' She pulled a little face. 'Inch-deep.'

'This not wanting to be alone with him –'

'It was such a tiny thing.'

'You've already proved you're telepathic.' She smiled again, her lips pressed tight. 'Were these bad vibes sexual ones?'

'Just that something was suppressed. Something . . .'

'Let it come out. However wild.'

'Something he might suddenly tell me. That he might break down. Not that he ever would. I can't explain.'

'But an unhappiness in him?'

'Not even that. Just someone else, behind it all. It's nothing, but I'm not quite making it up after the facts.' She shrugged. 'When it all happened, something seemed to fit. It wasn't quite the shock it ought to have been.'

'You think the someone else was very different from the man everyone knew?' She gave her slow, reluctant nod. 'Nicer or nastier?'

'More honest?'

'You never heard him say anything that suggested he was changing his politics? Moving leftward?'

'Absolutely not.'

'Did he seem to approve of you as a future daughter-in-law?'

She seemed faintly embarrassed at that.

220   'I'm not interested in getting married yet. It's not been that sort of relationship.'

'Which they understood?'

'They knew we were sleeping together. There wasn't any separate room nonsense when we stayed down there.'

'But he liked you in some way you didn't like? Or is that over-simplifying?'

Suddenly she gave him a strange look: a kind of lightning assessment of who he was. Then she looked away.

'Could we go and sit down a moment? Under that tree?' She went on before he could say anything. 'I'm holding out on you. There's something I should have told you before. The police. It's very minor. But it may help explain what I'm trying to say.'

Again that quickness: a little smile, that stopped him before he could speak.

'Please. Let's sit down first.'

She sat cross-legged, like a child. He took a cigarette packet out of his blazer pocket, but she shook her head and he put it away. He sat, then lay on an elbow opposite her. The tired grass. It was totally airless. Just the white dress with the small blue stripes, very simple, a curve off her shoulders down above her breasts, the skin rather pale, faintly olive; those eyes, the line of her black hair. She broke off a stalk of dry grass and fiddled with it in her lap.

'That last meal we had.' She smiled up. 'The last supper? Actually I was alone with him for a few minutes before Peter arrived. He'd been at some meeting at the L S E, he was a tiny bit late. Mr Fielding never was. So. He asked me what I'd been doing all week. We're doing a reprint of some minor late Victorian novels – you know, those campy illustrated ones, it's just cashing in on a trend – and I explained I'd been reading some.' She was trying to split the grass-stalk with a nail. 'It's just this. I did mention I had to go to the British Museum reading-room the next day to track one down.' She looked up at the sergeant. 'Actually in the end I didn't. But that's what I told him.'

He looked down from her eyes. 'Why didn't you tell us?'

'I suppose "no one asked me" isn't good enough?'

'Not from someone of your intelligence.'

She went back to the grass-stalk. 'Then sheer cowardice? Plus the knowledge that I'm totally innocent.'

'He didn't make a thing of it?'

'Not at all. It was just said in passing. I spent most of the time telling him about the book I'd been reading that day. That was all. Then Peter came.'

'And you never went to the Museum?'

'There was a panic over some proofs. I spent the whole of Friday in the office reading them.' She looked him in the eyes again. 'You could check. They'd remember the panic.'

'We already have.'

'Thank God for that.'

'Where everybody was that afternoon.' He sat up and stared away across the grass to Highgate Hill. 'If you're innocent, why keep quiet about it?'

'Purely personal reasons.'

'Am I allowed to hear them?'

'Just Peter. It's actually been rather more off than on for some time now. Since before. The real reason we didn't go down to Tetbury that weekend was that I refused to.' She glanced up at the sergeant, as if to see whether she had said enough; then down again into her lap. 'I felt the only reason he tried to get me down there was to put me in what you just said – the future daughter-in-law situation? Using something he pretends to hate to try and get me. I didn't like it. That's all.'

'But you still wanted to protect him?'

'He's so desperately confused about his father. And I thought, you know . . . whatever I said, it would seem fishy. And Mrs Fielding. I mean, I *know* I'm innocent. But I wasn't sure anyone else would. And I couldn't see, I still can't, that it proves anything.'

'If he did go to see you, what could he have wanted?'

She uncrossed her legs, and sat sideways to him, hands clasped round the knees. 'I thought at first something to do with me being in publishing. But I'm just a nobody. He knew that.'

'You mean some kind of book? Confession?'

She shook her head. 'It doesn't make sense.'

'You should have told us.'

'The other man didn't explain what he wanted. You have.'

'Thanks. And you've still been wicked.'

'Duly contrite.'

The head was bowed. He pressed a smile out of his mouth.

'This feeling he wanted to tell you something – is that based on this, or something previous?'

'There was one other tiny thing. Down at Tetbury in June. He took me off one day to see some new loose-boxes they'd just had put up. It was really an excuse. To give me a sort of pat on the back. You know. He said something about being glad Peter had hit it off with me. Then that he needed someone with a sense of humour. And then he said: *Like all us political animals.*' She spoke the words slowly, as if she were listing them. 'I'm sure of that. Those words exactly. Then something about, one sometimes forgets there are other ways of seeing life. That was all, but he was sort of trying to let me know he knew he wasn't perfect. That he knew Tetbury wasn't my scene. That he didn't despise my scene as much as I might think.' She added, 'I'm talking about tiny, very faint impressions. And retrospective ones. They may not mean anything.'

'Peter obviously didn't know about the Museum thing?'

'It didn't come up. Fortunately. Something in him always liked to pretend I didn't earn my own living.'

He noted that past tense.

'And he wouldn't have believed you – if he had known?'

'Do you?'

'You wouldn't be here now, otherwise. Or telling me.'

'No, I suppose I wouldn't.'

He leant back again, on an elbow; and tried to calculate how far he could go with personal curiosity under the cover of official duty.

'He sounds very mixed-up. Peter.'

'The opposite really. Unmixed. Like oil and water. Two people.'

'And his father could have been the same?'

'Except it's naked with Peter. He can't hide it.' She was talking with her head bent, rocking a little, hands still clasped around her knees. 'You know, some people – that kind of pretentious life, houseboys waiting at table and all the rest of it. Okay, one loathes it, but at least it's natural. Peter's mother.' She shrugged. 'She really believes in the formal hostess bit. Leaving the gentlemen to the port and cigars.' She glanced sideways at him again. 'But his father. He so obviously wasn't a fool. Whatever his political views.'

'He saw through it?'

'But something in him was also too clever to show it. I mean, he never sent it up. Apologized for it, the way some people do. Except for that one thing he said to me. It's just some kind of discrepancy. I can't explain.' She smiled at him. 'It's all so tenuous. I don't even know why I'm bothering to tell you.'

'Probably because you know I'm torn between arresting you for conspiracy to suppress evidence and offering you a cup of tea at Kenwood.'

She smiled and looked down at her knees, let three or four seconds pass.

'Have you always been a policeman?'

He told her who his father was.

'And you enjoy it?'

'Being a leper to most of your own generation?'

'Seriously.'

He shrugged. 'Not this case. No one wants it solved now. Sleeping dogs and all that. Between ourselves.'

'That must be foul.'

He smiled. 'Not until this afternoon, anyway.' He said quickly. 'That's not a pass. You're just about the first person I've seen who makes some kind of sense of it all.'

'And you're really nowhere nearer . . . ?'

'Further. But you may have something. There was someone else. Saying more or less what you've said. Only not so well.'

She left another pause.

'I'm sorry I said that thing just now. About police brutality.'

'Forget it. It does happen. Coppers also have small daughters.'

'Do you really feel a leper?'

'Sometimes.'

'Are all your friends in the police?'

'It's not that. Just the work. Having to come on like authority. Officialdom? Obeying people you don't always respect. Never quite being your own man.'

'That worries you?'

'When I meet people I like. Who can be themselves.'

She stared into the distance.

'Would it ever make you give it up?'

'Would what?'

'Not being your own man?'

'Why do you ask?'

'Just . . .' she shrugged. 'That you should use that phrase.'

'Why?'

She said nothing for a moment, then she looked down at her knees. 'I do have a private theory. About what happened. It's very wild.' She grinned at him. 'Very literary. If you want to hear it, it will cost you one cup of tea.' She raised the purse. 'I didn't bring any money.'

He stood and held out a hand. 'You're on.'

They walked towards the trees of Kenwood House. She kept obstinately to her bargain. Her 'theory' must wait till they had their tea. So they talked more like the perfect strangers, hazard-met, that they were; about their respective jobs, which required a disillusioning on both sides as to very much of the supposed glamour and excitement attached to them. She admitted, when he revealed that he knew about the children's stories, to a general literary ambition – that is, a more adult one. She was trying to write a novel, it was so slow, you had to destroy so much and start again; so hard to discover whether one was really a writer or just a victim of a literary home environment. He felt a little bit the same about his own work; and *its* frustrations and endless weeks of getting nowhere. They rather surprisingly found, behind the different cultural backgrounds, a certain kind of unspoken identity of situation. He queued up behind his witness at the tea-counter, observing the back of her head, that tender skin above the curve of the dress, the starchy blue stripes in its mealy whiteness; and he knew he had to see her again, off-duty. He had no problems with girls. It was not a physical thing, a lack of confidence sexually; not even a class or a cultural thing; but a psychological thing, a knowledge that he was – despite the gaffe, but even the gaffe had been a kind of honesty – dealing with a quicker and more fastidious mind in the field of emotions and personal relationships . . . that, and the traditional ineligibility of his kind for her kind, with the added new political bar, if the intelligence was also progressive, that he had referred to as a leprosy. Something about her possessed something that he lacked: a potential that lay like unsown ground, waiting for just this unlikely corn-goddess; a direction he could follow, if she would only show it. An honesty, in one word. He had not wanted a girl so fast and so intensely for a long time. Nevertheless, he made a wise decision.

They found a table to themselves in a corner. This time she accepted a cigarette.

'So let's have it.'

'Nothing is real. All is fiction.'

She bit her lips, lips without make-up, waiting for his reaction.

'That solves the case?'

'Lateral thinking. Let's pretend everything to do with the Fieldings, even you and me sitting here now, is in a novel. A detective story. Yes? Somewhere there's someone writing us, we're not real. He or she decides who we are, what we do, all about us.' She played with her teaspoon; the amused dark eyes glanced up at him. 'Are you with me?'

'By the skin of my teeth.'

'A story has to have an ending. You can't have a mystery without a solution. If you're the writer you have to think of something.'

'I've spent most of this last month –'

'Yes, but only in reality. It's the difference between I haven't many facts, so I can't decide anything – and I haven't many facts, but I've simply got to decide something.'

He felt a little redressment of the imbalance – after all a fault in this girl, a cerebral stillness. It would have irritated him in someone less attractive in other ways; now it simply relieved him. He smiled.

'We play that game too. But never mind.'

She bit her lips again. 'I propose to dismiss the *deus ex machina* possibility. It's not good art. An awful cheat, really.'

'You'd better . . .'

She grinned. 'The god out of the machine. Greek tragedy. When you couldn't work out a logical end from the human premises, you dragged in something external. You had the villain struck down by lightning. A chimney-pot fell on his head. You know?'

'I'm back on my feet.'

'Of course the British Museum thing may have been pure coincidence. On the other hand the vanished man might have been really determined to see that girl. So I think the writer would make him – when he found she wasn't in the reading-room after all – telephone the publishers where she works. There's a blank in her day. Between just after half-past five, when she left work, until about eight, when she met Peter Fielding to go to a rather ghastly party.'

And suddenly he felt more seriously out of his depth. He was being teased – which meant she liked him? Or he was being officially mocked – which meant she didn't?

'They met then?'

She raised a finger.

'The writer *could* have made them meet. He'd have to make it a kind of spur-of-the-moment thing. Obviously it could have been much better planned, if the missing man had had it in mind for some time. He'd have to say something like . . . I've just broken under all the hidden pressures of my life, I don't know who to turn to, you seem quite a sympathetic and level-headed girl, you –'

'This level-headed girl would be telling me all this?'

'Only if she was quite sure it couldn't be proved. Which she might be. Given that at this late date the police have apparently never even suspected such a meeting.'

'Correction. Found evidence of.'

'Same thing.'

'All right.'

'So he might just have made her pity him? This seeming hollow man pouring out all his despair. A hopelessness. Terribly difficult to write, but it could be done. Because it so happens the girl is rather proud of her independence. And her ability to judge people. And don't forget she really hasn't any time at all for the world he's running away from.' The real girl played with her plastic teaspoon, looked up at him unsmiling now; trying him out. 'And there's no sex angle. She'd be doing it out of the kindness of her heart. And not very much. Just fixing up somewhere for him to hide for a few days, until he can make his own arrangements. And being the kind of person she is, once she'd decided it was the right thing to do, nothing, not even rather dishy young policemen who buy her cups of tea, would ever get the facts out of her.'

He stared at his own cup and saucer. 'You're not by any chance . . . ?'

'Just one way the writer might have played it.'

'Hiding people isn't all that easy.'

'Ah.'

'Especially when they've acted on the spur of the moment and made no financial arrangements that one can discover. And when they're not spur-of-the-moment people.'

'Very true.'

'Besides, it's not how I read her character.'

'More conventional?'

'More imaginative.'

She leant away on an elbow, smiling.

'So our writer would have to tear this ending up?'

'If he's got a better.'

'He has. And may I have another cigarette?'

He lit it for her. She perched her chin on her hands, leant forward.

'What do you think would strike the writer about his story to date – if he re-read it?'

'He ought never to have started it in the first place.'

'Why?'

'Forgot to plant any decent leads.'

'Doesn't that suggest something about the central character? You know, in books, they do have a sort of life of their own.'

'He didn't mean evidence to be found?'

'I think the writer would have to face up to that. His main character has walked out on him. So all he's left with is the character's determination to have it that way. High and dry. Without a decent ending.'

The sergeant smiled down. 'Except writers can write it any way they like.'

'You mean detective stories have to end with everything explained? Part of the rules?'

'The unreality.'

'Then if our story disobeys the unreal literary rules, that might mean it's actually truer to life?' She bit her lips again. 'Leaving aside the fact that it *has* all happened. So it must be true, anyway.'

'I'd almost forgotten that.'

She set out her saucer as an ashtray.

'So all our writer could really do is find a convincing reason why this main character had forced him to commit the terrible literary crime of not sticking to the rules?' She said; 'Poor man.'

The sergeant felt the abyss between them; people who live by ideas, people who have to live by facts. He felt obscurely humiliated, to have to sit here and listen to all this; and at the same time saw her naked, deliciously naked on his bed. Her bed. Any bed or no bed. The nipples showed through the thin fabric; the hands were so small, the eyes so alive.

'And you happen to have it?'

'There was an author in his life. In a way. Not a man. A system, a view of things? Something that had written him. Had really made him just a character in a book.'

'So?'

'Someone who never put a foot wrong. Always said the right thing, wore the right clothes, had the right image. Right with a big r, too. All the roles he had to play. In the City. The country. The dull and dutiful member of parliament. So in the end there's no freedom left. Nothing he can choose. Only what the system says.'

'But that goes for –'

'Then one has to look for something very unusual in him. Since he's

done something very unusual?' The sergeant nodded. She was avoid-
228 ing his eyes now. 'All this dawns on him. Probably not suddenly.
Slowly. Little by little. He's like something written by someone else, a
character in fiction. Everything is planned. Mapped out. He's like a
fossil – while he's still alive. One doesn't have to suppose changes of
view. Being persuaded by Peter politically. Seeing the City for the
nasty little rich man's casino it really is. He'd have blamed everything
equally. How it had used him. Limited him. Prevented him.'

She tapped ash from her cigarette.

'Did you ever see his scrapbooks?'

'His what?'

'They're in the library down at Tetbury. All bound in blue morocco. Gilt-tooled. His initials. Dates. All his press cuttings. Right back
to the legal days. *Times* law reports, things like that. Tiniest things.
Even little local rag clippings about opening bazaars and whatnot.'

'Is that so unusual?'

'It just seems more typical of an actor. Or some writers are like that.
A kind of obsessive need to know . . . that they've been known?'

'Okay.'

'It's a kind of terror, really. That they've failed, they haven't
registered. Except that writers and actors are in far less predictable
professions. They can have a sort of eternal optimism about themselves. Most of them. The next book will be fabulous. The next part
will be a rave.' She looked up at him, both persuading and estimating.
'And on the other hand they live in cynical open worlds. Bitchy ones.
Where no one really believes anyone else's reputation – especially if
they're successful. Which is all rather healthy, in a way. But he isn't
like that. Tories take success so seriously. They define it so exactly. So
there's no escape. It has to be position. Status. Title. Money. And the
outlets at the top are so restricted. You have to be prime minister. Or a
great lawyer. A multi-millionaire. It's that or failure.' She said,
'Think of Evelyn Waugh. A terrible Tory snob. But also very shrewd,
very funny. If you can imagine someone like that, a lot more imagination than anyone ever gave him credit for, but completely without all
the safety valves Waugh had. No brilliant books, no Catholicism, no
wit. No drinking, no impossible behaviour in private.'

'Which makes him like thousands of others?'

'But we have a fact about him. He did something thousands of
others don't. So it must have hurt a lot more. Feeling failed and
trapped. And forced – because everything was so standard, so

conforming in his world – to pretend he was happy as he was. No creative powers. Peter's told me. He wasn't even very good in court, as a barrister. Just specialized legal knowledge.' She said, 'And then his cultural tastes. He told me once he was very fond of historical biography. Lives of great men. And the theatre, he was genuinely quite keen on that. I know all this, because there was so little else we could talk about. And he adored Winston Churchill. The biggest old ham of them all.'

A memory jogged the sergeant's distracted mind: Miss Parsons, how Fielding had 'nearly' voted Labour in 1945. But that might fit.

He said, 'Go on.'

'He feels more and more like this minor character in a bad book. Even his own son despises him. So he's a zombie, just a high-class cog in a phony machine. From being very privileged and very successful, he feels himself very absurd and very failed.' Now she was tracing invisible patterns on the top of the table with a fingertip: a square, a circle with a dot in it. The sergeant wondered if she was wearing anything at all beneath the dress. He saw her sitting astride his knees, her arms enlacing his neck, tormenting him; and brutality. You fall in love by suddenly knowing what past love hadn't. 'Then one day he sees what might stop both the rot and the pain. What will get him immortality of a kind.'

'Walking out.'

'The one thing people never forget is the unsolved. Nothing lasts like a mystery.' She raised the pattern-making finger. 'On condition that it stays that way. If he's traced, found, then it all crumbles again. He's back in a story, being written. A nervous breakdown. A nutcase. Whatever.'

Now something had shifted, little bits of past evidence began to coagulate, and listening to her became the same as being with her. The background clatter, the other voices, the clinging heat, all that started to recede. Just one thing nagged, but he let it ride.

'So it has to be for good?'

She smiled at him. 'God's trick.'

'Come again.'

'Theologians talk about the *Deus absconditus* – the God who went missing? Without explaining why. That's why we've never forgotten him.'

He thought of Miss Parsons again. 'You mean he killed himself?'

'I bet you every penny I possess.'

He looked down from her eyes.

'This writer of yours – has he come up with a scenario for that?'

'That's just a detail. I'm trying to sell you the motive.'

He was silent a moment, then sought her eyes. 'Unfortunately it's the details I have to worry about.'

His own eyes were drily held. 'Then your turn. Your department.'

'We have thought about it. Throwing himself off a night-ferry across the Channel. But we checked. The boats were crowded, a lot of people on deck. The odds are dead against.'

'You mustn't underrate him. He'd have known that was too risky.'

'No private boats missing. We checked that as well.'

She gave him a glance under her eyebrows; a touch of conspiracy, a little bathing in collusion; then looked demurely down.

'I could tell you a suitable piece of water. And very private.'

'Where?'

'In the woods behind Tetbury Hall. They call it the lake. It's just a big pond. But they say it's very deep.'

'How does he get there without being seen?'

'He knows the country round Tetbury very well. He owns a lot of it. Hunting. Once he's within walking distance from London, he's safe.'

'And that part of it?'

'Some kind of disguise? He couldn't have hired a car. Or risked the train. By bus?'

'Hell of a lot of changing.'

'He wasn't in a hurry. He wouldn't have wanted to be anywhere near home before nightfall. Some stop several miles away? Then cross-country? He liked walking.'

'He still has to sink himself. Drowned bodies need a lot of weight to stay down.'

'Something inflatable? An air mattress? Car-tyre? Then deflate it when he's floated far enough out?'

'You're beginning to give me nightmares.'

She smiled and leant back and folded her hands in her lap; then she grinned up and threw it all away.

'I also fancy myself as an Agatha Christie.'

He watched her; and she looked down, mock-penitent.

'How serious are you being about all this?'

'I thought about it a lot in Paris. Mainly because of the British

Museum thing. I couldn't work out why he'd have wanted to see me. I mean if he didn't, it was a kind of risk. He might have bumped into me. And you can't walk into the reading-room just like that. You have to show a pass. I don't know if that was checked.'

'Every attendant there.'

'So what I think now is that it was some kind of message. He never meant to see me, but for some reason he wanted me to know that I was involved in his decision. Perhaps because of Peter. Something for some reason he felt I stood for.'

'A way out he couldn't take?'

'Perhaps. It's not that I'm someone special. In the ordinary world. I was probably just very rare in his. I think it was simply a way of saying that he'd have liked to talk to me. Enter my world. But couldn't.'

'And why Tetbury Hall?'

'It does fit. In an Agatha Christie sort of way. The one place no one would think of looking. And its neatness. He was very tidy, he hated mess. On his own land, no trespassing involved. Just a variation on blowing your brains out in the gun-room, really.'

He looked her in the eyes. 'One thing bothers me. Those two hours after work of yours that day.'

'I was only joking.'

'But you weren't at home. Mrs Fielding tried to telephone you then.'

She smiled.

'Now it's my turn to ask how serious you're being.'

'Just tying ends up.'

'And if I don't answer?'

'I don't think that writer of yours would allow that.'

'Oh but he would. That's his whole point. Nice people have instincts as well as duties.'

It was bantering, yet he knew he was being put to the test; that this was precisely what was to be learnt. And in some strange way the case had died during that last half-hour; it was not so much that he accepted her theory, but that like everyone else, though for a different reason, he now saw it didn't really matter. The act was done; taking it to bits discovering how it had been done in detail, was not the point. The point was a living face with brown eyes, half challenging and half teasing; not committing a crime against that. He thought of a ploy, some line about this necessitating further questioning; and rejected it. In the end, he smiled and looked down.

She said gently, 'I must go now. Unless you're going to arrest me for
second sight.'

They came to the pavement outside the house in Willow Road, and
stood facing each other.

'Well.'

'Thank you for the cup of tea.'

He glanced at the ground, reluctantly official.

'You have my number. If anything else . . .'

'Apart from bird-brained fantasy.'

'I didn't mean that. It was fun.'

There was a little silence.

'You should have worn a uniform. Then I'd have remembered who
you were.'

He hesitated, then held out his hand. 'Take care. And I'll buy that
novel when it comes out.'

She took his hand briefly, then folded her arms.

'Which one?'

'The one you were talking about.'

'There's another. A murder story.' She looked past his shoulder
down the street. 'Just the germ of an idea. When I can find someone to
help me over the technical details.'

'Like police procedure?'

'Things like that. Police psychology, really.'

'That shouldn't be too difficult.'

'You think someone . . . ?'

'I know someone.'

She cocked her left sandal a little forward; contemplated it against
the pavement, her arms still folded.

'I don't suppose he could manage tomorrow evening?'

'How do you like to eat?'

'Actually I rather enjoy cooking myself.' She looked up. 'When I'm
not at work.'

'Dry white? About eight?'

She nodded and bit her lips, with a touch of wryness, perhaps a
tinge of doubt.

'All this telepathy.'

'I wanted to. But . . .'

'Noted. And approved.'

She held his eyes a moment more, then raised her hand and turned towards the front door; the dark hair, the slim walk, the white dress. At the door, after feeling in her purse and putting the key in the lock, she turned a moment and again raised her hand briefly. Then she disappeared inside.

The sergeant made, the next morning, an informal and unsuccessful application to have the pond at Tetbury Hall dragged. He then tried, with equal unsuccess, to have himself taken off the case, indeed to have it tacitly closed. His highly circumstantial new theory as to what might have happened received no credence. He was told to go away and get on with the job of digging up some hard evidence instead of wasting his time on half-baked psychology; and heavily reminded that it was just possible the House of Commons might want to hear why one of their number was still untraced when they returned to Westminster. Though the sergeant did not then know it, historical relief lay close at hand – the London letter-bomb epidemic of later that August was to succeed where his own request for new work had failed.

However, he was not, by the time that first tomorrow had closed, the meal been eaten, the Sauvignon drunk, the kissing come, the barefooted cook finally and gently persuaded to stand and be deprived of a different but equally pleasing long dress (and proven, as suspected, quite defenceless underneath, though hardly an innocent victim in what followed), inclined to blame John Marcus Fielding for anything at all.

The tender pragmatisms of flesh have poetries no enigma, human or divine, can diminish or demean – indeed, it can only cause them, and then walk out.

J. G. BALLARD

MEMORIES OF THE SPACE AGE

I

All day this strange pilot had flown his antique aeroplane over the abandoned space centre, a frantic machine lost in the silence of Florida. The flapping engine of the old Curtiss biplane woke Dr Mallory soon after dawn, as he lay asleep beside his exhausted wife on the fifth floor of the empty hotel in Titusville. Dreams of the space age had filled the night, memories of white runways as calm as glaciers, now broken by this eccentric aircraft veering around like the fragment of a disturbed mind.

From his balcony Mallory watched the ancient biplane circle the rusty gantries of Cape Kennedy. The sunlight flared against the pilot's helmet, illuminating the cat's cradle of silver wires that pinioned the open fuselage between the wings, a puzzle from which the pilot was trying to escape by a series of loops and rolls. Ignoring him, the plane flew back and forth above the forest canopy, its engine calling across the immense deserted decks, as if this ghost of the pioneer days of aviation could summon the sleeping titans of the Apollo programme from their graves beneath the cracked concrete.

Giving up for the moment, the Curtiss turned from the gantries and set course inland for Titusville. As it clattered over the hotel Mallory recognized the familiar hard stare behind the pilot's goggles. Each morning the same pilot appeared, flying a succession of antique craft – relics, Mallory assumed, from some forgotten museum at a private airfield nearby. There were a Spad and a Sopwith Camel, a replica of the Wright Flyer, and a Fokker triplane that had buzzed the NASA causeway the previous day, driving inland thousands of frantic gulls and swallows, denying them any share of the sky.

Standing naked on the balcony, Mallory let the amber air warm his skin. He counted the ribs below his shoulder blades, aware that for the first time he could feel his kidneys. Despite the hours spent foraging each day, and the canned food looted from the abandoned super-markets, it was difficult to keep up his body weight. In the two months since they set out from Vancouver on the slow, nervous drive back to Florida, he and Anne had each lost more than thirty pounds, as if their bodies were carrying out a reinventory of themselves for the coming world without time. But the bones endured. His skeleton seemed to grow stronger and heavier, preparing itself for the unnourished sleep of the grave.

Already sweating in the humid air, Mallory returned to the bedroom. Anne had woken, but lay motionless in the centre of the bed, strands of blond hair caught like a child's in her mouth. With its fixed and empty expression, her face resembled a clock that had just stopped. Mallory sat down and placed his hands on her diaphragm, gently respiring her. Every morning he feared that time would run out for Anne while she slept, leaving her for ever in the middle of a night-mare.

She stared at Mallory, as if surprised to wake in this shabby resort hotel with a man she had possibly known for years but for some reason failed to recognize.

'Hinton?'

'Not yet.' Mallory steered the hair from her mouth. 'Do I look like him now?'

'God, I'm going blind.' Anne wiped her nose on the pillow. She raised her wrists, and stared at the two watches that formed a pair of time-cuffs. The stores in Florida were filled with clocks and watches that had been left behind in case they might be contaminated, and each day Anne selected a new set of timepieces. She touched Mallory reassuringly. 'All men look the same, Edward. That's streetwalker's wisdom for you. But I meant the plane.'

'I'm not sure. It wasn't a spotter aircraft. Clearly the police don't bother to come to Cape Kennedy any more.'

'I don't blame them. It's an evil place. Edward, we ought to leave, let's get out this morning.'

Mallory held her shoulders, trying to calm this frayed but still handsome woman. He needed her to look her best for Hinton. 'Anne, we've only been here a week – let's give it a little more time.'

'Time? Edward . . .' She took Mallory's hands in a sudden show of affection. 'Dear, that's one thing we've run out of. I'm getting those headaches again, just like the ones I had fifteen years ago. It's uncanny, I can feel the same nerves . . .'

'I'll give you something, you can sleep this afternoon.'

'No . . . They're a warning. I want to feel every twinge.' She pressed the wrist-watches to her temples, as if trying to tune her brain to their signal. 'We were mad to come here, and even more mad to stay for a second longer than we need.'

'I know. It's a long shot but worth a try. I've learned one thing in all these years – if there's a way out, we'll find it at Cape Kennedy.'

'We won't! Everything's poisoned here. We should go to Australia, like all the other NASA people.' Anne rooted in her handbag on the floor, heaving aside an illustrated encyclopaedia of birds she had found in a Titusville bookstore. 'I looked it up – western Australia is as far from Florida as you can go. It's almost the exact antipodes. Edward, my sister lives in *Perth*. I knew there was a reason why she invited us there.'

Mallory stared at the distant gantries of Cape Kennedy. It was difficult to believe that he had once worked there. 'I don't think even Perth, Australia, is far enough. We need to set out into space again . . .'

Anne shuddered. 'Edward, don't say that – a *crime* was committed here, everyone knows that's how it all began.' As they listened to the distant drone of the aircraft she gazed at her broad hips and soft thighs. Equal to the challenge, her chin lifted. 'Noisy, isn't it? Do you think Hinton is here? He may not remember me.'

'He'll remember you. You were the only one who liked him.'

'Well, in a sort of way. How long was he in prison before he escaped? Twenty years?'

'A long time. Perhaps he'll take you flying again. You enjoyed that.'

'Yes . . . He was strange. But even if he is here, can he help? He was the one who started it all.'

'No, not Hinton.' Mallory listened to his voice in the empty hotel. It seemed deeper and more resonant, as the slowing time stretched out the frequencies. 'In point of fact, I started it all.'

Anne had turned from him and lay on her side, a watch pressed to each ear. Mallory reminded himself to go out and begin his morning search for food. Food, a vitamin shot, and a clean pair of sheets. Sex with Anne, which he hoped would keep them bickering and awake, had generated affection instead. Suppose they conceived a child, here at Cape Kennedy, within the shadow of the gantries . . . ?

He remembered the mongol and autistic children he had left behind at the clinic in Vancouver, and his firm belief – strongly contested by his fellow physicians and the worn-out parents – that these were diseases of time, malfunctions of the temporal sense that marooned these children on small islands of awareness, a few minutes in the case of the mongols, a span of micro-seconds for the autistics. A child conceived and born here at Cape Kennedy would be born into a world without time, an indefinite and unending present, that primeval paradise that the old brain remembered so vividly, seen both by those living for the first time and by those dying for the first time. It was curious that images of heaven or paradise always presented a static world, not the kinetic eternity one would expect, the roller-coaster of a hyperactive funfair, the screaming Luna Parks of LSD and psilocybin. It was a strange paradox that given eternity, an infinity of time, they chose to eliminate the very element offered in such abundance.

Still, if they stayed much longer at Cape Kennedy he and Anne would soon return to the world of the old brain, like those first tragic astronauts he had helped to put into space. During the previous year in Vancouver there had been too many attacks, those periods of largo when time seemed to slow, an afternoon at his desk stretched into days. His own lapses in concentration both he and his colleagues put down to eccentricity, but Anne's growing vagueness had been impossible to ignore, the first clear signs of the space sickness that began to slow the clock, as it had done first for the astronauts and then for all the other NASA personnel based in Florida. Within the last months the attacks had come five or six times a day, periods when everything began to slow down, he would apparently spend all day shaving or signing a cheque.

Time, like a film reel running through a faulty projector, was moving at an erratic pace, at moments backing up and almost coming to a halt, then speeding on again. One day soon it would stop, freeze forever on one frame. Had it really taken them two months to drive from Vancouver, weeks alone from Jacksonville to Cape Kennedy?

He thought of the long journey down the Florida coast, a world of immense empty hotels and glutinous time, of strange meetings with Anne in deserted corridors, of sex-acts that seemed to last for days. Now and then, in forgotten bedrooms, they came across other couples who had strayed into Florida, into the eternal present of this timeless

zone, Paolo and Francesca forever embracing in the Fontainebleau
Hotel. In some of those eyes there had been horror . . .

As for Anne and himself, time had run out of their marriage fifteen
years ago, driven away by the spectres of the space complex, and by
memories of Hinton. They had come back here like Adam and Eve
returning to the Edenic paradise with an unfortunate dose of VD.
Thankfully, as time evaporated, so did memory. He looked at his few
possessions, now almost meaningless – the tape machine on which he
recorded his steady decline; an album of nude Polaroid poses of a
woman doctor he had known in Vancouver; his Gray's *Anatomy* from
his student days, a unique work of fiction, pages still stained with
formalin from the dissecting-room cadavers; a paperback selection of
Muybridge's stop-frame photographs; and a psychoanalytic study of
Simon Magus.

'Anne . . . ?' The light in the bedroom had become brighter, there
was a curious glare, like the white runways of his dreams. Nothing
moved, for a moment Mallory felt that they were waxworks in a
museum tableau, or in a painting by Edward Hopper of a tired couple
in a provincial hotel. The dream-time was creeping up on him, about
to enfold him. As always he felt no fear, his pulse was calmer . . .

There was a blare of noise outside, a shadow flashed across the
balcony. The Curtiss biplane roared overhead, then sped low across
the rooftops of Titusville. Roused by the sudden movement, Mallory
stood up and shook himself, slapping his thighs to spur on his heart.
The plane had caught him just in time.

'Anne, I think that was Hinton . . .'

She lay on her side, the watches to her ears. Mallory stroked her
cheeks, but her eyes rolled away from him. She breathed peacefully
with her upper lungs, her pulse as slow as a hibernating mammal's. He
drew the sheet across her shoulders. She would wake in an hour's
time, with a vivid memory of a single image, a rehearsal for those last
seconds before time finally froze . . .

II

Medical case in hand, Mallory stepped into the street through the
broken plate-glass window of the supermarket. The abandoned store
had become his chief source of supplies. Tall palms split the sidewalks
in front of the boarded-up shops and bars, providing a shaded
promenade through the empty town. Several times he had been
caught out in the open during an attack, but the palms had shielded

his skin from the Florida sun. For a reason he had yet to understand, he liked to walk naked through the silent streets, watched by the orioles and parakeets. The naked doctor, physician to the birds . . . perhaps they would pay him in feathers, the midnight-blue tail-plumes of the macaws, the golden wings of the orioles, sufficient fees for him to build a flying machine of his own?

The medical case was heavy, loaded with packet rice, sugar, cartons of pasta. He would light a small fire on another balcony and cook up a starchy meal, carefully boiling the brackish water in the roof tank. Mallory paused in the hotel car-park, gathering his strength for the climb to the fifth floor, above the rat and cockroach line. He rested in the front seat of the police patrol car they had commandeered in a deserted suburb of Jacksonville. Anne had regretted leaving behind her classy Toyota, but the exchange had been sensible. Not only would the unexpected sight of this squad car confuse any military spotter planes, but the hotted-up Dodge could outrun most light aircraft.

Mallory was relying on the car's power to trap the mysterious pilot who appeared each morning in his antique aeroplanes. He had noticed that as every day passed these veteran machines tended to be of increasingly older vintage. Sooner or later the pilot would find himself well within Mallory's reach, unable to shake off the pursuing Dodge before being forced to land at his secret airfield.

Mallory listened to the police radio, the tuneless static that reflected the huge void that lay over Florida. By contrast the air-traffic frequencies were a babel of intercom chatter, both from the big jets landing at Mobile, Atlanta and Savannah, and from military craft overflying the Bahamas. All gave Florida a wide berth. To the north of the 31st parallel life in the United States went on as before, but south of that unfenced and rarely patrolled frontier was an immense silence of deserted marinas and shopping malls, abandoned citrus farms and retirement estates, silent ghettoes and airports.

Losing interest in Mallory, the birds were rising into the air. A dappled shadow crossed the car-park, and Mallory looked up as a graceful, slender-winged aircraft drifted lazily past the roof of the hotel. Its twin-bladed propeller struck the air like a child's paddle, driven at a leisurely pace by the pilot sitting astride the bicycle pedals within the transparent fuselage. A man-powered glider of advanced design, it soared silently above the rooftops, buoyed by the thermals rising from the empty town.

'Hinton!' Certain now that he could catch the former astronaut, **240** Mallory abandoned his groceries and pulled himself behind the wheel of the police car. By the time he started the flooded engine he had lost sight of the glider. Its delicate wings, almost as long as an airliner's, had drifted across the forest canopy, kept company by the flocks of swallows and martins that rose to inspect this timorous intruder of their air-space. Mallory reversed out of the car-park and set off after the glider, veering in and out of the palms that lifted from the centre of the street.

Calming himself, he scanned the side roads, and caught sight of the machine circling the jai alai stadium on the southern outskirts of the town. A cloud of gulls surrounded the glider, some mobbing its lazy propeller, others taking up their station above its wing-tips. The pilot seemed to be urging them to follow him, enticing them with gentle rolls and yaws, drawing them back towards the sea and to the forest causeways of the space complex.

Reducing his speed, Mallory followed three hundred yards behind the glider. They crossed the bridge over the Banana River, heading towards the NASA causeway and the derelict bars and motels of Cocoa Beach. The nearest of the gantries was still over a mile away to the north, but Mallory was aware that he had entered the outer zone of the space grounds. A threatening aura emanated from these ancient towers, as old in their way as the great temple columns of Karnak, bearers of a different cosmic order, symbols of a view of the universe that had been abandoned along with the state of Florida that had given them birth.

Looking down at the now clear waters of the Banana River, Mallory found himself avoiding the sombre forests that packed the causeways and concrete decks of the space complex, smothering the signs and fences, the camera towers and observation bunkers. Time was different here, as it had been at Alamagordo and Eniwetok, a psychic fissure had riven both time and space, then run deep into the minds of the people who worked here. Through that new suture in his skull time leaked into the slack water below the car. The forest oaks were waiting for him to feed their roots, these motionless trees were as insane as anything in the vision of Max Ernst. There were the same insatiable birds, feeding on the vegetation that sprang from the corpses of trapped aircraft . . .

Above the causeway the gulls were wheeling in alarm, screaming against the sky. The powered glider side-slipped out of the air, circled and soared along the bridge, its miniature undercarriage only ten feet above the police car. The pilot pedalled rapidly, propeller flashing at the alarmed sun, and Mallory caught a glimpse of blond hair and a woman's face in the transparent cockpit. A red silk scarf flew from her throat.

'Hinton!' As Mallory shouted into the noisy air the pilot leaned from the cockpit and pointed to a slip road running through the forest towards Cocoa Beach, then banked behind the trees and vanished.

Hinton? For some bizarre reason the former astronaut was now masquerading as a woman in a blond wig, luring him back to the space complex. The birds had been in league with him . . .

The sky was empty, the gulls had vanished across the river into the forest. Mallory stopped the car. He was about to step on to the road when he heard the drone of an aero-engine. The Fokker triplane had emerged from the space centre. It made a tight circuit of the gantries and came in across the sea. Fifty feet above the beach, it swept across the palmettos and saw-grass, its twin machine-guns pointing straight towards the police car.

Mallory began to re-start the engine, when the machine-guns above the pilot's windshield opened fire at him. He assumed that the pilot was shooting blank ammunition left over from some air display. Then the first bullets struck the metalled road a hundred feet ahead. The second burst threw the car on to its flattened front tyres, severed the door pillar by the passenger seat and filled the cabin with exploding glass. As the plane climbed steeply, about to make its second pass at him, Mallory brushed the blood-flecked glass from his chest and thighs. He leapt from the car and vaulted over the metal railing into the shallow culvert beside the bridge, as his blood ran away through the water towards the waiting forest of the space grounds.

III

From the shelter of the culvert, Mallory watched the police car burning on the bridge. The column of oily smoke rose a thousand feet into the empty sky, a beacon visible for ten miles around the Cape. The flocks of gulls had vanished. The powered glider and its woman pilot – he remembered her warning him of the Fokker's approach – had slipped away to its lair somewhere south along the coast.

Too stunned to rest, Mallory stared at the mile-long causeway. It would take him half an hour to walk back to the mainland, an easy target for Hinton as he waited in the Fokker above the clouds. Had the former astronaut recognized Mallory and immediately guessed why the sometime NASA physican had come to search for him?

Too exhausted to swim the Banana River, Mallory waded ashore and set off through the trees. He decided to spend the afternoon in one of the abandoned motels in Cocoa Beach, then make his way back to Titusville after dark.

The forest floor was cool against his bare feet, but a soft light fell through the leafy canopy and warmed his skin. Already the blood had dried on his chest and shoulders, a vivid tracery like an aboriginal tattoo that seemed more suitable wear for this violent and uncertain realm than the clothes he had left behind at the hotel. He passed the rusting hulk of an Airstream trailer, its steel capsule overgrown with lianas and ground ivy, as if the trees had reached up to seize a passing space craft and dragged it down into the undergrowth. There were abandoned cars and the remains of camping equipment, moss-covered chairs and tables around old barbecue spits left here twenty years earlier when the sightseers had hurriedly vacated the state.

Mallory stepped through this terminal moraine, the elements of a forgotten theme park arranged by a demolition squad. Already he felt that he belonged to an older world within the forest, a realm of darkness, patience and unseen life. The beach was a hundred yards away, the Atlantic breakers washing the empty sand. A school of dolphins leapt cleanly through the water, on their way south to the Gulf. The birds had gone, but the fish were ready to take their place in the air.

Mallory welcomed them. He knew that he had been walking down this sand-bar for little more than half an hour, but at the same time he felt that he had been there for days, even possibly weeks and months. In part of his mind he had always been there. The minutes were beginning to stretch, urged on by this eventless universe free of birds and aircraft. His memory faltered, he was forgetting his past, the clinic at Vancouver and its wounded children, his wife asleep in the hotel at Titusville, even his own identity. A single moment was a small instalment of forever – he plucked a fern leaf and watched it for minutes as it fell slowly to the ground, deferring to gravity in the most elegant way.

—

Aware now that he was entering the dream-time, Mallory ran on through the trees. He was moving in slow-motion, his weak legs carrying him across the leafy ground with the grace of an Olympic athlete. He raised his hand to touch a butterfly apparently asleep on the wing, embarking his outstretched fingers on an endless journey.

The forest that covered the sand-bar began to thin out, giving way to the beach-houses and motels of Cocoa Beach. A derelict hotel sat among the trees, its gates collapsed across the drive, Spanish moss hanging from a sign that advertised a zoo and theme park devoted to the space age. Through the waist-high palmettos the chromium and neon rockets rose from their stands like figures on amusement park carousels.

Laughing to himself, Mallory vaulted the gates and ran on past the rusting space ships. Behind the theme park were overgrown tennis courts, a swimming pool and the remains of the small zoo, with an alligator pit, mammal cages and aviary. Happily, Mallory saw that the tenants had returned to their homes. An overweight zebra dozed in his concrete enclosure, a bored tiger stared in a cross-eyed way at his own nose, and an elderly caiman sunbathed on the grass beside the alligator pit.

Time was slowing now, coming almost to a halt. Mallory hung in mid-step, his bare feet in the air above the ground. Parked on the tiled path beside the swimming pool was a huge transparent dragonfly, the powered glider he had chased that morning.

Two wizened cheetahs sat in the shade under its wing, watching Mallory with their prim eyes. One of them rose from the ground and slowly launched itself towards him, but it was twenty feet away and Mallory knew that it would never reach him. Its threadbare coat, refashioned from some old carpet bag, stretched itself into a lazy arch that seemed to freeze forever in mid-frame.

Mallory waited for time to stop. The waves were no longer running towards the beach, and were frozen ruffs of icing sugar. Fish hung in the sky, the wise dolphins happy to be in their new realm, faces smiling in the sun. The water spraying from the fountain at the shallow end of the pool now formed a glass parasol.

Only the cheetah was moving, still able to outrun time. It was now ten feet from him, its head tilted to one side as it aimed itself at Mallory's throat, its yellow claws more pointed than Hinton's bullets. But Mallory felt no fear for this violent cat. Without time it could never reach him, without time the lion could at last lie down with the lamb, the eagle with the vole.

He looked up at the vivid light, noticing the figure of a young woman who hung in the air with outstretched arms above the diving board. Suspended over the water in a swallow dive, her naked body flew as serenely as the dolphins above the sea. Her calm face gazed at the glass floor ten feet below her small, extended palms. She seemed unaware of Mallory, her eyes fixed on the mystery of her own flight, and he could see clearly the red marks left on her shoulders by the harness straps of the glider, and the silver arrow of her appendix scar pointing to her child-like pubis.

The cheetah was closer now, its claws picking at the threads of dried blood that laced Mallory's shoulders, its grey muzzle retracted to show its ulcerated gums and stained teeth. If he reached out he could embrace it, comfort all the memories of Africa, soothe the violence from its old pelt . . .

IV

Time had flowed out of Florida, as it had from the space age. After a brief pause, like a trapped film reel running free, it sped on again, rekindling a kinetic world.

Mallory sat in a deck chair beside the pool, watching the cheetahs as they rested in the shade under the glider. They crossed and uncrossed their paws like card-dealers palming an ace, now and then lifting their noses at the scent of this strange man and his blood.

Despite their sharp teeth, Mallory felt calm and rested, a sleeper waking from a complex but satisfying dream. He was glad to be surrounded by this little zoo with its backdrop of playful rockets, as innocent as an illustration from the children's book.

The young woman stood next to Mallory, keeping a concerned watch on him. She had dressed while Mallory recovered from his collision with the cheetah. After dragging away the boisterous beast she settled Mallory in the deck chair, then pulled on a patched leather flying suit. Was this the only clothing she had ever worn? A true child of the air, born and sleeping on the wing. With her over-bright mascara and blond hair brushed into a vivid peruke, she resembled a leather-garbed parakeet, a punk madonna of the airways. Worn NASA flashes on her shoulder gave her a biker's swagger. On the name-plate above her right breast was printed: *Nightingale*.

'Poor man – are you back? You're far, far away.' Behind the child-like features, the soft mouth and boneless nose, a pair of adult **245** eyes watched him warily. 'Hey, you – what happened to your uniform? Are you in the police?'

Mallory took her hand, touching the heavy Apollo signet ring she wore on her wedding finger. From somewhere came the absurd notion that she was married to Hinton. Then he noticed her enlarged pupils, a hint of fever.

'Don't worry – I'm a doctor, Edward Mallory. I'm on holiday here with my wife.'

'Holiday?' The girl shook her head, relieved but baffled. 'That patrol car – I thought someone had stolen your uniform while you were . . . out, Dear doctor, no one comes on holiday to Florida any more. If you don't leave soon this is one vacation that may last forever.'

'I know . . .' Mallory looked round at the zoo with its dozing tiger, the gay fountain and cheerful rockets. This was the amiable world of the Douanier Rousseau's *Merry Jesters*. He accepted the jeans and shirt which the girl gave him. He had liked being naked, not from any exhibitionist urge, but because it suited the vanished realm he had just visited. The impassive tiger with his skin of fire belonged to that world of light. 'Perhaps I've come to the right place, though – I'd like to spend forever here. To tell the truth, I've just had a small taste of what forever is going to be like.'

'No, thanks.' Intrigued by Mallory, the girl squatted on the grass beside him. 'Tell me, how often are you getting the attacks?'

'Every day. Probably more than I realize. And you . . . ?' When she shook her head a little too quickly, Mallory added: 'They're not that frightening, you know. In a way you want to go back.'

'I can see. Doctor, you ought to be worried by that. Take your wife and leave – any moment now all the clocks are going to stop.'

'That's why we're here – it's our one chance. My wife has even less time than I have. We want to come to terms with everything – whatever that means. Not much any more.'

'Doctor . . . The real Cape Kennedy is inside your head, not out here.' Clearly unsettled by the presence of this marooned physician, the girl pulled on her flying helmet. She scanned the sky, where the gulls and swallows were again gathering, drawn into the air by the distant drone of an aero-engine. 'Listen – an hour ago you were nearly killed. I tried to warn you. Our local stunt pilot doesn't like the police.'

'So I found out. I'm glad he didn't hit you. I thought he was flying your glider.'

'Hinton? He wouldn't be seen dead in that. He needs speed. Hinton's trying to join the birds.'

'Hinton . . .' Repeating the name, Mallory felt a surge of fear and relief, realizing that he was committed now to the course of action he had planned months ago when he left the clinic in Vancouver. 'So Hinton is here.'

'He's here.' The girl nodded at Mallory, still unsure that he was not a policeman. 'Not many people remember Hinton.'

'I remember Hinton.' As she fingered the Apollo signet ring he asked: 'You're not married to him?'

'To Hinton? Doctor, you have some strange ideas. What are your patients like?'

'I often wonder. But you know Hinton?'

'Who does? He has other things in his mind. He fixed the pool here, and brought me the glider from the museum at Orlando.' She added, archly: 'Disneyland East – that's what they called Cape Kennedy in the early days.'

'I remember – twenty years ago I worked for NASA.'

'So did my father.' She spoke sharply, angered by the mention of the space agency. 'He was the last astronaut – Alan Shepley – the only one who didn't come back. And the only one they didn't wait for.'

'Shepley was *your* father?' Startled, Mallory turned to look at the distant gantries of the launching grounds. 'He died in the Shuttle. Then you know that Hinton . . .'

'Doctor, I don't think it was Hinton who really killed my father.' Before Mallory could speak she lowered her goggles over her eyes. 'Anyway, it doesn't matter now. The important thing is that someone will be here when he comes down.'

'You're waiting for him?'

'Shouldn't I, doctor?'

'Yes . . . but it was a long time ago. Besides, it's a million to one against him coming down here.'

'That's not true. According to Hinton, Dad may actually come down somewhere along this coast. Hinton says the orbits are starting to decay. I search the beaches every day.'

Mallory smiled at her encouragingly, admiring this spunky but sad child. He remembered the news photographs of the astronaut's daughter, Gale Shepley, a babe in arms fiercely cradled by the widow outside the courtroom after the verdict. 'I hope he comes. And your little zoo, Gale?'

'Nightingale,' she corrected. 'The zoo is for Dad. I want the world to be a special place for us when we go.'

'You're leaving together?'

'In a sense – like you, doctor, and everyone else here.'

'So you do get the attacks.'

'Not often – that's why I keep moving. The birds are teaching me how to fly. Did you know that, doctor? The birds are trying to get out of time.'

Already she was distracted by the unswept sky and the massing birds. After tying up the cheetahs she made her way quickly to the glider. 'I have to leave, doctor. Can you ride a motorcycle? There's a Yamaha in the hotel lobby you can borrow.'

But before taking off she confided to Mallory: 'It's all wishful thinking, doctor, for Hinton too. When Dad comes it won't matter any more.'

Mallory tried to help her launch the glider, but the filmy craft took off within its own length. Pedalling swiftly, she propelled it into the air, climbing over the chromium rockets of the theme park. The glider circled the hotel, then levelled its long, tapering wings and set off for the empty beaches of the north.

Restless without her, the tiger began to wrestle with the truck tyre suspended from the ceiling of its cage. For a moment Mallory was tempted to unlock the door and join it. Avoiding the cheetahs chained to the diving board, he entered the empty hotel and took the staircase to the roof. From the ladder of the elevator house he watched the glider moving towards the space centre.

Alan Shepley – the first man to be murdered in space. All too well Mallory remembered the young pilot of the Shuttle, one of the last astronauts to be launched from Cape Kennedy before the curtain came down on the space age. A former Apollo pilot, Shepley had been a dedicated but likeable young man, as ambitious as the other astronauts and yet curiously naïve.

Mallory, like everyone else, had much preferred him to the Shuttle's co-pilot, a research physicist who was then the token civilian among the astronauts. Mallory remembered how he had instinctively disliked Hinton on their first meeting at the medical centre. But from the start he had been fascinated by the man's awkwardness and irritability. In its closing days, the space programme had begun to attract people who were slightly unbalanced, and he recognized that Hinton belonged to this second generation of astronauts, mavericks with complex motives of their own, quite unlike the disciplined service pilots who had furnished the Mercury and Apollo flight-crews. Hinton had the intense and obsessive temperament of a Cortez, Pizarro or Drake, the hot blood and cold heart. It was Hinton who had exposed for the first time so many of the latent conundrums at the heart of the space programme, those psychological dimensions that had been ignored from its start and subsequently revealed, too late, in the crack-ups of the early astronauts, their slides into mysticism and melancholia.

'The best astronauts never dream,' Russell Schweickart had once remarked. Not only did Hinton dream, he had torn the whole fabric of time and space, cracked the hour-glass from which time was running. Mallory was aware of his own complicity, he had been chiefly responsible for putting Shepley and Hinton together, guessing that the repressed and earnest Shepley might provide the trigger for a metaphysical experiment of a special sort.

At all events, Shepley's death had been the first murder in space, a crisis that Mallory had both stage-managed and unconsciously welcomed. The murder of the astronaut and the public unease that followed had marked the end of the space age, an awareness that man had committed an evolutionary crime by travelling into space, that he was tampering with the elements of his own consciousness. The fracture of that fragile continuum erected by the human psyche through millions of years had soon shown itself, in the confused sense of time displayed by the astronauts and NASA personnel, and then by the inhabitants of the towns near the space centre. Cape Kennedy and the whole of Florida itself became a poisoned land to be for ever avoided like the nuclear testing grounds of Nevada and Utah.

Yet, perhaps, instead of going mad in space, Hinton had been the first man to 'go sane'. During his trial he pleaded his innocence and then refused to defend himself, viewing the international media circus with a stoicism that at times seemed bizarre. That silence had unnerved everyone – how could Hinton believe himself innocent of a murder (he had locked Shepley into the docking module, vented his air supply and then cast him loose in his coffin, keeping up a matter-of-fact commentary the whole while) committed in full view of a thousand million television witnesses?

Alcatraz had been re-commissioned for Hinton, for this solitary prisoner isolated on the frigid island to prevent him contaminating the rest of the human race. After twenty years he was safely forgotten, and even the report of his escape was only briefly mentioned. He was presumed to have died, after crashing into the icy waters of the bay in a small aircraft he had secretly constructed. Mallory had travelled down to San Francisco to see the waterlogged craft, a curious ornithopter built from the yew trees that Hinton had been allowed to grow in the prison island's stony soil, boosted by a home-made rocket engine powered by a fertilizer-based explosive. He had waited twenty years for the slow-growing evergreens to be strong enough to form the wings that would carry him to freedom.

Then, only six months after Hinton's death, Mallory had been told by an old NASA colleague of the strange stunt pilot who had been seen flying his antique aircraft at Cape Kennedy, some native of the air who had so far eluded the half-hearted attempts to ground him. The descriptions of the bird-cage aeroplanes reminded Mallory of the drowned ornithopter dragged up on to the winter beach . . .

So Hinton had returned to Cape Kennedy. As Mallory set off on the Yamaha along the coast road, past the deserted motels and cocktail bars of Cocoa Beach, he looked out at the bright Atlantic sand, so unlike the rocky shingle of the prison island. But was the ornithopter a decoy, like all the antique aircraft that Hinton flew above the space centre, machines that concealed some other aim?

Some other escape?

V

Fifteen minutes later, as Mallory sped along the NASA causeway towards Titusville, he was overtaken by an old Wright biplane. Crossing the Banana River, he noticed that the noise of a second engine had drowned the Yamaha's. The venerable flying machine appeared above the trees, the familiar gaunt-faced pilot sitting in the open cockpit. Barely managing to pull ahead of the Yamaha, the pilot flew down to within ten feet of the road, gesturing to Mallory to stop, then cut back his engine and settled the craft on to the weed-grown concrete.

'Mallory, I've been looking for you! Come on, doctor!'

Mallory hesitated, the gritty backwash of the Wright's props stinging the open wounds under his shirt. As he peered among the struts Hinton seized his arm and lifted him on to the passenger seat.

'Mallory, yes . . . it's you still!' Hinton pushed his goggles back on to his bony forehead, revealing a pair of blood-flecked eyes. He gazed at Mallory with open amazement, as if surprised that Mallory had aged at all in the past twenty years, but delighted that he had somehow survived. 'Nightingale just told me you were here. Doctor Mysterium . . . I nearly killed you!'

'You're trying again . . . !' Mallory clung to the frayed seat straps as Hinton opened the throttle. The biplane gazelled into the air. In a gust of wind across the exposed causeway it flew backwards for a few seconds, then climbed vertically and banked across the trees towards the distant gantries. Thousands of swallows and martins overtook them on all sides, ignoring Hinton as if well-used to this erratic aviator and his absurd machines.

As Hinton worked the rudder tiller, Mallory glanced at this feverish and undernourished man. The years in prison and the rushing air above Cape Kennedy had leached all trace of iron salts from his pallid skin. His raw eyelids, the nail-picked septum of his strong nose and his scarred lips were blanched almost silver in the wind. He had gone beyond exhaustion and malnutrition into a nervous realm where the rival elements of his warring mind were locked together like the cogs of an overwound clock. As he pummelled Mallory's arm it was clear that he had already forgotten the years since their last meeting. He pointed to the forest below them, to the viaducts, concrete decks and blockhouses, eager to show off his domain.

They had reached the heart of the space complex, where the gantries rose like gallows put out to rent. In the centre was the giant crawler, the last of the Shuttles mounted vertically on its launching platform. Its rusting tracks lay around it, the chains of an unshackled colossus.

Here at Cape Kennedy time had not stood still but moved into reverse. The huge fuel tank and auxiliary motors of the Shuttle resembled the domes and minarets of a replica Taj Mahal. Lines of antique aircraft were drawn up on the runway below the crawler – a Lilienthal glider lying on its side like an ornate fan window, a Mignet Flying Flea, the Fokker, Spad and Sopwith Camel, and a Wright Flyer that went back to the earliest days of aviation. As they circled the launch platform Mallory almost expected to see a crowd of Edwardian aviators thronging this display of ancient craft, pilots in gaiters and overcoats, women passengers in hats fitted with leather straps.

Other ghosts haunted the daylight at Cape Kennedy. When they landed Mallory stepped into the shadow of the launch platform, an iron cathedral shunned by the sky. An unsettling silence came in from the dense forest that filled the once open decks of the space centre, from the eyeless bunkers and rusting camera towers.

'Mallory, I'm glad you came!' Hinton pulled off his flying helmet, exposing a lumpy scalp under his close-cropped hair – Mallory remembered that he had once been attacked by a berserk warder. 'I couldn't believe it was you! And Anne? Is she all right?'

'She's here, at the hotel in Titusville.'

'I know, I've just seen her on the roof. She looked . . .' Hinton's voice dropped, in his concern he had forgotten what he was doing. He began to walk in a circle, and then rallied himself. 'Still, it's good to see you. It's more than I hoped for – you were the one person who knew what was going on here.'

'Did I?' Mallory searched for the sun, hidden behind the cold bulk of the launch platform. Cape Kennedy was even more sinister than he had expected, like some ancient death camp. 'I don't think I –'

'Of course you knew! In a way we were collaborators – believe me, Mallory, we will be again. I've a lot to tell you . . .' Happy to see Mallory, but concerned for the shivering physician, Hinton embraced him with his restless hands. When Mallory flinched, trying to protect his shoulders, Hinton whistled and peered solicitously inside his shirt.

'Mallory, I'm sorry – that police car confused me. They'll be coming for me soon, we have to move fast. But you don't look too well, doctor. Time's running out, I suppose, it's difficult to understand at first . . .'

'I'm starting to. What about you, Hinton? I need to talk to you about everything. You look –'

Hinton grimaced. He slapped his lip, impatient with his under-nourished body, an atrophied organ that he would soon discard. 'I had to starve myself, the wingloading of that machine was so low. It took years, or they might have noticed. Those endless medical checks, they were terrified that I was brewing up an even more advanced psychosis – they couldn't grasp that I was opening the door to a new world.' He gazed round at the space centre, at the empty wind. 'We had to get out of time – that's what the space programme was all about . . .'

He beckoned Mallory towards a steel staircase that led up to the
252 assembly deck six storeys above them. 'We'll go topside. I'm living in
the Shuttle – there's a crew module of the Mars platform still inside
the hold, a damn sight more comfortable than most of the hotels in
Florida.' He added, with an ironic gleam: 'I imagine it's the last place
they'll come to look for me.'

Mallory began to climb the staircase. He tried not to touch the
greasy rivets and sweating rails, lowering his eyes from the tiled skin
of the Shuttle as it emerged above the assembly deck. After all the
years of thinking about Cape Kennedy he was still unprepared for the
strangeness of this vast, reductive machine, a Juggernaut that could
be pushed by its worshippers across the planet, devouring the years
and hours and seconds.

Even Hinton seemed subdued, scanning the sky as if waiting for
Shepley to appear. He was careful not to turn his back on Mallory,
clearly suspecting that the former N A S A physician had been sent to
trap him.

'Flight and time, Mallory, they're bound together. The birds have
always known that. To get out of time we first need to learn to fly.
That's why I'm here. I'm teaching myself to fly, going back through
all these old planes to the beginning. I want to fly without wings . . .'

As the Shuttle's delta wing fanned out above them, Mallory swayed
against the rail. Exhausted by the climb, he tried to pump his lungs.
The silence was too great, this stillness at the centre of the stopped
clock of the world. He searched the breathless forest and runways for
any sign of movement. He needed one of Hinton's machines to take
off and go racketting across the sky.

'Mallory, you're going . . . ? Don't worry, I'll help you through it.'
Hinton had taken his elbow and steadied him on his feet. Mallory felt
the light suddenly steepen, the intense white glare he had last seen as
the cheetah sprang towards him. Time left the air, wavered briefly as
he struggled to retain his hold on the passing seconds.

A flock of martins swept across the assembly deck, swirled like
exploding soot around the Shuttle. Were they trying to warn him?
Roused by the brief flurry, Mallory felt his eyes clear. He had been
able to shake off the attack, but it would come again.

'Doctor – ? You'll be all right.' Hinton was plainly disappointed as
he watched Mallory steady himself at the rail. 'Try not to fight it,
doctor, everyone makes that mistake.'

'It's going . . .' Mallory pushed him away. Hinton was too close to the rail, the man's manic gestures could jostle him over the edge. 'The birds –'

'Of course, we'll join the birds! Mallory, we can all fly, every one of us. Think of it, doctor, true flight. We'll live forever in the air!'

'Hinton . . .' Mallory backed along the deck as Hinton seized the greasy rail, about to catapult himself on to the wind. He needed to get away from this madman and his lunatic schemes.

Hinton waved to the aircraft below, saluting the ghosts in their cockpits. 'Lilienthal and the Wrights, Curtiss and Bleriot, even old Mignet – they're here, doctor. That's why I came to Cape Kennedy. I needed to go back to the beginning, long before aviation sent us all off on the wrong track. When time stops, Mallory, we'll step from this deck and fly towards the sun. You and I, doctor, and Anne . . .'

Hinton's voice was deepening, a cavernous boom. The white flank of the Shuttle's hull was a lantern of translucent bone, casting a spectral light over the sombre forest. Mallory swayed forward, on some half-formed impulse he wanted Hinton to vault the rail, step out on to the air and challenge the birds. If he pressed his shoulders . . .

'Doctor –?'

Mallory raised his hands, but he was unable to draw any nearer to Hinton. Like the cheetah, he was for ever a few inches away.

Hinton had taken his arm in a comforting gesture, urging him towards the rail.

'Fly, doctor . . .'

Mallory stood at the edge. His skin had become part of the air, invaded by the light. He needed to shrug aside the huge encumbrance of time and space, this rusting deck and the clumsy tracked vehicle. He could hang free, suspended forever above the forest, master of time and light. He would fly . . .

A flurry of charged air struck his face. Fracture lines appeared in the wind around him. The transparent wings of a powered glider soared past, its propeller chopping at the sunlight.

Hinton's hands gripped his shoulders, bundling him impatiently over the rail. The glider slewed sideways, wheeled and flew towards them again. The sunlight lanced from its propeller, a stream of photons that drove time back into Mallory's eyes. Pulling himself free from Hinton, he fell to his knees as the young woman swept past in her glider. He saw her anxious face behind the goggles, and heard her voice shout warningly at Hinton.

But Hinton had already gone. His feet rang against the metal staircase. As he took off in the Fokker he called out angrily to Mallory, disappointed with him. Mallory knelt by the edge of the steel deck, waiting for time to flow back into his mind, hands gripping the oily rail with the strength of the new-born.

VI

Tape 24: *August 17.*
Again, no sign of Hinton today.

Anne is asleep. An hour ago, when I returned from the drugstore, she looked at me with focused eyes for the first time in a week. By an effort I managed to feed her in the few minutes she was fully awake. Time has virtually stopped for her, there are long periods when she is clearly in an almost stationary world, a series of occasionally varying static tableaux. Then she wakes briefly and starts talking about Hinton and a flight to Miami she is going to make with him in his Cessna. Yet she seems refreshed by these journeys into the light, as if her mind is drawing nourishment from the very fact that no time is passing.

I feel the same, despite the infected wound on my shoulder – Hinton's dirty finger-nails. The attacks come a dozen times a day, everything slows to a barely perceptible flux. The intensity of light is growing, photons backing up all the way to the sun. As I left the drugstore I watched a parakeet cross the road over my head, it seemed to take two hours to fly fifty feet.

Perhaps Anne has another week before time stops for her. As for myself, three weeks? It's curious to think that at, say, precisely 3.47 p.m., 8 September, time will stop for ever. A single micro-second will flash past unnoticed for everyone else, but for me will last an eternity. I'd better decide how I want to spend it!

Tape 25: *August 19.*
A hectic two days, Anne had a relapse at noon yesterday, vaso-vagal shock brought on by waking just as Hinton strafed the hotel in his Wright Flyer. I could barely detect her heartbeat, spent hours massaging her calves and thighs (I'd happily go out into eternity caressing my wife). I managed to stand her up, walked her up and down the balcony in the hope that the noise of Hinton's aircraft might jolt her back on to the rails. In fact, this morning she spoke to me in a

completely lucid way, obviously appalled by my derelict appearance. For her it's one of those quiet afternoons three weeks ago.

We could still leave, start up one of the abandoned cars and reach the border at Jacksonville before the last minutes run out. I have to keep reminding myself why we came here in the first place. Running north will solve nothing. If there is a solution it's here, somewhere between Hinton's obsessions and Shepley's orbiting coffin, between the space centre and those bright, eerie transits that are all too visible at night. I hope I don't go out just as it arrives, spend the rest of eternity looking at the vaporizing corpse of the man I helped to die in space. I keep thinking of that tiger. Somehow I can calm it.

Tape 26: *August 25.*
3.30 p.m. The first uninterrupted hour of conscious time I've had in days. When I woke 15 minutes ago Hinton had just finished strafing the hotel – the palms were shaking dust and insects all over the balcony. Clearly Hinton is trying to keep us awake, postponing the end until he's ready to play his last card, or perhaps until I'm out of the way and he's free to be with Anne.

I'm still thinking about his motives. He seems to have embraced the destruction of time, as if this whole malaise were an opportunity that we ought to seize, the next evolutionary step forward. He was steering me to the edge of the assembly deck, urging me to fly, if Gale Shepley hadn't appeared in her glider I would have dived over the rail. In a strange way he was helping me, guiding me into that new world without time. When he turned Shepley loose from the Shuttle he didn't think he was killing him, but setting him free.

The ever-more primitive aircraft – Hinton's quest for a pure form of flight, which he will embark upon at the last moment. A Santos-Dumont flew over yesterday, an ungainly box-kite, he's given up his First World War machines. He's deliberately flying badly designed aircraft, all part of his attempt to escape from winged aviation into absolute flight, poetical rather than aeronautical structures.

The roots of shamanism and levitation, and the erotic cathexis of flight – can one see them as an attempt to escape from time? The shaman's supposed ability to leave his physical form and fly with his spiritual body, the psychopomp guiding the souls of the deceased and able to achieve a mastery of fire, together seem to be linked with those defects of the vestibular apparatus brought on by prolonged exposure to zero gravity during the space flights. We should have welcomed them.

That tiger – I'm becoming obsessed with the notion that it's on fire.

Tape 27: *August 28.*
An immense silence today, not a murmur over the soft green deck of Florida. Hinton may have killed himself. Perhaps all this flying is some kind of expiatory ritual, when he dies the shaman's curse will be lifted. But do I want to go back into time? By contrast, that static world of brilliant light pulls at the heart like a vision of Eden. If time *is* a primitive mental structure we're right to reject it. There's a sense in which not only the shaman's but all mystical and religious beliefs are an attempt to devise a world without time. Why did primitive man, who needed a brain only slightly larger than the tiger in Gale's zoo, in fact have a mind almost equal to those of Freud and Leonardo? Perhaps all that surplus neural capacity was there to release him from time, and it has taken the space age, and the sacrifice of the first astronaut, to achieve that single goal.

Kill Hinton . . . How, though?

Tape 28: *September 3.*
Missing days. I'm barely aware of the flux of time any longer. Anne lies on the bed, wakes for a few minutes and makes a futile attempt to reach the roof, as if the sky offers some kind of escape. I've just brought her down from the staircase. It's too much of an effort to forage for food, on my way to the supermarket this morning the light was so bright that I had to close my eyes, hand-holding my way around the streets like a blind beggar. I seemed to be standing on the floor of an immense furnace.

Anne is increasingly restless, murmuring to herself in some novel language, as if preparing for a journey. I recorded one of her drawn-out monologues, like some Gaelic love-poem, then speeded it up to normal time. An agonized 'Hinton . . . Hinton . . .'

It's taken her twenty years to learn.

Tape 29: *September 6.*
There can't be more than a few days left. The dream-time comes on a dozen stretches each day, everything slows to a halt. From the balcony I've just watched a flock of orioles cross the street. They seemed to

take hours, their unmoving wings supporting them as they hung above the trees.

At last the birds have learned to fly.

Anne is awake . . .

(*Anne*): Who's learned to fly?

(*EM*): It's all right – the birds.

(*Anne*): Did you teach them? What am I talking about? How long have I been away?

(*EM*): Since dawn. Tell me what you were dreaming.

(*Anne*): Is this a dream? Help me up. God, it's dark in the street. There's no time left here. Edward, find Hinton. Do whatever he says.

VII

Kill Hinton . . .

As the engine of the Yamaha clacked into life, Mallory straddled the seat and looked back at the hotel. At any moment, as if seizing the last few minutes left to her, Anne would leave the bedroom and try to make her way to the roof. The stationary clocks in Titusville were about to tell the real time for her, eternity for this lost woman would be a flight of steps around an empty elevator shaft.

Kill Hinton . . . he had no idea how. He set off through the streets to the east of Titusville, shakily weaving in and out of the abandoned cars. With its stiff gearbox and unsteady throttle the Yamaha was exhausting to control. He was driving through an unfamiliar suburb of the town, a terrain of tract houses, shopping malls and car parks laid out for the NASA employees in the building boom of the 1960s. He passed an overturned truck that had spilled its cargo of television sets across the road, and a laundry van that had careened through the window of a liquor store.

Three miles to the east were the gantries of the space centre. An aircraft hung in the air above them, a primitive helicopter with an overhead propeller. The tapering blades were stationary, as if Hinton had at last managed to dispense with wings.

Mallory pressed on towards the Cape, the engine of the motorcycle at full throttle. The tracts of suburban housing unravelled before him, endlessly repeating themselves, the same shopping malls, bars and motels, the same stores and used-car lots that he and Anne had seen in their journey across the continent. He could almost believe that he was driving through Florida again, through the hundreds of small towns that merged together, a suburban universe in which these identical liquor stores, car parks and shopping malls formed the building blocks of a strand of urban DNA generated by the nucleus of the space centre. He had driven down this road, across these silent intersections, not for minutes or hours but for years and decades. The unravelling strand covered the entire surface of the globe, and then swept out into space to pave the walls of the universe before it curved back on itself to land here at its departure point at the space centre. Again he passed the overturned truck beside its scattered television sets, again the laundry van in the liquor store window. He would forever pass them, forever cross the same intersection, see the same rusty sign above the same motel cabin . . .

'Doctor . . . !'

The smell of burning flesh quickened in Mallory's nose. His right calf was pressed against the exhaust manifold of the idling Yamaha. Charred fragments of his cotton trousers clung to the raw wound. As the young woman in the black flying suit ran across the street Mallory pushed himself away from the clumsy machine, stumbled over its spinning wheels and knelt in the road.

He had stopped at an intersection half a mile from the centre of Titusville. The vast planetary plain of parking lots had withdrawn, swirled down some cosmic funnel and then contracted to this small suburban enclave of a single derelict motel, two tract houses and a bar. Twenty feet away the blank screens of the television sets stared at him from the road beside the overturned truck. A few steps further along the sidewalk the laundry van lay in its liquor store window, dusty bottles of vodka and bourbon shaded by the wing-tip of the glider which Gale Shepley had landed in the street.

'Dr Mallory! Can you hear me? Dear man . . .' She pushed back Mallory's head and peered into his eyes, then switched off the still clacking engine of the Yamaha. 'I saw you sitting here, there was something – My God, your leg! Did Hinton . . . ?'

'No . . . I set fire to myself.' Mallory climbed to his feet, an arm around the girl's shoulder. He was still trying to clear his head, there was something curiously beguiling about that vast suburban world . . . 'I was a fool trying to ride it. I must see Hinton.'

'Doctor, listen to me . . .' The girl shook his hands, her eyes wide with fever. Her mascara and hair were even more bizarre than he remembered. 'You're dying! A day or two more, an hour maybe, you'll be gone. We'll find a car and I'll drive you north.' With an effort she took her eyes from the sky. 'I don't like to leave Dad, but you've got to get away from here, it's inside your head now.'

Mallory tried to lift the heavy Yamaha. 'Hinton – it's all that's left now. For Anne, too. Somehow I have to . . . kill him.'

'He knows that, doctor –' She broke off at the sound of an approaching aero-engine. An aircraft was hovering over the nearby streets, its shadowy bulk visible through the palm leaves, the flicker of a rotor blade across the sun. As they crouched among the television sets it passed above their heads. An antique autogyro, it lumbered through the air like an aerial harvester, its free-spinning rotor apparently powered by the sunlight. Sitting in the open cockpit, the pilot was too busy with his controls to search the streets below.

Besides, as Mallory knew, Hinton had already found his quarry. Standing on the roof of the hotel, a dressing gown around her shoulders, was Anne Mallory. At last she had managed to climb the stairs, driven on by her dream of the sky. She stared sightlessly at the autogyro, stepping back a single pace only when it circled the hotel and came in to land through a storm of leaves and dust. When it touched down on the roof the draught from its propeller stripped the gown from her shoulders. Naked, she turned to face the autogyro, lover of this strange machine come to save her from a time-reft world.

VIII

As they reached the NASA causeway huge columns of smoke were rising from the space centre. From the pillion seat of the motorcycle Mallory looked up at the billows boiling into the stained air. The forest was flushed with heat, the foliage glowing like furnace coals.

Had Hinton refuelled the Shuttle's engines and prepared the craft for lift-off? He would take Anne with him, and cast them both loose into space as he had done with Shepley, joining the dead astronaut in his orbital bier.

Smoke moved through the trees ahead of them, driven by the explosions coming from the launch site of the Shuttle. Gale throttled back the Yamaha and pointed to a break in the clouds. The Shuttle still sat on its platform, motors silent, the white hull reflecting the flash of explosions from the concrete runways.

Hinton had set fire to his antique planes. Thick with oily smoke, the flames lifted from the glowing shells slumped on their undercarts. The

Curtiss biplane was burning briskly. A frantic blaze devoured the engine compartment of the Fokker, detonated the fuel tank and set off the machine-gun ammunition. The exploding cartridges kicked through the wings as they folded like a house of cards.

Gale steadied the Yamaha with her feet, and skirted the glowing trees two hundred yards from the line of incandescent machines. The explosions flashed in her goggles, blanching her vivid make-up and giving her blonde hair an ash-like whiteness. The heat flared against Mallory's sallow face as he searched the aircraft for any sign of Hinton. Fanned by the flames that roared from its fuselage, the autogyro's propeller rotated swiftly, caught fire and spun in a last blazing carnival. Beside it, flames raced along the wings of the Wright Flyer, in a shower of sparks the burning craft lifted into the air and fell on to its back upon the red-hot hulk of the Sopwith Camel. Ignited by the intense heat, the primed engine of the Flying Flea roared into life, propelled the tiny aircraft in a scurrying arc among the burning wrecks, setting off the Spad and Bleriot before it overturned in a furnace of rolling flame.

'Doctor – on the assembly deck!'

Mallory followed the girl's raised hand. A hundred feet above them, Anne and Hinton stood side by side on the metal landing of the stairway. The flames from the burning aircraft wavered against their faces, as if they were already moving through the air together. Although Hinton's arm was around Anne's waist, they seemed unaware of each other when they stepped forward into the light.

IX

As always during his last afternoons at Cocoa Beach, Mallory rested by the swimming pool of the abandoned hotel, watching the pale glider float patiently across the undisturbed skies of Cape Kennedy. In this peaceful arbour, surrounded by the drowsing inmates of the zoo, he listened to the fountain cast its crystal gems on to the grass beside his chair. The spray of water was now almost stationary, like the glider and the wind and the watching cheetahs, elements of an emblematic and glowing world.

As time slipped away from him, Mallory stood under the fountain, happy to see it transform itself into a glass tree that shed an opalescent fruit on to his shoulders and hands. Dolphins flew through the air over the nearby sea. Once he immersed himself in the pool, delighted to be embedded in this huge block of condensed time.

Fortunately, Gale Shepley had rescued him before he drowned. Mallory knew that she was becoming bored with him. She was intent now only on the search for her father, confident that he would soon be returning from the tideways of space. At night the trajectories were ever lower, tracks of charged particles that soared across the forest. She had almost ceased to eat, and Mallory was glad that once her father arrived she would at last give up her flying. Then the two of them would leave together.

Mallory had made his own preparations for departure. The key to the tiger cage he held always in his hand. There was little time left to him now, the light-filled world had transformed itself into a series of tableaux from a pageant that celebrated the founding days of creation. In the finale every element in the universe, however humble, would take its place on the stage in front of him.

He watched the tiger waiting for him at the bars of its cage. The great cats, like the reptiles before them, had always stood partly out of time. The flames that marked its pelt reminded him of the fire that had consumed the aircraft at the space centre, the fire through which Anne and Hinton still flew forever.

He left the pool and walked towards the tiger cage. He would unlock the door soon, embrace these flames, lie down with this beast in a world beyond time.

WILLIAM TREVOR

A MEETING IN MIDDLE AGE

'I am Mrs da Tanka,' said Mrs da Tanka. 'Are you Mr Mileson?' The man nodded, and they walked together the length of the platform, seeking a compartment that might offer them a welcome, or failing that, and they knew the more likely, simple privacy. They carried each a small suitcase, Mrs da Tanka's of white leather or some material manufactured to resemble it, Mr Mileson's battered and black. They did not speak as they marched purposefully: they were strangers one to another, and in the noise and the bustle, examining the lighted windows of the carriages, there was little that might constructively be said.

'A ninety-nine-years' lease,' Mr Mileson's father had said, 'taken out in 1862 by my grandfather, whom of course you never knew. Expiring in your lifetime, I fear. Yet you will by then be in a sound position to accept the misfortune. To renew what has come to an end; to keep the property in the family.' The property was an expression that glorified. The house was small and useful, one of a row, one of a kind easily found; but the lease when the time came was not renewable – which released Mr Mileson of a problem. Bachelor, childless, the end of the line, what use was a house to him for a further ninety-nine years?

Mrs da Tanka, sitting opposite him, drew a magazine from an assortment she carried. Then, checking herself, said: 'We could talk. Or do you prefer to conduct the business in silence?' She was a woman who filled, but did not overflow from a fair-sized, elegant, quite expensive tweed suit. Her hair, which was grey, did not appear so; it was tightly held to her head, a reddish gold colour. Born into another class she would have been a chirpy woman; she guarded against her chirpiness, she disliked the quality in her. There was often laughter in her eyes, and as often as she felt it there she killed it by the severity of her manner.

'You must not feel embarrassment,' Mrs da Tanka said. 'We are beyond the age of giving in to awkwardness in a situation. You surely **263** agree?'

Mr Mileson did not know. He did not know how or what he should feel. Analysing his feelings he could come to no conclusion. He supposed he was excited but it was more difficult than it seemed to track down the emotions. He was unable, therefore, to answer Mrs da Tanka. So he just smiled.

Mrs da Tanka, who had once been Mrs Horace Spire and was not likely to forget it, considered those days. It was a logical thing for her to do, for they were days that had come to an end as these present days were coming to an end. Termination was on her mind: to escape from Mrs da Tanka into Mrs Spire was a way of softening the worry that was with her now, and a way of seeing it in proportion to a lifetime.

'If that is what you want,' Horace had said, 'then by all means have it. Who shall do the dirty work – you or I?' This was his reply to her request for a divorce. In fact, at the time of speaking, the dirty work as he called it was already done: by both of them.

'It is a shock for me,' Horace had continued. 'I thought we could jangle along for many a day. Are you seriously involved elsewhere?'

In fact she was not, but finding herself involved at all reflected the inadequacy of her married life and revealed a vacuum that once had been love.

'We are better apart,' she had said. 'It is bad to get used to the habit of being together. We must take our chances while we may, while there is still time.'

In the railway carriage she recalled the conversation with vividness, especially that last sentence, most especially the last five words of it. The chance she had taken was da Tanka, eight years ago. 'My God,' she said aloud, 'what a pompous bastard he turned out to be.'

Mr Mileson had a couple of those weekly publications for which there is no accurate term in the language: a touch of a single colour on the front – floppy, half-intellectual things, somewhere between a journal and a magazine. While she had her honest mags. *Harper's*. *Vogue*. Shiny and smart and rather silly. Or so thought Mr Mileson. He had opened them at dentists' and doctors', leafed his way through the ridiculous advertisements and aptly titled model girls, unreal girls in unreal poses, devoid it seemed of sex, and half the time of life. So that was the kind of woman she was.

'Who?' said Mr Mileson.

'Oh, who else, good heavens! Da Tanka I mean.'

Eight years of da Tanka's broad back, so fat it might have been padded beneath the skin. He had often presented it to her; he was that kind of man. Busy, he claimed; preoccupied.

'I shall be telling you about da Tanka,' she said. 'There are interesting facets to the man; though God knows, he is scarcely interesting in himself.'

It was a worry, in any case, owning a house. Seeing to the roof; noticing the paint cracking on the outside, and thinking about damp in mysterious places. Better off he was, in the room in Swiss Cottage; cosier in winter. They'd pulled down the old house by now, with all the others in the road. Flats were there instead: bulking up to the sky, with a million or so windows. All the gardens were gone, all the gnomes and the Snow White dwarfs, all the winter bulbs and the little paths of crazy paving; the bird-baths and bird-boxes and bird-tables; the miniature sandpits, and the metal edging, ornate, for flower-beds.

'We must move with the times,' said Mrs da Tanka, and he realized that he had been speaking to her; or speaking aloud and projecting the remarks in her direction since she was there.

His mother had made the rockery. Aubretia and sarsaparilla and pinks and Christmas roses. Her brother, his uncle Edward, bearded and queer, brought seaside stones in his motor-car. His father had shrugged his distaste for the project, as indeed for all projects of this nature, seeing the removal of stones from the seashore as being in some way disgraceful, even dishonest. Behind the rockery there were loganberries: thick, coarse, inedible fruit, never fully ripe. But nobody, certainly not Mr Mileson, had had the heart to pull away the bushes.

'Weeks would pass,' said Mrs da Tanka, 'without the exchange of a single significant sentence. We lived in the same house, ate the same meals, drove out in the same car, and all he would ever say was: "It is time the central heating was on." Or: "These windscreen-wipers aren't working."'

Mr Mileson didn't know whether she was talking about Mr da Tanka or Mr Spire. They seemed like the same man to him; shadowy, silent fellows who over the years had shared this woman with the well-tended hands.

'He will be wearing city clothes,' her friend had said, 'grey or nondescript. He is like anyone else except for his hat, which is big and black and eccentric.' An odd thing about him, the hat: like a wild oat almost.

There he had been, by the tobacco kiosk, punctual and expectant; gaunt of face, thin, fiftyish; with the old-fashioned hat and the weekly papers that somehow matched it, but did not match him.

'Now would you blame me, Mr Mileson? Would you blame me for seeking freedom from such a man?'

The hat lay now on the luggage-rack with his carefully folded overcoat. A lot of his head was bald, whitish and tender like good dripping. His eyes were sad, like those of a retriever puppy she had known in her childhood. Men are often like dogs, she thought; women more akin to cats. The train moved smoothly, with rhythm, through the night. She thought of da Tanka and Horace Spire, wondering where Spire was now. Opposite her, he thought about the ninety-nine-year lease and the two plates, one from last night's supper, the other from breakfast, that he had left unwashed in the room at Swiss Cottage.

'This seems your kind of place,' Mr Mileson said, surveying the hotel from its ornate hall.

'Gin and lemon, gin and lemon,' said Mrs da Tanka, matching the words with action: striding to the bar.

Mr Mileson had rum, feeling it a more suitable drink though he could not think why. 'My father drank rum with milk in it. An odd concoction.'

'Frightful, it sounds. Da Tanka is a whisky man. My previous liked stout. Well, well, so here we are.'

Mr Mileson looked at her. 'Dinner is next on the agenda.'

But Mrs da Tanka was not to be moved. They sat while she drank many measures of the drink; and when they rose to demand dinner they discovered that the restaurant was closed and were ushered to a grill-room.

'You organized that badly, Mr Mileson.'

'I organized nothing. I know the rules of these places. I repeated them to you. You gave me no chance to organize.'

'A chop and an egg or something. Da Tanka at least could have got us soup.'

In 1931 Mr Mileson had committed fornication with the maid in his parents' house. It was the only occasion, and he was glad that adultery was not expected of him with Mrs da Tanka. In it she would be more experienced than he, and he did not relish the implication. The

grill-room was lush and vulgar. 'This seems your kind of place,' Mr
Mileson repeated rudely.

'At least it is warm. And the lights don't glare. Why not order some
wine?'

Her husband must remain innocent. He was a person of importance, in the public eye. Mr Mileson's friend had repeated it, the friend
who knew Mrs da Tanka's solicitor. All expenses paid, the friend had
said, and a little fee as well. Nowadays Mr Mileson could do with little
fees. And though at the time he had rejected the suggestion downright, he had later seen that friend – acquaintance really – in the pub
he went to at half past twelve on Sundays, and had agreed to take part
in the drama. It wasn't just the little fee; there was something rather
like prestige in the thing; his name as co-respondent – now *there* was
something you'd never have guessed! The hotel bill to find its way to
Mrs da Tanka's husband who would pass it to his solicitor. Breakfast
in bed, and remember the face of the maid who brought it. Pass the
time of day with her, and make sure she remembered yours. Oh very
nice, the man in the pub said, very nice Mrs da Tanka was – or so he
was led to believe. He batted his eyes at Mr Mileson; but Mr Mileson
said it didn't matter, surely, about Mrs da Tanka's niceness. He knew
his duties: there was nothing personal about them. He'd do it himself,
the man in the pub explained, only he'd never be able to keep his
hands off an attractive middle-aged woman. That was the trouble
about finding someone for the job.

'I've had a hard life,' Mrs da Tanka confided. 'Tonight I need your
sympathy, Mr Mileson. Tell me I have your sympathy.' Her face and
neck had reddened: chirpiness was breaking through.

In the house, in a cupboard beneath the stairs, he had kept his
gardening boots. Big, heavy army boots, once his father's. He had
worn them at week-ends, poking about in the garden.

'The lease came to an end two years ago,' he told Mrs da Tanka.
'There I was with all that stuff, all my gardening tools, and the
furniture and bric-à-brac of three generations to dispose of. I can tell
you it wasn't easy to know what to throw away.'

'Mr Mileson, I don't like that waiter.'

Mr Mileson cut his steak with care: a three-cornered piece, neat and
succulent. He loaded mushroom and mustard on it, added a sliver of
potato and carried the lot to his mouth. He masticated and drank some
wine.

'Do you know the waiter?'

Mrs da Tanka laughed unpleasantly; like ice cracking. 'Why should I know the waiter? I do not generally know waiters. Do you know the waiter?'

'I ask because you claim to dislike him.'

'May I not dislike him without an intimate knowledge of the man?'

'You may do as you please. It struck me as a premature decision, that is all.'

'What decision? What is premature? What are you talking about? Are you drunk?'

'The decision to dislike the waiter I thought to be premature. I do not know about being drunk. Probably I am a little. One has to keep one's spirits up.'

'Have you ever thought of wearing an eye-patch, Mr Mileson? I think it would suit you. You need distinction. Have you led an empty life? You give the impression of an empty life.'

'My life has been as many other lives. Empty of some things, full of others. I am in possession of all my sight, though. My eyes are real. Neither is a pretence. I see no call for an eye-patch.'

'It strikes me you see no call for anything. You have never lived, Mr Mileson.'

'I do not understand that.'

'Order us more wine.'

Mr Mileson indicated with his hand and the waiter approached. 'Some other waiter, please,' Mrs da Tanka cried. 'May we be served by another waiter?'

'Madam?' said the waiter.

'We do not take to you. Will you send another man to our table?'

'I am the only waiter on duty, madam.'

'It's quite all right,' said Mr Mileson.

'It's not quite all right. I will not have this man at our table, opening and dispensing wine.'

'Then we must go without.'

'I am the only waiter on duty, madam.'

'There are other employees of the hotel. Send us a porter or the girl at the reception.'

'It is not their duty, madam —'

'Oh nonsense, nonsense. Bring us the wine, man, and have no more to-do.'

Unruffled, the waiter moved away. Mrs da Tanka hummed a popular tune.

'Are you married, Mr Mileson? Have you in the past been married?'

'No, never married.'

'I have been married twice. I am married now. I am throwing the dice for the last time. God knows how I shall find myself. You are helping to shape my destiny. What a fuss that waiter made about the wine!'

'That is a little unfair. It was you, you know –'

'Behave like a gentleman, can't you? Be on my side since you are with me. Why must you turn on me? Have I harmed you?'

'No, no. I was merely establishing the truth.'

'Here is the man again with the wine. He is like a bird. Do you think he has wings strapped down beneath his waiter's clothes? You are like a bird,' she repeated, examining the waiter's face. 'Has some fowl played a part in your ancestry?'

'I think not, madam.'

'Though you cannot be sure. How can you be sure? How can you say you think not when you know nothing about it?'

The waiter poured the wine in silence. He was not embarrassed, Mr Mileson noted; not even angry.

'Bring coffee,' Mrs da Tanka said.

'Madam.'

'How servile waiters are! How I hate servility, Mr Mileson! I could not marry a servile man. I could not marry that waiter, not for all the tea in China.'

'I did not imagine you could. The waiter does not seem your sort.'

'He is your sort. You like him, I think. Shall I leave you to converse with him?'

'Really! What would I say to him? I know nothing about the waiter except what he is in a professional sense. I do not wish to know. It is not my habit to go about consorting with waiters after they have waited on me.'

'I am not to know that. I am not to know what your sort is, or what your personal and private habits are. How could I know? We have only just met.'

'You are clouding the issue.'

'You are as pompous as da Tanka. Da Tanka would say issue and clouding.'

'What your husband would say is no concern of mine.'

'You are meant to be my lover, Mr Mileson. Can't you act it a bit?

My husband must concern you dearly. You must wish to tear him limb from limb. Do you wish it?'

'I have never met the man. I know nothing of him.'

'Well then, pretend. Pretend for the waiter's sake. Say something violent in the waiter's hearing. Break an oath. Blaspheme. Bang your fist on the table.'

'I was not told I should have to behave like that. It is against my nature.'

'What is your nature?'

'I'm shy and self-effacing.'

'You are an enemy to me. I don't understand your sort. You have not got on in the world. You take on commissions like this. Where is your self-respect?'

'Elsewhere in my character.'

'You have no personality.'

'That is a cliché. It means nothing.'

'Sweet nothings for lovers, Mr Mileson! Remember that.'

They left the grill-room and mounted the stairs in silence. In their bedroom Mrs da Tanka unpacked a dressing-gown. 'I shall undress in the bathroom. I shall be absent a matter of ten minutes.'

Mr Mileson slipped from his clothes into pyjamas. He brushed his teeth at the wash-basin, cleaned his nails and splashed a little water on his face. When Mrs da Tanka returned he was in bed.

To Mr Mileson she seemed a trifle bigger without her daytime clothes. He remembered corsets and other containing garments. He did not remark upon it.

Mrs da Tanka turned out the light and they lay without touching between the cold sheets of the double bed.

He would leave little behind, he thought. He would die and there would be the things in the room, rather a number of useless things with sentimental value only. Ornaments and ferns. Reproductions of paintings. A set of eggs, birds' eggs he had collected as a boy. They would pile all the junk together and probably try to burn it. Then perhaps they would light a couple of those fumigating candles in the room, because people are insulting when other people die.

'Why did you not get married?' Mrs da Tanka said.

'Because I do not greatly care for women.' He said it, throwing caution to the winds, waiting for her attack.

'Are you a homosexual?'

The word shocked him. 'Of course I'm not.'

WILLIAM TREVOR

'I only asked. They go in for this kind of thing.'

'That does not make me one.'

'I often thought Horace Spire was more that way than any other. For all the attention he paid to me.'

As a child she had lived in Shropshire. In those days she loved the country, though without knowing, or wishing to know, the names of flowers or plants or trees. People said she looked like Alice in Wonderland.

'Have you ever been to Shropshire, Mr Mileson?'

'No. I am very much a Londoner. I lived in the same house all my life. Now the house is no longer there. Flats replace it. I live in Swiss Cottage.'

'I thought you might. I thought you might live in Swiss Cottage.'

'Now and again I miss the garden. As a child I collected birds' eggs on the common. I have kept them all these years.'

She had kept nothing. She cut the past off every so often, remembering it when she cared to, without the aid of physical evidence.

'The hard facts of life have taken their toll of me,' said Mrs da Tanka. 'I met them first at twenty. They have been my companions since.'

'It was a hard fact the lease coming to an end. It was hard to take at the time. I did not accept it until it was well upon me. Only the spring before I had planted new delphiniums.'

'My father told me to marry a good man. To be happy and have children. Then he died. I did none of those things. I do not know why except that I did not care to. Then old Horry Spire put his arm around me and there we were. Life is as you make it, I suppose. I was thinking of homosexual in relation to that waiter you were interested in downstairs.'

'I was not interested in the waiter. He was hard done by, by you, I thought. There was no more to it than that.'

Mrs da Tanka smoked and Mr Mileson was nervous; about the situation in general, about the glow of the cigarette in the darkness. What if the woman dropped off to sleep? He had heard of fires started by careless smoking. What if in her confusion she crushed the cigarette against some part of his body? Sleep was impossible: one cannot sleep with the thought of waking up in a furnace, with the bells of fire brigades clanging a death knell.

'I will not sleep tonight,' said Mrs da Tanka, a statement which frightened Mr Mileson further. For all the dark hours the awful woman would be there, twitching and puffing beside him. *I am mad. I am out of my mind to have brought this upon myself.* He heard the words. He saw them on paper written in his handwriting. He saw them typed, and repeated again as on a telegram. The letters jolted and lost their order. The words were confused, skulking behind a fog. 'I am mad,' Mr Mileson said, to establish the thought completely, to bring it into the open. It was a habit of his; for a moment he had forgotten the reason for the thought, thinking himself alone.

'Are you telling me now you are mad?' asked Mrs da Tanka, alarmed. 'Gracious, are you worse than a homo? Are you some sexual pervert? Is that what you are doing here? Certainly that was not my plan, I do assure you. You have nothing to gain from me, Mr Mileson. If there is trouble I shall ring the bell.'

'I am mad to be here. I am mad to have agreed to all this. What came over me I do not know. I have only just realized the folly of the thing.'

'Arise then, dear Mileson, and break your agreement, your promise and your undertaking. You are an adult man, you may dress and walk from the room.'

They were all the same, she concluded: except that while others had some passing superficial recommendation, this one it seemed had none. There was something that made her sick about the thought of the stringy limbs that were stretched out beside her. What lengths a woman will go to to rid herself of a horror like da Tanka!

He had imagined it would be a simple thing. It had sounded like a simple thing: a good thing rather than a bad one. A good turn for a lady in need. That was as he had seen it. With the little fee already in his possession.

Mrs da Tanka lit another cigarette and threw the match on the floor.

'What kind of a life have you had? You had not the nerve for marriage. Nor the brains for success. The truth is you might not have lived.' She laughed in the darkness, determined to hurt him as he had hurt her in his implication that being with her was an act of madness.

Mr Mileson had not before done a thing like this. Never before had he not weighed the pros and cons and seen that danger was absent from an undertaking. The thought of it all made him sweat. He saw in the future further deeds: worse deeds, crimes and irresponsibilities.

Mrs da Tanka laughed again. But she was thinking of something else.

'You have never slept with a woman, is that it? Ah, you poor thing! What a lot you have not had the courage for!' The bed heaved with the raucous noise that was her laughter, and the bright spark of her cigarette bobbed about in the air.

She laughed, quietly now and silently, hating him as she hated da Tanka and had hated Horace Spire. Why could he not be some young man, beautiful and nicely-mannered and gay? Surely a young man would have come with her? Surely there was one amongst all the millions who would have done the chore with relish, or at least with charm?

'You are as God made you,' said Mr Mileson. 'You cannot help your shortcomings, though one would think you might by now have recognized them. To others you may be all sorts of things. To me you are a frightful woman.'

'Would you not stretch out a hand to the frightful woman? Is there no temptation for the woman's flesh? Are you a eunuch, Mr Mileson?'

'I have had the women I wanted. I am doing you a favour. Hearing of your predicament and pressed to help you, I agreed in a moment of generosity. Stranger though you were I did not say no.'

'That does not make you a gentleman.'

'And I do not claim it does. I am gentleman enough without it.'

'You are nothing without it. This is your sole experience. In all your clerkly subservience you have not paused to live. You know I am right, and as for being a gentleman – well, you are of the lower middle classes. There has never been an English gentleman born of the lower middle classes.'

She was trying to remember what she looked like; what her face was like, how the wrinkles were spread, how old she looked and what she might pass for in a crowd. Would men not be cagey now and think that she must be difficult in her ways to have parted twice from husbands? Was there a third time coming up? Third time lucky, she thought. Who would have her, though, except some loveless Mileson?

'You have had no better life than I,' said Mr Mileson. 'You are no more happy now. You have failed, and it is cruel to laugh at you.'

They talked and the hatred grew between them.

'In my childhood young men flocked about me, at dances in Shropshire that my father gave to celebrate my beauty. Had the fashion been duels, duels there would have been. Men killed and maimed for life, carrying a lock of my hair on their breast.'

'You are a creature now, with your face and your fingernails. Mutton dressed as lamb, Mrs da Tanka!'

Beyond the curtained windows the light of dawn broke into the night. A glimpse of it crept into the room, noticed and welcomed by its occupants.

'You should write your memoirs, Mr Mileson. To have seen the changes in your time and never to know a thing about them! You are like an occasional table. Or a coat-rack in the hall of a boarding-house. Who shall mourn at your grave, Mr Mileson?'

He felt her eyes upon him; and the mockery of the words sank into his heart with intended precision. He turned to her and touched her, his hands groping about her shoulders. He had meant to grasp her neck, to feel the muscles struggle beneath his fingers, to terrify the life out of her. But she, thinking the gesture was the beginning of an embrace, pushed him away, swearing at him and laughing. Surprised by the misunderstanding, he left her alone.

The train was slow. The stations crawled by, similar and ugly. She fixed her glance on him, her eyes sharpened; cold and powerful.

She had won the battle, though technically the victory was his. Long before the time arranged for their breakfast Mr Mileson had leaped from bed. He dressed and breakfasted alone in the dining-room. Shortly afterwards, after sending to the bedroom for his suitcase, he left the hotel, informing the receptionist that the lady would pay the bill. Which in time she had done, and afterwards pursued him to the train, where now, to disconcert him, she sat in the facing seat of an empty compartment.

'Well,' said Mrs da Tanka, 'you have shot your bolt. You have taken the only miserable action you could. You have put the frightful woman in her place. Have we a right,' she added, 'to expect anything better of the English lower classes?'

Mr Mileson had foolishly left his weekly magazines and the daily paper at the hotel. He was obliged to sit barefaced before her, pretending to observe the drifting landscape. In spite of everything, guilt gnawed him a bit. When he was back in his room he would borrow the vacuum cleaner and give it a good going over: the exercise would calm him. A glass of beer in the pub before lunch; lunch in the ABC; perhaps an afternoon cinema. It was Saturday today: this, more or less, was how he usually spent Saturday. Probably from lack of sleep he would doze off in the cinema. People would nudge him to draw attention to his snoring; that had happened before, and was not pleasant.

'To give you birth,' she said, 'your mother had long hours of pain.

Have you thought of that, Mr Mileson? Have you thought of that poor woman crying out, clenching her hands and twisting the sheets? Was it worth it, Mr Mileson? You tell me now, was it worth it?'

He could leave the compartment and sit with other people. But that would be too great a satisfaction for Mrs da Tanka. She would laugh loudly at his going, might even pursue him to mock in public.

'What you say about me, Mrs da Tanka, can equally be said of you.'

'Are we two peas in a pod? It's an explosive pod in that case.'

'I did not imply that. I would not wish to find myself sharing a pod with you.'

'Yet you shared a bed. And were not man enough to stick to your word. You are a worthless coward, Mr Mileson. I expect you know it.'

'I know myself, which is more than can be said in your case. Do you not think occasionally to see yourself as others see you? An ageing woman, faded and ugly, dubious in morals and personal habits. What misery you must have caused those husbands!'

'They married me, and got good value. You know that, yet dare not admit it.'

'I will scarcely lose sleep worrying the matter out.'

It was a cold morning, sunny with a clear sky. Passengers stepping from the train at the intermediate stations, muffled up against the temperature, finding it too much after the warm fug within. Women with baskets. Youths. Men with children, with dogs collected from the guard's van.

Da Tanka, she had heard, was living with another woman. Yet he refused to admit being the guilty party. It would not do for someone like da Tanka to be a public adulterer. So he had said. Pompously. Crossly. Horace Spire, to give him his due, hadn't given a damn one way or the other.

'When you die, Mr Mileson, have you a preference for the flowers on your coffin? It is a question I ask because I might send you off a wreath. That lonely wreath. From ugly, frightful Mrs da Tanka.'

'What?' said Mr Mileson, and she repeated the question.

'Oh well – cowparsley, I suppose.' He said it, taken off his guard by the image she created; because it was an image he often saw and thought about. Hearse and coffin and he within. It would not be like that probably. Anticipation was not in Mr Mileson's life. Remembering, looking back, considering events and emotions that had been at the time mundane perhaps – this kind of thing was more to his liking. For by hindsight there was pleasure in the stream of time. He could not establish his funeral in his mind; he tried often but ended up always with a funeral he had known: a repetition of his parents' passing and the accompanying convention.

'Cowparsley?' said Mrs da Tanka. Why did the man say cowparsley? Why not roses or lilies or something in a pot? There had been cowparsley in Shropshire; cowparsley on the verges of dusty lanes; cowparsley in hot fields buzzing with bees; great white swards rolling down to the river. She had sat among it on a picnic with dolls. She had lain on it, laughing at the beautiful anaemic blue of the sky. She had walked through it by night, loving it.

'Why did you say cowparsley?'

He did not know, except that once on a rare family outing to the country he had seen it and remembered it. Yet in his garden he had grown delphiniums and wallflowers and asters and sweet-pea.

She could smell it again: a smell that was almost nothing: fields and the heat of the sun on her face, laziness and summer. There was a red door somewhere, faded and blistered, and she sat against it, crouched on a warm step, a child dressed in the fashion of the time.

'Why did you say cowparsley?'

He remembered, that day, asking the name of the white powdery growth. He had picked some and carried it home; and had often since thought of it, though he had not come across a field of cowparsley for years.

She tried to speak again, but after the night there were no words she could find that would fit. The silence stuck between them, and Mr Mileson knew by instinct all that it contained. She saw an image of herself and him, strolling together from the hotel, in this same sunshine, at this very moment, lingering on the pavement to decide their direction and agreeing to walk to the promenade. She mouthed and grimaced and the sweat broke on her body, and she looked at him once and saw words die on his lips, lost in his suspicion of her.

The train stopped for the last time. Doors banged; the throng of people passed them by on the platform outside. They collected their belongings and left the train together. A porter, interested in her legs, watched them walk down the platform. They passed through the barrier and parted, moving in their particular directions. She to her new flat where milk and mail, she hoped, awaited her. He to his room; to the two unwashed plates on the draining board and the forks with egg on the prongs; and the little fee propped up on the mantelpiece, a pink cheque for five pounds, peeping out from behind a china cat.

IN THE HOURS OF DARKNESS

On a stretch of road from London and not yet in sight of Cambridge, Lena suddenly remarked that it was like Australia. There was more than one reason for this: the physical loneliness was exactly like that she had experienced in the countryside above Sydney one warm intoxicating Saturday and the road itself, devoid of houses or tillage, suggested a depopulated land. Also the high grass on either side was tawny, bleached no doubt by the long phenomenal English summer. The bridges too that flanked the motorways were ugly and graceless and reminded her of that other time.

Her son Iain said that any minute they would see the spires of Cambridge and already her mind ran on to her first view of the old historic town, the various university complexes, the stout walls, the stained-glass windows and the overall atmosphere of studiousness. She was intrigued. She envisaged going into the hotel bedroom and drawing curtains – they would be dark red and once drawn she would click on a light and sit in an armchair to read some of Jane Austen in order to re-discover through that woman reserve and perseverance.

Her youngest son was going up to Cambridge and she was facing the predicament she had read about in novels – that of a divorced woman, bereft of her children, having to grow old without these beloved props, having in some indescribable way to take the first steps into loneliness as if she were a toddler again.

Two signposts read the same mileage for Cambridge even though they were miles apart and she said that was typical, then instantly decided that she was becoming a shrew. Soon maybe she would be questioning bills, talking to herself and finding fault with any services that were to be done to her house. To save face she remarked on the beauty of a fairly ordinary little village in which she noticed a post office, an ale house, whimsy-looking cottages and an antique shop.

The hotel at Cambridge was not what she had imagined. The

entrance adjoined the car park and in the too huge lobby there were arrows pointing to several bars. Then hammering to testify that construction work was in progress. Would it stop at night? She was obsessed with noise and could, she believed, be wakened by an air bubble in her water pipes at night. She followed the porter and was dismayed to find that he lost his way. It was a big ramshackle place with various flights of stairs leading to different quarters. Her bedroom was on the first floor and just outside was a child's cot and a single mattress standing on its end. The room was everything she dreaded – a single bed with a stained orange coverlet, matching curtains, plastic lampshade, wardrobe with three empty metal hangers that moved slightly as if propelled by some shiver. The one summoning bell brought no response – no buxom girl, no doddery old man, no housekeeper with motherly smile came in answer to the ringing of the green oblong button. In fact there was no way of telling if it was connected, or if in fact a bell had rung somewhere in the bowels of that place and was being ignored with a shrug. 'Bad place to die', she thought, and as fervently as she had longed for the surprise and repose of that little room, she now longed to be out of it and safely at home.

She wanted tea. Her stockings were wet. She and Iain had had to walk the last bit of the journey carrying baskets, a record player, a drawing-board and loose bits of lighting flex. He had parked the car outside the town because it was against university rules to own one. On their walk it had begun to drizzle and by now it was raining heavily. Lifting the curtain she looked at the spatters as they crawled down the window-pane and lodged on the frame beneath. The view was of a football field empty except for its goal posts. She would make the best of it.

In the lobby the guests were being served with tea and everything about them suggested not an academic life but a life of commerce. She had to step over bags bursting with shopping, and at first glance every mouth seemed to be allied to a piece of oily chocolate cake. She sat at one empty table waiting for service, and in her restlessness began to eat the bits of damp ribbony lettuce that served as decoration on the plate of sandwiches that the previous occupant had devoured. The waiter strolled across and caught her in this nonsensical theft. She asked him to bring tea quickly as she was dining at seven. He spurned her to her face, he also spurned the entire human race and did both these offices in broken English. —

Dinner was in one of the most esteemed of the colleges and they foregathered in a small overheated sitting-room, that was full of furniture and pieces of china. Her host, a professor, had invited a younger professor and two freshmen. They sat and awkwardly sorted each other out, the young men laughing lightly at everything and constantly interjecting their remarks with bits of French as they bantered with each other about their sleeping habits and their taste for sherry or classical music. It was stiff. Her son should have had a different introduction, something much less formal, a bit of gaiety. The conversation centred for a long time on a professor who had the nickname of a woman and who received students in his long johns and thought nothing of it. Incongruously he was described as a hermit even though he seemed to be receiving students most mornings in his cluttered room. It was stifling hot. To calm herself, Lena thought of the beautiful mist like fine gauze sparkling on the courtyard outside, and above it a sky perfectly pictorial with its new moon and its thrilling stars.

They went down a short flight of stairs and then climbed some other steps to their early dinner. The host had done everything to make it perfect – smoked salmon, grouse, chantilly, different wines for each course and all this printed alongside each person's nameplace. The old servant was so nervous that he trembled as he stood over her and kept debating with his long hands whether to proffer the entrée dish or the gravy jug. It was touch and go. His master told him for God's sake to put the jug down. A movement that caused his neck to tremble like that of a half-dead cockerel's. Yes, 'It was so' that students were sent down but they had to be awfully bad or else awfully unlucky and of course it was an awfully amusing thing. 'I am in a modern English play,' she thought, the kind of play that portrayed an intelligent man or woman going to seed and making stoical jokes about it. Academic life was not for her. She would rather be a barbarian. She sucked on the word as if it were sherbet. Barbarian.

The grouse was impossible to tackle. Everyone talked too much and tried too eagerly and this all-round determination to be considerate caused them instead to be distracted and noisy. Little bright jets of blood shot up as knives vainly attacked the game. To conceal his embarrassment the young professor said it was too delicious. The host said it was uneatable and if young Freddie's was delicious to give it to Lena since hers was like a brick. She demurred, said it was lovely, while at the same time resolved that she would eat the sprouts and would drink goblets of wine. A toast was raised to her son and he went scarlet as he heard himself being praised. Looking downwards she saw that the various plates contained a heap of little bones, decked with bits of torn pink flesh, and true to her domestic instinct she said they would make good broth, those leavings. A most tactless slip. Everyone raved over the nice raspberry chantilly and quite huge portions of it rested on the young men's dessert plates.

Having dined so early she felt it was appropriate to leave early. Earlier, her host had confessed to being tired and yet in his bedroom where she went to fetch her coat, she felt that he wanted to talk, that he was avid to tell some little thing. He simply said that he had never married because he could not stand the idea of a woman saying 'we', organizing his thought, his time, his suits of clothing and his money. It was a small functional room with a washstand, an iron bed with a frayed paisley robe laid across it. Staring from the wall was a painting of a wolf with a man's eyes and she thought this professor is not as mild as he seems. On an impulse she kissed him and he seemed so childishly glad that she then became awkward and tripped over a footstool.

Out on the street they lingered, admiring the courtyard, the stone archways, and the beautiful formidable entrance. The town itself was just shops, and shut cafés, with cars whizzing up and down as on any high street. At the hotel she bade Iain good night and knew that the hour had come when they were parting more or less for ever. They made light of it and said they would cruise Cambridge on the morrow.

As she approached her bedroom she began to remonstrate with herself, began to laugh. The music she heard was surely phantom music because after all she had been insistent about securing a quiet room. But as she proceeded down the corridor the sound increased in volume and pitch and she wondered if anxiety could play such a thorough trick. When she put the key in her own door and entered, the furnishings were shaking from the implosion of the noise and she looked instinctively for men in white coats with hair oil, which was her outdated version of the members of a dance band. Yes, a dance was in progress. The metal hangers which she had forborne to use were almost doing a jig. The hotel telephonist could do nothing, was not even sympathetic.

She took her key and went down the stairs, then crossed the street to the college where her son was. The porter directed her and seemed to sense her dismay because he kept repeating the instructions, kept saying, 'If you walk down now, towards the rectangular buildings, and take the first turning on the left you will find your son will be the fifth staircase along, and you will find him there.' Walking along she thought only of the sleep that would 'knit up the ravelled' day and hoped that in one of those buildings a bed awaited her, a bed, an eiderdown and total silence.

Coming towards her was a young man wearing a motorcyclist's leather jacket that was too small for him. Something about the way he walked reminded her of restless youths that she had seen in an American film, of gangs who went out at night to have fights with other gangs, and inventing as a reason for murder their virility or their honour. This boy reminded her of that group. She wondered who he would be, thought that probably he had put on the jacket to give himself an image, was looking for friends. Four or five hundred young men were now installed in that college and she thought of the friendships that would ensue, of the indifferent meals they would all eat, the gowns they would buy, the loves and hatreds that would flourish as they became involved. She was glad not to be one of them. Just before the figure came level with her she realized that it was Iain and that obviously he was going in search of adventure. She lost heart then and could not tell him of her plan to find a bed in his house. She joked, pretended not to know him, walked past with her hips out and then in an affected voice said, 'Haven't we met somewhere.' Then she asked him if he was enjoying it and he said yes, but he always said yes at an awkward moment. They walked towards the gates and he said that his name was painted at the foot of the landing, his and three other names and how he had a little kitchen with a fridge and that there was a note informing him of a maid who would be at his service on Monday. How she wanted to be that maid. They said good night again, this time a little more gamely since there was a mutual suspicion that they might meet a third time.

In the lobby some people had come out from the dance and a drunken woman was holding up a broken silver shoe asking if the heel could be mended. The dance would go on till two. Lena felt like crying. The manager asked if she would like another hotel and she said yes then ran to her room and packed things quickly, viciously. In the lobby yet again she felt herself to be conspicuous, what with half her belongings falling out of the bag and a look of madness. In the taxi she thought of warm milk laced with whisky. Vain thought. The porter in the new hotel was fast asleep and stirred himself only when the black

Dalmatian dog bared his teeth at her legs which she quickly shielded with her suede bag. She had to pay there and then, and had to write the cheque by balancing the book against the wall as the counter space was taken up with various advertisement cards. Home, home, her heart begged. The last train for London had left an hour ago. She followed the porter down the corridor and herself let out a shriek when he admitted her to a room in which a shocked woman sat up in a bed-jacket screaming. In fact the two women's screams coincided.

'Sorry about that, Madam.' He had made a mistake. He made a similar mistake three times over, leaving some occupants of that wing in a state of anger and commotion. At last he conducted her to an empty room, that was weirdly identical to the one she had just vacated. He said not to open the window in case of burglary.

Such nights are not remarkable for their sound sleeping, but this one had extra impediments. The single bed was so narrow that each time she tried to turn over she had to stop herself from falling on to the floor. The tap let out involuntary groans and now and then the Dalmatian gave a watchdog's moan. She put her black cardigan over the telephone to blot out its faint luminous glow. She was fighting for sleep. She took two large two-toned capsules that were filled with barbiturate. Her son at that same hour had climbed up by means of scaffolding to the roof of Christ's College and with his friend was debating whether to pee on it or not, and make a statement that might result in their being rusticated. Up there they had brought the wine, the roast fillets of pork and the cheeses that she had given him for his first night's picnic. She could feel the sleeping pills starting to work as she put her hand out to assist herself in turning over. Nevertheless she tumbled, fell and conked her head on the bedside locker. It made her wide awake. The last sure little route to sleep was closed. It was a question of waiting till morning, so she dressed and then grappling with anger paced the room.

A hand-printed sign above the mirror caught her attention. It said, 'In the hours of darkness, if a client has an urgent need will he or she please ring *and wait* because due to security the night porter may be prowling the building and not find himself adjacent to the switchboard.' She took it down, re-read it with amazement, then wrote, 'You must be joking', and signed her name in full. Then she sank into the gaping armchair and waited stoutly for morning.

B. S. JOHNSON

A FEW SELECTED SENTENCES

Someone has to keep the records . . .

The Cacao is a fruite little lesse then Almonds, yet more fat, the which being roasted hath no ill taste. The chief use of this Cacao is in a drinke which they call Chocholate, whereof they make great accompt in that Country, foolishly, and without reason; for it is loathsome to such as are not acquainted with it, having a skum or froth that is very unpleasant to taste, if they be not very well conceited thereof. Yet it is a drinke very much esteemed among the Indians, wherewith they feast Noble men as they passe through their Country.

What are hands for, if not to hide the eyes?

Le Soixante-neuf est Interdit dans les Couloirs.

Eight years' penal servitude.

As a lorry driven by Croxley left the scene, the sound of a hunting horn was heard. Was it a warning? The police found the body of a stag in the bracken, still warm. Later, police came across Croxley, Ryman and Straker standing by the lorry at the place where the stag had been. Croxley said he was birdwatching, Ryman said his hobby was photography, and Straker, who was carrying a crossbow, said: 'I am interested in all forms of medieval weaponry.' In the lorry police found a quiver full of arrows, a pair of binoculars, two pairs of Sherwood Green tights, and five sheath knives. A broken arrowshaft corresponded to an arrowhead embedded in the dead stag. All three men said they were committee members of Bowmen for Britain, had been out seeking small vermin, and had been on a public footpath. Straker said: 'I saw a squirrel and fired at it but the stag which I did not know was there ran into it.'

A FEW SELECTED SENTENCES

A child left to himself bringeth his mother to shame.

I love anecdotes. I fancy mankind may come in time to write all aphoristically, except in narrative; grow weary of preparation and connection and illustration, and all those arts by which a big book is made.

The man had long white hands which he clasped tightly behind his back when not using them to eat several helpings of jellied eels. Most customers looked thoughtful.

One year, suspended.

All afternoon the girl threatened to jump. She said her husband had become converted to a religious sect which forbade her the use of her television. When she had wished to listen to the Queen's Xmas broadcast she had had to go into the bathroom. It was her radio. Because she used makeup her husband likened her to Jezebel, the painted woman of the Scriptures. It was accepted that he was sincere. As soon as they brought a priest to talk to her, she jumped.

Permission to laugh?

Have you heard what Cynon sang?
Beware of drunkards –
Drink unlocks the human heart.

The father appealed for witnesses to his son's death to come forward, not expecting to be overwhelmed by numbers. What had happened as far as they knew was that on Furse Bend he had crossed the inner edge on to the central reserve and in the resulting spill (which was not particularly dangerous in itself) the point of the clutch lever had entered his brain by way of the base of his skull. The father wished to know how designers of safety helmets had not taken this possibility into account. His colleagues said he should have had a ball on it.

But I am trying to be benign.

A rusty charlatan stated dogmatically that a discussion was an argument in which no one was particularly interested. He was reminded that every good deed is followed by the punishment of God. But, he insisted, one must have a proper regard for the ordinary.

The continuous process of recognizing that what is possible is not achievable.

A man taking pictures of a man taking pictures: there must be something in that.

At a wedding reception everyone was drunk, including the children. Indeed, one of the children became so affected as to seem ill, and it was considered advisable to take him to a hospital to have him seen to, stomach-pumped if necessary. They chose the receptor who seemed least drunk to drive the child, quickly. On the way the car was stopped by a policeman on a horse, who invited the driver to puff breath into a plastic bag. Crystals in the tube attached to this bag turned a certain colour which convinced the policeman that the driver was under the influence of alcohol and he informed him that he would be charged with an offence. 'Oh no,' said the driver, 'Your bags must be faulty. Perhaps indeed you have a batch of faulty bags. Why don't we test them by trying one out on this innocent child?'

A bard's land shall be free. He shall have a horse when he follows the king and a gold ring from the queen and the harp he shall never part with.

Do I want that to be the truth?

The Vice-Chancellor was killed when inspecting the progress of the building of Senate House. A technician was pushing a loaded wheelbarrow across a plank spanning a liftshaft. He saved himself, but the wheelbarrow was lost. The Vice-Chancellor was standing at the bottom of the liftshaft. Accommodate that mess.

Most of the time they look for things to want, schoolfriends.

Miceal and I would play snooker. He would generally win. His was always the same remark when he sank the green or the brown which would put him beyond being caught unless he gave away an unlikely number of penalty points: 'Now you haven't got enough balls. You'll have to put your own up.' I cannot say I laughed more than the first and second times, despite tradition. And 'No points for hard luck' was another saying of his that stuck.

– Who was there?
– The usual mess, of course. Baldies, hairies, collapsed faces, fallen women, who would you think?

Life.

—

Someone has to keep the records. I may even be thanked, in time.

MALCOLM BRADBURY

*C*OMPOSITION

I

We are, for the purposes of this story, in the courthouse square of a very small Middle Western town. It is a hot, sunny afternoon in the September of an old, tumultuous year, 1971. In the centre of the square stands the courthouse itself, a Victorian building of no distinction, with defensive cannon at every corner. In front of the courthouse stands a statue, of a soldier, his rifle in a negative position, a Henry Fleming who has been perpetuated as he ducks out of the Civil War. On the copper roof of the building, gone green, a row of pigeons stands, depositing, in some vague evolutionary gesture, quantities of new guano on top of the old guano. From a corner of the square there enters the one Greyhound bus of the day, which comes down from the state capital, two hundred miles to the north, where they keep all the money and the records of accurate time. The bus has aluminium sides, green glareproof windows, and a lavatory; it circles the square, slows, and stops at the depot, a telephone booth outside Lee's Diner. The driver, J. L. Gruner, safe, reliable, courteous, levers open the door; steps unfold; down the steps there descends, into the literal level of reality, in a brown suit, carrying a mackintosh on one arm, his hair long, his face lightly bearded, hot, but in good order, a person, a young English person named William Honeywell. His feet touch the board sidewalk, crisp with pigeon dung. He does not look around, or move far. Instead he stands close to the aluminium flank of the bus, which coughs diesel fumes at him, for the engine is still running, as J. L. Gruner gets down and unlocks the flaps under which this William's luggage is concealed. J. L. Gruner has been William's guide and conductor for most of the day, virtually ever since that early morning hour when William arrived, on the Boeing 727, after a transatlantic and then a transcontinental flight, in what pleases to call itself America. It is J. L. Gruner who took William's ticket as he stood in the bleak bus station, amid the lockers and the bums, in the state capital, two hundred miles to the north; it is J. L. Gruner who, his face reassuringly reflected in the driving mirror, has driven him for four hours over rough concrete highways that flipped rhythmically under the tyres, unravelled straight ahead into the haze, flashing him past fields containing withered corn-stalks and rooting hogs, past sorghum mills and Burmah shave signs, past the Wishy Washy and the Dreme-Ez Motel, to deposit him on this wooden sidewalk, here. 'Okay, pal, which is it?' asks J. L. Gruner. William points out his big Antler suitcase, his little boxed typewriter, with their new airline labels; Gruner puts them out onto the sidewalk. 'Thank you,' says William. 'Or righty,' says Gruner, then he climbs back into the bus and, from the operator's seat, clangs shut the big aluminium, or rather aluminum, for we are there not here, door. The diesel engine whirs; the bus moves, circles the square again, finds an exit, and takes off into the great American steppeland.

William stands, beside his luggage, on the pigeon dung, in the dust, in his brown suit, holding his mackintosh. He is there, here. This is his beginning. He sniffs the smell, tastes the air, of the town. It has a faded, dusty note, as if generations of farmhands have shaken out their coveralls in the little square. Around it are two-storey buildings in wood and brick. There is a J. C. Penney, a Woolworth, a Floresheim Shoe, a McDonald Hamburger, a gas station with a sign saying 'We really are very friendly' and no people, and seven parking meters. A big dog lopes down the gutter. A cat comes out of J. C. Penney. A person laughs somewhere in Lee's Diner. Somewhere out there Nixon is President. The marquee of the tiny movie house advertises *I Was a Teenage Embalmer*. The Pentagon Papers have appeared in the *New York Times*. A sign on the novelty store says 'Worms'. They are having a war in Vietnam. They are having a sale on hoes at J. C. Penney. William goes on standing; he is here, such as it is. Somewhere in this town, if it is the right town and not the wrong town, there is a state university; the university has many students and a library containing the papers of many famous writers, none of whom have ever lived here. At that university, if it is here, and not there, William will teach Freshman Composition, a course in existential awareness and the accurate use of the comma. But is it here? On the steps of the courthouse, in the sunlight, a row of elderly farmers in faded denim coveralls sits; they have been there all the time, watching William unblinkingly. William, one eye on his luggage left on the sidewalk, moves, crosses over to them. They inspect him as he comes: the suit, the mackintosh, the longish red hair. William stops before them; he says, to the oldest and so presumably the wisest, 'Excuse me, please.' 'What's that, boy?' asks the man, spitting into the dust. 'Do you know,' asks William, looking around, a mystification on his face, 'where I can find the university?' The man screws his eyes, thinks for a moment, spits again, and says: 'Didn't know it was lost, son.' His eyes glaze, cackles come from the others, and the courthouse pigeons drop dung around the outer edges of the encounter, plainspeaking America triumphing over fancy Europe.

William, standing there, knows himself. He is not a naïf. He has read widely in literature and profited emotionally from the experience. He has taken all the lesser drugs, has had two mistresses, and assisted one of them through a neurotic abortion. He has travelled as far as Turkey, has a good graduate student knowledge of structuralism; he has been hit by a policeman with a truncheon at a political demonstration in London, been in a sit-in, and written two pop songs. He has not been to America before, but has been Americanized, by cultural artefacts and universal modernization, and he knows it by image and by instinct. He has read America in many books. He has a part-written thesis in his luggage, on the disjunctive city in contemporary American fiction, and he has libertarian intentions. He has even come here hoping to find a little bit more of himself, to extend his being beyond its present circumscriptions and circumference. He has existential expectations, based on self-knowledge and sex. But he knows he is resident in a very old story: only I myself am novel, he thinks, the experience is not. Nixon is President. There are the Pentagon Papers. The Vietnam war, against which he has protested, goes on. There are black ghettos, poverty programmes, corruptions and conspiracies; actuality is continually outdoing our talents. History is moving apace, and is everywhere; the simple literary redemptions are hard to sustain. He wants more, deserves more, than a replay of old fictions, a plain and simple reality. 'Great, thanks,' he says, and walks back across the street to his lonely baggage on the sidewalk. But what, he thinks, next?

'Hey,' shouts one of the other farmers, pointing down the street. About half a block down, in front of Sears Roebuck, there is a cab, with a sign on the side saying 'Schuler Taxi'; it was not there before. The driver sits inside and watches William unmovingly; he watches as he carries his heavy bag and his little case, the mackintosh over the shoulder, down the sidewalk. He watches, through the mirror, as William opens the rear door and lifts the luggage inside. 'Baggage goes in the trunk,' he says, when William is finished. 'In the boot?' asks William. 'In the trunk,' says the man. It is an ancient terminological game they are playing, thinks William, as he heaves out the bag and puts it in the binominal place, the rehearsal, a million times in, of a traditional, weary encounter; the lousy part is it also strains the back. 'Whar to?' asks the man, when William is back in the cab. William hands him the slip of paper that has been sent to him, back in England, stating his dormitory reservation, exhausted with dialogue. The man starts the cab, tours the square, strikes out into the hinterland. They pass the Astoria Motel, which advertises two for the price of one, and through a residential section where housewives sit on frame porches in mail-order sportswear. 'Whar ya frum, boy?' asks the man. Now there are stone houses with Greek letters over the doors, and young men lying outside them in Ford Mustangs, with their feet over the side. 'England,' says William. There are Victorian semi-churches, covered in red ivy, a large football stadium, a television mast. 'England, huh? Hoity toity,' says the man. There is a long low building outside which students in sweatshirts are throwing a frisbee in great arcs. 'Five dollars,' says the man, 'You'll like it here better.' 'Will I?' says William, finding currency. 'Good.' 'One time we had a mayor of Chicago punched your King George right in the snoot,' says the cabbie. 'You did?' asks William. 'That's history, that's an accurate fact,' says the man, staring incredulously at the quarter William has pressed into his palm as a tip, 'You can look it up in all them books you guys has gotten in that library.' 'I will,' says William, collecting up his luggage. A frisbee whizzes past his ear. 'Some of those fraternity boys,' say the cabbie, admiringly, 'they lay eight, ten girls a week. They get prizes for it.' 'Well earned, no doubt,' says William. 'Don't forget now,' says the cabbie, 'It's better here, so if you don't like it go back where you came from.'

'Ting,' says a voice, as William, carrying his bags, pushes open the door of the graduate dormitory and walks into the hall, 'Ting.' 'I've just arrived from England, fresh to teach Freshman Composition, and I have a room booked here,' says William to a small oriental student in a collegiate sweater, who sits in a small wooden armchair in a cubicle, reading Lemon and Reis, eds., *Russian Formalist Criticism: Four Essays*. 'Ting,' says the student, getting up and shaking his hand. There is a metal bunk bed, an armchair, a small desk, and a lamp on a snaky spiral support, which looks capable of wrapping itself around the arm as you write under its light (a minor symbol, a serpent for the American Eden), in the first-floor room this student leads him to. 'Fine, thanks,' says William. 'Ting,' says the student. William begins to unpack: his clothes, his medicines, his teaching notes, his small flute, his part-thesis, the leather toilet-case given him, with tears at Heathrow, by the girl with the abortion. He sits on the bed. There is a knock at the door. 'Ting,' says the oriental student, 'I take you to where we eat.' But it is evening now: the sun has suddenly withdrawn, leaving a faint chill, and William has been awake for a ridiculous number of hours. He has culture-shock, jet-lag, a coffee hangover, the plasticized remnant of an airline meal knotted in his stomach. He says he will sleep. He finds a bathroom, with no doors on the stalls, and an Arab sitting on one of the bowls. He urinates, returns to his room, undresses, gets into the iron bed. There are a few brief, disorienting images in his head – of a girl in a caftan who sat across the aisle in the jet, of a man in the bus depot in the state capital who asked for a quarter and then, hearing his accent, raised it to fifty cents – such as travellers have to make them feel lonely; but they are purged by unconsciousness, and he is asleep, his red hair on an American pillow.

It is much later, in the middle of the American night, when he wakens to a curious noise. He gets up and, in Winceyette pyjamas, goes to the window. The landscape suddenly judders and explodes; the rural plain which stretches beyond the window is lit by a bright green glare. In it, white barns flash into existence, then expire. A torrential rain is falling. Blackness resumes. 'Cling, cling,' goes a noise. There is a strange hooting and a roaring. The noise, mobile, comes closer. On the right of the blank composition a slowly gyrating, long beam of light appears, its shifting angle casting itself first towards William, then away again. Another green flash lights up the fast-running sky; William realizes that this is abstract realism he is in, and he sees that the shrieking torch is his first American train. It grinds near; it says 'Cling, cling'; it passes hard by the dormitory. As it does so, a bolt snaps down and catches a power sub-station, mounted fecklessly on a pole across the street. It explodes with a flash and a roar. There is a scream, as of pleasure. In the flash, William has seen a human figure. On the grass below his window it stands, a fat naked girl, her legs wide apart, pushing up her loose large breasts to take onto them the impact of the rain. There is a knock at the door. 'Ting,' says a voice. 'Cling cling,' says the train. 'Who?' says William. 'You,' says a voice. 'What is it?' asks William. 'A visit,' says the voice. William goes and opens the door. The little oriental who met him stands there, in shortie pyjamas. 'Bill Ting, your counsellor,' he says. 'You must close lindow. Water coming through floor into my loom downstair.' 'I'm sorry,' says William. 'Also, offplint of article for loo to lead. For English opinion. Source, *Victorian Studies*.' Another pleasured scream shrills from outside. 'Who wrote it?' asks William. 'Ting,' says Ting, 'On Charlotte Blontë.' 'Look, I'll read it tomorrow,' says William, putting the offplint on his desk, 'Goodnight.' He goes back to the window, to shut it. It is entire black outside, too black to see the girl: the storm is subsiding. 'Okay, America,' says William to the dark world beyond the fly-screen, 'we'll let you know.'

William stands in a puddle and closes the window; but the truth is that, despite himself, he is at last impressed. He knows himself under the agency of divine comedians of a somewhat different stamp from those whose work he has always known, new gods with a fancier taste in apocalyptics, quite like those of the modern critics he reads. He is here. What will he do? He will teach freshmen composition, demonstrate the orderly economy of language, the complexities of *langue* and *parole*, cleanse the tools of speech and thought. He will teach wisdom, taste, cultural awareness. 'Ring,' goes the telephone. 'Ting,' says a voice down the wire. 'Lain still come in.' 'Leave me alone,' says William. He stands in the dark, thinking of the girl with the abortion, dark-haired, a little fat, someone he is not sure whether to remember or forget. It is an imperfect image: a photograph into which the light has been let. He stands in the puddle, he feels in a muddle. Somewhere below the typewriter clatters. He gets into bed, he puts down his head. The typewriter reaches the end of a line: 'Ping,' it says. He starts to weep, he goes to sleep.

II

'You seem to be a well set-up, morally earnest young man,' says Fardiman, 'The sort of person who takes literature seriously, and teaches it good. So why worry?' Outside the window, on the grass, blue jays screech offensively. A man with a leaf-collecting machine comes by under the trees, collecting a faint harvest from the first of the fall. Two dogs copulate over by the Business Building. It is a bright fall day; William can see all this from the screened wooden window of the office in Humanities Hall he shares with five other graduate assistants. He has a large desk by the window, a desk with inkstains in the drawers and a large, high-backed, swivel chair. William is grieving. He has been teaching now for just over a week, and has met all his classes, twice, in the Chemistry Building, his hands dangling loosely in the pedagogic sink, or absent-mindedly turning on the gas-taps, as he stares outward at the massive ethnic mix of the faces before him. Overcoming timidity, if not terror, he has begun work; he has told them where his office is, writing a map on the board so they can all find him, and where the library is, and where they are; he has asked them to write for him the first theme on the official schedule, on the demanding topic of 'My Home Town'. Now these themes have come in, deposited in a pocket outside his office door; he is marking them now. Fardiman sits at the next desk, writing a report for the graduate seminar on Milton he is taking; he keeps a copy of the *Kama Sutra* on his desk and a jar of apple cake on the bookcase. William is chewing apple cake as he reads. 'I am,' says William, turning to Fardiman, 'I'm a devotee of Leavis, though I disapprove of his culturally right-wing position, and also his interpretation of *Women In Love*. I'm also into semiotics, and I'm somewhat influenced by Frank Kermode.' 'I was reading his *What's the Sense of an Ending?*' says Fardiman, 'It stirred me in the gut. It gives me faith in my own clerkly scepticism. Now *that*'s what you could use some of, right now.' 'I've read and digested Roland Barthes and the *Tel Quel* school,' says William, 'I'm into Adorno and Horkheimer and revisionist Marxist esthetics. I'm interested in alternative education. I've got a part to play. But, Fardiman, what's it all got to do with essays about "My Home Town"?' 'It's all phenomenological discourse,' says Fardiman, 'Writing degree about twenty below. It has a beginning, a middle and an end, not usually in that order, but this it shares with most modern literature. It adds up to the cumulative fund of words in the universe; and, William, we want those words *right*.' William groans; he pushes the theme he has been reading across onto Fardiman's desk, which, in the cramped space, is up against his own. The theme begins: 'The people which lives in my home town is good folks, bad folks, rich folks, poor folks, white and some black, go to church and not go to church, and many other things.'

Fardiman puts down his apple cake and, picking up a red pen, he looks at the theme. While he reads, William swivels his chair and stares again through the screened window. Blue jays screech. The leaf-collector with the leaf-collector collects the leaves. The dogs are separate and distinct. Along the pathway between Humanities and Business, so ironically juxtaposed, as if by some cynically literary architect, a procession begins. The bells have rung in the classrooms and the students pour along the paths, in bright clothes, the girls making cradles of their arms to carry their textbooks and notecases in. Some of the students, a distinctive group, the girls without bras, the men with long hair and Afros, go by with anti-war placards; there is a political demonstration that day. William has a sense of his pointless little face staring through the dark grilled screens at what they are doing. But he is here to read what they have written, which seems to bear no resemblance to what they are doing, to have no connection with these minds and bodies. 'It's not a great start,' says Fardiman, putting down the theme, 'But how would you have started it?' 'It's not *my* home town,' says William, 'There are all kinds of ways to start a piece about a town, if you want to start one.' 'Talk to him,' says Fardiman, 'Try to get him to do it more personally. But there's real potential here.' 'There is?' asks William, staring at Fardiman. 'Sure there is. This kid is a comma artist. I know it doesn't sound much, with the world the way it is, and *Tel Quel* the way it is, but those are real good commas.' William looks at Fardiman, who has marched on the Pentagon, and reads Illich, and will refuse to be drafted; and he sees no light. 'Don't be anxious,' says Fardiman, 'It's your task to take these self-satisfied, super-sensual oafs and lead them, through the study of sentences, into becoming mature, questioning, critical, politically alert individuals like ourselves.' 'With better hang-ups,' says William. 'Right,' says Fardiman. 'Alternatively, I guess, you could move, yourself, in the other direction, and have fun.'

William looks out of the window. The trees on campus start to turn brown, orange, and maroon, in a brilliant fall display. The air grows colder. The leaf-collector collects many a leaf. William puts on thicker clothes, and goes out to the few student bars that serve the specially diluted beer that will protect them. He goes to the McDonald Hamburger stand, and to graduate student parties to smoke pot, and to political meetings. He writes letters home to the girl with the abortion, and washes his clothes in the laundry down in the basement of the graduate dormitory, shown the way by Ting. He eats Fardiman's apple cake and grades many themes. He stands behind his desk in the Chemistry Building, three days a week, and tells his students about Carnaby Street and the Portobello Road. He goes to the Teaching Round Table, where all the graduate assistants sit around a square table and discuss their problems, about grading themes, about flunking students who might be drafted, about why are we here, about the falling jobs market. Sensing an over-devotion to diurnal reality among his students, even the politically active ones, he tries to find his way to truth by perplexing them with complexity of fictions, reading them Nabokov, Coover, Barthelme, asking why writers write like that. 'Finks,' says one student, Miss Armfelt, an energetic little girl who interrupts his classes by asking him about their relevance, abusing Nixon, talking about the Third World, speaking for Women's Rights, condemning the conformity of the course, the use-lessness of education, the corruption of grades, 'Escapers.' William likes his students, more than he likes most of his colleagues; the trouble is he is unsure how close he should get to them. Taking one or two of the co-eds on dates, he feels a vague inhibition, a guilt: the start of a professional conscience. He does not touch them; they stare at him. Once he asks Miss Armfelt, but she tells him dates are a fake ritual, part of the heterosexual conformity she repudiates. For safety's sake, then, William redirects his emotional ambitions; he has an affair with a graduate girl, also teaching freshmen composition. Strangely, it seems that some diminution of sexual attractiveness is an entry qualification for graduate school. Miss Daubernethy is not like the co-eds; she is tough and fairly charmless, a dark girl with a mole on her cheek, whom he meets in the basement of the dormitory, while observing one night the whirl of his socks and undershorts as they spin behind the thick bubble of glass, and to whom he makes all unwit-tingly, an obscene suggestion: for he asks, as they stand drinking Coke together, on the wet floor in the windowless room, smelling of washing powder and drying clothes, whether she could possibly sew a button on his shirt. 'Christ,' says Miss Daubernethy, staring at him in anger, 'I'm not a homemaker. I'm a graduate student. I'm not a woman, pal. I'm a person.' 'Of course, right,' says William, 'I believe in all that. I wasn't trying to rôle-type you, honestly. I'd have asked anybody.' 'Oh, sure. Anybody who's historically supposed to be seen around with a needle,' the girl said, 'Like a woman. Come on, how come you picked on me?' William is aghast with his own guilt, glimpsing the darkness of his unconscious chauvinism. 'Oh God,' he says, 'I'm sorry.' It can of course only have one consequence: it is not very long after this – in fact later that night – that, person to person, with

William abased, they are making love on the metal bunk bed in his room, while Ting goes ping below.

The winter outside the office window gets colder, and all is not well. Miss Daubernethy, who comes from Florida, is shrill, tastes of Listerine, and not quite William's ideal type, or the sort of person he would have picked in the free and open market. He knows, and fears she does, that she is a surrogate for the fancy, fresh, forbidden bodies in his classes, for the flashing legs and mobile nipples under sweaters, such as Miss Armfelt's sweater, that he finds himself staring at as he stands over the sink in the Chemistry Building, and talks about the use and significance of tenses. Miss Daubernethy is thirty, tight around the jaw, and has cramps because of the tension of her PhD orals. She wears long dresses to hide her legs, and has exhibitionistic tastes in lovemaking, liking to pleasure herself, by seeing herself or doing things to herself, which is spiriting at first, but somehow basically uncooperative, and not very easy in her or William's dormitory room, or in the back of her Willy jeep. She has an overhung bottom, stout thighs and there are more moles round her waist. There is an old myth in these matters to which William has subscribed: that American women have outrun the world in establishing an intense level of sensation for themselves in sex. William, having had too much of the over-domesticated British variety, feels that this should have its potential for him, its high compensations. Yet, with Miss Daubernethy, as the weeks go by, it seems not to. He touches and rubs and kisses, they move and wriggle and sweat, but the challenging athletics gradually acquire not the tone of an existential liberation, a Reichian fulfilment, but rather of a vulgarly inflated achievement, like trying to play a Beethoven quartet with ten musicians, for better sound. A certain fleshly exhaustion begins to come over William, and something more: I'm a humanist, he thinks to himself. As he sits in his office by day, writing B, and D, and F on essays, and noting at the end of them 'Shows improvement', 'This could be better developed', 'You get to the point too quickly', he feels unease, knowing that his own beginnings, middles and ends, his paragraphing and spacing, his use of the colon, will be similarly flatly measured by Miss Daubernethy's idealized grading system. The students get very anxious about these grades: 'Do you grade on the curve?' they come and ask, 'Do you give As for the best work you get from us, or do you only give them for, like, *Middlemarch*?' Miss Daubernethy in the dormitory room, lying across his armchair, feet splayed and apart, crotch high, raises a similar problem in standards: 'You're okay, you're as good as anyone I've had, to be fair, but you're not as good as the ones I'll get.' William grows haunted by these Joyces, Prousts, and Manns of sex. Back in the office, he tells the kids who come and sit in his consultation chair, 'It's not an abstract best. There are rules and good habits, which I'm trying to teach you. But it's a humanist affair, the best from you, the fullest insight out of you.' Back in the dormitory room, William, lying naked on top of Miss Daubernethy's desk, the sweat on his brow, and the inexorable large thighs dominant above, says: 'Do you think sex can ever become personal?' 'I want you back up higher and your knees more together,' says Miss Daubernethy, monstrous against the light, ultimately and in all a teacher. 'I want your adjectives spaced out more and your verbs more together,' she is saying, in conference in her office, in the light of the snaky desk lamp, when William comes by to fetch her for a meal – for they eat too – the following night.

The winter grows colder still, and all is worse. One night, in her dormitory room, while Miss Daubernethy paints her nipples with silver nail varnish in the light of the desk lamp, William, naked on her bed, finds a large sharp knife under her pillow. 'What's this?' he asks. 'You shouldn't have found that,' says Miss Daubernethy, and starts to cry. William feels a little twinge of terror: 'What were you going to *do*?' he asks. 'I don't know, I think I must be going lesbian. I can't tell you how the shape of a man's body gets me disgusted. I hate you *there*.' Then her nails come flying across the room and she is lunging for the knife. The door is locked but William turns the knob, flies out into the corridor. Happily he still holds the knife. There are long, long corridors back to his room, on the other side of the building. But William makes it in a hurry, seen only by Mr Ting, a cool person, who stands contemplatively in the passage, evincing only a modest clerkly scepticism at the sight of his nudity, his knife, his panting terror. He locks his door and leans against it, feeling for the first time not the chance and arbitrary nature, but rather the utter precious sanctity, of his male equipment. Is this the lesson? 'You need to cut down your ending,' Miss Daubernethy, unchanged, is saying in her office next day, as William goes in, interrupting a conference, to ask for his clothes back. The clothes turn up in the garbage can in the basement, just by the washing machine where they had first met, back there when the weather was by no means so cold.

It is over; and William subsides into an extraordinary fleshy disgust, thinking over without pleasure the detailed, intimate construction of her body and sensing an ultimate deceit in what the flesh, with all its promises, actually contains. But it is not over, for Miss Daubernethy is omnipresent. She starts wearing sexy clothes, and appears by his side during the break in the Teaching Round Table, when they all stand in the corridor drinking Cokes, saying: 'It was nothing personal, William. It's not because I don't like you or anything. It was just because you're a man.' 'Anyone who's historically supposed to be seen around with a prick,' says William. 'That's chauvinism too.'

In the Victorian Novel seminar, on the very day he is due to read his paper on *Jane Eyre*, Miss Daubernethy comes into the class and sits beside him, though she is not enrolled for the seminar, being a medievalist. 'Any comments?' asks the professor, when he has finished. 'I just love your penis,' whispers Miss Daubernethy. 'Do we all agree about the symbolism of the blocked up window?' asks the professor. 'You can't have it,' whispers William. 'Narrative strategy?' asks the professor. 'I want to feel it inside me,' whispers Miss Daubernethy, looking heated. 'How do we relate this to the symbolic emasculation of Mr Rochester?' asks the professor. 'Now,' says Miss Daubernethy. 'Do you?' says William, looking around at the rest of the class taking notes. 'With or without me attached?'

At the faculty picnic in early December she appears round the other side of a tree by the icy lakeside, holds onto his coat, and says: 'Funny dark things can happen, William. I was crazy. But I'm through it now. You have to be with me again, because I think of you all the time.' William looks at her, thinks of her disgust, and then of his, inspects the body with no appeal, the body which is supposed to render us everything. 'I'm really sorry,' says William, 'But I'm really way into celibacy now. I want to try that for a bit.' 'No,' says Miss Daubernethy, pushing him into the lake. Two deans and three fully tenured professors are needed to get him dripping out. He is taken back by a Swinburne specialist and put into his dormitory bed. In the following days his throat seizes up and, after two croaking classes, speech becomes impossible. He goes to the campus hospital and lies feverish between clean, antiseptic sheets, while beautiful white-clad nurses inject penicillin into his bottom. Sometimes, hot, he thinks he sees Miss Daubernethy peering in through his room window, but only Fardiman comes inside, bearing the *New York Review of Books*. When he is better, it is Christmas, the festive season, and the students

298 have gone home; happily Fardiman is there, with his old Studebaker, proposing, for his family have gone east for the break to New York City, that they both go off on a healthy vacation together. They drive south, William's mind clearing under Spanish moss. They leave behind the cold and the snowfalls. On Christmas day he sits on the porch of a motel in the sunlight, watching pelicans, farcical birds, ungainly and unadapted, revelling in their own absurdity.

III

After Christmas, with only a little more of the semester still to go, the snow piles up on the window sill of William's office, from which the screens had gone, and there is a curious change of atmosphere in his classes. He has been, with his little English radicalism, and his fancy talk about fictions, a popular teacher, but now someone steals his nameplate from the door of the office, and the students come in to complain about grades he has been giving them. There is a politics about grades, but it is a curious politics. There is the problem of the draftees, which would have been simple (William has been putting brackets, and commas, in for them right through the course), were there not also, subjunctively, the problem of the girls, and the problem of the footballers, and the problem of the blacks, and the problem of the fraternity boys. 'What did she mean when she said she'd do anything to get an A?' asks William, as a girl who has plagiarized an essay, having submitted for him a copied-out article from *Reader's Digest*, entitled 'One of Nature's Wonders: The Mighty Bee', leaves his consultancy chair, right by his desk, and departs angrily from the office. 'She means *anything*,' says Fardiman, 'She'll use what she's got, and what she's got isn't in her head.' 'I thought that's what she meant,' says William. 'I wonder whether you could take a moment or two to talk to me about a few of my themes,' says Mr Krutch, coming in; Mr Krutch sits in the front row of William's class with his feet up on the teaching desk, sometimes with vaguely insulting messages – like 'Limey' – written on the soles. 'Sure,' says William. 'I wonder whether there's any rational explanation of the grades you gave them,' says Mr Krutch, 'Or whether you're just plain crazy.' 'I could be,' says William. 'Look,' says Mr Krutch, 'this theme was handed in by another guy to another teacher. He gave it a B, you gave it a D. How come?' 'Maybe you didn't copy it out very well when you were plagiarizing it,' says William. 'What do I have to do to get good grades from you?' asks Mr Krutch, 'Stand on my head? Play the piano with my ass? I'm just a nice, ordinary guy. I'm not so different than anyone else on this campus.' 'From,' says William, 'We did different from.' 'Tell him goodbye, and Happy New Year,' says Fardiman. An hour later the football coach is in to plead for Dubchek, who has submitted an essay called 'The Function of Criticism at the Present Time', an argument so complete that it even concludes with the name Matthew Arnold. Fortunately there is Miss Armfelt, who comes next, dark, intense, with no bra, a city girl. She has been getting As right through the course. 'Another A,' says William, handing her theme back to her with relief. 'So what?' says Miss Armfelt, putting her Mexican totebag down on the desk, and putting the folded theme, with William's red A on it, inside it, 'Grades are crap.' 'That's right,' says Fardiman, leaning back, 'Take Hester Prynne. She got an A, and look what happened to her.' Miss Armfelt looks coolly at him. 'Grades are repression,' she says, 'Grammar's repression. All true creativity transcends rules.' 'So does all true stupidity,' says Fardiman, eating apple cake. 'I wondered if I could have a private word with you, Mr Honeywell,' says Miss Armfelt. 'Sure, I'll go to the john for a minute,' says Fardiman, 'Since you're already getting As.' 'Oh, it's not about *grades*,' shouts Miss Armfelt after him, 'Screw grades.' When Fardiman has gone, she says: 'It's just a crazy thought. We were wondering – we is myself and Laura Ann Dix, she's my room-mate and she's in your section too, you know? – we thought you looked kind of bushed. We both enjoyed your classes. So, like to say thank you, we thought we'd ask if you'd like to stop round at our place sometime for a drink. And one thing we *won't* talk about is grades.' 'That's very human,' says William, 'Sure I'll come.' 'Tomorrow night around eight?' 'Fine,' says William. 'They're even crowding round the doors of the faculty john,' says Fardiman, when he comes back, 'Hoping to catch us unbuttoned.'

The next day William posts one set of his final grades on his office door and locks himself in. He can hear the students outside, reading the grades and banging on the door. He has been infinitely generous, a compromise between the system and his politics, but indignation is rife: 'We know you're in there,' voices shout. Towards evening he creeps out down the ill-lit hall and, his coat-collar turned up, eats a hamburger at the hamburger stand, before going to Miss Armfelt's. He crosses the campus. Some black students, sitting-in in the computer block, have started a fire. Outside a dormitory, boys in red Ford

Thunderbirds are shouting to girls to come away with them to the West Coast. William reaches the tree-shaded streets just off campus, with ploughed snow stacked on the sidewalk, and finds Miss Armfelt's place, a small basement entrance below a frame house. He taps on the door. 'Come on in,' someone shouts. Some freak music is on the record player. 'Hi,' says Miss Armfelt, wearing her swimsuit and sitting on an exercise bicycle in the middle of the room, pedalling busily, 'I'll be through in a minute.' Laura Ann Dix, whom William knows, sits on the sofa, next to a brown retriever, which growls at him. 'Stay, Fidel,' says Laura Ann. 'Fix some beer, eh?' says Miss Armfelt, peddling on, 'There's some in the icebox.' 'I'll get it,' says William. 'Let me, you talk to Ellie,' says Laura Ann. William leans against a bookcase and watches Miss Armfelt getting up real speed. 'You don't need exercise,' he says. 'I wish I had one of those exercise pogo sticks, with a pedometer on it,' says Miss Armfelt. 'And another one for the dog?' asks William, 'Why do you need exercise?' 'It's for the bodily pleasure,' says Miss Armfelt, 'Hey get me a cigar, will you? Right there in that box, Mr Honeywell.' 'William,' says William, getting a cigar and slipping it between Miss Armfelt's pert lips. 'How's that for symbolic action,' says William. 'They're illegal Havanas,' says Miss Armfelt, 'I guess it keeps *him* in business.'

'How come we have so much light?' says Laura Ann, bringing in the cans of beer. She switches lights out and others on, leaving a paper Japanese lampshade hanging low over the end of the sofa, and a tiny intense-light desklamp on the coffee table. William picks up a matchbook and lights Miss Armfelt's cigar. 'Get one,' says Miss Armfelt. 'She'll be through in a minute,' says Laura Ann, 'Come and sit on the sofa with me.' William sits down. 'Doesn't it drive you crazy, teaching this crazy course?' asks Laura Ann. 'It wouldn't, if all the kids were as bright as you.' 'I look at you sometimes, standing there, and I keep thinking, what he must be thinking! But you never get mad.' 'I really would just once like to see you really let fly,' says Ellie Armfelt. 'It'll happen,' says William. 'But you must have such a good level of consciousness,' says Laura Ann. William laughs and says: 'I'm a stranger. Maybe what sounds commonplace to you doesn't to me.' 'Oh, but the things they tell you,' says Laura Ann, 'They make up things because they think you'll believe it.' 'He knows that,' says Ellie, 'I keep wanting to interrupt, but I say to myself, he knows that.' 'I loved the way you put down that W A S P kid who was talking about dates,' says Laura Ann. 'What's that?' asks Ellie. 'Oh, she was saying she gave a boy her right breast on the first date, and her left breast on the second date, and he said, it was funny, what happens on the third, don't you run out of breasts?' They all laugh. 'We really enjoy your classes. You're the most interesting teacher I ever had.' 'You haven't had him,' says Laura Ann. '*You* haven't had him,' shouts Ellie Armfelt. Laura Anna laughs, and then pushes her face against William's. He kisses it. Miss Armfelt suddenly gets off the exercise bicycle and disappears into the kitchen space. Laura Ann surfaces out of William's arms and says: 'What are you doing, Ellie?'

'I just had a great idea, let's have some tequila,' shouts Ellie. Laura Ann's face pushes back into William's. 'She'll be a minute, let's have a first date and a second date.' William's hand goes in under her blouse and slides up over her right breast; she presses it into her and he feels the fluttering stir in his palm. 'Wait,' she says, and pulls off the blouse. Her brown body is under the light from the Japanese lantern, and William feels at last the waning of his physical aversion that Miss Daubernethy had left with him. His hands run up her, and then a voice says: 'Me too,' and there is Ellie Armfelt by him, swimsuit off, naked. William feels a splendid, relaxed sense of benison, of plurality of gifts. The record player switches over to Beethoven. Now Laura Ann is out of her skirt and her hands are on his body, pushing aside his shirt. Ellie Armfelt is working on the trousers. 'I thought,' says William, 'you were lesbian.' Miss Armfelt leans over Laura Ann and William and hugs them together, kissing both their faces. Laura Ann is pulling his body round to reach it with her mouth. Ellie Armfelt puts a breast against his face. William can hardly see, but he knows there is another girl in the room. The impression is so hazy that it almost drifts past him. But there she is, near the bicycle, holding up a square black box. 'Who's that?' asks William. 'That's our other room-mate,' whispers Ellie, 'She's in your class too.' The flashbulb goes off, leaving a glaring residue of light in William's retina, showing him, vividly, the breasts against his face, like the breasts of the fat girl he saw on the grass in the electric storm. She was graceless; he has an instinct of the gracelessness of these bodies too, but the shudder is coming up him. There is another flash of light, and another, and another. The girl with the camera comes nearer for a moment. She says, politely, 'Why, hi, Mr Honeywell,' and then she goes away.

IV

There is an envelope, almost expected, lying under the door of William's office when he gets there early the next morning. He has slept well in his dormitory bedroom, post-coitally tired, and then, waking up towards dawn, has thought of this, getting up soon after the light came to come over and check. But they have been up early too. He carries the envelope, with his name on it, the handwriting recognizable from themes, to his desk. He opens it up and takes out the single Polaroid print, with its whirl of bodies and its central, naked Honeywell, and then the sheet of folded theme-paper, with its long message. It says:

Dear William,

This is to thank you for last night. Oh boy are you a swinger. It really was a good scene. Take a look at the photo. Isn't it great? It was taken by a friend, Delise Roche, who shares our pad too. I guess you saw her when she stopped by. She's a really keen photographer, and a friend. Please remember. This is all part of the fun we have had, and a wonderful way of us all remembering it for all time. It was a swell evening, and I know I will always want to remember it. I hope you will come around again, 'for a drink', I mean it, you're really welcome. Next time we ought to make it a foursome. I mean, you really ought to meet Delise. She's a really good friend of Laura Ann and I. You will know her, she's in your Comp. class too, a different section than us. A great kid with a problem. Her problem is that she has been working really hard 'for the cause', active in Civil Rights, anti-war, Women's Lib, etc. and has just not made the grades. Like me, she thinks grades are crap, though I guess her parents would kill her or something if she flunked out of college. Anyway we need her around, on the political front, etc. A great girl. Photography's her bag right now. She says a photograph is truer than words, and I guess she's right. It's typical of her that she takes these photographs of us just for fun, and for keepsake. Not to do anything with them. Show them to anyone, I mean. What grade are you giving her in Comp, William? Hey, you have a great body, William. See you maybe? Yours with affection, really,

Ellie.

Williams sits at the desk. He scratches at a body bite and reads the letter through carefully, twice more, trying to penetrate it. It is a crisp and beautiful morning, and through the window he can see the sun bringing out red glitter on the new snow that has dusted the campus, in the small hours after he got back to his room. An innocent morning. The fire seems out now in the computing complex. He stares at the photograph, with its sticky surface and falsified colours, at the image of himself from outside, alienating, gross, yet retrieving the doings already hazy now in his head. There is a footstep out in the hallway. A key turns in the lock. 'I already opened it,' shouts William. 'My,' says Fardiman, coming inside in red earmuffs, 'And I thought I was early.' 'I couldn't sleep,' says William. 'I've got some more grades to turn in,' says Fardiman, hanging up his coat, 'I've been reading themes all night. I'm so tired. I start to think the way they do. In unattached subordinate clauses. Like this.'

'Can you bear to read one more?' asks William. 'Only for a real friend,' says Fardiman, sitting down at the desk and taking off the earmuffs. William throws the photograph and the letter onto the stack of papers on his desk. 'Look at the photograph first,' he says. Fardiman looks, and whistles. 'You should make the sex magazines with this one,' he says. 'I like it, but I'd question whether you can count it in your list of publications.' 'It was taken by a student,' says William. 'Well, I like the way the guy has got this bicycle wheel in the foreground, to give perspective.' 'Now the letter,' says William, 'Read it carefully, for tone.' 'For tone, heh?' says Fardiman, automatically picking up the red pen from his desk, and making marks as he goes through the document. When he has finished he says: 'Well, William, I think it's got a lot of tone. I told you if you taught these kids properly they'd learn to write relevant prose.' 'You did,' says William, 'What do you think it means?' 'Well,' says Fardiman, 'We could have a graduate seminar on this one. Indeed it's better than *Moll Flanders*. If read at the level of innocence, she likes you, William. She's a sentimental girl, given to reminiscence. If read for irony, with the methods of the New Criticism, hunting for paradox and ambiguity, I'd say she's got you. It's a rhetorical technique called blackmail.' 'How do we determine which?' 'I have a feeling it's one of those occasions where the intrinsic approach fails us. Where we turn to contextual factors, like are there more photographs.' 'I think she took four,' says William. 'Of course, they may not all have come out,' says Fardiman, 'but that would affect my reading of the text.' 'Yes,' says William, 'Fardiman, am I in a bad position?' Fardiman looks at the photograph: 'It looks quite a good position,' he says. 'With the university,' says William. 'Oh, with the university,' says Fardiman, 'That depends what you want to do, in the future. These are permissive times.' 'This permissive?' asks William. 'What *are* your career plans?' asks Fardiman. 'I'd like to stay on here a couple of years, and get my Master's, and then take a university post, if there are any around then. Here, or in England. I've been thinking about it a lot. I like teaching.' 'William,' says Fardiman, looking at Honewell in despair, 'why pick a future like that at a time like this?' 'No?' asks William. 'No,' says Fardiman.

William sits for a minute, and thinks. The sun is coming up over the snow, and the early students are going to eight o'clock class. He says: 'You really think if she sent these photographs to anyone, I'd be in difficulties.' 'There's still a professional code, especially for guys without tenure,' says Fardiman, 'If she sends them to our Department Chairman, I'd think your chances of a renewal next year, or a good reference on your placement file, sort of low. Like around zero. If she really papers the town, and sends them to the Regent and the President, it might be wise to have a booking on the next flight home. On the other hand, if she keeps them in her purse, and looks at them occasionally, with a fond smile for the teacher she once had, then you'll have a sweetness following you for the rest of your days.' 'I suppose I could, at a pinch, argue that I'm human like everyone else,' says William. 'What kind of an excuse is that?' asks Fardiman, 'The plea of the rogue throughout the ages.' 'It could happen to any of us,' says William, 'I didn't really do anything. It was all done to me. And it happens all over, Fardiman.' 'I know,' says Fardiman, 'But you got caught.' 'I could tell the whole story.' 'Then all four of you would get fired. You could run away and make blue movies together.' William sits and stares at his desk, at the list of grades he has given. He inspects the list; Delise Roche has a D. Not even an F. Just a D. 'Fardiman,' he says, 'How will it end?' Fardiman looks sadly at him. 'I'm sorry, William,' he says, 'You have to write your own ending.' 'Do you think,' says William tentatively, 'I should raise Miss Roche's grade? We raised grades for the draftees, for the blacks. She's been working for them.' 'I would never advise it under any circumstances,' says Fardiman, 'But my mother, that old fiend, my mother would raise Miss Roche's grade.' 'I'd never do it at home,' says William. 'You'd never do *that* at home, would you?' asks Fardiman, tapping the photograph, 'I guess we all do things away from home we wouldn't do at home. And since most of us are never at home we're always doing things we would never do.' 'Fardiman,' says William, 'if I do it, and keep my job, I wouldn't feel fit to keep the job I was keeping.' 'I said you were a well set-up, morally earnest fellow,' says Fardiman, 'and they always get screwed. Of course, we could be screwing ourselves.'

William looks at Fardiman, wondering. 'We're complex people,' says Fardiman, 'that's our training. We're always reading for necessity, design, structure, plot.' 'It's quite a plot,' says William. 'But are we missing innocence? Maybe it's contingent, not necessary, as Kermode would say. Maybe this letter's a pristine, guileless thing, all this while. A statement of modern love.' 'Can it be?' asks William. Fardiman gets up from his desk and goes to his jar of apple cake. 'We find it hard to believe. I mean, what's personal now? In bed my wife is a political agent, a minor functionary for the woman revolution. My kids rip off cookies from the refrigerator and call it an anti-capitalist gesture. But people *do* do loving things.' 'But how do we find out?' 'Well, how do we? Do we really know about ourselves? You could go and see her.' 'These grades go into the office at nine,' says William, 'then they go in the computer, unless it's all burned up.' 'There's always another computer,' says Fardiman, 'I'm sorry, William, I don't think you can know. Here we are: we've read Leavis and Kermode, and *Tel Quel* and Marcuse. We're lost souls on the historical turn. But, we say, we know how to read. Then here's a text, offering two worlds, one glowing with fleshy promiscuities, one tainted with the harsh corruption of interest, okay, radical interest, and what happens? We can offer multiple interpretations. We can see it psycho-linguistically and socio-linguistically. We can find the apocalyptic figure and the low mimetic type. We can note its thematic constituents, like Delise, photography, politics, grades. We can observe in it the post-modernist or the McLuhanite emphasis on the visual as opposed to the verbal or linear mode, right? We can read it as Sontagian erotics. The only thing we can't say is whether she got you round there to try a bit of Sontagian erotics herself on that nice British body of yours, or to shake you down for a safe passing B for this Delise. We can't *read* it, William. Or, in a phrase, penetrate the literal level of this reality.'

And so there sits William Honeywell, who came here on the Greyhound bus and stood in the courthouse square, in his high-back swivel chair, looking out at the snow. It has been the coldest night on record in this little Mid-Western town, with its rich folks and its poor folks, its go to church and its not go to church, two hundred miles south of the state capital, where they keep all the money and the record of accurate time. On the literal level of William's reality, it is seventeen minutes past or after eight, and his grades are due at nine. Can there be a knock on the door, Miss Armfelt come by to say that it is all for love? He sits and sits, staring at the path between Humanities and Business. Fardiman, with a red pen, marks.

V A

There is a knock at the door. Fardiman goes and opens it. 'Happy New Year,' he says to whomever is outside. 'Is Mr Honeywell there?' asks a voice. 'He's gone to Chicago, Mr Krutch,' says Fardiman, 'the Windy City.' 'I have to see him about my grades,' says Krutch. 'Come back another day, when once more he's not here,' says Fardiman. 'There's someone breathing back there,' says Krutch, 'He's there.' 'No, there's no one breathing,' says Fardiman, 'If I let you in here, you wouldn't see anybody, but I won't. You've got to learn to take words on trust.' 'Oh, *sure*, Mr Fardiman,' says Krutch, unconvinced. 'Goodbye now,' says Fardiman. William breathes: he reads, and then rereads, the letter. He takes up the red marking pen from his desk. From under the letter he takes out the computerized mark-sheet. He runs his eye down it, finds a name and, with the pen, he makes a small alteration. Then he picks up the letter, tears it, and throws it into the wastebasket. 'How about keeping the photograph?' asks Fardiman, 'A sweet reminiscence. Something gained, however momentary.' William reaches in his pocket and brings out a matchbook. It has the name of a motel in Saratoga Springs, N Y, 12866, on it. William stares at it, for he has never in his life been to Saratoga. Then he recalls that he picked it up in Miss Armfelt's basement apartment, to light her cigar. He strikes a match on the matchbook, closing the cover as instructed, and puts the little match to the photograph. It flares, with a smell of chemicals. 'You must come back to New York City and meet my mother,' says Fardiman, coughing in the polluted smoke.

V B

There is a knock at the door. Fardiman crosses the room and opens it. 'Mr Honeywell in?' asks a voice. 'He's gone to Chicago,' says Fardiman, 'Hog butcher, stacker of wheat.' 'I need to talk to him right now about my grades,' says the voice. 'Try again some other time, Mr Krutch,' says Fardiman. 'There are papers rustling in there,' says Krutch, 'I know he's there.' 'It's the wind,' says Fardiman, 'The local mistral. I'm all alone. Okay?' 'I don't know whether I believe you, Mr Fardiman.' 'What's truth?' asks Fardiman, 'What's lies? What are fictions? Where is the literal level of reality? You just go away, huh, Mr Krutch.' 'Metaphysician,' says Mr Krutch, and goes. William releases the papers he is holding: he reads, and reads again, the letter. He takes up the red marking pen from his desk. He goes carefully through the letter once more, making professional markings on it. He underlines the phrase 'a really good friend of Laura Ann and I' and writes 'error in case'; he underlines the phrase 'a different section than us' and writes 'Not a comparative: different . . . from'. On the bottom he writes: 'You get to the point too slowly' and then 'Two errors carrying full penalization: F.' From his desk drawer, he takes a clean envelope and addresses it to Miss Ellie Armfelt, at her apartment address. 'Sell me a stamp, Fardiman,' he says. Fardiman, marking, reaches in his back pocket and pulls out his black wallet. 'Have it on me,' says Fardiman, and then, 'Let me go down the corridor and mail it. That guy could still be waiting out there, puzzling through the metaphysics.' Fardiman goes, and William sits at his desk, and looks out of the window.

Vc

There is a knock at the door. Fardiman steps across and opens it. 'Oh, hi,' he says. 'Is Mr Honeywell there?' asks a voice. 'He's gone to Pittsburgh,' says Fardiman. 'Oh, I'm sorry,' says a voice, 'My name's Krutch. I just wanted to tell him he's the best teacher I ever had. I really learned from his course. I didn't understand it, but it was really good, you know what I mean? It's funny, there are some teachers who just make everything seem really interesting. I mean, I'm a dull, ordinary guy. I got these terrible grades from him. I may flunk. But who cares? That's not what matters. I'll never forget being taught by him. You know?' 'I'm sure he'll be really glad to have that message,' says Fardiman, 'I'll tell him when I see him.' 'You won't forget?' asks Krutch, 'I mean, if a guy's great, he ought to be told, right?' 'Right, Mr Krutch,' says Fardiman. 'Oh, and a Happy New Year,' says Krutch. 'And to you.' says Fardiman. William reads, and then re-reads, the letter. He takes up the red marking pen from his desk. He takes up a clean sheet of paper and begins writing. 'Dear Ellie,' he writes,

> I can't tell you how good it was to get your letter. It was under my
> door first thing this morning, when I arrived, just what I needed to
> hear. I'd been wondering all night, with the snowstorm going on

outside my window, just how you felt, you and Laura Ann. I mean, it could have been something just casual. Like *Blow Up* or something – did you see that great film? What it meant to me was a breaking down of distances, a real getting close. How these artificial rôles, teacher and student, block out real relationships. I accept your invitation, who wouldn't? I'll be round tomorrow night (I have a paper tonight to finish for my graduate course; I wonder what grade I'll get!). Certainly I'd like to meet Delise. She's right, of course; photography is better than words, as involvement is better than analysis, life better than writing about life. And you're right too, about grades being crap. In fact that whole academic factory atmosphere is crap too. Petty research by petty minds evading everything that's real and alive. Well, you're alive, and you've taught me something. Do you know what your letter made me do? Burn my grade sheets. I guess that's the end of my contract, but who cares? What kind of life is that? I wanted to write songs anyway. Don't take too much exercise before I come. Do you know what I'm doing? I sit at my desk, in a high-back swivel chair, looking out at the snow. I have an incredible, fresh sense of reality. It's a really crisp, beautiful morning, and out through the window I can see people walking in all their peopleness, and the sun bringing out red glitter. . .

'Hey, William, William,' says Fardiman, marking, 'what's all that stuff you're writing?'

*W*EEKEND

By seven-thirty they were ready to go. Martha had everything packed into the car and the three children appropriately dressed and in the back seat, complete with educational games and wholewheat biscuits. When everything was ready in the car Martin would switch off the television, come downstairs, lock up the house, front and back, and take the wheel.

Weekend! Only two hours' drive down to the cottage on Friday evenings: three hours' drive back on Sunday nights. The pleasures of greenery and guests in between. They reckoned themselves fortunate, how fortunate!

On Fridays Martha would get home on the bus at six-twelve and prepare tea and sandwiches for the family: then she would strip four beds and put the sheets and quilt covers in the washing machine for Monday: take the country bedding from the airing basket, plus the books and the games, plus the weekend food – acquired at intervals throughout the week, to lessen the load – plus her own folder of work from the office, plus Martin's drawing materials (she was a market researcher in an advertising agency, he a freelance designer) plus hairbrushes, jeans, spare T-shirts, Jolyon's antibiotics (he suffered from sore throats), Jenny's recorder, Jasper's cassette player and so on – ah, the so on! – and would pack them all, skilfully and quickly, into the boot. Very little could be left in the cottage during the week. ('An open invitation to burglars': Martin) Then Martha would run round the house tidying and wiping, doing this and that, finding the cat at one neighbour's and delivering it to another, while the others ate their tea; and would usually, proudly, have everything finished by the time they had eaten their fill. Martin would just catch the BBC2 news, while Martha cleared away the tea table, and the children tossed up for the best positions in the car. 'Martha,' said Martin, tonight, 'you ought to get Mrs Hodder to do more. She takes advantage of you.'

Mrs Hodder came in twice a week to clean. She was over seventy. She charged two pounds an hour. Martha paid her out of her own wages: well, the running of the house was Martha's concern. If Martha chose to go out to work – as was her perfect right, Martin allowed, even though it wasn't the best thing for the children, but that must be Martha's moral responsibility – Martha must surely pay her domestic stand-in. An evident truth, heard loud and clear and frequent in Martin's mouth and Martha's heart.

'I expect you're right,' said Martha. She did not want to argue. Martin had had a long hard week, and now had to drive. Martha couldn't. Martha's licence had been suspended four months back for drunken driving. Everyone agreed that the suspension was unfair; Martha seldom drank to excess: she was for one thing usually too busy pouring drinks for other people or washing other people's glasses to get much inside herself. But Martin had taken her out to dinner on her birthday, as was his custom, and exhaustion and excitement mixed had made her imprudent, and before she knew where she was, why there she was, in the dock, with a distorted lamp-post to pay for and a new bonnet for the car and six months' suspension.

So now Martin had to drive her car down to the cottage, and he was always tired on Fridays, and hot and sleepy on Sundays, and every rattle and clank and bump in the engine she felt to be somehow her fault.

Martin had a little sports car for London and work: it could nip in and out of the traffic nicely: Martha's was an old estate car, with room for the children, picnic baskets, bedding, food, games, plants, drink, portable television and all the things required by the middle classes for weekends in the country. It lumbered rather than zipped and made Martin angry. He seldom spoke a harsh word, but Martha, after the fashion of wives, could detect his mood from what he did not say rather than what he did, and from the tilt of his head, and the way his crinkly, merry eyes seemed crinklier and merrier still – and of course from the way he addressed Martha's car.

'Come along, you old banger you! Can't you do better than that? You're too old, that's your trouble. Stop complaining. Always complaining, it's only a hill. You're too wide about the hips. You'll never get through there.'

Martha worried about her age, her tendency to complain, and the width of her hips. She took the remarks personally. Was she right to do so? The children noticed nothing: it was just funny lively laughing Daddy being witty about Mummy's car. Mummy, done for drunken driving. Mummy, with the roots of melancholy somewhere deep beneath the bustling, busy, everyday self. Busy: ah so busy!

Martin would only laugh if she said anything about the way he spoke to her car and warn her against paranoia. 'Don't get like your mother, darling.' Martha's mother had, towards the end, thought that people were plotting against her. Martha's mother had led a secluded, suspicious life, and made Martha's childhood a chilly and a lonely time. Life now, by comparison, was wonderful for Martha. People, children, houses, conversations, food, drink, theatres – even, now, a career. Martin standing between her and the hostility of the world – popular, easy, funny Martin, beckoning the rest of the world into earshot.

Ah, she was grateful: little earnest Martha, with her shy ways and her penchant for passing boring exams – how her life had blossomed out! Three children too – Jasper, Jenny and Jolyon – all with Martin's broad brow and open looks, and the confidence born of her love and care, and the work she had put into them since the dawning of their days.

Martin drives. Martha, for once, drowses.

The right food, the right words, the right play. Doctors for the tonsils: dentists for the molars. Confiscate guns: censor television: encourage creativity. Paints and paper to hand: books on the shelves: meetings with teachers. Music teachers. Dancing lessons. Parties. Friends to tea. School plays. Open days. Junior orchestra.

Martha is jolted awake. Traffic lights. Martin doesn't like Martha to sleep while he drives.

Clothes. Oh, clothes! Can't wear this: must wear that. Dress shops. Piles of clothes in corners: duly washed, but waiting to be ironed, waiting to be put away.

Get the piles off the floor, into the laundry baskets. Martin doesn't like a mess.

Creativity arises out of order, not chaos. Five years off work while the children were small: back to work with seniority lost. What, did you think something was for nothing? If you have children, mother, that is your reward. It lies not in the world.

Have you taken enough food? Always hard to judge.

Food. Oh, food! Shop in the lunch-hour. Lug it all home. Cook for the freezer on Wednesday evenings while Martin is at his car-maintenance evening class, and isn't there to notice you being unrestful. Martin likes you to sit down in the evenings. Fruit, meat, vegetables, flour for home-made bread. Well, shop bread is full of pollutants. Frozen food, even your own, loses flavour. Martin often remarks on it. Condiments. Everyone loves mango chutney. But the expense!

London Airport to the left. Look, look, children! Concorde? No, idiot, of course it isn't Concorde.

Ah, to be all things to all people: children, husband, employer, friends! It can be done: yes, it can: super woman.

Drink. Home-made wine. Why not? Elderberries grown thick and rich in London: and at least you know what's in it. Store it in high cupboards: lots of room: up and down the step-ladder. Careful! Don't slip. Don't break anything.

No such thing as an accident. Accidents are Freudian slips: they are wilful, bad-tempered things.

Martin can't bear bad temper. Martin likes slim ladies. Diet. Martin rather likes his secretary. Diet. Martin admires slim legs and big bosoms. How to achieve them both? Impossible. But try, oh try, to be what you ought to be, not what you are. Inside and out.

Martin brings back flowers and chocolates: whisks Martha off for holiday weekends. Wonderful! The best husband in the world: look into his crinkly, merry, gentle eyes; see it there. So the mouth slopes away into something of a pout. Never mind. Gaze into the eyes. Love. It must be love. You married him. *You.* Surely *you* deserve true love?

Salisbury Plain. Stonehenge. Look, children, look! Mother, we've seen Stonehenge a hundred times. Go back to sleep.

Cook! Ah cook. People love to come to Martin and Martha's dinners. Work it out in your head in the lunch-hour. If you get in at six-twelve, you can seal the meat while you beat the egg white while you feed the cat while you lay the table while you string the beans while you set out the cheese, goat's cheese, Martin loves goat's cheese, Martha tries to like goat's cheese – oh, bed, sleep, peace, quiet.

Sex! Ah sex. Orgasm, please. Martin requires it. Well, so do you. And you don't want his secretary providing a passion you neglected to develop. Do you? Quick, quick, the cosmic bond. Love. Married love.

Secretary! Probably a vulgar suspicion: nothing more. Probably a fit of paranoics, à la mother, now dead and gone.
　At peace.
　RIP.
　Chilly, lonely mother, following her suspicions where they led.

Nearly there, children. Nearly in paradise, nearly at the cottage. Have another biscuit.

Real roses round the door.

Roses. Prune, weed, spray, feed, pick. Avoid thorns. One of Martin's few harsh words.

'Martha, you can't not want roses! What kind of person am I married to? An anti-rose personality?'

Green grass. Oh, God, grass. Grass must be mown. Restful lawns, daisies bobbing, buttercups glowing. Roses and grass and books. Books.

Please, Martin, do we have to have the two hundred books, mostly twenties' first editions, bought at Christie's book sale on one of your afternoons off? Books need dusting.

Roars of laughter from Martin, Jasper, Jenny and Jolyon. Mummy says we shouldn't have the books: books need dusting!

Roses, green grass, books and peace.

Martha woke up with a start when they got to the cottage, and gave a little shriek which made them all laugh. Mummy's waking shriek, they called it.

Then there was the car to unpack and the beds to make up, and the electricity to connect, and the supper to make, and the cobwebs to remove, while Martin made the fire. Then supper – pork chops in sweet and sour sauce ('Pork is such a *dull* meat if you don't cook it properly': Martin), green salad from the garden, or such green salad as the rabbits had left ('Martha, did you really net them properly? Be honest now!': Martin) and sauté potatoes. Mash is so stodgy and ordinary, and instant mash unthinkable. The children studied the night sky with the aid of their star map. Wonderful, rewarding children!

Then clear up the supper: set the dough to prove for the bread: Martin already in bed: exhausted by the drive and lighting the fire. ('Martha, we really ought to get the logs stacked properly. Get the children to do it, will you?': Martin) Sweep and tidy: get the TV aerial right. Turn up Jasper's jeans where he has trodden the hem undone. ('He can't go around like *that*, Martha. Not even Jasper': Martin)

Midnight. Good night. Weekend guests arriving in the morning. Seven for lunch and dinner on Saturday. Seven for Sunday breakfast, nine for Sunday lunch. ('Don't fuss, darling. You always make such a fuss': Martin) Oh, God, forgotten the garlic squeezer. That means ten minutes with the back of a spoon and salt. Well, who wants *lumps* of garlic? No one. Not Martin's guests. Martin said so. Sleep.

Colin and Katie. Colin is Martin's oldest friend. Katie is his new young wife. Janet, Colin's other, earlier wife, was Martha's friend.

Janet was rather like Martha, quieter and duller than her husband. A nag and a drag, Martin rather thought, and said, and of course she'd let herself go, everyone agreed. No one exactly excused Colin for walking out, but you could see the temptation.

Katie versus Janet.

Katie was languid, beautiful and elegant. She drawled when she spoke. Her hands were expressive: her feet were little and female. She had no children.

Janet plodded round on very flat, rather large feet. There was something wrong with them. They turned out slightly when she walked. She had two children. She was, frankly, boring. But Martha liked her: when Janet came down to the cottage she would wash up. Not in the way that most guests washed up – washing dutifully and setting everything out on the draining board, but actually drying and putting away too. And Janet would wash the bath and get the children all sat down, with chairs for everyone, even the littlest, and keep them quiet and satisfied so the grown-ups – well, the men – could get on with their conversation and their jokes and their love of country weekends, while Janet stared into space, as if grateful for the rest, quite happy.

Janet would garden, too. Weed the strawberries, while the men went for their walk; her great feet standing firm and square and sometimes crushing a plant or so, but never mind, oh never mind. Lovely Janet; who understood.

Now Janet was gone and here was Katie.

Katie talked with the men and went for walks with the men, and moved her ashtray rather impatiently when Martha tried to clear the drinks round it.

Dishes were boring, Katie implied by her manner, and domesticity was boring, and anyone who bothered with that kind of thing was a fool. Like Martha. Ash should be allowed to stay where it was, even if it was in the butter, and conversations should never be interrupted.

Knock, knock. Katie and Colin arrived at one-fifteen on Saturday morning, just after Martha had got to bed. 'You don't mind? It was the moonlight. We couldn't resist it. You should have seen Stonehenge! We didn't disturb you? Such early birds!'

Martha rustled up a quick meal of omelettes. Saturday nights' eggs. ('Martha makes a lovely omelette': Martin) ('Honey, make one of your mushroom omelettes: cook the mushrooms separately, remember, with lemon. Otherwise the water from the mushrooms gets into the egg, and spoils everything.') Sunday supper mushrooms. But ungracious to say anything.

Martin had revived wonderfully at the sight of Colin and Katie. He brought out the whisky bottle. Glasses. Ice. Jug for water. Wait. Wash up another sinkful, when they're finished. 2 a.m.

'Don't do it tonight, darling.'
'It'll only take a sec.' Bright smile, not a hint of self-pity. Self-pity can spoil everyone's weekend.
Martha knows that if breakfast for seven is to be manageable the sink must be cleared of dishes. A tricky meal, breakfast. Especially if bacon, eggs, and tomatoes must all be cooked in separate pans. ('Separate pans mean separate flavours!': Martin)

She is running around in her nightie. Now if that had been Katie – but there's something so *practical* about Martha. Reassuring, mind; but the skimpy nightie and the broad rump and the thirty-eight years are all rather embarrassing. Martha can see it in Colin and Katie's eyes. Martin's too. Martha wishes she did not see so much in other people's eyes. Her mother did, too. Dear, dead mother. Did I misjudge you?

This was the second weekend Katie had been down with Colin but without Janet. Colin was a photographer: Katie had been his accessorizer. First Colin and Janet: then Colin, Janet and Katie: now Colin and Katie!

Katie weeded with rubber gloves on and pulled out pansies in mistake for weeds and laughed and laughed along with everyone when her mistake was pointed out to her, but the pansies died. Well, Colin had become with the years fairly rich and fairly famous, and what does a fairly rich and famous man want with a wife like Janet when Katie is at hand?

On the first of the Colin/Janet/Katie weekends Katie had appeared out of the bathroom. 'I say,' said Katie, holding out a damp towel with evident distaste, 'I can only find this. No hope of a dry one?' And Martha had run to fetch a dry towel and amazingly found one, and handed it to Katie who flashed her a brilliant smile and said, 'I can't bear damp towels. Anything in the world but damp towels,' as if speaking to a servant in a time of shortage of staff, and took all the water so there was none left for Martha to wash up.

The trouble, of course, was drying anything at all in the cottage. There were no facilities for doing so, and Martin had a horror of clothes lines which might spoil the view. He toiled and moiled all week in the city simply to get a country view at the weekend. Ridiculous to spoil it by draping it with wet towels! But now Martha had bought more towels, so perhaps everyone could be satisfied. She would take nine damp towels back on Sunday evenings in a plastic bag and see to them in London.

On this Saturday morning, straight after breakfast, Katie went out to the car – she and Colin had a new Lamborghini; hard to imagine Katie in anything duller – and came back waving a new Yves St Laurent towel. 'See! I brought my own, darlings.'

They'd brought nothing else. No fruit, no meat, no vegetables, not even bread, certainly not a box of chocolates. They'd gone off to bed with alacrity, the night before, and the spare room rocked and heaved: well, who'd want to do washing-up when you could do that, but what about the children? Would they get confused? First Colin and Janet, now Colin and Katie?

Martha murmured something of her thoughts to Martin, who looked quite shocked. 'Colin's my best friend. I don't expect him to bring anything,' and Martha felt mean. 'And good heavens, you can't protect the kids from sex for ever: don't be so prudish,' so that Martha felt stupid as well. Mean, complaining, and stupid.

Janet had rung Martha during the week. The house had been sold over her head, and she and the children had been moved into a small flat. Katie was trying to persuade Colin to cut down on her allowance, Janet said.

'It does one no good to be materialistic,' Katie confided. 'I have nothing. No home, no family, no ties, no possessions. Look at me! Only me and a suitcase of clothes.' But Katie seemed highly satisfied with the me, and the clothes were stupendous. Katie drank a great deal and became funny. Everyone laughed, including Martha. Katie had been married twice. Martha marvelled at how someone could arrive in their mid-thirties with nothing at all to their name, neither husband, nor children, nor property and not mind.

Mind you, Martha could see the power of such helplessness. If Colin was all Katie had in the world, how could Colin abandon her? And to what? Where would she go? How would she live? Oh, clever Katie.

'My teacup's dirty,' said Katie, and Martha ran to clean it, apologizing, and Martin raised his eyebrows, at Martha, not Katie.

'I wish *you'd* wear scent,' said Martin to Martha, reproachfully. Katie wore lots. Martha never seemed to have time to put any on, though Martin bought her bottle after bottle. Martha leapt out of bed each morning to meet some emergency – miaowing cat, coughing child, faulty alarm clock, postman's knock – when was Martha to put on scent? It annoyed Martin all the same. She ought to do more to charm him.

Colin looked handsome and harrowed and younger than Martin, though they were much the same age. 'Youth's catching,' said Martin in bed that night. 'It's since he found Katie.' Found, like some treasure. Discovered; something exciting and wonderful, in the dreary world of established spouses.

On Saturday morning Jasper trod on a piece of wood ('Martha, why isn't he wearing shoes? It's too bad': Martin) and Martha took him into the hospital to have a nasty splinter removed. She left the cottage at ten and arrived back at one, and they were still sitting in the sun, drinking, empty bottles glinting in the long grass. The grass hadn't been cut. Don't forget the bottles. Broken glass means more mornings at the hospital. Oh, don't fuss. Enjoy yourself. Like other people. Try.

But no potatoes peeled, no breakfast cleared, nothing. Cigarette ends still amongst old toast, bacon rind and marmalade. 'You could have done the potatoes,' Martha burst out. Oh, bad temper! Prime sin. They looked at her in amazement and dislike. Martin too.

'Goodness,' said Katie. 'Are we doing the whole Sunday lunch bit on Saturday? Potatoes? Ages since I've eaten potatoes. Wonderful!'

'The children expect it,' said Martha.

So they did. Saturday and Sunday lunch shone like reassuring beacons in their lives. Saturday lunch: family lunch: fish and chips. ('So much better cooked at home than bought': Martin) Sunday. Usually roast beef, potatoes, peas, apple pie. Oh, of course. Yorkshire pudding. Always a problem with oven temperatures. When the beef's going slowly, the Yorkshire should be going fast. How to achieve that? Like big bosom and little hips.

'Just relax,' said Martin. 'I'll cook dinner, all in good time. Splinters always work their own way out: no need to have taken him to hospital. Let life drift over you, my love. Flow with the waves, that's the way.'

And Martin flashed Martha a distant, spiritual smile. His hand lay on Katie's slim brown arm, with its many gold bands.

'Anyway, you do too much for the children,' said Martin. 'It isn't good for them. Have a drink.'

So Martha perched uneasily on the step and had a glass of cider, and wondered how, if lunch was going to be late, she would get cleared up and the meat out of the marinade for the rather formal dinner that would be expected that evening. The marinaded lamb ought to cook for at least four hours in a low oven; and the cottage oven was very small, and you couldn't use that and the grill at the same time and Martin liked his fish grilled, not fried. Less cholesterol.

She didn't say as much. Domestic details like this were very boring, and any mild complaint was registered by Martin as a scene. And to make a scene was so ungrateful.

This was the life. Well, wasn't it? Smart friends in large cars and country living and drinks before lunch and roses and bird song – 'Don't drink *too* much,' said Martin, and told them about Martha's suspended driving licence.

The children were hungry so Martha opened them a can of beans and sausages and heated that up. ('Martha, do they have to eat that crap? Can't they wait?': Martin)

Katie was hungry: she said so, to keep the children in face. She was lovely with children – most children. She did not particularly like Colin and Janet's children. She said so, and he accepted it. He only saw them once a month now, not once a week.

'Let me make lunch,' Katie said to Martha. 'You do so much, poor thing!'

And she pulled out of the fridge all the things Martha had put away for the next day's picnic lunch party – Camembert cheese and salad and salami and made a wonderful tomato salad in two minutes and opened the white wine – 'not very cold, darling. Shouldn't it be chilling?' – and had it all on the table in five amazing competent minutes. 'That's all we need, darling,' said Martin. 'You are funny with your fish-and-chip Saturdays! What could be nicer than this? Or simpler?'

Nothing, except there was Sunday's buffet lunch for nine gone, in place of Saturday's fish for six, and would the fish stretch? No. Katie had had quite a lot to drink. She pecked Martha on the forehead. 'Funny little Martha,' she said. 'She reminds me of Janet. I really do like Janet.' Colin did not want to be reminded of Janet, and said so. 'Darling, Janet's a fact of life,' said Katie. 'If you'd only think about her more, you might manage to pay her less.' And she yawned and stretched her lean, childless body and smiled at Colin with her inviting, naughty little girl eyes, and Martin watched her in admiration.

Martha got up and left them and took a paint pot and put a coat of white gloss on the bathroom wall. The white surface pleased her. She was good at painting. She produced a smooth, even surface. Her legs throbbed. She feared she might be getting varicose veins.

Outside in the garden the children played badminton. They were bad-tempered, but relieved to be able to look up and see their mother working, as usual: making their lives for ever better and nicer: organizing, planning, thinking ahead, side-stepping disaster, making preparations, like a mother hen, fussing and irritating: part of the natural boring scenery of the world.

On Saturday night Katie went to bed early: she rose from her chair and stretched and yawned and poked her head into the kitchen where Martha was washing saucepans. Colin had cleared the table and Katie had folded the napkins into pretty creases, while Martin blew at the fire, to make it bright. 'Good night,' said Katie.

Katie appeared three minutes later, reproachfully holding out her Yves St Laurent towel, sopping wet. 'Oh dear,' cried Martha. 'Jenny must have washed her hair!' And Martha was obliged to rout Jenny out of bed to rebuke her, publicly, if only to demonstrate that she knew what was right and proper. That meant Jenny would sulk all weekend, and that meant a treat or an outing mid-week, or else by the following week she'd be having an asthma attack. 'You fuss the children too much,' said Martin. 'That's why Jenny has asthma.' Jenny was pleasant enough to look at, but not stunning. Perhaps she was a disappointment to her father? Martin would never say so, but Martha feared he thought so.

An egg and an orange each child, each day. Then nothing too bad would go wrong. And it hadn't. The asthma was very mild. A calm, tranquil environment, the doctor said. Ah, smile, Martha smile. Domestic happiness depends on you. 21 × 52 oranges a year. Each one to be purchased, carried, peeled and washed up after. And what about potatoes. 12 × 52 pounds a year? Martin liked his potatoes carefully peeled. He couldn't bear to find little cores of black in the mouthful. ('Well, it isn't very nice, is it?': Martin).

Martha dreamt she was eating coal, by handfuls, and liking it.

Saturday night. Martin made love to Martha three times. Three times? How virile he was, and clearly turned on by the sounds from the spare room. Martin said he loved her. Martin always did. He was a courteous lover; he knew the importance of foreplay. So did Martha. Three times.

Ah, sleep. Jolyon had a nightmare. Jenny was woken by a moth. Martin slept through everything. Martha pottered about the house in the night. There was a moon. She sat at the window and stared out into the summer night for five minutes, and was at peace, and then went back to bed because she ought to be fresh for the morning.

But she wasn't. She slept late. The others went out for a walk. They'd left a note, a considerate note: 'Didn't wake you. You looked tired. Had a cold breakfast so as not to make too much mess. Leave everything 'til we get back.' But it was ten o'clock, and guests were coming at noon, so she cleared away the bread, the butter, the crumbs, the smears, the jam, the spoons, the spilt sugar, the cereal, the milk (sour by now) and the dirty plates, and swept the floors, and tidied up quickly, and grabbed a cup of coffee, and prepared to make a rice and fish dish, and a chocolate mousse and sat down in the middle to eat a lot of bread and jam herself. Broad hips. She remembered the office work in her file and knew she wouldn't be able to do it. Martin anyway thought it was ridiculous for her to bring work back at the weekends. 'It's your holiday,' he'd say. 'Why should they impose?' Martha loved her work. She didn't have to smile at it. She just did it.

Katie came back upset and crying. She sat in the kitchen while Martha worked and drank glass after glass of gin and bitter lemon. Katie liked ice and lemon in gin. Martha paid for all the drink out of her wages. It was part of the deal between her and Martin – the contract by which she went out to work. All things to cheer the spirit, otherwise depressed by a working wife and mother, were to be paid for by Martha. Drink, holidays, petrol, outings, puddings, electricity, heating: it was quite a joke between them. It didn't really make any difference: it was their joint money, after all. Amazing how Martha's wages were creeping up, almost to the level of Martin's. One day they would overtake. Then what?

Work, honestly, was a piece of cake.

Anyway, poor Katie was crying. Colin, she'd discovered, kept a photograph of Janet and the children in his wallet. 'He's not free of **323** her. He pretends he is, but he isn't. She has him by a stranglehold. It's the kids. His bloody kids. Moaning Mary and that little creep Joanna. It's all he thinks about. I'm nobody.'

But Katie didn't believe it. She knew she was somebody all right. Colin came in, in a fury. He took out the photograph and set fire to it, bitterly, with a match. Up in smoke they went. Mary and Joanna and Janet. The ashes fell on the floor. (Martha swept them up when Colin and Katie had gone. It hardly seemed polite to do so when they were still there.) 'Go back to her,' Katie said. 'Go back to her. I don't care. Honestly, I'd rather be on my own. You're a nice old fashioned thing. Run along then. Do your thing, I'll do mine. Who cares?'

'Christ, Katie, the fuss! She only just happens to be in the photograph. She's not there on purpose to annoy. And I do feel bad about her. She's been having a hard time.'

'And haven't you, Colin? She twists a pretty knife, I can tell you. Don't you have rights too? Not to mention me. Is a little loyalty too much to expect?'

They were reconciled before lunch, up in the spare room. Harry and Beryl Elder arrived at twelve-thirty. Harry didn't like to hurry on Sundays; Beryl was flustered with apologies for their lateness. They'd brought artichokes from their garden. 'Wonderful,' cried Martin. 'Fruits of the earth? Let's have a wonderful soup! Don't fret, Martha. I'll do it.'

'Don't fret.' Martha clearly hadn't been smiling enough. She was in danger, Martin implied, of ruining everyone's weekend. There was an emergency in the garden very shortly – an elm tree which had probably got Dutch elm disease – and Martha finished the artichokes. The lid flew off the blender and there was artichoke purée everywhere. 'Let's have lunch outside,' said Colin. 'Less work for Martha.'

Martin frowned at Martha: he thought the appearance of martyrdom in the face of guests to be an unforgivable offence.

Everyone happily joined in taking the furniture out, but it was Martha's experience that nobody ever helped to bring it in again.

Jolyon was stung by a wasp. Jasper sneezed and sneezed from hay fever and couldn't find the tissues and he wouldn't use loo paper. ('Surely you remembered the tissues, darling?': Martin)

Beryl Elder was nice. 'Wonderful to eat out,' she said, fetching the cream for her pudding, while Martha fished a fly from the liquefying Brie ('You shouldn't have bought it so ripe, Martha': Martin) – 'except it's just some other woman has to do it. But at least it isn't *me*.' Beryl worked too, as a secretary, to send the boys to boarding school, where she'd rather they weren't. But her husband was from a rather grand family, and she'd been only a typist when he married her, so her life was a mass of amends, one way or another. Harry had lately opted out of the stockbroking rat race and become an artist, choosing integrity rather than money, but that choice was his alone and couldn't of course be inflicted on the boys.

Katie found the fish and rice dish rather strange, toyed at it with her fork, and talked about Italian restaurants she knew. Martin lay back soaking in the sun: crying, 'Oh, this is the life.' He made coffee, nobly, and the lid flew off the grinder and there were coffee beans all over the kitchen especially in amongst the row of cookery books which Martin gave Martha Christmas by Christmas. At least they didn't have to be brought back every weekend. ('The burglars won't have the sense to steal those': Martin)

Beryl fell asleep and Katie watched her, quizzically. Beryl's mouth was open and she had a lot of fillings, and her ankles were thick and her waist was going, and she didn't look after herself. 'I love women,' sighed Katie. 'They look so wonderful asleep. I wish I could be an earth mother.'

Beryl woke with a start and nagged her husband into going home, which he clearly didn't want to do, so didn't. Beryl thought she had to get back because his mother was coming round later. Nonsense! Then Beryl tried to stop Harry drinking more home-made wine and was laughed at by everyone. He was driving, Beryl couldn't, and he did have a nasty scar on his temple from a previous road accident. Never mind.

'She does come on strong, poor soul,' laughed Katie when they'd finally gone. 'I'm never going to get married,' – and Colin looked at her yearningly because he wanted to marry her more than anything in the world, and Martha cleared the coffee cups.

'Oh don't *do* that,' said Katie, 'do just sit *down*, Martha, you make us all feel bad,' and Martin glared at Martha who sat down and Jenny called out for her and Martha went upstairs and Jenny had started her first period and Martha cried and cried and knew she must stop because this must be a joyous occasion for Jenny or her whole future would be blighted, but for once, Martha couldn't.

Her daughter Jenny: wife, mother, friend.

DAVID LODGE

HOTEL DES BOOBS

'Hotel des Pins!' said Harry. 'More like Hotel des Boobs.'

'Come away from that window,' said Brenda. 'Stop behaving like a Peeping Tom.'

'What d'you mean, a Peeping Tom?' said Harry, continuing to squint down at the pool area through the slats of their bedroom shutters. 'A Peeping Tom is someone who interferes with someone else's privacy.'

'This is a private hotel.'

'Hotel des Tits. Hotel des Bristols. Hey, that's not bad!' He turned his head to flash a grin across the room. 'Hotel Bristols, in the plural. Geddit?'

If Brenda got it, she wasn't impressed. Harry resumed his watch. 'I'm not interfering with anyone's privacy,' he said. 'If they don't want people to look at their tits, why don't they cover them up?'

'Well go and look, then. Don't peep. Go down to the pool and have a good look.' Brenda dragged a comb angrily through her hair. 'Hold an inspection.'

'You're going to have to go topless, you know, Brenda, before this holiday's over.'

Brenda snorted derisively.

'Why not? You've nothing to be ashamed of.' He turned his head again to leer encouragingly at her. 'You've still got a fine pair.'

'Thanks very much, I'm sure,' said Brenda. 'But I intend to keep them covered as per usual.'

'When in Rome,' said Harry.

'This isn't Rome, it's the Côte d'Azur.'

'Côte des Tits,' said Harry. 'Côte des Knockers.'

'If I'd known you were going to go on like this,' said Brenda, 'I'd never have come here.'

For years Harry and Brenda had taken family holidays every summer in Guernsey, where Brenda's parents lived. But now that the children were grown up enough to make their own arrangements, they had decided to have a change. Brenda had always wanted to see the South of France, and they felt they'd earned the right to treat themselves for once. They were quite comfortably off, now that Brenda, a recent graduate of the Open University, had a full-time job as a teacher. It had caused an agreeable stir in the managerial canteen at Barnard Castings when Harry dropped the name of their holiday destination in among the Benidorms and Palmas, the Costas of this and that, whose merits were being debated by his colleagues.

'The French Riviera, Harry?'

'Yes, a little hotel near St Raphael. Brenda got the name out of a book.'

'Going up in the world, aren't we?'

'Well, it *is* pricey. But we thought, well, why not be extravagant, while we're still young enough to enjoy it.'

'Enjoy eyeing all those topless birds, you mean.'

'Is that right?' said Harry, with an innocence that was not entirely feigned. Of course he knew in theory that in certain parts of the Mediterranean girls sunbathed topless on the beach, and he had seen pictures of the phenomenon in his secretary's daily newspaper, which he filched regularly for the sake of such illustrations. But the reality had been a shock. Not so much the promiscuous, anonymous breast-baring of the beach, as the more intimate and socially complex nudity around the hotel pool. What made the pool different, and more disturbing, was that the women who lay half-naked around its perimeter all day were the same as those you saw immaculately dressed for dinner in the evening, or nodded and smiled politely at in the lobby, or exchanged small talk about the weather with in the bar. And since Brenda found the tree-shaded pool, a few miles inland, infinitely preferable to the heat and glare and crowdedness of the beach (not to mention the probable pollution of the sea), it became the principal theatre of Harry's initiation into the new code of mammary manners.

Harry – he didn't mind admitting it – had always had a thing about women's breasts. Some men went for legs, or bums, but Harry had always been what the boys at Barnard's called a tit-fancier. 'You were weaned too early,' Brenda used to say, a diagnosis that Harry accepted with a complacent grin. He always glanced, a simple reflex action, at the bust of any sexually interesting female that came within his purview, and had spent many idle moments speculating about the shapes that were concealed beneath their sweaters, blouses and brassieres. It was disconcerting, to say the least, to find this harmless pastime rendered totally redundant under the Provençal sun. He had scarcely begun to assess the figures of the women at the Hotel des Pins before they satisfied his curiosity to the last pore. Indeed, in most cases he saw them half-naked before he met them, as it were, socially. The snooty Englishwoman, for instance, mother of twin boys and wife to the tubby stockbroker never seen without yesterday's *Financial Times* in his hand and a smug smile on his face. Or the female partner of the German couple who worshipped the sun with religious zeal, turning and anointing themselves according to a strict timetable and with the aid of a quartz alarm clock. Or the deeply tanned brunette of a certain age whom Harry had privately christened Carmen Miranda, because she spoke an eager and rapid Spanish, or it might have been Portuguese, into the cordless telephone which the waiter Antoine brought to her at frequent intervals.

Mrs Snooty had hardly any breasts at all when she was lying down, just boyish pads of what looked like muscle, tipped with funny little turned-up nipples that quivered like the noses of two small rodents when she stood up and moved about. The German lady's breasts were perfect cones, smooth and firm as if turned on a lathe, and never seemed to change their shape whatever posture she adopted; whereas Carmen Miranda's were like two brown satin bags filled with a viscous fluid that ebbed and flowed across her rib-cage in continual motion as she turned and twisted restlessly on her mattress, awaiting the next phone call from her absent lover. And this morning there were a pair of teenage girls down by the pool whom Harry hadn't seen before, reclining side by side, one in green bikini pants and the other in yellow, regarding their recently acquired breasts, hemispheres smooth and flawless as jelly moulds, with the quiet satisfaction of housewives watching scones rise.

'There are two newcomers today,' said Harry. 'Or should I say, four.'

'Are you coming down?' said Brenda, at the door. 'Or are you going to spend the morning peering through the shutters?'

'I'm coming. Where's my book?' He looked around the room for his Jack Higgins paperback.

'You're not making much progress with it, are you?' said Brenda sarcastically. 'I think you ought to move the bookmark every day, for appearance's sake.'

A book was certainly basic equipment for discreet boob-watching down by the pool: something to peer over, or round, something to look up from, as if distracted by a sudden noise or movement, at the opportune moment, just as the bird a few yards away slipped her costume off her shoulders, or rolled on to her back. Another essential item was a pair of sunglasses, as dark as possible, to conceal the precise direction of one's gaze. For there was, Harry realized, a protocol involved in toplessness. For a man to stare at, or even let his eyes rest for a measurable span of time upon, a bared bosom, would be bad form, because it would violate the fundamental principle upon which the whole practice was based, namely, that there was nothing note-worthy about it, that it was the most natural, neutral thing in the world. (Antoine was particularly skilled in managing to serve his female clients cold drinks, or take their orders for lunch, stooping low over their prone figures, without seeming to notice their nakedness.) Yet this principle was belied by another, which confined toplessness to the pool and its margins. As soon as they moved on to the terrace, or into the hotel itself, the women covered their upper halves. Did bare tits gain and lose erotic value in relation to arbitrary territorial zones? Did the breast eagerly gazed upon, fondled and nuzzled by husband or lover in the privacy of the bedroom, become an object of indiffer-ence, a mere anatomical protuberance no more interesting than an elbow or kneecap, on the concrete rim of the swimming pool? Obviously not. The idea was absurd. Harry had little doubt that, like himself, all the men present, including Antoine, derived considerable pleasure and stimulation from the toplessness of most of the women, and it was unlikely that the women themselves were unaware of this fact. Perhaps they found it exciting, Harry speculated, to expose themselves knowing that the men must not betray any sign of arousal; and their own menfolk might share, in a vicarious, proprietorial way in this excitement. Especially if one's own wife was better endowed than some of the others. To intercept the admiring and envious glance of another man at your wife's boobs, to think silently to yourself, '*Yes, all right matey, you can look, as long as it's not too obvious, but only I'm allowed to touch 'em, see?*' That might be very exciting.

Lying beside Brenda at the poolside, dizzy from the heat and the consideration of these puzzles and paradoxes, Harry was suddenly transfixed by an arrow of perverse desire: to see his wife naked, and lust after her, through the eyes of other men. He rolled over on to his stomach and put his mouth to Brenda's ear.

'If you'll take your top off,' he whispered, 'I'll buy you that dress we saw in St Raphael. The one for twelve hundred francs.'

The author had reached this point in his story, which he was writing seated at an umbrella-shaded table on the terrace overlooking the hotel pool, using a fountain pen and ruled foolscap, as was his wont, and having accumulated many cancelled and rewritten pages, as was also his wont, when without warning a powerful wind arose. It made the pine trees in the hotel grounds shiver and hiss, raised wavelets on the surface of the pool, knocked over several umbrellas, and whirled the leaves of the author's manuscript into the air. Some of these floated back on to the terrace, or the margins of the pool, or into the pool itself, but many were funnelled with astonishing speed high into the air, above the trees, by the hot breath of the wind. The author staggered to his feet and gaped unbelievingly at the leaves of foolscap rising higher and higher, like escaped kites, twisting and turning in the sun, white against the azure sky. It was like the visitation of some god or daemon, a pentecost in reverse, drawing words away instead of imparting them. The author felt raped. The female sunbathers around the pool, as if similarly conscious, covered their naked breasts as they stood and watched the whirling leaves of paper recede into the distance. Faces were turned towards the author, smiles of sympathy mixed with *Schadenfreude*. Bidden by the sharp voice of their mother, the English twins scurried round the pool's edge collecting up loose sheets, and brought them with doggy eagerness back to their owner. The German, who had been in the pool at the time of the wind, came up with two sodden pages, covered with weeping longhand, held between finger and thumb, and laid them carefully on the author's table to dry. Pierre, the waiter, presented another sheet on his tray. '*C'est le petit mistral*,' he said with a *moue* of commiseration. '*Quel dommage!*' The author thanked them mechanically, his eyes still on the airborne pages, now mere specks in the distance, sinking slowly down into the pine woods. Around the hotel the air was quite still again. Slowly the guests returned to their loungers and mattresses. The women discreetly uncovered their bosoms, renewed the application of Ambre Solaire, and resumed the pursuit of the perfect tan.

'Simon! Jasper!' said the Englishwoman, 'Why don't you go for a walk in the woods and see if you can find any more of the gentleman's papers?'

'Oh, no,' said the author urgently. 'Please don't bother. I'm sure they're miles away by now. And they're really not important.'

'No bother,' said the Englishwoman. 'They'll enjoy it.'

'Like a treasure hunt,' said her husband. 'Or rather, paperchase.' He chuckled at his own joke. The boys trotted off obediently into the woods. The author retired to his room, to await the return of his wife, who had missed all the excitement, from St Raphael.

'I've bought the most darling little dress,' she announced as she entered the room. 'Don't ask me how much it cost.'

'Twelve hundred francs?'

'Good God, no, not as much as that. Seven hundred and fifty, actually. What's the matter, you look funny?'

'We've got to leave this hotel.'

He told her what had happened.

'I shouldn't worry,' said his wife. 'Those little brats probably won't find any more sheets.'

'Oh yes they will. They'll regard it as a challenge, like the Duke of Edinburgh Award. They'll comb the pine woods for miles around. And if they find anything, they're sure to read it.'

'They wouldn't understand.'

'Their parents would. Imagine Mrs Snooty finding her nipples compared to the nose tips of small rodents.'

The author's wife spluttered with laughter. 'You are a fool,' she said.

'It wasn't my fault,' he protested. 'The wind sprang out of no-where.'

'An act of God?'

'Precisely.'

'Well, I don't suppose He approved of that story. I can't say I cared much for it myself. How was it going to end?'

The author's wife knew the story pretty well as far as he had got with it, because he had read it out to her in bed the previous night.

'Brenda accepts the bribe to go topless.'

'I don't think she would.'

'Well, she does. And Harry is pleased as Punch. He feels that he and Brenda have finally liberated themselves, joined the sophisticated set. He imagines himself telling the boys back at Barnard Castings about it, making them ribaldly envious. He gets such a hard-on that he has to lie on his stomach all day.'

DAVID LODGE

'Tut, tut!' said his wife. 'How crude.'

332

'He can't wait to get to bed that night. But just as they're retiring, they separate for some reason I haven't worked out yet, and Harry goes up to their room first. She doesn't come at once, so Harry gets ready for bed, lies down, and falls asleep. He wakes up two hours later and finds Brenda is still missing. He is alarmed and puts on his dressing gown and slippers to go in search of her. Just at that moment, she comes in. *Where the hell have you been?* he says. She has a peculiar look on her face, goes to the fridge in their room and drinks a bottle of Perrier water before she tells him her story. She says that Antoine intercepted her downstairs to present her with a bouquet. It seems that each week all the male staff of the hotel take a vote on which female guest has the shapeliest breasts, and Brenda has come top of the poll. The bouquet was a mark of their admiration and respect. She is distressed because she left it behind in Antoine's room.'

'Antoine's room?'

'Yes, he had coaxed her into seeing his room, a little chalet in the woods, and gave her a drink, and one thing led to another, and she ended up letting him make love to her.'

'How improbable.'

'Not necessarily. Taking off her bra in public released some dormant streak of wantonness in Brenda that Harry had never seen before. She is rather drunk and quite shameless. She taunts him with graphic testimony to Antoine's skill as a lover, and compares Harry's genital equipment unfavourably to the Frenchman's.'

'Worse and worse,' said the author's wife.

'At that point Harry hits her.'

'Oh, nice. Very nice.'

'Brenda half undresses and crawls into bed. A couple of hours later, she wakes up. Harry is standing by the window staring down at the empty pool, a ghostly blue in the light of the moon. Brenda gets out of bed, comes across and touches him gently on the arm. *Come to bed*, she says. *It wasn't true, what I told you.* He turns his face slowly towards her. *Not true? No*, she says, *I made it up. I went and sat in the car for two hours with a bottle of wine, and I made it up. Why?* he says. *I don't know why*, she says. *To teach you a lesson, I suppose. But I shouldn't have. Come to bed.* But Harry just shakes his head and turns back to stare out of the window. *I never knew*, he says, in a dead sort of voice, *that you cared about the size of my prick. But I don't*, she says. *I made it all up.* Harry shakes his head disbelievingly, gazing down at the blue, breastless margins of the pool. That's how the story was going to end, with those words, "the blue, breastless margins of the pool."'

As he spoke these words, the author was himself standing at the window, looking down at the hotel pool from which all the guests had departed to change for dinner. Only the solitary figure of Pierre moved among the umbrellas and tables, collecting bathing towels and tea-trays.

'Hmm,' said the author's wife.

'Harry's fixation on women's breasts, you see,' said the author, 'has been displaced by an anxiety about his own body from which he will never be free.'

'Yes, I see that. I'm not stupid, you know.' The author's wife came to the window and looked down. 'Poor Pierre,' she said. 'He wouldn't dream of making a pass at me, or any of the other women. He's obviously gay.'

'Fortunately,' said the author, 'I didn't get that far with my story before the wind scattered it all over the countryside. But you'd better get out the Michelin and find another hotel. I can't stand the thought of staying on here, on tenterhooks all the time in case one of the guests comes back from a walk in the woods with a compromising piece of fiction in their paws. What an extraordinary thing to happen.'

'You know,' said the author's wife. 'It's really a better story.'

'Yes,' said the author. 'I think I shall write it. I'll call it "Tit for Tat".'

'No, call it "Hotel des Boobs",' said the author's wife. 'Theirs and yours.'

'What about yours?'

'Just leave them out of it, please.'

Much later that night, when they were in bed and just dropping off to sleep, the author's wife said:

'You don't really wish I would go topless, do you?'

'No, of course not,' said the author. But he didn't sound entirely convinced, or convincing.

*C*LAP *H*ANDS, *H*ERE *C*OMES *C*HARLIE

Two weeks before Christmas, Angela Bisson gave Mrs Henderson six tickets for the theatre. Mrs Henderson was Angela Bisson's cleaning lady.

'I wanted to avoid giving you money,' Angela Bisson told her. 'Anybody can give money. Somehow the whole process is so degrading . . . taking it . . . giving it. They're reopening the Empire Theatre for a limited season. I wanted to give you a treat. Something you'll always remember.'

Mrs Henderson said, 'Thank you very much.' She had never, when accepting money, felt degraded.

Her husband, Charles Henderson, asked her how much Angela Bisson had tipped her for Christmas.

Mrs Henderson said not much. 'In fact,' she admitted, 'nothing at all. Not in your actual pounds, shillings and pence. We've got tickets for the theatre instead.'

'What a discerning woman,' cried Charles Henderson. 'It's just what we've always needed.'

'The kiddies will like it,' protested Mrs Henderson. 'It's a pantomime. They've never been to a pantomime.'

Mrs Henderson's son, Alec, said *Peter Pan* wasn't a pantomime. At least not what his mother understood by the word. Of course, there was a fairy-tale element to the story, dealing as it did with Never-Never land and lost boys, but there was more to it than that. 'It's written on several levels,' he informed her.

'I've been a lost boy all my life,' muttered Charles Henderson, but nobody heard him.

'And I doubt,' said Alec, 'if our Moira's kiddies will make head nor tail of it. It's full of nannies and coal fires burning in the nursery.'

'Don't talk rot,' fumed Charles Henderson. 'They've seen coal fires on television.'

'Shut up, Charlie,' said Alec. His father hated being called Charlie.

'Does it have a principal boy?' asked Mrs Henderson, hopefully. **335**

'Yes and no,' said Alec. 'Not in the sense you mean. Don't expect any singing or any smutty jokes. It's allegorical.'

'God Almighty,' said Charles Henderson.

When Alec had gone out to attend a union meeting, Mrs Henderson told her husband he needn't bother to come to the theatre. She wasn't putting up with him and Alec having a pantomime of their own during the course of the evening and spoiling it for everyone else. She'd ask Mrs Rafferty from the floor above to go in his place.

'By heck,' shouted Charles Henderson, striking his forehead with the back of his hand, 'why didn't I think of that? Perish the thought that our Alec should be the one to be excluded. I'm only the blasted bread-winner.' He knew his wife was just mouthing words.

Mrs Rafferty's answer to such an outlandish invitation was a foregone conclusion. She wouldn't give it houseroom. Mrs Rafferty hadn't been out of the building for five years, not since she was bashed over the head coming home from Bingo.

All the same, Charles Henderson was irritated. His wife's attitude, and the caustic remarks addressed to him earlier by Alec brought on another attack of indigestion. It was no use going to his bed and lying flat. He knew from experience that it wouldn't help. In the old days, when they had lived in a proper house, he could have stepped out of the back door and perambulated up and down the yard for a few minutes. Had there been anything so exalted as a back door in this hell-hole, going out of it certainly wouldn't improve his health. Not without a parachute. He couldn't even open the window for a breath of air. This high up there was generally a howling gale blowing in from the river – it would suck the Christmas cards clean off the sideboard. It wasn't normal, he thought, to be perpetually on a par with the clouds. People weren't meant to look out of windows and see nothing but sky, particularly if they weren't looking upwards. God knows how Moira's kiddies managed. They were stuck up in the air over Kirby. When Moira and Alec had been little they'd played in the street – Moira on the front step fiddling with her dolly, Alec on one roller-skate scooting in and out of the lamp-posts. Of course there was no denying that it had been nice at first to own a decent bathroom and have hot water coming out of the tap. After only a few weeks it had become unnecessary to scrub young Alec's neck with his toothbrush; the dirt just floated off on the towel. But there was surely more to life than a clean neck. Their whole existence, once work was over for the day, was lived as though inside the cabin of an aeroplane. And they weren't going anywhere – there wasn't a landing field in sight. Just stars. Thousands of the things, on clear nights, winking away outside the double glazing. It occurred to Charles Henderson that there were too many of them for comfort or for grandeur. It was quality that counted, not quantity.

At the end of the yard of the terraced house in which he had once lived, there had been an outside toilet. Sitting within the evil-smelling little shed, its door swinging on broken hinges, he had sometimes glimpsed one solitary star hung motionless above the city. It had, he felt, given perspective to his situation, his situation in the wider sense – beyond his temporary perch. He was earthbound, mortal, and a million light-years separated him from that pale diamond burning in the sky. One star was all a man needed.

On the night of the outing to the theatre, a bit of a rumpus took place in the lift. It was occasioned by Moira's lad, Wayne, jabbing at all the control buttons and giving his grandmother a turn.

Alec thumped Wayne across the ear and Charles Henderson flared up. 'There was no cause to do that,' he shouted, though indeed there had been. Wayne was a shocking kiddie for fiddling with things.

'Belt up, Charlie,' ordered Alec.

Alec drove them to the Empire theatre in his car. It wasn't a satisfactory arrangement as far as Charles Henderson was concerned but he had no alternative. The buses came and went as they pleased. He was forced to sit next to Alec because he couldn't stand being parked in the back with the children and neither Moira nor Mrs Henderson felt it was safe in the passenger seat. Not with Alec at the wheel. Every time Alec accelerated going round a corner, Charles Henderson was swung against his son's shoulder.

'Get over, can't you?' cried Alec. 'Stop leaning on me, Charlie.'

When they passed the end of the street in which they had lived a decade ago, Mrs Henderson swivelled in her seat and remarked how changed it was, oh how changed. All those houses knocked down, and for what? Alec said that in his opinion it was good riddance to bad rubbish. The whole area had never been anything but a slum.

'Perhaps you're right, son,' said Mrs Henderson. But she was pandering to him.

Charles Henderson was unwise enough to mention times gone by.

He was talking to his wife. 'Do you remember all the men playing football in the street after work?'

'I do,' she said.

'And using the doorway of the Lune Laundry for a goal-post? It was like living in a village, wasn't it?'

'A village,' hooted Alec. 'With a tobacco warehouse and a brewery in the middle of it? Some village.'

'We hunted foxes in the field behind the public house,' reminisced Charles Henderson. 'And we went fishing in the canal.'

'You did. You were never at home,' said Mrs Henderson, without rancour.

'What field?' scoffed Alec. 'What canal?'

'There was a time,' said Charles Henderson, 'when we snared rabbits every Saturday and had them for Sunday dinner. I tell no lies. You might almost say we lived off the land.'

'Never-Never land, more like,' sneered Alec, and he drove, viciously, the wrong way down a one way street.

When they got to the town centre he made them all get out and stand about in the cold while he manoeuvred the Mini backwards and forwards in the underground car park. He cursed and gesticulated.

'Behave yourself,' shouted Charles Henderson, and he strode in front of the bonnet and made a series of authoritative signals. Alec deliberately drove the car straight at him.

'Did you see what that madman did?' Charles Henderson asked his wife. 'He ran over my foot.'

'You're imagining things,' said Mrs Henderson, but when he looked down he saw quite clearly the tread of the tyre imprinted upon the Cherry Blossom shine of his Sunday left shoe.

When the curtain went up, he was beginning to feel the first twinges of his indigestion coming on again. It wasn't to be wondered at all that swopping of seats because Moira had a tall bloke sitting in front of her, and the kiddies tramping back and forth to the toilet, not to mention the carry-on over parking the car. At least he hadn't got Alec sitting next to him. He found the first act of *Peter Pan* a bit of a mystery. It was very old-fashioned and cosy. He supposed they couldn't get a real dog to play the part. Some of the scenery could do with a lick of paint. He didn't actually laugh out loud when Mr Darling complained that nobody coddled him – oh no, why should they, seeing he was only the bread-winner – but he did grunt sardonically; Mrs Henderson nudged him sharply with her elbow. He couldn't for the life of him make out who or what Tinkerbell was, beyond being a sort of glow-worm bobbing up and down on the nursery wall, until Wendy had her hair pulled for wanting Peter to kiss her, and then he more or less guessed Tinkerbell was a female. It was a bit suggestive, all that. And at the end of the first scene when they all flew out of the window, something must have gone wrong with the wires because one of the children never got off the ground. They brought the curtain down fast. Wayne was yawning his head off.

During Acts Two and Three, Charles Henderson dozed. He was aware of loud noises and children screaming in a bloodthirsty fashion. He hoped Wayne wasn't having one of his tantrums. It was confusing for him. He was dreaming he was fishing in the canal for tiddlers and a damn big crocodile crawled up the bank with a clock ticking inside it. Then he heard a drum beating and a voice cried out 'To die will be an awfully big adventure.' He woke up then with a start. He had a pain in his arm.

In the interval they retired to the bar, Moira and himself and Alec. Mrs Henderson stayed with the kiddies, to give Moira a break. Alec paid for a round of drinks. 'Are you enjoying it then, Charlie?' he asked.

'It's a bit loud for me,' said Charles Henderson. 'But I see what you mean about it being written on different levels.'

'You do surprise me,' said Alec. 'I could have sworn you slept through most of it.'

Moira said little Tracy was terrified of the crocodile but she loved the doggie.

'Some doggie,' muttered Charles Henderson. 'I could smell the moth balls.'

'But Wayne thinks it's lovely,' said Moira. 'He's really engrossed.'

'I could tell,' Charles Henderson said. 'They must have heard him yawning in Birkenhead.'

'It's one of his signs,' defended Moira. 'Yawning. He always yawns when he's engrossed.' She herself was enjoying it very much, though she hadn't understood at first what Mr Darling was doing dressed up as Captain Hook.

'It's traditional,' Alec told her.

'What are you on about?' asked Charles Henderson. 'That pirate chappie was never Mr Darling.'

'Yes it was, Dad,' said Moira. 'I didn't cotton on myself at first, but it was the same man.'

'I suppose it saves on wages,' Charles Henderson said. Alec explained it was symbolic. The kindly Mr Darling and the brutal Captain Hook were two halves of the same man.

'There wasn't more than a quarter of Mr Darling,' cried Charles Henderson, heatedly. 'That pirate was waving his cutlass about every time I opened my eyes. I can't see the point of it, can you, Moira?'

Moira said nothing, but her mouth drooped at the corners. She was probably thinking about her husband who had run off and left her with two kiddies and a gas bill for twenty-seven quid.

'The point,' said Alec, 'is obvious. Mr Darling longs to murder his offspring.' He was shouting quite loudly. 'Like fathers in real life. They're always out to destroy their children.'

'What's up with you?' asked Mrs Henderson, when her husband had returned to his seat.

'That Alec,' hissed Charles Henderson. 'He talks a load of codswallop. I'd like to throttle him.'

During Act Four Charles Henderson asked his wife for a peppermint. His indigestion was fearsome. Mrs Henderson told him to shush. She too seemed engrossed in the pantomime. Wayne was sitting bolt upright. Charles Henderson tried to concentrate. He heard some words but not others. The lost boys were going back to their Mums, that much he gathered. Somebody called Tiger Lily had come into it. And Indians were beating tom-toms. His heart was beating so loudly that it was a wonder Alec didn't fly off the handle and order him to keep quiet. Wendy had flown off with the boys, jerkily, and Peter was asleep. It was odd how it was all to do with flying. That Tinkerbell person was flashing about among the cloth trees. He had the curious delusion that if he stood up on his seat, he too might soar up into the gallery. It was a daft notion because when he tried to shift his legs they were as heavy as lead. Mrs Darling would be pleased to see the kiddies again. She must have gone through hell. He remembered the time Alec had come home half an hour late from the Cubs – the length of those minutes, the depth of that fear. It didn't matter what his feelings had been towards Alec for the last ten years. He didn't think you were supposed to feel much for grown-up children. He had loved little Alec, now a lost boy, and that was enough.

Something dramatic was happening on stage. Peter had woken up and was having a disjointed conversation with Tinkerbell, something to do with cough mixture and poison. *Tink, you have drunk my medicine . . . it was poisoned and you drank it to save my life . . . Tink dear, are you dying?* . . . The tiny star that was Tinkerbell began to flicker. Charles Henderson could hear somebody sobbing. He craned sideways to look down the row and was astonished to see that his grandson was wiping at his eyes with the back of his sleeve. Fancy Wayne, a lad who last year had been caught dangling a hamster on a piece of string from a window on the fourteenth floor of the flats, crying about a light going out. Peter Pan was advancing towards the audience, his arms flung wide. *Her voice is so low I can hardly hear what she is saying. She says . . . she says she thinks she could get well again if children believed in fairies. Say quick that you believe. If you believe, clap your hands. Clap your hands and Tinkerbell will live.*

At first the clapping was muted, apologetic. Tinkerbell was reduced to a dying spark quivering on the dusty floorboards of the stage. Charles Henderson's own hands were clasped to his chest. There was a pain inside him as though somebody had slung a hook through his heart. The clapping increased in volume. The feeble Tinkerbell began to glow. She sailed triumphantly up the trunk of a painted tree. She grew so dazzling that Charles Henderson was blinded. She blazed above him in the skies of Never-Never land.

'Help me,' he said, using his last breath.

'Shut up, Charlie,' shouted Mrs Henderson, and she clapped and clapped until the palms of her hands were stinging.

PSYCHOPOLIS

Mary worked in and part-owned a feminist bookstore in Venice. I met her there lunchtime on my second day in Los Angeles. That same evening we were lovers, and not so long after that, friends. The following Friday I chained her by the foot to my bed for the whole weekend. It was, she explained to me, something she 'has to go into to come out of'. I remember her extracting (later, in a crowded bar) my solemn promise that I would not listen if she demanded to be set free. Anxious to please my new friend, I bought a fine chain and diminutive padlock. With brass screws I secured a steel ring to the wooden base of the bed and all was set. Within hours she was insisting on her freedom, and though a little confused I got out of bed, showered, dressed, put on my carpet slippers and brought her a large frying-pan to urinate in. She tried on a firm, sensible voice.

'Unlock this,' she said. 'I've had enough.' I admit she frightened me. I poured myself a drink and hurried out on to the balcony to watch the sun set. I was not at all excited. I thought to myself, if I unlock the chain she will despise me for being so weak. If I keep her there she might hate me, but at least I will have kept my promise. The pale orange sun dipped into the haze, and I heard her shout to me through the closed bedroom door. I closed my eyes and concentrated on being blameless.

A friend of mine once had analysis with an elderly man, a Freudian with a well-established practice in New York. On one occasion my friend spoke at length about his doubts concerning Freud's theories, their lack of scientific credibility, their cultural particularity and so on. When he had done the analyst smiled genially and replied, 'Look around you!' And indicated with his open palm the comfortable study, the rubber plant and the begonia rex, the book-lined walls and finally, with an inward movement of the wrist which both suggested candour and emphasized the lapels of his tasteful suit, said, 'Do you really think I would have got to where I am now if Freud was wrong?'

In the same manner I said to myself as I returned indoors (the sun now set and the bedroom silent), the bare truth of the matter is that I am keeping my promise.

All the same, I felt bored. I wandered from room to room turning on the lights, leaning in doorways and staring in at objects that already were familiar. I set up the music stand and took out my flute. I taught myself to play years ago and there are many errors, strengthened by habit, which I no longer have the will to correct. I do not press the keys as I should with the very tips of my fingers, and my fingers fly too high off the keys and so make it impossible to play fast passages with any facility. Furthermore my right wrist is not relaxed, and does not fall, as it should, at an easy right angle to the instrument. I do not hold my back straight when I play, instead I slouch over the music. My breathing is not controlled by the muscles of my stomach. I blow carelessly from the top of my throat. My embouchure is ill-formed and I rely too often on a syrupy vibrato. I lack the control to play any dynamics other than soft or loud. I have never bothered to teach myself notes above top G. My musicianship is poor, and slightly unusual rhythms perplex me. Above all I have no ambition to play any other than the same half-dozen pieces and I make the same mistakes each time.

Several minutes into my first piece I thought of her listening from the bedroom and the phrase 'captive audience' came into my mind. While I played I devised ways in which these words could be inserted casually into a sentence to make a weak, light-hearted pun, the humour of which would somehow cause the situation to be elucidated. I put the flute down and walked towards the bedroom door. But before I had my sentence arranged, my hand, with a kind of insensible automation, had pushed the door open and I was standing in front of Mary. She sat on the edge of the bed brushing her hair, the chain decently obscured by blankets. In England a woman as articulate as Mary might have been regarded as an aggressor, but her manner was gentle. She was short and quite heavily built. Her face gave an impression of reds and blacks, deep red lips, black, black eyes, dusky apple-red cheeks and hair black and sleek like tar. Her grandmother was Indian.

'What do you want?' she said sharply and without interrupting the motion of her hand.

'Ah,' I said. 'Captive audience!'

'What?' When I did not repeat myself she told me that she wished to be left alone. I sat down on the bed and thought, If she asks me to set her free I'll do it instantly. But she said nothing. When she had finished with her hair she lay down with her hands clasped behind her head. I sat watching her, waiting. The idea of asking her if she wished to be set free seemed ludicrous, and simply setting her free without her permission was terrifying. I did not even know whether this was an ideological or psycho-sexual matter. I returned to my flute, this time carrying the music stand to the far end of the apartment and closing the intervening doors. I hoped she couldn't hear me.

On Sunday night, after more than twenty-four hours of unbroken silence between us, I set Mary free. As the lock sprang open I said, 'I've been in Los Angeles less than a week and already I feel a completely different person.'

Though partially true, the remark was designed to give pleasure. One hand resting on my shoulder, the other massaging her foot, Mary said, 'It'll do that. It's a city at the end of cities.'

'It's sixty miles across!' I agreed.

'It's a thousand miles deep!' cried Mary wildly and threw her brown arms about my neck. She seemed to have found what she had hoped for.

But she was not inclined to explanations. Later on we ate out in a Mexican restaurant and I waited for her to mention her weekend in chains and when, finally, I began to ask her she interrupted with a question. 'Is it really true that England is in a state of total collapse?'

I said yes and spoke at length without believing what I was saying. The only experience I had of total collapse was a friend who killed himself. At first he only wanted to punish himself. He ate a little ground glass washed down with grapefruit juice. Then when the pains began he ran to the tube station, bought the cheapest ticket and threw himself under a train. The brand new Victoria line. What would that be like on a national scale? We walked back from the restaurant arm in arm without speaking. The air hot and damp around us, we kissed and clung to each other on the pavement beside her car.

'Same again next Friday?' I said wryly as she climbed in, but the words were cut by the slam of her door. Through the window she waved at me with her fingers and smiled. I didn't see her for quite a while.

—

I was staying in Santa Monica in a large, borrowed apartment over a hire shop which specialized in renting out items for party givers and, strangely, equipment for 'sickrooms'. One side of the shop was given over to wineglasses, cocktail shakers, spare easy chairs, a banqueting table and a portable discotheque, the other to wheelchairs, tilting beds, tweezers and bedpans, bright tubular steel and coloured rubber hoses. During my stay I noticed a number of these stores throughout the city. The manager was immaculately dressed and initially intimidating in his friendliness. On our first meeting he told me he was 'only twenty-nine'. He was heavily built and wore one of those thick drooping moustaches grown throughout America and England by the ambitious young. On my first day he came up the stairs and introduced himself as George Malone and paid me a pleasant compliment. 'The British,' he said, 'make damn good invalid chairs. The very best.'

'That must be Rolls-Royce,' I said. Malone gripped my arm.

'Are you shitting me? Rolls-Royce make . . .'

'No, no,' I said nervously. 'A . . . a joke.' For a moment his face was immobilized, the mouth open and black, and I thought, He's going to hit me. But he laughed.

'Rolls-Royce! That's neat!' And the next time I saw him he indicated the sickroom side of his shop and called out after me, 'Wanna buy a Rolls?' Occasionally we drank together at lunchtime in a red-lit bar off Colorado Avenue where George had introduced me to the barman as 'a specialist in bizarre remarks'.

'What'll it be?' said the barman to me.

'Pig oil with a cherry,' I said, cordially hoping to live up to my reputation. But the barman scowled and turning to George spoke through a sigh.

'What'll it be?'

It was exhilarating, at least at first, to live in a city of narcissists. On my second or third day I followed George's directions and walked to the beach. It was noon. A million stark, primitive figurines lay scattered on the fine, pale, yellow sand till they were swallowed up, north and south, in a haze of heat and pollution. Nothing moved but the sluggish giant waves in the distance, and the silence was awesome. Near where I stood on the very edge of the beach were different kinds of parallel bars, empty and stark, their crude geometry marked by silence. Not even the sound of the waves reached me, no voices, the whole city lay dreaming. As I began walking towards the ocean there were soft murmurs nearby, and it was as if I overheard a sleep-talker. I saw a man move his hand, spreading his fingers more firmly against the sand to catch the sun. An icebox without its lid stood like a gravestone at the head of a prostrate woman. I peeped inside as I passed and saw empty beercans and a packet of orange cheese floating in water. Now that I was moving among them I noticed how far apart each solitary sunbather was. It seemed to take minutes to walk from one to another. A trick of perspective had made me think they were jammed together. I noticed too how beautiful the women were, their brown limbs spread like starfish; and how many healthy old men there were with gnarled muscular bodies. The spectacle of this common intent exhilarated me and for the first time in my life I too urgently wished to be brown-skinned, brown-faced, so that when I smiled my teeth would flash white. I took off my trousers and shirt, spread my towel and lay down on my back thinking, I shall be free, I shall change beyond all recognition. But within minutes I was hot and restless, I longed to open my eyes. I ran into the ocean and swam out to where a few people were treading water and waiting for an especially huge wave to dash them to the shore.

Returning from the beach one day I found pinned to my door a note from my friend Terence Latterly. 'Waiting for you,' it said, 'in the Doggie Diner across the street.' I had met Latterly years ago in England when he was researching a still uncompleted thesis on George Orwell, and it was not till I came to America that I realized how rare an American he was. Slender, extraordinarily pallid, fine black hair that curled, doe eyes like a Renaissance princess, long straight nose with narrow black slits for nostrils, Terence was unwholesomely beautiful. He was frequently approached by gays, and once, in Polk Street San Francisco, literally mobbed. He had a stammer, slight enough to be endearing to those endeared by such things, and he was intense in his friendships to the point of occasionally lapsing into impenetrable sulks about them. It took me some time to admit to myself I actually disliked Terence and by that time he was in my life and I accepted the fact. Like all compulsive monologuists he lacked curiosity about other people's minds, but his stories were good and he never told the same one twice. He regularly became infatuated with women whom he drove away with his labyrinthine awkwardness and consumptive zeal, and who provided fresh material for his monologues. Two or three times now quiet, lonely, protective girls had fallen hopelessly for Terence and his ways, but, tellingly, he was not interested. Terence

cared for long-legged, tough-minded, independent women who were
346 rapidly bored by Terence. He once told me he masturbated every day.

He was the Doggie Diner's only customer, bent morosely over an
empty coffee cup, his chin propped in his palms.

'In England,' I told him, 'a dog's dinner means some kind of
unpalatable mess.'

'Sit down then,' said Terence. 'We're in the right place. I've been so
humiliated.'

'Sylvie?' I asked obligingly.

'Yes yes. Grotesquely humiliated.' This was nothing new. Terence
dined out frequently on morbid accounts of blows dealt him by
indifferent women. He had been in love with Sylvie for months now
and had followed her here from San Francisco, which was where he
first told me about her. She made a living setting up health food
restaurants and then selling them, and as far as I knew, she was hardly
aware of the existence of Terence.

'I should never've come to Los Angeles,' Terence was saying as the
Doggie Diner waitress refilled his cup. 'It's O K for the British. You
see everything here as a bizarre comedy of extremes, but that's
because you're out of it. The truth is it's psychotic, totally psychotic.'
Terence ran his fingers through his hair which looked lacquered and
stiff, and stared out into the street. Wrapped in a constant, faint blue
cloud, cars drifted by at twenty miles an hour, their drivers propped
their tanned forearms on the window ledges, their car radios and
stereos were on, they were all going home or to bars for happy hours.

After a suitable silence I said, 'Well . . . ?'

From the day he arrives in Los Angeles Terence pleads with Sylvie
over the phone to have a meal with him in a restaurant, and finally,
wearily, she consents. Terence buys a new shirt, visits the hairdresser
and spends an hour in the later afternoon in front of the mirror, staring
at his face. He meets Sylvie in a bar, they drink bourbon. She is
relaxed and friendly, and they talk easily of Californian politics, of
which Terence knows next to nothing. Since Sylvie knows Los
Angeles she chooses the restaurant. As they are leaving the bar she
says, 'Shall we go in your car or mine?'

Terence, who has no car and cannot drive, says, 'Why not yours?'

By the end of the *hors d'oeuvres* they are starting in on their second
bottle of wine and talking of books, and then of money, and then of
books again. Lovely Sylvie leads Terence by the hand through half a
dozen topics; she smiles and Terence flushes with love and love's

wildest ambitions. He loves so hard he knows he will not be able to resist declaring himself. He can feel it coming on, a mad confession. The words tumble out, a declaration of love worthy of the pages of Walter Scott, its main burden being that there is nothing, absolutely nothing in the world Terence would not do for Sylvie. In fact, drunk, he challenges her now to test his devotion. Touched by the bourbon and wine, intrigued by this wan, *fin de siècle* lunatic, Sylvie gazes warmly across the table and returns his little squeeze to the hand. In the rarefied air between them runs a charge of goodwill and daredevilry. Propelled by mere silence Terence repeats himself. There is nothing, absolutely nothing, in the etc. Sylvie's gaze shifts momentarily from Terence's face to the door of the restaurant through which a well-to-do middle-aged couple are now eating. She frowns, then smiles.

'Anything?' she says.

'Yes, yes, anything.' Terence is solemn now, sensing the real challenge in her question. Sylvie leans forward and grips his forearm.

'You won't back out?'

'No, if it's humanly possible I'll do it.' Again Sylvie is looking over at the couple who wait by the door to be seated by the hostess, an energetic lady in a red soldier-like uniform. Terence watches too. Sylvie tightens her grip on his arm.

'I want you to urinate in your pants, now. Go on now! Quick! Do it now before you have time to think about it.'

Terence is about to protest, but his own promises still hang in the air, an accusing cloud. With drunken sway, and with the sound of an electric bell ringing in his ears, he urinates copiously, soaking his thighs, legs and backside and sending a small, steady trickle to the floor.

'Have you done it?' says Sylvie.

'Yes,' says Terence. 'But why . . . ?' Sylvia half-rises from her seat and waves prettily across the restaurant at the couple standing by the door.

'I want you to meet my parents,' she says. 'I've just seen them come in.' Terence remains seated for the introductions. He wonders if he can be smelled. There is nothing he will not say to dissuade this affable, greying couple from sitting down at their daughter's table. He talks desperately and without a break ('as if I was some kinda bore'), referring to Los Angeles as a 'shithole' and its inhabitants as 'greedy devourers of each other's privacy'. Terence hints at a recent prolonged

mental illness from which he had hardly recovered, and he tells
Sylvie's mother that all doctors, especially women doctors, are
'assholes' (arseholes). Sylvie says nothing. The father cocks an eye-
brow at his wife and the couple wander off without farewell to their
table on the far side of the room.

Terence appeared to have forgotten he was telling his story. He was
cleaning his nails with the tooth of a comb. I said, 'Well, you can't stop
there. *What happened?* What's the explanation for all this?' Around us
the diner was filling up, but no one else was talking.

Terence said, 'I sat on a newspaper to keep her car seat from getting
wet. We didn't speak much and she wouldn't come in when we got to
my place. She told me earlier she didn't like her parents much. I guess
she was just fooling around.' I wondered if Terence's story was
invented or dreamed for it was the paradigm of all his rejections, the
perfect formulation of his fears or, perhaps, of his profoundest
desires.

'People here,' Terence said as we left the Doggie Diner, 'live so far
from each other. Your neighbour is someone forty minutes' car ride
away, and when you finally get together you're out to wreck each other
with the frenzy of having been alone.'

Something about that remark appealed to me and I invited Terence
up to my place to smoke a joint with me. We stood about on the
pavement a few minutes while he tried to decide whether he wanted to
or not. We looked across the street through the passing traffic and into
the stores where George was demonstrating the disco equipment to a
black woman. Finally Terence shook his head and said that while he
was in this part of town he would go and visit a girl he knew in Venice.

'Take some spare underwear,' I suggested.

'Yeah,' he called over his shoulder as he walked away. 'See you!'

There were long pointless days when I thought, Everywhere on earth
is the same. Los Angeles, California, the whole of the United States
seemed to me then a very fine and frail crust on the limitless,
subterranean world of my own boredom. I could be anywhere, I could
have saved myself the effort and the fare. I wished in fact I was
nowhere, beyond the responsibility of place. I woke in the morning
stultified by oversleep. Although I was neither hungry nor thirsty, I
ate breakfast because I dared not be without the activity. I spent ten
minutes cleaning my teeth knowing that when I finished I would have
to choose to do something else. I returned to the kitchen, made more

coffee and very carefully washed the dishes. Caffeine aided my growing panic. There were books in the living room that needed to be studied, there was writing that needed completion but the thought of it all made me flush hot with weariness and disgust. For that reason I tried not to think about it, I did not tempt myself. It hardly occurred to me to set foot inside the living room.

Instead I went to the bedroom and made the bed and took great care over the 'hospital corners'. Was I sick? I lay down on the bed and stared at the ceiling without a thought in my head. Then I stood up and with my hands in my pockets stared at the wall. Perhaps I should paint it another colour, but of course I was only a temporary resident. I remembered I was in a foreign city and hurried to the balcony. Dull, white, box-shaped shops and houses, parked cars, two lawn sprinklers, festoons of telephone cable everywhere, one palm tree teetering against the sky, the whole lit by a cruel white glow of a sun blotted out by high cloud and pollution. It was as obvious and self-explanatory to me as a row of suburban English bungalows. What could I do about it? Go somewhere else? I almost laughed out loud at the thought.

More to confirm my state of mind than change it, I returned to the bedroom and grimly picked up my flute. The piece I intended to play, dog-eared and stained, was already on the music stand, Bach's Sonata No. 1 in A minor. The lovely opening Andante, a series of lilting arpeggios, requires a flawless breathing technique to make sense of the phrasing, yet from the beginning I am snatching furtively at breaths like a supermarket shoplifter, and the coherence of the piece becomes purely imaginary, remembered from gramophone recordings and super-imposed over the present. At bar fifteen, four and a half bars into the Presto, I fumble over the octave leaps but I press on, a dogged, failing athlete, to finish the first movement short of breath and unable to hold the last note its full length. Because I catch most of the right notes in the right order, I regard the Allegro as my showpiece. I play it with expressionless aggression. The Adagio, a sweet thoughtful melody, illustrates to me every time I play it how out of tune my notes are, some sharp, some flat, none sweet, and the semi-demi quavers are always mis-timed. And so to the two Minuets at the end which I play with dry, rigid persistence, like a mechanical organ turned by a monkey. This was my performance of Bach's Sonata, unaltered now in its details for as long as I could remember.

I sat down on the edge of the bed and almost immediately stood up again. I went to the balcony to look once more at the foreign city. Out on one of the lawns a small girl picked up a smaller girl and staggered a few steps with her. More futility. I went inside and looked at the alarm clock in the bedroom. Eleven forty. Do something, quick! I stood by the clock listening to its tick. I went from room to room without really intending to, sometimes surprised to find that I was back in the kitchen again fiddling with the cracked plastic handle of the wall can-opener. I went into the living room and spent twenty minutes drumming with my fingers on the back of a book. Towards the middle of the afternoon I dialled the time and set the clock exactly. I sat on the lavatory a long time and decided then not to move till I had planned what to do next. I remained there over two hours, staring at my knees till they lost their meaning as limbs. I thought of cutting my finger-nails, that would be a start. But I had no scissors! I commenced to prowl from room to room once more, and then, towards the middle of the evening, I fell asleep in an armchair, exhausted with myself.

George at least appeared to appreciate my playing. He came upstairs once, having heard me from the shop, and wanted to see my flute. He told me he had never actually held one in his hands before. He marvelled at the intricacy and precision of its levers and pads. He asked me to play a few notes so he could see how it was held, and then he wanted me to show him how he could make a note for himself. He peered at the music on the stand and said he thought it was 'brilliant' the way musicians could turn such a mess of lines and dots into sounds. The way composers could think up whole symphonies with dozens of different instruments going at once was totally beyond him. I said it was beyond me too.

'Music,' George said with a large gesture of his arm, 'is a sacred art.' Usually when I wasn't playing my flute I left it lying about collecting dust, assembled and ready to play. Now I found myself pulling it into its three sections and drying them carefully and laying each section down like a favourite doll, in the felt-lined case.

George lived out in Simi Valley on a recently reclaimed stretch of desert. He described his house as 'empty and smelling of fresh paint still'. He was separated from his wife and two weekends a month had his children over to stay, two boys aged seven and eight. Impercept-ibly George became my host in Los Angeles. He had arrived here penniless from New York city when he was twenty-two. Now he made almost forty thousand dollars a year and felt responsible for the city and my experience in it. Sometimes after work George drove me for miles along the freeway in his new Volvo.

'I want you to get the feel of it, the insanity of its size.'

'What's that building?' I would say to him as we sped past an illuminated Third Reichian colossus mounted on a manicured green hill. George would glance out of his window.

'I dunno, a bank or temple or something.' We went to bars, bars for starlets, bars for 'intellectuals' where screenwriters drank, lesbian bars and a bar where the waiters, little, smooth-faced young men, dressed as Victorian serving-maids. We ate in a diner founded in 1947 which served only hamburgers and apple pie, a renowned and fashionable place where waiting customers stood like hungry ghosts at the backs of those seated.

We went to a club where singers and stand-up comedians performed in the hope of being discovered. A thin girl with bright red hair and sequined T-shirt reached the end of her passionately murmured song on a sudden shrill, impossible top note. All conversation ceased. Someone, perhaps maliciously, dropped a glass. Halfway through, the note became a warbling vibrato and the singer collapsed on the stage in an abject curtsy, arms held stiffly in front of her, fists clenched. Then she sprang to her tiptoes and held her arms high above her head with the palms flat as if to forestall the sporadic and indifferent applause.

'They all want to be Barbra Streisand or Liza Minnelli,' George explained as he sucked a giant cocktail through a pink plastic straw. 'But no one's looking for that kind of stuff any more.'

A man with stooped shoulders and wild curly hair shuffled on to the stage. He took the microphone out of its rest, held it close to his lips and said nothing. He seemed to be stuck for words. He wore a torn, muddied denim jacket over bare skin, his eyes were swollen almost to the point of closing and under the right there ran a long scratch which ended at the corner of his mouth and gave him the look of a partly made-up clown. His lower lip trembled and I thought he was going to weep. The hand that was not holding the microphone worried a coin and looking at that I noticed the stains down his jeans, yes, fresh wet vomit clung there. His lips parted but no sounds came out. The audience waited patiently. Somewhere at the back of the room a wine bottle was opened. When he spoke finally it was to his fingernails, a low, cracked murmur.

'I'm such a goddamn mess!'

The audience broke into fallabout laughter and cheering, which after a minute gave way to footstamping and rhythmic clapping. George and I, perhaps constrained by each other's company, smiled. The man reappeared by the microphone the moment the last clapping died away. Now he spoke rapidly, his eyes still fixed on his fingers. Sometimes he glanced worriedly to the back of the room and we caught the flash of the whites of his eyes. He told us he had just broken up with his girl-friend, and how, as he was driving away from her house, he had started to weep, so much so that he could not see to drive and had to stop his car. He thought he might kill himself but first he wanted to say goodbye to *her*. He drove to a call box but it was out of order and this made him cry again. Here the audience, silent till now, laughed a little. He reached his girl-friend from a drug store. As soon as she picked up the phone and heard his voice she began to cry too. But she didn't want to see him. She told him, 'It's useless, there's nothing we can do.' He put the phone down and howled with grief. An assistant in the drug store told him to leave because he was upsetting the other customers. He walked along the street thinking about life and death, it started to rain, he popped some amyl nitrate, he tried to sell his watch. The audience was growing restless, a lot of people had stopped listening. He bummed fifty cents off a bum. Through his tears he thought he saw a woman aborting a foetus in the gutter and when he got closer he saw it was cardboard boxes and a lot of old rags. By now the man was talking over a steady drone of conversation. Waitresses with silver trays circulated the tables. Suddenly the speaker raised his hand and said, 'Well, see you,' and he was gone. A few people clapped but most did not notice him leave.

Not long before I was due to leave Los Angeles George invited me to spend Saturday evening at his house. I would be flying to New York late the following day. He wanted me to bring along a couple of friends to make a small farewell party, and he wanted me to bring along my flute.

'I really want to sit,' said George, 'in my own home with a glass of wine in my hand and hear you play that thing.' I phoned Mary first. We had been meeting intermittently since our weekend. Occasionally she had come and spent the afternoon at my apartment. She had another lover she more or less lived with, but she hardly mentioned him and it was never an issue between us. After agreeing to come, Mary wanted to know if Terence was going to be there. I had recounted to her Terence's adventure with Sylvie, and described my own ambivalent feelings about him. Terence had not returned to San Francisco as he had intended. He had met someone who had a friend 'in screenwriting' and now he was waiting for an introduction. When I phoned him he responded with an unconvincing parody of Semitic peevishness. 'Five weeks in this town and I'm invited out already?' I decided to take seriously George's wish to hear me play the flute. I practised my scales and arpeggios, I worked hard at those places in the Sonata No. 1 where I always faltered and as I played I fantasized about Mary, George and Terence listening spellbound and a little drunk, and my heart raced.

Mary arrived in the early evening and before driving to pick up Terence we sat around on my balcony watching the sun and smoked a small joint. It had been on my mind before she came that we might be going to bed for one last time. But now that she was here and we were dressed for an evening elsewhere, it seemed more appropriate to talk. Mary asked me what I had been doing and I told her about the night club act. I was not sure whether to present the man as a performer with an act so clever it was not funny, or as someone who had come in off the street and taken over the stage.

'I've seen acts like that here,' said Mary. 'The idea, when it works, is to make your laughter stick in your throat. What was funny suddenly gets nasty.' I asked Mary if she thought there was any truth in my man's story. She shook her head.

'Everyone here,' she said, gesturing towards the setting sun, 'has got some kind of act going like that.'

'You seem to say that with some pride,' I said as we stood up. She smiled and we held hands for an empty moment in which there came to me from nowhere a vivid image of the parallel bars on the beach; then we turned and went inside.

Terence was waiting for us on the pavement outside the house where he was staying. He wore a white suit and as we pulled up he was fixing a pink carnation into his lapel. Mary's car had only two doors. I had to get out to let Terence in, but through a combination of sly manoeuvring on his part and obtuse politeness on my own, I found myself introducing my two friends from the back seat. As we turned on to the freeway Terence began to ask Mary a series of polite, insistent questions and it was clear from where I sat, directly behind Mary, that as she was answering one question he was formulating the next, or falling over himself to agree with everything she said.

'Yes, yes,' he was saying, leaning forwards eagerly, clasping
354 together his long, pale fingers, 'That's a really good way of putting it.'
Such condescension, I thought, such ingratiation. Why does Mary
put up with it? Mary said she thought Los Angeles was the most
exciting city in the USA. Before she had even finished Terence was
outdoing her with extravagant praise.

'I thought you hated it,' I interjected sourly. But Terence was
adjusting his seat belt and asking Mary another question. I sat back
and stared out the window, attempting to control my irritation. A
little later Mary was craning her neck trying to find me in her mirror.

'You're very quiet back there,' she said gaily. I fell into sudden,
furious mimicry.

'That's a really good way of putting it, yes, yes.' Neither Terence
nor Mary made any reply. My words hung over us as though they were
being uttered over and over again. I opened my window. We arrived at
George's house with twenty-five minutes of unbroken silence behind
us.

The introductions over, the three of us held the centre of George's
huge living room while he fixed our drinks at the bar. I held my flute
case and music stand under my arm like weapons. Apart from the bar
the only other furniture was two yellow, plastic sag chairs, very bright
against the desert expanse of brown carpet. Sliding doors took up the
length of one wall and gave on to a small back yard of sand and stones
in the centre of which, set in concrete, stood one of those tree-like
contraptions for drying clothes on. In the corner of the yard was a
scrappy sagebrush plant, survivor of the real desert that was here a
year ago. Terence, Mary and I addressed remarks to George and said
nothing to each other.

'Well,' said George when the four of us stood looking at each other
with drinks in our hands, 'Follow me and I'll show you the kids.'
Obediently we padded behind George in single file along a narrow,
thickly carpeted corridor. We peered through a bedroom doorway at
two small boys in a bunk bed reading comics. They glanced at us
without interest and went on reading.

Back in the living room I said, 'They're very subdued, George.
What do you do, beat them up?' George took my question seriously
and there followed a conversation about corporal punishment. George
said he occasionally gave the boys a slap on the back of the legs if
things got really out of hand. But it was not meant to hurt them, he
said, so much as to show them he meant business. Mary said she was

dead against striking children at all, and Terence, largely to cut a figure I thought, or perhaps to demonstrate to me that he could disagree with Mary, said that he thought a sound thrashing never did anyone any harm. Mary laughed, but George, who obviously was not taking to this faintly foppish, languid guest sprawled across his carpet, seemed ready to move into the attack. George worked hard. He kept his back straight even when he sat in the sag chair.

'You were thrashed when you were a kid?' he asked as he handed round the scotch.

Terence hesitated and said, 'Yes.' This surprised me. Terence's father died before he was born and he had grown up with his mother in Vermont.

'Your mother beat you?' I said before he had time to invent a swaggering bully of a father.

'Yes.'

'And you don't think it did you any harm?' said George. 'I don't believe it.'

Terence stretched his legs. 'No harm done at all.' He spoke through a yawn that might have been a fake. He gestured towards his pink carnation. 'After all, here I am.'

There was a moment's pause then George said, 'For example, you never had any problem making out with women?' I could not help smiling.

Terence sat up. 'Oh yes,' he said. 'Our English friend here will verify that.' By this Terence referred to my outburst in the car. But I said to George, 'Terence likes to tell funny stories about his own sexual failures.'

George leaned forwards to catch Terence's full attention. 'How can you be sure they're not caused by being thrashed by your mother?'

Terence spoke very quickly. I was not sure whether he was very exited or very angry. 'There will always be problems between men and women and everyone suffers in some way. I conceal less about myself than other people do. I guess you never had your backside tanned by your mother when you were a kid, but does that mean you never have any hang-ups with women? I mean, where's your wife . . . ?'

Mary's interruption had the precision of a surgeon's knife.

'I was only ever hit once as a kid, by my father, and do you know why that was? I was twelve. We were all sitting round the table at suppertime, all the family, and I told everyone I was bleeding from between my legs. I put some blood on the end of my finger and held it up for them all to see. My father leaned across the table and slapped my face. He told me not to be dirty and sent me up to my room.'

George got up to fetch more ice for our glasses and muttered 'Simply grotesque' as he went. Terence stretched out on the floor, his eyes fixed on the ceiling like a dead man's. From the bedroom came the sound of the boys singing, or rather chanting, for the song was all on one note. I said to Mary something to the effect that between people who had just met, such a conversation could not have taken place in England.

'Is that a good thing do you think?' Mary asked.

Terence said, 'The English tell each other nothing.'

I said, 'Between telling nothing and telling everything there is very little to choose.'

'Did you hear the boys?' George said as he came back.

'We heard some kind of singing,' Mary told him. George was pouring more Scotch and spooning ice into the glasses.

'That wasn't singing. That was praying. I've been teaching them the Lord's Prayer.' On the floor Terence groaned and George looked round sharply.

'I didn't know you were a Christian, George,' I said.

'Oh, well, you know . . .' George sank into his chair. There was a pause, as if all four of us were gathering our strength for another round of fragmentary dissent.

Mary was now in the second sag chair facing George. Terence lay like a low wall between them, and I sat cross-legged about a yard from Terence's feet. It was George who spoke first, across Terence to Mary.

'I've never been interested in church-going much but . . .' He trailed off, a little drunkenly, I thought. 'But I always wanted the boys to have as much of it as possible while they're young. They can reject it later, I guess. But at least for now they have a coherent set of values that are as good as any other, and they have this whole set of stories, really good stories, exotic stories, believable stories.'

No one spoke so George went on. 'They like the idea of God. And heaven and hell, and angels and the Devil. They talk about that stuff a whole lot and I'm never sure quite what it means to them. I guess it's a bit like Santa Claus, they believe it and they don't believe it. They like the business of praying, even if they ask for the craziest things. Praying for them is a kind of extension of their . . . their inner lives. They pray about what they want and what they're afraid of. They go to church every week, it's about the only thing Jean and I agree on.'

George addressed all this to Mary who nodded as he spoke and stared back at him solemnly. Terence had closed his eyes. Now that he had finished, George looked at each of us in turn, waiting to be challenged. We stirred. Terence lifted himself on to his elbow. No one spoke.

'I don't see it's going to hurt them, a bit of the old religion,' George reiterated.

Mary spoke into the ground. 'Well, I don't know. There's a lot of things you could object to in Christianity. And since you don't really believe in it yourself we should talk about that.'

'O K,' said George. 'Let's hear it.'

Mary spoke with deliberation at first. 'Well, for a start, the Bible is a book written by men, addressed to men and features a very male God who even looks like a man because he·made man in his own image. That sounds pretty suspicious to me, a real male fantasy . . .'

'Wait a minute,' said George.

'Next,' Mary went on, 'women come off pretty badly in Christianity. Through Original Sin they are held responsible for everything in the world since the Garden of Eden. Women are weak, unclean, condemned to bear children in pain as punishment for the failures of Eve, they are the temptresses who turn the minds of men away from God; as if women were more responsible for men's sexual feelings than the men themselves! Like Simone de Beauvoir says, women are always the "other", the real business is between a man in the sky and the men on the ground. In fact women only exist at all as a kind of divine afterthought, put together out of a spare rib to keep men company and iron their shirts, and the biggest favour they can do Christianity is not to get dirtied up with sex, stay chaste, and if they can manage to have a baby at the same time then they're measuring up to the Christian Church's ideal of womanhood – the Virgin Mary.' Now Mary was angry, she glared at George.

'Wait a minute,' he was saying, 'you can't impose all that Women's Lib stuff on to the societies of thousands of years ago. Christianity expressed itself through available . . .'

At roughly the same time Terence said, 'Another objection to Christianity is that it leads to passive acceptance of social inequalities because the real rewards are in . . .'

IAN McEWAN

And Mary cut in across George in protest. 'Christianity has provided an ideology for sexism now, and capitalism . . .'

'Are you a communist?' George demanded angrily, although I was not sure who he was talking to. Terence was pressing on loudly with his own speech. I heard him mention the Crusades and the Inquisition.

'This has nothing to do with Christianity.' George was almost shouting. His face was flushed.

'More evil perpetrated in the name of Christ than . . . this has nothing to do with . . . to the persecution of women herbalists as witches . . . Bullshit. It's irrelevant . . . corruption, graft, propping up tyrants, accumulating wealth at the altars . . . fertility goddess . . . bullshit . . . phallic worship . . . look at Galileo . . . this has nothing to . . .' I heard little else because now I was shouting my own piece about Christianity. It was impossible to stay quiet. George was jabbing his finger furiously in Terence's direction. Mary was leaning forwards trying to catch George by the sleeve and tell him something. The whisky bottle lay on its side empty, someone had upset the ice. For the first time in my life I found myself with urgent views on Christianity, on violence, on America, on everything, and I demanded priority before my thoughts slipped away.

'. . . and starting to think objectively about this . . . their pulpits to put down the workers and their strikes so . . . objective? You mean male. All reality now is male rea . . . always a violent God . . . the great capitalist in the sky . . . protective ideology of the dominant class denies the conflict between men and women . . . bullshit, total bullshit . . .'

Suddenly I heard another voice ringing in my ears. It was my own. I was talking into a brief, exhausted silence.

'. . . driving across the States I saw this sign in Illinois along Interstate 70 which said, "God, Guts, Guns made America great. Let's keep all three."'

'Hah!' Mary and Terence exclaimed in triumph. George was on his feet, empty glass in hand.

'That's right,' he cried. 'That's right. You can put it down but it's right. This country has a violent past, a lot of brave men died making . . .'

'Men!' echoed Mary.

'All right, and a lot of brave women too. America was made with the gun. You can't get away from that.' George strode across the room to the bar in the corner and drew out something black from behind the bottles. 'I keep a gun here,' he said, holding the thing up for us to see.

'What for?' Mary asked.

'When you have kids you begin to have a very different attitude towards life and death. I never kept a gun before the kids were around. Now I think I'd shoot at anyone who threatened their existence.'

'Is it a real gun?' I said. George came back towards us with the gun in one hand and a fresh bottle of Scotch in the other. 'Dead right it's a real gun!' It was very small and did not extend beyond George's open palm.

'Let me see that,' said Terence.

'It's loaded,' George warned as he handed it across. The gun appeared to have a soothing effect on us all. We no longer shouted, we spoke quietly in its presence. While Terence examined the gun George filled our glasses. As he sat down he reminded me of my promise to play the flute. There followed a bleary silence of a minute or two, broken only by George to tell us that after this drink we should eat dinner. Mary was far away in thought. She rotated her glass slowly between her finger and thumb. I lay back on my elbows and began to piece together the conversation we had just had. I was trying to remember how we arrived at this sudden silence.

Then Terence snapped the safety catch and levelled the gun at George's head.

'Raise your hands, Christian,' he said dully.

George did not move. He said, 'You oughtn't to fool around with a gun.' Terence tightened his grip. Of course he was fooling around, and yet I could see from where I was that his finger was curled about the trigger, and he was beginning to pull on it.

'Terence!' Mary whispered, and touched his back gently with her foot. Keeping his eyes on Terence, George sipped at his drink. Terence brought his other hand up to steady the gun which was aimed at the centre of George's face.

'Death to the gun owners.' Terence spoke without a trace of humour. I tried to say his name too, but hardly a sound left my throat. When I tried again I said something in my accelerating panic that was quite irrelevant.

'Who is it?' Terence pulled the trigger.

From that point on the evening collapsed into conventional, labyrinthine politenesses at which Americans, when they wish, quite outstrip the English. George was the only one to have seen Terence

remove the bullets from the gun, and this united Mary and I in a state
of mild but prolonged shock. We ate salad and cold cuts from plates
balanced on our knees. George asked Terence about his Orwell thesis
and the prospects of teaching jobs. Terence asked George about his
business, fun party hire and sickroom requisites. Mary was questioned about her job in the feminist bookshop and she answered
blandly, carefully avoiding any statement that might provoke
discussion. Finally I was called on to elaborate on my travel plans,
which I did in great and dull detail. I explained how I would be
spending a week in Amsterdam before returning to London. This
caused Terence and George to spend several minutes in praise of
Amsterdam, although it was quite clear they had seen very different
cities.

Then while the others drank coffee and yawned, I played my flute. I
played my Bach sonata no worse than usual, perhaps a little more
confidently for being drunk, but my mind ran on against the music.
For I was weary of this music and of myself for playing it. As the notes
transferred themselves from the page to the end of my fingers I
thought, Am I still playing *this*? I still heard the echo of our raised
voices, I saw the black gun in George's open palm, the comedian
reappear from the darkness to take the microphone again, I saw
myself many months ago setting out for San Francisco from Buffalo in
a drive-away car, shouting out for joy over the roar of the wind
through the open windows, It's me, I'm here, I'm coming . . . where
was the music for all this? Why wasn't I even looking for it? Why did I
go on doing what I couldn't do, music from another time and
civilization, its certainty and perfection to me a pretence and a lie, as
much as they had once been, or might still be, a truth to others? What
should I look for? (I tooled through the second movement like a piano
roll.) Something difficult and free. I thought of Terence's stories
about himself, his game with the gun, Mary's experiment with
herself, of myself in an empty moment drumming my fingers on the
back of a book, the vast, fragmented city without a centre, without
citizens, a city that existed only in the mind, a nexus of change or
stagnation in individual lives. Picture and idea crashed drunkenly one
after the other, discord battened to bar after bar of implied harmony
and inexorable logic. For the pulse of one beat I glanced past the music
at my friends where they sprawled on the floor. Then their after-image
glowed briefly at me from the page of music. Possible, even likely, that
the four of us would never see each other again, and against such

commonplace transience my music was inane in its rationality, paltry in its over-determination. Leave it to others, to professionals who could evoke the old days of its truth. To me it was nothing, now that I knew what I wanted. This genteel escapism . . . crossword with its answers written in, I could play no more of it.

I broke off in the slow movement and looked up. I was about to say, 'I can't go on any more', but the three of them were on their feet clapping and smiling broadly at me. In parody of concert-goers George and Terence cupped their hands round their mouths and called out 'Bravo! Bravissimo!' Mary came forward, kissed me on the cheek and presented me with an imaginary bouquet. Overwhelmed by nostalgia for a country I had not yet left, I could do no more than put my feet together and make a bow, clasping the flowers to my chest.

Then Mary said, 'Let's go. I'm tired.'

ANGELA CARTER

FLESH AND THE MIRROR

It was midnight – I chose my times and set my scenes with the precision of the born artiste. Hadn't I gone eight thousand miles to find a climate with enough anguish and hysteria in it to satisfy me? I had arrived back in Yokohama that evening from a visit to England and nobody met me, although I expected him. So I took the train to Tokyo, half an hour's journey. First, I was angry; but the poignancy of my own situation overcame me and then I was sad. To return to the one you love and find him absent! My heart used to jump like Pavlov's dogs at the prospect of such a treat; I positively salivated at the suggestion of unpleasure, I was sure that *that* was real life. I'm told I always look lonely when I'm alone; that is because, when I was an intolerable adolescent, I learned to sit with my coat collar turned up in a lonely way, so that people would talk to me. And I can't drop the habit even now, though, now, it's only a habit and, I realize, a predatory habit.

It was midnight and I was crying bitterly as I walked under the artificial cherry blossom with which they decorate the lamp standards from April to September. They do that so the pleasure quarters will have the look of a continuous carnival, no matter what ripples of agitation disturb the never-ceasing, endlessly circulating, quiet, gentle, melancholy crowds who throng the wet web of alleys under a false ceiling of umbrellas. All looked as desolate as Mardi Gras. I was searching among a multitude of unknown faces for the face of the one I loved while the warm, thick, heavy rain of summer greased the dark surfaces of the streets until, after a while, they began to gleam like sleek fur of seals just risen from the bottom of the sea.

The crowds lapped round me like waves full of eyes until I felt that I was walking through an ocean whose speechless and gesticulating inhabitants, like those with whom medieval philosophers peopled the countries of the deep, were methodical inversions or mirror images of the dwellers on dry land. And I moved through these expressionist perspectives in my black dress as though I was the creator of all and of myself, too, in a black dress, in love, crying, walking through the city in the third person singular, my own heroine, as though the world stretched out from my eye like spokes from a sensitized hub that galvanized all to life when I looked at it.

I think I know, now, what I was trying to do. I was trying to subdue the city by turning it into a projection of my own growing pains. What solipsistic arrogance! The city, the largest city in the world, the city designed to suit not one of my European expectations, this city presents the foreigner with a mode of life that seems to him to have the enigmatic transparency, the indecipherable clarity, of dream. And it is a dream he could, himself, never have dreamed. The stranger, the foreigner, thinks he is in control; but he has been precipitated into somebody else's dream.

You never know what will happen in Tokyo. Anything can happen.

I had been attracted to the city first because I suspected it contained enormous histrionic resources. I was always rummaging in the dressing-up box of the heart for suitable appearances to adopt in the city. That was the way I maintained my defences for, at that time, I always used to suffer a great deal if I let myself get too close to reality since the definitive world of the everyday with its hard edges and harsh light did not have enough resonance to echo the demands I made upon experience. It was as if I never experienced experience *as* experience. Living never lived up to the expectations I had of it – the Bovary syndrome. I was always imagining other things that could have been happening, instead, and so I always felt cheated, always dissatisfied.

Always dissatisfied, even if, like a perfect heroine, I wandered, weeping, on a forlorn quest for a lost lover through the aromatic labyrinth of alleys. And wasn't I in Asia? Asia! But, even though I lived there, it always seemed far away from me. It was as if there were glass between me and the world. But I could see myself perfectly well on the other side of the glass. There I was, walking up and down, eating meals, having conversations, in love, indifferent, and so on. But all the time I was pulling the strings of my own puppet; it was this puppet who was moving about on the other side of the glass. And I eyed the most marvellous adventures with the bored eye of the agent with the cigar watching another audition. I tapped out the ash and asked of events: 'What else can you do?'

So I attempted to rebuild the city according to the blueprint in my imagination as a backdrop to the plays in my puppet theatre, but it sternly refused to be so rebuilt; I was only imagining it had been so rebuilt. On the night I came back to it, however hard I looked for the one I loved, she could not find him anywhere and the city delivered her into the hands of a perfect stranger who fell into step beside her and asked why she was crying. She went with him to an unambiguous hotel with mirror on the ceiling and lascivious black lace draped round a palpably illicit bed. His eyes were shaped like sequins. All night long, a thin, pale, sickle moon with a single star pendant at its nether tip floated upon the rain that pitter-pattered against the windows and there was a clockwork whirring of cicadas. From time to time, the windbell dangling from the eaves let out an exquisitely mournful tinkle.

None of the lyrical eroticism of this sweet, sad, moon night of summer rain had been within my expectations; I had half expected he would strangle me. My sensibility wilted under the burden of response. My sensibility foundered under the assault on my senses.

My imagination had been pre-empted.

The room was a box of oiled paper full of the echoes of the rain. After the light was out, as we lay together, I could still see the single shape of our embrace in the mirror above me, a marvellously unexpected conjunction cast at random by the enigmatic kaleidoscope of the city. Our pelts were stippled with the fretted shadows of the lace curtains as if our skins were a mysterious uniform provided by the management in order to render all those who made love in that hotel anonymous. The mirror annihilated time, place and person; at the consecration of this house, the mirror had been dedicated to the reflection of chance embraces. Therefore it treated flesh in an exemplary fashion, with charity and indifference.

The mirror distilled the essence of all the encounters of strangers whose perceptions of one another existed only in the medium of the chance embrace, the accidental. During the durationless time we spent making love, we were not ourselves, whoever that might have been, but in some sense the ghosts of ourselves. But the selves we were not, the selves of our own habitual perceptions of ourselves, had a far more insubstantial substance than the reflections we were. The magic mirror presented me with a hitherto unconsidered notion of myself as I. Without any intention of mine, I had been defined by the action reflected in the mirror. I beset me. I was the subject of the sentence written on the mirror. I was not watching it. There was nothing whatsoever beyond the surface of the glass. Nothing kept me from the fact, the act; I had been precipitated into knowledge of the real conditions of living.

Mirrors are ambiguous things. The bureaucracy of the mirror issues me with a passport to the world; it shows me my appearance. But what use is a passport to an armchair traveller? Women and mirrors are in complicity with one another to evade the action I/she performs that she/I cannot watch, the action with which I break out of the mirror, with which I assume my appearance. But *this* mirror refused to conspire with me; it was like the first mirror I'd ever seen. It reflected the embrace beneath it without the least guile. All it showed was inevitable. But I myself could never have dreamed it.

I saw the flesh and the mirror but I could not come to terms with the sight. My immediate response to it was, to feel I'd acted out of character. The fancy-dress disguise I'd put on to suit the city had betrayed me to a room and a bed and a modification of myself that had no business at all in my life, not in the life I had watched myself performing.

Therefore I evaded the mirror. I scrambled out of its arms and sat on the edge of the bed and lit a fresh cigarette from the butt of the old one. The rain beat down. My demonstration of perturbation was perfect in every detail, just like the movies. I applauded it. I was gratified the mirror had not seduced me into behaving in a way I would have felt inappropriate – that is, shrugging and sleeping, as though my infidelity was not of the least importance. I now shook with the disturbing presentiment that he with his sequin eyes who'd been kind to me was an ironic substitute for the other one, the one I loved, as if the arbitrary carnival of the streets had gratuitously offered me this young man to find out if I *could* act out of character and then projected our intersection upon the mirror, as an objective lesson in the nature of things.

Therefore I dressed rapidly and ran away as soon as it was light outside, that mysterious, colourless light of dawn when the hooded crows flap out of the temple groves to perch on the telegraph poles, cawing a baleful dawn chorus to the echoing boulevards empty, now, of all the pleasure-seekers. The rain had stopped. It was an overcast morning so hot that I broke out into a sweat at the slightest movement. The bewildering electrographics of the city at night were all switched off. All the perspectives were pale, gritty grey, the air was full of dust. I never knew such a banal morning.

The morning before the night before, the morning before this oppressive morning, I woke up in the cabin of a boat. All the previous day, as we rounded the coast in bright weather, I dreamed of the

reunion before me, a lovers' meeting refreshed by the three months
I'd been gone, returning home due to a death in the family. I will come
back as soon as I can – I'll write. Will you meet me at the pier? Of
course, of course he will. But he was not at the pier; where was he?

So I went at once to the city and began my desolate tour of the
pleasure quarters, looking for him in all the bars he used. He was
nowhere to be found. I did not know his address, of course; he moved
from rented room to rented room with the agility of the feckless and
we had corresponded through accommodation addresses, coffee
shops, poste restante, etc. Besides, there had been a displacement of
mail reminiscent of the excesses of the nineteenth-century novel, such
as it is difficult to believe and could only have been caused by a
desperate emotional necessity to cause as much confusion as possible.
Both of us prided ourselves on our passionate sensibilities, of course.
That was *one* thing we had in common! So, although I thought I was
the most romantic spectacle imaginable as I wandered weeping down
the alleys, I was in reality at risk – I had fallen through one of the holes
life leaves in it; these peculiar holes are the entrances to the counters at
which you pay the price of the way you live.

Random chance operates in relation to these existential lacunae; one
tumbles down them when, for the time being, due to hunger, despair,
sleeplessness, hallucination or those accidental-on-purpose misread-
ings of train timetables and airline schedules that produce margins of
empty time, one is lost. One is at the mercy of events. That is why I
like to be a foreigner; I only travel for the insecurity. But I did not
know that, then.

I found my self-imposed fate, my beloved, quite early that morning
but we quarrelled immediately. We quarrelled the day away assidu-
ously and, when I tried to pull the strings of my self and so take control
of the situation, I was astonished to find the situation I wanted was
disaster, shipwreck. I saw his face as though it were in ruins, although
it was the sight in the world I knew best and, the first time I saw it, had
not seemed to me a face I did not know. It had seemed, in some way, to
correspond to my idea of my own face. It had seemed a face long
known and well remembered, a face that had always been imminent in
my consciousness as an idea that now found its first visual expression.

So I suppose I do not know how he really looked and, in fact, I
suppose I shall never know, now, for he was plainly an object created
in the mode of fantasy. His image was already present somewhere in
my head and I was seeking to discover it in actuality, looking at every

face I met in case it was the right face – that is, the face which corresponded to my notion of the unseen face of the one I should love, a face created parthenogenetically by the rage to love which consumed me. So his self, and, by his self, I mean the thing he was to himself, was quite unknown to me. I created him solely in relation to myself, like a work of romantic art, an object corresponding to the ghost inside me. When I'd first loved him, I wanted to take him apart, as a child dismembers a clockwork toy, to comprehend the inscrutable mechanics of its interior. I wanted to see him far more naked than he was with his clothes off. It was easy enough to strip him bare and then I picked up my scalpel and set to work. But, since I was so absolutely in charge of the dissection, I only discovered what I was able to recognize already, from past experience, inside him. If ever I found anything new to me, I steadfastly ignored it. I was so absorbed in this work it never occurred to me to wonder if it hurt him.

In order to create the loved object in this way and to issue it with its certificate of authentication, as beloved, I had also to labour at the idea of myself in love. I watched myself closely for all the signs and, precisely upon cue, here they were! Longing, desire, self-abnegation, etc. I was racked by all the symptoms. Even so, in spite of this fugue of feeling, I had felt nothing but pleasure when the young man who picked me up inserted his sex inside me in the blue-movie bedroom. I only grew guilty later, when I realized I had not felt in the least guilty at the time. And was I in character when I felt guilty or in character when I did not? I was perplexed. I no longer understood the logic of my own performance. My script had been scrambled behind my back. The cameraman was drunk. The director had a *crise de nerfs* and been taken away to a sanatorium. And my co-star had picked himself up off the operating table and painfully cobbled himself together again according to his own design! All this had taken place while I was looking at the mirror.

Imagine my affront.

We quarrelled until night fell and, still quarrelling, found our way to another hotel but this hotel, and this night, was in every respect a parody of the previous night. (That's more like it! Squalor and humiliation! Ah!) Here, there were no lace drapes nor windbells nor moonlight nor any moist whisper of lugubriously seductive rain; this place was bleak, mean and cheerless and the sheets on the mattress they threw down on the floor for us were blotched with dirt although, at first, we did not notice that because it was necessary to pretend the urgent passion we always used to feel in one another's presence even if we felt it no longer, as if to act out the feeling with sufficient intensity would re-create it by sleight of hand, although our skins (which knew us better than we knew ourselves) told us the period of reciprocation was over. It was a mean room and the windows overlooked a parking lot with a freeway beyond it, so that the paper walls shuddered with the reverberations of the infernal clamour of the traffic. There was a sluggish electric fan with dead flies caught in the spokes and a single strip of neon overhead lit us and everything up with a scarcely tolerable, quite remorseless light. A slatternly woman in a filthy apron brought us glasses of thin, cold, brown tea made from barley and then she shut the door on us. I would not let him kiss me between the thighs because I was afraid he would taste the traces of last night's adventure, a little touch of paranoia in *that* delusion.

I don't know how much guilt had to do with the choice of this décor. But I felt it was perfectly appropriate.

The air was thicker than tea that's stewed on the hob all day and cockroaches were running over the ceiling, I remember. I cried all the first part of the night, I cried until I was exhausted but he turned on his side and slept – he saw through that ruse, though I did not since I did not know that I was lying. But I could not sleep because of the rattling of the walls and the noise of traffic. We had turned off the glaring lamp; when I saw a shaft of light fall across his face, I thought: 'Surely it's too early for the dawn.' But it was another person silently sliding open the unlocked door; in this disreputable hotel, anything can happen. I screamed and the intruder vanished. Wakened by a scream, my lover thought I'd gone mad and instantly trapped me in a stranglehold, in case I murdered him.

We were both old enough to have known better, too.

When I turned on the lamp to see what time it was, I noticed, to my surprise, that his features were blurring, like the underwriting on a palimpsest. It wasn't long before we parted. Only a few days. You can't keep *that* pace up for long.

Then the city vanished; it ceased, almost immediately, to be a magic and appalling place. I woke up one morning and found it had become home. Though I still turn up my coat collar in a lonely way and am always looking at myself in mirrors, they're only habits and give no clue at all to my character, whatever that is.

The most difficult performance in the world is, acting naturally, isn't it? Everything else is artful.

LET ME COUNT THE TIMES

Vernon made love to his wife three and a half times a week, and this was all right.

For some reason, making love always averaged out that way. Normally – though by no means invariably – they made love every second night. On the other hand Vernon had been known to make love to his wife seven nights running; for the next seven nights they would not make love – or perhaps they would once, in which case they would make love the following week only twice but four times the week after that – or perhaps only three times, in which case they would make love four times the next week but only twice the week after that – or perhaps only once. And so on. Vernon didn't know why, but making love always averaged out that way; it seemed invariable. Occasionally – and was it any wonder? – Vernon found himself wishing that the week contained only six days, or as many as eight, to render these calculations (which were always blandly corroborative in spirit) easier to deal with.

It was, without exception, Vernon himself who initiated their conjugal acts. His wife responded every time with the same bashful alacrity. Oral foreplay was by no means unknown between them. On average – and again it always averaged out like this, and again Vernon was always the unsmiling ring master – fellatio was performed by Vernon's wife every third coupling, or 60.8333 times a year, or 1.1698717 times a week. Vernon performed cunnilingus rather less often: every fourth coupling, on average, or 45.625 times a year, or .8774038 times a week. It would also be a mistake to think that this was the extent of their variations. Vernon sodomized his wife twice a year, for instance – on his birthday, which seemed fair enough, but also, ironically (or so *he* thought), on hers. He put it down to the expensive nights out they always had on these occasions, and more particularly to the effects of champagne. Vernon always felt

desperately ashamed afterwards, and would be a limp spectre of
embarrassment and remorse at breakfast the next day. Vernon's wife
never said anything about it, which was something. If she ever did,
Vernon would probably have stopped doing it. But she never did. The
same sort of thing happened when Vernon ejaculated in his wife's
mouth, which on average he did 1.2 times a year. At this point they
had been married for ten years. That was convenient. What would it
be like when they had been married for eleven years – or thirteen.
Once, and only once, Vernon had been about to ejaculate in his wife's
mouth when suddenly he had got a better idea: he ejaculated all over
her face instead. She didn't say anything about that either, thank God.
Why he had thought it a better idea he would never know. He didn't
think it was a better idea now. It distressed him greatly to reflect that
his rare acts of abandonment should expose a desire to humble and
degrade the loved one. And she was the loved one. Still, he had only
done it once. Vernon ejaculated all over his wife's face .001923 times a
week. That wasn't very often to ejaculate all over your wife's face, now
was it?

Vernon was a businessman. His office contained several electronic
calculators. Vernon would often run his marital frequencies through
these swift, efficient, and impeccably discreet machines. They always
responded brightly with the same answer, as if to say, 'Yes, Vernon,
that's how often you do it,' or 'No, Vernon, you don't do it any more
often than that.' Vernon would spend whole lunch-hours crooked
over the calculator. And yet he knew that all these figures were in a
sense approximate. Oh, Vernon knew, Vernon knew. Then one day a
powerful white computer was delivered to the accounts department.
Vernon saw at once that a long-nursed dream might now take flesh:
leap years. 'Ah, Alice. I don't want to be disturbed, do you hear?' he
told the cleaning lady sternly when he let himself into the office that
night. 'I've got some very important calculations to do in the accounts
department.' Just after midnight Vernon's hot red eyes stared up
wildly from the display screen, where his entire sex life lay tabulated
in recurring prisms of threes and sixes, in endless series, like mirrors
placed face to face.

Vernon's wife was the only woman Vernon had ever known. He
loved her and he liked making love to her quite a lot; certainly he had
never craved any other outlet. When Vernon made love to his wife he
thought only of her pleasure and her beauty: the infrequent but highly
flattering noises she made through her evenly parted teeth, the divine

plasticity of her limbs, the fever, the magic, and the safety of the moment. The sense of peace that followed had only a little to do with the probability that tomorrow would be a night off. Even Vernon's dreams were monogamous: the women who strode those slipped but essentially quotidian landscapes were mere icons of the self-sufficient female kingdom, nurses, nuns, bus-conductresses, parking wardens, policewomen. Only every now and then, once a week, say, or less, or not calculably, he saw things that made him suspect that life might have room for more inside – a luminous ribbon dappling the under-curve of a bridge, certain cloudscapes, intent figures hurrying through changing light.

All this, of course, was before Vernon's business trip.

It was not a particularly important business trip: Vernon's firm was not a particularly important firm. His wife packed his smallest suitcase and drove him to the station. On the way she observed that they had not spent a night apart for over four years – when she had gone to stay with her mother after that operation of hers. Vernon nodded in surprised agreement, making a few brisk calculations in his head. He kissed her goodbye with some passion. In the restaurant car he had a gin and tonic. He had another gin and tonic. As the train approached the thickening city Vernon felt a curious lightness play through his body. He thought of himself as a young man, alone. The city would be full of cabs, stray people, shadows, women, things happening.

Vernon got to his hotel at eight o'clock. The receptionist confirmed his reservation and gave him his key. Vernon rode the elevator to his room. He washed and changed, selecting, after some deliberation, the more sombre of the two ties his wife had packed. He went to the bar and ordered a gin and tonic. The cocktail waitress brought it to him at a table. The bar was scattered with city people: men, women who probably did things with men fairly often, young couples secretively chuckling. Directly opposite Vernon sat a formidable lady with a fur, a hat, and a cigarette holder. She glanced at Vernon twice or perhaps three times. Vernon couldn't be sure.

He dined in the hotel restaurant. With his meal he enjoyed half a bottle of good red wine. Over coffee Vernon toyed with the idea of going back to the bar for a crème de menthe – or a champagne cocktail. He felt hot; his scalp hummed; two hysterical flies looped round his head. He rode back to his room, with a view to freshening up. Slowly, before the mirror, he removed all his clothes. His pale body was inflamed with the tranquil glow of fever. He felt deliciously raw, tingling to his touch. What's happening to me? he wondered. Then, with relief, with shame, with rapture, he keeled backwards on to the bed and did something he hadn't done for over ten years.

Vernon did it three more times that night and twice again in the morning.

Four appointments spaced out the following day. Vernon's mission was to pick the right pocket calculator for daily use by all members of his firm. Between each demonstration – the Moebius strip of figures, the repeated wink of the decimal point – Vernon took cabs back to the hotel and did it again each time. 'As fast as you can, driver,' he found himself saying. That night he had a light supper sent up to his room. He did it five more times – or was it six? He could no longer be absolutely sure. But he was sure he did it three more times the next morning, once before breakfast and twice after. He took the train back at noon, having done it an incredible 18 times in 36 hours: that was – what? – 84 times a week, or 4,368 times a year. Or perhaps he had done it 19 times! Vernon was exhausted, yet in a sense he had never felt stronger. And here was the train giving him an erection all the same, whether he liked it or not.

'How was it?' asked his wife at the station.

'Tiring. But successful,' admitted Vernon.

'Yes, you do look a bit whacked. We'd better get you home and tuck you up in bed for a while.'

Vernon's red eyes blinked. He could hardly believe his luck.

Shortly afterwards Vernon was to look back with amused disbelief at his own faint-heartedness during those trail-blazing few days. Only in bed, for instance! Now, in his total recklessness and elation, Vernon did it everywhere. He hauled himself roughly on to the bedroom floor and did it there. He did it under the impassive gaze of the bathroom's porcelain and steel. With scandalized laughter he dragged himself out protesting to the garden tool shed and did it there. He did it lying on the kitchen table. For a while he took to doing it in the open air, in windy parks, behind hoardings in the town, on churned fields; it made his knees tremble. He did it in corridorless trains. He would rent rooms in cheap hotels for an hour, for half an hour, for ten minutes (how the receptionists stared). He thought of renting a little love-nest somewhere. Confusedly and very briefly he considered running off with himself. He started doing it at work, cautiously at first, then with nihilistic abandon, as if discovery was the very thing he secretly craved. Once, giggling coquettishly before and afterwards (the danger, the danger), he did it while dictating a long and tremulous letter to the secretary he shared with two other senior managers. After this he came to his senses somewhat and resolved to try only to do it at home.

'How long will you be, dear?' he would call over his shoulder as his wife opened the front door with her shopping-bags in her hands. An hour? Fine. Just a couple of minutes? Even better! He took to lingering sinuously in bed while his wife made their morning tea, deliciously sandwiched by the moist uxoriousness of the sheets. On his nights off from love-making (and these were invariable now: every other night, every other night) Vernon nearly always managed one while his wife, in the bathroom next door, calmly readied herself for sleep. She nearly caught him at it on several occasions. He found that especially exciting. At this point Vernon was still trying hectically to keep count; it was all there somewhere, gurgling away in the memory banks of the computer in the accounts department. He was averaging 3.4 times a day, or 23.8 times a week, or an insane 1,241 times a year. And his wife never suspected a thing.

Until now, Vernon's 'sessions' (as he thought of them) had always been mentally structured round his wife, the only woman he had ever known – her beauty, the flattering noises she made, the fever, the safety. There were variations, naturally. A typical 'session' would start with her undressing at night. She would lean out of her heavy brassière and submissively debark the tender checks of her panties. She would give a little gasp, half pleasure, half fear (how do you figure a woman?), as naked Vernon, obviously in sparkling form, emerged impressively from the shadows. He would mount her swiftly, perhaps even rather brutally. Her hands mimed their defencelessness as the great muscles rippled and plunged along Vernon's powerful back. 'You're too big for me,' he would have her say to him sometimes, or 'That hurts, but I like it.' Climax would usually be synchronized with his wife's howled request for the sort of thing Vernon seldom did to her in real life. But Vernon never did the things for which she yearned, oh no. He usually just ejaculated all over her face. She loved that as well of course (the bitch), to Vernon's transient disgust.

And then the strangers came.

One summer evening Vernon returned early from the office. The car was gone: as Vernon had shrewdly anticipated, his wife was out somewhere. Hurrying into the house, he made straight for the bedroom. He lay down and lowered his trousers – and then with a sensuous moan tugged them off altogether. Things started well, with a compelling preamble that had become increasingly popular in recent weeks. Naked, primed, Vernon stood behind the half-closed bedroom door. Already he could hear his wife's preparatory truffles of shy arousal. Vernon stepped forward to swing open the door, intending to stand there menacingly for a few seconds, his restless legs planted well apart. He swung open the door and stared. At what? At his wife sweatily grappling with a huge bronzed gypsy, who turned incuriously towards Vernon and then back again to the hysteria of volition splayed out on the bed before him. Vernon ejaculated immediately. His wife returned home within a few minutes. She kissed him on the forehead. He felt very strange.

The next time he tried, he swung open the door to find his wife upside down over the headboard, doing scarcely credible things to a hairy-shouldered Turk. The time after that, she had her elbows hooked round the back of her knee-caps as a 15 stone Chinaman feasted at his leisure on her imploring sobs. The time after that, two silent, glistening negroes were doing what the hell they liked with her. The two negroes, in particular, wouldn't go away; they were quite frequently joined by the Turk, moreover. Sometimes they would even let Vernon and his wife get started before they all came thundering in on them. And did Vernon's wife mind any of this? Mind? She liked it. Like it? She *loved* it! And so did Vernon, apparently. At the office Vernon soberly searched his brain for a single neutrino of genuine desire that his wife should do these things with these people. The very idea made him shout with revulsion. Yet, one way or another, he didn't mind it really, did he? One way or another, he liked it. He loved it. But he was determined to put an end to it.

His whole approach changed. 'Right, my girl,' he muttered to himself, 'two can play at that game.' To begin with, Vernon had affairs with all his wife's friends. The longest and perhaps the most detailed was with Vera, his wife's old school chum. He sported with her bridge-partners, her co-workers in the Charity. He fooled around with all her eligible relatives – her younger sister, that nice little niece of hers. One mad morning Vernon even mounted her hated mother. 'But Vernon, what about . . . ?' they would all whisper fearfully. But Vernon just shoved them on to the bed, twisting off his belt with an imperious snap. All the women out there on the edges of his wife's world – one by one, Vernon had the lot.

Meanwhile, Vernon's erotic dealings with his wife herself had continued much as before. Perhaps they had even profited in poignancy and gentleness from the pounding rumours of Vernon's nether life. With this latest development, however, Vernon was not slow to mark a new dimension, a disfavoured presence, in their bed. Oh, they still made love all right; but now there were two vital differences. Their acts of sex were no longer hermetic; the safety and the peace had gone: no longer did Vernon attempt to apply any brake to the chariot of his thoughts. Secondly – and perhaps even more crucially – their love-making was, without a doubt, *less frequent*. Six and a half times a fortnight, three times a week, five times a fortnight . . . : they were definitely losing ground. At first Vernon's mind was a chaos of back-logs, short-falls, restructured schedules, recuperation schemes. Later he grew far more detached about the whole business. Who said he had to do it three and a half times a week? Who said that this was all right? After ten nights of chaste sleep (his record up till now) Vernon watched his wife turn sadly on her side after her diffident goodnight. He waited several minutes, propped up on an elbow, glazedly eternalized in the potent moment. Then he leaned forward and coldly kissed her neck, and smiled as he felt her body's axis turn. He went on smiling. He knew where the real action was.

For Vernon was now perfectly well aware that any woman was his for the taking, any woman at all, at a nod, at a shrug, at a single convulsive snap of his peremptory fingers. He systematically serviced every woman who caught his eye in the street, had his way with them, and tossed them aside without a second thought. All the models in his wife's fashion magazines – they all trooped through his bedroom, too, in their turn. Over the course of several months he worked his way through all the established television actresses. An equivalent period took care of the major stars of the Hollywood screen. (Vernon bought a big glossy book to help him with this project. For his money, the girls of the Golden Age were the most daring and athletic lovers: Monroe, Russell, West, Dietrich, Dors, Ekberg. Frankly, you could keep your Welches, your Dunaways, your Fondas, your Keatons.) By now the roll-call of names was astounding. Vernon's prowess with them epic, unsurpassable. All the girls were saying that he was easily the best lover they had ever had.

One afternoon he gingerly peered into the pornographic magazines that blazed from the shelves of a remote newsagent. He made a mental note of the faces and figures, and the girls were duly accorded brief membership of Vernon's thronging harem. But he was shocked; he didn't mind admitting it: why should pretty young girls take their clothes off for money like that, like *that*? Why should men want to buy pictures of them doing it? Distressed and not a little confused, Vernon conducted the first great purge of his clamorous rumpus rooms. That night he paced through the shimmering corridors and becalmed ante-rooms dusting his palms and looking sternly this way and that. Some girls wept openly at the loss of their friends; others smiled up at him with furtive triumph. But he stalked on, slamming the heavy doors behind him.

Vernon now looked for solace in the pages of our literature. Quality, he told himself, was what he was after – quality, quality. Here was where the high-class girls hung out. Using the literature shelves in the depleted local library, Vernon got down to work. After quick flings with Emily, Griselda, and Criseyde, and a strapping weekend with the Good Wife of Bath, Vernon cruised straight on to Shakespeare and the delightfully wide-eyed starlets of the romantic comedies. He romped giggling with Viola over the Illyrian hills, slept in a glade in Arden with the willowy Rosalind, bathed nude with Miranda in a turquoise lagoon. In a single disdainful morning he splashed his way through all four of the tragic heroines: cold Cordelia (this was a bit of a frost, actually), bitter-sweet Ophelia (again rather constricted, though he quite liked her dirty talk), the snake-eyed Lady M. (Vernon had had to watch himself there) and, best of all, that sizzling sorceress Desdemona (Othello had *her* number all right. She *stank* of sex!). Following some arduous, unhygienic yet relatively brief dalliance with Restoration drama, Vernon soldiered on through the prudent matrons of the Great Tradition. As a rule, the more sedate and respectable the girls, the nastier and more complicated were the things Vernon found himself wanting to do to them (with lapsed hussies like Maria Bertram, Becky Sharp, or Lady Dedlock, Vernon was in, out, and away, darting half-dressed over the rooftops). Pamela had her points, but Clarissa was the one who turned out to be the true co-artist of the oeuvres; Sophie Western was good fun all right, but the pious Amelia yodelled for the humbling high points in Vernon's sweltering repertoire. Again he had no very serious complaints about his one-night romances with the likes of Elizabeth Bennett and Dorothea

Brooke; it was adult, sanitary stuff, based on a clear understanding of his desires and his needs; they knew that such men will take what they want; they knew that they would wake the next morning and Vernon would be gone. Give him a Fanny Price, though, or better, much better, a Little Nell, and Vernon would march into the bedroom rolling up his sleeves; and Nell and Fan would soon be ruing the day they'd ever been born. Did they mind the horrible things he did to them? Mind? When he prepared to leave the next morning, solemnly buckling his belt before the tall window – how they howled!

The possibilities seemed endless. Other literatures dozed expectantly in their dormitories. The sleeping lion of Tolstoy – Anna, Natasha, Masha, and the rest. American fiction – those girls would show even Vernon a trick or two. The sneaky Gauls – Vernon had a hunch that he and Madame Bovary, for instance, were going to get along just fine . . . One puzzled weekend, however, Vernon encountered the writings of D. H. Lawrence. Snapping *The Rainbow* shut on Sunday night, Vernon realized at once that this particular avenue of possibility – sprawling as it was, with its intricate trees and their beautiful diseases, and that distant prospect where sandy mountains loomed – had come to an abrupt and unanswerable end. He never knew women behaved like *that* . . . Vernon felt obscure relief and even a pang of theoretical desire when his wife bustled in last thing, bearing the tea-tray before her.

Vernon was now, on average, sleeping with his wife 1.15 times a week. Less than single figure love-making was obviously going to be some sort of crunch, and Vernon was making himself vigilant for whatever form the crisis might take. She hadn't, thank God, said anything about it, yet. Brooding one afternoon soon after the Lawrence débâcle, Vernon suddenly thought of something that made his heart jump. He blinked. He couldn't believe it. It was true. Not once since he had started his 'sessions' had Vernon exacted from his wife any of the sly variations with which he had used to space out the weeks, the months, the years. Not once. It had simply never occurred to him. He flipped his pocket calculator on to his lap. Stunned, he tapped out the figures. She now owed him . . . Why, if he wanted, he could have an entire week of . . . They were behind with *that* to the tune of . . . Soon it would be time again for him to . . . Vernon's wife passed through the room. She blew him a kiss. Vernon resolved to shelve these figures but also to keep them up to date. They seemed to balance things out.

He knew he was denying his wife something she ought to have; yet at the same time he was withholding something he ought not to give. He began to feel better about the whole business.

For it now became clear that no mere woman could satisfy him – not Vernon. His activities moved into an entirely new sphere of intensity and abstraction. Now, when the velvet curtain shot skywards, Vernon might be astride a black stallion on a marmoreal dune, his narrow eyes fixed on the caravan of defenceless Arab women straggling along beneath him; then he dug in his spurs and thundered down on them, swords twirling in either hand. Or else Vernon climbed from a wriggling human swamp of tangled naked bodies, playfully batting away the hands that clutched at him, until he was tugged down once again into the thudding mass of membrane and heat. He visited strange planets where women were metal, were flowers, were gas. Soon he became a cumulus cloud, a tidal wave, the East Wind, the boiling Earth's core, the air itself, wheeling round a terrified globe as whole tribes, races, ecologies fled and scattered under the continent-wide shadow of his approach.

It was after about a month of this new brand of skylarking that things began to go rather seriously awry.

The first hint of disaster came with sporadic attacks of *ejaculatio praecox*. Vernon would settle down for a leisurely session, would just be casting and scripting the cosmic drama about to be unfolded before him – and would look down to find his thoughts had been messily and pleasurelessly anticipated by the roguish weapon in his hands. It began to happen more frequently, sometimes quite out of the blue: Vernon wouldn't even notice until he saw the boyish, tell-tale stains on his pants last thing at night. (Amazingly, and rather hurtfully too, his wife didn't seem to detect any real difference. But he was making love to her only every ten or eleven days by that time.) Vernon made a creditable attempt to laugh the whole thing off, and, sure enough, after a while the trouble cleared itself up. What followed, however, was far worse.

To begin with, at any rate, Vernon blamed himself. He was so relieved, and so childishly delighted, by his newly recovered prowess that he teased out his 'sessions' to unendurable, unprecedented lengths. Perhaps that wasn't wise . . . What was certain was that he overdid it. Within a week, and quite against his will, Vernon's 'sessions' were taking between thirty and forty-five minutes; within two weeks, up to an hour and a half. It wrecked his schedules: all the lightning strikes, all the silky raids, that used to punctuate his life were reduced to dour campaigns which Vernon could perforce never truly win. 'Vernon, are you ill?' his wife would say outside the bathroom door. 'It's nearly *tea*-time.' Vernon – slumped on the lavatory seat, panting with exhaustion – looked up wildly, his eyes startled, shrunken. He coughed until he found his voice. 'I'll be straight out,' he managed to say, climbing heavily to his feet.

Nothing Vernon could summon would deliver him. Massed, maddened, cart-wheeling women – some of molten pewter and fifty feet tall, others indigo and no bigger than fountain-pens – hollered at him from the four corners of the universe. No help. He gathered all the innocents and subjected them to atrocities of unimaginable proportions, committing a million murders enriched with infamous tortures. He still drew a blank. Vernon, all neutronium, a supernova, a black sun, consumed the Earth and her sisters in his dead fire, bullocking through the solar system, ejaculating the Milky Way. That didn't work either. He was obliged to fake orgasms with his wife (rather skilfully, it seemed: she didn't say anything about it). His testicles developed a mighty migraine, whose slow throbs all day timed his heartbeat with mounting frequency and power, until at night Vernon's face was a sweating parcel of lard and his hands shimmered deliriously as he juggled the aspirins to his lips.

Then the ultimate catastrophe occurred. Paradoxically, it was heralded by a single, joyous, uncovenanted climax – again out of the blue, on a bus, one lunchtime. Throughout the afternoon at the office Vernon chuckled and gloated, convinced that finally all his troubles were at an end. It wasn't so. After a week of ceaseless experiment and scrutiny Vernon had to face the truth. The thing was dead. He was impotent.

'Oh my God,' he thought, 'I always knew something like this would happen to me some time.' In one sense Vernon accepted the latest reverse with grim stoicism (by now the thought of his old ways filled him with the greatest disgust); in another sense, and with terror, he felt like a man suspended between two states: one is reality, perhaps, the other an unspeakable dream. And then when day comes he awakes with a moan of relief; but reality has gone and the nightmare has replaced it: the nightmare was really there all the time. Vernon looked at the house where they had lived for so long now, the five rooms through which his calm wife moved along her calm tracks, and he saw it all slipping away from him forever, all his peace, all the fever and the safety. And for what, for what?

'Perhaps it would be better if I just told her about the whole thing and made a clean breast of it,' he thought wretchedly. 'It wouldn't be easy, God knows, but in time she might learn to trust me again. And I really *am* finished with all that other nonsense. God, when I . . .' But then he saw his wife's face – capable, straightforward, confident – and the scar of dawning realization as he stammered out his shame. No, he could never tell her, he could never do that to her, no, not to her. She was sure to find out soon enough anyway. How could a man conceal that he had lost what made him a man? He considered suicide, but – 'But I just haven't got the guts,' he told himself. He would have to wait, to wait and melt in his dread.

A month passed without his wife saying anything. This had always been a make-or-break, last-ditch deadline for Vernon, and he now approached the coming confrontation as a matter of nightly crisis. All day long he rehearsed his excuses. To kick off with Vernon complained of a headache, on the next night of a stomach upset. For the following two nights he stayed up virtually until dawn – 'preparing the annual figures,' he said. On the fifth night he simulated a long coughing fit, on the sixth a powerful fever. But on the seventh night he just helplessly lay there, sadly waiting. Thirty minutes passed, side by side. Vernon prayed for her sleep and for his death.

'Vernon?' she asked.

'Mm-hm?' he managed to say – God, what a croak it was.

'Do you want to talk about this?'

Vernon didn't say anything. He lay there, melting, dying. More minutes passed. Then he felt her hand on his thigh.

Quite a long time later, and in the posture of a cowboy on the back of a bucking steer, Vernon ejaculated all over his wife's face. During the course of the preceding two and a half hours he had done to his wife everything he could possibly think of, to such an extent that he was candidly astonished that she was still alive. They subsided, mumbling soundlessly, and slept in each other's arms.

Vernon woke up before his wife did. It took him thirty-five minutes to get out of bed, so keen was he to accomplish this feat without waking her. He made breakfast in his dressing-gown, training every cell of his concentration on the small, sacramental tasks. Every time his mind veered back to the night before, he made a low growling sound, or slid his knuckles down the cheese-grater, or caught his tongue between his teeth and pressed hard. He closed his eyes and he could see his wife crammed against the headboard with that one leg sticking up in the air; he could hear the sound her breasts made as he two-handedly slapped them practically out of alignment. Vernon steadied himself against the refrigerator. He had an image of his wife coming into the kitchen – on crutches, her face black and blue. She couldn't very well not say anything about *that*, could she? He laid the table. He heard her stir. He sat down, his knees cracking, and ducked his head behind the cereal packet.

When Vernon looked up his wife was sitting opposite him. She looked utterly normal. Her blue eyes searched for his with all their light.

'Toast?' he bluffed.

'Yes please. Oh Vernon, wasn't it lovely?'

For an instant Vernon knew beyond doubt that he would now have to murder his wife and then commit suicide – or kill her and leave the country under an assumed name, start all over again somewhere, Romania, Iceland, the Far East, the New World.

'What, you mean the –?'

'Oh yes. I'm so happy. For a while I thought that we . . . I thought you were –'

'I –'

'– Don't, darling. You needn't say anything. I understand. And now everything's all right again. Ooh,' she added. 'You were naughty, you know.'

Vernon nearly panicked all over again. But he gulped it down and said, quite nonchalantly, 'Yes, I was a bit, wasn't I?'

'Very naughty. So *rude*. Oh Vernon . . .'

She reached for his hand and stood up. Vernon got to his feet too – or became upright by some new hydraulic system especially devised for the occasion. She glanced over her shoulder as she moved up the stairs.

'You mustn't do that too often, you know.'

'Oh really?' drawled Vernon. 'Who says?'

'*I* say. It would take the fun out of it. Well, not *too* often, anyway.'

Vernon knew one thing: he was going to stop keeping count. Pretty soon, he reckoned, things would be more or less back to normal. He'd had his kicks: it was only right that the loved one should now have hers. Vernon followed his wife into the bedroom and softly closed the door behind them.

ROSE TREMAIN

MY WIFE IS A WHITE RUSSIAN

I'm a financier. I have financial assets, world-wide. I'm in nickel and
pig-iron and gold and diamonds. I like the sound of all these words.
They have an edge, I think. The glitter of saying them sometimes
gives me an erection.

I'm saying them now in this French restaurant, where the table-
cloths and the table-napkins are blue linen, where they serve sea-food
on platters of seaweed and crushed ice. It's noisy at lunch-time. It's
May and the sun shines in London, through the open restaurant
windows. Opposite me, the two young Australians blink as they wait
(so damned courteous, and she has freckles like a child) for me to
stutter out my hard-word list, to manipulate tongue and memory so
that the sound inside me forms just behind my lips and explodes with
extraordinary force above my oysters: '*Diamonds!*'

But then I feel a soft, perfumed dabbing at my face. I turn away
from the Australians and there she is. My wife. She is smiling as she
wipes me. Her gold bracelets rattle. She is smiling at me. Her lips are
astonishing, the colour of claret. I've been wanting to ask her for some
time, 'Why are your lips this terrible dark colour these days? Is it a
lipstick you put on?'

Still smiling at me, she's talking to the Australians with her odd
accent: 'He's able to enjoy the pleasures of life once more, thank God.
For a long time afterwards I couldn't take him out. Terrible. We
couldn't do one single thing, you know. But now – he enjoys his wine
again.'

The dabbing stops. To the nurse I tried to say when I felt a
movement begin: 'Teach me how to wipe my arse. I cannot let my wife
do this because she doesn't love me. If she loved me, she probably
wouldn't mind wiping my arse, and I wouldn't mind her wiping my
arse. But she doesn't love me.'

The Australian man is talking now. I let my hand go up and take hold of my big-bowled wine glass into which the waiter has poured the expensive Chablis my wife likes to drink when she eats fish. Slowly, I guide the glass across the deadweight distance between the table and my mouth. I say 'deadweight' because the spaces between all my limbs and the surfaces of tangible things have become mighty. To walk is to wade in waist-high water. And to lift this wine glass . . . 'Help me,' I want to say to her, 'just this once.' Just this once.

'Heck,' says the Australian man, 'we honestly thought he'd made a pretty positive recovery.' His wife, with blue eyes the colour of the napkins, is watching my struggles with the glass. She licks her fine line of a mouth, sensing I suppose, my longing to taste the wine. The nurse used to stand behind me, guiding the feeding-cup in my hand. I never explained to her that the weight of gravity had mysteriously increased. Yet often, as I drank from the feeding-cup, I used to imagine myself prancing on the moon.

'Oh, this is a very positive recovery,' says my wife. 'There's very little he can't do now. He enjoys the ballet, you know, and the opera. People at Covent Garden and the better kind of place are very considerate. We don't go to the cinema because there you have a very inconsiderate type of person. Don't you agree? So riff-raffy. Don't you agree?'

The Australian wife hasn't listened to a word. The Australian wife puts out a lean freckled arm and I watch it come towards me, astounded as usual these days by the speed with which other people can move parts of their bodies. But the arm, six inches from my hand holding the glass, suddenly stops. 'Don't help him!' snaps my wife. The napkin-blue eyes are lowered. The arm is folded away.

Heads turn in the restaurant. I suppose her voice has carried its inevitable echo round the room where we sit: 'Don't help him! Don't help him!' But now that I have an audience, the glass begins to jolt, the wine splashing up and down the sides of the bowl. I smile. My smile widens as I watch the Chablis begin to slop onto the starched blue cloth. WASTE. She of all people understands the exquisite luxury of waste. Yet she snatches the glass out of my hand and sets it down by her own. She snaps her fingers and a young bean pole of a waiter arrives. He spreads out a fresh blue napkin where I have spilled my wine. My wife smiles her claret smile. She sucks an oyster into her dark mouth.

The Australian man is, I was told, the manager of the Toomin

Valley Nickel Consortium. The wife is, as far as I know, just a wife. I own four-fifths of the Toomin Valley Nickel Consortium. The Australian man is here to discuss expansion, supposedly with me, unaware until he met me this lunch-time that despite the pleasing cadences of the words I'm unable to say Toomin Valley Nickel Consortium. I can say 'nickel'. My tongue lashes around in my throat to form the click that comes in the middle of the word. Then out it spills: *Nickel!* In my mind, oddly enough, the word 'nickel' is the exact greyish-white colour of an oyster. But 'consortium' is too difficult for me. I know my limitations.

My wife is talking again: 'I've always loved the ballet, you see. This is my only happy memory of Russia – the wonderful classical ballet. A little magic. Don't you think? I would never want to be without this kind of magic, would you? Do you have the first-rate ballet companies in Australia? You do? Well, that's good. *Giselle*, of course. That's the best one. Don't you think? The dead girl. Don't you think? Wonderful.'

We met on a pavement. I believe it was in the Avenue Matignon, but it could have been the Avenue Montaigne. I often get these muddled. It was in Paris, anyway. Early summer, as it is now. Chestnut candle blooms blown along the gutters. I waited to get into the taxi she was leaving. But I didn't get into it. I followed her. In a bar, she told me she was very poor; her father drove the taxi I had almost hired. She spoke no English then, only French with a heavy Russian accent. I was just starting to be a financier at that time, but already I was quite rich, rich by her standards – she who had been used to life in post-war Russia. My hotel room was rather grand. She said in her odd French: 'I'll fuck for money.'

I gave her fifty francs. I suppose it wasn't much, not as much as she'd hoped for, a poor rate of exchange for the white, white body that rode astride me, head thrown back, breasts bouncing. She sat at the dressing-table in the hotel room. She smoked my American cigarettes. More than anything, I wanted to brush her gold hair, brush it smooth and hold it against my face. But I didn't ask her if I could do this. I believe I was afraid she would say, 'You can do it for money.'

The thin waiter is clearing away our oyster platters. I've eaten only three of my oysters, yet I let my plate go. She lets it go. She pretends not to notice how slow I've been with the oysters. And my glass of wine still stands by hers, untasted. Yet she's drinking quite fast. I hear her order a second bottle.

The Australian man says: 'First rate choice, if I may say so. We like Chably.'

I raise my left arm and touch her elbow, nodding at the wine. Without looking at me, she puts my glass down in front of me. The Australian wife stares at it. Neither she nor I dare to touch it.

My wife is explaining to the Australians what they are about to eat, as if they were children: 'I think you will like the turbot very much. *Turbot poché hollandaise*. They cook it very well. And the hollandaise sauce – you know this, of course? Very difficult to achieve, the lightness of this sauce. But here they do it very well. And the scallops in saffron. Again, a very light sauce. Excellent texture. Just a little cream added. And fresh scallops, naturally. We never go to any restaurant where the products are frozen. So I think you will like these dishes very much . . .'

We have separate rooms. Long before my illness, when I began to look (yet hardly to feel) old, she demanded her privacy. This was how she put it: she wanted to be private. The bedroom we used to share and which is now hers is very large. The walls are silk.

She said: 'There's no sense in being rich and being cooped up together in one room.'

Obediently, I moved out. She wouldn't let me have the guest room, which is also big. I have what we call 'the little room', which I always used to think of as a child's room.

I expect in her 'privacy' that she is smiling: 'The child's room is completely right for him. He's a helpless baby.' Yet she's not a private person. She likes to go out four or five nights a week, returning at two or three in the morning, sometimes with friends, and they sit and drink brandy. Sometimes, they play music. Elton John. She has a lover (I don't know his name) who sends her lilies.

I'm trying to remember the Toomin Valley. I believe it's an immense desert of a place, inhabited by no one and nothing except the mining machinery and the Nickel Consortium employees, whose clusters of houses I ordered to be whitewashed to hide the cheap grey building blocks. The windows of the houses are small, to keep out the sun. In the back yards are spindly eucalyptus trees, blown by the scorching winds. I want to ask the Australian wife, did you have freckles before you went to live in the Toomin Valley, and does some

wandering prima ballerina dance *Giselle* on the gritty escarpment
above the mine?

My scallops arrive, saffron yellow and orange in the blue and white
dish – the colours of a childhood summer. The flesh of a scallop is firm
yet soft, the texture of a woman's thigh (when she is young, of course,
before the skin hardens and the flesh bags out). A forkful of scallop is
immeasurably easier to lift than the glass of wine, and the Australian
wife (why don't I know either of their names?) smiles at me approving-
ly as I lift the succulent parcel of food to my mouth and chew it
without dribbling. My wife, too, is watching, ready with the little
scented handkerchief, yet talking as she eats, talking of Australia as
the second bottle of Chablis arrives and she tastes it hurriedly with a
curt nod to the thin waiter. I exist only in the corner of her eye, at its
inmost edge, where the vulnerable triangle of red flesh is startling.

'Of course, I've often said to Hubert' (she pronounces my name
'Eieu-bert', trying and failing with what she recognizes as the upper
class *h*), 'that it's very unfair to expect people like you to live in some
out-of-the-way place. I was brought up in a village, you see, and I
know that an out-of-the-way village is so dead. No culture. The same
in Toomin, no? Absolutely no culture at all. Everybody dead.'

The Australian wife looks – seemingly for the first time – straight at
my wife. 'We're outdoor people.'

I remember now. A river used to flow through the Toomin Valley.
Torrential in the rainy season, they said. It dried up in the early
'forties. One or two sparse willows remain, grey testimony to the
long-ago existence of water-rich soil. I imagine the young Australian
couple, brown as chestnuts, swimming in the Toomin River, resting
on its gentle banks with their fingers touching, a little loving nest of
bone. There is no river. Yet when they look at each other – almost
furtively under my vacant gaze – I recognize the look. The look says:
'These moments with strangers are nothing. Into our private
moments together – only there – is crammed all that we ask of
life.'

'Yes, we're outdoor folk.' The Australian man is smiling. 'You can
play tennis most of the year round at Toomin. I'm president of the
tennis club. And we have our own pool now.'

I don't remember these things: tennis-courts and swimming-pools.

'Well, of course, you have the climate for these things.' My wife is
signalling our waiter to bring her Perrier water. 'And it's something to

do, isn't it? Perhaps when the new expansions of the company are made, a concert hall could be built for you, or a theatre.'

'A theatre!' The Australian wife's mouth opens to reveal perfect, freshly-peeled teeth and a laugh escapes. She blushes.

My wife's dark lips are puckered into a sneer.

But the Australian man is laughing too – a rich laugh you might easily remember on the other side of the world – and slapping his thigh. 'A theatre! What about that, ay?'

She wanted, she said, as she smoked my American cigarettes, to see *Don Giovanni*. Since leaving Russia with her French mother and her Russian father, no one had ever taken her to the opera. She had seen the posters advertising *Don Giovanni* and had asked her father to buy her a ticket.

He had shouted at her: 'Remember whose child you are! Do you imagine taxi drivers can afford seats at the Opéra?'

'Take me to see *Don Giovanni*,' she said to me, 'and I will fuck for nothing.'

I've never really appreciated the opera. The Don was fat. It was difficult to imagine so many women wanting to lie with this fat man. Yet afterwards, she leant over to me and put her head on my shoulder and wept. Nothing, she told me, had ever moved her so much – nothing in her life had ever touched the core of her being – as this had done, this production of *Don Giovanni*.

'If only,' she said, 'I had money as you have money, then I would go to hear music all the time and see the classical ballet and learn from these what is life.'

The scallops are good. She never learned what is life. I feel emboldened by the food. I put my hand to my glass, heavier than ever now because the waiter has filled it up. The sun shines on my wine and on my hand, blotched (splattered, it seems) with the oddly repulsive stains of old age. For a second, I see my hand and the wine glass as a still-life. But then I lift the glass. The Australian wife lowers her eyes. My wife, for a moment, is silent. I drink. I smile at the Australian wife because I know she wants to applaud.

I'm talking. The words are like stones weighing down my lower jaw. *Nickel*. I'm trying to tell the Australian man that I dream about the nickel mine. In my dreams, the Australian miners drag wooden carts loaded with threepenny bits. I run my hands through the coins as though through a sack of wheat, and the touch of them is pleasurable and perfect. I also want to say to the Australian man: 'I hope you're happy in your work. When I was in control, I visited all my mines and all my subsidiaries at least once a year. Even in South Africa, I made sure a living wage was paid. I said to the men underground, "I hope you're happy in your work."'

But now I have a manager, a head-manager to manage all the other managers, including this one from the Toomin Valley. I am trundled out in my chair to meet them when they come here to discuss redundancy or expansion. My wife and I give them lunch in a restaurant. They remind me that I still have an empire to rule, if I were capable, if indeed my life had been different since the night of *Don Giovanni*.

When I stopped paying her to sleep with me, her father came to see me. He held his cap in his hands. 'We're hoping for a marriage,' he said. And what more could I have given – what less – to the body I had begun to need? The white and the gold of her, I thought, will ornament my life.

Yet now I never touch her. The white and the gold of her lies only in the lilies they send, the unknown lovers she finds in the night, while I lie in the child's room and dream of the nickel mines. My heart is scorched dry, like the dry hills of the Toomin Valley. I am punished for my need of her while her life stalks my silence; the white of her, the gold of her, the white of Dior, the gold of Cartier. Why did she never love me? In my dreams, too, the answer comes from deep underground: it's the hardness of my words.

THE PROPHET'S HAIR

Early in 19—, when Srinagar was under the spell of a winter so fierce it could crack men's bones as if they were glass, a young man upon whose cold-pinked skin there lay, like a frost, the unmistakable sheen of wealth was to be seen entering the most wretched and disreputable part of the city, where the houses of wood and corrugated iron seemed perpetually on the verge of losing their balance, and asking in low, grave tones where he might go to engage the services of a dependably professional thief. The young man's name was Atta, and the rogues in that part of town directed him gleefully into ever-darker and less public alleys, until in a yard wet with the blood of a slaughtered chicken he was set upon by two men whose faces he never saw, robbed of the substantial bank-roll which he had insanely brought on his solitary excursion, and beaten within an inch of his life.

Night fell. His body was carried by anonymous hands to the edge of the lake, whence it was transported by shikara across the water and deposited, torn and bleeding, on the deserted embankment of the canal which led to the gardens of Shalimar. At dawn the next morning a flower-vendor was rowing his boat through water to which the cold of the night had given the cloudy consistency of wild honey when he saw the prone form of young Atta, who was just beginning to stir and moan, and on whose now deathly pale skin the sheen of wealth could still be made out dimly beneath an actual layer of frost. The flower-vendor moored his craft and by stooping over the mouth of the injured man was able to learn the poor fellow's address, which was mumbled through lips which could scarcely move; whereupon, hoping for a large tip, the hawker rowed Atta home to a large house on the shores of the lake, where a painfully beautiful girl and her equally handsome mother, neither of whom, it was clear from their eyes, had slept a wink from worrying, screamed at the sight of their Atta – who was the elder brother of the beautiful girl – lying motionless amid the funereally stunted winter blooms of the hopeful florist. The flower-vendor was indeed paid off handsomely, not least to ensure his silence, and plays no further part in our story. Atta himself, suffering terribly from exposure as well as a broken skull, entered a coma which caused the city's finest doctors to shrug helplessly. It was therefore all the more remarkable that on the very same evening the most wretched and disreputable part of the city received a second unexpected visitor. This was Huma, the sister of the unfortunate young man, and her question was the same as her brother's, and asked in the same low, grave tones: 'Where may I hire a thief?'

The story of the rich idiot who had come looking for a burglar was already common knowledge in those insalubrious gullies, but this time the girl added: 'I should say that I am carrying no money, nor am I wearing any jewels; my father has disowned me and will pay no ransom if I am kidnapped; and a letter has been lodged with the Commissioner of Police, my uncle, to be opened in the event of my not being safe at home by morning. In that letter he will find full details of my journey here, and he will move Heaven and Earth to punish my assailants.' Her extraordinary beauty, which was visible even through the enormous welts and bruises disfiguring her arms and forehead, coupled with the oddity of her inquiries, had attracted a sizable group of curious onlookers, and because her little speech seemed to them to cover just about everything, no one attempted to injure her in any way, although there were some raucous comments to the effect that it was pretty peculiar for someone who was trying to hire a crook to invoke the protection of a high-up policeman uncle. She was directed into ever-darker and less public alleys until finally in a gully as dark as ink an old woman with eyes which stared so piercingly that Huma instantly understood she was blind motioned her through a doorway from which darkness seemed to be pouring like smoke. Clenching her fists, angrily ordering her heart to behave normally, the girl followed the old woman into the gloom-wrapped house.

The faintest conceivable rivulet of candle-light trickled through the darkness; following this unreliable yellow thread (because she could no longer see the old lady), Huma received a sudden sharp blow to the shins and cried out involuntarily, after which she instantly bit her lip, angry at having revealed her mounting terror to whatever waited there shrouded in black. She had, in fact, collided with a low table on which a single candle burned and beyond which a mountainous figure could be made out, sitting crosslegged on the floor. 'Sit, sit,' said a man's calm, deep voice, and her legs, needing no more flowery invitation, buckled beneath her at the terse command. Clutching her left hand in her right, she forced her voice to respond evenly: 'And you, sir, will be the thief I have been requesting?'

Shifting its weight very slightly, the shadow-mountain informed her that all criminal activity originated in this zone was well organized and also centrally controlled, so that all requests for what might be termed freelance work had to be channelled through this room. He demanded comprehensive details of the crime to be committed, including a precise inventory of items to be acquired, also a clear statement of all financial inducements being offered with no gratuities excluded, plus, for filing purposes only, a summary of the motives for the application. At this, Huma, as though remembering something, stiffened both in body and resolve and replied loudly that her motives were entirely a matter for herself; that she would discuss details with no one but the thief himself; but that the rewards she proposed could only be described as 'lavish'. 'All I am willing to say to you, sir, since this appears to be some sort of employment agency, is that in return for such lavish rewards I must have the most desperate criminal at your disposal, a man for whom life holds no terrors, not even the fear of God. The worst of fellows, I tell you – nothing less will do!'

Now a paraffin storm-lantern was lighted, and Huma saw facing her a grey-haired giant down whose left cheek ran the most sinister of scars, a cicatrice in the shape of the Arabic letter 'S'. She had the insupportably nostalgic notion that the bogymen of her childhood nursery had risen up to confront her, because her ayah had always forestalled any incipient acts of disobedience by threatening Huma and Atta: 'You don't watch out and I'll send that one to steal you away – that Sheikh Sín, the Thief of Thieves!' Here, grey-haired but unquestionably scarred, was the notorious criminal himself – and was she crazy, were her ears playing tricks, or had he truly just announced that, given the circumstances, he himself was the only man for the job?

Struggling wildly against the newborn goblins of nostalgia, Huma warned the fearsome volunteer that only a matter of extreme urgency and peril would have brought her unescorted into these ferocious streets. 'Because we can afford no last-minute backings-out,' she continued, 'I am determined to tell you everything, keeping back no secrets whatsoever. If, after hearing me out, you are still prepared to proceed, then we shall do everything in our power both to assist you and to make you rich.' The old thief shrugged, nodded, spat. Huma began her story.

Six days ago, everything in the household of her father, the wealthy moneylender Hashim, had been as it always was. At breakfast her mother had spooned khichri lovingly onto the moneylender's plate; the conversation had been filled with those expressions of courtesy and solicitude on which the family prided itself. Hashim was fond of pointing out that while he was not a godly man he set great store by 'living honourably in the world'. In that spacious lakeside residence, all outsiders were greeted with the same formality and respect, even those unfortunates who came to negotiate for small fragments of Hashim's great fortune, and of whom he naturally asked an interest rate of 71 per cent, partly, as he told his khichri-spooning wife, 'to teach these people the value of money: let them only learn that, and they will be cured of this fever of borrowing, borrowing all the time – so you see that if my plans succeed, I shall put myself out of business!' In their children, Atta and Huma, the moneylender and his wife had sought, successfully, to inculcate the virtues of thrift, plain dealing, perfect manners and a healthy independence of spirit.

Breakfast ended; the family wished each other a fulfilling day. Within a few hours, however, the glassy contentment of that household, of that life of porcelain delicacy and alabaster sensibilities, was to be shattered beyond all hope of repair.

The moneylender summoned his personal shikara and was on the verge of stepping into it when, attracted by a glint of silver, he noticed a small phial floating between the boat and his private quay. On an impulse, he scooped it out of the glutinous water: it was a cylinder of tinted glass cased in exquisitely wrought silver, and Hashim saw within its walls a silver pendant bearing a single strand of human hair. Closing his fist around this unique discovery, he muttered to the boatman that he'd changed his plans, and hurried to his sanctum where, behind closed doors, he feasted his eyes on his find. There can be no doubt that Hashim the moneylender knew from the first that he was in possession of the famous holy hair of the Prophet Muhammad, whose theft from the shrine at Hazratbal the previous morning had created an unprecedented hue and cry in the valley. The thieves – no doubt alarmed by the pandemonium, by the procession through the streets of the endless ululating crocodiles of lamentation, by the riots, the political ramifications and by the massive police search which was commanded and carried out by men whose entire careers now hung upon this single lost hair – had evidently panicked and hurled the phial into the gelatine bosom of the lake. Having found it by a stroke of good fortune, Hashim's duty as a citizen was clear: the hair must be restored to its shrine, and the state to equanimity and peace.

But the moneylender had formed a different notion. All about him in his study was the evidence of collector's mania: great cases full of impaled butterflies from Gulmarg, three dozen miniature cannons cast from the melted-down metal of the great gun Zam-zama, innumerable swords, a Naga spear, ninety-four terracotta camels of the sort sold on railway-station platforms and an infinitude of tiny sandalwood dolls, which had originally been carved to serve as children's bathtime toys. 'And after all,' Hashim told himself, 'the Prophet would have disapproved mightily of this relic-worship: he abhorred the idea of being deified, so by keeping this rotting hair from its mindless devotees, I perform – do I not? – a finer service than I would by returning it! Naturally, I don't want it for its religious value: I'm a man of the world, of this world; I see it purely as a secular object of great rarity and blinding beauty – in short, it's the phial I desire, not the hair. There are American millionaires who buy stolen paintings and hide them away – they would know how I feel. I must, must have it!'

Every collector must share his treasures with one other human being, and Hashim summoned – and told – his only son Atta, who was deeply perturbed but, having been sworn to secrecy, only spilt the beans when the troubles became too terrible to bear. The youth left his father alone in the crowded solitude of his collections. Hashim was sitting erect in a hard chair, gazing intently at the beautiful phial.

It was well known that the moneylender never ate lunch, so it was not until evening that a servant entered the sanctum to summon his master to the dining-table. He found Hashim as Atta had left him. The same, but not the same: because now the moneylender looked swollen, distended, his eyes bulged even more than they always had, they were red-rimmed and his knuckles were white. It was as though he was on the point of bursting, as though, under the influence of the misappropriated relic, he had filled up with some spectral fluid which might at any moment ooze uncontrollably from his every bodily opening. He had to be helped to the table, and then the explosion did indeed take place. Seemingly careless of the effect of his words on the carefully constructed and fragile constitution of the family's life, Hashim began to gush, to spume streams of terrible truths. In horrified silence, his children heard their father turn upon his wife, and reveal to her that for many years their marriage had been the worst of his afflictions. 'An end to politeness!' he thundered. 'An end to hypocrisy!' He revealed to his family the existence of a mistress; he informed them of his regular visits to paid women. He told his wife that, far from being the principal beneficiary of his will, she would receive no more than the seventh portion which was her due under Islamic law. Then he turned upon his children, screaming at Atta for his lack of academic ability – 'A dope! I have been cursed with a dope!' – and accusing his daughter of lasciviousness, because she went around the city barefaced, which was unseemly for any good Muslim girl to do: she should, he commanded, enter purdah forthwith. He left the table without having eaten and fell into the deep sleep of a man who has got many things off his chest, leaving his children stunned, his wife in tears, and the dinner going cold on the sideboard under the gaze of an anticipatory bearer.

At five o'clock the next morning the moneylender forced his family to rise, wash and say their prayers; from that time on, he began to pray five times daily for the first time in his life, and his wife and children were obliged to do likewise. Before breakfast, Huma saw the servants, under her father's direction, constructing a great heap of books in the garden and setting fire to it. The only volume left untouched was the Quran, which Hashim wrapped in a silken cloth and placed on a table in the hall. He ordered each member of his family to read passages from this book for at least two hours per day. Visits to the cinema were also forbidden. And if Atta invited male friends to the house, Huma was to retire to her room.

By now, the family had entered a state of wild-eyed horror; but there was worse to come. That afternoon, a trembling debtor arrived at the house to confess his inability to pay the latest instalment of interest owed, and made the mistake of reminding Hashim, in somewhat blustering fashion, of the Quran's strictures against usury. The moneylender, flying into a rage, attacked the fellow with one of his large collection of bull-whips. By mischance, later the same day a second defaulter came to plead for time, and was seen fleeing Hashim's study with a great gash on his arm, because Huma's father had called him a thief of other men's money and had tried to cut off the fellow's right hand with one of the thirty-eight kukri knives hanging on the study walls. These breaches of the family's laws of decorum alarmed Atta and Huma, and when, that evening, their mother attempted to calm Hashim down, he struck her on the face with an open hand. Atta leapt to his mother's defence and he, too, was sent flying. 'From now on,' Hashim bellowed, 'there's going to be some discipline around here!'

The moneylender's wife began a fit of hysteria which continued throughout the night and the following day, and which so provoked her husband that he threatened her with divorce, at which she fled to her room, locked the door and subsided into a raga of sniffling. Huma now lost her composure, challenged her father openly, announced (with that same independence of spirit which he had encouraged in her) that she would wear no cloth over her face: apart from anything else, it was bad for the eyes. On hearing this, her father disowned her at once and gave her one week in which to pack her bags.

By the fourth day, the fear in the air of the house had become so thick that it was difficult to walk around. Atta told his shock-numbed sister: 'We are descending to gutter-level – but I know what must be done.'

That afternoon, Hashim left home accompanied by two hired thugs to extract the unpaid dues from his two insolvent clients. Atta went immediately to his father's study. Being the son and heir, he possessed his own key to the moneylender's safe, which he now used, and removing the little phial from its hiding-place, he slipped it into his trouser pocket and re-locked the safe door.

Now he told Huma the secret of what his father had found in Lake Dal, and cried: 'Maybe I'm crazy – maybe the awful things that are happening have made me cracked – but I am convinced there will be no peace in our house until this hair is out of it.' His sister instantly agreed that the hair must be returned and Atta set off in a hired shikara to Hazratbal mosque. Only when the boat had delivered him into the throng of the distraught faithful which was swirling around the desecrated shrine did Atta discover that the relic was no longer in his pocket. There was only a hole, which his mother, usually so attentive to household matters, must have overlooked under the stress of recent events . . . Atta's initial surge of chagrin was quickly replaced by a feeling of profound relief. 'Suppose,' he imagined, 'I had already announced to the mullahs that the hair was on my person! They would never have believed me now – and this mob would have lynched me! At any rate, it's gone, and that's a load off my mind.' Feeling more contented than he had for days, the young man returned home.

Here he found his sister bruised and weeping in the hall; upstairs, in her bedroom, his mother wailed like a brand-new widow. He begged Huma to tell him what had happened, and when she replied that their father, returning from his brutal business trip, had once again noticed a glint of silver between boat and quay, had once again scooped up the errant relic, and was consequently in a rage to end all rages, having beaten the truth out of her – then Atta buried his face in his hands and sobbed that, in his opinion, that hair was persecuting them, that it had come back to finish the job.

Now it was Huma's turn to think of a way out of their troubles. While her arms turned black and blue and great stains spread across her forehead, she hugged her brother and whispered to him her determination to get rid of the hair *at all costs*: she repeated this last phrase several times. 'The hair,' she then declared, 'must be stolen. It was stolen from the mosque; it can be stolen from this house. But it must be a genuine robbery, carried out by a real thief, not by one of us who are the hair's victims – by a thief so desperate that he fears neither capture nor curses.' Of course, she added, the theft would be ten times harder to pull off now that their father, knowing that there had already been one attempt on the relic, was certainly on his guard.

'Can you do it?' Huma, in a room lit by candle and storm-lantern, ended her account with this question: 'What assurances can you give that the job holds no terrors for you still?' The criminal, spitting, stated that he was not in the habit of providing references, as a cook might, or a gardener, but he was not alarmed so easily, not by any children's djinn of a curse. The girl had to be content with this boast, and proceeded to describe the details of the proposed burglary. 'Since my brother's failure to restore the hair to the mosque, my father has taken to sleeping with his precious treasure under his pillow. However, he sleeps alone and very energetically: only enter his room without waking him, and he will certainly have tossed and turned quite enough to make the theft a simple matter. When you have the phial, come to my room,' and here she handed Sheikh Sin a plan of her home, 'and I will hand over all the jewellery owned by my mother and by myself. You will find . . . It is worth . . . You will be able to get a fortune for it . . .' It was clear that her self-control was weakening and that she was on the point of physical collapse. 'Tonight,' she burst out finally, 'you must come tonight!'

No sooner had she left the room than the old criminal's body was convulsed by a fit of coughing: he spat blood into an old tin can. The great Sheikh, the 'Thief of Thieves', was also an old and sick man, and every day the time drew nearer when some young pretender to his power would stick a dagger in his stomach. A lifelong addiction to gambling had left him as poor as he had been when, decades ago, he had started out in this line of work as a mere pickpocket's apprentice: in the extraordinary commission he had accepted from the money-lender's daughter he saw his opportunity of amassing enough wealth, at a stroke, to leave the valley and acquire the luxury of a respectable death which would leave his stomach intact.

As for the Prophet's hair, well, neither he nor his blind wife had ever had much to say for prophets – that was one thing they had in common with the moneylender's clan. It would not do, however, to reveal the nature of this, his last crime, to his four sons: to his consternation, they had all grown up into hopelessly devout fellows, who even spoke absurdly of making the pilgrimage to Mecca some day. 'But how will you go?' their father would laugh at them, because, with the absolutist love of a parent, he had made sure they were all provided with a lifelong source of high income by crippling them at birth, so that, as they dragged themselves around the city, they earned excellent money in the begging business. The children, then, could look after themselves; he and his wife would be off with the jewel-boxes of the moneylender's women. It was a timely chance indeed that had brought the beautiful bruised girl into his corner of the town.

That night, the large house on the shore of the lake lay blindly waiting, with silence lapping at its walls. A burglar's night: clouds in the sky and mists on the winter water. Hashim the moneylender was asleep, the only member of his family to whom sleep had come that night. In another room, his son Atta lay deep in the coils of his coma with a blood-clot forming on his brain, watched over by a mother who had let down her long greying hair to show her grief, a mother who placed warm compresses on his head with gestures redolent of impotence. In yet a third bedroom Huma waited, fully dressed, amidst the jewel-heavy caskets of her desperation. At last a bulbul sang softly from the garden below her window and, creeping down-stairs, she opened a door to the bird, on whose face there was a scar in the shape of the Arabic letter 'S'. Noiseless now, the bird flew up the stairs behind her. At the head of the staircase they parted, moving in opposite directions along the corridor of their conspiracy without a glance at one another.

Entering the moneylender's room with professional ease, the burglar, Sin, discovered that Huma's predictions had been wholly accurate. Hashim lay sprawled diagonally across his bed, the pillow untenanted by his head, the prize easily accessible. Step by padded step, Sin moved towards the goal. It was at this point that young Atta, without any warning, his vocal cords prompted by God knows what pressure of the clot upon his brain, sat bolt upright in his bed, giving his mother the fright of her life, and screamed at the top of his voice: 'Thief! Thief! Thief!'

It seems probable that his poor mind had been dwelling, in these last moments, upon his own father, but it is impossible to be certain, because having uttered these three emphatic words the young man fell back on his pillow and died. At once his mother set up a screeching and a wailing and a keening and a howling so ear-splittingly intense as to complete the work which Atta's cry had begun – that is, her laments penetrated the walls of her husband's bedroom and brought Hashim wide awake.

Sheikh Sin was just deciding whether to dive beneath the bed or brain the moneylender good and proper when Hashim grabbed the tiger-striped swordstick which always stood propped up in a corner beside his bed, and rushed from the room without so much as noticing the burglar who stood on the opposite side of the bed in the darkness. Sin stooped quickly and removed the phial containing the Prophet's hair from its hiding-place.

Meanwhile Hashim had erupted into the corridor, having unsheathed the sword inside his stick; he was waving the blade about dementedly with his right hand and shaking the stick with his left. Now a shadow came rushing towards him through the midnight darkness of the passageway and, in his somnolent anger, the moneylender thrust his sword fatally through its heart. Turning up the light, he found that he had murdered his daughter, and under the dire influence of this accident he found himself so persecuted by remorse that he turned the sword upon himself, fell upon it and so extinguished his life. His wife, the sole surviving member of the family, was driven mad by the general carnage and had to be committed to an asylum for the insane by her brother, the city's Commissioner of Police.

Sheikh Sin had quickly understood that the plan had gone awry: abandoning the dream of the jewel-boxes when he was but a few yards from its fulfilment, he climbed out of Hashim's window and made his escape during the awful events described above. Reaching home before dawn, he woke his wife and confessed his failure: it would be necessary, he said, for him to vanish for a while. Her blind eyes never opened until he had gone.

The noise in the Hashim household had roused their servants and even awakened the night-watchman, who had been fast asleep as usual on his charpoy by the gate; the police were alerted and the Commissioner himself informed. When he heard of Huma's death, the mournful officer opened and read the sealed letter which his niece had given him, and instantly led a large detachment of armed men into the light-repellent gullies of the most wretched and disreputable part of the city. The tongue of a malicious cat-burglar named Huma's fellow conspirator; the finger of an ambitious bank-robber pointed at the house in which he lay concealed; and although Sin managed to crawl through a hatch in the attic and attempt a roof-top escape, a bullet from the Commissioner's own rifle penetrated his stomach and brought him crashing messily to the ground at the feet of the enraged uncle. From the dead man's ragged pockets rolled a phial of tinted glass, cased in filigree silver.

The recovery of the Prophet's hair was announced at once on All-India Radio. One month later, the valley's holiest men assembled at the Hazratbal mosque and formally authenticated the relic. It sits to this day in a closely guarded vault by the shores of the loveliest of lakes in the heart of the valley which is closer than any other place on earth to Paradise.

But before its story can properly be concluded, it is necessary to record that when the four sons of the dead Sheikh awoke on that morning of his death, having unwittingly spent a few minutes under the same roof as the holy hair, they found that a miracle had occurred, that they were all sound of limb and strong of wind, as whole as they might have been if their father had not thought to smash their legs in the first hours of their lives. They were, all four of them, very properly furious, because this miracle had reduced their earning powers by 75 per cent, at the most conservative estimate: so they were ruined men.

Only the Sheikh's widow had some reason for feeling grateful, because although her husband was dead she had regained her sight, so that it was possible for her to spend her last days gazing once more upon the beauties of the valley of Kashmir.

JULIAN BARNES

ONE OF A KIND

I always had this theory about Romania. Well, not a proper theory; more an observation, I suppose. Have you ever realized how, in various fields, Romania has managed to produce one – but only one – significant artist? It's as if the race only has enough strength for one of anything – like those plants which channel all their energy into a single bloom. So: one great sculptor – Brancusi; one playwright – Ionesco; one composer – Enuscu; one cartoonist – Steinberg. Even one great popular myth – Dracula.

I once mentioned this theory at a literary party to a Romanian writer in exile. Marian Tiriac was a sallow, plump, combative man, and I had got off on the wrong foot with him by referring to the question of 'dissidents'. It's always an awkward word to use with Eastern European exiles, as I should have realized. Some of them take the high political line of 'It is the Government who are the dissidents'; others the personal, practical one of 'I am not a dissident; I am a writer.' I had idly asked Tiriac whether there were any dissidents in Romania. He swished the remnants of some publisher's white wine round in the bottom of his glass, as aggressively as he could without losing any of it, and replied:

'There are no dissidents in Romania. There are merely a few people who are unavailable for comment to the foreign press. In any case, they live some way from Bucharest. The roads aren't too good up near the Hungarian border; nor are your journalists very inquisitive.'

He said it with irony, but also with a sort of funny pride, as if I didn't have the right to an opinion – or even a question – on the subject of his homeland. Not wishing to give in, but also not wishing to irritate him further, I then brought up my Romanian Theory; which I did with due English meekness and hesitancy and pleading of ignorance. Tiriac smiled at me genially enough, and reached for another stuffed olive.

'You forget poetry,' he said. 'Eminescu.' It was a name I had vaguely encountered, so I gave a nod of disgraced recognition. 'And **401** tennis – Nastase.' Another nod; was he sending me up? 'And party leadership – Ceausescu.' Now he was.

'What about novelists?' I persisted. 'Is there one I should have heard of?'

'No,' he replied, with a doleful shake of the head. 'There are none. We have no novelists.'

I forgot this conversation for almost a year, when I was invited to attend a conference of young writers in Bucharest. The occasion was as pleasant as it was pointless – I listened to dozens of vague if well-intentioned speeches about the duty of the writer towards mankind, and about the power of the written word to shape men's souls – but at least it got me to a country I wouldn't otherwise have visited. There were banquets with plum brandy, and an excursion to the Danube delta where we strained our eyes for distant flights of pelican, and parties at which local officials asked you serious questions about the craft of writing – questions which made you feel slightly ashamed, as if you ought to take your vocation more earnestly than you did.

The last morning of the trip was designated free time, and I strolled round the city with an Italian writer of experimental verse. We looked into small, dark churches, silent except for the crackling of beeswax candles and the shuffling of old people. We visited the Art Museum of the Socialist Republic of Romania, where we saw a Van Eyck portrait of an olive-skinned burgher in a blue headdress; the nameplate had been worn away by reverent fingers, as if this, the finest painting in the gallery, had become an icon to be touched no less usefully than the sculpted feet of Mary. Finally, we strolled along the Calea Victoriei and looked into the shops. On a corner of the Palatul Republicii, opposite the Headquarters of the Central Committee, we found a bookshop. One of the windows was devoted to a single work, a novel by someone called Nicolai Petrescu; we stared at the pyramid of copies for a while, wondering if we had met the author in the previous seven days. A small photograph at the corner of the display – showing a plump, white-bearded man with rimless spectacles – confirmed that we hadn't. Since this appeared to be one of the main bookshops in the country, and Petrescu, presumably, one of its more important writers, it struck us as slightly odd that he hadn't been wheeled out for some free plum brandy along with all the others.

My companion and I looked briefly into the Western languages section of the shop – if you're foreign, it's best to be dead as well if you plan to sell in Bucharest – and moved on. Later that day we were driven to Otopeni airport and flew home.

I didn't see Marian Tiriac for some months afterwards, but when I did I offered to give him my impressions of the country he hadn't seen in thirty years of exile. He seemed discouragingly unexcited by the idea, and informed me that since he would certainly never return, he made a point of not finding out what had become of the place. During his first few years of exile, he had been bitter and nostalgic, and had kept up a plaintive correspondence with many friends; but this had made things worse rather than better, and he had now severed all contact.

'Well, in any case,' I went on. 'You weren't telling me the truth. There *are* novelists in Romania.'

'Oh, perhaps. You mean Rebreanu. Or maybe Sadoveanu. I'm afraid they're only thesis material nowadays. They are not the Brancusi and Nastase you seek.'

'No, I wasn't saying that.' I hardly could have been, since I hadn't recognized either of the names. 'I just meant there were a few around. A few we met.' I mentioned three or four. He shook his head.

'You must remember, I do not have much interest in these things nowadays.'

'And there was someone else – we saw a lot of copies of something of his in a window. Petrescu; Nicolai Petrescu.'

'Ah,' he said sharply. 'Ah. Nicolai; you saw Nicolai. They are still selling his book? And how is he?'

I explained that we hadn't actually met him. I described the bookshop in Calea Victoriei, the window display, and the small picture in the corner. I said that as far as one could tell from a photo, the writer seemed to be well.

'And did he have anything in his buttonhole? A little decoration of some sort?'

'You mean a flower?'

'Of course not. A decoration. A badge.'

I said I couldn't remember. Tiriac settled himself further down into the sofa, and balanced his glass on the arm.

'I will tell you about Nicolai Petrescu if you like.' I did like. 'But you must not necessarily believe everything I say because I knew him very well. You must – what is that expression in shooting? – you must aim off. You must aim off for truth, I think.

'Nicolai and I are about the same age – our middle fifties. We were both just young enough to miss the war, for which we used to give many thanks. Fighting for the Germans against the Russians, and then changing ends and fighting for the Russians against the Germans was not particularly pleasant by all accounts. The bullets could come from either direction, or even both at the same time. But we missed much of that, fortunately.

'We were about eighteen or so when what the present administration likes to refer to as "the national anti-fascist and anti-imperialist insurrection" took place. Two men and a dog and a home-made flag, plus the fraternal Russian army – that's what that means. The Russians came in, drove out the Germans, and looked around for the local Communists. The only trouble was, they couldn't find any. Do you know how big the Communist party was in Romania in 1944? Two football teams. So, the Russians stayed around for a bit, helping to build socialism – or at least party membership – until they thought it was more or less safe to go. They sort of went in 1947. Sort of.

'Nicolai and I were at polytechnic together at that time. We were – how shall I put it? – good middle-class boys. We weren't fascists or anything; we just weren't from the working class. What's more, we both wanted to be writers. You see the problem?'

I nodded. I thought how much better he had aged than Petrescu. Tiriac looked to be in his mid-forties; Petrescu could have been over sixty from his photo.

'I suppose, when it comes down to it, it's a question of temperament more than talent, which way a writer goes. In that sort of place, anyway. We talked about it a lot. Not when we went along to the Writers' Union, of course; but between the two of us. I'm – well, you could say I was idealistic if you wanted to, but maybe it's just that I'm despairing by temperament. I only thought of the difficulties; I only thought of what they wouldn't let you write, not of what they would. I took a rather hard line on everything in those days: I believed – well, perhaps I still do – that if you can't write exactly what you want to, then you shouldn't write anything. Silence, or exile, you could say. Well, I chose exile. I lost my language, and half my talent. So I still have a lot to be despairing about.

'Nicolai, well, he was of a different temperament. No – not a collaborator at all. He was a nice man; he was my friend. He was very intelligent, I remember, and just as despairing as me, but somehow more cynical in his mind. Perhaps I don't mean cynical – perhaps I just mean he had a sense of humour. I chose silence and exile; he chose cunning.

'You know what they call wedding-cake architecture?' I nodded. I'd seen quite enough of it on my few brief trips to Eastern Europe. 'Well, the very worst examples you can see – outside Russia, I mean – the biggest, the nastiest, the ones in the most overpowering positions in the cities, are the ones which were imposed by Stalin. Gifts of the Soviet people, they were called, to Warsaw, or wherever. Monstrosities they are. People walk past on the opposite side of the road and have a quiet spit just when they come level with them. The street-cleaners are more busy opposite these wedding-cake monstrosities than anywhere else in the whole city.

'Nicolai one day conceived this plan to write what he called the wedding-cake novel. We'd been at a particularly foul and depressing meeting of the Writers' Union, and went for a walk afterwards in Cismigiu park, and I remember Nicolai turning to me as we reached the edge of the lake and saying, "If that's what they want, then that is what I shall give them." I might have pushed him in the lake, except that I saw he was smiling at me, very broadly. And then he began to explain his idea.

'The wedding-cake novel was also to be a sort of Trojan horse. Leave it outside the city and let them wheel it in; that way they'll be even more pleased. So Nicolai started working on his book. It was, of course, an epic: epically historical, epically sentimental, epically improving, epically realistic. And at the same time he began to speak at meetings of the Writers' Union. "I have this problem, comrades . . ." he would begin, and he would refer to his novel, and explain some difficulty he had come across – the problem of realistically conveying the point of view of fascist anti-patriots, for instance, or the question of handling sexual experience without offending the intrinsic good taste of the bookbuying steel-worker of Ploesti. That sort of thing. He would act troubled, and then slowly allow the clodheads and buffoons of the Union to guide him into their way of thinking, to lead him towards the light. "I have this problem, comrades . . ." Every time I heard him say it, I thought, They'll see through him this time, surely. But then irony is not a mode with which the committee were too familiar.

'And so Nicolai continued with his book, and by suggesting all these problems he was having with it, managed to create within the Union a certain apprehension. You can imagine how it is – they don't want anyone to rock the boat. If one writer steps out of line, it places everyone else in jeopardy. Nicolai was very good at playing on this fear, and the fact that he never brought any of his book along to read worried them a bit too. He kept saying that he needed to do another draft to correct a few final errors. "I have this problem, comrades . . ."

'He showed me bits of it, though he had to be careful, because I was getting into disfavour by now. Too despairing, they said of me. The few scraps of work I offered to publish were held to be insufficiently uplifting to the human spirit. Uplifting . . . ha. As if writing were a brassière and the human spirit were a pair of bosoms.

'Nicolai was a very good writer. The parts he let me see were wonderful. I mean, they were entirely awful as well, but they were wonderful too. They weren't satirical – he didn't want to do it that way. What he did was to put on a false heart and then write from the bottom of it. This false heart was intensely patriotic, sentimental and documentary. There was a lot about how little food people had, and much reference to Romanian history and the sturdiness of the national character. The history, of course, had to be vetted by the Union. "Comrades – I have another little problem . . ." I can see him now.'

Tiriac gave a chuckle as he thought of his friend, a sad chuckle. I could see how easily he appeared despairing, even when he was amused.

'And then?'

'And then he finished it, and he called it, naturally, *The Wedding Cake*. He couldn't resist the title, and he put in a long passage of facile symbolism about a wedding cake, just to back it up. He wanted the book to be like one of Stalin's presents to his slave nations. He wanted it to stand there, grand and half-admired at first, but always unignorable. And then gradually, just by standing there, it would begin to make people wonder about it. And the longer it stood there and the more it had been praised, the more it would end by shaming and embarrassing those who had revered it.

'I asked him what he would do after it was published; if his plan worked. "I shall do nothing," he said. "I shan't write another word. That will make the joke clearer as the years go by." "But they might try and make you," I said to him, "they don't let people not work, you know." "Well, maybe I'll be too famous by then. Besides, I shall tell them I have put all my heart and all my soul into *The Wedding Cake*. 'If you want to read a second book by me,' I shall say, 'Read the first one again.' And then I shall sit back and try and look as distinguished as possible."

'I left the country in 1951, when Nicolai still had some way to go with his book; he had about thirty-five strands of narrative, and they all had to be tied off in neat granny knots. We never wrote to one another after I left, because it would have been difficult for him. Instead I wrote to . . . unimportant people. My mother, a few harmless friends. As you know, I haven't ever been back; I haven't heard any news for almost a quarter of a century. But in one of her last letters to me before she died, my mother told me that *The Wedding Cake* had been published with enormous success. She had not read the book – her eyesight was poor and she didn't want to make it worse – but she wrote and told me about it. "And to think," she said, "If you had stayed, my Marian, you might have been the success that Nicolai now is."'

He turned back towards me, and took another swig of wine. He seemed depressed by his story. Then he smiled.

'Actually, if I'd known, I'd have got you to bring me a copy of *The Wedding Cake*,' he said. 'It might have been – what? – good for a laugh.'

'I'm not sure I saw a copy.'

'. . . ? But you told me . . . in the window.'

'No, the book I saw in the window just had a woman's name for a title. *Emanuella, Maria*, something like that; with a picture of a girl in a headscarf.' I asked him the Romanian for wedding-cake; he told me. 'Well, I don't remember that one. But there must have been six or seven other titles by Petrescu and I didn't look at them very carefully. Perhaps it was there.'

Then we both paused, and looked at one another, and held the pause. I could imagine some of what he was thinking.

'Well,' he finally said. 'There you have it. Another piece of evidence for your Romanian theory. Another single bloom. One great ironist – Petrescu.'

'Of course,' I replied quickly, and gave him my most agreeing smile.

*P*HILOMELA

Before I married, when we lived in Athens, the bright emptiness of the long days was made bearable by my sister Philomela, who spoke the thoughts I hardly knew I had.

Why permit yourself to be taken off like a slave? We can leave Athens and go and live in the mountains. We will be free. And if we die, anything better than the life that lies ahead of us.

I knew she was right, but I couldn't find the courage to go. The nights are cold in the mountains, and we would almost certainly perish. Tereus came and married me and we went to Thrace in a procession of such magnificence that I knew I would never come back. When my son Itylus was born, I felt as if I had been buried in a soft tomb.

I'll come and live with you, Philomela said. You won't have to wait long.

She never came. I moped, like the birds my children bring back when they go out for a walk. Tereus noticed, but he didn't care. The palace, as it is now, was always full of young men singing, and preparations for war, and the bustle of sandalled feet going aimlessly back and forth on the worn marble. I stayed on my couch, almost pleased that my beauty was going and that I was unable to sleep at night. It was a slow death, but no one who is buried alive dies quickly.

Then one day Tereus said he would go and find my sister. There had been no wars for two years, and the festivities were palling. He was looking older himself; perhaps only bloodshed kept him young; at any rate he wanted to travel, and he liked the idea of doing something gallant and slightly ridiculous. To his delight, everyone laughed when he said he was going to rescue my sister from her monotonous life in Athens.

It was at the height of summer that he set off. When he had gone I went down into the gardens for the first time for years and looked in an interested way at the flowers and the strolling peacocks. My children even smiled at me when I went up to them. I pretended to myself that my health had changed, that I had been ill for a long time and was now quite naturally better, but I knew that it was really because Philomela was coming that I saw these things in a different way. Her face and her voice kept flowing through me as I paced out the rest of the day, glancing foolishly at the position of the sun in the sky. It was a long journey, and it might be weeks before Tereus brought her back.

Tereus came back one winter day. The air was clear and I could see a huddle of people galloping across the plain. My throat ached, as if I had tried to shout to them across that distance, and my hands kept flying to my neck and pulling at the gold chains I wore. Then I felt I was going to cry, and I sent for Coda to bring me a herb drink that soothes my mind. I even thought for a moment of climbing to the temple. But I restrained myself, in case Philomela should climb the wide steps when I wasn't there to see her. And I wanted to show her the garden we had made, to take her into the house of which I felt suddenly proud.

Tereus' head seemed larger, I remember that. And the young men with him hung back, which they don't usually do – no one ran past me with a quick salute on the way to the courtyard and the refreshing wine. Tereus' head loomed over me like a round polished shield. His tongue moved thickly in his dry lips.

Philomela is dead, he said.

I spent a year in that room. When the sun lurked in the courtyard, beyond the hangings, which it did in the morning early when the slaves were washing the stone-fruited floors, I lifted my goblet of wine and poured it down my throat. All day long I called for more wine – and Coda and Dita brought it with lowered eyes.

I gave birth to another child. Itylus came and sat with me sometimes, but he was learning to go out with his father more. He had a horse of his own. When I asked him about the garden we had made, he was embarrassed and changed the subject. I began to suspect that it was overgrown, or that Tereus had got rid of it altogether. Not that I really cared. The garden had been for Philomela, and she would never come now.

When the new child was beginning to learn how to crawl about on the soft rugs in my room, I got up for the first time and went onto the wide porch that looks over the plain. It was summer, and birds were singing in the thicket of olives. My eyes were tired from crying: they had changed their shape now and slanted down in the corners instead of being round.

I gazed out at all the empty expanses around me. Sky. Earth. Distant mountain. None of them contained anything at all.

I leant back against a pillar and sighed. My back was weak after so long in my room. A slave came up the steps towards me. He stopped, surprised to see me there, and then prostrated himself.

He had something for me: it seemed to be a bundle of cloth. I took it listlessly – a present no doubt from one of the noble women I no longer consented to see. The slave glanced anxiously at me once, and then ran into the house. I opened the bundle, yawning.

A tapestry. My eyes were blurred, and I had to bring it up close to my face to see what scenes were depicted. Chariots in Thrace, I thought at first, and noble warriors under a spiky sun. Then I saw that the chief figure was Tereus himself.

This is amusing, I said aloud. Is Tereus worth this? I looked closer.

In the first scene, Tereus was embracing a woman passionately. Her face was obscured; I smiled. In the second, I saw it. The owner of the face was cringing at Tereus' feet and she was pleading for mercy. Philomela. In the next scene he had advanced on her. He cut out her tongue. In the following scene Philomela, imprisoned in a castle, looked out as Tereus galloped away into the distance. That was all. I looked again. There was no doubt about it. Philomela.

I went to my room and sat holding the tapestry. Tereus' feet sounded in the courtyard outside: I pushed the tapestry under the couch and sat there as I had for so long, doing nothing. But he didn't come in.

So I was able to form my plan. I sent for Coda and Dita. I told them my suspicions and I gave the last of my gold for the search. Somewhere, between here and Athens, Philomela suffered alone. Secretly, men were found and set out on their horses. It was late at night when they left, and my heart beat loudly as I listened to the hooves growing fainter on the plain.

They found her and brought her back. Poor, dumb Philomela. And we all feasted, the smoke from the burning flesh of the animals went up into the sky for hours before we ate, the fountain was fed with wine, Tereus kept laughing and saying he must have made a mistake. He was so frightened he couldn't even find an excuse. So we ate and drank, and the wild boars on our gold cups chased themselves endlessly round as the gold glinted in the light from the torches and the round heads of Tereus' friends shone the same bright colour. Philomela never once looked reproach.

We lay together in my room, and I whispered in her ear. Her eyes could always answer me. And we knew we would avenge ourselves on Tereus.

Philomela lay in the prow of the boat. Her black hair just touched the water. I watched her all the time – for signs of happiness, or discontent, or simply to see what her eyes would say to me. Today she was smiling, and we glided at the rhythm of her breathing over water so clear that the smallest pebbles on the bottom looked as big and white as rocks.

We were there because a war was raging inland. On the shore, brightly coloured as victory, were Tereus' tents. From the beach little wisps of black smoke went up: the slaves were preparing the evening meal.

Tereus comes back from the war tonight. His fingers will pull at roasted meat. His mouth will be red with juice. The singing will start in a dull roar, and torches will be lit on the sand. Dancing figures, giants inside the tents but small in the great expanse outside, will run from every angle to the edge of the sea. Because of the wine, the moon will shine brilliantly.

The four curved paddles of our boat guided us gently back to land. I stepped out, with Philomela in my arms, and set her down on the stones. We both stood for a moment, looking at the tents and the blade of blue which carves out the clumsy shapes of the mountains; but we saw only the evening ahead. It was months since Tereus had gone to the war. We had almost forgotten his face. He had gone, probably, because the embarrassment was too great for him at home – and he hoped, while he was away, that we would forget what he had done. We thought of him as we walked up to the encampment. And without glancing at each other again, we went to lie down until the heat of the day had passed.

The sun lay to one side of the sky and our shadows were long when we left the great tent and went inland to the olive groves. The preparations for the banquet were growing more frantic – and it was only when we were surrounded by bushes of myrtle and thyme that we were able to go on without vomiting on the ground. The smell of burning meat was so strong.

Philomela saw Itylus first. I followed the line of her pointing finger and could just make out, in the gloom where the trees were thicker, a group of boys playing at war. Itylus had a bow and arrow, and was run-

ning importantly from tree to tree calling out commands. As Tereus'
son he was obeyed: this had made him arrogant, but charming still;
already he had taken on the pompous, exaggerated stride of his father.

Now he sent a shower of arrows over our heads and the other boys
ran laughing towards us to retrieve them. They all liked Philomela,
and made a pretence of searching in the glade at her feet so she could
stroke them and smile. And she did! While my heart beat heavily and
slowly, and my legs felt as rooted and shapeless as the lines of trees that
marched out to all sides of us.

Itylus!

I had to call him, of course – but if only it could have been
Philomela! What do you want?

Anything to have been spared the sound of his voice. As I made no
sign of moving, he came reluctantly forward. He knew I had come to
spoil his game. It's nearly dark, I said. Your father is coming. We
must go back to the tents.

He shrugged, then followed. We went in single file down to the
beach.

Tereus will come down the mountain pass as the sun is setting.
Taking advantage of the glory; wearing the flaming sky like a cloak he
has picked up on the battlefield. Boasting as he tramps through the
encampment. Flinging himself down, the exhausted warrior, and
waiting for us, my tongueless sister and his wife to shower our praise
on him.

On the pretext of showing him a big sea animal that had been caught
in the nets that morning, we took Itylus into the cave at the other end
of the beach. It was dark there, with a rancid smell: the colour of the
air was the same deep grey all the way up to the roof of the cave and the
rocks were thin and sharp like the teeth of a rotting fish. The children
made piles of the fragile sea anemones and we crunched them under
foot as we walked, the shells the faint pink-blue of an earlobe.
Philomela and I stood silently by as Itylus, with controlled excitement, examined the monster.

A great eye lay in a network of tentacles. The confused limbs,
sprawled now on the stale sand at the back of the cave, had evidently
put up a fight – here and there they had been hacked by men's hands
and were crushed like a reed that someone has tried to break off and
then abandoned. Perhaps because of the eye, which seemed, wherever
we stood, to be watching us, we were afraid to go too near. Only
Itylus, to show his courage and manhood, picked up a piece of

driftwood and advanced on it cautiously. It was dead since morning; but the glare of the black pupil in the pool of white suggested hidden power and energy. In our minds, we saw it rise and attack. The limbs, although twisted and battered, had a febrile strength. We felt them crush our ribs and wind themselves round our necks.

We lifted a boulder and came up on Itylus from behind. He fell without a sound. Philomela's eyes spoke terror. I was the only one to cry out.

The sound I made was flung back by the walls of the cave in anger and contempt. It took a long time to die, lingering in a whimper in the wet stone.

The eye still watched us as we lifted the body of Itylus and crept to the mouth of the cave with it. I looked out first. The sun was setting, the sky was red. I could see nothing of the black mountains, but a contingent of men, torches lit in preparation for the sudden descent of night, were moving like fiery beetles from the beach to the foothills. Tereus must be on his way down, then.

How quick and how slow our dragging on the great pot from its hiding place in the entrance of the cave, our pyre of dry wood, the heating of the water. But when we looked out at the sea, we saw his floating hair. And the sand in the red glow from the sinking sun was the colour of his poor boiling flesh. How slow!

Years and years will pass, and these minutes will still be longer than them all. Every hour will be made up out of them. And we will be standing by the staring eye in the back of the cave and Tereus will be coming down the hill and we will be standing at the mouth of the cave and looking out at the sea to shift the time. How quickly the years will pass!

When the meat was ready we drained the water away until there was only a little at the bottom of the pot. We had tried to find fresh water – there was an old well just above the beach – but seawater had seeped in. Tiny limpets and shreds of sour weed clung to the flesh. We threw in herbs and animal fat. Philomela made a dough with her agile fingers, which she used for speaking now, holding them up and flashing combinations of numbers when she had to make it clear what she wanted. I watched her hands as she laid the fine crust over the pot. We built up the fire, and waited.

It was a fine banquet. I sat at Tereus' side, my eyes down, my face flushed with pride for him. Philomela, as always on these occasions, was a ghost, a shadow that fell only occasionally across his face if he should look round and see her. I was his wife; and I celebrated his victories with him.

The men shouted and sang. When the moon rose, some of them ran drunkenly to the entrance to the tent, and gazed up at it as if it had appeared for the first time. Like Tereus, I laughed indulgently at them. Like Tereus, I applauded when the captive slave girls danced, their bodies greased and jewels shining between their eyes. With Tereus I rose and walked to the great table where the wine and food was laid out. On the glistening fig leaves, grapes and pomegranates stood in mounds. Great sides of roasted ox were garlanded with fast-wilting flowers.

The pie was brought in. Tereus sat down like a child and ate. When he had eaten a few mouthfuls, he nodded his approval. He offered some to his favourites, and they swaggered forward, holding out their hands. Then he turned to me.

Eat! – he said. You have done well.

I shook my head. Black, dizzy sickness. Inside me an ill-tempered sea rolled violently. I had to look up. Eyes looked back at me with a mixture of curiosity and dislike. Where is Philomela?

But her eyes had gone. And I half fell, as all the eyes there in that room merged together and one eye, lidless, staring shone out at me. Tereus, the juice from the pie dribbling down his chin, pulled me back on the seat beside him with astonishment. He thrust a tender morsel in my face. Eat! he said laughing. What's the matter with you?

Philomela came forward from the back of the tent. Because she was dumb the men were afraid of her, and they fell back easily enough to let her through. I felt Tereus wince.

Take that woman away! he muttered. But his voice lacked conviction: like the others, he was afraid of her. She had become, in the camp, like the priestess of an oracle without a voice. She was the unconscious avenger of every sin. If only Tereus knew the barbarity she had suffered, the others guessed at it.

She reached my side and took my hand so I could rise with new strength. Except for distant shouting outside, her silence had spread. The eyes looked at us now with fear and unease. They were waiting: waiting for me to speak.

I turned to Tereus.

It is for you to eat your son Itylus, I said. You destroyed us long ago.

(How slow! Tereus' long years of exile and grief. How quickly the years will pass.)

*B*EDBUGS

During the night I have a vision of bedbugs in congress. A concrescence of male and female. The polluted mass pulsates, masculine organs pullulate, grow into dangerous spikes that, blinded by passion, miss the proffered orifices and stab deep into the soft bellies of their consorts. While I thus dream my blood is sucked and the satiated bugs, too bloated to return to their hiding places, excrete their waste upon the sheets and make their getaway. When I awake I observe the tell-tale black stains and become conscious of new islands of itchiness erupting upon my body. Life has taken a turn for the better for the dispossessed bedbugs, homeless since the demolition of the ancient slums, with the construction of the concrete college. Here at last the flat-bodied bugs have found sanctuary in the snug crevices, and plenty of food in the beds. Even during the long summer vacation, when the abandoned beds are filled by foreign students and their teachers; the former having come to Cambridge to improve their English, the latter to improve their finances. I am among the latter.

Some weeks previously I had been telephoned by a director of Literature & Linguistics Ltd, hitherto unknown, and been offered a job as a tutor at their Cambridge Summer School, held annually in the vacated university. He was frank. He said that they had been let down at the last minute and that someone had given him my name; he apologized for the short notice and enquired if I knew anything about the poets of the Great War, the course set by the deserter, for which books had already been purchased and despatched to the students; he added that these students tended to be young, German, intelligent, fluent, and – with a chuckle – female; he said by way of conclusion that Literature & Linguistics Ltd was a reputable company and that the salary was equally respectable. I promised to let him know the following day. Here was irony! Teaching First World War poetry to Germans, who had cut short the careers of most of the poets. Being

Jewish I also felt a more personal thin-skinned irony. But was such irony justified? After all neither I nor the students were even born in the days of the Third Reich, so could I blame them for the fact that had their parents proved victorious I would never have been born at all? Easily. Then what made me take the position? Money? Of course. But even more persuasive was Isaac Rosenberg. On account of a little known biographical detail: his affair with my grandmother. He was ten and she was seven. They kissed one fine afternoon outside the Rosenbergs' house in Stepney, a few doors down from my great-grandfather's green-grocery. Furthermore, when Rosenberg decided to enlist he ran away from home and joined a bantam battalion in Bury St Edmunds. You can see his barracks from our bedroom window. The grotesque red-brick pastiche of a castle looms over me as I call the director to announce my acceptance. I do not mention that I have re-named the course Rosenberg's Revenge.

However, the German girls completely disarm me. They are charming, receptive and funny. Above all they seem so innocent. Our first class began in a tentative way, polite, giggly, until one of the girls demanded to know why we were studying such poetry. 'The concerns of the poets are out of date, they do not mean anything to us,' she said, 'especially since we are mostly girls here and not interested in war one bit. So why do you make us read about these horrible things?' Other girls snorted, to be interpreted as derisive. In that parallel course running in my head, Rosenberg's Revenge, I rubbed the cow's nose in Nazi atrocities, but in our Cambridge classroom I was patient, persuasive. I did not mention the pink stain on her neck which I took to be a love bite, sign of her preoccupations. 'Why? Because the poetry transcends its environment,' I said. 'War becomes the inspiration. A source of destruction, but also creation. A paradox to contemplate. The proximity of death added to the intensity of the poet. Their minds were consecrated wonderfully.' My allies moved in to attack. Women not interested in war? What nonsense! War involves everybody. My enemy was routed, isolated, leaving the rest of us clear to commence the course. In that introductory meeting relationships were established, and I was pleased to note that foremost among my supporters was the most attractive girl in the room. Vanity also is an inspiration.

There are two tutors for the twenty students; myself for literature, the other for linguistics, with composition shared. Although Bury St Edmunds is only thirty miles from Cambridge I am expected to sleep in the college, since my duties include evening entertainment. Tonight my colleague is giving a lecture on phonemes, freeing me to telephone my wife. As I listen to the ringing tone I consider the fact that while each peal is identical, subsequent conversation gives it a retrospective value; from phony, wrong number, to euphony for a lover. 'Hello love,' says my wife, 'miss me?' 'Lots,' I say. So our catechism continues, a pleasant exchange of self-confidences, until I realize with alarm that my answers are counterfeit. I am not thinking about her. I do not miss her. I am a liar. Second sight suddenly reveals this peccadillo as prophetic and I foresee the wreck of our marriage. Doubtless this is a romantic fallacy to be dismissed as easily as the psychosomatic cramp that has gripped my stomach. What harm can there be in euphemism if it makes her happy? 'Sleep well,' says my wife, 'sweet dreams.'

But the belly-ache won't go away. Back in my room I stretch upon the bed. My room is modernistic, without extraneous matter; for example, there are no handles on the drawers, just holes for fingers to pull them open. Being double the room is a duplex, and in the steps that connect the levels the style reaches its apotheosis. Granted that only 50 per cent of a regular staircase is used, since just one foot presses on each step, what does the architect do? Lop off the redundant half, of course. Leaving steps that alternate, right, left, right, left, etcetera. True the residents have tried to impress their personalities upon this chamber, by decorating the walls with posters, but in their absence, devoid of their possessions, these emphasize the emptiness. Nor are there any books on the shelves, save my war poems, and a book marked with a single yellow star. The ghetto journal of a Warsaw Jew. The diary was discovered after the war, his body never was. Actually, I did not bring the book along to read, rather as a reminder of an evil that cannot be exorcized. Nevertheless, flat out with colic I read it from cover to cover. What can I say? In class we talk of literature, but this is not art. The writer chronicles everything as dispassionately as possible, a record for future historians, until in the end he can restrain himself no longer. 'Daughter of Germany!' he curses. 'Blessed is he who will seize your babes and smash them against the Rock!'

Sweet dreams! I dream of flesh in torment and awaken to find my body in a rash. No stranger to hives I blame my brain, never suspecting the true culprits. But instead of fading the hives swell so that by mid-morning, my class in full swing, they are throbbing in sympathy with the soldiers in the trenches. Fighting the temptation to scratch I ask my enemy to read Rosenberg's *Louse Hunting*. Blushing she begins, **417**

> *Nudes, stark and glistening,*
> *Yelling in lurid glee. Grinning faces*
> *And raging limbs*
> *Whirl over the floor on fire;*
> *For a shirt verminously busy*
> *Yon soldier tore from his throat*
> *With oaths*
> *Godhead might shrink at, but not the lice . . .*

And gets no further. Bursting into tears she cries, 'You mock me! You see the bites on my neck and you think I am dirty! But only here have I got them! There are bugs in my bed!' 'She means Franz,' says someone, referring to my only male student, likewise bitten. 'My dictionary tells me that a bug is a ghost, a bogeyman, a night prowler,' says another, 'so Franz could be defined as a bed-bug.' 'But they are not the only ones who have been bitten,' I say, 'look at my arms.' Whereupon my enemy regards me with something like gratitude. 'You see,' I say, 'the poems are relevant to our condition after all.'

Tonight it is my turn to amuse the students. So I have arranged a visit to the Cambridge Arts Theatre. Since the play is Ionesco's *The Lesson*, which ends with the pedagogue stabbing his pupil and donning Nazi uniform, we have made attendance voluntary. In the event I am accompanied only by my erstwhile enemy, Franz, and my most attractive acolyte. Naturally I am curious to see how my charges will react to the drama. Franz and Monika fidget as the dead girl drops immodestly into a chair and her professor pulls on his swastika armband. On the other hand Inge is impressed. 'Such a play explains much about fascism,' she says, 'and about Germany.' 'Perhaps Germany as it was,' says Franz, 'but today things are different.' 'Nonsense,' says Inge, 'we remain a nation of *hausfraus* who thrive on order. We didn't like the Jews so we made them disappear. Just like dust. We were frightened by the Baader-Meinhof gang so we killed them. Pouf! No more terrorism. We adore neatness. That is why Monika is horrified by her bed-bugs. They leave marks. So she cannot forget them. She cannot sweep them under the carpet – is that what you say?' 'Suicide,' says Franz, 'they killed themselves.' 'That is what we are told,' says Inge, 'what you are pleased to believe.' Monika looks at Franz. 'We must go,' he says, 'we are tired.' 'Not me,' says Inge, 'the play has given me an appetite.'

The Castle, an unexceptional pub on the road back to college. We request drinks and curries. The landlord motions us to a table. It is midweek and the pub is deserted save for a couple sitting in a darkened corner. The man is not in his right mind. 'Tell me, George,' he says to the landlord, 'now the season is a fortnight old what do you think of our esteemed football team?' 'My name is not George,' says the landlord. 'No spunk, that's their problem,' he says, 'not enough aggression.' 'They've only lost two games,' says the landlord. 'But how many more?' says the man. 'Listen, George, you know everyone in Cambridge. You tell the manager I've got some advice for him. A bastard I may be, pardon my French – father was killed in the war before he had time to do the honourable thing – but I'm related to lords, the highest in the land. Therefore the manager will listen to me. Did you hear about that Aussie coach who showed his team newsreels of Nazi war crimes before a big match? That got their blood up! Went straight out and thrashed the opposition. I've plenty of ideas as good as that. I'm counting on you, George. Tell the manager the bastard wants to see him.' 'Wash your mouth out,' shouts the landlord, 'I won't have bad language in this pub. Not when there's ladies present. If you won't behave you can clear off.' But Inge is not embarrassed. 'That was a fine play we saw tonight,' she says, 'perhaps we could produce something like that in our composition class?' 'Good idea,' I say, 'but it will be difficult with so many people. You and Monika will never agree about anything. You'll argue over every word and nothing will get written.' 'You are right of course,' says Inge. 'Maybe we could do something with a smaller group,' I say, 'you, me and one or two others.' 'But then those who are left out might become envious,' says Inge, 'they will accuse us of élitism.' 'Then we must arrange a cabaret for the last night,' I say, 'everyone will be invited to help. I'll advertise for poets, singers, even stripteasers. Our contribution will be the play.' Inge laughs. Her shoulders tremble. Not for the first time I observe the body beneath the shirt.

Two plates of curry stand in the serving hatch growing cold. We watch them while the landlord sulks. Finally I deliver them myself. But before we can begin our meal the loony snatches Inge's plate and scurries to his table. 'You've taken our dinner,' he yells, 'we were here before you!' His companion looks miserable, but remains silent. As if awaiting this opportunity the landlord reappears. 'You have gone too far,' he bellows, 'apologize to these people at once!' The man is outraged. He puckers his lips as if about to blow a kiss. 'Sir,' he says, 'it is they who should apologize to us for stealing our food.' The landlord's wrath descends upon the lunatic who flees for his life. 'I might be illegitimate,' he cries into the night, 'but I do not copulate with Germans.' Now I am angry. But I am a hypocrite, the half-wit is a prophet. **419**

Brushing my teeth in preparation for bed there is a knock on the door. Foaming at the mouth I admit Inge. 'This afternoon I purchased equipment to purge your bedbugs,' she says, 'I planned to tell you after the theatre but the events in the pub drove it from my mind.' I rinse out the toothpaste. Inge meanwhile is crumbling a firelighter into a large metal fruit-bowl, and mixing the fragments with charcoal chips. The result is ignited. Flames leap from the bowl like tongues ravenous for bedbugs. 'Now we must wait,' says Inge, 'until the charcoal becomes red hot.' We sit looking at one another. 'You are married?' says Inge. 'Yes,' I say. 'I am not married, though I have a man in Germany,' she says, 'here I am free, there I am a prisoner. You understand? Always we must do what he wants. Do you know the word "eudemonism"? It means you act for another's happiness. It is your moral duty. That is always the role of women, don't you think? Your wife, does she work?' 'No,' I say. 'Why not?' says Inge. 'She was pregnant,' I say, 'but she lost the baby. She is going back to work soon.' 'Is she – how do you say? – in a depression?' asks Inge. 'She is over it now,' I say, 'we don't talk about it any more.' We feel the heat from the glowing coals. 'Let us hope the bowl does not crack,' says Inge, 'it isn't mine, it comes from my room.' As if casting a spell she pours yellow powder on to the embers. Asphyxiating fumes immediately fill the room. 'Sulphur,' she says, 'the gas it makes will kill all the bugs.' Coughing I lead her upstairs.

We stare into the underworld. 'Look,' says Inge, 'as I said.' Sure enough, bugs are dropping lifelessly from crannies in the ceiling. Suddenly an unexpected twang! The bowl has split. 'Oh no,' cries Inge. Brilliant as the steps are in conception it is dangerous to descend them at speed, as Inge learns. She tumbles, hits the floor with a thump, and remains utterly inert. Spreadeagled, supine. There is no blood, but I do not know if this is a good or a bad sign. Her hand is limp. I feel for the pulse, but it is either stopped or I have my thumb in the wrong spot. Her heart. Situated, of all places, beneath her left breast. It is warm certainly. But I can feel no heartbeat, though the nipple tantalizingly hardens. However, for all I know this may be a posthumous reflex action or even the beginnings of *Rigor mortis*. I am no doctor. At a loss I rock forward upon my knees and part her lips with my tongue, intending to administer the kiss of life. But as I begin to blow into her mouth I feel Inge's right arm curl around my neck. And as she presses me closer I realize that my hand is still upon her breast.

Bugs continue to fall as Inge glides out of her pants. Possessed now, I turn out the light so that Inge's naked body is illuminated only by the smouldering charcoal, a serpentine shape, splashed with red, an undulant stream of lava into which I fling myself. 'Take me,' hisses Inge, 'here, as I am, on the floor.' While the madness lasts I pump my body into her, aware only of our sweat and the uncontrollable pleasure, dimly conscious of the mocking parody the dying embers cast upon the wall. Spent, prone upon Inge's salty body, I gasp for breath in the sulphurous air. 'Please,' whispers Inge, 'I am not finished.' She directs my hand down her belly to a damper place. Slowly my senses settle as I watch Inge's spectre writhe, and listen to her ecstatic groans, which dissolve as a deeper voice fills my ear:

> *Soon like a demons' pantomime*
> *This plunge was raging.*
> *See the silhouettes agape,*
> *See the gibbering shadows*
> *Mix with the baffled arms on the wall.*

A man emerges from the shadows. He is dressed in khaki and puttees, but looks too delicate to be a soldier. 'Do you like my poem?' he says. 'Yes,' I say, 'you were a genius.' 'Tell that to the Germans,' he says. I nod. I am. 'Do you hate them?' I ask. 'You cannot hate the dead,' he says, 'and you lose touch with the living.' Inge, oblivious, cavorts on the end of my finger. 'I'm doing this for you,' I say. He shrugs. 'Why bother with humbug when you've got bedbugs?' he says. 'Jews, Germans, we're all the same to them. They have cosmopolitan sympathies. We destroy one another and the bedbugs take revenge.' 'Not here,' I say, 'they're all dead.' 'So am I,' he says. 'Do you remember my grandmother?' I ask. 'Eva Zelinsky, she lived near you in Oxford Street.' 'What does she look like?' he asks. 'An old lady, white hair, in her eighties,' I say. He smiles. 'Everything changes,' he

says, 'except the dead.' 'Aaaaaaaah!' cries Inge. She comes, he goes.
There is quiet in the room. Inge is drowsy with delight. The charcoal
has burned itself out. 'Come,' I say, 'let's go to bed.' During the night
I have a vision of bedbugs in congress.

Throughout the day Inge wears a silk scarf to conceal the bites upon
her neck. Likewise, when I telephone my wife, I hide the truth from
her. Better keep quiet and skip the consequences. In two weeks Inge
will be back in Germany with her jailer. At the moment, however, she
is in my room again. We are awaiting another girl, selected to
complete our playwriting team. 'When you took off your clothes,' says
Inge, 'I saw something. That you are a Jew. Please, you must tell me.
When you fucked me, was it for revenge?' I shake my head. 'No,' I
say, 'I did it because I wanted you. I forgot you were a German.' 'I am
glad,' says Inge. 'You know, I have always admired the Jewish people.
You have read Martin Buber?' 'Buber? Sure,' I say. 'I know my
melancholy fate is to turn every *thou* into an *it*, every person into a
thing. Last night you were a *thou*, this afternoon already you are an *it*,
last night we had intercourse, a real spiritual dialogue, this afternoon
we must write dialogue.' Inge grins. 'And do you have any ideas?' she
says. 'No,' I say, 'I am the producer. Ideas are not my responsibility.
Do you?' 'Only simple ones,' she says, 'like a husband and wife, eating
dinner, watching television, talking but not communicating. Just one
twist, a girl will be the husband and you must play the wife.' The other
girl arrives and accepts the idea with enthusiasm. We work on the play
through the evening and into the night. The other girl goes. Inge
stays. Martin Buber? A *boobe-myseh!*

On the last Saturday I escort all the students to Bury St Edmunds. A
coach has been hired and I sit up beside the driver holding a
microphone. As we approach the town along the Newmarket Road I
indicate, to the left, the barracks where Rosenberg trained, on the
right, my house. The coach halts in the large square at the top of Angel
Hill. 'Okay,' I say, 'I'll tell you what there is to see in Bury St
Edmunds. Opposite are the walls of the Abbey, behind are the ruins
and a park. There is a cathedral. Go up Abbeygate Street and you'll
come to the market. Fruit. Vegetables. Junk. Beyond the market is
Moyses Hall. Built by a Jew in 1180. Unfortunately for him all the
Jews were expelled from Bury in 1190. Now off you go. Back here at
three o'clock.' Gradually the others slip away until I am left with only
Inge for company. It is a hot day, dusty with heat. The locals look

white and sweaty, like creatures unused to the light. The women wear drab moth-proofed frocks that show off the freckles on their breasts; the men roll up their shirt-sleeves to reveal the tattoos upon their arms. It is a mystery, this abundance of sample-book tattooing, all of course applied by choice. By contrast Inge's spectacular sexuality stops people in their tracks; her black scarf, her red tee-shirt, clinging like a second skin, her denim shorts and – this I know – no underwear. 'I feel so good today,' says Inge, 'I should like a souvenir. Is there perhaps a booth where we can have our photograph taken together?' 'There's one in Woolworth's,' I say. A photograph! Thus far the affair has been vague, nothing to do with my real life, as insubstantial as a dream. It will be a simple trick to persuade myself that it never happened. But a photograph! Our faces fixed, cheek by cheek, our relationship projected into the foreseeable future. Proof snatched from the lethal fingers of time.

The booth is already occupied by three small boys. We can see their legs, and hear their excited giggling. Then as the first flash fades we hear, above their laughter, the screech of a creature in terror. Inge tears back the curtain and exposes the boys, including one who is dangling a kitten by its tail in front of the camera. The kitten flails about uselessly, tensing and squealing with horror at each flash, only to redouble its efforts in the lacuna. 'You monsters,' cries Inge, 'stop torturing that poor animal.' The boys grin. The kitten swings. Faster and faster. Until the boy lets go. The kitten lands on Inge's shoulder. Seeking to steady itself it raises its paw and sinks its claw into her ear. Inge gently lifts the kitten so her ear is not torn although the lobe is pierced and bleeding profusely, staining her tee-shirt a deeper red. I give her my handkerchief to press against the wound. 'It looks worse than it is,' says Inge, 'it does not hurt.' 'Nevertheless, you must come back to our house,' I say, 'you must wash and change. You can't go around covered in blood.' Once again a curious accident has left me with no choice. Inge will meet my wife.

We surprise my wife sunbathing naked in the garden. 'Hello love,' she says, 'I didn't know you were bringing somebody back with you.' 'Only one of my students,' I say, 'she's been wounded.' My wife, wrapping a towel around herself, approaches Inge and leads her off to the bathroom. They reappear in identical cotton shirts, bargains from the market. A stranger might take them for sisters. I cook omelettes for lunch, with a few beans from the garden, and serve them on the lawn where my wife had been alone less than an hour before. I am astonished how relaxed we all are. Inge rattles off examples of her lover's male chauvinism. We all laugh. I feel no guilt, my wife feels no pain. She suspects nothing. She waves the flies from our food and throws breadcrumbs down for the sparrows. 'Are you enjoying the course?' she asks. 'Very much,' says Inge, 'especially our little playwriting group. Has Joshua told you about our play? Yes? Of course. You must come to our cabaret and see it performed.' 'I shall look forward to that,' says my wife. She removes the plates and returns with a bowl of peaches. They are sweet and juicy and attract many wasps. Our fingers become sticky. 'I am glad everything is going so well,' says my wife, 'without any problems.' 'Only the bedbugs.' I say, 'look what they've done to my arms.' 'Poor thing,' says my wife, 'can't you move into a different room?' 'No need,' I say, 'they've been exterminated.' My wife smiles. What contentment! I realize now why I feel so untroubled; I do not really believe that I have made love to Inge. She is what she seems, just a visitor. My wife is my wife. We belong. Cambridge is a foreign city. To which I must return, however. I kiss my wife. 'See you on Wednesday,' I say. 'What a nuisance,' says Inge as the coach passes our house, 'I have left my scarf behind.' 'Never mind,' I say, 'I'll pick it up on Wednesday. Besides you can hardly see the bites now.'

On Tuesday we complete the play. In the evening the heatwave breaks with a tremendous storm. Knowing how much my wife dreads thunder I telephone her. She does not answer. Later, when the rain has stopped, Inge and I stroll to the Castle to toast our success. Afterwards we return to my room, where Inge now sleeps as a matter of course. In the morning I telephone my wife again. No reply. Probably shopping. Lunch over, teaching being at an end, I drive home to collect her. There are three milk bottles on the doorstep, the first already sour. Its top is off, filling the stagnant air with its nauseous odour. Within is a different smell, naggingly familiar. I shout my wife's name. But there is no response. The house seems deserted. Bedrooms, bathroom, dining room, all empty. On the table is Inge's black scarf, neatly folded, and a note:

> Don't forget this, Love Rachel
> P S. Hope the bedbugs have stopped biting Inge.

Then in the kitchen I realize what the smell reminds me of. A butcher's shop. Naked, legs splayed, my wife sits upon the kitchen floor with the wooden handle of our carving knife protruding from her belly. Her back rests against the wall, her arms hang stiffly down, her eyes are open wide. The blood is dry. It flowed down from her wound, between her thighs, and formed puddles on the floor. The only sound is the buzzing of flies. They walk upon her breasts, mass around her vagina where the hair is matted with blood. This horror is too shocking to be true! It is a phantasmagoria produced by my conscience. Art, not life.

'Your face is very white,' says Inge, 'is everything all right?' 'I'm just nervous about this evening,' I say. We have gathered all the props we require; cutlery, crockery, sauce bottles, and a starting pistol loaded with blanks. And while Monika – of all people – strips down to her underwear in front of the directors of Literature & Linguistics Ltd Inge and I exchange clothes. A suit and tie for her, a dress for me. 'This is Cambridge,' I think, 'this is my life. There is nothing else.' We hear Franz sing his folk songs. Then applause. We are joined by the third member of the cast. We walk out to cheers and laughter. 'Your wife is in the audience?' asks Inge. 'I hope so,' I say, 'she is coming by train.' The play begins.

Inge – my husband – is a bank clerk. I am a housewife. The other girl is a television set. Inge orders me to switch her on. We hear the news. I serve dinner to my husband and our two children who are invisible. An argument develops between us over the boy's long curls. 'You'll turn your son into a pansy with your ways of bringing him up,' yells Inge. 'They're always my children when there is something the matter,' I shout, 'I don't think you really wanted them. I won't forget how you treated me when I was pregnant. You didn't even try to hide your disgust. But you're the one who's disgusting!' What am I talking about? Why am I pretending to be my wife? Wife? I have no wife. How these silly words have confused me! What next? Oh yes, I am supposed to take the gun from my handbag. I point the gun at Inge. Why? Because I hate her. But why? Because she seduced me? Because she murdered my wife? Wife? I can't even remember her name. With her shirt and tie and pencil moustache Inge looks like a creature from pre-war Berlin. I hate her because she is German. A Nazi! I fire the gun. The blast fills my head. 'Daughter of Germany!' I scream. 'Daughter of Germany!' I shoot at her until the gun is empty.

*S*ERAGLIO

In Istanbul there are tombs, faced with calligraphic designs, where the dead Sultan rests among the tiny catafalques of younger brothers whom he was obliged, by custom, to murder on his accession. Beauty becomes callous when it is set beside savagery. In the grounds of the Topkapi palace the tourists admire the turquoise tiles of the Harem, the Kiosks of the Sultans, and think of girls with sherbet, turbans, cushions, fountains. 'So were they just kept here?' my wife asks. I read from the guide-book: 'Though the Sultans kept theoretical power over the Harem, by the end of the sixteenth century these women effectively dominated the Sultans.'

It is cold. A chill wind blows from the Bosphorus. We had come on our trip in late March, expecting sunshine and mild heat, and found bright days rent by squalls and hail-storms. When it rains in Istanbul the narrow streets below the Bazaar become torrents, impossible to walk through, on which one expects to see, floating with the debris of the market, dead rats, bloated dogs, the washed up corpses of centuries. The Bazaar itself is a labyrinth with a history of fires. People have entered, they say, and not emerged.

From the grounds of the Topkapi the skyline of the city, like an array of upturned shields and spears, is unreal. The tourists murmur, pass on. Turbans, fountains; the quarters of the Eunuchs; the Pavilion of the Holy Mantle. Images out of the Arabian Nights. Then one discovers, as if stumbling oneself on the scene of the crime, in a glass case in a museum of robes, the spattered kaftan in which Sultan Oman II was assassinated. Rent by dagger thrusts from shoulder to hip. The thin linen fabric could be the corpse itself. The simple white garment, like a bathrobe, the blood-stains, like the brown stains on the gauze of a removed elastoplast, give you the momentary illusion that it is your gown lying there, lent to another, who is murdered in mistake for yourself.

We leave, towards the Blue Mosque, through the Imperial Gate, past the fountain of the Executioner. City of monuments and murder, in which cruelty seems ignored. There are cripples in the streets near the Bazaar, shuffling on leather pads, whom the tourists notice but the inhabitants do not. City of siege and massacre and magnificence. When Mehmet the Conqueror captured the city in 1453 he gave it over to his men, as was the custom, for three days of pillage and slaughter; then set about building new monuments. These things are in the travel books. The English-speaking guides, not using their own language, tell them as if they had never happened. There are miniatures of Mehmet in the Topkapi Museum. A pale, smooth-skinned man, a patron of the arts, with a sensitive gaze and delicate eyebrows, holding a rose to his nostrils . . .

It was after I had been explaining to my wife from the guide-book, over lunch in a restaurant, about Mehmet's rebuilding of the city, that we walked round a corner and saw a taxi – one of those metallic green taxis with black and yellow chequers down the side which cruise round Istanbul like turquoise sharks – drive with almost deliberate casualness into the legs of a man pushing a cart by the kerb. A slight crunch; the man fell, his legs at odd angles, clothes torn, and did not get up. Such things should not happen on holiday. They happen at home – people cluster round and stare – and you accommodate it because you know ordinary life includes such things. On holiday you want to be spared ordinary life.

But then it was not the fact of the accident for which we were unprepared but the reactions of the involved parties. The injured man looked as if he were to blame for having been injured. The taxi driver remained in his car as if his path had been deliberately blocked. People stopped on the pavement and gabbled, but seemed to be talking about something else. A policeman crossed from a traffic island. He had dark glasses and a peaked cap. The taxi driver got out of his car. They spoke languidly to each other and seemed both to have decided to ignore the man on the road. Beneath his dark glasses the policeman's lips moved delicately and almost with a smile, as if he were smelling a flower. We walked on round the corner. I said to my wife, even though I knew she would disapprove of the joke: 'That's why there are so many cripples.'

Our hotel is in the new part of Istanbul, near the Hilton, overlooking the Bosphorus, across which there is a newly built bridge.

Standing on the balcony you can look from Europe to Asia. Uskudar, on the other side, is associated with Florence Nightingale. There are few places in the world where, poised on one continent, you can gaze over a strip of water at another.

We had wanted something more exotic. No more Alpine chalets and villas in Spain. We needed yet another holiday, but a different holiday. We had had this need for eight years and it was a need we could afford. We felt we had suffered in the past and so required a perpetual convalescence. But this meant, in time, even our holidays lacked novelty; so we looked for somewhere more exotic. We thought of the East. We imagined a landscape of minarets and domes out of the Arabian Nights. However, I pointed out the political uncertainties of the Middle East to my wife. She is sensitive to such things, to even remote hints of calamity. In London bombs go off in the Hilton and restaurants in Mayfair. Because she has borne one disaster she feels she should be spared all others, and she looks upon me to be her guide in this.

'Well Turkey then – Istanbul,' she said – we had the brochures open on the table, with their photographs of the Blue Mosque – 'that's not the Middle East.' I remarked (facetiously perhaps: I make these digs at my wife and she appreciates them for they reassure her that she is not being treated like something fragile) that the Turks made trouble too; they had invaded Cyprus.

'Don't you remember the Hamiltons' villa? They're still waiting to know what's become of it.'

'But we're not going to Cyprus,' she said. And then, looking at the brochure – as if her adventurousness were being tested and she recognized its limits: 'Besides, Istanbul is in Europe.'

My wife is beautiful. She has a smooth, flawless complexion, subtle, curiously expressive eyebrows, and a slender figure. I think these were the things which made me want to marry her, but though they have preserved themselves well in eight years they no longer have the force of a motive. She looks best in very dark or very pale colours. She is fastidious about perfumes, and tends devotedly our garden in Surrey.

She is lying now on the bed in our hotel bedroom in Istanbul from which you can see Asia, and she is crying. She is crying because while I have been out taking photos, in the morning light, of the Bosphorus, something has happened – she has been interfered with in some way – between her and one of the hotel porters.

I sit down beside her. I do not know exactly what has happened. It is difficult to elicit details while she is crying. However, I am thinking: She only started to cry when I asked, 'What's wrong?' When I came into the room she was not crying, only sitting stiller and paler than usual. This seems to me like a kind of obstructiveness.

'We must get the manager,' I say, getting up, 'the police even.' I say this bluffly, even a little heartlessly; partly because I believe my wife may be dramatizing, exaggerating (she has been moody, touchy ever since that accident we witnessed: perhaps she is blowing up some small thing, a mistake, nothing at all); partly because I know that if my wife had come out with me to take photos and not remained alone none of this would have occurred; but partly too because as I stare down at her and mention the police, I want her to think of the policeman with his dark glasses and his half-smiling lips and the man with his legs crooked on the road. I see that she does so by the wounded look she gives me. This wounds me in return for having caused it. But I had wanted this too.

'No,' she says, shaking her head, still sobbing. I see that she is not sobered by my remark. Perhaps there is something there. She wants to accuse me, with her look, of being cold and sensible and wanting to pass the matter on, of not caring for her distress itself.

'But you won't tell me exactly what happened,' I say, as if I am being unfairly treated.

She reaches for her handkerchief and blows her nose deliberately. When my wife cries or laughs her eyebrows form little waves. While her face is buried in the handkerchief I look up out of the window. A mosque on the Asian side, its minarets like thin blades, is visible on the skyline. With the morning light behind it, it seems illusory, like a cut-out. I try to recall its name from the guide-book but cannot. I look back at my wife. She has removed the handkerchief from her eyes. I realize she is right in reproaching me for my callousness. But this process of being harsh towards my wife's suffering, as if I blamed her for it, so that I in turn will feel to blame and she will then feel justified in pleading her suffering, is familiar. It is the only way in which we begin to speak freely.

She is about to tell me what happened now. She crushes the handkerchief in her hand. I realize I really have been behaving as if nothing had happened.

When I married my wife I had just landed a highly sought-after job. I am a consultant designer. I had everything and, I told myself, I was in love. In order to prove this to myself I had an affair, six months after my marriage, with a girl I did not love. We made love in hotels. In the West there are no harems. Perhaps my wife found out or guessed what had happened, but she gave no sign and I betrayed nothing. I wonder if a person does not know something has happened, if it is the same as if nothing had happened. My affair did not affect in any way the happiness I felt in my marriage. My wife became pregnant. I was glad of this. I stopped seeing the girl. Then some months later my wife had a miscarriage. She not only lost the baby, but could not have children again.

I blamed her for the miscarriage. I thought, quite without reason, that this was an extreme and unfair means of revenge. But this was only on the surface. I blamed my wife because I knew that, having suffered herself without reason, she wanted to be blamed for it. This is something I understand. And I blamed my wife because I myself felt to blame for what had happened and if I blamed my wife, unjustly, she could then accuse me, and I would feel guilty, as you should when you are to blame. Also I felt that by wronging my wife, by hurting her when she had been hurt already, I would be driven by my remorse to do exactly what was needed in the circumstances: to love her. It was at this time that I realized that my wife's eyebrows had the same attractions as Arabic calligraphy. The truth was we were both crushed by our misfortune, and by hurting each other, shifting the real pain, we protected each other. So I blamed my wife in order to make myself feel bound towards her. Men want power over women in order to be able to let women take this power from them.

This was seven years ago. I do not know if these reactions have ever ceased. Because we could have no children we made up for it in other ways. We began to take frequent and expensive holidays. We would say as we planned them, to convince ourselves: 'We need a break, we need to get away.' We went out a lot, to restaurants, concerts, cinemas, theatres. We were keen on the arts. We would go to all the new things, but we would seldom discuss, after seeing a play for instance, what we had watched. Because we had no children we could afford this; but if we had had children we could still have afforded it, since as my career advanced my job brought in more.

This became our story: our loss and its recompense. We felt we had justifications, an account of ourselves. As a result we lived on quite neutral terms with each other. For long periods, especially during those weeks before we took a holiday, we seldom made love – or when we did we would do so as if in fact we were not making love at all. We would lie in our bed, close but not touching, like two continents, each with its own customs and history, between which there is no bridge. We turned our backs towards each other as if we were both waiting our moment, hiding a dagger in our hands. But in order for the dagger thrust to be made, history must first stop, the gap between continents must be crossed. So we would lie, unmoving. And the only stroke, the only wound either of us inflicted was when one would turn and touch the other with empty, gentle hands, as though to say, 'See, I have no dagger.'

It seemed we went on holiday in order to make love, to stimulate passion (I dreamt, perhaps, long before we actually travelled there, and even though my wife's milky body lay beside me, of the sensuous, uninhibited East). But although our holidays seldom had this effect and were only a kind of make-believe, we did not admit this to each other. We were not like real people. We were like characters in a detective novel. The mystery to be solved in our novel was who killed our baby. But as soon as the murderer was discovered he would kill his discoverer. So the discovery was always avoided. Yet the story had to go on. And this, like all stories, kept us from pain as well as boredom.

'It was the boy – I mean the porter. You know, the one who works on this floor.'

My wife had stopped crying. She is lying on the bed. She wears a dark skirt; her legs are creamy. I know who she is talking about, have half guessed it before she spoke. I have seen him, in a white jacket, collecting laundry and doing jobs in the corridor: one of those thick-faced, crop-haired, rather melancholy-looking young Turks with whom Istanbul abounds and who seem either to have just left or to be about to be conscripted into the army.

'He knocked and came in. He'd come to repair the heater. You know, we complained it was cold at night. He had tools. I went out onto the balcony. When he finished he called out something and I came in. Then he came up to me – and touched me.'

'Touched you? What do you mean – touched you?' I know my wife will not like my inquisitorial tone. I wonder whether she is wondering if in some way I suspect her behaviour.

'Oh, you know,' she says exasperatedly.

'No. It's important I know exactly what happened, if we're –'

'If what?'

She looks at me, her eyebrows wavering.

I realize again that though I am demanding an explanation I really don't want to know what actually happened or, on the other hand, to accept a story. Whether, for example, the Turk touched my wife at all; whether if he did touch her, he only touched her or actually assaulted her in some way, whether my wife evaded, resisted or even encouraged his advances. All these things seem possible. But I do not want to know them. That is why I pretend to want to know them. I see too that my wife does not want to tell me either what really happened or a story. I realize that for eight years, night after night, we have been telling each other the story of our love.

'Well?' I insist.

My wife sits up on the bed. She holds one hand, closed, to her throat. She has this way of seeming to draw in, chastely, the collar of her blouse, even when she is not wearing a blouse or her neck is bare. It started when we lost our baby. It is a way of signalling that she has certain inviolable zones that mustn't be trespassed on. She gets up and walks around the room. She seems overwhelmed and avoids looking out of the window.

'He is probably still out there, lurking in the corridor,' she says as if under siege.

She looks at me expectantly, but cautiously. She is not interested in facts but reactions. I should be angry at the Turk, or she should be angry at me for not being angry at the Turk. The truth is we are trying to make each other angry with each other. We are using the incident to show that we have lost patience with each other.

'Then we must get the manager,' I repeat.

Her expression becomes scornful, as if I am evading the issue.

'You know what will happen if we tell the manager,' she says. 'He will smile and shrug his shoulders.'

I somehow find this quite credible and for this reason want to scoff at it harshly. The manager is a bulky, balding man, with stylish cuff-links and a long, aquiline nose with sensitive nostrils. Every time trips have been arranged for us which have gone wrong or information been given which has proved faulty he has smiled at our complaints and shrugged. He introduces himself to foreign guests as Mehmet, but this is not significant since every second Turk is a Mehmet or Ahmet. I have a picture of him listening to this fresh grievance and raising his hands, palms exposed, as if to show he has no dagger.

My wife stares at me. I feel I am in her power. I know she is right; that this is not a matter for the authorities. I look out of the window. The sun is glinting on the Bosphorus from behind dark soot-falls of approaching rain. I think of what you read in the guide-books, the Arabian Nights. I should go out and murder this Turk who is hiding in the linen cupboard.

'It's the manager's responsibility,' I say.

She jerks her head aside at this.

'There'd be no point in seeing the manager,' she says.

I turn from the window.

'So actually nothing happened?'

She looks at me as if I have assaulted her.

We both pace about the room. She clasps her arms as if she is cold. Outside the sky is dark. We seem to be entering a labyrinth.

'I want to get away,' she says, crossing her arms so her hands are on her shoulders. 'This place' – she gestures towards the window. 'I want to go home.'

Her skin seems thin and luminous in the fading light.

I am trying to gauge my wife. I am somehow afraid she is in real danger. All right, if you feel that bad, I think. But I say, with almost deliberate casualness: 'That would spoil the holiday, wouldn't it?' What I really think is that my wife should go and I should remain, in this unreal world where, if I had the right sort of dagger, I would use it on myself.

'But we'll go if you feel that bad,' I say.

Outside a heavy shower has begun to fall.

'I'm glad I got those photos then,' I say. I go to the window where I have put the guide-books on the sill. A curtain of rain veils Asia from Europe. I feel I am to blame for the weather. I explain from the guide-book the places we have not yet visited. Exotic names. I feel the radiator under the window ledge. It is distinctly warmer.

My wife sits down on the bed. She leans forward so that her hair covers her face. She is holding her stomach like someone who has been wounded.

The best way to leave Istanbul must be by ship. So you can lean at the stern and watch that fabulous skyline slowly recede, become merely two-dimensional; that Arabian Nights mirage which when you get close to it turns into a labyrinth. Glinting under the sun of Asia, silhouetted by the sun of Europe. The view from the air in a Turkish **433** Airlines Boeing, when you have had to cancel your flight and book another at short notice, is less fantastic but still memorable. I look out of the porthole. I am somehow in love with this beautiful city in which you do not feel safe. My wife does not look; she opens a magazine. She is wearing a pale-coloured suit. Other people in the plane glance at her.

All stories are told, like this one, looking back at painful places which have become silhouettes, or looking forward, before you arrive, at scintillating façades which have yet to reveal their dagger thrusts, their hands in hotel bedrooms. They buy the reprieve, or the stay of execution, of distance. London looked inviting from the air, spread out under clear spring sunshine; and one understood the pleasures of tourists staying in hotels in Mayfair, walking in the morning with their cameras and guide-books, past monuments and statues, under plane trees, to see the soldiers at the Palace. One wants the moment of the story to go on for ever, the poise of parting or arriving to be everlasting. So one doesn't have to cross to the other continent, doesn't have to know what really happened, doesn't have to meet the waiting blade.

KAZUO ISHIGURO

A FAMILY SUPPER

Fugu is a fish caught off the Pacific shores of Japan. The fish has held a special significance for me ever since my mother died through eating one. The poison resides in the sexual glands of the fish, inside two fragile bags. When preparing the fish, these bags must be removed with caution, for any clumsiness will result in the poison leaking into the veins. Regrettably, it is not easy to tell whether or not this operation has been carried out successfully. The proof is, as it were, in the eating.

Fugu poisoning is hideously painful and almost always fatal. If the fish has been eaten during the evening, the victim is usually overtaken by pain during his sleep. He rolls about in agony for a few hours and is dead by morning. The fish became extremely popular in Japan after the war. Until stricter regulations were imposed, it was all the rage to perform the hazardous gutting operation in one's own kitchen, then to invite neighbours and friends round for the feast.

At the time of my mother's death, I was living in California. My relationship with my parents had become somewhat strained around that period, and consequently I did not learn of the circumstances surrounding her death until I returned to Tokyo two years later. Apparently, my mother had always refused to eat fugu, but on this particular occasion she had made an exception, having been invited by an old schoolfriend whom she was anxious not to offend. It was my father who supplied me with the details as we drove from the airport to his house in the Kamakura district. When we finally arrived, it was nearing the end of a sunny autumn day.

'Did you eat on the plane?' my father asked. We were sitting on the tatami floor of his tea-room.

'They gave me a light snack.'

'You must be hungry. We'll eat as soon as Kikuko arrives.'

My father was a formidable-looking man with a large stony jaw and furious black eyebrows. I think now in retrospect that he much resembled Chou En-lai, although he would not have cherished such a comparison, being particularly proud of the pure samurai blood that ran in the family. His general presence was not one which encouraged relaxed conversation; neither were things helped much by his odd way of stating each remark as if it were the concluding one. In fact, as I sat opposite him that afternoon, a boyhood memory came back to me of the time he had struck me several times around the head for 'chattering like an old woman'. Inevitably, our conversation since my arrival at the airport had been punctuated by long pauses.

'I'm sorry to hear about the firm,' I said when neither of us had spoken for some time. He nodded gravely.

'In fact the story didn't end there,' he said. 'After the firm's collapse, Watanabe killed himself. He didn't wish to live with the disgrace.'

'I see.'

'We were partners for seventeen years. A man of principle and honour. I respected him very much.'

'Will you go into business again?' I asked.

'I am – in retirement. I'm too old to involve myself in new ventures now. Business these days has become so different. Dealing with foreigners. Doing things their way. I don't understand how we've come to this. Neither did Watanabe.' He sighed. 'A fine man. A man of principle.'

The tea-room looked out over the garden. From where I sat I could make out the ancient well which as a child I had believed haunted. It was just visible now through the thick foliage. The sun had sunk low and much of the garden had fallen into shadow.

'I'm glad in any case that you've decided to come back,' my father said. 'More than a short visit, I hope.'

'I'm not sure what my plans will be.'

'I for one am prepared to forget the past. Your mother too was always ready to welcome you back – upset as she was by your behaviour.'

'I appreciate your sympathy. As I say, I'm not sure what my plans are.'

'I've come to believe now that there were no evil intentions in your mind,' my father continued. 'You were swayed by certain – influences. Like so many others.'

'Perhaps we should forget it, as you suggest.'

'As you will. More tea?'

Just then a girl's voice came echoing through the house.

'At last.' My father rose to his feet. 'Kikuko has arrived.'

Despite our difference in years, my sister and I had always been close. Seeing me again seemed to make her excessively excited and for a while she did nothing but giggle nervously. But she calmed down somewhat when my father started to question her about Osaka and her university. She answered him with short formal replies. She in turn asked me a few questions, but she seemed inhibited by the fear that her questions might lead to awkward topics. After a while, the conversation had become even sparser than prior to Kikuko's arrival. Then my father stood up, saying: 'I must attend to the supper. Please excuse me for being burdened down by such matters. Kikuko will look after you.'

My sister relaxed quite visibly once he had left the room. Within a few minutes, she was chatting freely about her friends in Osaka and about her classes at university. Then quite suddenly she decided we should walk in the garden and went striding out onto the veranda. We put on some straw sandals that had been left along the veranda rail and stepped out into the garden. The daylight had almost gone.

'I've been dying for a smoke for the last half-hour,' she said, lighting a cigarette.

'Then why didn't you smoke?'

She made a furtive gesture back towards the house, then grinned mischievously.

'Oh I see,' I said.

'Guess what? I've got a boyfriend now.'

'Oh yes?'

'Except I'm wondering what to do. I haven't made up my mind yet.'

'Quite understandable.'

'You see, he's making plans to go to America. He wants me to go with him as soon as I finish studying.'

'I see. And you want to go to America?'

'If we go, we're going to hitch-hike.' Kikuko waved a thumb in front of my face. 'People say it's dangerous, but I've done it in Osaka and it's fine.'

'I see. So what is it you're unsure about?'

We were following a narrow path that wound through the shrubs and finished by the old well. As we walked, Kikuko persisted in taking unnecessarily theatrical puffs on her cigarette.

'Well. I've got lots of friends now in Osaka. I like it there. I'm not sure I want to leave them all behind just yet. And Suichi – I like him, but I'm not sure I want to spend so much time with him. Do you understand?'

'Oh perfectly.'

She grinned again, then skipped on ahead of me until she had reached the well. 'Do you remember,' she said, as I came walking up to her, 'how you used to say this well was haunted?'

'Yes, I remember.'

We both peered over the side.

'Mother always told me it was the old woman from the vegetable store you'd seen that night,' she said. 'But I never believed her and never came out here alone.'

'Mother used to tell me that too. She even told me once the old woman had confessed to being the ghost. Apparently she'd been taking a short cut through our garden. I imagine she had some trouble clambering over these walls.'

Kikuko gave a giggle. She then turned her back to the well, casting her gaze about the garden.

'Mother never really blamed you, you know,' she said, in a new voice. I remained silent. 'She always used to say to me how it was their fault, hers and Father's, for not bringing you up correctly. She used to tell me how much more careful they'd been with me, and that's why I was so good.' She looked up and the mischievous grin had returned to her face. 'Poor Mother,' she said.

'Yes. Poor Mother.'

'Are you going back to California?'

'I don't know. I'll have to see.'

'What happened to – to her? To Vicki?'

'That's all finished with,' I said. 'There's nothing much left for me now in California.'

'Do you think I ought to go there?'

'Why not? I don't know. You'll probably like it.' I glanced towards the house. 'Perhaps we'd better go in soon. Father might need a hand with the supper.'

But my sister was once more peering down into the well. 'I can't see any ghosts,' she said. Her voice echoed a little.

'Is Father very upset about his firm collapsing?'

'Don't know. You can never tell with Father.' Then suddenly she straightened up and turned to me. 'Did he tell you about old Watanabe? What he did?'

'I heard he committed suicide.'

'Well, that wasn't all. He took his whole family with him. His wife and his two little girls.'

'Oh yes?'

'Those two beautiful little girls. He turned on the gas while they were all asleep. Then he cut his stomach with a meat knife.'

'Yes, Father was just telling me how Watanabe was a man of principle.'

'Sick.' My sister turned back to the well.

'Careful. You'll fall right in.'

'I can't see any ghost,' she said. 'You were lying to me all that time.'

'But I never said it lived down the well.'

'Where is it, then?'

We both looked around at the trees and shrubs. The light in the garden had grown very dim. Eventually I pointed to a small clearing some ten yards away.

'Just there I saw it. Just there.'

We stared at the spot.

'What did it look like?'

'I couldn't see very well. It was dark.'

'But you must have seen something.'

'It was an old woman. She was just standing there, watching me.'

We kept staring at the spot as if mesmerized.

'She was wearing a white kimono,' I said. 'Some of her hair had come undone. It was blowing around a little.'

Kikuko pushed her elbow against my arm. 'Oh be quiet. You're trying to frighten me all over again.' She trod on the remains of her cigarette, then for a brief moment stood regarding it with a perplexed expression. She kicked some pine needles over it, then once more displayed her grin. 'Let's see if supper's ready,' she said.

We found my father in the kitchen. He gave us a quick glance, then carried on with what he was doing.

'Father's become quite a chef since he's had to manage on his own,' Kikuko said with a laugh. He turned and looked at my sister coldly.

'Hardly a skill I'm proud of,' he said. 'Kikuko, come here and help.'

For some moments my sister did not move. Then she stepped forward and took an apron hanging from a drawer.

'Just these vegetables need cooking now,' he said to her. 'The rest just needs watching.' Then he looked up and regarded me strangely for some seconds. 'I expect you want to look around the house,' he said eventually. He put down the chopsticks he had been holding. 'It's a long time since you've seen it.'

As we left the kitchen I glanced back towards Kikuko, but her back was turned.

'She's a good girl,' my father said quietly.

I followed my father from room to room. I had forgotten how large the house was. A panel would slide open and another room would appear. But the rooms were all startlingly empty. In one of the rooms the lights did not come on, and we stared at the stark walls and tatami in the pale light that came from the windows.

'This house is too large for a man to live in alone,' my father said. 'I don't have much use for most of these rooms now.'

But eventually my father opened the door to a room packed full of books and papers. There were flowers in vases and pictures on the walls. Then I noticed something on a low table in the corner of the room. I came nearer and saw it was a plastic model of a battleship, the kind constructed by children. It had been placed on some newspaper; scattered around it were assorted pieces of grey plastic.

My father gave a laugh. He came up to the table and picked up the model.

'Since the firm folded,' he said, 'I have a little more time on my hands.' He laughed again, rather strangely. For a moment his face looked almost gentle. 'A little more time.'

'That seems odd,' I said. 'You were always so busy.'

'Too busy perhaps.' He looked at me with a small smile. 'Perhaps I should have been a more attentive father.'

I laughed. He went on contemplating his battleship. Then he looked up. 'I hadn't meant to tell you this, but perhaps it's best that I do. It's my belief that your mother's death was no accident. She had many worries. And some disappointments.'

We both gazed at the plastic battleship.

'Surely,' I said eventually, 'my mother didn't expect me to live here for ever.'

'Obviously you don't see. You don't see how it is for some parents. Not only must they lose their children, they must lose them to things they don't understand.' He spun the battleship in his fingers. 'These little gunboats here could have been better glued, don't you think?'

'Perhaps. I think it looks fine.'

'During the war I spent some time on a ship rather like this. But my ambition was always the air force. I figured it like this. If your ship was struck by the enemy, all you could do was struggle in the water hoping for a lifeline. But in an aeroplane – well – there was always the final weapon.' He put the model back onto the table. 'I don't suppose you believe in war.'

'Not particularly.'

He cast an eye around the room. 'Supper should be ready by now,' he said. 'You must be hungry.'

Supper was waiting in a dimly lit room next to the kitchen. The only source of light was a big lantern that hung over the table, casting the rest of the room into shadow. We bowed to each other before starting the meal.

There was little conversation. When I made some polite comment about the food, Kikuko giggled a little. Her earlier nervousness seemed to have returned to her. My father did not speak for several minutes. Finally he said:

'It must feel strange for you, being back in Japan.'

'Yes, it is a little strange.'

'Already, perhaps, you regret leaving America.'

'A little. Not so much. I didn't leave behind much. Just some empty rooms.'

'I see.'

I glanced across the table. My father's face looked stony and forbidding in the half-light. We ate on in silence.

Then my eye caught something at the back of the room. At first I continued eating, then my hands became still. The others noticed and looked at me. I went on gazing into the darkness past my father's shoulder.

'Who is that? In that photograph there?'

'Which photograph?' My father turned slightly, trying to follow my gaze.

'The lowest one. The old woman in the white kimono.'

My father put down his chopsticks. He looked first at the photograph, then at me.

'Your mother.' His voice had become very hard. 'Can't you recognize your own mother?'

'My mother. You see, it's dark. I can't see it very well.'

No one spoke for a few seconds, then Kikuko rose to her feet. She took the photograph down from the wall, came back to the table and gave it to me.

'She looks a lot older,' I said.

'It was taken shortly before her death,' said my father.

'It was the dark. I couldn't see very well.'

I looked up and noticed my father holding out a hand. I gave him the photograph. He looked at it intently, then held it towards Kikuko. Obediently, my sister rose to her feet once more and returned the picture to the wall.

There was a large pot left unopened at the centre of the table. When Kikuko had seated herself again, my father reached forward and lifted the lid. A cloud of steam rose up and curled towards the lantern. He pushed the pot a little towards me.

'You must be hungry,' he said. One side of his face had fallen into shadow.

'Thank you.' I reached forward with my chopsticks. The steam was almost scalding. 'What is it?'

'Fish.'

'It smells very good.'

In amidst soup were strips of fish that had curled almost into balls. I picked one out and brought it to my bowl.

'Help yourself. There's plenty.'

'Thank you.' I took a little more, then pushed the pot towards my father. I watched him take several pieces to his bowl. Then we both watched as Kikuko served herself.

My father bowed slightly. 'You must be hungry,' he said again. He took some fish to his mouth and started to eat. Then I too chose a piece and put it in my mouth. It felt soft, quite fleshy against my tongue.

'Very good,' I said. 'What is it?'

'Just fish.'

'It's very good.'

The three of us ate on in silence. Several minutes went by.

'Some more?'

'Is there enough?'

'There's plenty for all of us.' My father lifted the lid and once more steam rose up. We all reached forward and helped ourselves.

'Here,' I said to my father, 'you have this last piece.'

'Thank you.'

When we had finished the meal, my father stretched out his arms and yawned with an air of satisfaction. 'Kikuko,' he said. 'Prepare a pot of tea, please.'

My sister looked at him, then left the room without comment. My father stood up.

'Let's retire to the other room. It's rather warm in here.'

I got to my feet and followed him into the tea-room. The large sliding windows had been left open, bringing in a breeze from the garden. For a while we sat in silence.

'Father,' I said, finally.

'Yes?'

'Kikuko tells me Watanabe-San took his whole family with him.'

My father lowered his eyes and nodded. For some moments he seemed deep in thought. 'Watanabe was very devoted to his work,' he said at last. 'The collapse of the firm was a great blow to him. I fear it must have weakened his judgement.'

'You think what he did – it was a mistake?'

'Why, of course. Do you see it otherwise?'

'No, no. Of course not.'

'There are other things besides work.'

'Yes.'

We fell silent again. The sound of locusts came in from the garden. I looked out into the darkness. The well was no longer visible.

'What do you think you will do now?' my father asked. 'Will you stay in Japan for a while?'

'To be honest, I hadn't thought that far ahead.'

'If you wish to stay here, I mean here in this house, you would be very welcome. That is, if you don't mind living with an old man.'

'Thank you. I'll have to think about it.'

I gazed out once more into the darkness.

'But of course,' said my father, 'this house is so dreary now. You'll no doubt return to America before long.'

'Perhaps. I don't know yet.'

'No doubt you will.'

For some time my father seemed to be studying the back of his hands. Then he looked up and sighed.

'Kikuko is due to complete her studies next spring,' he said. 'Perhaps she will want to come home then. She's a good girl.'

'Perhaps she will.'

'Things will improve then.'

'Yes, I'm sure they will.'

We fell silent once more, waiting for Kikuko to bring the tea.

*S*TRUCTURAL *A*NTHROPOLOGY

Structural anthropology is psychoanalysis on a basis broader than the individual. Both techniques seek to discover the workings of the human mind by examining its unconscious productions, but while psychoanalysis studies patterns inside a single skull, awake or asleep, structural anthropology concentrates on the communal dream that is ritual behaviour. Then, too, psychoanalysis confines itself by and large to its own culture, while anthropology operates by preference at a distance conducive to objectivity, among tribes whose conscious carapace offers relatively little resistance to the anthropologist's scientific tools. But these are self-imposed limits, and a degree of overlap is common enough; though based in Vienna, Freud felt free to discuss the mental workings of his contemporary, Woodrow Wilson, distant in space, of his European neighbour, Leonardo da Vinci, distant in time, and of course of Oedipus, at a considerable remove of both time and space. In the same way, the techniques of structural anthropology pioneered by Lévi-Strauss can uncover much that is startling in our own culture, if applied with care and thoroughness.

But let us pass from introduction to example. Nurses in a provincial hospital recently took charge of a man who had been bizarrely punished by his wife for infidelity. She had returned unexpectedly to the family home, and could hear him misbehaving. He was engaged in sexual congress that was both noisy and enthusiastic, characteristics which had been missing for some time from his dealings with his wife. She herself made no noise, let herself out of the flat, and returned at her usual time. She cooked a fine dinner, taking care to grind up some sleeping-pills and include them in the mashed potatoes. Her husband retired early to bed, pleading tiredness, and a little later on she stripped him as he slept, and stuck his hand to his penis with Super Glue.

The doctors and nurses faced the problem of separating manual and genital flesh from their tangle, and they had moreover to improvise an arrangement to enable the patient to urinate; plastic surgery was eventually required to restore the appearance of the parts.

And there it is, a little sordid, a little amusing, a story of no great distinction, promising no great yield of insight. But this story moves faster than any story can on its own merits, it *travels* at high speed, and suddenly it is everywhere; it satisfies a need that runs unexpectedly deep, and someone can even be heard claiming it was current years ago, in another town. It is therefore a myth, even if it happened, and can be guaranteed to explain itself if asked the right questions. But its music will remain mysterious until it is struck with the subtle mallet of structural anthropology, which gives resonances priority over mere sound.

I. NATURE/CULTURE

The crucial opposition, as ever, is nature/culture. Sexuality is *wild*, *tamed* in marriage, revealed as *wild* all along in adultery. The dangerous animal is transformed into a social adhesive, but breaks loose again. The animal parts boiled down into glue threaten no such resurrection; hence the woman's choice of instrument for her revenge. The actual composition of glue in modern times is rarely organic, but the collective unconscious always is; it refers to the constants of human experience, and not to mere life 'as it is lived'. The collective unconscious exists independently of chronological sequence, and doesn't keep pace with developments in glue technology. Nor for that matter is a man excused by his ignorance of Greek mythology from desiring his father's death and his mother's body.

2. LIMP/STIFF

The secondary axis of oppositions in our chosen myth is limp/stiff; the married man undertakes to be *stiff* with his wife, *limp* in all other contexts. Impotence in the marriage-bed and tumescence elsewhere are symmetrical threats to social order and the next generation. But here, the adulterer is punished for his criminal stiffness with *more*, with a stiffness he cannot control, for it is precisely his lack of control which is stigmatized. The betrayed woman betrays *him* to the castrating laughter of the world by parodying his virility, source of his transgression; the permanent erection she gives him nevertheless shows him to be impotent. Hardness and softness are equally laughable, equally disgusting, when they are constant pathological states, unmediated by contract and by alternation.

3. FOOD/DRUG

The married man sacrifices excitement and variety, distraction and unpredictability, in the interests of a higher set of values; he enters an economy of duties and pleasures. He signs a contract to stop playing the field, and to start cultivating it; he must reduce his erotic options to one before he can reproduce himself in the next generation. Energy invested in marriage accrues as capital; in promiscuity it is dissipated and comes to nothing. The married man renounces sex as a drug and binds himself to a life of intimate affection, of sex as food; from this point on, his hunger will be satisfied rather than stimulated. But the adulterous husband violates the metabolism of marriage by continuing to demand excitement instead of sustenance. Very well then; the woman whose power to satisfy appetite he has scorned will retaliate by *drugging his food*. And she will make use of drugs in their narcotic rather than stimulant aspect; instead of excitement she will deliver sedation, and helplessness instead of a heightened awareness. For her, adultery is, like alcohol, a 'sedative hypnotic with paradoxical stimulation', a down that only masquerades as an up; and her revenge necessarily dramatizes her attitudes to betrayal.

4. PRIVATE/PUBLIC

When two people combine as husband and wife, and no longer define themselves as their parents' children, their changed status must be marked by a ritual; as they move from separate establishments into a shared household they pass through a kind of sacred corridor, which irreversibly differentiates the past from the future. Although they are private individuals making a private decision, they must declare it in public, and though they are drastically loosening their ties with their parents, their wedding is traditionally attended by all the people from whom they are, in effect, receding.

Whether they choose to be married in church or opt for the ceremonial minimum in front of a Registrar, their act is no less ritual, and as such it cannot simply be dropped and not mentioned again. It must be renounced; a formula must be found which symbolically inverts the ritual of binding. Even though the magic has died, the spell must be said backwards for the release of the participants. Their disenchantment must be fully enacted.

And we can see this process at work in our myth. The original ritual impels the couple through a solemn public space and towards the marriage-bed; the counter-ritual starts in that same bed, now a trap for the sinner and not a nest, and expels the guilty party towards a public space purged of all solemnity. The husband drugged in the marriage-bed is already paying the price for his transgression; having preferred excitement to security, he must abide by his choice, and forfeits safety absolutely. But there is more in store for him.

His wife's selection, for her symbolic inverse of a *church*, of a *hospital*, is a masterstroke on the part of the collective unconscious. They are respectively the homes of a mystery resistant to analysis and an analysis resistant to mystery; a suggestive darkness, and an inescapable light.

We may add in passing that only structural anthropology increases mystery in the process of explaining it. Here at last science and religion marry and settle down.

And there is a further excellence to the patterning, in that a man who has spurned his chosen bed and sought sex elsewhere, is immobilized in a bed he hasn't chosen; a bed in which the body is examined and treated clinically, without a moment's consideration for the sensual component he has rated so highly. He occupies an asexual bed, then, lying there in limbo, defined by no relationships, and sharing the premises with other transients who at least have the prospect of returning to their interrupted lives. He, however, has sought to combine freedom of action with the security of the hearth, and has been brusquely deprived of both.

5. COMEDY/TRAGEDY

In our study of structural elements we have so far considered the glue, the sleeping-pills, the bed, and the hospital. There remain the hand and the penis. By her sarcastic conjunction of these two organs the wife insists on the comic rather than the tragic aspects of her predicament; she makes the dissolution of her marriage a matter for public laughter rather than private heartbreak. She represents her husband as caught in the act, but the act itself is ironically diminished; his posture convicts him not of adultery but self-abuse. The enforced junction of hand and penis yokes man's highest ambitions and his betraying weakness.

(It is obviously his dominant hand that she so mockingly cements in place; impossible to imagine her spoiling the symbolism by insulting the left hand of a right-hander. That would be quite foreign to the exhaustive brilliance of a mind that doesn't even know it is operating!)

She juxtaposes the opposable thumb, which was such an achievement of evolution, with the third leg – those guilty tissues which threaten to slide Man back into the swamp of undifferentiation. The woman declares the marital atrocity simply waste, the crime against herself mere self-indulgence.

In her construction of a counter-ritual the woman has developed a persona whose trademark is *the ironic fulfilment of wishes*; she has metamorphosed from one folk-tale character into another, from Captive Maiden into Witch. Her husband wants to be stiff elsewhere than in her bed? She can arrange it. He wants an adventure? She will see what she can do.

With her glue she ensures their separation, with the hardness she contrives for him she parodies his virility. But her final coup is her magical ability to use others to work her revenge; there is a superficial mercy to her actions with the tube of glue, but the surgeons must exercise their skills unstintingly. The way in which these members of the community seem to carry out the betrayed woman's commands gives the punishment an air of impersonality; the woman herself refrains from the knife, but hands him over to her agents for surgery. They collaborate in his humiliation.

The knife is in fact being used to repair damage, but this is not apparent to the victim, except at that lowermost level where words mean two opposite things (compare Freud on the binary meanings of basic words). The patient's hand *cleaves* to his penis, the doctors must *cleave* them apart again.

But the women in the hospital are essentially more important than the men. The surgeons are predominantly male, the nurses by and large female, and it is the nurses who make up the hospital community as perceived by the patient. The doctors pay visits, but the nurses seem to live on the wards. And so the final phase of the adulterer's punishment is accomplished. With her woman's laughter his wife hands him over to the laughter of women who re-enact the transformation of the female from subservient employee to ambiguous manipulator: women who touch him without tenderness, who are intimate

with him but not interested, who tend without establishing a
relationship with the man in their care; who confirm his exile from a
world where the female can be taken for granted, and who may even
be laughing behind their hands.

What remains of our original story? Certainly nothing of the sordid
or trivial; these elements have been absorbed into their opposites. And
simplicity too has yielded the complex, without losing its shape. For
just below the surface of story, like the succulent separate threads
beneath the skin of a perfectly cooked vegetable-spaghetti, lies the
tangled richness of myth.